João Klein was born in Santo Ângelo, Rio Grande do Sul, Brazil. He grew up with his roots fixed on the horizon. He is the father of two wonderful boys.

To God, who loved me first.

To Mariana, my eternal sister.

To the courageous João Gabriel, for I have loved you deeply from the moment of your conception, and I always will.

To little Benaiah, your smiles saved me.

João Klein

THE FELLOWSHIP OF THE SWORD

Book I – The Father Sword

AUSTIN MACAULEY PUBLISHERS™

LONDON * CAMBRIDGE * NEW YORK * SHARJAH

Ordering Information
Quantity sales: Special discounts are available on quantity purchases by corporations, associations, and others. For details, contact the publisher at the address below.

Publisher's Cataloging-in-Publication data
Klein, João
The Fellowship of the Sword

ISBN 9781643784250 (Paperback)
ISBN 9781643784267 (Hardback)
ISBN 9781645367789 (ePub e-book)

Library of Congress Control Number: 2021908866

www.austinmacauley.com/us

First Published (2021)
Austin Macauley Publishers LLC
40 Wall Street, 33rd Floor, Suite 3302
New York, NY 10005
USA

mail-usa@austinmacauley.com
+1 (646) 5125767

To Lord Jesus, for he loved the most.

"And he shall burn all his fat upon the altar, as the fat of the sacrifice of peace offerings: and the priest shall make an atonement for him as concerning his sin, and it shall be forgiven him."

– Leviticus 4:26

Why

The most important thing anywhere, ever, is perspective. All other things pale in comparison.

One needs to have a clear view of what perspective really is in order to understand anything at all.

Down on the ground lays the earth. Standing over it is your foot. Your foot is kept alive through nourishment. Before it, is the drive to find such sustenance. Above it, is the reason why. Commanding it, is the will to know why. Ruling all those things, your soul – a mystery.

Containing the soul, the Ether – the spiritual world. Comprehending the Ether, the multiverse of necessary dimensions that stabilize, represent, and, for lack of a better term, dignify reality.

Controlling the Ether, there are many larger perspectives dancing (in the purest form) with each other. Those cosmic beings, although sentient, are so high in existence and have devised and merged themselves in so many ways, that they could hardly be properly perceived, understood, or even represented as individual presences. Above the multitude of those powerful beings, there is the one necessary and absolute perspective that contains everything.

In every facet and level of the existential ladder described above, there are a plethora of perspectives. Up and down, right and left, they surround reality from directions that transcend description.

It is through a perspective that things, including life, come to be. Perspective is the creative mold within the conscious mind. It is the multidimensional shaper of the awakened consciousness. It is through perspective that all things are fashioned into existence. Perspective is the theme that a creator gives to everything it creates. It is the necessary pillar of conception, and it is also what gives the structural design to all things created.

The creator's mind is the resting place of a perspective. It is the nest where it lays. It is what gives its character. Both are so connected that it is virtually impossible to establish where one begins and the other ends. They are fused together. Parted, but indivisible. And, within their dynamics, are secrets regarding the very nature of the universe.

Conceptually, perspective is what it is, holding its meanings by itself. A mind is what a perspective will come to be through existence inside a manifestation. Both are not of a substantive nature as immediately apparent, but of a verbal essence — while being they exist. Without both of them, there is no fruition. No movement. Therefore, no end. Hence, no beginning. No creation. Without them, there are only the infinite solitudes of eternal nothingness.

Even the highest things need to be created through perspective. Even the First Creator, through a perspective of his own design and infinite complexity, created himself. In a single flash of boundlessness, he came to be. Beyond the most indivisible unit of measurement, and within an interconnected paradox of necessities that were caused to meant to be, he came into existence. From the void, he came forth and everything started.

As all things needed a perspective to be designed upon, and he needed an existence to be a perspective in, the First Creator, through a union of eternal and indivisible love, married his creation in the moment of its conception, marking his togetherness within the very structure of reality precisely inside the dynamic between mind and perspective.

His first act of love was to make himself infinite, for he could not limit himself in his desire to contain all things under the guard of his care. Although yet unrevealed, with him, through him, within him, everything was instantly dragged into existing at that moment when he decided to be the father of all.

However, by definition, completeness is reserved and contained only in the First Creator and his highest perspective, but due to the affectionate nature he chose to be his own, he desired, above all else, to share many aspects of himself with his creation. For that intent, he kept his mind, but he shattered his being in many smaller perspectives, setting them free to be co-creators with him.

Moved by the most profound devotion, he made all things free for the sake of truly relating to them. Only with separation and the universal gift of freedom, the First Creator could now be in its creation, and, at the same time, he could avoid his creation to be in him. Which was an absolute necessity, due to the consequent enslavement and resulting entropy suffered by a smaller perspective when in contact with his wholeness.

He, thus, freed them to be whatever they wished. To be unrestricted. To be themselves while pursuing their own creative interest according to their own desires and talents.

And so they did, and although some decided to be forever connected with the Higher One, cosmically mixed with his overruling perspective, many chose to have a taste of their own creative pursuits.

They went forward forming many things, even other co-creators, who, by themselves, produced other co-creators and so forth. They all gladly toiled until existence was full and inhabited. Yet, they soon learned that no creature could craft a perspective broader than their own, for a work is contained by the boundaries of its creator's mind's conceptions. Consequently, the more the creators refined and disseminated themselves, increasing their distance from the light of the First Creator, narrower, less meaningful, and less capable were their sons' and daughters' perspectives.

Their labor was pure, good, and plentiful, though. They populated empty spaces, gave reason to countless things, and the whole of creation matured in their purpose. Those days were called The Days of Eternity, for they contained the countless eras before the formation of the material world.

It was a period of unmatched delight and incomparable generosity, and the works of those days pleased the First Creator greatly, for although all things were in him already, its revelation is the true facet of existence.

Together, through the devise of great happiness, the total of the first co-creators' work culminated into the weaving of time and the material universe.

Time, for the organizing, beautification, and final fulfillment of all revelations; and matter, to anchor the results of the sum of all their works in one single actuality, connecting all planes of existence in one continuous destiny. For, until then, their making, although wonderful, was dispersed in many dimensions and in many larger perspectives in distant corners of the multiverse, and that dispersion of their now plentiful works felt erratic from their perspectives. For that reason, they all cheered in great joy when they first contemplated the latter creation, realizing the whole magnitude of the blessings of the First Creator when he himself gave the final push to unify and objectify all things in matter and time.

Existence, thus, expressed in matter, became hence the utmost representation of all things coming together as they unfold through time while the First Creator reveals his totality to and within all things.

The First Creator loved material existence more than anything else. Upon contemplating it, he considered it the prime jewel of his creation, for the destiny of all things was bound to it.

Matter was stablished as the most refined form of creation. In many respects, it is the conclusion of everything. Every particle's position, state, and interactions are reflexed and anchored in all dimensions, serving the purpose of a greater design and balancing the dance of existence.

In some aspects, the material world can be compared to the sum of all the shadows cast by all the parallel existences. Anything can happen in the multiverse, but only in the material world are those things truly happening omnipresently.

It is at the same time a perfectly stabilized neat agglutination of inter-cosmic results, as well as a conduit for perpetual changes. For, like a key in a piano, if one touches a particle or influence a force in the material actuality, it would echo its tones throughout the multiverse of dimensions by the means of its fastened strings.

Remarkably, and despite its intricate doors and secret pathways, this is a two-way interaction. The higher dimensions form and guide the material world, but the opposite is also possible.

Once time and matter were created, the whole universe was touched by change. Nevertheless, creative perspectives continued to refine their work. Now, however, inside the constraints of time, but even so they masterfully used it in their favor, laboring until the material universe was rich and established.

Incidentally, matter was finite, and upon facing this reality some co-creators, drunk from their own vanity and pride, felt their working space was now limited and unglorified. A friction was born, but the works continued.

Within the ages, all matter felt the clashes of the infinite interests of extra-dimensional beings. The material world became a battlefield of perspectives. Through it, divisions and many repugnancies came to be. In time, the angles that separate some perspectives grew too obtuse. Clashes invariably happened and the main theme of many works was abandoned, forgotten, or even distorted by many creators. In countless places, free creation was set aside and dispute took its place.

Many, falsely believing they were now limited, turned to themselves and started to blindingly overvalue their own perspectives. This clouded the truth greatly. To a point that great works could not be done anymore due to lack of cooperation and the narrowing of important perspectives.

The collective and perfect communion gave way to increasing selfishness and fanaticism. That, by its turn, brought oceans of chaos and conflict into existence.

Slowly, a sense of proportion was deemed evermore necessary in the Ether. The moment arrived when there was a clear distinctiveness in existence – it was called evil. And every act that had a meaning and a purpose in the following quarrels came from this original perceived insufficiency.

From the multitude of interests that came from the struggles of jealousy, many co-creators lost their way. With them, their portion of co-created reality fell from grace. Some even manifested in matter with nothing but destructive designs in their hearts, causing confusion and pain.

The things boiling in the Ether eventually overflowed, infesting time and matter and casting a shadow over the sentient beings that were already inhabiting the material world at that point. This caused them to lose the connections they once had with higher existences. Being carnal beings and spiritual creatures at the same time only added more complexity to the problem. In some of them, their carnal roots were so deep that they even lost their regards to the Ether.

As time went by, that unawareness increased. Some reached the point of absurdly denying its very existence, and to increase their problems, their cultural and social complexity expanded over time, causing them to blindly face their own growing mundane existential needs.

One day, they woke to find themselves indirectly involved and entrapped in a complex net of higher turmoils with no or little consciousness of what was really happening around them. Confused and scared, they turn against each other not knowing what they were actually doing.

Eventually, the world became filled with creatures and even entire civilizations that walked the world with meek perspectives and nothing but pieces of true knowledge. Henceforth interacting with each other with little understanding and minor love. Many started arguing that everything was pointless and that these interactions among perspectives should be seen as random connections.

However, the keepers of truth knew that the very origins of the universe prove that a higher meaning and greater destiny is behind every single one of those exchanges. A mystery is within even the worst or the smallest of them, and, in the end, they will be the only thing that has ever mattered.

They kept alive the hope that although a sea of difficulties and confusion was now stablished across the universe, the First Creator was and would always be the keeper of the way back, and that all the ways were, ultimately, his. Everything indeed mattered, and all things were bound to end where they had begun.

Thus, perspective is everything. Truly, perspective and its effects are what the whole of creation is about. Its clashes are the unfolding of the revelation of everything to all things. This is the secret of the ages, the secret of existence, the big "why." The world of Fabula exists through this secret.

Fabula

The world of Fabula is a world of wishes. If you wish for something hard enough, it will come true.

In this world, reality can be altered by the power of will. It does not matter how impossible something may seem; in Fabula, anything can happen if you really want it to.

This fact has a dramatic effect on everything there, bringing a lot of distinctiveness to this world. The sense of wonder brought by this deep freedom increased the disposition of all living beings. Many took the opportunity to leave their mark on creation, causing a multitude of wonderful and terrible stories to come to life, turning the world of Fabula into a world of high adventure.

Some acts of willpower are so extravagant, unique, and fundamentally transcendent of the apparent reality that it is called magic.

In Fabula, as in most worlds, existence tends to exist – it is a necessity. As a result, almost all things contain the logical fruit of this tendency, holding it in their utmost essence. Thus, a wisher can create or alter anything with magic by understanding and manipulating these essences through this tendency.

Although the level of exposure and use of magic varies drastically in both intensity and quality, there are, likewise, groups of creatures that are so bound by and so immersed in the effects of it, that they just see it as another force of nature. Which, in fact, it is.

Most of these beings are at peace with it, not excluding magic and its effects from their personal definition of normality. However, because of its mystic, transgressive, dangerous, and passionate nature, many are also scared of magic. Too scared to even try it. Too scared to wish. Too scared to dare. Too scared to live.

For these reasons, most individuals go along with their daily routines trying to avoid it. Victims of their self-imposed limitations, these creatures simply fixate their attention on ordinary things, giving themselves only to the unrefined perceptible that they can grasp and shallowly understand. Therefore, although magic is ever-present and can be manifested in most places, the majority live and die ordinary lives with no magic in them whatsoever.

Nevertheless, there are some who do wish. Among them, there are those who do it passionately and fiercely. Then there are some who deeply, sincerely, and powerfully wish. Those, more often than not, live through extraordinary things and absolutely amazing moments, for they live to see their will become reality. They live to see their dreams come true.

The end result of this arrangement is that after tens of thousands of years of wishes, visions, and dreams of many different co-creators, the world of Fabula is full of life. Vivid, beautiful, artsy, unexpected, romantic, and splendid life.

Granted, there are also, of course, a great many number of terrors, but life always prevails.

Life in Fabula is expressed in an extensive number of different colors, forms, and shapes. But, surprisingly contradicting common sense, as truth normally does, these parameters are not the most important things about life in this world.

The most important thing about life in this world is the most important thing ever: perspective.

There are many perspectives among Fabula's incarnated creatures, but they are mainly divided into two categories: the minds who are aware of their own self, and the ones who are not.

The "existing beings" are the ones totally unaware of their own identity. They are named as so, for they do just that – they just exist. Blameless and innocent, they travel through reality guiltless.

They are aware of the creation surrounding them, but not of themselves. Their ego sleeps through their whole existence, and they are mostly driven by instincts. These, are the most prolific kind of sentient beings. The bugs in the fields, most of the fish in the oceans, and the majority of common critters are examples of this kind.

There are also, of course, the "existential beings."

These living creatures are the ones whose egos are "awakened." Therefore, they are not only aware of the world around them but are also aware of their own selves. Their own identities.

Existing with the need to deal with their ever-present conscience mirrors, these beings tend to bear much more refined minds. They generally are the possessors of a distinct and acute perception of the world around them, for they use it in their daily battles over the laboring fields between their material and their spiritual existences – which is precisely where they live.

Due to the fact that they do not only exist, but they rather perceive their own existence, they approach awareness through their own unique perspectives by using their complex mental processes. Humans, dwarves, and elves are the primal examples. Although, there are surely more, much more.

Their "awakening," and the freedom to wish that these existential beings enjoy, are the major cause of most of the perceived chaos and the observable tragedies that plague this world. However, it has also certainly inspired infinite expressions of beauty and magnificent acts of love, and in this conflictual duality, life in Fabula, from the lowest definition to its highest meaning, went on.

Elaroth

Fabula is composed far more of water than earth. It has only a few major continents and, although there is a great number of colossal islands, most of its surface is covered by water.

Though many have tried (and some still are) there is no supreme king overseeing Fabula. As the diffusion of the use of magic empowers individuals against centralized political regimes, there is an infinite variety of kingdoms, realms, and independent collective organizations.

This world is truly ruled by the currents and the winds of its many oceans. As veins and arteries circulate blood in a body, the uncountable invisible roads made of water and air circulates fleets of merchant and exploring vessels throughout the seas.

Commerce, in its many expressions and types, is what keeps the world together. To and fro brave men go, spreading their trades of wonderfulness and novelties elsewhere.

As life in Fabula is very colorful, highly interesting, and worth living, there is no shortage of adventure all over. Anyone who looks for it will most certainly find it.

In this exciting world, the continent of Elaroth is at the center of it all, either geographically, commercially, or politically. If you want to trade or go anywhere, you eventually pass through Elaroth. Most of the maritime commercial routes pass through its shores, enriching their inhabitants with life-changing business opportunities and strange magic.

Elaroth is a large continental landmass right in the center of the known world. Therefore, it naturally became a very "dynamic" place. A place for disputes and reckoning. A place for profit and loss. A place for adventure and for homecoming. A place for love, and a place for war.

As it now stood, it was divided into five major areas: the ancient Elven Realm, occupying all the territories north of the Fire Mountains; the Fire Mountains in the middle, dividing the land; the Barbarian Territories over the southwestern part; the Valkarian Empire in the southeast; and the Coronian Trade Federation to the South.

The ancient Elven Realm is where most of the elves who love the woods, fields, valleys, and mountains reside.

The elves are one of the most prolific and powerful races in Fabula. They enjoy great intimacy with magic and are the possessors of a very long lifespan. Their bodies age ten times slower than humans do, and they keep their vigor well into their old days.

Incredibly artistic, they are the elders of the world, the keepers of many secrets, and warders of profound wisdom.

Countless wonderful tales and songs are told and sung about its crystal cities, magic water lakes, and healing flowers. Nonetheless, those songs and tales have aged now for it has been a long time since any outsider has entered the elven lands and lived to tell a tale or sing a song.

Very little is known about it, but a quarantine was decreed by the Elf King some time ago. Since its inception, no one has been allowed to enter or exit their kingdom. Folks who venture too close to its borders, or dare cross it, are never to be seen again.

The ones who get out without the king's authorization are banned forever. They are not allowed to return, however noble or important they might be. Merciless and everlasting banishment is their fate.

Groups of explorers who live to tell about their encounters on the borders and shores claim they are not the merry and magical people they once were. Instead, a bitter shadow lingers in the depths of their huge and expressive eyes. Visitors are largely unwanted and treated coldly and unmercifully. Instead of warm gathers in fanciful treehouses, they are received by hunter packs and soldiers on military patrols.

Leave or die are the only choices they give foreigners nowadays. No matter how needy they are. This is in stark contrast to former times, when they would invite passersby to freely make merry and drink wine with them. They even gave them presents without any formalities.

By interacting with the exiled dissidents, the general population face a deep contradiction thinking how such a wonderful, musical, loving, and poetic folk could come out of such a stern and edgy place.

From a human standpoint, there has been so much time since the realm has suffered this transformation that it is now a blank spot on most maps. Just a massive amount of shorelines and forests with the words "do not enter" written in big and alarming letters all over it.

Although the best libraries still hold maps detailing their long wood roads, magic ponds, and the many wonderful things therein on their ancient lands, it has become increasingly hard to find geographical references now. Either way, most ship captains make sure the elfish mainland is never within sight over the horizon. The world, having enough problems as it is, generally left the elves alone to deal with whatever gloomy business they have put themselves into.

The Fire Mountains are located just south of the Elven Realm, sharing a long land border with it. They stretched from the east to the west coast all the way through Elaroth, dividing the continent in two.

These mountains are a very dangerous place, maybe the most dangerous place in Elaroth. The skies are unsafe, the land is crawling in treachery, and the subterranean, well, the subterranean is even worse.

It is a place plagued by the foulest creatures in the world. There, dragons, giants, ogres, orcs, runaways, rebels, defectors, criminals, creatures with aversion to civilization, civilizations aversive to creatures, and all sorts of perils await. Danger is always watching over high peaks and lurking under their deep valleys.

The problems that plague the Fire Mountains does not end in the earth beneath their feet though, they start there. For underneath the mountains' peaks and beneath their rocky pillars, lay the three Dwarven Reigns.

Originally known as the birthplace of the dwarves, the Dwarven Reigns are reminiscent of ancestral times. There, this stubborn folk managed to survive, hiding inside their impenetrable fortress and wonderful homes.

They are very proud of their craftsmanship, and there are still some feats of enchantment that can only be accomplished by them. The deep knowledge they hold about the structure of matter, and the wonders they have created because of it, made them a target for many of the world's powers. Through the centuries, the dwarves' enemies have tried to acquire by force what they couldn't peacefully buy from them.

Since time immemorial, dwarves have also faced an almost constant war.

There are, however, independent cities across the mountains. They are isolated islands of "progress" that barely managed to survive this treacherous land. They are mostly self-ruling and renegade cities, fortified mines manned by tough pioneers, or other sorts of highly tense and isolated communities. Most of them are composed of expatriate folks and special interest groups that live out of some profitable dangerous business or some common ideal.

The surface of the Fire Mountains resembles, in a great measure, the world of the past. With giant and ancient beasts still buzzing around freely, forbidden cults hiding themselves from the forces of order, and colorful and secluded communities. It resembled the world before the races had organized themselves in larger kingdoms, enforcing their law and civilization over the land.

While in precariously isolated conditions and holding little or no land around themselves, most of these independent cities are very rich from all the business they mediate between the dwarfs and the world. They enjoy a prosperity hard to come by anywhere else, attracting many people of initiative and action.

These cities are great places for competent mercenaries and bold adventurers to find work. Most, but not all, are located over or next to a dwarf city, working as a business station, offering relative protection and shelter services for bold merchants. In the limit of their interest, they also organize the logistics of the trading caravans seeking to protect them from the unlimited number of vicious raiders who plague this part of the world.

The Barbarian Territories are in the western part of the south portion of Elaroth. Most of it is covered by a seemingly endless and utterly cruel forest that is commonly known as the Dire Woods. Its fauna and flora are so aggressive towards civilized life that the only humans who have survived there are scattered tribes and clans of tenacious wild men. Their tribes are sparse and devised by the totem they worship, uniting in a colossal horde in the eventual case when their common survival is at stake.

These hardened men do not see themselves and are not perceived by others human groups as "common humans." Many specialists consider them a sub-race of human beings. Some say they are the purest kind of humans – the primal humans, descendants of the original men before they interbred with the others races in Fabula.

There are a few Coronian scholars that have classified them as "Dire Men" for their overly muscular bodies, their superior bone structure, their primitive guttural rites, and their familiarity with their animalistic instincts. The rest of the world, much less interested in literacy, simply call them Barbarians.

Life in the wild domains has indeed imbued in them a certain kind of ruthless resilience though. A very refined and powerful survival instinct that could bring them to trigger a powerful and focused temper in combat, making them very dangerous enemies, and even more terrible friends.

Generally, they hold a great aversion to the outside world, preferring to be in the heart of their woodlands, living their dire lives to the fullest. However, they occasionally, but not commonly, circulate among civilized lands. Yet, when they do so, it is not uncommon for them to be frowned upon and discriminated against. This happens due to the memory of the many bloody wars they have fought with their neighbors and the raids that aggressive and corrupt tribes organize randomly. Consequently, a lot of resentments and generalizations are still lingering in people's memory. Especially considering that civilized men have a different perception of war, seeing it as a catastrophe that should be avoided. Barbarians, on the other hand, see it as a celebration of their manhood and something that is a part of life – a natural thing. "A Long Hunt" as they call it.

As they seldom care to explain themselves, tending to be very introspective, the cultural shocks caused by the Barbarian's divergences in so many matters easily lead to deadly conflicts and other problems when they interact with outsiders.

They share an eastern border with the Valkarian Empire, holding a relatively steady frontier now. Although it was forged with much-spilled blood from both sides throughout the centuries.

In the south, things are not so stable. There is a much disputed and unstable frontier with the Coronian Federation, who refuse to acknowledge the dispersed tribes and clans as a real government. Rather, they treat and deal with the Barbarians as if they were savages to be tamed. Due to this arrogance, the Coronians have never really succeeded in any real "domestication" attempt, but instead, they have been constantly bashed and humiliated in the battles they drag the Barbarian tribes into.

Traditionally, the Barbarians enforce no rule but their own natural law, and do it passively, over any coincidental occasion. Therefore, their lands run wild and unmarked. Add that to the chaos of the Fire Mountains and you have a scenario that describes their northern frontier. It is plain mayhem, and this is pretty much it – no further efforts are needed to describe it.

There, the only law is of the stronger, making the western portion of the Fire Mountains, by a long shot, the most lawless region of Elaroth. Even mighty emperors and kings have limited reach and power projection there. All this is further aggravated by the far distance to civilized lands and the elven quarantine to the North. For these reasons, this region is home to numerous evils in search of discretion and isolation.

Guarding the southwest of Elaroth lays the beautiful and fair Coronia. A land that inspired more minstrels than any lady in the history of the world.

Blessed with reasonable weather and with a terrain of mostly highly fertile soft hills, its golden cereal fields and flower gardens go on for endless miles.

Politically it is nothing but a huge cluster of very rich and refined human principalities, which are controlled by aristocratic families related to trade and finance.

Founders and keepers of most of the trade throughout Fabula, the Coronians are a smart and passionate folk. They are very keen and sleek in all their doings, as well as always ready on their feet. Although shorter boned than the Valkarians, they own warmer hearts, using them extensively in life and all its significances of love and glory.

Beautiful, vain, and proud owners of an extraordinary talent for commerce, diplomacy, art, and navigation, they stablished Coronia as the single largest known naval and commercial power in Fabula.

It is said that the real Coronia is not found on their bucolic hill's mansions, but rather at sea – everywhere and elsewhere, over their perpetual horizon. There, their innumerable vessels dare and explore; always looking for a profit to be made and a new mystery to be unfolded.

It is a common saying that the world is the Coronian's mirror. For they can only see themselves through their relation to it. They are souls in perennial need of new interlocutors and new interactions. They are, indeed, hungry social creatures, living on the edge and loving to know and to explore.

They enjoy investing their time and efforts in everything that represent progress and knowledge. Navigational instruments, libraries, and new technologies are not seen there as a luxury or curiosity, but rather what dignifies life. Slaves of their own egos, they tend to value things more for its adjective elements than for its substantive content. For that reason, they enjoy novelties with greater joy than most folks.

For them, to expose themselves to the unknown and to untold uniqueness is to breathe in. To share it, is to breathe out. And like so they live. With fast and wandering hearts, and with minds dripping with an audacious curiosity.

With their powerful cruisers, the Galleons, they sail the seas to wherever they can reach. Sometimes, even to where they cannot. They sail from the colorful Sultanates of the Deepsouth to the Dragon Lands in the Highnorth. They sail trading the silk from the Ansan Empire, past the Magical Islands in the far west. They take peoples and goods to the Blood Reefs and the Colossus Sea in the East. Their bold ships ignore frontiers, legends, and fears. They transport possessions and interests to wherever they are needed, reaching all the many corners of the world, and beyond.

Finally, in the southeastern portion of Elaroth lay the realm where this tale has its origins and where most of it unfolds: the Valkarian Empire.

No Sacrifice

The only way to truly understand the Land of Valkar is to understand what its people are about. The very best way to accurately comprehend what its people are about is to hear the tale of The Last Battle. Which is, naturally, a tale of a battle. A battle that took place in The First War.

The First War was a war of cataclysmic proportions that encompassed the whole world. Almost every creature had to choose a side, and, in one way or the other, everyone fought in it. That war marked and changed Fabula deeply, that is why all life calls it The First War.

During those bleak times, there was no peace over the land, only war. Many heroes had surfaced during that period; some, from the most surprising origins and manners. Countless legends are still being told to the inhabitants of Fabula about the glorious things that occurred in that era.

Many horrors came to be as well. Horrors of such deep vileness that it destroyed not only lives, but much of the world's innocence, scarring it forevermore.

It was a long war and it was a tough war. As simplistic as it may sound, ultimately, it was a confrontation between good and evil. It was the first open and widespread confrontation between the forces of creation, the legions of destruction, and everything between.

In the Ether, these perspectives' distances, focus, and angles had moved away from each other for too long, causing this long-standing opposition to materialize suddenly and ferociously in a generalized open warfare.

The conflict started when creatures from a lower dimension somehow managed to open what mortals call "a portal" and entered Fabula. In doing so, they started conveying their chaotic energies all over, crushing and corrupting creation beyond any hope of repair.

They incarnated into powerful bodies, existing for the sole purpose of creating turmoil and devastation to feed their bottomless souls. The visible and palpable forms of those beings were called demons. If a cruelty never saw before, they advanced throughout the land and sea, contaminating, in many forms, all life systems with their destructive evil drives.

Their depravity was so intense, that the whole world came together and fought the invading forces. Struggling at first, the forces of good assembled a resistance. In time, they established a firm opposition and a front. With countless sacrifices, they turned the tables and took initiative, hunting the demons as an inquisition.

At some point, however terrible the war was, it was about to end. After a long campaign, the races of Fabula and their many armies managed to push The Chaos Legions to where everything had begun: the doorsteps of the demons' main inter-dimensional gate.

After they laid siege to the Fortress of Despair – the demons' last standing stronghold, built around their last portal – the forces of order pushed back the dreadful troops. Paying dearly for each dead enemy, they destroyed all of their wicked bodies. An arduous effort was also allocated into the undoing of the demons' dreadful works of corruption. At a great cost, victory was near.

Exhausted by the very nature of their skirmish, the forces of good could sense that the war and the destiny of the world were on the brink of a conclusion. Weary and desperate, The First Alliance prepared the last attack to destroy the gate. They deployed their forces and called the remaining demons for a last battle. They threw everything they had, knowing that the result of the scuffle would decide who would rule Fabula. Winning or losing, either way, fate decided that everything would be defined where it all had started.

The First Alliance army displayed their forces by the high cliffs that held the river valley where the Demon Portal was located. Among them, in the vanguard, were the warriors of the land of Valkar.

Taller, stronger, and nobler than most folks, they were born, lived, and died with a profound self-reliant and martial spirit. By then, those warriors were still not an empire, but were definitively an imperial people. They had always been strong and united, believing in freedom above everything else, rarely constituting authority over themselves, living as free men.

All the way through that horrific period they suffered the worst and showed the best. The war had been too long and too draining of an undertaking, even for the Valkarians. They were still in the fight but were truly drained from it. Yet, they were there. They were all there. After pushing back the demonic multitudes one by one in a lengthy bloodshed, they were there. In their infancy as a nation, leading the world in their most desperate moment – the pioneers of glory.

Their plate armors, swords, and shields were shining under a deranged sky. Their hosts were surrounded by a silvery blue light reflected by the result of the extensive use of the ancient and magical Palladium in their steel works. They resembled pinnacles of light in a sea of dark ashes.

Although they were many, they acted like a single man, supporting each other beside their struggles. Never lowering their heads or standing submissive. Disciplined and united, under the banner of honor, over the flag of splendor, they were the nation of glory.

In one of the most dramatic and heroic blockades that the world had ever seen, they gave it all, but when it was all done, they still struggled to see hope.

In that moment, they exceeded everything by sacrificing everything. At that point, they had destroyed all their enemy's legions, but victory still seemed far for the leaders of all remaining things.

Now, at the shadow of the demons' last gate, they still had one last foe to defeat.

There he was – the one undestroyed. His captains and his personal guard laid dead in the waste beneath his feet. There he was, surrounded and alone, over the cliff that led to the Demon Portal. There he was, on the literal edge of the abyss.

The very air around him was fearful of him, escaping his presence. The touch of his feet burned the field's herbs for many miles in all directions.

His body was fury, his face was his kingdom – eternal rebellion.

The sun never shone in his presence, for he was the denial of light. The sky was never blue when he was under it.

He had no name to be called upon, as he was lower than evil itself. Lower than destruction, his right arm. Lower than death, his tool. When there was a need to name him, he was regretfully called The Lord of the Low.

Still, there he was: apparently, on the verge of defeat.

To impose that on him, the people of Fabula paid a price in blood that left an eternal scar on their souls. The whole world lost its innocence. Its creatures, people, kingdoms, nations, and races sacrificed like never before, or after.

They all fought for their lives in a truly total war. Kingdoms were consumed until exhaustion. Entire races went extinct. Mountains fell and valleys rose. It changed the world completely and fundamentally. Traditions were forgotten and legends forged. In the end, there were no more strong, brave, or cunning men. No more kings and princes, servants or slaves, they learned by force and pain to place themselves beyond all that. Among the few lives that remained, there were no more awards or penalties. There were no more first or last – there were only heroes.

Among those, in the spear tip, facing the enemy of everything and everyone, a man. Brave as lions, he faced wickedness itself. A man that had a vision of hope regardless of all the chaos and death. A man that, in this needy moment, against all chance, understood the purpose of his life. A man that, transporting himself for a broader understanding and a greater meaning, beheld and saw. He looked into the bottomless pit and spotted light, and he did that precisely when every single one of them had lost faith. When all shared the same hopeless despair, forming a wasteland of broken souls, the waters of faith broke from his eyes. They shone for an instant only, and it was enough.

There was not a single drop of defeat in him, there had never been. He was cleansed from the sin of loss. He was the incarnation of victory; he was destined to win, and now, he understood it. It was revealed unto him, into his soul. It came down from every bit of his body. The discharge of energy was so magnificent, that the air around him flickered and burst with sparks of an unseen splendor.

This man, as a man of destiny, had always been a man of few words, but now he knew exactly what to say. Even on that day, and at that moment. A moment where the whole world was soundless, and there was not even an echo to be heard over the face of the Ether, and all things were waiting for a decisive manifestation of fate.

When he turned around, all the seasoned marching armies behind him stopped at once. There was a silence that hushed all things – purpose was on the brink of manifesting itself in the writing of destiny. The voice of chance could not be heard at all.

All things were being dragged in a net of decisiveness. It was too much for mortal creatures to bear witness. The warrior's arms loosened strength, the bowman's bow loosened its tension, the wizard's staff lacked its reverberating magical light of his focus. The elves cried in anguish. The legs of the dwarfs stumbled and failed. Over the highest peak, there was fear in the heart of the proudest dragon. The fortune of the world was hanging by a thread as the strain reached its climax.

Precious and beautiful, the man's soul became clear as a diamond. He took the lead and went forth, shouting with his mighty breath,

'Oh hear me all! All there is!' they heard him.

'I have waged war on everything, against everything! From the smallest things to the highest meanings!' he shouted. Then, as if lamenting, he lowered his head.

'And I am victorious!' he said for himself, but even the clouds in the skies listened.

His words were, in that moment, magical. As he spoke, a new and unforeseen hope entered reality.

'Brothers!' he shouted. A ray of light escaped the unnatural disturbance of the skies and fell over them.

'Before us, something that cannot be defeated!' he pointed to the lord of the demons.

'He has always lived within, and now...now he has contaminated the mortals with the temptation of his essence.' Uncontrollable tears of despise and repulsion rolled bravely over his face as he said those words.

Then, he rested a gaze of disgust over the Lord of the Low.

'No!' he shouted in a strange despair as if he himself was contaminated by the tainted evil he was committed against. 'No one or nothing can defeat it!' His eyes froze in a fanatical stare full of doomed humane despair.

'But I have already defeated him!' His voice lowered as he unfolded his irresistible revelation.

Another ray of sunlight hit them. He was speaking in words that transcended rational understanding, but their souls were in a position where they could receive his truth. Magic was all around them.

'Alas! I have defeated it already!' he cried in such a terrible despair that it seemed that his soul was being ripped from his spirit.

He wept, and he had never wept before.

Although many could not understand the powerful emotions he was going through, so dominant was the momentum of his will that all hearts lamented with him. In communion, they shared the weight that was on his shoulders. In doing so, their hearts were taken out of their immediate reality and followed him to a place of higher sensations. When they got there, they shared, in total harmony, whatever was in him. Spontaneously and majestically, they all wept with him.

'Oh, hear me all!' He raised his voice once again to the skies and cried with even greater furor.

'I complete the impossible! For I am the Impossible Warrior!' With the echoes of those words, they all understood what a thousand poets could not tell them. They understood that the key to destiny was with him, even in him.

'Not yet,' as the voice of evil spoke, the war was upon all of them again.

The nightmarish voice waged war and uproar in the Ether itself. It opposed all things from within. It reverberated into the material world in horrific tunes of disturbances.

'Fool!' the obliterating voice continued.

'Submit yourself to me…there is no sacrifice that can save this world,' the Lord of the Low had spoken.

The mere sound of his speech made all substances which were not anchored under a heavy and complex equation to be disrupted, distorted, and altered horrifically around him. Rocks as big as castles shattered like river pebbles, iron objects deformed and lit on fire like wood sticks, flowers died on the other side of the world.

Ignoring his enemy's evil words, the man turned to his adversary and laughed innocently while further tears rolled down his face. He looked right past him. Even through the great many things within the creature's essence, and the great and vast complex geometry that composed what he truly was, the warrior set his mind above it all.

The man's eyes showed that his heart was redeemed. That brought fear deep within the multidimensional heart of the Lord of the Low.

The many legends about that moment say that the Impossible Warrior had eyes like the purest child, that his stare was docile and beautiful, as if he truly believed his vision and embodied it with all his being.

He raised his perfect sword in the air.

'No sacrifice!' he shouted a war cry that echoed forever in the hearts of the world's heroes.

They all listened incapable of doing anything, for his completion was not yet stablished.

With the power of his soul and his impetus, his cry altered very complex and broad equations throughout the spiritual world forevermore – before his act, his will prevailed.

'Glory!!!' The long shout sent a shockwave of invisible energy that agitated and renewed all legions. They gathered momentum like a falling mountain.

The Lord of the Low doubted and hesitated for the first time since eternity began.

'Oh, hear me all!' Not even the demon lord dared to interrupt him now.

'No sacrifice!' he shouted again, possessed by prophecy.

'I do not deliver my life! I confirm it!' A jubilation raptured all hearts to a state of emotions far beyond ecstasy.

'No sacrifice!!!' he repeated, sounding as the ultimate lion roar.

They were now all involved in a glorious daze as if they were powerfully daydreaming. Their souls were over their skins, energizing them beyond rational words could describe. In perfect communion, they all believed in him. Down, deep in themselves, they were one with him.

Nothing in this world, neither wild animal, nor dread fish, nor dragon, nor any serpent, no warrior, not even any elf had ever charged like that man did. Nor they ever will, till the end of time. Everything became prophetic in that moment when all things came together and that man held the fortune of the world in his grip.

With a single jump, he charged evil. His focus was as profound as it could be. Actually, by the very nature of the things that were unfolding, it was beyond that, for his prophetic will reached a point of transcendence, breaking through reality, inverting existing polarities. His acts changed the laws of the Multiverse while molding it at the same time, inverting things deeply rooted in the first creation. With and within his actions, he took total control of the actuality and re-wrote reality. It was a surprising thing, a new thing, and no one was expecting it.

He attacked, and his foe couldn't resist him. With destiny itself fueling his wits, he sliced the head and a large portion of the avatar's thorax, just as the Ancient Ones had instructed him to do. When his blade went through the demon's chest, it gutted the Lord of the Low's Soul Binder in two.

The creature's body, as all bodies that exist in the material world, must be connected with their spiritual architecture. As so, the lord's body had no heart for his spirit was devoid of mercy. He also had no blood as his soul always stood as an enemy of life since creation came forth. To kill it, it was necessary to separate the head from the body and to physically destroy the fountain of his existing energy – a phylactery shaped in a form of a jewel called Soul Binder.

Still driven by the same energy, and as if in a single movement, the man went down the Abyss below. In one hand his sword and in the other the demon lord's head and part of its torso. He held it by one of the creature's horns, like a brute savage fiercely griping a piece of mauled hunt.

It was a splendid image, and the creatures witnessing it knew that they were watching something out of the ordinary. It was the perfect physical picture of what was happening in the higher dimensions, for this time the forces of the universe had been inverted, and reality, a sincere shadow of the spiritual world, had projected and changed the high heavens, forcing the floods of existence to run in the opposite direction.

Through the anchorage of his act, all life on Fabula kept on existing. Because of him, Fabula had won. The physical world had won. Reality had won.

His deed summarized a symbol to all further existence's destiny. It showcased that all things were really possible, and that nothing was truly impossible. The consequence of his attack became a very capable and broad equation. It changed everything, and a new hope in a new creation echoed throughout the Ether.

While the man fell, the portal retracted. The power to keep it open was bound to the demon's existential mind, therefore it shrunk as his conscience left the world due to the death of his material body and the destruction of his Soul Binder.

While they fell, the impure interference of the hectic energies that were being poured from the dimension of pure chaos on the other side of the portal was gradually substituted by the natural and harmonic sounds of the running water of the Rowdy River.

The edges of the portal were full of existential instability, for it takes immense paradoxes to keep it open. The window between the two dimensions took a finite but hyper-complex amount of equational realignments in other to stabilize and exist. The balance of equations that kept the inter-world door within the realm of possibilities was generating a flux of chaotic and fluid trans-dimensional energy that could alter and create anything. As the Impossible Warrior touched that area during his fall, his matter and spirit transmuted and realigned itself in a unique way. With his will, he forced the theme of this transmutation to be the very essence of his act and the intensity of his own courage. He held his destiny, fulfilling it to the last molecule. His essence was fused with the mighty spirit and the equations contained in his sword.

As he vanished inside the disappearing portal, he used the infinite energy contained in the portal paradox to stamp himself in many dimensions, becoming a powerful, stable, and beautiful equation. That equation was his legacy, and the true legacy of the Land of Valkar. He blessed that land with fragments of his soul, for the balance that stabilizes the universe did not allow him to fade away, and his spirit survived.

He conquered death, confirming his vision, fulfilling his life. He won his path out of existence, and on that day, in that hour, he completed himself by becoming greater than himself – an eternal champion.

Faithful to his words, therefore, he had not delivered himself, he had not become a sacrifice. His body and spoils transcended into the Ether, but his sword escaped that destiny and the closing of the portal. After a disturbing gather of air by an unnatural vacuum, the portal collapsed and an explosion followed.

Driven by the power of the blast the sword flew across the air. Under the light of the undiscovered dawn of a new world, it flew across the air. Followed by the gaze of all the world's heroes, it flew across the air. Under the first pure and true sun ray in a long time, it flew across the air. It flew high in the sky, and all eyes followed it as it started to descend furiously. It landed with a firm and boisterously metallic sound. As if giving pursuit to the dark forces, hitting firmly right where the Demon Portal had the base of its focal point.

The blade penetrated deeply in the top of the gigantic boulder. The supernatural sparks that poured from the impact lit the waters of the river on fire, so powerful was the collateral energy when the sword magically sealed the gate with its last stroke. As the matter around it was still unstable when it landed on the rock, it merged itself with it, enchanting the land with aspects of its essence, and blessing its people with the strength to exercise a watchful peace over all good things in the world.

From that day forward, the blade remained there, symbolizing the unquestionable gratitude and admiration they held for what the Impossible Warrior achieved. It became the real foundation of their nation, and the Valkarians treasured it as their most precious possession. It was the true north of their aspirations as a people, and the source of their luck, their power, their legends and, eventually, their empire.

The Valkarian Empire and the Sons of the Impossible Warrior

Valkar was at peace.

Following the struggles it went through after The First War, it was at peace. After the bloody expansion and colonization period that hardened its people's hearts, it was at peace. After centuries of useless and regrettable internal conflicts for power, it was at peace. After the consumption of a whole generation fighting a devastating dragon army in their last war, it was at peace. Although Valkar was now known as the nation of countless battles, it was, now, at peace.

With the centuries, the realm became too big to be called a kingdom. It was too large, it had too many powerful lords, and an excess of giant fortresses and mighty warriors. Upon understanding this, shortly after the frontiers stabilized and its expansion era came to an end, the Valkarians named their claimed land an empire.

The most powerful among its lords was elected Emperor. However, his authority was very weak in the beginning, consisting mostly of solving minor disputes among the lords. In time, its powers grew tremendously, mostly due to the necessity of a strong centralized government to deal with the many external threats they faced.

It is well recognized that it wasn't by chance that the Valkarian Empire became an empire. This fact was due too, in great measure, to its people's imperious attitude. After all, since the beginning, the Valkarians were destined to manifest a boldness toward the way they dealt with their political and social matters – they were (and still are) deeply noble folks.

This nobility was profoundly rooted in their characters and had naturally passed from generation to generation. For, in general, they cannot tolerate evil or tyranny, valuing freedom above everything else. They are eager to enjoy peace, but never hesitate waging war. And, once they do it, they do it with unrestful disposition and cold discipline until they see it to conclusion.

The descendants of the Impossible Warrior faced many problems during the times of the first frontiers and the expansion. So many, that they became avid and open-minded regarding the adoption of solutions for their many problems. Their predispositions for action and practicalities were forged through their harsh history during that period. In time, they came to be a tough, open, and pragmatic people who knew what to value and when not to waste their time.

Demographically, the Valkarian Empire was populated predominantly, but not only, by the human race. Humans, in all its varieties, were one of the most adaptable and definitely the most prolific race in Fabula. Their ways were fundamental to the empire's foundation, but overtime there were also many different influences that formed the Valkarian Empire.

Since its inception, the folks that established the first Valkarian kingdoms were accessible and open to anyone who would help them defend their land. The constant state of emergency caused by the ever-present danger of the surrounding hostile creatures gave them no option but to accept and welcome any help they might find. Because of sheer necessity, racial prejudices were expunged very early in their history. It was sacrificed in the altar of necessity. Whoever wanted to join in and abide by the few laws they enforced were accepted and welcomed into their villages, towns, and armies, regardless of their race and cultural differences.

Although Valkarians tended to be quick in drawing their sharp blades, tolerance was high across their cities. Having no time for small problems, everything and everyone that were not an immediate menace to their wellbeing and freedom were gladly left alone or pushed into a favorable friendship. They were quick to notice that the advantage of amalgamation offered an obvious advantage for their collective security.

The result of centuries of this open-minded non-declared friendly policy caused them to completely integrate many different tribes, races, and nations into their own nation. Thus, until this day, there are many pockets of exotic populations throughout the empire, most of them considering themselves a part of it as any human would.

These populations, although living under the direct authority of the Emperor, and being susceptible to a call to arms to fight in the empire's wars, are allowed a great amount of independence among their kept territories. Nevertheless agreements vary, these communities are taxed regularly as any other protectorate or realm under the guard of the Emperor. Even if those groups live under an apparent isolation, most non-human folks have been fused with the general population to the point that there are no clear discernible differences among them and a human citizen's civil life. They plow fields, do business, fall in love, hunt orcs, are hunted by dragons, and commit crimes just as any Valkarian human would do.

Geographically, the Valkarian Empire sits mostly over silent long plains, but there are many types of irregular and mystic terrains all over the land.

In the north, in the high plateaus that border the Fire Mountains, there is an extensive and profitable trade. The Valkarians forged, and have carefully kept, strong alliances with all the dwarf kingdoms and most of the independent cities in the Fire Mountains. Therefore, the dwarves' cities under the mountains are one of the most close trading partner of the empire.

Centuries of friendship among the Valkarians and the short folks have created a unique relationship between them. The citizens of the Under Realm have free transit in the imperial lands and are welcome to settle down everywhere in the empire. In the same way, the citizens of the empire are treated with fairness in the deep forts of the forge's masters.

It is well known, and proven, that the dwarves and Valkarians share much more than just trade. Their interests and ambitions fall in the same place more often than not, and it is not rare for them to march to war together, but one thing that they truly share in great friendship, is their hatred for the malicious dragons that plague the Fire Mountains.

In the East lies the rocky Valkarian coast. It is a place of high adventure where waves and pirates constantly clash over the empire's shores. There, through the centuries, the Emperors have conquered and built great port-cities. Valkar was one of them. It was the empire's capital and was the starting point of the establishment of the Valkarian Empire. It is not exactly on the seaside, but it is considered a coastal city for its easy and close connection to the sea through the Rowdy River.

The Capital, as it is known, is the most northern point of the empire. It faces the dreadful Lava Peak – a fire spiting mountain deep and high in the Fire Mountains. The city stands vigilant over the Lava Peak, faithfully guarding its perpetual fiery turmoil as a bastion.

Throughout the rich history of the many accomplishments of the Valkarian Empire, the backbones of their reputation and the reason why they are well known and respected around the world, were their boldness and their intense will power. The stories and legends about it are loud enough for its echo to be heard many hundreds of miles along the horizon of the high seas.

Since its inception, the empire was created through, with, and for the destruction of enemies seated in the vast fertile lands of its interior and for the neutralization of the legions that menaced its frontiers from the exterior. The hundreds of years of forced colonization among its violent territory indoctrinated the Valkarians in the deepest military mindset. They train their children for war as soon as they can stand. They learn to read books first and foremost to study military manuals. The Cavalry is the ecstasy of the youth, and sports that simulate war are the favorite pastime of the population. In Valkarian, "home" and "fortress" are expressed by the same word.

Destiny allowed the Valkarians no peaceful choice. For them, to make war and to make living was not much different. This culture of conflict had already reached its peak several hundred years ago, and war always was and still is lurking throughout the empire.

Since its foundation, the Valkarian Empire wasn't more than an ever-expanding melting pot of powerful baronies with a relatively feeble central government. During the first centuries, it was not much more than an alliance of vast kingdoms united under the same banner when in need.

In time they prevailed, and their many sacrifices paid off. They thrived with the relative stability brought by the establishment of large fortress-cities in strategic locations throughout the territory, the reduction of internal conflicts for power, and the construction of a long-paved road system with an efficient communication outposts scheme. The impacts of the utility of mail and transport systems across the vast tracts of land were felt in trade, which grew exponentially, pushing for greater integration, forming a circle of development that solidified and institutionalized the establishment of the empire as it is today. With that, and at the same time, the central government got stronger and stronger, until one day the barons woke up with a real emperor on their hands.

Two generations ago, desperate over the threat of an invasion from massive and powerful hordes of a clan of red dragons from the Lava Peak, the Emperor Kassius III reorganized the Baronies, centralizing the economy and the military to an extent never seen before. He then named brave men to see the Emperor's interests across the territory. A caste of foreseers selected among the cream of the crop. Men of sober minds, noble hearts, and legendary fighting skills were recruited amid the army lines and were subjected to an oath of loyalty to the Emperor himself. They were called the Black Lions and were supposed to act as the eyes, ears and, especially, the heart of the Emperor throughout the land.

For the first time, there was reasonable political stability, allowing the Emperor to fully focus the strength of Valkar, directing it to destroy its external enemies one by one.

With nothing in their way, one after the other, the vast and well-supported imperial troops systematically eliminated the dragons, the remaining ancestral beasts and the rogue creatures that still lingered inside the empire's borders.

The more the empire strengthened, the more enemies it gathered though. But the energy mustered by the Emperor proved to be irresistible and could not be defeated. Anyone that opposed the Valkarians were defeated battle after battle, and the Valkarian Imperial flag became the standard of victory.

The top of this historical moment was The War of the Flame. It was a war that lasted generations, letting behind deep marks and endless tales of heroism. In it, the tyrannical red dragons from the Lava Peak gathered all the empire's enemies over their mighty claws, and under the lawless banner of the Red Legions, they waged a cruel war against the Valkarians and their allies.

Gradually and painfully, the invading dragon's armies were persecuted, besieged, and destroyed. Then, Heironeus II, the grandson of Kassius III, fielded one of the most formidable armies that had ever marched on mortal lands and charged the Lava Peak, challenging the dragons to a final and decisive battle.

At the Battle of Broken Bones, Xshisrahil, the great enemy of Valkar, the matriarch of the red dragons and supreme commander of the Red Legions, accepted the Emperor's challenge and joined the fight. With an immense cost, and aided by many powers that had an interest in Xshisrahil's destruction and the preservation of the empire, Heironeus II prevailed on the battlefield. The Red Legions were destroyed and the remaining red dragons were forced to retreat, seeking shelter in dark caves away from the Valkarian's borders.

In time, Valkar's wounds were healed, and under the wise government of Heironeus II, the empire enjoyed a period of peace and prosperity that lasted more than twenty years. In it, a whole new generation came to be. These young men and women grew up isolated from desperation, with the true meaning of war feebly floating among old stories. This, however, was about to change.

Unlearning to End Things

The perennial sounds of clashing and bashing were all around them. It was the typical background noise of a Valkarian training camp.

As they practiced from sunset to dawn, the clamor went the whole day on. As they trained from the first to the last day of the year, it resonated all year around. It was part of the landscape, a perpetual vibration that filled the air around the camp – it never went quiet.

The students trained tirelessly. Whether it was sunny, snowing, or raining, they trained. Blood and sweat.

Swords clashed with daggers, their sisters. Spears with shields, cousins. Darts and arrows hit their targets with great force and precision while sweat dripped on the ground like rain, seasoning it with different colors and a contrasting texture. Blood and sweat.

Platoons of young men and women divided into age groups obsessively trained under the watchful eyes of their instructors. Day after day they never stopped fighting, loving every second of it. Blood and sweat was their motto.

It was late in the afternoon when, gradually, the background noise of the skirmishing weapons diminished slowly but surely. A feeling of novelty spread across the camp.

A static electricity grew in the air. A blue bird that happened to be nearby stopped what it was doing, interrupting its flight midair. With a piece of hay still in its beak, it settled down on a tree branch. Scared, it pushed its senses trying to spot a given sudden catastrophe.

The blue bird was not alone in his silence and tension, for all the birds and the critters that lured nigh got so accustomed to the noise, that they became apprehensive and oddly quiet when, for some reason, the racket ceased.

In the middle of the strange quietness, a new fuss took the stage. From a sea of innumerable knocks and bangs, a single sequence came forth. It was similar to the previous for it was also combat, but it was undoubtedly more refined, carrying a singularity and a muteness on itself. It was somewhat less methodical, uneventful. The sounds were quite innovative, full of spontaneous emotions and expertise.

In the area where the advanced level students trained, two senior pupils faced each other in close combat. Noticing the unusual agitation, the younger warriors stopped whatever they were doing and ran to see the fighters. A mob quickly formed around them. Some of the younger students, willing to witness the fight, placed themselves between the legs of the taller, older colleagues. A few climbed over their friend's shoulders, for everything was valid to watch what was coming to pass.

Instructors were silently observing it, struggling not to show signs of excitement and to keep their professionalism. They whispered their impressions in hushed tones amongst themselves. Sometimes openly covering their mouths to hide the content of their arguments.

In the middle of it all, within a circle of people, there were two fine examples of young Valkarians. They were fiercely competing for each inch of ground in a ferocious yet highly disciplined brawl.

Strong, broad-shouldered, and tall, they could now be mistaken for grown men, but their eyes gave their immaturity away upon a lingering boyish light that still rested upon their gazes.

Despite the beautiful techniques both were displaying, what really caught the attention of the audience was the way they fought. Everyone knew them and were aware of their antagonistic competitiveness and fond friendship.

They both were very talented, but, at the same time, they were different in every conceivable way. One was emotional, the other cold and distant. One was focused, the other a true provocateur. One was insecure, the other arrogantly confident. One was an attacker, the other a counter-attacker. Although representing two distinct things, together, at that moment, they reflected one thing only: dispute. And the audience loved that.

They were best friends, always had been since they were small children. In different ways, both had habitually found comfort in their friendship, but when competing, even the teachers admired their unusual determination to win. It was as if both were, for different reasons, fighting some ghost that had claimed their peace. As if an invisible hated enemy that haunted their souls surfaced over their thoughts every time they fought. They never seemed to really fight each other, but glimmers of their most profound and intimate feelings – dark presences on their minds. Every time they were in combat, a possession changed their disposition, bringing them to their real edges, demanding the very best out of them and putting one hundred percent of themselves in the present.

'Give up, farm boy, the last one is mine,' Lucien said with a struggling smile on his face, as he forced the handle of his wooden sword down against Bastian's.

'The first one was not yours, nor will be the last,' replied Bastian, willing to distract his friend.

Bastian grasped the momentum trying to get rid of his unfavorable position. He knew that Lucien was dangerous with his counterattacks and defenses combined with attack, especially with the hand-and-a-half sword, ideal weapon for this. Willing to counter that, Bastian directed Lucien's sword to the course he needed by letting it slide through his. Then he deployed a brief feint and a kick in Lucien's stomach. They disengaged.

'Hum! The outcome of that battle was never clear, peasant!' said Lucien ironically, struggling with pain. 'However, you affirm that victory was yours?' Lucien threw a provocative look, looking for any distraction in Bastian's defense so he could recover from the stomach kick.

Lucien kept himself in a defensive position while he formulated a strategy that could provide him an advantage. He was searching for any words that would tingle Bastian's ego and diminish his focus on the fight, creating an attack window for him. Bastian, however, remained concentrated as a lion. His eyes, his mind, his everything was fixed in his target.

His technique is very good, they both thought, trying to find ways to get the upper hand over each other. Although they were both aware of the mind battle, the two of them knew better, hiding their impressions in the back of their eyes as deep as they could, for mirroring their intentions over their eyes was the same as broadcasting their next move, a sure way for defeat. A battlefield is not a place for sincerity, and they both knew that.

'I did not say that I won, gentleman. I meant that you didn't!' At the very moment Lucien's brain was processing Bastian's response, at the time of his maximum distraction, Bastian attacked directly with his great sword. The distraction and the attack were effective; Bastian managed to flank Lucien. He even found time to resettle his weapon up straight. A fundamental necessity, as his two-handed sword was heavier and slower. This type of sword was so complex in its handling, that it demanded Bastian to always overthink his next move so he could keep the initiative. And that was also the reason why he got used to never executing a single attack. He would always present a preconceived combination of blows. Lucien knew that, and Bastian knew that he knew.

Things were running fast now. Leg wise, Bastian put himself in a much better position, but he needed far more space to hit with his two-handed sword blade. Willing to do just that, Bastian anticipated and slap-kicked Lucien in the torso with a lightning-fast round kick before he could attack.

Surprised once again, Lucien flew several feet before regaining equilibrium. Struggling with the pain of a second direct blow, Lucien jumped into the air to recover his leg control. He landed in the dust, sliding, standing like a cat. Lucien was very agile, but Bastian had the mind of a real warrior, managing to surprise him for a second time now.

Lucien was now in his own personal hell, he was in the place he hated the most – he got his pride hurt. All his being was now committed to make Bastian pay for the formidable disengaging kick and sequences of blows he suffered. In Lucien's eyes, a strange glow was now sparkling. Many had learned to fear it during the years he had spent in the camp. Throughout his time in the training camp, students and teachers knew that he was terribly daring and intensively careless about any damage to his body, but his ego was another story. Bitter and malicious, he leaned to the left keeping his legs firm.

Bastian, knowing that he had far more reach than Lucien due to his longer blade, and knowing also about Lucien's aggressive nature, took advantage of this situation and decided to move forward and attack. He was willing to unleash a flurry of blows, taking the initiative out of Lucien and leaving his weapon out of range. Bastian knew that he had to keep Lucien under relentless pressure or he might not resist his friend's dangerous counter-attacks and lose the fight. However, when Bastian ran to execute his attack plan, Lucien followed his movements as he was reading and timing them. Demonstrating a great knowledge of tempo, sensing a hint on Bastian's feet that indicated he was preparing to make a long throw with a spin attack, Lucien discreetly leaned his sword straight in the back of his forearm, pointing it up, aligning it with his torso. Then he threw his weight to the left, spinning with Bastian in the same direction as him, stretching his legs in the largest arch he could make, practically jumping furtively into the position he deemed correct. He completed a movement that was very similar to a long and jumpy boxing dodge, using his core as a swivel. It was a vicious and unexpected move, and it wrenched smiles of satisfaction from some of the blade masters that were watching.

With great agility and excellent timing, Lucien managed to infiltrate Bastian's attack, neutralizing his reach advantage and subverting his guard to the right on his left flank. When Bastian finished his attack spin, he did not find Lucien where he hoped he would. Bastian was not even aware of Lucien's position for a split second.

Lucien, perfectly positioned behind Bastian, applied a blow on his knee, forcing Bastian to kneel out of balance. Then he mercilessly, and even dangerously, went to strike Bastian's neck with the wrist of his sword. Yet, Bastian learned very well to keep his vitals protected against adversaries equipped with lighter weapons than his. He had studied with great precision the two-perimeter defense technique, which was created by no one less than Lankan the Strong. Therefore, in the second he lost Lucien's position from sight, he intuitively lowered his head, forcing a bearing, thus recovering the guard and his defensive capabilities even if he was now in a disadvantageous squatting position.

Surprised by the emptiness in which his strike had fallen, Lucien changed the direction of his blade with the speed of someone who had trained his very instincts to battle. He managed to follow Bastian, denying him space to maneuver his big, heavy sword. Then he raised his blade behind his head, in the scorpion position, and started using piercing attacks with the tip of his sword. His impressive footwork kept Bastian in check, forcing him to systematically retreat at every one of Lucien's blows.

Realizing the difficult situation, he found himself in, Bastian took an instantaneous field decision: he would force a defense from Lucien's piercing attacks, letting him move up his weapon to the height of his wrist and then he would disarm his friend. In doing so, Bastian did not take into consideration the agility of Lucien's hips, and when he turned to finish his sequence with a hook attack, Lucien was already out of range.

In a single fluent movement, Bastian then hurled himself backward with the force generated when he tried to grip his friend's weapon. While at it, Bastian barely dodged the deadly hook instantly deployed by Lucien's opportunistic style.

Immediately after rolling together, they simultaneously perceived that their advantageous positions were re-established, finding themselves into a full-fledged exchange. They were openly and brutally engaging in a furious sequence of attacks, counter-attacks, defenses, and feints that made experienced spectators nurture great respect for the talent that the young men were showing.

As the fight became more and more impulsive, Lucien had a moment of illumination. In a counterattack charge, he left Bastian in an awful position, creating a lateral opening on Bastian's flank. Then, he did a very precise and fast frontal attack, stopping his blade at Bastian's neck.

'Aha! The sweet taste of victory!' Sweat ran down Lucien's beautiful face, covering his long dark brown hair. His dilated eyes were still fogged by the overcoming insanity of his revenge. He had the smile of a contained madman and was breathing heavily.

'Attention, my good man.' With his eyes, Bastian pointed to Lucien's chest. There, rested the tip of Bastian's sword. His knees hinted the efficiency of his attack. Lucien read the situation and his eyes collapsed on an abyss of surprise and doubt.

'Have we managed to reach another draw?' asked Bastian after he made sure Lucien saw his under-the-guard little trick.

'Irony? This is not your specialty…farm boy,' said Lucien, disappointed, as he lowered his blade.

Neither noticed the applause and cheering from the audience. It all felt like background noise to them, for their minds were still deep into the fight. The spectators dispersed and went back to whatever they had been doing before, but the two friends continued to discuss the outcome of the match, although knowing all too well that it had been a draw.

'Don't be like that, Lucien.' Bastian tried to give him some space. 'You defend yourself as if you are excusing your defeat, but it was just another tie. Calm down.' he said while massaging his own damaged knee. Knowing his friend as he did, Bastian was willing to irritate Lucien beyond his limits, so he would drop the subject. Often, this was the only way to bring Lucien out of a discussion without damaging their relation.

'If I ever lose to you, I'd lay down on my own sword,' said Lucien, willing to end the subject. 'You're as slow as my grandmother.' He smiled a light pretentious smile, recovering a little humor as he put his equipment away, finally letting the argument go.

'Oh, come on! What were you thinking?' Bastian fueled the argument even more while removing the leather protection from his own legs. 'That you were finally going to defeat me before the end of our last year?' Bastian smiled, willing to provoke Lucien's ego, pushing him again into the discussion.

'My friend, the mere fact that you are still breathing depends on my victory in life. Know your place and cheer for me,' Lucien said, not willing to give Bastian an inch, as he noticed what his friend was trying to do.

'My noble victory over my own self,' he continued. 'On the contrary! My noble consciousness, weakened by all the small competitive and brutal nature of our inner lower man, would have placed yourself into your RIGHTEOUS berth, peasant!' Lucien liked to speak as a proper nobleman just to arrogantly rub his high-born education and, therefore, position, over Bastian's face.

'Is it so? And what did you get out of it?' Bastian laughed carefreely. He knew well how to deal with some of Lucien's tactics at this point.

'I avoid conflicts between classes in this poor training camp,' said Lucien while sipping some water and looking around. His eyes were provocatively arrogant. His gaze kept a mix of irony and smugness with a hint of humor. Although he had an overall charming personality, he could be altogether terrible in his intentions.

'What are you going to do after graduation?' asked Bastian trying to change the subject, as none of them seemed to be capable of annoying each other to peace anymore.

'I don't know,' Lucien answered, and started considering it. Upon reflecting on Bastian's question, he changed expression completely.

'I have not thought about it much really,' he said, trying not to mind it, but showing signs he was hit hard by the mere thought it.

'Probably will be a squire for one of my dad's political allies,' he said resentfully, as if he was vomiting the words rather than saying them. His face reflected the awful taste they left in his mouth.

'Want to join me?' asked Bastian softly, sensing the tension, and knowing he was bringing up a delicate issue.

'You're a stubborn little meathead, aren't you?' Really irritated, Lucien instantly changed his expression and the tone of his voice.

Bastian instantly knew he touched a nerve or two.

'I cannot take it out of my head,' Bastian excused himself, looking away. There was a misplaced tiredness in his gaze. 'I have been dreaming about it. A lot,' revealed Bastian, as if he was confessing some secret to his friend. His voice indicated a heavy emotional burden.

'I think you are putting too much thought into it,' said Lucien trying to take his friend's mind off the topic. 'Come, let us go to town. I'm paying. As usual,' he said, attempting to cheer Bastian up.

'No. Not this time, Lucien.' Bastian was dead serious, and although he was too young for bitterness, a shadow lingered over his face. When Lucien noticed it, he got a little scared.

'Thank you, brother, but I'm going home.' Bastian collected his things and gave his friend a firm handshake and an honest smile, making sure to show that he cared about Lucien. The emotional momentum was such that even the cold Lucien was speechless. Bastian hung his canvas backpack over his right shoulder and quietly walked away. He disappeared among the clouds of dust and the late-afternoon low-angle golden sunrays that showered the training camp.

Lucien was immobilized by the reality stroke that had just hit him. He found himself too confused to even call Bastian back and try to convince him out of his plans. He stood there alone. His thoughts were his sole companions, but he despised most of them. Empty and shocked, he looked at the Dire Woods in the distance.

At first, he worried about his friend and felt nostalgic for the first time in his life. It was a powerful feeling, even for someone who had avoided them during most of his brief existence.

Only now he faced the fact that his training was complete. The last minute of his last day was finally upon him. His routine was broken, and the life he knew with it also. His stubborn heart avoided thinking about this moment for a long time and now it was here. Now, it was his immediate reality, and it was utterly terrifying to him.

He desperately tried to gather why he found himself so depressed and scared. Quickly he found the answer: it was their last day of school and he had no place to go. Rather, no place he was willing to be in. And so, he sat in the first place he found. For even his mighty legs failed him.

His life appeared interrupted, gutted. The new perspective he now had to put forth seemed to be too heavy of a burden. Not finding any answer within him, he raised his eyes and turned his head, looking around. Yet, he was, in reality, looking inside himself.

The air was thick with the excitement of the younger students that were about to go on their yearly break. It was the end of a high summer afternoon. The atmosphere around him was lingering that kind of dense heat that accumulates throughout a hot day. The sun was flooding the place with an orange horizontal light, lengthening the shadows to its limits. The intense landscape mixed with the dust raised by all the running around, playing, and fighting of hundreds of very energetic young pupils. It all looked surreal to him, he no longer had a place to belong to, and the wistfulness was overwhelming.

Lucien watched it all with mirrored eyes. He felt like he was the only one paying attention. Everything seemed to be at a different speed now. Life was passing by in slow motion. His eyes, as his heart, were capturing all the small moments that were unfolding around him in this once deeply familiar place. A group of young children playing with each other, a couple of instructors laughing at a joke, and a dog chasing a blue bird. He looked around in vain, trying to connect himself to that place one more time. It was all for nothing, for although he noticed all moments that normally went by hidden under the clouds of routine, he couldn't find his place there.

The training ground was the only world he knew, only there he had control. He felt a sudden, clear, and cold limit between him and the life he knew there. Suddenly, they cut his umbilical cord, but they forgot to warn him. An emotional barrier was pushing him out. It was the end of an era, but he was having a hard time accepting it.

Looking around, he realized that most of the things he had lived there were now only memories. That world seemed so different from what he was seeing around him now that his life there could have happened a thousand years ago. It wouldn't matter. He did not matter.

There were so many new faces. He felt like the place was rejecting him. As if his time was due and there was now this cruel necessity to leave, to make space for others, to change. And he hated change.

The worst thing about this crushing feeling was that it was true. He felt disconnected, directionless, lost.

Lucien was not good at dealing with emotions, he suppressed them whenever he could. Now, a terrible anxiety made his stomach ache. He was the kind of person who could not stand melancholy or intense feelings. When he had no alternative, he would either deny it with irony and cynicism, or eagerly search for relief in alcohol or worse.

The anxiety he was now feeling was making him truly sick – there was no relief or escape from it this time. He had to face the moment he was denying for a long time. He had to leave, but where to? He felt truly alone for the first time. Only now, at the last minute of the last day, when forced to face the truth that his training there ended, he finally started accepting that it was over. It was all over.

Bastian easily and unceremoniously left, and Lucien was now all by himself, with nothing but a terrible solitude to keep him company. He found it impossible to leave, so he stood there. Sat. Watching the golden sun dive on the horizon and the long kids' shadows dancing around in the dust.

What you going to do after graduation? Bastian's words kept ringing in his head like a bell.

Lucien had thought about it, obviously, but when the moment to turn the page and close the book finally came, a load of unexpected emotions hit him hard. He suddenly found himself in a world of shattered routines and void meanings. Nothing was holding him to that place anymore, he could leave now and never come back, but still he lingered around. That thought of leaving that place seemed violent and brutal to him somehow. He hated above all to be a victim, but, alone, he braced himself and took the full blow of those feelings.

At home or on the training grounds, Lucien was always surrounded by many people, but he hid himself from everyone, even his siblings. Pride and fear of looking weak had made him mask his feelings. He concealed himself by forcing part of him to the back of his mind. That part of him, maybe his best, lived isolated from the world deep inside his heart. However, the old snow finally melts and the old seeds eventually bloom. And, as long as he could remember, anger grew within him because of this self-imposed repression, filling his personality with many dangerous things, making him prone to infatuation. Still, Lucien was extremely intelligent and sensible in his own way, and deep down he was perfectly aware of who he was. He also knew that Bastian was conscious of his flaws, but Bastian had a heart full of empathy, being, still, a surprisingly innocent person. For that reason, even if subconsciously, Lucien knew that Bastian would never really hurt him, and he was the only one Lucien dared to hang around, despising everybody else.

In that instant, however, upon contemplating his empty future, he had nothing to hate and a lot to fear. Thus, situation forced him to deal with his exposed self, a thing he had avoided his whole life. More so now, when his ego was shaken by the realization that he had always carried all that weakness inside of him.

This was the first time Lucien looked behind in his life. Like a broken dam, the weight of his overflowing emotions was unbearable, and he hated feeling vulnerable like that.

He had spent most of his time on the training grounds, always using it as an excuse for not having to deal with his family problems and his future. Now, thinking about them, he perceived he had always been in denial. Lucien was a very intelligent and sensitive person, he was capable of self-criticism, and, upon his contemplations, he concluded that his whole life was nothing more than a culmination of his efforts to disconnect himself from his own life. He felt like almost everything he had ever done was pointless. He tasted the most bitter defeat, for he had no enemy but himself and he was still losing. It all felt like a waste.

After ruminating on that for a time, he suddenly noticed that the fear and anxiety that were tormenting him were about, above all, his future. He trembled as he looked forward, feeling how dark of an abyss uncertainty really was.

Now that he had lost his safe place he felt disoriented and hopeless, clueless about his direction in life. Watching those young kids fighting in the middle of this golden particle-filled air just increased his sadness, as he remembered his first years.

There were so many memories! he thought. *Good memories,* he corrected himself. *Great memories,* he corrected again.

He tried to make sense of all that for a moment. Until he realized he needed to decide what to do with his life and needed to do it right now. He then wished. He wished that if he could, he would have kept it the same. He desired he could stay there endlessly, trapped in the secure routines he knew so well. He felt so strong about making all those lost moments go on forever, but he couldn't, or could he? He concluded and accepted that his nature could not bear otherwise. He would not change. If he was going to live his life, he would do it his own way. No matter what. He would affirm himself and fight for what he wanted. There was no other way for him.

In the training fields he was successful, he had control over his life. He had control over the world around him. He had no responsibility and he liked it that way. He knew that out there, in the real world, he was nobody. It was a wild world and he was frightened by it. In a perfectly accurate epiphany, he understood he was scared of it because he had no control over it at all.

Then, after a sincere recollection, he concluded that this was the thing that was in fact disturbing him the whole time. He measured it for a while and as the last sun rays began disappearing in the horizon, he sealed it. Not in his head, but in his heart. He made his heart, and in that instant a feeling was born into his soul that would fuel him for the rest of his life, through the brightest or the darkest moments. It was far more than mere rationality. He made peace with the idea that the only way for him to be himself, in a world that eagerly demanded changes from him, was to not change his ways at all. Rather, he would change his surrounding realities. He would change the world.

Propelled by an immense fear, he decided that he would take charge of his fate, and he was not going to be a subject of the will of others. He was not sure if he was going to do something meaningful with his life, but he was most certainly not abiding by others' rules.

This was the one thing he decided. This was the one thing that gave him peace. This was the one thing he found that gave him purpose and made life bearable for him. This was the one thing he could not go without even if it cost him his life. He would live his life on his own terms, no matter what.

No matter what, he said to himself, really meaning it. His heart was as bitter as one's could be. Its acidity sealed his wounds.

When he had produced all his resolutions and rooted them deep in his soul, and there was nothing more to think about, he stood up and left. The last daylight disappeared in the horizon while he speedily rode his horse home.

Leeroy

As the seventh child of a well-placed family in the imperial society, Leeroy had the luxury of a lot of freedom. From his older brothers and sisters much was requested, but from him very little. Mostly, to stay out of the way.

His perspective was different from the norm, very unique. It is enough to say that his vision of the world fell short of his parent's opinion.

His proud and pragmatic family had little patience for him and his constantly distant mind. Over the years, they themselves paid him no attention. He became nothing but an idling shadow that roamed his family mansion's gardens. He silently went around, minding what everybody ignored and ignoring what everyone minded.

Apparently, no one could or cared to understand him, and he had never felt the need to explain himself. He lived isolated in his mind, alone inside his own world, shaping his own ideas of reality. Daydreaming while answering himself the questions of his own making.

Repressed by his aristocratic, competitive, and strong-willed siblings, he created his own universe inside his head, living there as much as he could. He considered the world, and the people on it, cruel things and learned to enjoy his time alone.

When observed in public places, he was thought by all as an oppressed boy. Some went as far as to suggest that he was "mildly underdeveloped," so far his ways went from a regular Valkarian lad. This label, however, was far from the truth. Leeroy was highly intelligent and superbly sensible to all things around him. However, it was true that his blossoming mind could not concentrate on something objective for a long time. Not because he couldn't, but because of his sheer lack of interest in pure materialism. He loved his mind games and everything subjective about them. He didn't know then, but he was meant to see the broader picture.

Owner of an eager mind, Leeroy considered all the things he could understand to be unbearably tedious. Learning, for him, was not an instant action. It was a constant, multifaceted, never-ending hunger. His personality was the mask he wore to interact with the world he observed. Reserving his true self only for his fantasies. He lived in true loneliness, and he was perfectly fine with it.

His mind did not flourish linearly, but exponentially. He could only be dragged forward by nothing but the winds of his intimal passion. Leeroy couldn't bare the common selfish desires for power that propelled people. He couldn't motivate himself through the simple accumulation of knowledge, or the mere achieving of rather illusional positions in other people's worlds and schemes. He was one of those rare cases when one's motivated by the love of truth.

He was not an athlete, but he was dangerous with a quarterstaff – his favorite weapon to defend himself from the older boys who bullied him. It was the perfect defensive weapon, and he was reasonably good with it. He learned to stand his ground and defend himself until the bullies left him alone. Despite appearances, the Valkarian seed was strong in Leeroy, but his particularities were even stronger. Thus, he enjoyed far more to be himself than to be his legacy. Unlike his brothers and sisters though, and also to his father's distaste, he had never had the discipline or the desire to train and entirely master his combat skills.

Affected by the social rejection and awkward solitude, he had little motivation to face the boredom of academic subjects, and even though the teachers who homeschooled him considered him highly intelligent, he did not obtain particularly great results in his early studies. His insensible tutors were quick to judge him as lazy and distracted. They were even quicker to make his severe father aware of that untrue statement, conveniently hiding their incompetence and the limitations of their methods, thinking of nothing but to justify their payments.

Leeroy could spend days in a library devouring the subjects that interested him. The compass of his interest though was wild and erratic, following his mood. He was also very quick to tedium, jumping from book to book with little regards for formalities. He read about everything with great joy but rarely got to the end of a book after grasping the spirit of it. His mind was indeed meant to see the broader picture.

Because of his uniqueness, and to his great sorrow, his father denied him affection. The rest of his family, due to tradition, respect, and jealousy, blindly followed their patriarch in his cruel attitude toward Leeroy. They all seemed happy to relegate him to be the family scapegoat.

In his innocence, he cried many nights over this tacit condemnation. They were all insensible to the fact that he was just insisting upon being what he was. Leeroy could not understand the stares, the general unkindness, and the overall repudiation he suffered every day.

For his misery, even if he tried, he could not manage to be anything else. He could not bear to be anything that would please them. For the love for the hidden truths that he saw everywhere was stronger than him. Somehow, he also knew his nature was connected to his destiny, and that this feeling he carried inside of him was above all other personality traits that he might possess. He couldn't explain, but he knew it was bigger them him, and it was him at the same time. He knew it was his destiny.

Leeroy was mature enough to understand that they were more agreeing with society and the head of the family than rejecting him. He, however, reserved the right to despise them a little because of how they so easily submitted to be objects of their own fears, denying so many things to its rightful place. He was not ambitious, but felt that his heart was full of qualities that everyone seemed to ignore. This saddened him deeply and isolated him even more. He was often miserable about how people, in general, had rather superficial understandings, or worse, acceptance, of one's motivations. Even at an early age, he really believed that people were highly paradoxical and unwise. Constantly putting, with its non-reflexive actions and hasty thoughts, a great distance between them and any truth there was.

All that caused him great misery, but he always carried a strange hope in his heart. Through his struggles, he kept alive inside of him an overwhelming hope that could not stop telling him that eventually, completion would come – even to him. In his solitude and in his silence, he decided to wait.

As he could not find comfort in anyone, he grew up being the master of his own emotions. He kept his courage, enjoying the wonders of the simplicity and of the complexity, loving whatever beauty he could find in them. He spent his days, therefore, toddling around his family's house, reflecting and doing whatever amused him the most.

At the dinner table though, Leeroy was a proper ghost. Everyone ignored him as if he was the unpleasant remains of a sad story, a failed anomaly in a council of proud champions, or even some past mistake that, if forgotten, might disappear.

All his brothers and sisters were engaged in many sorts of highly visible social activities, conquering titles and awards in everything they did. They were respected inside the family and recognized by society. Leeroy, on the other hand, barely finished his studies, achieving no merits at all.

To his father, he was a total disgrace – a living nightmare of shame. The seeming lack of cherishing he had for his son's introspection morphed over time into a vindictiveness and cold disdain. He saw Leeroy as an old war wound that constantly hurt and bothered him, or a heavy anchor that was slowing down his work over his family heritage.

Thus, on a certain morning, even before breakfast, the young man was met by his own luggage. It was pre-packed for him and waiting by his doorsteps. In the hand of a servant, a cold letter signed by his father. It informed him that he was assigned to "a course of further education." It commanded him very objectively and firmly to be absolutely obedient to his new mentor, ending with a dry and formal good luck at the end.

Leeroy could not believe what he had read when the name Eliaroth'kull came up. Apparently, his father had made a sort of deal with the mysterious and legendary archmage, and it somehow involved Leeroy's education. Apparently, the mage would have Leeroy as his new apprentice, probably in exchange for some political favor.

Accustomed to flying free into crystal clear skies, Leeroy's winged mind had now crashed in the mud of the valley of sorrows. His broken heart had weighed it down, sinking him deep in the mud of his immediate reality.

The surprise of the new situation should have made a panic come up his spine like a lightning bolt, but it didn't. Leeroy was fully aware of the wizard's reputation, but he was not thinking about that. Leeroy knew that the wizard was known in Valkar and beyond to be powerful, enigmatic, and extremely harsh with his apprentices, and that in recent years they all ended up suffering various inexplicable accidents of furtive and deadly nature under his tutelage. However, this was also not what was troubling Leeroy right now.

What concerned Leeroy was, as usual, the bigger picture. What troubled his mind now was a very personal and immediate realization: his family had no love for him indeed. No love at all.

He knew that he was not his father's favorite, and there were many reservations regarding him, but this was too much. To use his life as a bargain for political or material gains as if he was an object was too much. Deep inside, he had always hoped for something. A turning point, a moment, a hug, but nothing ever come by. He got nothing, and it hurt.

Awful words and excruciating emotions echoed in him now. The way his father had used and abandoned him in a political horse trade had him paralyzed. His imagination fainted and his fingers failed. The thick official paper on which the letter was written slipped through them, falling to the floor. Leeroy was in shock.

The servant who had packed his things could not stand to look at the kid and his lost hopes. She looked back at the wall to sob discreetly. She dried her tears and hurried the boy up, helping him with his belongings.

He couldn't feel his legs or the ground under him as he walked down the main patio. The young man could not understand how a child could be generated and so easily dismissed by the very ones who were supposed to love him. By suffering that malignant and cruel disregard, Leeroy lost his innocence that day.

As he climbed up into the carriage, he was not thinking about his frightening destination, but the fact that no one came to say goodbye. In the end, it was too much to absorb through reason, and certainly was too much for him, or any kid, to endure. With no choice, he just let the overwhelming feelings of abandonment that were upon him to sink in.

Leeroy finally had to face the circumstances of how the people that surrounded him really saw him. He arrived at the conclusion that his life simply did not have enough value for them. Apparently, he was not valuable enough to be loved. Everyone he knew had rejected him. The world he knew had rejected him, and this was too much to take.

As he absorbed all these unsaid things that were now being said out loud, he felt his heart plummet into a bottomless pit that had been mercilessly opened in his chest.

Before that cruel morning, Leeroy was deluded by the idea that, beneath the cloak of discord, deep down, even by blood ties, everyone accepted him. He still believed he was part of the family, that there was a place for him there. However, he found, in the worst possible way, that the love of men lies in the representations and not in the content of qualities.

That silent morning brought the truth that fell as heavy and undesired on him as the copious and cold winter rain that was pouring over the wagon's horses by the entrance of the atrium.

Much of his boyhood and the gleam of his eyes died on that trip. Through dark forests and deserted roads, he traveled indeed. Even the hardened guards that were scouting him felt pity for him as he silent, paled, and numbed the whole way in.

The image of the pre-packed bags and the memory of that morning's letter stretched for long days afterwards. In time, those memories faded, but those feelings of rejection and abandonment never went away. They stood out in his mind during his whole life, molding his character. Always present, always vivid.

Those dark days have permanently left a sorrowful impression in his soul. Its outcome would make all the difference during, and after the end of his life, and, before it was all over, the destiny of the world would be changed by it.

The Hens Hear It All

'Hello, Mrs. Swaizz,' said Lucien distractedly while trying to look over the house in search of his friend.

The small Swaizz family ranch was an adorable place, but no more than a tiny farm lost in the plains a few miles east of Westgate.

'He is in the back, feeding the chickens,' she said, guessing Lucien's purpose here.

Bastian's mother, continuing her work, kneeled behind a very fragrant row of red roses. When Lucien passed by her side, she tilted the huge straw hat down to hide the expression of disapproval that she had on her face. She was a polite woman but was not very fond of Lucien.

Bastian was in the middle of the ranch's very large chicken coop. He was looking rather funny wearing an old and oversized leather apron. In his arms there was a huge bowl full of corn. He was feeding the chickens by throwing the corn in the air, so it would spread over a large area and they would not need to fight for it, avoiding injuries among them.

His efforts were useless though. The chickens, with an incredibly stupid expression, ran around in a random direction, stumbling over each other while corn fall over their heads, agitated by the imminent feast or whatever crazy thought that went through a chicken's mind.

Lucien got closer and settled over the wooden fence with much familiarity. He was chewing on a bush stick and was avoiding looking directly to Bastian. No word was said by neither of them.

After some time looking down, Lucien finally faced Bastian, who was still throwing corn in the air. Bastian was really having difficulties trying to dodge all the madness caused by the unnecessary chicken's frenzy. Once every two seconds or more, a fight would break out among them and the others would get extra crazy, jumping in the air, losing some feathers and squawking loudly.

After a while, Lucien gave up and decided to break the silence.

'So, what about an insane warm-up of five days and five nights before the Shields Bashing festival?' he asked, using his magic beans salesman voice. 'Wine, girls, music, girls, the most filthy and cheap taverns in Westgate. One little fight from time to time to keep the spirit. Oh, did I mention girls?' Lucien was trying really hard, but he could not get a reaction from Bastian.

'And don't give me the old excuse of lack of money. I will take care of it this time. It's like the bards say: when you have the heart, money appears.' Lucien was really hoping he could have a taste of his old life back. At least for a while, until he could clarify what to do next.

'This time your gold, better yet, your father's gold, will not make me change my mind, Lucien,' said Bastian without interrupting what he was doing or looking at Lucien.

'You know very well that I have to leave in the next two days if I hope to return before the winter starts,' said Bastian.

Lucien constrained his teeth. He knew by Bastian's voice that he was committed to his plans. Lucien knew that Bastian had made his heart. He knew that even if that expedition would cost Bastian his life (and it probably would), he would risk it anyway. Bastian had promised it in front of so many people, so many times. He said all the time that when his training was complete, he would not rest until he finds it. Even if the search led him to the sixth circle of the Abyss. He would claim it, he would search it, he would find it and he would have it – his father's sword.

'This time I will ignore your lack of enthusiasm about my sponsors,' said Lucien, trying to take some tension out of the conversation. 'But will you really be stupid enough to miss the best party of the year?' Lucien placed all the emphasis he could on that phrase, claiming Bastian's memories of previous Shield Bashing Festival, where both had had so much fun. Lucien used hand gestures and all his breath to emphatically display the immanent logic of his reasoning, but he was not used to trying to convince people, so all his efforts ended in him looking stupid. And so he felt.

'Especially now that we are free, and don't have to go back to that smelly farm to beat the crap out of those talentless boys?' he tried an extra push.

'Lucien, for the last time,' said Bastian, already a little nervous by the mayhem the chickens were making and the annoyance that Lucien's silly arguments were causing in him. 'My grandfather forged that sword himself. He did it from the blue metal extracted from a comet that fell precisely over his forge. He believed the blade was destined to be in my family. It is destined to me. I WILL find it,' Bastian looked exhausted for having to deal with the chickens and Lucien at the same time.

'I told you that story so many times…you know he was a famous master artisan, but what I have not told you is that he learned to forge weapons directly from one of the greatest weapon masters among the northern dwarf: Dimbo Firerock.' Bastian was narrating it with a lot of emotion and pausing at every sentence.

Lucien rolled his eyes, bored.

'To melt the incredibly hard metal my grandfather used rare Dwarven Fire Crystals and worked restlessly in the treacherous Iron Mountain. Following Dimbo's instruction, he found a place only a handful of dwarves know about, a sacred place – the Magma Slit. There, the matter from the innards of the world pours into the surface through a crack before they make their way back into a bottomless abyss. The ores rise crested with crude energies of the very first creations, and the heat of their state cannot hide the fumes of pure magic they radiate,' Bastian said, clearly quoting someone else's words that he probably heard a long time ago.

'My grandpa,' he continued, 'camped there for almost a year to work on the blade. Sleeping out in the open and against the wind in a region infested by beasts. He fought to survive numerous times to finish his masterpiece. He told my father that because of his open wounds, he bled over the blade while working on it, mixing the tempering fluid with his own blood. My grandfather used to say that the sword's metal was tainted with so much of his blood that it became part of the family. The reality was that an unexpected magical effect sprouted in the sword, attaching it to my family lineage. To my blood,' said Bastian solemnly.

'The comet fell on the same night my father was born. The heat was so intense that the whole oven evaporated completely. It was a forgery oven, Lucien, it was made to stand intense heat,' he said. 'Even on those days Star Ore was more valuable than gold, but my grandpa was not interested in money,' he said proudly. 'He decided to forge a weapon with it, for he knew that weapons made of this metal have the best characteristics, not only for strength and edge retention but because the metal is mysteriously bursting with Mana particles, it multiplies several folds any magical energy imbued in it,' said Bastian.

'Yeah, don't lecture me about the value of Star Ore. My family has weapons made of it. You, however, never yielded a magic weapon,' said Lucien, pushily.

'But I will. One day I will,' said Bastian, wandering.

'My mother told me that my grandfather used to say that the metal was so concentrated with Mana particles that the magic energy simply poured from it,' said Bastian.

'My grandfather thought long and hard before deciding what to build with this gift from above. He studied a lot before starting the forge. My mother told me that Dimbo himself made many visits to my grandfather's forge to advise him and help him with his work. My father told her, and she told me that their relationship went from pupil and master to great friends. She said that they worked on many projects together, and that they constantly debated the details about the sword's project,' said Bastian, unconvinced.

'There is more to it than what they told me, Lucien. I'm telling you, I can feel it. I know it,' said Bastian, determined.

Lucien started searching for a strategy to convince Bastian out of his plans, but before he could think of something, Bastian started again.

'My grandparents lived in a border village, next to the Fire Mountains. You know well how the northern territories are, but they were even more unstable then. Fate decided that my father would be my grandfather's only descendant. Upon seeing his son, his only son, his most precious treasure, growing into the world full of wars and violence, he realized he had to do something to protect his family, his seed. He set to the mountainside and returned a winter later with a bunch of scars and a sword in his hands,' said Bastian.

'On one night, the old man placed the sword in my father's lap. He told him the story of the blade, and gravely uttered these words: "Woe my son! This is your father, your mother, your brother, your sister, your best friend, and your heritage – honor them. With it, you must learn to defend against all that oppresses you. Together, never apart. I have forged this sword, but tonight, you must forge a true Fellowship. A fellowship of steel and blood. A fellowship between you and your weapon. A fellowship of the sword."'

Even with all his artificial emotional distance and his selfishness, Lucien was still a Valkarian, and as so, he felt the hair on the back of his neck rising when he heard Bastian's grandfather's words. It was in that moment that

Lucien was sure that Bastian was a true Valkarian and a legitimate descendant of true Valkarians.

'The impact of these words deeply shaped my father's character, you know?' Bastian looked straight into Lucien's eyes now, asking for emotional support and comprehension in what he was about to say. 'When he reached the age, he became a soldier in the army. A natural-born leader, who fought for much higher things than himself, but also for the pleasure of sporting his legacy proudly. A true Valkarian they say.' Bastian lamented his father's reputation instead of welcoming it. Although he always tried to do the right thing, he had his reservations about not growing up with his old man by his side.

'It was part of him,' he continued, 'of us really. My family's pride was all in that.' He stopped for a second.

'Hell, IT was that! And it still is, Lucien. The jewel of any honored warrior, my inheritance!' Bastian looked away like he had spotted something on the horizon. His eyes beamed with pride and were very expressive now.

The chickens were still making a chaotic mess around them, absolutely ignoring the solemnity of the moment.

'Father was the youngest field sergeant in Westgate history. He was taken away before his time, but to this day I still get the respect of hundreds of men whose lives he saved,' Bastian said.

Lucien couldn't argue with that. He couldn't even look at his friend in the eyes right now. Instead, he stared at the havoc the chickens were raising, spitting a feather out of his mouth.

'You must understand, Lucien. How can I go on with my life? Everyone expects it from me. If I die trying to find that sword, it will be only natural. I will die doing the right thing, trying to rescue what represented and still represents what I am as a person. That thing is far more than a sword to me.' Bastian paused a little, swallowed dry, and then continued.

'Besides, this farm would kill me over time.' Bastian expressed a sad and resigned side look. He looked around frustrated, analyzing his surroundings as if he had done it a million times before.

Suddenly, a strange thing made its presence notable to him. His mind suddenly stroked him with the feeling that something was out of place. He looked around, his eyes rolling frantically.

The chickens were unusually silent, but they were also very thrilled. Strangely, they were all frozen, immovable. All of their heads were leaning toward his direction, forming a bizarre audience. The expressionless eyes were wide open and fixed on Bastian, making him feel awkward and out of place. The way they stared somehow seemed that they were deeply involved in Bastian's tale.

It was a weird scene, even for Bastian who had lived on the farm his whole life. Somehow, the chickens were weirded out too, for throughout their whole existence they had done nothing but random and inexplicable chicken things. Now, an unnatural conjunction was over them.

Bastian's tale had indeed touched Lucien, who was completely unaware of the chickens' situation. He was looking down and considering everything with himself.

The late afternoon sun was intensely fatiguing the high plains around them. Time seemed to stop for both while they considered.

'Damn, Lucien, you already know the story!' said Bastian, turning back to the argument at hand, deciding to completely ignore the chicken phenomenon.

'I WILL find it.' Bastian's voice showed that he was not willing to continue the conversation anymore.

Lucien laughed while still looking down. Then he looked up in the direction of Bastian, finally facing him.

'And what are you planning to do?' he asked Bastian.

'Depart the day after tomorrow, before sunrise. There is a path up the Dire Woods, then go up the Hunters' Old Road until the Rocky River, then climb up to the Valley of Bones,' said Bastian.

'And once there? If once there?' asked Lucien raising one eyebrow.

'Well, Star Ore weapons do not rust or decay with the passage of time. It has probably not been undone by the Barbarians, orcs, or goblins as it takes much more than a normal furnace to melt it. Only a few of the best blacksmith masters could have worked on it. Not counting that it is possible that the ones who have it will not feel inclined to destroy this unique work,' he reckoned. 'It must be there somewhere, lost or maybe even found,' he said looking to the West. 'One thing is certain: an object like that does not go by unnoticed,' Bastian concluded his speculations.

'OK, assuming you overcome the robbers of the prairies, who, according to the last report of the city guard, are particularly dangerous and active lately. After that, let us suppose you could defeat all the wild and hungry giant beasts that lurk behind every Dire Woods' shadow. Also, that you surpass the wildest, hungriest, and even more gigantic beasts that patrol the high banks of the Rocky River. And then, you reach the historically dangerous, and, by the way, haunted, Valley of Bones, which is located, let us not forget, on the border of the territory of the Wolverine tribe, which is recognized as one of the most bloodthirsty eastern Barbarian tribe,' Lucien paused to breathe some air in.

'And let us not forgot for a moment of the not-so-friendly Red Claw orc tribe. Remembering that, according to the last report of Westgate's intelligence, through its new and ridiculously cruel leader, they are looking to rescue their old glory and their ancient custom of mixing their already bad blood with the blood of demons?!' Lucien stopped, hoping his words would sink in his friend's brain.

Still with the same face, Bastian kept throwing corn in the air.

'We also must take into consideration the huge possibility of getting lost in the difficult terrain and dangerous vegetation. And, you must also figure out a plan not only to get there but also to pull out. Probably through all of that, again!!!' he said emphatically, but to no avail.

'Of course, we cannot simply teleport in or out, because magic, my dear, dear friend, is not really our trade.' Lucien made his habitual "is that not obvious?" sarcastic expression. A little extra exaggerated this time though.

'Yes. I know,' answered Bastian with a firm voice.

'Demons, Bastian! I said demons! Are you listening to me?!' Lucien was now exasperated.

'I still have a lot to do before sunset and tomorrow will be a very important day, so I would like you to leave or help me out with the chores, please,' said Bastian calmly.

He felt uncomfortable with the fact that, for the first time, he was asking Lucien to leave his house (it was, in fact, the first time he was asking anyone to leave his house), but he wouldn't let anything stand in the way of his plan.

'Aaaaaahhhh!' Lucien jumped from the fence and kicked a wooden bucket. His action scared the chickens, who ran in panic, but, upon realizing they knew not where they were going, they returned frantically from whence they came. When they arrived there, they paradoxically remembered that they had forgotten why they were there in the first place, in doing so, they slowed down their pace, but kept a watchful stance, even though they had forgotten what had scared them before.

'What the hell, Bastian?! This year's Shields Bashing will be the best it's ever been! Besides, we are far too young for these things you are proposing.' Although irritated, Lucien was being sincere.

'Lucien, it is him when I look in the mirror,' Bastian said sharply, glancing straight at Lucien.

Bastian's words hit Lucien like an arrow to the heart. Fear and amazement flooded Lucien's eyes. He stared right through Bastian, past what he wanted his friend to be to finally see what his friend have decided to become. His eyes became wet. Ashamed and defeated, Lucien lowered his head.

'We are never too young to stand for what we believe. Besides, you have no need to worry, after the first glass of anything or at the first dose of anyone you will forget we ever had this conversation,' said Bastian, really willing to be alone and in peace with his resolution.

'I believe this would be impossible, my stupid, cheap, and inopportune friend.' Lucien smiled, resigned. His shoulders were down.

'Why?' Bastian questioned with little interest while concentrating on the chickens.

Bastian had no idea of what was going through Lucien's head, but he now cared to know a little.

'Because I am going with you,' Lucien said conclusively, and a little furious.

'But –' Totally surprised, Bastian was caught off guard by Lucien's answer.

'No buts!' Lucien interrupted sharply. 'Or do you really think I would let you take all the fame and leave me behind?' he smiled malevolently at Bastian. 'I will be the hero of the year! I am already seeing my painting on the walls of Westgate. Under my painting a saying: "Hero helps mentally disabled friend recover his father's lost sword."' Lucien was all sarcasm now, but Bastian knew that he was using humor to mitigate the tension of the serious circumstance.

'I will be very famous! Besides, I have trained you, so I just know very well that you have a tiny, but possible, chance of getting out alive from this one. If that happened, and I had no participation in it, I would feel a moral obligation of throwing myself off the North Tower, or something dramatic of the genre,' Lucien said ironically.

'But –' Bastian protested.

'I could go on all day,' Lucien sharply interrupted him again.

'But –'

'BUT I will spare you to use your atrophied peasant brain, making excuses that only reflect pity on yourself. Very common in second-hand losers by the way. I am going with you,' said Lucien willing to end the topic.

Before Bastian could say anything, he jumped off the fence to wash the dust and the feathers off his face on the wheel a few yards from him.

With a nervous smile, not knowing what to think or feel, Bastian shook his head in denial and mumbled while preparing an answer for when Lucien returned. He instinctively continued feeding the chickens by throwing corn around in a large arch. Suddenly, he noticed that all of them were gone, and that he had been pointlessly throwing the grains on an empty floor, like a perfect idiot.

The Tower

Still disoriented and deeply sad, as a child should never be, Leeroy found himself facing a "small," old, and robust Valkarian observation tower. The place looked abandoned and oppressively desolated.

The escorts that had taken him there were quick to unload his luggage and get back to the road from where they had come. The experienced guards knew that that region was dangerous and haunted. They were all seasoned warriors, so it was unlikely that they were afraid, but they were not stupid either, making sure they got out of there as soon as possible in order to avoid unwelcome encounters.

By analyzing the structure's details, Leeroy saw that it was little different from a standard small Valkarian outpost. Certain nuances suggested it was built in a different era, but it was clearly an imperial work nonetheless. The only thing that caught his attention, besides the utter lack of maintenance in the exterior, was a small beautiful stone fountain surrounded by an old abandoned garden. Leeroy's sharp eyes could notice hints that indicated that the surroundings used to be cared by skillful hands. All around him, but hidden in details, Leeroy could notice leads that indicated that, in a distant past, the place was probably quite pleasant. The atmosphere around the tower still contained remains of an unusual warmness, and the air was full of a deserted but very clear nostalgia.

Fancy details and sculptured art covered the whole extent of the site. Abandoned structures hidden behind tall bushes were here and there. He thought it was a huge waste to see such an admirable place fall into that level of neglect.

The architecture was somehow odd, even considering its age. Although clearly built by Valkarians, the mix of themes in the tower itself and in the ruins around it gave the impression that the site had been repurposed many times before. The whole place was a pile of concluded stories.

The structure was doubtlessly human, but eventually, a careful observer could catch alien traces here and there. Traces that were way too dynamic and subtle for simple minds to perceive. They were all around the tower and its surroundings, filling the air with a massive amount of misplaced assertiveness.

Leeroy sat in his leather stash and started analyzing the surroundings a little more. He instantly noticed that the tower had a remarkable characteristic: it did not have doors nor windows whatsoever.

While he reflected upon that mystery, a citric and incredible refreshing odor came with the wind. It was sweet beyond measure and completely new to him. Leeroy was instantly fascinated by it, even raising himself high so his nose could capture more of it.

Ignoring the immediate enigma over the tower's lack of doors and windows, he digressed from his purpose there and got into calculating the fragrance's origins. He concluded it came from somewhere behind the structure.

Still holding one of his bags, he was now on his toe's tips trying to sniff more of the wonderful scent. While he was still trying to identify the source of such an amazing and altogether different perfume, he was also determining the compensation generated by a passing butterfly's wings and crossing it with the wind speed. His mind was floating freely once more after many days of darkness. The relief of being him again made him forget his precarious situation.

Suddenly, he felt a growing numbness in his stomach. At first, he thought he was growing hungry, then, he realized it was not his stomach. He somehow serialized that he knew, that he knew, that he knew, that it was coming from his body's vertical equilibrium point.

It unapologetically spread to his whole body, and then to the space around him. Following, he found himself in a circumstance of most unusual nimbleness as reality changed quickly. He lost the initiative of thinking. There was no more unknown opinions, just certainties. His mind was not existing in a rational world anymore, but rather in a transitional space where real reality is and where the mind's perceptions prevail over carnal reasoning.

Taken by an overwhelming feeling of immateriality that was sensed on every atom of every nerve on his body, all his notion of dimension and space initiated an intensifying reshaping processes in which his conscience was an involuntary partaker – he felt forced into it.

However, Leeroy could not say with certainty if the things that were happening with him originated or not from his free will. It was a massively confusing situation to him, as if his brain was discovering a new sense. Which, in fact, it was.

At some point, even though it was an immense load of information, Leeroy could understand the definition of his position in space. When that happened, he had become deeply aware of his body's interaction with its surroundings' dimensions and depths. All the world was reduced to vectors and force exchanging particles, but before he had time to absorb all that information, he observed something that he could only be called "an anomaly pivot." For there were many things he was feeling and seeing that could not be defined or reduced by words.

The anomaly denied every possibility around him, and, with an unstoppable force, reorganized his vectors and his matter, forcing his whole being into its direction.

Absolutely stunned and without thinking about the consequences, Leeroy instinctively tried to interfere with that force. In the moment he set his mind to it, he saw that the force was not natural or gentle as he had first imagined. It had a will of its own, and when he tried to resist, a dry pull tracked him down, and in a mathematical and fluid way, all his movements' vectors were dragged inside the empty space from where the anomaly was originated.

However, the complex and involuntary planar trip he was now in, and even though he was still surprised and stupefied by the surreal experience, Leeroy managed to organize himself. His mind and body sensed the space around him very naturally and instinctively. So much so that when reality presented itself suddenly, as he was materialized inside the tower, he was standing up and was in the position he had to choose to be during the trip. This was very rare among first-time teleporters. Most people just made a mess of it, and not rarely, they materialized themselves upside down or in some weird angle high above the ground. It took a lot of practice to acquire a proper control over the planar jump, for there were few people that had the combination of the right instincts and the proper mindset to perform the trick correctly.

Leeroy had been teleported for the first time and somehow he was aware of all that. He knew he had just accomplished a hard thing, and he knew he had done it well. Surprisingly, he found no questions in his mind afterwards, he just knew what had happened and that he enjoyed the experience very much.

The room where he and his luggage were now in had granite walls and a large fireplace. It was very well furnished, and, strangely, still felt empty.

From nowhere and everywhere at the same time a very particular, clear, and ever-present light arose. It gave the place a quite inspiring atmosphere. A sense of magic.

What a weird place, he said to himself over his first impressions. However, somehow and for his own surprise, he was enjoying that fact.

The air inside the tower was very unusual also. Although there was no aperture to be seen, it was as fresh as in an open field during a spring night. Rather than just filling their lungs, it refreshed them with every single breath. Leeroy found it very invigorating, but a little disturbing also, since, when he closed his eyes, he was under the impression that he was outside, exposed.

Although the tower was not broad enough to contain even the room Leeroy was now standing in, and there was no material proof to make the case that he was in the tower, a strange and newfound discernment gave him a strong conviction that he was inside it. That feeling intrigued him at that time, and after he gave it some thought, he laughed about the wonderful absurdity of it – it was the first time Leeroy laughed in several days.

The room could be described as very cozy and having just the right amount of space to be called comfortable. It had a relativity high ceiling and, overall, it seemed to have been clearly organized by a wise mind with higher purposes.

The tower's interior was confusing to most people, and it was full of rooms that connected with other rooms that connected with other rooms that were not supposed to be there. Leeroy instead found it fascinating. Above all, he enjoyed the subtle smartness and the rebellious utility of the architecture and the designs.

With his mind still broadly opened to the many different layers of reality by the planar trip he had just been forced through, and still sensing things in different levels, he came to understand and feel that the space inside the tower behaved differently than it did outside.

While having these wonderful realizations, he was suddenly called back to reality when he stumbled upon the thought that because of the intimacy and proximity of the spaces of the tower's interior, he would, sooner or later, meet someone. Including, and especially, his new mentor.

He had not put a lot of thought on this first encounter, but he now had to, as the meeting seemed imminent. An anxiety grew profusely throughout his guts when he thought about it. In fear, and unconsciously taking possession of his newfound space, he closed the door of what he now called "his room."

He decided to take his mind out of this fearful thought by investigating the large and deep hardwood wardrobes that populated the room. In them, he found many clothes and other objects that had, apparently, belonged to his predecessors. That freaked him out a little bit.

He also noticed a set of suitcases that had not even been undone. That freaked him out a little more than a little bit.

Cautiously but diligently, he continued to explore the room. In doing so, he continued finding many interesting and appalling things. The stubborn silence that echoed throughout there was the scariest of them. Even the sound of his breath seemed to disturb it. Inside the tower, one could easily hear their own thoughts as if they were screams in a quiet forest. The silence was so deep that it exposed you to yourself – a scary thing to most people.

After a while, the silence became more of a background noise and it ceased to be a source of anxiety for him. Rather, it strangely calmed him down. Leeroy learned a long time ago to enjoy solitude and praised the time alone with his thoughts.

Once he cleaned a section in one of the wardrobes, he started to unpack. When he was already in the socks, the door suddenly opened. He felt his arms and legs freezing in cold hopeless panic.

For his amazement and terror, he saw a flying golem rushing into the room. It had the form of a large silvery hawk with blue agate eyes. It dropped two objects over the bed and flew away as quickly as it had fled in. The door closed by itself behind it.

A few minutes after the hawk left, Leeroy's heart started to slow down to a bearable pace. Blood came back to his legs and arms and he could feel them again. Only then, he started to process what had just happened.

Warily, he went to examine the objects left by the bed. There, he found two tubular scroll holders. They were both made of a fine and light silver alloy.

Upon opening one of them, he extracted a narrow scroll with the inscription "CHORES" above a bright sun wax seal. Although that was the only word written on the outside, Leeroy noticed that the calligraphy was refined, perfectly executed, very elegant, and at the same time of a purist style.

After a few minutes of thinking it through, and a final moment of hesitation, Leeroy broke the seal and gave the paper a wrist jolt to unroll it properly. To his amazement, the paper unfolded uncontrollably, rolling down for several yards until it reached the wall on the other side of the room.

As the unconscious silly expression on his face was clearly telling, Leeroy's notion of proportion was embarrassed for a while by the unexpected long unroll. After realizing that there was not much to be done about it but to read the list, he read the list.

It was not a bad joke though, it was a real list. On it, there were all kinds of duties and chores that he was supposed to perform. Some, he thought, were quite domestic. Others seemed plain bizarre and senseless to him. Many he could not even comprehend, for they were talking about things Leeroy still did not know about.

Get the rust out of the Iron Golems, polish the Crystal Sphere exclusively with a blue satin cloth, look for and neutralize any paradox shifts next to the library's special shelf with the wand number 17, prepare dinner, regulate the air, were some of the tasks that seemed bizarre to him, and the meaningless list went on forever, ever more senseless.

What in the world is a Crystal Sphere? Where is it? And where the heck would I find a blue satin cloth?! he thought, feeling overwhelmed. To take his head out of it, he decided to examine the second list.

This one looked exactly as the first one. Right away he noticed the word "RULES" in the same place and with the same excellent calligraphy. The only difference was that it got an exclamation point drawn with red ink on the right side of it. Leeroy couldn't avoid the thought that this emphasis was quite disturbing.

This time, armed with a good dose of caution, he positioned himself in front of an empty space, and unrolled the scroll as a mat, preparing himself for a massive expansion. However, this time, the piece of paper was short and narrow. It was no longer than half-palm. On it, he could easily read a set of five brief rules:

"1. Never do enchants without supervision;

2. Never do anything other than the chores contained in the Chore List;

3. Never touch my Grimoire;

4. Under any hypothesis execute any unauthorized spells;

5. Execute all the chores in the Chores List with care and appropriate frequency."

Thinking about them, Leeroy found that the rules were very strange. Especially considering that, in theory, he was there to study and learn how to do magic, and that he needed to use magic to do some of the crazy chores on the other list.

During the countless hours he spent meditating about the odd purpose of those lists, his mind jumped from possibility to possibility, flying ever away from the rules, the chores, the paper, and tower, away from it all.

Westgate

Westgate was among the most important strongholds of the Valkarian Empire. It protected the center-west access to the empire's central plains. Its patrols reached long and deep in all directions. It was strategically located in the middle of the Great West Road that bordered the Dire Woods and the Barbarians Territories from the utmost north to the lowest south.

Located barely a day of march away from the Dire Woods tree line, the immense fortress was seated on a large monolithic hill made of a single gigantic granite boulder that was shaped into a rectangular block. Its towers were the perfect observation point to guard the east-central plains, the north, east, and south road, and the forest on the West.

The natural granite cliffs that bordered the empire's western frontier from North to South seldom led to an access to the central plains. Westgate guarded one the largest of those accesses, therefore protecting the empire from major incursions.

After centuries of being constantly sieged and occasionally overran by massive Barbarian hordes or worse, the city had endured many reconstructs and improvements. Every time it got damaged, the Valkarians rebuilt it to be larger and more powerful. In doing so, they had mastered how to fight a defensive siege war and had evolved their tactics to a degree next to perfection.

The quality of the dark gray granite chosen for its walls was praised and respected even by the dwarves, who were the world's greatest stones workers. The natural high position of the monolith in relation to the plains below allowed its watchtowers a deep field of observation, which stretched for dozens of miles in every direction.

Its defense systems included the base rock itself, which was filled with hidden traps, deadly pitfalls, and a fair amount of creative and concealed passive siege weapons.

There was a good thirty yards of curved rock after the traps, that practically would make useless any efforts of taking the first line of walls by the deployment of mobile towers. The shape of the round rock bellow it helped the spreading and the containment of the burning of oil into big shallow pools. This had a devastating effect on any troops trying to breach the outer wall.

The outer wall was the first structure of the fortress itself. Carved deep into the base rock, it was a silky-smooth barrier that was fifty yards high and ten yards deep. It was independent and had dedicated garrisons located inside solid granite bunkers that were imbued in it throughout the wall's extension.

The bunkers protected the city's defenders against any enemy's artillery or air attacks. These fortifications were built with the extensive help of dwarven war engineers, making them positioned for excellent defensive fighting in every aspect.

From the grass of the plain until the first sentinel eyes, one hundred yards were counted. It was well known that around it, the thick of any clash would be felt harder. Thus, the best defenses were around its structures. The vertical angle of the outer wall was perfect, and its surface was immaculately flat. It was loaded full of trickeries, deadly combat schemes, and retractable loopholes installed in hollow walls where troops could move unnoticed and securely. These were just some of the tricks that the fortress made available as combat options.

Any army marching against that bastion of one square mile of massive rock would know they had a real obstacle to overcome. A detailed review of the fortress city revealed several layers upon layers of walls, towers, and defense mechanisms. Its five imposing towers sported many defensive crew weapons that could be defined by foreigners as "an almost ridiculous exaggeration."

Some of these magic crew weapons were magic, relics plundered from old wars. Almost all had magic directly or indirectly involved in its working mechanisms, and in its ammunitions.

The specialized soldiers that would operate them trained daily in their handling. The crews reached a proficiency level where they could fight in perfect harmony with all the other defensive systems, becoming flexible and aggressive enough to deploy great effect on any target in any battlefield condition.

Aided by combat engineers and gnome math-masters, all systems could deliver incredible precision. The fields around the city were previously mapped, gridded, and divided into areas for easy targeting coordination. The weapons were upgraded with the best aiming instruments and they all carry wind and elevation tables for final compensation.

The number of gates was limited to five, each defended by independent counter-fort in a deep tunnel nicknamed Death Trap. Defensive troops and schemes were particularly concentrated on those as they were the most vulnerable parts of the outer wall.

The city was also divided into five fully hermetic levels, each possessing its own defensive battle plans. Those, for obvious reasons, were kept in great secret by the city council.

All the important logistical and combat multipliers had many redundancies in the fortress. Its subterranean shelters were able to house several legions of soldiers or refugees safely. Highly protected water cisterns, several water fountains, giant silos full of grains, and many kinds of other foods made sure they could sustain a siege for a long time, even without the help of magic.

Lakes of oil, seas of arrows, and many other abundantly stocked supplies were in place, allowing the city not only to defend itself, but to launch operations and sorties to ambush, flank, and destroy invading armies.

In a defensive operation, to equip all Westgate positions to the maximum, a force of at least ten thousand soldiers was required. However, the excellence of its design was so efficient that just over three thousand well-trained combatants could defend it well. Be that as it may, in the case of reinforcements, the city walls and towers could effectively accommodate and direct the combat energy of tens of thousands of soldiers.

In peace times however, for reasons related to cost, the city maintained only two battalions of heavy infantry and two battalions of bowmen, directing most of its efforts to keep a full garrison of light infantry serving as heavy weapons specialists at the ready.

When on patrol duty, the heavy infantry was equipped with heavy siege shields and long pikes. Although they were still primarily field infantry, they were particularly well trained in defensive techniques and in collective discipline inside an urban environment. They constantly practiced maneuvers in the city streets and towers as realistically as they possibly could. They did guard duties on the city walls and patrolled sensitive areas to avoid infiltrators and sabotage. They were mentally toughed in preparation for chewy fights. They knew all too well that whatever might overcome the city's primary defenses wouldn't be easy to defeat once they were inside. Thus their tactics went way beyond holding a shield line, and they trained to master the use of pressure inside the city's choking points.

The bowmen, in the same manner, learned to share their fighting space with the heavy infantry, supporting and defending them in a possible tridimensional battlefield. When on guard duty, they were issued ultra-heavy crossbows that were unpractical for field use, but when shot through an arrow slit, they could go through a hill giant's skull from a few hundred feet away.

Although the Westgate focus was heavy infantry, archery, and artillery (typical defensive forces), the city had a relatively large cavalry unit. In peacetime, it was used for periodic long-range patrols across the territory. In wartime, they scouted or, more rarely, they performed shock attacks on enemy formations. As the main function of Westgate's cavalry force was highly mobile low-intensity operations aimed at intelligence gathering, they were mostly deployed as light cavalry units. Though most of them eagerly dreamed of the day when they could set heavy armor over their horses and themselves and charge the enemy full on.

Westgate looked like a fortress, but it was fundamentally also a city. However, its stone houses possessed an architecture that was integrated into the combative environment. Westgate houses were designed to be little strongholds inside a fort, inside a stronghold. They were all a part of the defense plan and resembled small castles. They all had its individual design, but were positioned in a fashion clearly planned to stall the advance of invading forces as much as possible, making the attacking army pay a dear price for every yard of soil they grasped. Their walls and ceilings were made of thick granite and no wood was used externally, making the entire city very

72

close to fireproof. All the doors were heavy and the windows were made into loopholes. Heavy implements used to seal them shut were considered part of the furniture.

The streets were narrow, irregular in length and height, and confusing on purpose. They were projected to ambush and confuse an invading force, buying time for the defenders to regroup and reorganize in the successive level.

There were many towers in Westgate, but five of them were fundamental to the city security, being an integral part of the defense tactics. They were, each one of them, an independent vertical fortress capable of fighting a war on their own. Impossible to flank, they were built to fight in three hundred and sixty degrees and to repeal either land or air attacks.

Four of them were inside the second layer of walls, each one located in the city four corners. They were called "Porcupines" because of the sheer number of weapons they held.

The fifth one, much taller and larger than the others, was in the geometrical center of the city. This one was called the "Watch Tower." It was much more robust and carried heavier and more powerful weapons than the Porcupines.

They were all part of an intrinsic, multiphase battle strategy. The Watch Tower's main job was to protect the Porcupines. Those protected the walls, which, by their turn, guarded the city.

The Watch Tower possessed four massive balconies equipped with monstrous trebuchets that were built with the gigantic and solid timber gathered in the Dire Woods. In combat, they could, with just one shot, launch rocks the size of a small house, a salvo of hundreds of rocks the size of a man's chest, or even, they could launch dozens of oil barrels capable of setting several sectors of the battlefield on fire.

These powerful weapons were positioned under turning platforms. They turned in every direction, in such a way, that three of them could engage the same target at the same time for better effect. Its operation was formidable, including gnomic optic instruments for precision and complex automatic reloading mechanisms.

The high position of the Watch Tower's weapons gave them a formidable range, making the enemy pay a very high price way before they even get close to the city walls.

The highest point of the Watch Tower was the base of The Observatory, a high stone pillar that went as high as the engineers deemed safe. In its interior a small circular stair that conducted to a top floor that contained a small room of a few square yards where day and night four men kept a watch over the border, expecting the unexpected.

The internal communication system played an important role in this capability, being so efficient that once an order was given at the command center, it was almost instantly fulfilled by the designated troop. Weapon operators simply had to choose the right type of ammunition, compensate for wind, speed, and distance from the target and engage.

The collective training of the city's defenders was so synchronized that the whole city fought as a single living organism, adapting to many types of foe, various types of attacks and changing battlefield situations.

In general, and considering the needs of each different area of the empire, all Valkarian city-fortresses worked in a similar manner. Their strength and resolve were instrumental in enabling the people of Valkar to maintain their territory over the centuries. They defended the land and protected the people, keeping their inner territories relatively safe from external threats.

Anxiety

Leeroy woke up and found himself in an uncomfortable emotional state again.

His particular situation regarding his new life in the tower was being affected by many things, but mainly by the daily uncertainty of his outcomes – he never knew what would happen to him.

Death and its worst friends were always close to him, at every corner and inside of every second. Leeroy lived every day under the pressure of not knowing if this was the day he would turn into a cockroach or disappear into a pink mist.

He was constantly facing the fact that he could not manage to do all the tasks that he was asked to perform without using magic. He found that it was impossible to go through the chores list without exercising a dexterous control of the many magically enchanted objects in the tower. His chores were the only thing he had to distract his mind, but his diligence turned into frustration at every step of the way.

He felt scared the whole time, always afraid of doing something wrong that would result in a punishment by his allegedly terrifying and certainly elusive master. The tension of constantly finding himself in challenging situations grew rapidly, flooding his days with anxiety.

To make matters worse, he simply couldn't find the courage, focus, motivation, or even the peace of mind to learn magic by himself. He had no idea from where to start, was not even sure if he was able to learn it, and doubted he was capable of one day do it.

Leeroy caught himself truly arrested in between days. Nothing seemed to progress in those days. Nothing went forward and a solid frustration settled in.

Exhausted and bitter, one day he found himself reluctant to get out of bed. In the night before, he had an epic battle with an animated broom, so he had to spend the whole night fixing and cleaning the resultant big mess. The fight left him covered in bruises and it gave him even more work to do. They had almost destroyed half the kitchen dueling over a "disagreement" about the cleanliness of the golem's room.

For what? he thought. *Everything is pointless anyway,* he concluded to himself and rolled over, staring at the unlit fireplace.

There is no way out of this, he thought. *Either I learn to do some magic, or I will be punished for not doing my tasks right.* He cringed his teeth.

Frustrated, Leeroy lay there, ruminating about it for hours. He remembered all the things he had heard and saw regarding magic. From his father's boasting that there was a high number of spellcasters in their bloodlines, to the many things he had sensed inside the tower, and everything in between.

It was for no vail, for all Leeroy could recollect about magic was sparse knowledge. It was unclear to him whether special talent was needed, or if it was something that you could learn by studying and practicing, or perhaps a little of both. He didn't know.

Thinking about it stressed him a good measure, and he decided to give himself a break from his thoughts on the subject. He chose to protest by staying in bed for the whole day. No more hard and unproductive work, no more worrying the whole time, and, especially, no more feeling like he was trying to make a river run against its own course.

However, he was now completely engaged in an imaginary adventure through the frontier of his metaphysic perceptions. He could not hold his mind from the quiet quest to understand what magic was, and far too many questions were popping in his head. Most came and went away unanswered, but some created smaller, refined versions of themselves, and others even opened new keyhole horizons that were fun to explore.

When Leeroy had depleted his mind of new arguments for his meditations, he closed his eyes and started concentrating on everything around him and in his perceptions of it all. Like in the mental games he like to play alone in his house on Westgate, he allowed no thought to have a clear form in his mind, he just let everything flow. He gathered his mental energies and put them to dance inside his head. Gently, he toyed with these four-dimensional things with the infinite possibilities of his imagination, as one would with his three-dimensional fingers in a thick cloud of smoke in a still air room.

After a long time of tripping and flowing with the colorful and geometrical projections on his mind, he opened his eyes and looked at the neatly piled wood inside the fireplace. In that moment, some instinct inside of him told him he should not allow what he was seeing to restrain what he was thinking, or even feeling. Instead, he felt he should let his will flow through what he was seeing while doing the dance of energies he loved.

Leeroy had done this a thousand times before, but always with his eyes closed and never with such focus. At that moment it all came together and he naturally felt that was the right thing to do. He was instantly overwhelmed by a feeling of deep peace with the present, and finally understood that he was now far from his rational mind. Unbeknownst to him, he reached somewhere else.

Leeroy found himself in a place where his rational thoughts were limited. Once there, the first thing he noticed was that his anxiety had vanished, for this new focal plane allowed him to grasp that most of his feelings were the product of his rational mind.

He instantly became a better person when he saw that most of his emotional distractions were not really a part of him, but cultural reactions that were the result of a socially indoctrinated persona. He felt impossibly relaxed when finally liberated from the illusion of his emotions. His ego was forever jeopardized – his perspective became broader.

Later in his life, he would laugh at the fact that although many regarded it as the pillar of civilization, rationality was not only a conceptual myth, but it had the power to parasitize a personality up to the point of becoming a barrier for self-growth, even shortening one's wisdom.

Leeroy never forgot this first experience with what he then didn't even know to be the limits of the spirit world. It was then that he understood why most legendary spellcasters are described as disconnected from so many aspects of reality, even considered dysfunctional and crazy, when in reality they are the most capable and lucid individuals that Fabula produced.

Although he could not yet vocalize it, it was during this first contact that Leeroy understood in depth that creation is not reason, thus why magic is so wild and hard to contain and control.

While Leeroy was still staring at the fireplace absorbing all that was happening to him, the diverse flows of multiform and inexplicable energies he had allowed to grow in his mind, had, somehow, became more real. With a consuming flick of his mind, in a subtle but still decisive act, a new thing came forth – a transmutation.

Leeroy felt like this presence that he did not even know he created had just entered reality itself. Immediately, he felt connected with his misshapen creation and saw that the need to adjust it was there, but in ways he could not say or seize yet. In that moment, within that process, a new sense awoke in his mind.

He could now see elements that had always been there, but were outside his objective mentality, and therefore forgotten by his regular senses. However, in that epiphany, Leeroy remembered it.

In this new sense, things were now being revealed to him, explaining much about the nature of the world. It was a new level of interconnectedness that fed information about the meaning and purpose of all things. It was a path to true understanding.

He didn't know then, but he was reading reality inside out. He was seeing the next level of everything. His mind was existing in a broader perspective now. In it, he could grasp the existential reasoning of the material things around him. It had many levels, but he was now only capable of dealing with the simple objects around him.

Moved by a gutsy curiosity, Leeroy stepped up and induced a perception of himself connecting him with everything around him in a deeper way. With it, the explanations were inexplicable. He quickly became overloaded with information, especially when he saw metaphysical things. His feelings, his mental projections, and the references his mind threw on objects were now naked to him; he could now see all the motivations of his subconsciousness and the truths and falsehoods of some of those interactions and references. In this paradigm-shifting experience, he learned that colors had a taste, sounds had shapes, and that all the textures had inherent smells.

In this vision, light seemed to be a numerical organizer and the substructure of all matter. Their equations were as beautiful as the deepest artistic insights. They were full of inspiration waiting to be gathered and an intrinsic universal glory that forced itself out of its hiding place. Everything was infinitely beautiful and tastefully magnetic.

Leeroy was completely astonished when he saw that he could acknowledge the lines made out of hard light that held everything together, not only for its beauty, but for the stimulating flawless dynamics of its designs. He was hooked.

The number of things he saw on this day could not be counted, named, or classified by his conscious mind. It was almost an insufferable amount of information, but he absorbed it like a sponge. His mind and his perspective were never the same again.

Amazed by it all, he surprisingly found strength in himself to continue ignoring his preconceived concepts of fear. To Leeroy, the fear of not experimenting all that again was greater. His analytical mind kept a small echo in the background, pushing for a sudden break from all that new clasped reality. He felt like a blind man who, once healed, was now afraid to close his eyes and miss the newfound world of wonders. Leeroy, then, let this persistence flow, and it manifested itself through him, growing as it was also part of him now. Then, out of something deeper than nothingness, he acknowledged that all the things around him could be touched by his mind. Yet touched in an unexplainable way, for this touch required the hold of a higher essence and many other modalities. They were available, but outside of him.

After he had absorbed that acknowledgement completely, his conscience reduced itself to a single focus, a beam of light, an energy more alive and real than anything in the room. He stared at it with his mind's eyes and appreciated it. He fed off its geometrical brightness until he was satisfied. Then, he decided to touch it.

When he did, he was suddenly ejected from that state of mind, returning to being in his rationality, pushed away with a blow of force, changing his mindset in a split second. He felt as if he had lived a totally different life and was now back to the moment he left.

Slowly, his mind returned to its previous state. He blinked because they were dry from being opened all this time. When he breathed, he felt something deep in his mind, like a lump inside his head. However, it looked detachable, ready to go.

There was no need for someone to tell him what it was. He looked at the top log in the fireplace and unloaded that energy. With a spark, a flame appeared on it. The fire spread through the wood and the place quickly felt warm and cozy. Mentally exhausted, and with his body accommodated by the comfort of his bed, he lazily looked at the flames, thought about what happened, smiled, rolled over, and fell asleep. His anxiety had left him.

A Ball in Westgate

Inside the gigantic and static war machine the Valkarians called Westgate, there was life, and people who lived it to its fullest.

In a certain night, one of the many small fortresses that served as mansion for a local powerful family was brighter than the others. There, a ball was taking place.

Most of the local nobility, foreigners, envoys, and special guests were gathered in its gardens and rooms. They were all suited in their best garments, pretending to have fun and faking merriness. There was an undeniable climate of general restraint and theatrical pomposity, and a bitter and contained aggressiveness perfumed the air. It was obvious that everybody was pursuing their own political agendas. The fight for dominance was being exercised in the open and at a professional level in every corner of that mansion. In every room, a thousand elephants.

In this particular night, the party's pretext was to receive and meet Iana, the Kronn family's patriarch's first daughter, second in the lineage. She had returned from Adinaf, which was one of the magic schools located in the far west, across the ocean where most of the Valkarian nobility sent their second sons to be educated in the arts of spellcasting.

Iana left as little more than a girl, but returned as a full wizard. She was now proud and mighty, young and beautiful, lacking nothing but restraint.

That night, she had everybody's attention, and not because of her beauty, but because of the political shift her remarkable achievement would cause.

Westgate's politicians and authorities were all anxious to appreciate where she would be accommodated on their political scene.

On the contrary of what many would claim, Valkarians had great respect for the magic arts, although it was true that they tended to exclusively weaponize it, using it mostly as a combat multiplier. Regardless, magicians were feared and respected everywhere, but especially in politics. Therefore, a great deal of public praise was being shed over Iana's graduation. The ball was an act of political passive aggressiveness. It was a demonstration of force by her family, and everything was designed to impress allies and enemies altogether.

Iana, of course, was aware of it, and knew that she could not show any sign of weakness. She was well instructed by her father and her house counselors, and she carried herself that night as if she had the entire city at her feet. However, the honesty of her youth was still prevalent in her, and when the night was still fresh and the guests were still arriving, she was already tired of swallowing herself down her own throat.

Having the favors of a wizard was indeed a thing to procure, it was only natural that Iana would receive far more attention than she could manage, but the kind of attention she was getting was consuming and horrible. She was being read, scrutinized, and tested in every bit of her demeanor.

She kept as she was told and stood by her father's side, for the message her family was sending was being transmitted through her. She was now expected to be counseling and "helping" her family's patriarch in his doings, which meant a lot. They were unequivocally showing off the Kronn family's new and powerful asset, and for those who could read between the lines, the evening was more of a saber-rattling than a welcome home ball.

Everyone was treating her very carefully and respectfully, meticulously giving her the space she was requiring, but also calculating every move, mood, and word as so to explore and/or register any weakness. They were all analyzing her positions and the strengths of her personality. It was an open warfare for power, and Iana did enjoy it at first, even showing a lot of unexpected disposition for it. She was not a shy girl by any measure, and since a young age she had been leading groups of boys (Bastian and Lucien included) in simulated battles in the streets of Westgate. She always had a noticeable drive for significance and power. She was a natural born leader, and her years in Adinaf and the adventures she lived there could fill up a book or two.

After the reception, the speech, and the welcome dinner that came soon after, she decided to take a break from the ego war and recharge her batteries.

As soon as she had fulfilled a good chunk of the protocol expected of her, she went to do something she was treasuring in the back of her mind for a long time. Since her return, she was eager to spend some time with her favorite brother and, of course, Bastian.

In her pride, she would not admit it, but she did miss them terribly. The three shared many stories together on all their summers together year after year.

After locating them and skillfully dodging at least a half-a-dozen of attention hungry aristocrats, she set to the balcony where she knew Lucien and Bastian were chatting.

Bastian was leaning at the balcony wall with his back to the party. He was looking to the Dire Woods and thinking about his father when Lucien hit him with his elbow. The hit surprised him.

Lucien leaned over the balcony too, but giving his back to the view and his face toward the party. When Bastian looked at him to see what was going on, Lucien pointed at something without saying a word. When Bastian turned to see what had caught Lucien's attention, he saw Iana climbing the brief but ample steps that lead to the balcony area.

Iana was Bastian's first love, and he was still very much in the years of his firsts. Although he was now despairingly looking at his future, she had been part of some of his sweetest memories from his early age and he was still very connected to those.

The last time he saw her was more than three years ago, during her last dismiss. It was a hot summer, and they kissed next to the waterfalls. They had always flirted and he was always excited with the prospects of seeing her, but now things were clearly different. She was not the girl from his memories anymore. She had always been older than him, but now she looked mature, stronger, complete. Also, he had his hands now full and the same old situation seemed intimidating and inconvenient to him now.

He peeked at her earlier, but as she came into his direction with her attention locked on him, Bastian saw a full-grown woman. She was adorned as nobility (which she was) and was occupying a place in society that was too far from Bastian's. Iana was young, talented, charming, rich, and had already won a reputation for herself. Threatened, Bastian wanted to believe that the memories of her were stuck in their past, a distant past. Now, there were too many things about her that he was not a part of. A destructive sadness convinced him that he could not find himself in her eyes anymore. He felt small, and was instantly oppressed by the feeling that there was no more space for him in her life. Everything he was feeling seemed convenient to him for he now had his own destiny to claim.

Maybe I was just the boy around, he thought. *It probably was just a childish thing,* he told himself while half-looking at her getting closer.

Still, there she was: a beautiful woman with amazing tights. Full of neat forms and stimulating curves. Her magnificent reinforced wizard dress was tailor-made and could not hide her shapes. She was as tall as Lucien and had a beautiful slightly curly dark brown hair that went all the way to the end of her back. She had a steady chin, impacting eyes, and a perfect posture. For sure she was something more than another nobleman's daughter.

As he looked at her, Bastian began to wonder if he still had an emotional connection with her, or if it had all become a naked physical attraction. He caught himself desiring her not only for her femininity, but for the powerful status she now represented. When she got closer, he looked away, hiding his desires and shame.

His soul was divided at this moment in his life, and the roots of his heart resisted all indulgences firmly. His spirit was burning with the necessity to leave all the things from his old life behind and press into his necessary future. Duty should be more important than his selfish wishes.

'I bet you appreciate my invitation now, hum?' provoked Lucien, noticing the way Bastian had looked away from his sister. 'I told you a couple of days won't make a difference,' he added, still trying to divert his friend from his plan.

'Have you finally set the date for the marriage?' she asked, joking about the inseparable friends.

'Funny, Iana, very funny,' said Lucien, annoyed and ironic. He was clearly jealous of the attention his sister was receiving.

'So, a big wizard, hum?' said Bastian, a little out of place by her presence.

It didn't take much for both to see that a different Bastian was meeting a different Iana. This made things instantly more awkward than both would have liked it to be.

'Congratulations,' he followed, now embarrassed to be under her direct attention.

With just a glimpse, Bastian noticed that her eyes had changed a lot.

'Yeah,' she said that just for saying. There was clearly something else behind her eyes. 'I have been around these politicians for two hours and I already cannot stand them,' she said, pretending she did not care, trying to put herself above it all and also finding herself surprisingly intimidated by Bastian's presence.

He had also changed. He was now as strong and tall as her brothers. She saw that there was still insecurity and doubt in him, but he was more confident than ever. She saw something all over him that made her hesitate too. He was not the boy she once knew. On his chin, neck, hair, forearm, legs, and shoulders, there were now undeniable aspects of a man. The strengths that would carry him through the prime of his life were already showing.

'Yeah, like you are not enjoying all this attention,' said Lucien.

'Why? Are you jealous, Lucien?' Iana said through her joyful and a little evil smile while raising her glass of wine.

Iana and Lucien had a good connection, but neither missed the opportunity to be belligerent with each other and more often than not that would lead to an argument and fight.

'What now?' Bastian asked her, changing the subject to avoid a fight.

It is summer vacation all over again, he thought, already seeing himself between them.

'Well, thinking about an adventure in the Dire Woods,' she said. 'But I cannot get into details with you guys. It involves other people, powerful people,' she said with a subtle and charming distaste.

'Yeah, right,' said Lucien, not willing to make a great deal out of it.

'Funny you said that, I'm thinking about it too,' said Bastian. 'You know, my father's…remains.' He looked down.

'Yes, I remember,' she said respectfully. 'You do know though that the chances are very much against you, right?' she said with an overmastering care, trying not to step on his feelings and remaining positive.

'Yes. I know,' he said, looking down again as if he was constantly battling his own thoughts.

'Iana dear, your father requires your presence,' her mother called from the edge of the party.

From the look on her face, her mother clearly disapproved that Iana was talking to unimportant young boys. This could be perceived as a sign of immaturity, and therefore weakness.

'They have a saying in Adinaf: "fewer chances, higher glory,"' she said kindly, after noticing Bastian's burden.

Iana pierced him with her intelligent eyes again before she left. She saw many things, more than everything Bastian knew about himself. She noticed he was fighting to become a man now. He was taking responsibility and being brave. The boy she knew was in the past and he was starting to become the man she knew deep inside he would somehow be. She actually found herself a little aroused by Bastian, but she had to leave. As did he, she had her whole life ahead of her.

'Make sure you have a good guide with you,' she touched him on the shoulder and forced his gaze up, 'or at least a very good friend,' she said with a sincere and broad smile, throwing her eyes at Lucien.

As an older and more experienced sister, Iana had always looked after the boys, and that was exactly what she was doing now, even if it was just one stare. With her relentless charm and natural influence, she was telling them something with her gaze. They knew she had been through many adventures in her last years, and noticed that her face contained more than just a goodbye. There was counseling in her eyes.

It was then that Bastian realized for the first time that she had become an incredibly strong and self-sufficient woman. She no longer had a great future ahead, her future had already come to her and she was living the great things she was supposed to live.

When she left, Bastian reflected on what she meant. Eventually, he caught himself turning his back to the party again and leaning over the balcony once more. In silence, he stared at the dark horizon, losing himself over his troubled thoughts again. His eyes pierced deep inside Dire Woods' night.

Leeroy's Food

Time passed uncounted in the tower. Slowly, Leeroy adapted himself to its environment. After the fireplace incident, his mind was somehow set free, and from then on, all things prospered before him.

The never-ending tasks and the necessary amount of concentration and ability needed to complete them properly forced him to fix his discipline issues. His attention span improved greatly, becoming excellent as he took possession of the space around him.

Leeroy was now in charge of things, and it could be said that he now loved his life in the tower. He learned to master all the tower's magic objects that were deemed necessary to complete his tasks efficiently. The rooms in the tower were now kept in perfect order, the Iron Golems were shining like silver, the books in the library were properly organized, and there was almost no fairy dust or any other unwanted magical particles on the laboratory floor.

He was alone all the time, learning to deal with things in his own time and manner. Sometimes, he admittedly exacerbated and expanded the use of magic items way beyond someone could call a regular use, but in the process, he developed a lot of skills through it.

One of his favorite things to do was to broom fairy dust off the lab floor. It was a job of great precision, for when the dust was touched, it generated random effects that he found wonderful to watch, hard to clean, and impossible to reverse. But he liked looking at them anyway, even if sometimes he was not happy with what it resulted in.

Upon noticing his experiments with the fairy dust, the magic broom, once his greatest enemy in the tower, showed him how to manipulate it to create a desired effect. From that day on they had a great time playing with it together. With the passing of time, mutual respect grew between them, and after Leeroy repaired some of its damaged parts, the magic broom became more docile and a friendship was born.

With the spirit of his boyhood still very much in him, Leeroy was always trying different things with the tower's magic gateways. His skill level increased until he transformed the daily task of navigating through them into a sport. He developed more than just a few neat tricks when transitioning through their inter-dimensional trips. He would not miss a chance to use them, sometimes, just for fun. More than once, while playing with it, he found secret passages and hidden places that he was not quite sure he was supposed to learn about. Among these places, Leeroy made a wonderful discovery: a secret garden.

The garden quickly became his favorite place to be. He found it in some hidden dimensional space over the tower's backyard.

Although abandoned, the place was absolutely fantastic. It had the clear technical touch of a botanic collection, and it was mightily artistic wherever it could. The way in which it was set, gave the impression that it was rather a personal reserve of rare and important plants instead of a garden. Nevertheless, it was still an incredibly agreeable place for leisure. Every corner reserved surprising shadows, shapes, and colors.

It had many white stone runways on which to navigate and access individual exhibition venues. At times, they also led to larger inventive dwellings that presented the viewer amidst a large and particular variety of strange plant species.

Some plants were displayed alone, but some were impossibly integrated with several other species, and, although the confusion of the lack of care, Leeroy could suppose that it resembled their original ecospheres.

There was a good amount of fruit trees and aromatic herbs. Most were clearly enchanted and all appeared to be of rare and delicate provenance.

Even considering all the amazing rooms and things in the tower, Leeroy found more good surprises in the garden than in any other place there. In the garden he discovered countless new shapes, flavors, and smells. His senses regarded most of them as highly improbable, and his brain had no name to express their tastes and smells in known words. Most provided the rare experience of being something entirely new.

Its constantly renewing novelties would never cease to astonish and please him. Exploring the garden was like discovering a completely new world.

As the place was truly wonderful to investigate, Leeroy started spending all his free time among its flowers and leaves. Overflowed with satisfaction, he cleaned, restored, and wandered in it until exhaustion. Year after year he continuously took care of the plants. From the largest to the smallest, he gardened them all, showing no favoritism.

The plants became his friends and he grew very enthusiastic about them, connecting with each and every one in a special manner. In time, all of them knew him and most accepted his care. Some, at least the most social and grateful ones, greeted him happily every time he went down the garden lane. Sometimes with a magnificent blossom, sometimes with a merry shake of its leaves, and, sometimes, with the gift of a healing or strengthening nectar.

There was an old elven tree that was particularly fond of Leeroy, and every single time he passed by it or rested in its shadows, it matured one of its fruit and offered him.

There was also an extremely aromatic bush with little bright colorful flowers and small soft leaves that loved him. It insisted on showing Leeroy gratitude every time he went by. In a clear expression of appreciation for his care, it would rub itself on him, embedding its sweet and intense perfume in his clothing and skin, dropping its little flowers in his hair. Leeroy noticed that every time that happened, his clothes would smell good for weeks and they would retain a strange cleanness that would make them resistant to dirt and actively repel dust in an almost magnetic way.

Even the most vicious species held their distresses and dangers away from Leeroy. Mostly, of course, in the selfish interest of receiving some of the custody they perceived him depositing all over.

Although the obvious abandon, Leeroy could easily deduct the old disposition of things and the original arrangements intended by the place's designer. It wasn't long before he fully recovered the garden to what it seemed to be its former glory.

Leeroy soon put many of the edible plants and its delicious, exotic, and inexplicable flavors to good use. Fair to the stomach, and light to the palate, most of them were true nutritious powerhouses. It was also not uncommon for them to cause incredible effects on the metabolism and body functions. Armed with an excellent botanic compendium from the library, he learned that almost all the plants were magically enhanced and/or even magically created. He studied and learned a lot about each and every one of them.

All over the garden there were also sculptures, fountains, and many works of art. Their shapes were too strange for the eyes to get used to, but also too ingenious to make no impact and to be understood. They were shaped by a mind clearly alienated to the common concept of form and beauty, but the powerful familiarity of tis undertones made them bizarrely universal while communicating their complex themes. The hypnotic effect they exerted over the observer was borderline magical, as if their sheer aspect allowed them to radiate obvious secrets from higher dimensions.

These truly artistic structures were always set in a disposition where they integrated their space with ancestral trees of majestic appearance and flowers of exotic curves. Their position and setup gave the garden's architecture a general argument of grandness.

In the center of the garden, there was a meeting point with a circle of stone benches and, in its middle, there was a very, very old fountain. It seemed to be much older than the tower itself, and it did not look like it had been built through the use of any discernible technique.

Its shape suggested that it had grown from the rock it was seated upon. The best way Leeroy could describe it was that it was as if the boulder had blossomed into a flower and water was being produced from it.

Upon tasting the water, Leeroy noticed that it had an unusual earthy taste of a mild sweet and sour suggestion. It caused a profound and instant freshness to all senses once ingested. It was the most refreshing and pure water Leeroy could imagine himself drinking, and from the moment he drank it, he somehow knew it was the right kind of water the plants would enjoy. It did not take him a long time to find out he was right.

The water miraculously maintained the same temperature throughout the year. It was cool in summer and would not freeze in the bitterness of the winter.

Leeroy utilized it in all his irrigation jobs, for the water made even dead plants and broken seeds flourish again. The more he took it from the fountain, the more it gushed, and he used it profusely, spreading colors, life, and strength all over the garden.

The effects of the water were also felt by his body too. He got used to the taste and drank it all day. Leeroy soon noticed that he could accomplish more work, perform his tasks with much more focus, and his body would require less rest when the day was done. After only a few days of drinking it, he would sleep only a few hours a night and feel totally rested afterward.

He also started using it for cooking, and the water made all the perfumes, colors, and nuances of whatever food he was preparing to get a renewed outcome. It enhanced the flavors to exquisite and almost unreachable tones. With this, he became motivated to cook ever more, constantly experimenting different recipes and ingredients. Over time, the garden, the tower kitchen, and Leeroy's body flourished, becoming extremely full of life.

Since everything in and around the tower seemed to have an infinite number of surprises and new things to teach him, Leeroy never took notice of how lonely and isolated he constantly was, and in this spirit of perennial novelty, the years passed him by.

In his solitariness he was not made aware, but, because of his rather special magical diet, his energy levels and physique developed to paragon levels as he came close to the edges of his adulthood.

The more he intensified his odd connection with the garden and the tower's magic, the more he was curious about them. As a result, by need, and by his own initiative, he started dedicating a few hours of his day to study their nature with books he retrieved from the tower's library. Increasingly, Leeroy was forced to spend a lot of time there, looking for solutions to the hundreds of problems he himself created. When facing a new question, he would work restlessly until he retained a deep amount of knowledge about everything around him. It took him more than a few years to reach a level he deemed comfortable, but he was not counting them.

The tricky part was that the best books were written in Arama, a language used by those who use magic. For Leeroy, the ability to read and speak Arama was also a quotidian need because most of the runes seen all over the tower were written in it. Some magical objects that he needed to manipulate to fulfill Eliaroth's task list were also full of it, demanding specific words in Arama to activate and deactivate. Learning that language was not a choice to him. Initially though, he had no knowledge of it, but by consulting a very good dictionary and practicing a fair amount daily, he gradually became proficient with it, and, eventually, fluent. Sleeping only two hours a night helped him a lot too.

By the appropriating and practical way in which he first approached such an important language, Leeroy developed a deep intimacy with its terminologies and etymologies. Without realizing it, he gained considerable proficiency with it, and this proved decisive many times later.

It was only when he could distinguish with absolute certainty what was edible and what was lethal in the garden, he began to really cook. He actually liked the magically created food that appeared in the kitchen every morning, but it was too impersonal for a person like Leeroy.

Since an early age, he had a will to express his inner fillings and a drive to create and alter things that surrounded him. As the tower was limited in providing materials for hobbies, he expressed himself in the kitchen, cooking.

During those first years in that place, Leeroy had never saw his alleged master. And he was quite happy with that arrangement. The mention or the memory of tales about Eliaroth'kull made him very nervous and anxious. Sometimes he could hear strange noises at a distance and heavy steps here and there, but he would never successfully locate the source or spot someone. For most of the time, silence reigned absolute around him.

In a beautiful spring afternoon, while colorful birds flew in through the kitchen's window to eat the breadcrumbs Leeroy always left by the large wooden windowsill, a lovely red garlic soup bubbled nearby the argyle cooker. The air was particularly light that day, and the open windows created a wind tunnel that flowed gently through the tower's rooms, transporting the wonderful aroma of Leeroy's food. The smell went everywhere, bringing life to otherwise cold stone, making the tower just a little bit cozier and homey.

While sitting in his favorite oak chair and absolutely immersed in *General Introduction to Magic, Volume 17*, Leeroy, without taking his eyes from inside the book or even blinking, rolled his index finger up in the air, guiding the magic spoon to gently mix the yummy soup that rested over the cooker, on the other side of the room.

'What is happening here?' a mighty voice asked.

Leeroy could have sworn his heart collided with his brain as they both tried to escape his body upon hearing the sound of those words. Regardless, like two very heavy wagons crashing on a crossroad, both his organs were paralyzed.

His whole body trembled in panic, not only because these were the first words he'd heard in a long, long time, but also because they came from a mouth used to command fire, water, air, and the very structure of the spaces between spaces. It was a voice that did not pronounce vain words or refer to ordinary things. A voice that came from a mind used to conceive only the highest of thoughts. A voice young in pitch, but ancient in tone. Decisive and authoritative, it filled the room.

Tizz Tizz. The magic spoon, imitating Leeroy's shaking fingers, trembled over the pan, spilling the soup over the cooker's hot iron.

Frozen by the shock, sitting in his favorite spot of the dining table, Leeroy was trying to raise his eyes over his glasses, and point them to the kitchen's entrance, where the voice came from. When he finally managed to gather the courage to do it, he faced a figure that somehow was exactly what he was not expecting.

An aesthetically handsome half-elf male stood at the kitchen door. He was dressed in a very refined velvet and silk garment, colored with a seamless infinite number of tonalities of yellows, oranges, and reds. His presence, like his voice, filled the room.

He was unarmed and was apparently not using any armor. Yet, his garments presented heavy reinforcements in the forearms, shoulders, hands, shin, and feet. Nothing that could compromise his dexterity and grace, nor tire his temper beforehand.

He was tall for an elf, which were normally as tall as the Coronians or the men from the high seas. His long bones, robust structure, and his expressive maxilla exposed the prominence of the Valkarian blood running in his veins. His long hair was as dense as a human's and as silky as a high elf's. It glowed rare tonalities of yellow, orange, and red that belonged exclusively to the royal linage of the sun elves. His pointy ears were too salient for a half-elf, looking as if they belonged to a pureblood deep wood elf.

He was a strange breed. He had inherited remarkable features of both races. Instead of diminishing them or mingling them together, his aspect enhanced them, creating very uncommon accentuations. He completely contradicted the general rule for half-elves, which was to fuse both races' characteristics, softly accommodating them together. He was neither the most human of the half-elves nor the most elf like half-human. He was just an intensified version of both. Apparently, neither halves of him made concessions to the other, hence his appearance showed that both his bloodlines had fought hard to be represented in his semblance.

Although he was the owner of a mighty body, by far, the most extraordinary thing about him was his noble eyes and his severe posture. He was a royal person, and his ever-present focus resembled someone that knew precisely what he wanted and where he stood all the time.

'Wh–Who a–are you?' Leeroy asked when he remembered how to speak.

Every word was a mental battle for him, and every syllable felt heavy in his mouth, but Leeroy managed to insert a somewhat menacing tone in his question. Fueled by a territorial instinct, and the fact that he was used to being alone, he was willing to push back the intruder from his intimate space.

'I'm Eliaroth'kull, possessor of this tower,' said the wizard.

The weight of his many centuries added a momentum to his voice that was impossible to imitate.

Confused, Leeroy was speechless. The amount of information popping into his mind at that point blocked his thoughts and reactions. All the hundreds of thoughts, questions, and failed illusions that were entering his head all at once almost made it explode. Over the years, Leeroy had made a completely different mental figure of his master, and now nothing made sense to him anymore, and, for a couple of seconds, he was benumbed.

With his mouth open, his eyes popped out of their orbs, his book still over his face and his shaking hand still stubbornly stirring the soup over the cooker, he continued to look at Eliaroth without knowing what to do.

'Is this red garlic soup?' Eliaroth asked in a smoother, but still very present voice. He was dry but interested.

'Y-ye-yes.' Leeroy had another epic mental collapse.

'Serve me dinner in my room,' the wizard said.

Before Leeroy's brain could process what his master had just said, and long before he could find out whether "yes, sir" or "yes, master" was an appropriate response, Eliaroth had already left the kitchen atrium. Leeroy was alone once again.

When he came to his senses, and with the agility of a person whose life depended on it, Leeroy went on to fulfill that man's request. He was trying so hard not to give space to the tide of reasoning flooding through his mind that he forgot that he had no idea where "Eliaroth's room" was.

Leeroy thought he already knew every inch of the tower and that it didn't include a "master's room," but he had a lot in his hands right now, and decided to leave logic to the side and focus on the task at hand.

Leeroy served a double portion of the soup over the finest bowl he could find in his hurry. Then he warmed a piece of the Sky Lentil bread he had made for the day. This time, he had also added to the bread recipe some of that strange Elven Corn he had collected from the garden a few days ago. It was the first time those plants had brought forth their fruits ever since Leeroy started caring for the garden. They were sweet to the nose, soft and velvety to the touch, and the grains were colorful in such a way that even when grounded into flour they would keep a bright multicolored aspect. The bread baked with it invariably turned so colorful it looked like a cake made for a child's birthday, and Leeroy thought it tasted even better.

Leeroy went to the tavern and chose a good wine, not that he was particularly knowledgeable in the subject, but he chose what seemed to be appropriate. He set everything on a tray and walked down the corridor without knowing exactly where he was going.

In the second he stepped outside of the kitchen, he noticed a massive door (considering the tower's standards) staring at him at the other end of the corridor.

He instantly stopped, feeling surprised and scared. His body language and gestures became even more misplaced and clumsy when he received the full blow of perplexity upon looking at this new door after years of seeing a wall there. Everything seemed surreal to him now, and it was such a confusing change in a very intimal space, that he felt wary of his surroundings although they were extremely familiar to him. He then instinctively started to look around checking if this was really the place he had spent all those last years in.

He was not sure of anything anymore. All the comfortable security and the sense of routine that took him so long to develop had vanished, and he was now a stranger in the tower again. The thought that that place had tricks that he had not yet unveiled, would normally improve Leeroy's disposition to learn and discover, but now he was dealing with people and rooms appearing out of nowhere, and that filled his bones with anxiety.

Throughout his whole life in Westgate, Leeroy had difficulty dealing with people. During his years in the tower he forgot that, but, on that afternoon, he remembered. Memories of the past were coming back as his long-lasting peace came to an end, and the unknown was again upon him.

He remembered how he had no patience for people's boring habits and soul-crushing social conventions, and how they resented everything about him too. His last interaction with them was not the most pleasant one and he had grown fond of his quiet days in the tower. Going back to meet people, especially Eliaroth, a wizard of ill fame, looked not only terrifying, but also frustrating. Deep inside, all that Leeroy wanted at this point of his life was to be left alone.

Anxious, frustrated, and mostly scared, he stepped into the direction of the newfound door. Before he could reach the knob, it opened by itself. On the other side, a very large room flooded with candle lights and a subtle and odd mix of sea waves, cinnamon, and tree bark filled the air.

Wow. Now this is A ROOM, thought Leeroy as his eyes drained his first impressions of Eliaroth's chambers.

The place was filled with what Leeroy deducted to be trophies from the wizard's countless adventures and endeavors. Everything in that room was the finest of its kind, and although most of the items were elvish, the exquisite collection of goods came from all over Fabula. Rare and unique magic instruments shared space with art from distant cultures and objects of elusive utility. Powdery parts of historical furniture from various ages and peoples completed the exclusiveness of the environment.

Leeroy's sharp eyes were quick to notice signs indicating that Eliaroth spent a lot of time there. He observed that there was bed with silk sheets which was undone, a collection of dirty wine goblets over a table, and lots of objects thrown here and there, clearly out of place.

For a second or two, Leeroy was distracted away from his original purpose there due to his well-trained instinct to tidy and organize the everything around him. The years constantly cleaning and organizing the tower's facilities created a habit in him that was borderline an addiction. He resisted the urge though, and pressed on with the tray on hands.

The room was truly huge, but the incredible number of objects made it look smaller. Between spears, crystal thrones and giant helmets, the chamber looked almost crowded. It looked more like a museum's deposit rather than a wizard's quarter, whatever that was.

Leeroy's subjective mind quickly noticed that there was a certain order in that chaos. Although it was too elusive for his inexperienced mind to distinguish with depth, he was able to see that things there were submitted to a higher, but very present geniality.

Although apparently unorganized, the room was very well lit and almost everything was impeccably clean. Including the huge dragon skull bone that was placed near an uncanny window. The skull certainly belonged to a specimen big enough to devour a man with just one bite. Leeroy felt a cold chill down his spine as he passed near it. He felt that, somehow, the skull was watching him. Little did he know that this was not very far from the truth.

Since Leeroy entered the room, he was trying to keep one eye on the way ahead while the other one was checking all the wonderful new things in there. Soon enough, however, both his eyes were scanning the place, and after stepping over a crystal frog, he struggled to balance the bottle of wine on the tray and almost spilled the wizard's dinner on the ground. After that, he decided to put his eyes together and fix his attention on what he was doing, so Eliaroth's dinner could reach its destination intact.

On the other side of the room, seated against a very large writing table entirely made of Darkwood, he found Eliaroth poured over an old scroll.

The wizard was in a deep state of concentration. Unaware of his surroundings, he murmured mysterious words while his eyes blinked frenetically as his mind considered a thousand of different perspectives. After standing for a long time in front of him without noticing any change in his state, Leeroy decided to politely intervene:

'Here it is, sir. As you asked.' Leeroy did not stutter, but the words felt like lead on his tongue.

Nothing changed, and the wizard continued hypnotized by his high meanings. Leeroy left the food in a vacant spot on the table and turned with the intention to leave. Eliaroth interrupted his analysis and looked down at what Leeroy had placed on his desk.

'What is it?' Eliaroth'kull pointed to the colored bread.

'Bre–bre–bread, my lord,' Leeroy panicked.

The mage tasted a little bit, but commented nothing. His severe expression didn't change an inch.

'Where did you find the Elven Corn needed to bake such bread?' Eliaroth interrogated Leeroy with such severity that the young man went one step back before he could, reluctantly, answer the wizard.

'In t–the gardens, o–outside.' Leeroy didn't notice but his left arm was raised and he had turned his body slightly to the right as in a defensive position. His eyes were wide open with fear.

Eliaroth took a silver spoon, dipped in the broth, and then brought it to his mouth. After a small pause, he raised an eyebrow and looked at Leeroy. He really looked at him this time, and it was the first time the wizard did that. In fact, it was the first time anyone did that, and even without completely understanding what was going on, Leeroy felt a little emotional.

Leeroy was not capable of reading Eliaroth's facial expression. Therefore, he thought that either his food had nauseated him, or it had brought old and intense memories. Anyway, the tension of the moment grew to a peak, and Leeroy was about to burst in emotions as he felt that his life depended on the feeblest thing, such as the right flavor of a recipe.

After so many years accustomed to being away from what he considered to be the evil outside world, hidden in a safe place, reality struck him and he remembered his sufferings.

Leeroy instantly felt overwhelmed by the memory of the days in which his life had no value. He suddenly felt a knot in his stomach and became very depressive, for he recollected how men were cruel, especially when confronting their selfish interests over his life. He still had no appetite for confrontation or dispute and knew that he could only lose in this kind of situation, because overcoming them would require part of his kind soul.

'As of today, you will fix my meals. Now leave me,' said the mage as he seeped his spoon a second time.

As if struck by another lighting, Leeroy became even more confused by what the wizard said. The whole confrontational scenario he was building inside of him was dismantled. Eliaroth liked his food.

Coming to his senses, Leeroy involuntarily opened a smile and started to move his feet in the door's direction, leaving the room.

On his way to the door, while still smiling and holding the tray tight in his chest, Leeroy stopped, turned, and, fueled by an overwhelming joy, dared to ask the wizard a question,

'Will you be here tomorrow, sir?' he asked, this time firmly and a little proud.

'I am ALWAYS here,' the wizard answered, looking a second time to Leeroy as he casually broke the bread and dipped it into the soup.

Their eyes crossed, and, again, Leeroy could not read Eliaroth's expression, but he could see a thousand unnamed mysteries in his eyes, and that was enough.

Confused but calm, Leeroy turned slowly and almost ran to the door. When he arrived in the kitchen, he had even more questions than when he left.

One Step Too Far

On a cold night in the stables of Bastian's farm, the young men saddled their horses and loaded them with provisions. Not much, because they both knew how to hunt and live off the land, but still a good amount. Sugar, coffee, salt, jerky, spices, travel bread, flour, a pot, two wooden plates, a canteen, a fire kit, oil, two wool and canvas sleeping bags, two long and thick military blankets, backpacks and some fresh vegetables and eggs in a bag.

When everything was ready, they started their favorite part: loading their weapons and arming themselves. They were packing a lot of weapons, and were proficient with many more. They were quiet, but were trembling with excitement for what was to come, for now there was nothing between them and the freedom and the adventures they had always dreamt of. Everything was before them.

Bastian was using a mix of his toughest travel clothes and parts of Lucien's old leather armor. It was a used piece, but of a good quality and far better than nothing.

His thorax's protection was composed by a continuous amalgamation of a few hardened leather plates. Considering that Bastian was a striker, his arms and shoulders were covered by thin steel plates, and hard layers of leather reinforced the parts that were attacked more frequently.

On the left forearm, he was using an armguard that was built-in in a leather gauntlet. His padded gloves ended right at the middle of the fingers, allowing a lot of dexterity for archery and whatnot.

At the last minute, they managed to find a solution to protect Bastian's calf and thigh tendons using bits and pieces they sourced here and there.

Topping all that, he threw an old army green wool cape that had belonged to his father. It matched him perfectly and made him a little proud.

By his right shoulder, arrows jutted toward his favorite draw angle. In his belt, there was a long sword and his father's war dagger. His mother had bought him that sword a few winters ago, so he would not be unarmed as he grew old enough to walk around by himself. It was a good enough blade, of quality but ordinary.

The war dagger was the last remaining piece of his father's combat kit. He had left it behind, for he had disassembled it for a hilt repair before he set off to what would be his last combat mission. The weapon was a massive Valkarian war dagger, so large that many foreigners would have trusted it to be a small sword. Bastian's grandfather had it made himself, engraving the family symbol on its pommel to look like a set along with his Star Ore two-handed sword. It was a heavy knife, with a thick blade made of the best alloy he could afford at the time. Bastian did not know what the metal was, but it would pierce through a steel plate without bending or breaking its tip, and it kept itself razor-sharp for a long time.

Bastian heard some rumors that his father's grip was so strong that, in some situations, he would use his two-handed sword with just one hand and his war knife in the other, attacking and defending with them both. He took a lot of pride in that and always gave special attention to strengthening exercises, becoming very strong ever since he was a teenager.

On his horse, at exactly four inches from his left hand, there was another quiver of arrows and the wooden longbow he used to hunt. It was a very good bow, fast and accurate, but it was built for a strong teenager, and Bastian was pulling with the man's strength now. However, it shot for real and Bastian compensated the lighter pull with faster shots.

There was another quiver on the horse's hip on the right side, a larger one, made for Javelins. Javelins were "small" throwing spears developed by the Valkarians throughout centuries of war. They were perfectly balanced and weighted for throwing, and were deadly in the hands of any Valkarian.

In his left flank there was an old, but still functional, wooden shield. In his right foot, strapped to his boot, Bastian had a flat hilt dagger, designed for piercing and balanced for throwing.

Even while armed to his teeth, and thankful for the options he had, Bastian felt naked without being equipped with a two-hand sword, his weapon of choice. It was one the most expensive weapons in the battlefield, and he could not allow himself this luxury.

At the last minute, he decided to take his father's long hunting spear. He thought that anything that served well in killing boars would do for killing everything else.

Lucien, in turn, looked like the knight of whom Bastian was the squire. He was dressed in his tailor-made breastplate, over his high-quality green and brown hunting clothes. His armor had a deep gray color and a matte brushed steel texture. As well as every other Valkarian that could afford it, Lucien chose every detail of his armor. After all, it mirrored his technique, his favorite tactics, and his fighting personality. It was quite common through the Valkarian ranks that a warrior would customize his gear. For them, especially for the professional mercenaries or the military career men, it was essential that once they've learned the fundamentals, they would naturally improve and grow their own style, developing their strong points and, in time, become one with it. This individual warrior mentality was not a doctrine, rather, it was part of their cultural package. To be the best warrior that you could be was part of how they perceived manhood. Their warrior abilities were, ultimately, an intrinsic part of their personalities, and so was their armor.

Unlike Bastian's improvised armor, Lucien's had a protection for the neck and shoulder joints. Its legs and arms were shielded by excellent steel and his left arm was specially reinforced considering his recursive parry movements.

His right gauntlet had spikes and a sharp thick blade in it, and his armor kit had a jaw shaped little helmet with four sharp teeth protruding from it, making a statement about the overall aggressiveness and the vicious style of sword fighting Lucien was pursuing.

On his right knee, he managed to make a fix curved blade on his steel kneepad. It was welded at the proper angle to give a lethal tone to Lucien's famous knee kicks.

His boots were integrated into the armor and its soles were made of metal, having spikes in tactical places.

Over everything, he was using a very rustic but sharp and well-made gray cloak.

As Lucien enjoyed the benefits of having a house guard equipped with military-grade weaponry, he armed himself very well. He "borrowed" a Valkarian steel longbow from his house's armory. The weapon was identical to the ones made for the deadly Empire's Archers. He would also carry with him arrows and javelins of very good quality. In his belt, he had two steel war knives firmly crossed. On his back, also crossed, a bastard sword and a sober medium size steel shield with his family crest on it.

After Lucien was done arming himself and loading his supplies, he got up on his horse. It was then that Bastian saw for the first time how majestic his friend was. Lucien's noble posture and high gaze made Bastian humble and insecure a second time.

Unlike Bastian, Lucien had no fear of staring at other people directly in the eyes. He was very sure of himself, but Bastian was the opposite, overthinking all his steps and always afraid of stumbling over people's feelings.

By watching his friend, Bastian considered how Lucien, like so many other noble people he knew, always seemed to be daring everything around them. The reason for such behavior was intriguing and alien to Bastian, and he was always fascinated by the fact that people like Lucien had a kind of dominant charisma that lingered around their presence. It was a sort of deifying entitlement that caused men to follow and obey.

Lucien had always been a secret to Bastian and he could not say if his friend was a rebel soul or just a person that knew exactly what he wanted and was not afraid of taking it. However, in that unique moment the very nature of Lucien's character was made clearer to him. Bastian understood what had been always there, but somehow he failed to conceptualize it in his own context. He saw Lucien's potential for leadership and admired the marvelous future ahead of him, but didn't include himself in this future.

He will be an army officer one day, he thought. *Maybe even an important knight,* he concluded while fixing his saddle and mounting it.

Bastian started thinking about how different they both were and why they were friends anyway. He was also now intrigued by why, somehow, this difference among them was one of the things that attracted them together.

Bastian secretly admired how Lucien was so keen and smart about everything, making everything look easy. Bastian wasn't like this at all, constantly expressing a displaced and fearful nature, restraining himself before every move he made. When really needed, Bastian could be decisive – especially when fighting. But in most subjects, he showed a hesitating character. Bastian admired Lucien and was thankful for having him as his friend, but deep inside he actually feared him for his cleverness and charm.

Bastian's life circumstances made him an indecisive young man. Growing up under a heavy self-imposed yoke of humility caused by a need of being approved had always sabotaged him, staining his soul. The need of getting other people to corroborate his actions made him vulnerable and a little socially clumsy. At the same time, it made his introspective, empathic, and non-invasive personality to be regarded as pleasant by other people, and he was generally considered a "good guy."

Bastian was raised by his mother, alone on the quiet farm his father built for them on the outskirts of Westgate. The young man believed that serving something better and larger than he was the true north of honor. Joining the Infantry and becoming a sergeant in the Imperial Army was his greatest dream.

Lucien, instead, was born in a powerful, rich, and influential family, and was one of the youngest sons of the head of his house. He grew up already used to certain honor, but hating it and tired of all the pomp around it. The reception dinners and the intrigues of the local government annoyed him to his core.

Bastian didn't even dare to imagine himself a knight, mainly because he believed he would never be able to enter the cavalry or achieve the fighting skills he understood the knights of the empire possessed. Lucien was raised to represent his family's interest in the empire's High Society. Although he was freed from the pressure and attention devoted to the firstborn, he was still expected to present himself with usefulness. As a result, he received a lot of specialist education from private teachers to supplement his instruction in the training camps. But he hated these classes and used his keen mind to ostracize his teachers at every opportunity he had. Though powerfully intelligent, from an early age he showed little interest in anything but fighting, and as his time approached he was not considered for any serious position by his family.

Therefore, there they were: different, disconnected, free, and about to make their own way in the world.

It was still dark in the early day when Bastian looked up at his friend once again with admiration. Lucien was all dressed and armed for a real mission and for the first time, Bastian really felt that they would ride in the direction of things far larger than what they experimented in the training grounds, or any other place they had ever been to.

'What?' reacted Lucien, perceiving Bastian's gazes. 'I want to look elegant on my death bed. Like a proper hero,' said Lucien while he settled in his horse, pretending he had not guessed his friend's thoughts and faking he did not notice Bastian's fears and doubts.

'Return as heroes? We are not exactly saving the world here, Lucien. We will only just be searching for a lost heirloom,' said Bastian turning to the passive-aggressive mode he would use to deal with Lucien's provocations.

'True, my truly mono-thoughted friend,' said Lucien, 'but few have returned from the Valley of Bones. Hell, few didn't even get there,' said Lucien, laughing at the pathetic logic of that reality. 'And I shall add that I'm certain that will do for a hero's merits,' Lucien concluded as he stretched his spine upon sitting on his horse, satisfied with his own logic.

Bastian felt his stomach sink when he heard those words about the Valley of Bones. He knew they were true, and he anxiously looked to the West.

When Lucien saw the fear on Bastian's face in the first light of dawn, he looked away and hardened his heart, determined not to be contaminated by it.

'I'm tired of this city anyways,' said Lucien, 'and I'm done playing boy games. It is time for us to see life. Or death. Or both. I am not going to sit my behinds in a chair and wait for the next war to burst! I want to see some action now. I don't care.' he said, resolute.

Lucien's words had such a decisive tone that Bastian's troubled heart ceased from troubling and regained its faith.

'Besides,' Lucien changed the tone for imminent irony, 'I liked how the words "the only one to return" sound after my name,' he said, directly provoking his friend.

Bastian smiled a little, then jumped on his horse's back without saying a word. He spurned his horse who jumped in the air before started running. Lucien followed him in the same manner.

The two friends rode away, leaving their lives and routines behind. In a single act, they embraced their destinies.

By the time they hit the road, the night was gone and it was no longer dark. All at once, the daylight conquered the heavens and the sun shone in the empire's sky.

The Apprentice

Although he never spoke of it, the wizard had grown very fond of Leeroy's food. And Leeroy knew it.

The continuous creative innovation, the genial mix of spices, the point of temper of the many and complex foods, the ingredients, and the overall balance of the menu hooked Eliaroth, who now secretly expected each meal with a much-restrained interest.

The wizard secretly admired how Leeroy managed to understand and to explore the nuances of some very specific recipes with a high level of precision and good taste without any external input. Eliaroth knew well which culinary book the young man had access to (they were his), and, being raised in the Elf Lands, he knew also what the dishes were supposed to taste like, but Leeroy was working out of sheer dedication.

However, the thing that really kept the wizard wondering was how the human would not never cease to push the barrier forward, despite having no training or guidance at all. What Leeroy had, the wizard noticed, were good instincts, a comfort in self-expressing himself, and, clearly, a certain geniality on how he approached things.

In time, the mere fact that he could cook ceased to interest Eliaroth. The wizard understood that Leeroy's applied intelligence was ever-growing, and its refinement knew no boundaries and wouldn't stop. Soon, he knew, it would spill out of control.

Eliaroth knew that, although many people ignored that fact, it took a lot of non-conventional and conventional intelligence plus a good amount of sensibility to be a good, consistent cook. The wizard knew all too well that this rule was also true for spell-crafting. Slowly, he exposed Leeroy more and more to his world while paying close attention to him.

With their daily encounters over the meals and whatnots, Leeroy got used to Eliaroth's imperious presence. Routine eliminated the fear he felt when the wizard was present, which was the last ingredient missing in his life's recipe. It was as if his last insecurity was removed. He was happy, and happy years came in.

Leeroy embraced his life in the tower completely, and he now felt truly content all the time. Provided all the tasks were properly executed, he had a great deal of freedom, doing everything he wanted when he wanted. He decided what to plant in the garden every year, he cooked whatever he felt like cooking, he read the books he felt like reading, and he spent his nights how and where he wanted. Invariably though, he always ended his days watching the stars.

On the tower's top or on the garden floor near the fountain, he would lie down and all the let gratitude for another day of wonder and peace burn in his heart. In harmony, he thanked the universe as he looked at the night sky. Over time, he learned to learn what his eyes witnessed and, partially unconscious, he began to study the Astros with strange affection and deep inspiration.

Although Leeroy would live to see many wonderful things, he would always regard those as the best days of his life, and he would treasure them and desired them back for the rest of his life.

Over the years, Leeroy grew strong and his mind matured. He regretted nothing, only that he wasn't practicing much magic – a subject he became increasingly interested in.

Considering he had no one's routine to compare his to, he wasn't aware of it, but he became an avid reader. Over the years, he felt it was getting harder and harder to find a book in the library that he had not read at least twice.

In a particularly cold winter, Eliaroth went away for a longer time than he would normally go. When he got back, he was even more fixated than he normally would be about his research. The wizard was going whole nights without sleeping, eating, or drinking.

After watching the wizard's struggles for a few nights, Leeroy could not sleep too. This time he got really worried about Eliaroth's fanatical attitude toward his researches, and the noises from the extensive use of the tower's equipment coming from Eliaroth's experiments would not help either.

With nothing to do besides surrender to the situation, Leeroy decided to serve his master a cup of wild orange tea infused with a mix of powerful calming herbs. He sided them with some cream and honey cookies he had baked the day before.

Upon entering Eliaroth's chambers, he heard the wizard mumbling, whispering, and oscillating the upper part of his torso, in complete absorption. The wizard crossed his hands in front of his chest as if he was feeling physical pain from his thinking process. It looked like he was immersed in some sort of a trance.

Just by noticing the number of objects, books, and scrolls that were out of place or on the ground, Leeroy knew that Eliaroth had lost it. The wizard was sitting on a small stool, his chair was being used as the foundation for a small hill of books. There were four open books floating around him, the one right in front of him was a volume of "Advanced Meta-magic." Leeroy knew that book well. It was written by maybe the most famous duelist mage of his era, Ashtair, The Invincible.

Ashtair claimed being capable of altering the fundamental properties of any material or being, whether it was magical or not, subdued or not to enchants of any nature. He claimed that a sufficiently powerful mind would not know limits inside the magical possibilities and probabilities. This was highly controversial among the academia, as most of the wizards subscribed to the theory of the "mana limit." Yet very controversial, Ashtair's work was a major contributor to the field of meta-magic and set the ground for many new lines of enchants.

Leeroy loved Ashtair's arguments, but deep down he knew something was out of place with his theories. There was a shadow of incompletion in his knowledge, and Leeroy could sense it, even if in a very subconscious level.

Although Leeroy had indeed not done a lot of magic by himself, he was deeply familiar with a lot of its theory and philosophy. He was perfectly capable of dealing the concepts contained in books such as this, and more. Much more.

Leeroy was a natural. However, he didn't know it, for he had nothing to compare himself to. His mind and education were set in a way that allowed him the cumulation of a lot of mental reach. Further, no competitive ego was found in him to draw him into the ways of some misleading fake universal truth when dealing with individual subjects. In other words: his mind grew in freedom with the right internal positive motivations that led to perfect intellectual attributes, and potent sensibilities.

When Leeroy studied, he always kept an impression in the back of his mind. This impression was about a strange and unusual thing for him. He noticed that every time he read about magic, he did it as if he could guess the next paragraph or chapter. Everything looked extremely intuitive for him. It was almost as if he didn't need to read those books to know their content. It seemed to him that he was not getting new knowledge, but clarifying some old and forgotten subject that had always lingered in the back of his mind.

Leeroy could distinguish the substance and pinpoint the magical nature of a published work very well. With no social mirror to look himself into and evaluate his position, he had no idea how knowledgeable he had become, and how this was already implying in greater things in his path.

For now, his main concern was serving the tea before it got cold. While doing it, he worried even more about the mental state of Eliaroth. The wizard continued to mumble things without apparently even noticing that Leeroy was right in front of him.

By listening to what the delirious half-elf was saying to himself, Leeroy started to make sense of some words, and, incredibly, distinguishing what his master was mumbling about.

He could understand everything although Eliaroth was using the language of the High Elves with some words of Arama here and there.

'It cannot be, it cannot be…it cannot be undone, it cannot be undone…control the five laws? Five? At least three! IF we could suppress two

– if the innate imperfection of a moment is to be connected to the fluxional structure of destiny by a semi-infinite number of dimensions of possibilities…so the expression of thoughts can indeed give birth to the materialization of will…it is a matter of focus, which of course is fueled by mana, but if…yes, of course, relativism again,' he murmured, looking through the book to some deep place inside his mind.

'There is one major thing to consider when reasoning about materialization in general,' added Leeroy, thinking out loud in the automatic mode of the scholars. 'Most minds ignore the process because of the influence of the veil of reality in their rationale. If one reverses that thought and considers the materialization and the focus element a fact, even if counter-intuitively, so there will be no necessity to suppress any number of laws. There is a factor or reason that is being ignored, thus the incidence of the five laws is artificially blurring the identification of this factor. This is not a relativism argument, it is about the very structure of magic power,' concluded Leeroy gently and slightly distracted by his sleepy mind.

He was so used to Eliaroth's presence by now that he finished the sentence while putting the second sugar block in his master's tea, as he would routinely do.

Constrained, Eliaroth dropped down from a high plane of understanding he had arrested himself to, unexpectedly and traumatically getting out of the daze he was into. He completely lost his line of thought by stopping to consider Leeroy's unexpected intromission, turning to face Leeroy while he readjusted to reality.

Leeroy panicked over the wizard's reaction when he understood what he had done, instinctively hiding himself behind the tea tray. He became terrorized by the fact that he may have forgotten his place.

'What reason?' the half-elf asked.

Although the wizard seemed to be beyond tired, in his face there was an expression that made Leeroy shiver, but somehow Leeroy knew it was not directed at him. This thought made him relax a little.

'Ye-yes, s-sir. More than reason. The Lush Theory,' he said, feeling that his own words were not making a lot of sense.

'Go on,' said Eliaroth with a calmer face.

'Yes, sir. More than simple reason: a pur–purpose, sir. Emotional energy. The Lush Theory…aah, you know. I think. I am sorry for interrupting you.'

Leeroy swiftly turned around and set himself in the direction of the door, leaving the room to a safe place. He almost ran his way out, wishing that a lightning bolt wouldn't hit him in the back and cut him in half. He gripped his tray firmly and contracted himself as if at any moment a blast of energy would hit him in the back. He only turned around to look behind and breathe again when he was in the kitchen. His heart was beating so hard he could feel the blood rushing through his body. No one followed him though. No wizard, nor any spell. Nothing.

In the next day, he was preparing breakfast when he was surprised by Eliaroth's presence in the kitchen. There was notably far more color in his face now. The wizard's eyes looked rested, and the fixations and the edginess he saw yesterday were gone.

Well, I'm still alive, that has to be a good sign, thought Leeroy, *he is looking good, maybe he had a full night's sleep. My chances to survive in this place just went up.* Leeroy was used to measuring Eliaroth's humor just by his looks, as they seldom talked.

'Prepare me a reinforced breakfast. I shall be leaving for a long journey,' said the wizard in a surprisingly mild tone.

'Yes, master,' said Leeroy. *Well, he talked to me. Point,* he thought, smiling inside while he took his cakes out of the oven.

'After you have served mine and eaten yours, go to the laboratory, to the vault, and to my studio. Gather me these items.' Eliaroth pointed to a small handwritten list over the table.

'Yes, master,' answered Leeroy diligently. *He trusted me a task!! Things are getting better by the minute!* he thought, almost incapable of hiding his excitement.

Ten minutes later, he entered the kitchen holding all the objects that were in Eliaroth's list inside two big cloth bags.

Ingredient belt? he thought. *Who needs an ingredient BELT?! Can he not use a bag? Why does he need everything at hand the whole time? Are really all wizards prone to a neurotic behavior as people believe they are? Jee, by the amount of bat guano, blue crystal, and sulfur, it looks like he is going to war or something.* Although happy and motivated, Leeroy was mentally questioning Eliaroth's purposes so he could cope with the tension of a new and refreshing level of interaction with the wizard.

Wand I, III and VIII? he thought while carefully displaying them over the table he was using to organize everything. *Wow, this is heavy artillery right here,* he thought while examining one of the wands. *You can feel the Mana dripping out of those. What or who is he going against? A dragon?!* Leeroy stopped and listened to his own words. After he had answered himself, concluding that this was an actual possibility, he thought best to hurry up.

When he was halfway into the second bag, Eliaroth appeared in the kitchen.

'Display them in the main room, over the long table, I will get ready there,' he said and left.

A few minutes later, it was done. Leeroy had never used that room, now he felt it was strange to be standing in there as he basically would only go there to clean the floor, to polish the Iron Golems, and to remove the bizarre static mold that grew around the protective runes.

Leeroy noted that every time Eliaroth left the tower, he prepared his kit very carefully and was very systematic in choosing his equipment. The wizard would dress the best he could, customizing his outfit for each of his adventures. Since he was the one who dusted and kept all the magic items in Eliaroth's collection, Leeroy realized that he always selected the most powerful equipment when going on a field trip. However, sometimes he would come back missing some of them, and sometimes he would come back with new ones.

Once done, Leeroy noticed that this time Eliaroth outdid himself. This time he seemed to be going to war or the most dangerous expedition.

Integrated into his heavy velvet garments, he was using a nimble chain mail made of elvish silver. Leeroy noticed that it was as light a soft cloth, but harder than steel.

Leeroy noticed that Eliaroth inserted the objects in the discreet pockets of his clothing very methodically and carefully, apparently following an ingenious order. The scrolls were in certain places, potions in others. Certain special ingredients in hidden pockets on the sleeves and so on.

He also noticed that it did not matter how much he filled those pockets, they never changed their volume or shape. They were magic, and could continually receive more and more things without getting bulkier or heavier. Leeroy found it amusing when a large or long object was inserted into these compartments and simply disappeared as they entered them. It looked like a trick of cheap magic, but it wasn't. In reality it was very expensive to enchant clothing like that.

There were beautiful rings on Eliaroth's fingers, made of several different metals and exquisite-colored gems. Leeroy had the impression they were not decorative, and that they all had a magical function. He knew that most magical rings were protective. These had the power to warn the wearer of an incoming attack, helping him dodge it or even involve the wear of an invisible magical inconsistency that would work as barriers against hostilities. Some of the rings were, of course, offensive, and could blast people and things out of existence with outstanding efficiency. It all depended on the amount of energy invested in its individual dimensional design.

In that morning, Leeroy knew that Eliaroth meant business for he was wearing his golden headband. It was one of the wizard's most powerful and useful equipment. It had two massive rubies on its forefront that worked as potent mental amplifiers, pulsing Mana when worn as if they were about to manifest all of Eliaroth's thoughts. That magic item was of ancient and mysterious origins that Leeroy could not trace. He knew, however, that the headband was particularly powerful and unique because it was placed on a special shelf in the vault, and Eliaroth only used it around the tower when he was faced with a very difficult problem in his research or studies.

Over his headband, still on his forehead, he had some gems that magically attached to his forehead and wouldn't fall no matter what. Later, Leeroy would discover that those were imbued with magic to enhance his physical and mental attributes.

Around his neck he was using the Amulet Number I, a beautiful silver swan with pearly wings attached to a silver chain. A stunning elven sword was neatly strapped to his back, and two thick ancient dwarf daggers, full of enchanted runes, laid on his adorned waist belt. In his right hand, he was holding a steel staff with a remarkably thin shaft of a very minimalistic and contained design, and a majestic blue and black heavy cloak made of Ansan Silk covered his back.

When Eliaroth was ready, Leeroy could feel, rather intensely, the energy from of all of those activated magical objects emanating from the wizard. It was a strange feeling. It was like a micro-vibration was coming from Eliaroth and hitting Leeroy's skin. The best way Leeroy could describe it, if he ever had the need to, was that it seemed like a pulsation that you could only feel with your most sensible mind instincts. It couldn't be sensed with the biological animalistic instincts, but only with a kind of instinct that is dormant in the back of the conscience, a kind of instinct that you need to awaken in your awareness – it was not a rational thing.

Leeroy had unquestionably awaked that instinct for he had manipulated to exhaustion the fleet of animated dust mops, brooms, pans, and the many other enchanted objects in the tower. Having to deal with them every day, hundreds of times per day, for years and years, made him a specialist on the subject. However, at that moment, as he watched Eliaroth, the next level of this awareness was born in him. As he concentrated on the artificial geometry (or magic, as most people would say) of those objects, he was increasingly getting the certainty that he could individualize them. Leeroy was almost tempted to jump to the next dimension so he could admire the moving beauty of their energy's designs.

Suddenly, he noticed that he had let himself get carried away by his thoughts and the wizard was staring at him. He also noted that, for the first time, Eliaroth had a different expression on his face than his usual elegant and severe dissatisfaction. Leeroy's fast eyes saw that it resembled a discreet smart smile. Leeroy diverted his eyes, playing them around trying to find something to do to avoid being under the wizard's gaze. Looking toward the table, he noticed that the wizard took everything that was over it but the books he ordered from the vault.

Scared and not knowing what to say and do, and willing to use any escape route to change that uncomfortable situation, Leeroy gathered his courage and pointed to the table.

'The books, my lord,' he said with the sweetest and most humble voice he could formulate.

For his despair, the strange expression remained on Eliaroth's face.

'Study them,' said the wizard. 'When I get back, I shall question you over the subjects,' Eliaroth answered.

'Bu-but, master, I have never done any magic besides activating some small objects in the tower to keep with my shores,' said Leeroy, unsure.

'Exactly,' the mage answered drily but also content, transmitting confidence.

The wizard looked at him straight in the eyes, and, with his presence, Eliaroth forced Leeroy into the understanding of his answer.

Leeroy, truly touched and humbled, lowered his head for one second, looking down his toes trying to find something to say.

He did. And, out of nowhere, the perfect words stroke him. Leeroy simply knew precisely what to say on that moment. Yet, when he looked up, his perfect words died on his lips and vanished. Startled, he saw that there was no one there.

Violence

Bastian and Lucien advanced easily through Westgate's western plains. They rapidly and without incident reached the tree line that served as the border between the empire and the Dire Woods.

The moment they entered the forest, they instantly felt that they were on an adventure. As if obeying a tacit command from the tall trees, their moods changed dramatically from high excitement to constant vigilance.

Within the forest, the whole environment oppressed them and they simply did not feel safe there. Everything there was dominated by a suffocated light of green tonalities that looked beautiful at first, but it became immensely annoying after a couple of days. Sooner than they would have liked to imagine, they became restless, moving on as if a subtle and ever-observant presence were always around them, hiding in some shadow.

The deeper they got inside the Dire Woods, the more they felt as if they were into a whole new world. It was astonishing how sudden the whole landscape changed. The bushes were as large as trees, and the ancient trees were so enormous that their exposed roots formed small hills. Some of the roots stems were so large that many of the trails and forest roads were built over them. More than once they served as bridges through some of the many creeks present there.

Most tree trunks were so colossal that a man standing on the forest floor could not define how high their tops reached. Their crowns were so dense, intertwined and multifaceted that they let in little light, creating a twilight atmosphere all over the forest floor. Even when the sun was high in the sky, there were large spots never touched by the day.

The gigantic and ancient trees were the foundation of the Dire Woods ecosystem, sustaining most life there and housing many unique species. Initially, Bastian and Lucien only had problems with some of them. Since day one they would be attacked by the tainted squirrels that lived in deep holes in the trunks. They were very territorial and furious in their instincts, and although they kept the accelerated metabolism and speed of their small and more docile cousins, they grew up to be as large as wolverines, making them terrible enemies.

Although the wildlife in the forest was very predatorial and aggressive, one of their main concerns were the evil owls and other sinister birds that hunted whatever moved on the forest floor, but specially travelers. They did their hunt by dropping down like meteors from their watching spots on the highest branches, silently ambushing unprepared victims. Their beautifully symmetric wings made no sound when they flapped, and some stories told their claws were able to pierce armor.

Because of this and many other common knowledge and stories regarding the forest's fauna and flora, Bastian and Lucien progressed with great caution. Occasionally, they spotted a white or gray shadow passing fast high above or a moving hill far in the horizon, but they failed to identify what exactly they were spotting. The creatures' keenness had a major part in it, but their eyes were not on their side either, for they were yet untrained and therefore incapable of telling sizes and shapes inside the Dire Woods. Dimensions and distances were as misleading as they could be between its surreal horizons.

From time to time, all background noise ceased. All the bug, critters, and even the trees made an active silence that was creeping to the bone. Once or twice a day, in a random manner, all the forest seemed to be holding their breath, as if anxiously waiting for something to happen. On these occasions, the two friends became nervous and apprehensive, and could not stop feeling that it was as if the Dire Woods had begun to test their nerves.

After the second day, by the shadows of the great trees, they started discussing about letting the horses go back home. They had been hard to control since day one, but now they were so constantly scared that the two friends had to invest a huge amount of energy to make them obey their commands. Besides, the path that they would take required some climbing, making it impossible for the horses to be useful for much longer.

Bastian planned to take the Rough Bushes' trail. In his preparation for his quest, he consulted with experienced hunters and famous scouts in Westgate. It was a common report among them that although it was much hard to cross and navigate through it, it was a quicker access to the Valley of Bones, and, more importantly, it was a much less used road. Apparently, deep wood hunters, orcs, and most of the vicious beasts didn't like the climb needed to get across that path.

Bastian's plan was working well until now: a quick and deep penetration by horse until the edge of the Rough Bushes, and then, avoiding all contacts, advance west through the relative safety of its dense vegetation until they get into the Valley of Bones. Bastian was willing to minimize the travel time and maximize the search time, but his plan also included their safe return, therefore a small footprint was fundamental.

When they got closer to the Rough Bushes, sunlight was far more present, and the forest's vertical horizon diminished significantly. The terrain was more inclined against them, but the air was lighter. They relaxed and lowered their guard, even risking some chat or jokes while trekking.

Minding they would have to carry all the equipment and food on their backs, which was not an easy task even with the nice backpacks they brought, they waited till the last minute to send the horses home. Only when they reached the edge of the Rough Bushes did they regretfully dispense them.

After an initial climb, they started walking a steep path while looking for a trail to enter the dense bushy vegetation. They could see now that it was undeniable that they were about to transpose to yet another biome. The trees were much smaller, the colors and textures were lighter, there was more light everywhere, and the air was cleaner.

The change in their surroundings was welcomed, and they immediately started feeling better. They relaxed, and the better mood made them walk faster and even chat along the way.

Suddenly, they saw themselves right in front of a low cave among some rocks embedded in several dead tree roots. Almost at the same time, the pungent and foul smell of death hit their noses. Instinctively, both immediately stopped.

In the front part of the cavern entrance, there was a small rustic camp populated with rubbish. Above the fire pit, in a wooden spike, still warm, there were the remains of what seemed to be a semi-devoured humanoid body.

Nasty flies, dark flesh-eating beetles, and all sorts of horrid bugs were everywhere around them. Chaos tormented that place and several random objects were scattered throughout the cave entrance. Old or new, they were on the floor, suspending from a tree branch, or even over some rocks here and there. A recently opened barrel of wine was turned over. A small red pool was being created around it as wine was still dripping from it.

After seeing all of that, they looked at each other. Both knew they were too much into whatever that situation was to get back from it now. Whatever the evil that inhabited that cave, he had smelled and heard their approach a long time ago.

With just a positive glance at one another, they agreed with that assessment. Almost at the same time, they initiated their line of action based on their training.

Silently and smoothly, they searched for cover and silently dropped their backpacks to the ground, readying their weapons and tactically positioning themselves over the terrain while scouting the surroundings with their eyes.

'Go check the cave, I will cover for you,' whispered Lucien with a surprisingly authoritarian voice while drawing his bow.

'YOU go ahead, I will cover for you!' Bastian returned, quietly shouting at his friend. Apparently, he was not happy with the frontline position Lucien was so quick to send him into.

'Now it is not the best time to argue, peasant,' said Lucien, taking cover behind a large boulder a few steps back. 'Besides, look at the size of this cavern. It must be just a couple of hill goblins or something,' he said.

In the exact moment Lucien finished his words, a primal and brutal shout came from inside the cavern. The little rocks around them trembled a little, and the ashes from the fire pit were agitated into a tiny cloud that flew away slowly – it was not a goblin.

'That is definitely not a goblin,' Bastian unconsciously declared his thought aloud while he nodded and squeezed the shaft of his spear.

'Well, you were so despaired to see some action. Now you got some action right there. And it is coming for us,' said Lucien sarcastically, scared, and a little bit angry.

Like a flower blooming out of its bottom, an immense wild ogre projected his upper body out of the cavern. His size doubled the aperture in the rock.

'I know, but it had to be that big?' Bastian answered Lucien while Lucien transformed the ogre's chest into a pork pine, shooting his bow frenetically.

The creature struggled to raise himself and his massive club out of the cavern. His heavy weapon was made out of an entire oak trunk and it was full of nodules, therefore he was moving slowly, and, prior he could stand completely up and left the cavern, several arrows from Lucien's bow reached his chest. The ogre roared fearlessly and charged Bastian, but before he could take two steps, two more arrows hit his exposed abdomen.

Lucien was an excellent archer and was trained to shooting his bow under pressure too. He had spent a lot of time hunting wild hogs with the men of his family ever since he was a boy. He knew how to shoot to kill and to keep the focus and the aim on the target even in extreme situations.

Because of the size of his opponent and the short distance between him and his target, Lucien was shooting two arrows at a time. Using a technique learned in the training fields and applied in many hunts, he hit the creature in different parts, prying for vitals and studying its reactions.

When the creature surpassed the glade in front of the cavern and got closer to their position, Bastian had already consolidated a defensive perimeter to counter the ogre's charge. When he got close enough, Lucien shot one well aimed arrow right in his forehead. It was a tricky shot, but he nailed it. However, the ogre's skull was so hard that even the long and sharp arrows that Lucien was using were not capable of penetrating it sufficiently to instantly kill him. Although, the shot generated pain and annoyance enough to distract him long enough so that Bastian could execute an anti-charge maneuver with his lance, fixing it against a rock in the ground and aiming the other extremity against the trajectory of the charging ogre.

The quick tactical thinking, dense combat knowledge, and the synchrony between the two friends were fundamental for the result of the fight – their extensive training had finally paid off.

The weight and the speed of the ogre's massive body were just enough for Bastian's ambush to work. His sharp spear trespassed skin, muscle, organs, and even bones before the robust shaft broke with a powerful snap.

They knew they got him good by the horrifying and all too real smell of rotten feces that came from the exposed laceration of the ogre's intestines. But they had no time to think about it now, for only one hit from the ogre's club would turn them into a pulp worse than what was throbbing out of the ogre's open belly.

The smart angle used by Bastian to set his spear, the ogre's momentum, and Lucien's distractions were enough to make their defense work effectively. The heavy trauma inflicted by the spear caused the ogre to hesitate and loose initiative.

After the rolling ogre passed him, Bastian threw himself to the left with a controlled roll, getting onto his feet with sword in hand, ready. Bastian was surprised by how his innate emotional drive to win was fundamental to keep himself in control of the combat zone.

While the dizzy ogre was still assimilating what had been done to him, arrows were continually being put into his face and eyes. However, Lucien had become an easy target now, for the ogre was close enough from him to reach him with his club.

When the creature raised his weapon to strike Lucien, Bastian, keeping a secure distance from his leg, unleashed a powerful lateral attack, slicing his unprotected right foot in half.

In great pain, the ogre turned his attention to Bastian, but before he could establish a way to deal with him or even prepare an attack, he was made functioning blind by more arrows from Lucien's frantic bow.

Despaired by the relentless sequence of successful attacks from different directions by the two Valkarians, the creature got into a desperate frenzy. Now, he had no alternative but to kick and punch everything around him hoping that his strikes would hit the authors of his increasingly painful hell.

However, much before he started that, Bastian and Lucien had already relocated and established new angles to hit him efficiently from a safe position.

Because of his furious panic, his heart was beating with a powerful and uncontrollable force, causing him to lose blood by the gallons through his open wounds. The increasing number of injuries he was getting from all cuts and piercings Bastian and Lucien were making sure he received, increased the bleeding even more.

The ogre's blasting blood splashed all around them. Over rocks, grass, trees, and Bastian and Lucien, it painted a picture of violence. Soon, small pools were forming under him, making him slide and fall on them while in agonizing pain.

In an uncontrollable hysteria typical of dying things, his heavy body fell multiple times, hitting the floor and the large boulders around him with great violence, pushing some of the arrows deeper into his flesh, making him shout louder in an increasing anguish over his excruciating agony.

Bastian was getting all the attacks of opportunities he could from a safe distance, changing his position every time to avoid being caught. With precise and well thought out hits, Bastian had cut functional pieces of the creature's hands and fingers, also severing leg tendons and inflicting many terrible lacerations.

Lucien, relentlessly kept up a barrage of arrows. He was now aiming at the heart to make the muscle collapse and end the whole thing quicker. Feeling that, the ogre desperately tried to protect his chest by crossing his arms over it. To avoid that, Lucien would first shoot an arrow in his face to distract him, and a second one would follow to his heart while what was left of his hands and arms were instinctively over the most recent wound. For the ogre's further desperation, this strategy worked more than once, but failed to surpass the ogre's thick rib case.

Blind, disabled, and overwhelmed by his injuries, the ogre contracted into a fetal position, bending over his stomach but keeping his knees up. Spotting an opportunity, Bastian tried to pierce his spine right behind his neck. Somehow, however, the ogre noticed him and punched in his direction trying to hit him. He failed, but he made Bastian slip and fall into the ground due to the high angle he had to put himself into to dodge the powerful blow.

The creature miserably tried to find where Bastian had fallen, but shrunk back to his nest of blood after one of Lucien's arrows went deep into his ear.

This time, the attack had good effect and it was clear that he was now dying. Lucien, however, continued to attack him. As the ogre bent down, he tried to reach his heart through the boneless part of his shoulder. After he had deployed two broad-headed arrows, the flux of blood had shown that he hit the heart. The creature threw up blood and pieces of flesh and passed out while at it. His bowels relaxed as he collapsed. It was an ugly scene.

Ogres, especially the wild ones, were terribly vigorous. Knowing that, they decided it was too dangerous to get close to give him a mercy blow. Lucien was not willing to waste any more arrows on him and Bastian's spear was broken with most of it still inside the ogre, so they decided to stand off and wait for him to expire. They had no choice but to leave him there, lying in his own blood. Deprived of strength and breathing his last breaths. Eventually, he started to show signs of heart failure and shortly after he would stop any remaining convulsions. When all signs of life ceased, they got closer to make it positive and Bastian used his sword one last time that day.

Immediately after Bastian cut the ogre's head off, although he didn't know why, he looked at Lucien.

'What are you looking at, squire?' asked Lucien, still catching his breath from the fight. 'Fetch me the water. Killing ogres makes me thirsty,' he said.

Too shaken to laugh at Lucien's dark humor, Bastian started searching the camp and the cave while he waited for his blood to cool off.

'Goblins, hum? I should be thankful that your aim is way better than your clueless deductions,' Bastian murmured without taking his eyes off his search.

'Next time I cover you and YOU will be the one almost run over by a charging ogre, OK?' he added, nervous but contained.

'Oh my,' started Lucien theatrically. 'You really cannot find good employees nowadays, can you? You do the best you can for them and they always complain anyway.'

Bastian said nothing, he thought the moment was far too dreadful to even answer him now.

'Well, whatever,' continued Lucien. 'Let me check this place to see if I find something valuable.'

Refusing to connect himself with what just happened to them, Lucien deepened himself in his disconnected humor and went to check a pile of stuff. It was not long before he concluded that most objects there probably belonged to the ogre's victims. The ogre might have had traps on the side of a nearby forest road, but in reality, they would never know what happened, he could only deduce, and from one deduction to the next, Lucien decided to explore the cave.

Bastian seemed unusually interested in the ogre's body. He had his mind fixed on it, as if his unconscious mind was sounding an alarm.

With the help of a shaft and a rock, he turned the carcass of the diseased ogre and examined it carefully.

'I've found it! I have found it!' he shouted when he saw it.

His voice was way too louder than it should be in that part of the Dire Woods. Lucien came running out of the cave, scared.

'What? More gold?' asked Lucien with a nasal voice, pressing his nose with his fingers while he approached the smelly ogre's corpse.

'No. Way better,' said Bastian excited.

Bastian's eyes were shining like the ones of an innocent boy feeling true happiness over his birthday's gift.

'Nothing is better than more gold,' disappointed, Lucien muttered to himself as he still tried to deal with the fear his friend had put him through.

'Diamonds?' he tried Bastian, interested after reading Bastian body language. 'Rubies? What?!' Anxious, he threw his head over Bastian's shoulder to see what he was looking at.

'An old Red Claw tribe mark!' Bastian was agitated, almost shouting in excitement.

Lucien shrugged and nodded, puzzled and a little irritated while keeping his handkerchief on his nose.

'It is possible that he had taken part in the Battle of the Cursed Stones, where my dad was ambushed!' said Bastian.

'Yes, yes, but that does not say a lot about what we are here to find. This is not what I would call a clue, Bastian,' said Lucien trying to emulate a balanced temper.

'Yes, I know, but it is something. A good start maybe!' said Bastian.

'OK, next time we come with presents and wait for the ogre to invite us for tea. Then we bring the matter up while we all sit down comfortably and chat about the good old days. We are all going to have a good time for sure.' The emphasis Lucien gave to the last two words loaded the already highly sarcastically sentence with irony.

Lucien was not willing to admit it, but he was still nervous from all the adrenalin released in their fight. He was then trying to suppress his feelings more than the usual, and that was causing him to express even more cynicism. Both dealing with contradictory emotions of reward and loss.

'What have you found in the cave?' asked Bastian truly interested, completely ignoring Lucien's attempt to downgrade his intents. A vivid curiosity burned in his eyes.

'Well,' surrendered Lucien, willing to get into the job they were there to do, and trying to keep his mind out of the adrenaline low that was now hitting his veins. 'Besides the most bizarre smell I have ever smelled in my whole life, some jewelry, some gold and silver, travel food, a few weapons we can use, and other objects of small valor,' he said, willing to look distracted, but still feeling his heart beating strangely.

'I'll take a second look,' said Bastian while gladly entering the cavern.

Lucien stood out, sitting on a rock to count the gold coins he found. He stopped for a second to think about what had happened when he noticed that it was hard to keep his finger from shaking.

Later, by the campfire, they remembered the agonizing scene with the ogre and all the blood and the guts. With nowhere to escape from their minds, they reflected about it. About the parts that they do not tell you on the training grounds. About those moments in combat where you need to promote death in such a brutal way, and how ruthlessly technical the vocation of warfare truly was. And about the possibility that, someday, they might have to do that with creatures more relatable than forest critters and ogres.

On that night they were made aware by their consciences that the path they chose, in reality, would fundamentally contradict all poetry and romanticism they were expecting to take out of it. There was no return from acts of lethal violence like that, and it was impossible to live it without causing your soul to take part in its destructive ends.

Although they were thought to fight energetically and efficiently, they were never told that the blow in the center of the brain, or the severed head that neutralizes the enemy instantly, were seldom possible. And that most fights went down gruesomely slow like that one did.

No one told them how long twenty seconds were when you are doing the dirty business yourself, and that normally you are going to have to watch your enemy die slowly of blood loss, and, as a matter of fact, you are going to have to apply the most vicious techniques in pursuance of causing just that while protecting yourself at the same time, reducing what it is imagined to be a great warrior into a coward butcher.

They had killed many animals and beasts up to that moment, but never a sentient creature. Ogres were not champions when it came to empathy, but they were not wolfs or bears, they were capable of feelings and speech. Now, they had to face the reality that they had killed someone, not something. Although certainly a terrible and rough someone, but still a someone.

That thought remained in them, creating a shadow around their faces as they thought about it by the fire. After feeling saturated and exhausted with the sinister perspectives on violence, they started to worry about what else they had not been told.

The Thing Within All Things

It was now routine for Leeroy that Eliaroth often came back from his business awfully tired, mentally drained, and disturbed.

More than once, he would find the wizard senseless in some random place in the tower. He would never talk about where he went and what he did in his trips, but Leeroy was pretty sure the wizard was not going around selling vegetables in some town market.

Although he could heal instantly and repair any physical object in the blink of an eye, Eliaroth would often return to the tower seriously injured and with his clothes torn. Sometimes he brought home strange symptoms, as if he was being affected by powerful supernatural disorders that defied understanding.

One day, he returned to the tower badly smoked in sulfur and had nightmares for weeks. Although the magical barriers isolated the rooms in the tower, Leeroy could still hear him screaming at night. The entire tower trembled with his mind's projections involuntarily and the echoes of his multidimensional agonies ejected during his night horrors.

After his last expedition things were different though. Leeroy noticed that something was different in the wizard's face. There was a clear and perceptible tonality of satisfaction escaping his eyes.

Leeroy would never ask about the wizards' problems and restrained himself from even speaking too much in his presence. Leeroy liked his space and knew Eliaroth liked his even more, but that change in his humor was palpable and that made Leeroy very curious.

Eliaroth was still acting very severe, very focused, and very reserved, but there was a higher sense of easiness around him now. Something had gone well since their last conversation.

'Have you read the books?' Eliaroth asked, leaning in the kitchen chair, savoring the exquisite welcome dinner Leeroy prepared for him.

'Yes, master,' Leeroy answered.

'Which ones?' asked the wizard.

'All of them. I reread all of them,' replied Leeroy hesitatingly, not understanding why this was not obvious.

'Reread?' For the first time Leeroy saw real doubt in Eliaroth's face.

'Yes, master,' Leeroy couldn't still understand why that wasn't obvious.

Eliaroth gave him a second look, making Leeroy quite uncomfortable.

'Very well, let us start,' said Eliaroth, pointing to the chair in front of him.

Surprisingly, the magician accepted Leeroy's answer and tilted his chair back, straightening his legs and relaxing.

'Start, master?' Leeroy asked with fear, not exactly knowing what Eliaroth was referring to.

'What is Mana?' asked the wizard haltingly and solemnly ignoring Leeroy's question.

After a brief pause, just enough for him to understand that this was it and that he would not escape from it, Leeroy sat down on the opposite side of the table and organized in his head all that he had been studying relentlessly since Eliaroth had left.

'Mana is the trans-dimensional energy that promotes alterations in the geometry of things,' Leeroy gave him a textbook answer.

'Is Mana energy?' Eliaroth asked half a second after Leeroy finished his answer.

'It is an energy. But it transcends the structure of reality enough to be categorized as more than just that. In fact, it is a higher form of energy, for it allows many designs of energies to enter or exit reality, whether in form of organized matter, a thought, an emotion, or a pure energy haze. However, the nature of its possibilities is not the point of it. Rather, the infinite number of possibilities that it brings from the higher dimensions, allowing those probabilities to occur in the material world is the main element of its nature. It is the flux that allows and determines the manifestation of transported possibilities and impossibilities throughout inter-dimensional occurrences. Its transcending and mobile nature can be executed to improve or to degrade any living or nonliving cre –'

'Is Mana magic?' the wizard abruptly interrupted Leeroy with his next question.

'For a long time and by many academics, Mana was considered the substantiation of magic. But, with the identification of worlds where the geometry of things was considered immutable (The Anchoring Dimensions – where the laws of the multiverse are fixed), magic was defined as the act of geometry modification and not the energy or energies that allow this alteration.'

Leeroy thought he was being too instinctive, opinionated, and not very terminologically accurate. He felt like he was running a lot of risks with the way he was presenting his arguments. Nonetheless, this was the only way he could express this kind of knowledge. He had to believe what he was saying through his own experience so he could declare it. It was how his intelligence worked and Leeroy felt willing to be himself at that important moment.

'What is geometry?' asked Eliaroth cold and unremittingly.

'Geometry is the multidimensional concept, or design, the "shape" of all things. It is reflected in all the dimensions above and below. It is an existential element's footprint represented in the higher and lower dimensions. It contains, and in fact it is, every aspect of that existence. All things need it to exist, from a giraffe to an emotion and all the interconnections and contexts in them, and between them.' Leeroy paused to reflect.

'The existence of something is a result of its geometry and not the contrary, for it was there before. A thought or a diamond needs to be designed and forcefully represented by the expense of energy in other to exist materially inside time.' He stopped as if meditating deeper before continuing. His eyes were distant, pointed to a random object at the table.

'After reading about it, I have noticed that, by the lingering in the inter-dimensional space when I use the teleportation devices in the tower, the geometries are also variable in value. There, I've…understood it. Everything is movement, everything is evolving and decaying. And this is most relevant because when we talk about a dynamic world, the dynamic itself had to have a geometry too, so refined, perfect, so integrated, and so complex that it held all the equations of existence in its design. In fact, if you look at the mathematics of it, it needs to be as complex as this universe's definition of infinity. Therefore, a true infinite equation. No, THE true infinite equation. Thus, unreachable – the key to all things.' A rare smile of appreciation hung over Leeroy's eyes and lips.

'The physical laws that kept the universe together, the free will of all consciousness, and the ultimate trajectory and fate of every particle, wave, and force are flowing inexorably united in one infinite continuous constant – a completely self-contained, self-perfecting, dynamical existence. It is a complex, balanced, interconnected, stable, ever-changing statement. Much like a work of art.' He pointed out with a surprising conviction.

'If one has the stomach to look it up, the supreme geometry maybe the most beautiful multidimensional painting any perspective can contemplate, as it contains all things.' Leeroy said.

He stopped for a few seconds. There was a beautiful and intense light in Leeroy's eyes, and a true smile on his lips. He shook himself as to get out of a trance, and turned back to the subject at hand.

'But I digress, master. Everything has a geometry. Even magical vortexes and paradoxes have a geometry or at least a mirror image of higher design, as some say. Material words are bounded by three or four dimensions and less complex laws. When a mind is in a dimension where the geometries can be "visualized," then the conscience can touch and/or change the design if the right amount of energy and focus is provided. Thus, changing reality from the outside, or even the inside, depending on the perspective. The dimensional manipulation of the geometry of things is how most magic is done in this world.' Leeroy ended as if he was resting a case of law.

'What is magic?' the mage asked keenly.

Leeroy did not need to go to another dimension to feel the pressure of that question in the air.

'It depends on the perspective, nature, and power, of the act named magic. Although generally, in this world, is the effects of the projection of a mind, or consciousness, in some of the higher dimensions (mostly, but not always, the closest ones). Then, in some cases, when there is the necessary focus, intent, and the talent needed, a new design is perpetrated through a mixture of the strength of that mind's will, it's creativity/ingenuity in design shaping, and its Mana flux and availability. Some describe it to play an absurdly active, demanding, and complex puppet show with actuality. I prefer to say that it is simply to move the strings of reality to get a particularly desired effect.' Leeroy finished his answer with a self-satisfied smile on his face.

He was getting very excited with his own, mainly because he was surprising himself with the amount of knowledge he had accumulated throughout his casual studies and experiences in the tower. But also due to how prolific he had become from being exposed to all those books and reflections.

'What is magic?' Eliaroth questioned him as if it was the first time.

The wizard was clearly not satisfied, and the smile vanished from Leeroy's face as he urged to provide his master with a proper answer.

'Magic is the multidimensional manipulation of reality by a consciousness through the use of Mana and the understanding of the living equations that reside in those dimensions.' Leeroy paused to read Eliaroth's face to see if his answer was sufficient.

He could not read what he was looking at, so he decided to continue.

'It is made possible by a mind operating in higher levels of existence. The –'

'What is manipulation?' the wizard continued his barrage, interrupting Leeroy abruptly again.

Leeroy babbled as his words died on his lips. He was full of doubts now and all sense of security was gone. He had not understood the relevance of the question, so he decided to interpret his query inside the limits of the debated subject.

'Magic manipulation is the –'

'What is manipulation?' the wizard interrupted him again.

Leeroy was intimidated, but also intrigued and decided to continue.

'General manipulation is when someone provokes an interference with things, events, and people in order to achieve an agenda,' he answered, certain that his answer was insufficient and weak.

'What is magic?' Eliaroth's eyes were full of resolve as he asked yet again. This time though, the wizard's posture fueled Leeroy and inspired him.

'It is an…interference…' he answered it reluctantly, pausing for a bit as if waiting for the wizard approval.

'Go on,' the wizard approved.

'It is an interference in the natural order of things,' Leeroy answered hoping for the best.

'Is magic natural?' the wizard asked milliseconds after Leeroy finished his phrase.

'Many new designs create chaos and distress, but some biospheres have so much magic integrated into them for so long, that they have become dependent of it, being impossible for them to stay balanced or even survive without magic,' Leeroy answered.

'It is true that a psychopathically irresponsible user of magic can stop the due flow of the soul after the death of its body, thus creating abominations, and an evil creature can create new diseases. However, one can also end famine by blessing a field, amplify a mind's reach, regenerate the arm of a worker, heal a child, and so on. We live in a world that was, and still is, molded by those decisions,' Leeroy concluded.

He looked at Eliaroth and seemed ready to move on with his arguments, but now he had a grim expression on his face, as if he was disgusted by what he was about to say. Before starting, he briefly read the wizard's face one last time.

'The almost philosophical debate of what is natural and what is magical is not logical. One of the certainties of the universe is that all things must have a drawing in the higher planes before they can exist. So, although some designs are much different from other and conscious creatures can acquire the power to alter things from the material plane, there are no fundamental differences between a rock and a fairy.

'Therefore, it is impossible to distinguish "magical" creations from "natural" creations. There is, however, a distinction between "new" design and "old" design, with the distance between them being measured by the way they blend into the background of the universe. The more ordinary something seems to be, the more it is integrated within reality. Consequently, older, taller, and more stable that creation tends to be.

'This characteristic can be spotted throughout the multiverse, even on "alien" designs, in the case of creations derived from a different material existence. A few scholars argue that it is possible to know from what plane of existence a creature or a thing was designed by only analyzing its dimensional shape. Especially if the nature of the perspective that created it is considered, but I digressed.

'In conclusion, rigid or malleable, established or infrequent, ordinary or extraordinary, all things were brought into existence through said "magic." So, even though magic is perceived as an artificial intervention (which it is at certain instance), all material existence, including what the common people understand as "natural reality" came to be through magic.' Leeroy paused as if hesitating, and then restarted as if he was touching a risky subject.

"In the books to which I have access and through my own observations of "nature" and "magic," it seems that all the debates and arguments about life, the universe, and magic end in a fundamental question". He stopped himself for a second.

Before continuing, Leeroy actually looked at Eliaroth. This time, not as a frightened servant who hid his gaze all the time, but as a sincere person who needed space to speak frankly, demanding to be excused from saying what Eliaroth probably knew he would say.

The wizard nodded in approval, and Leeroy knew he got his pass.

'It seems to me,' Leeroy started his argument, 'that the real question is: what is the true nature of The First Creator?' he concluded, satisfied with himself.

Upon saying those words Leeroy was not afraid anymore, he opened his mind completely to Eliaroth's scrutiny, and in doing so, the full extent of his understanding unfolded. He felt free of all guilt when he honestly opened his mental reach to the wizard.

With only but a single stare, Eliaroth showed that he was sensible to all the nuances of the moment. Leeroy felt secure and stimulated by this intellectual freedom. The wizard then leaned his body forward, giving the moment an exhilarating edge.

'What is magic, Leeroy?' using his powerful voice to load every word with meaning, the wizard asked one last time. Somehow, however, to Leeroy it sounded as if it was the first.

For the first time, Leeroy felt connected with his master, and all things came together for him. Leeroy could now finally understand what Eliaroth was meaning and doing. The wizard's eyes burned with the need for a deep conclusion. It was clear that Eliaroth would accept nothing shorter than the expression of a higher perception. He needed more than an answer from Leeroy, he needed a realization.

'Magic is…magic is creation, master.' And that was precisely what he got from Leeroy.

Robbers in the Bushes

After many days fighting against all kinds of ferocious wild animals and strange beasts that considered humans tasty, Bastian and Lucien felt lucky.

They also felt that their training had paid off. By this time, their understanding of combat had improved considerably, and they became proficient in applying their tactics, managing to deal with everything they have faced so far without suffering serious injuries.

There were plenty of all sorts of small games in the Rough Bushes and it was easy to hunt there because of the short engagement distances. Fat and abundant, roasted wild chicken on a stick was their favorite meal after a long day of scouting and fighting. There were also rabbits, deer, hogs, a variety of birds, and others. To eat freshly roasted meat was worth the extra fight they had to endure with the carnivorous beasts that smelled their cooking at the campsite. To deal with those, they quickly learned to camp in narrow places and to build big defensive traps before the night came. Hence, they advanced slowly, carefully defending themselves and exploring the uncanny vegetation of the Rough Bushes.

Invariably, they finally reached what the Valkarian rangers called the "Deep Forest." There, everything around them seemed to be much more untouched, more primitive. The fauna was more aggressive and worse things lurked.

They could distinguish the moment when they crossed the invisible natural barrier into the "Deep Forest." Everything was instantly quieter. Slowly but surely, the owl's hoot lowered its pitch, the deer became as elusive as they could, bears hesitated before growling, and wolves were more cautious, roaming around more like preys than predators.

The atmosphere was one of constant fear. The very forest and its critters seemed to be afraid of what was lurking beyond every shadow. A strange trouble was carried by the tremulous and chaotic winds that blew inconstant from time to time. The old trees were disturbed, and the two friends could feel the fear in the leaves and branches. A deeper shadow lingered ever close as the land became wilder.

They knew that the risk of facing an orc or a Barbarian patrol that deep in the Dire Woods was high. The boys knew that if either the orcs or the Barbarians would pick their trail, they would encircle them and attack in great numbers. Terms were maybe possible with the Barbarians, varying by tribe, but with the orcs death was certain.

Lucien and Bastian were increasingly apprehensive about the possibilities of having their scent chosen by an orc patrol. They had already gone through some skirmishes and were young and skilled, but now they were alone, deep in the forest.

Mentally, they were carrying the weight of knowing that a proper martial battle was very much different from fighting wild animals, but the experience they had defending themselves from the beasts increased greatly their confidence and aggressiveness to deal with any violent encounter. Although alone and scared, they were ready.

On a sunny day, when they were going up along the Rocky River, looking forward to reaching the Valley of Bones, they stopped on a small rocky beach to fill their canteens. Lucien went first. Tired, he aggressively dropped his backpack and kneeled to reach the water line.

Bastian took his time. After slowly releasing his backpack where Lucien had left his, he stretched for a couple of minutes before going for some fresh water. When he kneeled to fill his canteen, Lucien was already up, stretching his back and legs ritualistically.

Unexpectedly, while leaning to have some water, Bastian felt the hair on the back of his neck rising. With water still in his mouth, he gradually lifted his eyes to the woods. He felt everything, but saw nothing.

Slowly, he looked behind only to find Lucien as alert as he could be. Lucien's eyes were scanning the bushes and trees and his hand was already on the handle of his sword – he had felt it too.

Gradually, Bastian released his canteen and grabbed his sword, but kept it sheathed. His stare was fixed into the woods above them.

'What?' Bastian asked in a whisper. 'What is it?' he insisted, clearly anxious.

While speaking, he furtively took a defensive position, preparing his weapons and a few lines of actions.

'Have you seen something? Lucien?' he whispered again, this time with more energy.

Their eyes were trembling fast with the struggle to cover every inch of the trees in front of them, but still, they saw nothing.

Without saying a word or straying his eyes from the forest, Lucien pointed with his chin for a footprint in a muddy spot only a few feet from them. Inside it, there was a crushed green leaf. The footprint was as fresh as it could be, and it clearly wasn't theirs.

Bastian drew two javelins and kept his head down while he intuitively protected Lucien's flanks. Lucien did the same, protecting Bastian's back.

'We are too exposed here. Let us cross the river, maybe they will lose our track,' whispered Lucien.

'Do you think they have found us by now?' asked Bastian with the quietest voice he could make.

'HAHAHAHA!' a spine-chilling evil laughter emerged from the woods.

'No Bastian, I am sure,' Lucien answered Bastian's question.

The echoes of that voice were too profuse for them to identify where it came from. Their impressions of the environment changed rapidly as they sank with fear. The soft air of the wood was invaded by bestial screams and animalistic grunts. Before they could react, indistinguishable shadows were moving at the edge of the tree line and coming dangerously close.

Due to the sleek way they moved, Bastian was having difficulty identifying a target for his javelins. He hesitated, protecting himself behind his shield while his nervous eyes kept trying to find something to shoot at.

Then he had an epiphany about how that situation reminded him of his father's death. It was then that all fear left him and his heart was filled by a powerful feeling of revenge, for he would gladly give his life if it meant that he would take at least one orc with him.

'OK,' he said to Lucien without taking his eyes from the woods. 'This time I cover you, and you attack,' he said, determined.

Lucien did not respond. Bastian quickly looked behind him to see what was going on, but Lucien was not there. Surprised, Bastian raised his eyes in the direction of the river only to find his friend already halfway through it, jumping rock to rock. Apparently, Lucien had chosen a tactical retreat instead of Bastian's plan.

'Shit!' Bastian "hesitated" for a second, but came to his senses and ended up following Lucien across the river.

Bastian still wanted to kill orcs, but from the noise they were making as they progressed through the forest, it made the impression that there were too many for him to even stand a chance. Furthermore, the terrain they were in was the worst possible and they had no chance to acquire the initiative from there. "Backing down" now seemed like a viable option.

In the exact moment Bastian turned to run, a dirty and precarious black arrow hit the tree in the exact spot where his head had been a fraction of a second before, but the urge to escape the ambush left him no time to think about it.

Pumped by adrenaline, they ran until they lost any track of time, distance, and direction. Eventually, they committed a mistake, and, after taking a narrow path that led upward, they found themselves cornered on a plateau above the forest ground.

Fear stroke them when they understood they had reached a dead end and they started to look around for alternatives, there were none. There was nothing last to do but to stand and fight.

With a quick exchange of looks, they agreed upon that. The plateau was a good place to fight defensively, for not only it provided protection for their backs with its high rocky wall, but its access ramp would allow the passing of just one human-size attacker at a time.

It also favored them that the plateau rose considerably from the forest floor, making the horizons very short and thus preventing the enemy from advancing on them with the cover of archers or spear throwers. The distances were so short at the top of the plateau, that they would be able to easily engage most of the attackers in melee, even if an archer scaled their walls from the sides.

They got rid of their heavy backpacks and all the excessive weight. Lucien got his sword and shield ready. Bastian fixed some of his javelins on the ground right in front of him and also readied his sword and shield.

They both knew they would have to fight in a defensive half-moon arrangement. In it, each one would have to protect each other's flank, advancing and retreating together as the enemy made contact, avoiding an undesirable compression over the wall on their back.

'HAHAHAHA.' Again, the disturbing laughter full of madness echoed through the woods.

The two young warriors were on alert, watching the banks of the plateau closely. Their hands were sweaty and the tension around them increased as the noise of their pursuers grew louder and louder.

On the forest floor around the plateau, away from their eyes, there was a tremendous noise of dry leaves being crushed and sticks being broken. They knew that they were slowly being surrounded, and their expectations peaked.

"At least twenty," Lucien whispered to Bastian, while the skin on their faces paled.

By the number of sources, they knew they had little chance to get out of there alive, but their hands were still firmly gripping their weapons. Valkarians do not get into fights to die, they do it to live. The warrior instinct was rooted deep in their hearts, too deep for their hands to fail now.

'Lucien,' Bastian turned to his friend. 'Thank you for coming with me all the way until here. You are a true friend. Dying by your side will be an honor,' said Bastian, and swallowed dry.

'"Dying by your side will be an honor?!" Do you have any idea how much you sound like a loser right now?!' Lucien unexpectedly and smartly used his sarcasm to break the tension and raise Bastian's moral.

It worked.

'You know what? You're right,' replied Bastian. 'Let us take this bull by the horns,' he said with a smile on the corner of his lips.

His expression was sincere, but not enough to hide the fear that haunted his face completely. He kept his eyes fixed on the edge of the plateau as the noises of the approaching enemies were getting closer and closer.

'Yeah. Why not?' Lucien answered, doing a beak with his lips and bouncing his head. 'I have a free afternoon anyway.' He gave his shoulders a shrug and looked at Bastian, and then smiled. Bastian smiled back, nodding while he did.

When Lucien turned his face away from Bastian, he let the feelings he was truly holding in his chest come out, and his face became like a desperate man.

Abruptly, all noise ceased.

The tension in the air could be cut with a knife. They were both sweating profusely at this point. All the muscles of their bodies were contracted. They felt ready for a fight, even if it would probably be their last one.

'IIIIAAAAAAAAAAAA.' With a war shout, more than twenty Forest Goblins jumped on the plateau at the same time, confidently presenting themselves to battle.

Forest Goblins are the lower species of goblins. Destructive, persistent, dumb, and incredibly fertile, they were to forests what rats were to city sewers.

They were the lesser and wilder cousins of an inventive and astute race. However, the only inventiveness of this group was the fact that its leader had repurposed a small iron pan as a helmet – and that was all.

However, perspective is an interesting thing, and the goblin leader was under the impression that, through his magical powers, he had developed the perfect intimidating laugher. He was convinced that his magical properties scared his enemies and gave his warriors mystical fighting skills. That's why he felt so good all the time, and especially now that, because of his "magic powers" his scoundrels managed to corner these insolent humans. To show how good he felt, he proudly entered the plateau. He presented himself lastly, with a swollen chest, making sure he was standing taller among his lackeys. The body language he used while he walked through the narrow entrance of the plateau clearly showed beyond any doubt that he was convinced of his supernatural abilities and his superior strategist mind. His high chin and defying stare gave away the impressions he had about himself.

Like his lackeys, he had a terribly stinking brown war paint on his rotten pale green skin. Considering that the Forest Goblins were not exactly famous for their intrinsically refined manufacturing methods, thinking about what raw materials they used to make this war paint was not a task for the faint of stomach.

The image was embarrassing: although certainly showcasing a certain hysterical fury, confidence, and apparent alertness, none of the goblins carried a proper weapon – not a single one of them. Not even the "leader," who carried a rusty, semi-sharp shovel.

The others had a mixture of rustic short bows made of green branches (some still with leaves on them), oak twigs, bone maces, rock hammers, or even a single heavy stone.

Apparently, most of them climbed the granite walls that surrounded the plateau and, in order to keep their hands free to facilitate the climb, they left their "weapons" on the forest floor, now they were mainly armed with improvised sticks and stones.

Of those who picked stones, some, energized by their immense stupidity, overestimated their own strengths, and, excited by the idea of scaring humans, they raised their "weapons" high above their ugly, disproportionate and smelly heads, while grimacing at their enemies. On these occasions, some found their arms failing, causing the stones to fall on their heads, crushing them into unconsciousness. The scene was so pathetic that it initially left Bastian and Lucien confused, unable to believe what was happening.

The true weapon of these creatures, however, was their numbers. Breeding like rabbits, large groups would appear almost overnight, and entire hordes popped up from nowhere every spring. They grew up fast, too fast to learn anything constructive (not that time would help them in any manner). They died even faster, too quickly to create or transmit enough cultural-sustaining knowledge to the next generation. With no alternative (or anything else), they turned against those who knew how to do things. Thus living, since birth, in a state of constant hysteria and thievery.

Although of small intellect, these creatures could cooperate to some extent, with a reasonable amount of success (if it can be called that) in the execution of slightly more complex tasks. However, in general, their cooperation involved only the achievement of three main objectives: to kill, steal, and destroy.

'Shining things! Now!!! Me!!!' the goblin leader demanded from the top of his four feet.

The others kept smiling a sadistic smile that was borderline insane. Their master's request seemed to fill them with so much excitement that they started to sway in to a trance while standing. Their hectic and chaotic stance was a transparent reminder of their nature, of what their minds and souls contained. They oscillated while scrubbing their little weapons with their hands, incapable of containing themselves over the excitement of the killing that was about to happen.

When Bastian and Lucien could give their eyes credit, they relaxed, looked at each other and laughed. Lucien was the first to decide to seize the moment.

'I'm sorry, what?' he asked the leader.

'Shining things! Me, now!' the poor creature, doubting himself for a second, repeated his claim.

He stretched the limits of his high-pitched voice, trying to make himself understood. Clearly, he was struggling with the task of repeating himself, as it was not in his nature to even explain himself once.

Forest Goblins usually communicated with each other with hand signals, noise, and head bangs. With most of their vocabulary was composed of the latter modality. Lucien knew that.

'I'm so sorry, my gentle sir. Your servants, if you accept them to serve your highness, cannot understand the royal words that are coming out of thy graceful mouth. Thus, my lord, we beg you for you to repeat your royal command so we can vow our lives to make it happen.' Lucien ended with a theatrical and comical bow.

Bastian, leaned over his sword to watch that ridiculous scene, hiding his face to laugh at large.

Confused, the leader looked to one of its colleagues with an interrogation mark on his face. The consulted goblin got out of his position in the line they had formed to encircle the humans and came close to his chief. He whispered something in his ear while describing everything he was saying with his hand. In this manner, everyone could understand what he was whispering. Then, he returned to his position with the others, proud of his smartness.

The others waited, still erotically touching their "weapons" while fanatically oscillating their hips. The lengthening of their mind's moment revealed a terrible lack of options. The goblins continued where they were mentally simply because they could not conceive anything else. They felt safe on their mindless greed.

Part of them had no idea what was happening, part didn't care, and the rest was incapable of doing both.

'RRuuummrummm,' the tall goblin cleared his throat. Determined to control the situation, he openly calmed himself and energetically pointed to Lucien.

'Me?' Lucien displayed a staged pickiness worthy of any cheap tavern failed actor.

The goblin shook his head, satisfied.

'Shinneng thingss! Gold! I!' he said, pointing at himself, shaking himself so hard that the pot on his head moved a little, blocking his view.

Lucien turned his face, hiding his laughter. He barely managed to bite his lips and nod in agreement.

'Me! Me!' the goblin insisted while shaking his head and opening his eyes and mouth wide, anxiously waiting for the humans to give him what he wanted.

'Aaaahhhh!' Lucien, with an exaggerated gesture, showed them that he understood now.

The creatures followed his hands with an open mouth, exploding in collective satisfaction when they saw that Lucien responded to their demand. They laughed at each other and shook their heads energetically.

Lucien looked at Bastian to make sure he understood too. Bastian could not help but laugh at Lucien's little show. The goblins seemed very pleased with Lucien's assistance, temporarily forgetting the whole nature of their encounter.

Bastian got into the game and started waving his arms in all directions in a dramatic way. He pointed at Lucien and then to the goblins' leader, making huge gestures with his arms representing giant coins and the act of giving. Both warriors made sure that the goblin's message was passed and assimilated, making them even happier.

The two friends devoted themselves so much to the bluff, that they looked at each other and made comical and exaggerated expressions of "it was obvious" and "what an easier thing to do." The goblins began to interact with them, shrugging their shoulders and imitating the warriors as best they could, acting as if everything were just a silly formality. Soon, they were all a crowd of happy campers, laughing and agreeing with each other like good old friends.

At some point, everybody in the plateau was partaker of Lucien's little theater. Some even started reprehending others with slaps on their heads and faces for allegedly not having understood the whole point from the beginning. The truth, however, was that a part of them had no idea what was going on, another part did not care, and the rest were unable to do either.

That scene lingered for a few minutes because, for different reasons, they seemed to be having fun with all that. When they all finished laughing, the "chief," at this point looking at Bastian and Lucien with a friendly expression, raised his hand and made the universal gesture of "give it to me."

Laughing and nodding, Lucien lowered his head, hiding his face. When he revealed it again, a fire burned in his eyes. His lips carried an expression that could be read as a smile, but even the goblins knew it was a death promise.

Counting Existence

'What are your impressions on the subject of the book?' Eliaroth asked methodically, pausing as if considering every word of his own question.

'I would be lying if I said it was an easy reading, master,' Leeroy answered honestly, for he learned quickly that Eliaroth didn't tolerate any self-pity and preferred when Leeroy was transparent and direct about his thoughts and weakness.

'Linear math could work for engineers, builders, and artisans, but I see little use in magic,' he finished his answer, fearing for his sake.

The wizard's cold distance and demanding instructions kept the apprentice still very fearful of him.

'Why?' asked Eliaroth formally.

'Well, it is just not there,' Leeroy answered.

'How can we calculate and direct the vectors when our minds are in the upper dimensions then?' challenged Eliaroth.

'There is no way a rational mind can deal with the amount of information and details to calculate and alter the geometry of a particular object with the purpose to present a directed and feasible effect over it. It is just too much information,' said Leeroy.

Before Leeroy could understand what had happened, Eliaroth touched the space between his eyebrows and suddenly his essence left his body, or at least he felt as if.

Leeroy was now in a state of nimbleness, fluctuating into a parallel dimension at the same exact position his body was before. He was still in the kitchen, but the way he perceived everything had been altered. The only way he could explain in words was that reality was really real now.

He understood every aspect of everything around him. Information was not perceived through senses and then filtered by an acculturated mind, everything was what it really was. There was no veil covering any truth – everything was instantly revealed, with the mind and soul passively receiving the original facts of all things. Leeroy felt connected with everything, little or big, close or away. It was too much information to verbalize in any way possible that a three-dimensional world could provide. He knew he could write thousands and thousands of books just about the apple over the table.

Although briefly and superficially, the apprentice had already been in that frame of mind. In an intense dream, while being teleported, or when profoundly manipulating a magical object, part of his perspective had reached that dimension before. However, Leeroy had not experienced anything like the actual submersion he was now in. Right now, he was completely aware of his actions and totally immersed in whatever that was. He could see and understand everything in a way that he could never express with words. In fact, after that experience, he realized how limited words were to express the true nature of things, thereafter altering how he dealt with them.

The exposure of his consciousness to that reality forever changed him, and his mind was never the same again. The fact that he deliberately existed in such a realm, caused his whole being to become unable to go back to a narrow-angle perspective. He couldn't ignore even a second of what he saw, for he did it with his mind's eye and therefore the content of those understandings was now eternally printed in the very essence of what he was. Everything he saw was now part of him. Through his mind's expansion, he inherited a more dignified perception and a glorified intelligence, which completely contaminated him with a higher knowledge.

Concordantly, his whole being was also made open to his exploration with all his memories becoming readily available to him. Many things that were shadowed in the back of his mind simultaneously came to the light of his conscious thoughts, building a bridge between him and the realm of superintelligence. Leeroy could now experience what he had only imagined through reading those dense books, and many obscure and unreachable things he had read in them suddenly made sense.

From this day on, when possible, he would always return to that state of mind. Not only because analyzing the footprint of creation by observing every single detail of everything became a necessity to him, but because he felt like it was the perfect place for his ever-wandering mind to be entertained and inspired. By exploring the tower of truth, he would find his second secret garden.

He immediately knew that there was no turning back for him. He became addicted to be there, and the sense of completion he got from his explorations of that realm was absurd, insulting the very concept of limitless satisfaction.

He venerated the fact that there was little or no fear in that place, for these feelings are mostly fruit of many illusions born in the material plane. In that dimension, everything was available, clarified and demystified by the instantaneous "reading" of the geometries and essences. Although he found some equations hard to read in one sitting, there was nothing really shadowed there. He observed that even elusive and hard to pinpoint things like lies and illusions were just negative equations with a strange magnetism over them, being fundamentally not a part of anything, but connected and spread through everything like a virus.

The most comforting understanding he acquired was that there was no true chaos; everything was purpose, even frightening seemly chaotic things. This helped him to cope with his shaken philosophies, although it invariably changed many of his positions over many ethical issues.

With more than a few shocking moments, he discovered that the perspective alterations he suffered were inevitable and merciless, crushing his believes and ideas ruthlessly. He became unable to convince his own mind through rational logic, or to act, or even think, on the verge of a social understanding to justify something that was not accurate. He simply couldn't deny reality as he was now receiving its very pieces directly into his being. The infected processes of perception were now substituted by a clean connection. No lies, just crude truths. No illusions, just revelations.

Leeroy also learned that things like light and darkness had surprising meanings and functions. Darkness was a semi-illusion caused by the withdrawing of light, and, although it claimed its existence, was empty in its spaces, and doomed to be taken and fulfilled. Weak in its nature, empty in its substance. That caught Leeroy's attention, and he spent a long-time meditating over this dynamic. In doing so, he learned many wise things. One of which was that nothingness was in no place to be found, therefore everything was "dancing" under the one theme that ruled the universe. Everything was connected, everything was prophetic, everything was one – separation was the most melancholic lie ever created.

After this genuine rebirth, every time Leeroy found a new thing, whether a sensation, a rock, or a possibility, he would immediately meditate on it through the logic of the Ether. By doing so, again and again, he confirmed that the thesis known as "The Eternal Music" as the least flawed explanation for the mystery of the centuries. It said that although there was a first creator, and therefore one music that flowed throughout the whole of creation, there were many themes emulated and played by beings that would write new geometries. Co-creators that amplified or even caused divisions on the universe's harmonies.

With all this in mind, Leeroy repeatedly observed that, by analyzing the origin and motivations of a geometry, it was possible to trace the motives and nature of its creator. Because of it, and to his amazement, he also saw that everything narrowed down to the understanding of good and evil, hence his immediate fascination with light and darkness. He became convinced that the acceptance, or belief, of how good and evil worked would establish the shape and direction of a consciousness perspective on all things. Every perspective was either looking for truth, or controlled by lies at some level. That, by its turn, directed the angle of the power of will of the subject. The will to seek truth or to spread lies.

He understood the meaning of being called "star" or "bright," because the more aligned with the truth of how the universe and its hypercomplex dynamics worked, the easier a mind would increase its energy, reach, and focus over everything. This also determined the amount of energy a perspective could gather to express itself in the upper dimension and, by consequence, how profoundly its designs would affect material reality. In short terms, he learned firsthand that: truth was knowledge, knowledge was awareness, awareness was power. Thus, good and truth would fundamentally always be superior to evil and lies.

However, since its creation, "evil" seemed to be an ever-increasing and spreading force in its corruptions, diminishing the world's perspectives' clarity and cohesion. As reality traveled time, marking space and time with its revelation, evil was also evolving and spreading with it. Observing that anomaly, Leeroy understood in depth how that shuffling of the perspectives caused by the dissemination and intermingling of evil held the creation of great things. This, he found, was the reason why the wizards and enchanters of old had such tremendous power, and why it was so difficult for today's magician to acquire the same level of creation. Leeroy was utterly surprised when he found out that purity of purpose was what empowered a mind to reach the ability to do great things.

Thus, the dynamics of light and darkness were the first thing that called Leeroy's attention when he first entered the Ether consciously. That was not a coincidence, and this fact would greatly favor Leeroy as a spellcaster. For, since the beginning, as the innocent, sensible, and open person he was, Leeroy would always believe and pursue the notion that the universe was fundamentally good, and that evil was an illusion caused by the rebellious, jealous, destructive, and hateful minds.

Luckily, he was right. Profoundly right. He was as acutely right as existence could be, and that was precisely the secret of his talent. Without even knowing, Leeroy trusted to align himself with one of the greatest secrets in the universe. He deeply rooted in his soul the precise and truthful notion of good and evil, allowing his perspective the potential to be stretched very broadly and yet kept pure, reaching, therefore, high places of power.

The description of all the experiences Leeroy had in that lesson could not be translated into a lifetime of transcriptions. Plus, there are no words to describe most of the things revealed to him there. Though, when he finished absorbing all the information around him, and his mind got used to being open, he turned his perceptions to himself and felt a burning energy inside of him.

The feeling of power became overwhelming. When he was about to let the fire of his essence burn, he sensed a hand on what he could only call "shoulder." He looked at it and "saw" Eliaroth. However, he perceived him as he truly was.

Immediately Leeroy understood why his presence was so intimidating in the material world, for he could now see the majestic and immense energy that burned into the half-elf's soul. It was indescribable, and Leeroy was struck by the inevitable feeling that a multitude of powerful souls lived in Eliaroth at the same time. There were so many rich and important things connected and contained in Eliaroth's being, that Leeroy couldn't avoid thinking that the distances between them were hopelessly large.

The apprentice was also stunned by the constant distortions caused by the powerful magic objects that the wizard was wearing, and how the mighty spells that were cast over him flowed. All that, plus his experiences and powers acquired throughout the centuries, contributed to creating an energy field so strong that it transcended into reality, reverberating in the substances around him as a quiet noise of multiple effects. These vibrations were identifiable only by the most inner instincts of the sensible, but its effects were over everything around him. Leeroy could now understand that in many unexplainable levels.

Regardless of all the great things about Eliaroth's image in the Ether, Leeroy could not avoid focusing in a greater power reflected by the wizard's being. Leeroy saw something in his master that was truly terrible, and he knew that it was much greater than the things that composed Eliaroth's persona. Naturally curious, Leeroy projected all his attention to it, but was fully repelled and forced into a different direction.

The wizard started to control the section, sitting both on the table and pointing to an apple over it.

'Transform it into a pear,' he said.

Eliaroth did not really "say" it to Leeroy, for words were little things in that place. He expressed the feeling to the apprentice by having his intention naturally transmitted through a mind's connection. In it, there was also all the information on how to do it. Eliaroth communicated a complex concept with his mind, and it was impossible for Leeroy not to receive it because the whole concept of his request was entirely and wholesomely conveyed. Everything was so wonderful and truthful for Leeroy that he felt encouraged to try and immediately focused on the apple.

At first, he focused on the fruit as revealed unto him, becoming amazed by how he could be given every detail of it. He "saw" all the days of that fruit, from its inception until now. He understood it as all its interactions between it and the world around it. He even "saw" the tree from where it came, enjoying every little detail of its existence. Every curve on the bark, every lost leave, and every ray of sun and particle of water that fed it.

In time, he had counted all the apple's interactions, from its conception, to that very moment. Only by appreciating the total amount of information he could gather about such a simple object, he understood that time behaved differently on the Ether. The faster the distortion he was capable to create or participate, the more information he could gather. However, everything he was receiving contained much more energy that his time bounded body could withstand. Therefore, he had to be in a timeless plane to absorb all that true reality without having his brain burst into flames.

After his mind had engulfed and exhausted all the apple's elements, following Eliaroth's transmission, he drew a picture of all its particles and its vectors as it stood. After, he started a process that many wizards call "to draw" or "to design." He started to use his mind and energy to change the position and nature of the particles that composed the apple.

While struggling with that process, Leeroy came to understand that day's lesson. He learned about the need of an immense knowledge of advanced multi-dimensional mathematics (the very subject of the book discussed previously with his master) was fundamental to rearrange the particles of the apple. At the same time, he understood that the same math that was unbelievably hard to master in the slower speed or material existence, was just an available detail in the Ether. Everything was vectored there and nothing could be really destroyed but changed, with all interactions calculated to infinitesimal precision. When a mind existed there, it instantly perceived all the math of all the substances around it to a quantum level. For that reason, all the concepts and calculus described in many math manuals were just guides, just particles of water in the surface of a deep sea of interconnected equations that, bonded together, formed the universe and the all art on it.

Much before he could form a pear of any kind, Leeroy reached the intrinsic point of Eliaroth's lesson: the need to be objective and to think linearly when studying the universe was pointless. You must see and change reality from a place where reality is bare and changeable.

The class continued even after Leeroy came back to the "real" world, for he brought part of this perception with him, making him an absolute master of any linear math or any other mathematics that a tridimensional mind could produce.

The lesson was not over though, for the apple on the table was still not a pear. Pressed by his master, the apprentice concentrated on the task at hand.

Nevertheless, his mind was enlarged much beyond common geniality, Leeroy was still struggling with elements of shape, form, and substance to balance the equations that composed a simple pear.

In the kitchen window, a few colorful birds that would look for food there at that time of the day were waiting for some leftover bread that Leeroy would regularly serve them. Impatient, they would tweet tirelessly to a seemingly hypnotized Leeroy. Then, moved by the natural and fascinating effects of the changing of color and shape that were affecting the apple, they became silent and, amazed, they observed the phenomenon.

Exhausted and knowing that he reached his limits, Leeroy called it over.

In a split second, Eliaroth retracted him back to the "real" world. It took a certain time for his mind to get used to existing in such a suppressed reality again. Parts of it, he knew, would never come back to be like they were, for he brought elements of what he saw with him, making him an absolute master of any linear math and many other quantifiable sensibilities that a tridimensional mind could produce only in once in a lifetime epiphanies.

Although scarred, blurry, and dizzy, his mind dragged back from the Ether most of the knowledge and awareness he was exposed to, for only the remembrance of it made it real. From that day on, every time he reentered the Ether, the barrier between both realities got thinner and thinner. In time, he learned to feed from the energies thereof, keeping his mind running at the necessary speed and energy levels for him to navigate both as he pleased, or needed to.

It took him some time until he felt ready to open his eyes in the material world again, and when he did, they were different. Leeroy's eyes were as different as his soul now was. Her gaze now had more in common with Eliaroth's than with the people of Westgate.

The wizard anticipated this, making sure that the first thing Leeroy saw would be his wide, golden-yellow elven eyes. When Leeroy met his master's gaze, he could feel Eliaroth's distant comfort and dry empathy flowing through them. With elegance and power, the magician's face guided the apprentice to a peaceful conclusion to that extraordinary experience.

When most of the agitation of the experience had left the apprentice, and he was calm enough, the wizard used his eyes once more to guide Leeroy's to the pear over the table.

The fruit resembled a perfectly formed pear. Leeroy studied it for a few moments, and then he looked to Eliaroth. Clueless to what was to come, the apprentice smiled, trying to ease the tension.

Eliaroth kept looking straight to the pear with a serious and severe expression on his face as if he was seeing more than normal eyes could see.

'Eat it,' he said to Leeroy, dead serious.

Without thinking about it, Leeroy grabbed it and took a bite. Its juices tasted like fish left in the sun for two days, and it smelled like fish left in the sun for four days.

Leeroy almost threw the first bite, but Eliaroth frowned in such a menacing manner that he had no option but to swallow it. The wizard made it clear that he would not tolerate anything but his order obeyed.

Leeroy had no choice, he ate the whole thing. He painfully ate it all, controlling his vomit every step of the way. Bit by bit, he forcefully chewed and swallowed the awful fruit until every piece of it was inside of him.

'You ought to deal with your own creation,' said the wizard when Leeroy was over.

The intensity and seriousness of the Eliaroth's words marked the moment with a profound solemnity, tattooing them on the apprentice's heart.

Discreetly, and only when he was sure that his lesson sunk in, Eliaroth left the kitchen.

"You ought to deal with your creation." Those words would forevermore echo in Leeroy's mind. On that day, Eliaroth taught Leeroy more than he could ever imagine about respect and responsibility.

With a lot to deal with, Leeroy sat in his chair, collecting himself for hours. His mind was so energized and the number of things he had to digest was so vast, that he was unable to sleep for days after.

"Well, another day in school…" he said to himself, struggling not to lose faith.

He looked around the silent kitchen searching for something to distract or even anchor his mind. He saw the birds anxiously tweeting to him and suddenly realized that they were calling him for hours. He grabbed a piece of bread and went to finally feed the annoyed little things by the window. Once there, he raised his intensified eyes and contemplated the first stars that began to appear in the evening sky. The birds, impatient by hunger, overcame their natural fear and crawled over his hands and arms, pecking the bread vigorously from his fingers. Yet, Leeroy would not mind them at all, for he was now gazing at the stars with his new eyes. To him now, the stars were never so beautiful and his eyes never felt so wide and fierce.

The apprentice spent the whole night by the window, submerged in the emotions and thoughts of his new perspective of the universe. Exhausted, but refreshed. Lost, but also found.

Still in the Plateau

'Grashgraushumpgrrrrrraaaaush,' the goblin growled like a wild animal while desperately trying to free himself from the weight of Lucien's boot.

Lucien, still pumped by the adrenaline of the killing spree, was enjoying himself a little bit while questioning the poor creature.

Bastian was methodically checking one by one of the two dozen bodies on the plateau, tirelessly searching for any clue that could point him in some direction.

'Bi-big blue sword! Yes! Me saw it! Big orco!!! Yes, big orc!' the goblin barely managed to throw out these words through his raging teeth and his lack of breath.

'I can't believe I'm doing this,' Lucien thought out loud. 'This is as insane as asking a dog if he saw a needle in the haystack,' he concluded, shaking his head frustrated with the apparent frugality and pointlessness of it all.

'Me know! Me know!' The goblin tried to simulate a pathetic smile to draw some mercy from Lucien. His eyes were almost dropping from their sockets and his skin had changed color to a paler tonality. The goblin had many broken bones that crackled as Lucien step on him and blood was uncontrollably spilling out of his mouth.

'Big blue sword?' asked Lucien while he looked at the horizon as if asking an invisible being for patience.

'Hum'hum! Big sword! Hum'hum!' The fear and the anxiety in the poor creature's voice was pitiful.

The hill goblins were not smart, but he could see the impatience in Lucien's eyes and understand what was going to happen next. Seeing this, Lucien moved his blade casually, adding to the psychological terror imposed on the already terrified goblin. It worked and he began to panic.

'Yes! Yes! Me knows! Me knows! Big sky sword! Big warrior! Big orc warrior! Red Clawn!' the miserable creature shouted with his last breath.

Lucien saw his interest in the goblin renewed by his last words.

'Red Claw?' he asked the goblin, releasing a little of the pressure over the creature's chest and neck.

'Yes! Yes! Orcos bang with ax,' the goblin was breathing heavily through his teeth and blood, 'but big warrior bang with sword! Big bang!'

'Where is this warrior? Where can I find him? Speak!'

Lucien released the pressure over the creature torso a little more so the goblin wouldn't pass out from the lack of air. However, he pressed his face and head further, increasing the goblin's agony greatly.

'Red Claw! Red Claw!' the agonizing creature shouted.

'No, you piece of filth, the warrior's name!' Lucien rested the tip of his sword over the goblin chest.

'If Luggy say, war chief master king let Luggy go?' The tone of the goblin's voice was childish and pitiful.

'Luggy go?' Lucien asked cynically. 'Yes, I will let you go,' he promised.

'Big orc warrior! Big war chief!' the goblin started at once.

He looked sideways, trying to retrieve information from his brain, but it was a very short round trip and he promptly looked back at Lucien with nothing.

'And where is this big warrior at? Where is his clan?' asked Lucien.

'Red Claw! Red Clawn! Me knows! Great tribe, where the moon touch the water! Big water!' screamed Luggy.

'The Moon Lake?!' asked Lucien.

'Yes! Yes! Doom Blake! Yes! Yes!' Luggy was smiling desperately, analyzing every inch of Lucien's face trying to find if what he was saying had pleased him.

'You are not lying to us, are you, you little bastard?' Lucien made the creature savor the full taste of his boot's tip.

'No! No! Luggy is true!' he insisted. 'Big water after the white bang hole!'

'White bang hole?' asked Lucien.

'Yes! Yes! Many sticks, white sticks, good for the bang!' he pointed to a mace made of a human femur that was on the ground a few yards from them. It was still held by its wielder's severed hand.

'The Valley of Bones?' asked Lucien unsure.

'Yes, yes! Boones! Good to make the bang!' Luggy was doing his best to look useful.

'How far west after the Valley of Bones is this tribe's camp?' asked Lucien speculatively.

'Wha–what?'

Lucien's sentence was too complicated, and Luggy's motivation to live was not enough to make him understand it.

Frustrated with the goblin's limitations, Lucien mercilessly supported most of his weight over his right boot on the goblin, almost cracking his skull.

'Aaah!' the goblin screamed miserably. 'You said let Luggy go!' he said and started to cry.

'Yes, I did.' Lucien leaned to look at him straight in the eye, letting the goblin know his true intentions.

'Go.' Lucien pressed all his weight against the creature's head and plumed the tip of his sword into Luggy's naked chest.

The poor creature shook violently from the sharp pain when his heart was split in two. The shake turned to a convulsion when the flow of blood to his brain was interrupted. Then it stopped moving completely. When that happened, Lucien removed his sword from him and went to talk with Bastian, who was on the other side of the plateau still searching the bodies.

'You have got to be kidding me!' Bastian complained. 'What IS that smell?!' Disgusted, he vigorously rubbed his fingers in a three trunk full of damp moss.

Extenuated, as if he had a sudden physical relief, Lucien approached his friend slowly.

'Have you found something?' he asked Bastian.

'Maybe.' The frustration in Bastian's voice could not be contained. 'Some of them had some jerk that looks orcish,' he said, showing the beef jerk to Lucien. 'It seems that they did some trade with a local tribe. Probably the Red Claw,' he risked. 'I saw some small totems with their symbol too,' he resumed his case.

'You lucky bastard,' Lucien said with a smart smile on the corner of his lips.

Bastian did not understand.

In the kitchen, cobwebs grew where once the pots made good food. In the garden, unharvested fruits were rotting away and the place began to show signs that it had known better days. Throughout the tower, in the golems of the corridor, around the books in the library, inside the laboratory instruments, dust accumulated.

As Eliaroth caused his apprentice to suffer a deeper initiation to the magic arts, and quickly the young man found out he had no idea what it took to be a spellcaster. Everything was radically different from what he had imagined. The real experience was much, much more profound.

No projection or arrangements could have prepared him for what he was now daily facing. As sudden as the conceptual years of his formation had come, they were gone. A deeper engagement cornered the apprentice in the world of wonder he had always dreamed of. The theoretical phase was gone, the practical period was up and running deep. Without warning, the apprentice found himself doing fantastic magic in no time, all the time.

He now expended all his time meditating, conjuring, and pouring his mind into paradoxes on purposes. He was truly fixated and completely immersed in the idea of exploring the forces that kept the universe together, and, sometimes, apart.

He now had only one desire: to explore, manipulate, and transform the huge painting made of living art called reality, and, in the process, discover the limits of his soul by tasting, experiencing, and mingling with everything he could.

The greatness of the Cosmos and its architecture alone was enough fuel to inspire him to explore and gather his magic powers until and beyond the biological limits of his physical body.

He particularly liked to use his time studying the composition of the Astros, especially the stars, his favorites. Their subtle but basilar influences on all things did not cease to amaze the apprentice.

In surrendering to this newfound passion, he changed. His outlook on life was so altered that he no longer recognize himself, but he didn't care. In fact, his carelessness was so acute that it reflected upon his rational personality, causing him to lose interest in most things, including himself. In time, he lost track of who he was.

The only thing he knew for sure now was that whoever he was becoming, he had little to do with the frightened boy he used to be. The infinity and power of his new horizons set the past on the past; now, every day, life was new.

Things that had been stale to his eyes were now full of colors, shining under the daylight of his new revelations. He now stared reality in depth, sometimes reading it more than he could bear to care for. His soul's fire was lit, and it burned with a strength that startled, excited, and stimulated him at the same time. He was absolutely hooked, minding little else than to expand his perspective even further.

The apprentice had restlessly immersed himself into an impressive spiral of self-knowledge and self-improvement through the scanning of the Ether. Neither food, work, leisure, nor any other three-dimensional concept mattered to him anymore. He was seeing the material world through his inner being now, filtered thru the magic sight he was able to store in his spirit. Everything was geometry and everywhere was art. Art waiting to be discovered, art waiting to be admired, art waiting to be accomplished.

Every day he hungered excruciatingly to reach his self-purpose. He felt like his soul was an immense pool that had been empty since its construction, but now, after discovering what water was, it desired, above all else, to be filled.

He was willing. Willing in the edges of despair. Willing to know the limits of his own consciousness' expansion until it exploded throughout the stars. He was on a path that obeyed a different law from the world he was born in, for the more he ran, the more breath he had. There was nothing to stop him and he spent years on this acceleration in the direction of the unknown, and the only thing he found was the desire for more and more, and then some more. He finally found what power was.

As regular young men consumed themselves with their youth's passions, he found his, finally becoming infatuated with it. Beginning with the deflowering of his cognizance, his thirst for power became the one thing that eventually gave him focus.

Instead of sophisticated plates, he now ate whatever he found at hand – mostly magically created food. He now seldom slept or did anything else besides exploring and studying the Ether. His clothes were dirty and full of holes. His nails, hair, and beard were neither trimmed nor tended, and his hygiene habits were far less than ideal. He now lived only to feel Mana flowing through him.

He lost track of the seasons and of time itself, he transcended preconceived social notions, and his sense of attachment was completely lost and forgotten somewhere – everything was consumed by his soul's quest.

During this time, he reached the true origin of many things, maturing immensely as an individual, greatly surpassing most folks in wisdom and knowledge. Without noticing, he acquired that intense and concentrated expression of the wizards. It was an ever-present focus, a real drive that only a spellcaster possessed. A tension so transcending that would drench in the very air around them, revealing and stating that their mind's trigger was about to break, bursting their will throughout reality.

His thoughts were now like arrows; his will, a swinging axe; his ire, destruction. He was becoming a spellcaster, a pretty good one.

On a cloudless night, after a long day, he was meditating at the top of the tower. As it was now his costume, he was watching the stars, but not with his eyes of flesh.

After studying and admiring them for long hours, he went into a deep trance. A cold mountain wind was blowing into his bare chest, but he was not affected by it. He elevated his mind and splinted his consciousness in two, placing them in different "locations." Then, he started to manipulate and experiment with the energies that he found in these places, crossing the angles, molding existential junctions, rewriting complex equations, and watching the creations that laid in the space between spaces.

When he received the understanding that theme was everything, a pale golden light decanted from his head and naked thorax. It was the residual Mana that was coming into existence as it was farmed by his experimentations. Random sparks of discharged energies orbited and sparkled around him.

Although his conscious mind was not aware of it, he was levitating. Evolved in a unique and subtle vibration, he was fluctuating a few inches above the tower's top.

Affected by the field of magic around him, some small rocks rebelled against gravity, moving into strange patterns and lining themselves into all kinds of formations. Some were brought into being as moving symbols and silhouettes that represented equations and certain aspects of the "spiritual" world. The contours and transformative shapes of these formations could mesmerize an untrained mind into madness even over a quick stare. As the sculptures in the garden below him, these disturbances crudely revealed what was kept hidden in the higher dimensions, effectively communicating universal things. Things that directly affected reality when manifested, pouring an aura of irresistible magic around them. Their mere materialization was an open portal between two different realities, and that was exactly what the apprentice was searching for and experimenting with. His investigations were to determine what kind of door he could be, and what kind of energy and things he could, would, or should bring forth.

While he was still immersed in his meditations, something moved between two mountain peaks high above the tower. Unapologetically cutting the air of the night sky, a shadow quickly flew on a straight trajectory directly to the tower. It traveled with a tremendously unnatural speed, diving aggressively but keeping its altitude high above the treetops.

As the shadow approached, it gradually became a pale light. It was Eliaroth. When he was close enough to the tower, he deactivated the spell that made him fly faster than an angry dragon and, just as unnaturally, he slowed down.

As he got closer the tower top, he saw his apprentice in the middle of his meditation. The wizard approached carefully and silently, for he wished not to disturb the student. He stayed there, assessing the human. Silently, he stopped in middle air, observing.

Eliaroth was highly interested in his apprentice's recent progresses. Careful not to disturb him, he delicately let his feet touch the tower's wall. From there, he watched the human absorbed in his explorations.

The scenery made an even grander figure out of what was happening there. The mighty wizard was illuminated by the trans-dimensional lights poured by his apprentice. His lengthy mantle, his weapons, his majestic garments, and his magnificent long hair were agitated by the strong mountain breeze. His face was severe and undisturbed, but a faint and smart gladness was shown on the corner of his eyes.

In his hand, he was carrying a huge cloth bag. It was drenched in a dense bright blue liquid that seemed to escape from the round object the bag was containing. In his other hand, he was holding his graceful sword, unsheathed still. Its blade was stained by the same self-moving and sticky blue liquid. There was so much of it, that it was seeping into his hand and dropping from the tip of his sword. The wizard was clearly still in the middle of something, however, in that moment, his attention was turned over to his pupil.

Ignoring his own doings, he stood there, witnessing his apprentice's flows. When Eliaroth felt he saw what he needed to see, he smiled a very discreet smile with his eyes. The Valkarian, however, was deeply immersed in his research and did not notice his master.

'Child,' the wizard called using a calming voice.

He had never used such voice with his apprentice before. No answer came from the apprentice.

'Pupil!' he called with a voice full of power that echoed high in the Ether, reaching him.

The apprentice slowly and gradually got out of his daze. While he did so, the aura around him progressively disappeared. He set himself upright while still suspended in the air by his magical symptoms. When he opened his eyes, the same light of the aura around him was shining from them, but with a stronger intensity. He then blinked, adjusting his eyes to that reality. The light faded and disappeared. Yet, the stronger soul that conjured it was still there in his new gaze.

'Yes, master,' he finally answered Eliaroth.

His voice was now a man's voice. Like his eyes, it was deep and harmonic. Harmony of the lucky ones who find themselves in life.

Now he was as tall as Eliaroth, but he grew up to be of a more robust making. His body was very vigorous and his shoulders were broad and strong. His Valkarian bones had been strengthened by years of hard and passionate work around the tower. The long-term exposure of the magically enhanced foods from the garden and the healthy enchanted water consumed over the years played a major role in the formation of his exceptionally strong body. The supernatural nutrition he obtained from them while maturing into adulthood profoundly affected his metabolism and anatomy, giving him physical and mental advantages that went far beyond what was considered typical for a human.

The apprentice didn't know, but he was twice as strong as men of the same body complexion, and needed very little rest for a full recovery. His health was not easily compromised with diseases, his senses were refined, and his vision was sharper. His skin was flawless, and his hair and beard became dense and sturdy, his hands were as firm as of a trained spearman, and the many traces of

152

his journey were visible all over him. The dirty rags he was using, his mighty chest, his oily hair, and his peaceful face's expression attested that. Above all, there was a lot of contemplative maturity in him now, making his young eyes shine bright like jewels.

For a split second, Eliaroth looked at his aspect as if he was measuring something invisible. Then the wizard completely changed his facial expression, hinting that he had made his mind over a subject, but deciding to keep it in the back of his mind.

The apprentice was not sure what had just happened, nevertheless, after all things he'd been through, he still found it very hard to read his master.

'Clean the sword,' said the wizard. 'It is Slash blood,' he warned. 'You still remember how to clean Slash blood, right?' he asked rhetorically.

'Yes, master,' he said serenely, while his body was still vibrating with unbalanced magic energies.

'And put that in my lab over the Black Table,' Eliaroth said emphatically and gave him the bag and the sword at once.

The apprentice noticed that the wizard strangely chose the stairs over teleporting himself to his room, as he would normally do. He seemed tired. Not only physically for lack of rest or Mana, but by the cumulative stresses he was submitting himself to for decades now. Eliaroth's insistence over his goals was taking his toll on him.

'There is a large group of orcs on the Southern Trail, a day's walk away from us,' Eliaroth said, turning around as if he had almost forgotten to mention it. 'They are clearly advancing toward us,' he said dryly. 'Another attack, apparently,' his tone changed to mild frustration. 'I want you to deal with them, after dinner,' he commanded casually and went down the stairs.

'Yes, master,' said the apprentice.

When he saw himself alone again, he silently raised his eyes at the stars one more time.

Klunk

Around them, day and night, there were new sounds wherever they cared to listen. Bastian and Lucien were now so deep inside the Dire Woods that new species of birds and insects created a completely different sound sphere around them. Even the way the thunder reverberated on the rocks and trees was different for them – it was an entirely different world.

One such noise was the waters of the Rocky River and its many effluents. It rumbled loudly as it crashed and fell into its steep streams. They were now in a region of many cliffs and bodies of water, and its noises as it ran and fell was always in the background.

The precipitous terrain around them was marked by waterfalls every now and then. The trails were narrow and hard to hike. Most of the time they were going up or down, seldom in a straight line. This took a toll on their legs and their pace slowed.

The vegetation was more varied and denser, but the trees were shorter and smaller and far more numerous. There was a larger variety of plants in general, especially of herbs and flowers, which was noticeable by the higher number of shapes and sizes of leaves and petals.

Both, in the air and on the ground, the number of bugs was also sensibly greater. However, they noticed that their disposition was benign and their rhythms slower.

Fading old hunting trails were the only way to move around the region's high slopes and sudden canyons. They were the forest's roads and the two friends quickly noticed that they were highly used. Because of it, they'd been feeling insecure about every step they took now. They navigated on the trails very nervously, stopping and hiding from every minimum noise they heard.

Their plan was to move westward as fast and as straight as possible, resting as little as possible, hoping to reach the Valley of Bones as quietly as possible. They soon discovered that this was not an easy task.

The number of trails seemed infinite and they went everywhere, the dense vegetation hid sharp and sudden abysses. Barbarians and orcs hunting parties lurked up and down the slopes. Bones and other signs of battle were spotted all the time. Some were old, and some were very recent. That made them become extra careful, vigilant as owls and as sneaky as foxes, always hoping to get by unnoticed.

At a certain point, they faced an open trail between two cliffs. Its openness made them reluctant to cross it, for just a few hours ago they had found fresh orc tracks coming in that direction. They hesitated and took shelter in a thick bush to make plans.

Even after analyzing the pathway and calculating their odds carefully, for some unseen reason they could not verbalize, the two friends were still very nervous about going over that glade.

After observing the trail for a while, they finally compelled themselves to advance. They did so in a hurry and soon after they reached the other side of the clearing without incident. There, the vines that fell from the trees were so dense that they could barely see beyond their steps. Progress was very slow, and they found themselves holding the sword and shield in their hands as if they were being haunted by a spirit of insecurity.

Bastian was attentive to every step, but he was still diligently pressing forward. Shortly after they entered the vegetation cover again, just ahead of him, he found a majestic white leaf blocking the path. It belonged to a remarkable climbing plant that fell from a dying tree that guarded the trail. The leaves of the vine were incredibly succulent and as large and thick as a large shield. Due to their weight, they were hanging low around the tree. As they were trying to make the footprint as faint as possible and be as invisible as they could, Bastian decided not to cut the leaf. He raised his left hand to push the leaf out of the way. When he did that, he found himself face to face with an orc.

The orc's rugged face expressed a mad fury, his eyes were jumping from its orbs and his mouth was completely open as if he was shouting a potent war cry.

The adrenalin rush Bastian felt was so intense, that he instinctively and promptly stabbed the creature in the heart before he could even realize what he had done.

Strangely, the fury in the creature's face never became an attack, its eyes were not moving or blinking in pain from Bastian's puncture, and there was no war cry to be heard but in Bastian's imagination.

The orc remained where he was, immovable, unaltered and silent – frozen in a perennial state of aggressive rage. The first orc Bastian had killed was already dead.

Suspended by his rustic shoulder bag, the inert body quickly became a mystery to Bastian and Lucien. Blood was still dripping from his ragged "clothes." His eyes were really jumping out from their orbs, but not from rage or madness, but from an impact that smashed the backside of his head into the front side of his head. The skin on his back was bluntly snatched and they saw that its backbones were turned into crumbles. The stiffness of the arms and shoulder muscles gave away the impression that, apparently, the creature was charging someone or something when it died.

Whatever had killed that orc had done it in such a sudden and violent way, that the creature died before it could realize it. The face and body's muscle mass had been frosted stiff by the sudden trauma, remaining preserved exactly as it was the second before the creature ceased to live. Its right hand was still holding a powerful mace high above its head. The hand had such a strong muscular contraction, that Bastian and Lucien could not break the grip. They had to cut its fingers off to inspect the weapon.

Nevertheless, and although the many alarming things surrounding the dead orc, the element that scared them the most was that the death was fresh. So fresh that they were scared at the fact that none of them had heard any mayhem as they approached the area. Fearing for their lives, they stored their impressions and questions about the orc's death in the back of their minds, and with a firm defensive stance, they carefully observed the area around them as the overall tension peaked high.

'Up there,' whispered Lucien, who had the sharpest eyes.

Bastian followed as he pointed with his sword at another orc's body hanging from a tree a few dozen yards in front of them. In a terribly casual way, the distorted mass of flesh was swinging by the nimble of the cold morning breeze. Blood was also and still slowly trickling from it.

'Left, by the rock,' Bastian whispered.

This time it was him who located another one, although the body was barely recognizable for it was crushed and folded like a pancake, armor and all.

'What happened here?' Lucien asked himself, shushing in the lowest voice possible.

Bastian ignored him, for there were too many things going over his mind, and he suddenly found another body, and then another one.

'That one in the tree must be dangling from at least twenty yards high. What could possibly have thrown him there?' Lucien asked while they advanced carefully scanning their surroundings and with their guards up, protecting their flanks.

'Well, I officially have no clue on what is going on here,' said Bastian.

156

'Yeah, but staying here might help us to find out,' Lucien completed. 'Let's get out of here.'

Lucien took the lead and risked more noise moving faster through the vegetation with his shield up in front of him. Bastian followed.

Despite their active willingness to stay out of trouble, soon they would find out that they ran straight toward it.

As the trees and bushes grew sparser while they advanced, the body count grew unavoidably plentiful, and after a few minutes in that direction, they felt surrounded by the trail of the massacre that took place there.

The scene was utterly unbelievable, and the only scenario they could fathom was that the orcs had literally rained down from the skies, crashing into the earth like raindrops.

Up until that point, they had found no sign of life. Still, they advanced as if in the range of enemies' arrows. With admirable combat discipline, they went onward side by side with their shields up, protecting themselves and one another.

When they reached a large boulder that embraced a sharp turn on the trail, they carefully and stealthy spied through the curve to verify what lay beyond.

They were aware that due to the increasing concentration of dead orcs around them, they would find some answers around that corner. However, while what they found on the other side of the rock answered some of their questions, it created a few more.

Sitting in the middle of the trail, over a small orc, and surrounded by the dozens of corpses and countless parts of corpses of orcs, there was a very particular creature.

It was huge. His head was turned toward the sun, and he smiled while enjoyed its warmth over his face. The little orc was desperately trying to free his legs from the creature's "grip." The colossus, however, rested without any care in the world, placidly ignoring the terrible image around him.

If a human had to give an opinion on his appearance, it would say that he was a giant dwarf. If a giant had to define him, it would say he was the closest thing to a big human-dwarf hybrid. If a dwarf had to say something about him, it would say that he looked like a wicked offspring of a giant with an ugly human. However, very few people in Fabula could say precisely what he really was. Much less, who he was.

The most relevant thing about him, however, was that he loved to make friends. In fact, he had just caught the scent of two.

'Hehe, friends.' Like a child, he laughed by himself spontaneously.

He then lifted the heavy body forward, leaning his weight on the massive bone club and, with a strange mixture of fluidity and clumsiness, he stood up. Without hesitating, he went straight to where the boys were.

Bastian and Lucien panicked. Knowing that there was no chance of escape, they assembled the best combat formation they could in the few seconds before the "giant" showed himself by the boulder's corner.

When the brute appeared in front of them, they could appreciate how massive his legs and shoulders were. Bastian looked at him and then to his sword and then back at him again.

'We are going to need larger weapons,' he said.

The young man lined their shields and readied their spears while the living hill approached. They noticed that he had a childlike posture and an innocent smile on his face. Like a toddler holding a toy, he casually dragged his huge club made of an entire dragon's femur bone. Slowly and unconcernedly, tumbling upon his own tediousness he came closer until he stopped in front of their formation.

His back was broad and his torso was short. He kept his shoulders and eyes down most of the time, almost never looking directly at anyone. His large brown eyes, a perfect match for his unusual light brown hair, shone with a charismatic light that inspired confidence in a sensible observer.

He had a particularly pronounced but very smooth chin, which he kept high, and his thick lips permanently outlined a very particular smile. A smile as expected from a naughty child. His hair was cut straight into the bangs, just above the eyebrow, in the same way that Valkarian mothers used to cut their son's hair.

His body was entirely made of muscle. Its lean mass was highly developed and extremely dense, to the point of appearing exaggerated in its bulges. Although he was about ten feet high, his massive built made him look somehow much larger. Shoulder to shoulder, his back lengthened for about seven feet. His arms were as thick as tree logs and his hands were clearly disproportional for his overall size, but at the same time they looked like perfectly natural ends for his overly muscular arms.

He was wearing a rustic tunic made of bearskin that leaned over his left shoulder. For holding the few belongings he considered valuable, he had a very simple shoulder bag that appeared to be made from the same bear as his tunic. He carried the bag like a boy would his lunchbox, freely shaking the thing around his waist while he walked, ignoring his clumsiness and weight.

He walked barefoot.

'What do we do now?' blabbered Bastian to Lucien while he kept his guard high.

'I don't know. You're the diplomat. Do something!' said Lucien.

'What?!' Bastian quietly shouted at Lucien.

'I don't know. Do something!' Lucien said it nervously.

By his voice, it was clear to Bastian that Lucien's fears were overcoming his reason and that he was feeling pressed to preemptively strike. Bastian knew that most likely they would lose that fight, so he felt pushed to act quickly and do something decisive to save their lives.

Fighting against all the instincts in his body and soul, Bastian reluctantly lowered his spear, relaxed his posture, and stepped half a step forward.

'Hi,' he said, fighting his urge to keep his weapon ready.

'Hhhiiiiiiiiiiiiiiiiiiiiiiiiiiiii!' the semi-giant responded and, although he was being caricaturally sympathetic, the strong reverberation of his powerful lungs and the depth of his large vocal cords intimidated the humans, who retreated, hiding behind their shields.

When they raised their heads again, Bastian and Lucien looked at each other to check if they were still alive, then they turned back to their original postures, restarting from where they left.

The creature suddenly raised his left arm to clean the saliva that was dripping from the corner of his mouth. The unexpected movement made the two friends duck again.

Alienated from their feelings, the brute smiled widely at them with joy in his eyes. He seemed to be enjoying the conversation.

'I'm Bastian, and this is my friend Lucien,' said Bastian, pointing and gesturing, making sure the creature would understand him.

'Frieeend,' the brute said it as if he liked the sound of that word.

He raised his arm to scratch his back calmly. Bastian and Lucien ducked again.

'Yes. Friend,' said Bastian.

'Friennnd,' the creature seemed to be enjoying himself.

'Yes. Friend,' Bastian repeated, a little embarrassed now.

'Friiieeend,' he repeated after Bastian.

'Yes… Friend.' Bastian started worrying how he would move the conversation forward.

'Frienddd. D. D.' The brute kept a smile in his face and a great enthusiasm while experimenting with one of his favorite words.

'We are getting nowhere fast, Bastian,' Lucien interrupted irritated.

Again, the giant raised his left arm, and again, they ducked. And then again, and they ducked again. This time he scratched his back a little more energetically, a little distracted by it.

'What is your name?' Bastian was clearly running out of ideas on how to make it work.

'Hum?' the brute answered with a genuine doubtful expression on his face.

'Name. What is your naaame?' Bastian made sure he was being loud and clear.

'Naaame?' he played with the word, fascinated by how it sounded.

'Yes, your name,' Bastian confirmed.

'Hehe.' The brute giggled really fast.

'What is your name?' Bastian tried again.

'Hehe. Name.' He giggled again.

'Tell. Us. Your. Name,' Bastian said it as slowly and theatrically as he could.

'Naaa-me. Hehe.' This time he giggled so fast, he hiccupped.

'My suggestion is that we abandon the retarded baby giant and continue our way.' Lucien cut the attempted conversation dryly.

'Calm down, Lucien. Let me try to cal –' Once again the brute raised his massive arm to scratch his back. Once again they ducked behind their shields.

'Hey, hum, friend,' Bastian continued. 'Hum…hi! We are friends. I Bastian. He Lucien. You?' he asked.

The "giant," however, couldn't avoid ignoring Bastian. Distracted by his itching, his face changed from merry to concerned. He was now completely committed to bringing an end to it.

He started to stretch his arms and twist his shoulder trying to reach some elusive spot, but he was not having any success reaching it. Really bothered by the incessant tickling, the immense humanoid started using his club to rub his back where his arms were not reaching.

In the first scratch using the club, a little orc (in fact, THE little orc from before) was hit and fell into the ground behind him. On the orc's hand there was a knife bathed in blood.

The scene was surreal and the two friends could not believe what they were seeing. They hesitated for a moment, but then recovered their wits.

'Behind you!' Bastian shouted at the brute while pointing to his own back.

'Behind!' the brute repeated, smiling compassionately and emphatically.

With a surprising affection and incredible speed, he captured Bastian with one hand and used his club to "scratch" his back too. Even though Bastian wore armor, he felt as if his skin was being ripped from his flesh and that all the joints that could have snapped had snapped.

Lucien tried to free his friend from his agony by punching the colossus' hands and arms and pulling Bastian by his feet. The brute was laughing gladly, satisfied he'd been useful to his new friends somehow.

'Now you!' With real enthusiasm, he dropped Bastian and grabbed Lucien, scratching him in the same way. He smiled apologetically at Bastian, suggesting with his face that he had to take care of Lucien now, and compensate for the jealousy he was feeling for the special attention Bastian had enjoyed.

While all that was happening, the little orc, waking up from the knockout blow he received from the brute's "scratch," lifted his knife into the air and plunged it with all his strength into the colossus backside.

The orc's stab hit the spot, and he felt it this time. Instantly, the expression on the brute's face changed completely. He turned fast as lightning, as if he now understood that he had been stabbed all along. So fast, in fact, that he bumped into the orc before he could notice him. The impact was so sudden and blunt, that the orc flew in a straight trajectory just like a hummingbird. After the orc's impact on a nearby oak, the now enraged giant charged at him with the same unbelievable speed. When the brute finished hitting the orc's body, it was impossible to distinguish what was orc and what was forest floor.

The little earthquake created by the brute's blows caused leaves to rain on the whole area as if an autumn wind had just blown them down.

Tired, the brute dried the sweat from his forehead and gusted away a leaf that had fallen in the space between his nose and his mouse. He looked at the stain of goo on the ground and made a "you had been warned" grin. He then turned his back on his victim and went straight to where Bastian and Lucien were.

The moment he turned and faced the lads, he smiled broadly and frankly to the two Valkarians as if he was thrilled to continue the conversation where he had left it. It appeared that, beside the interruption, he was really enjoying his new friends and all the great interaction that he was getting from them.

Lucien and Bastian were completely actionless before that demonstration of strength and power. Creatures his size shouldn't be moving that fast. In doing so, he created an illusion of disproportionality that was difficult to accept and even more difficult to defend against.

'I think it is better for us to get on our way,' concluded Bastian, apprehensive.

'Agreed,' Lucien answered in no time.

Pretending they did not acknowledge the brute, the Valkarians simply crossed the clearing. The colossus, however, followed them happily. After a few moments of that nervous deadlock, Lucien stopped and turned around.

'Hiiiiii,' Lucien mimicked him sarcastically.

'We are going for our business and you must be on yours. OK, friend?' Lucien was very energetic, determined to get rid of him once and for all.

'Friiiend!' The brute's eyes shined full of love and happy expectations.

The humans turned their backs and kept walking. Whistling, the giant continued to follow them closely.

They knew that, from the amount of noise he was making, it wouldn't be long before an entire tribe of something bad attacked them. They ignored him as much as they could, but after a while, Lucien lost his temper.

'Hey, you stupid pile of gunk! Go away! Go away!' Lucien was being deliberately rude, even keeping his hand on the sword.

'Get out of here! Go home!' Lucien risked shooing him like a dog. He even tried to physically push the colossus, being absolutely unsuccessful, of course.

'Friend?' the giant asked in a low and sad tone.

'No! No friend! We do not want to be your friend! Go away! Go away now! Leave us alone!' shouted Lucien.

'Friend?' he asked again in an even more sorrowful tone.

'No, you imbecile creature! I do not want to be your friend! I want you to get lost! Go away! Be gone!' Lucien screamed while pushing him with all his strength.

Demoralized, the hulk gave way and moved a little. As if hurt by Lucien's words, he became as emotional as a child, but still he wouldn't leave his new friends.

While waiting for Lucien to stop talking and somehow trying to run away from his words, the brute "hid" behind Bastian. He continued to avoid Lucien as he ran around Bastian, asking for his support with his sad eyes.

'No friend. No friend,' he cried at Bastian and pointed at Lucien, complaining while he alternatively cleaned his nose on their cloaks.

Lucien was shouting all the insults he could think of while trying to poke the brute away with the unsharpened tip of his spear as they ran in circles around Bastian in a sort of cat and mouse chase. Trying to escape Lucien's blows, the brute pivoted Bastian as a piece of wood, placing him in front of Lucien as if he was a barrier.

'Enough!' Bastian shouted at both of them both.

Both obeyed immediately, stopping the running around, but the brute took Lucien's helmet and threw it in a bush. He pivoted Bastian one more time and raised his hand as if he had done nothing, begging protection against a probable revenge from Lucien.

'No! Bad giant! Bad giant! Can't!' Bastian reprehended him as an infant.

'I'm truly going to kill him now!' said Lucien while drawing his sword.

'Lucien!' shouted Bastian. 'Shut up!'

'Look, I am on a very important journey to retrieve a family treasure, OK? My friend Lucien here is helping me. We cannot take you with us, OK?' Bastian was being as polite and as incisive as he could.

'Treasure?' the hulk asked, explosively mystified and captivated as a child.

'Yes, a family treasure,' answered Bastian casually and nervously.

'Help,' the giant said resolutely, crossing his arms.

'We are sorry, but we cannot accept your help,' said Bastian, already regretting having revealed too much.

'Friends?' full of hope, the brute insinuated.

'Yes, we are your friends, OK. But we don't want your help today, okay?' answered Bastian.

'Help.' Stubbornly resolute, the brute crossed his arms even tighter and raised his chin.

'Look,' Bastian said and stopped to breathe in some patience and, hopefully, a little inspiration. Without knowing what to do or say, he looked at Lucien, who looked at him and pointed at his drawn sword with his eyes. Bastian disapproved of Lucien's suggestion with a discreet negative sign, then took a deep breath again and looked at the brute one more time.

'How can you stay with us if we don't know you? I mean, we don't even know your name,' he said logically and conclusively.

'My name is Klunk,' responded Klunk proudly, lethargically, and happily. He then casually grabbed Bastian's cloak again and cleaned his nose one more time.

A Wizard's Test

After barely washing his face, the apprentice went off to prepare Eliaroth's dinner. He was quite aware that the wizard always came back from his "field trips" with a spent body and an improved appetite.

"A recharging feast then," the apprentice said these words to himself as he entered the kitchen.

With impressive skill and admirable swiftness, he immediately activated the magical objects by the stove and the sink. He was now capable of controlling many of them at the same time, achieving with a great degree of precision whatever he needed from them.

Since explicitly allowed to use spells by Eliaroth, he had incorporated magic into all aspects of his life. Daily, he explored the limits of what he could get done with it. His immersion in the passion of his experiences sharpened his spell-crafting skills in an impressively short amount of time. On that night, the practical result of all this was that it didn't take long for him to be floating from the kitchen directly to the magician's quarters, in perfect order, four hot main courses, a dozen side dishes, three desserts, snacks, and appetizers.

After eating, Eliaroth melted down over his large studio chair, and it wasn't long until he started flirting with his dreams. The apprentice, also full, took the leftovers to the kitchen and went to see his master's will be done regarding the orcs.

To face an orc war party was no job for an apprentice. Nevertheless, he had at his disposition the powerful magic items from Eliaroth's own personal arsenal. They were game changers, and even a goblin shaman could blow up an entire city with them.

Let me see, he pondered while choosing his weapons amongst Eliaroth's stash.

With the Cloak of Flight I can fly over them out of the range of their arrows and spears. A Fireball wand would do the thick part of the job while I am still out of range, he said to himself while establishing his plan and collecting the items.

A Magic Missile Wand to finish the job. Definitely Sword number IV. Confident and excited, he laughed at himself while tapping the large blade on his body.

A healing potion because you never know, but no scroll, I won't need it. The strength, protection, dexterity, constitution, and resistance spells I need I will cast here over the Capacitator. Gosh, that thing is fascinating, he thought.

The apprentice found no pleasure in combat, facing this kind of job with relative monotony and tediousness. The only thing he got from it was a great thrill while "field using" all the powerful magic stored in Eliaroth's items during those sorties. Therefore, although a little bored, he felt distractedly confident when he left the tower.

The orc camp was exactly where the wizard said it would be. And although it was night, the apprentice found it easily, seeing it from a great distance, as it was unusually lit by hundreds of tall torches and large fires.

As soon as he saw it, he went down to the forest floor and hid behind a rock. There, with the help of a scroll, he cast upon himself a lesser kind of invisibility magic. Although it was still a wonderful and very useful spell, it was not particularly powerful or stable enough, for it left some visual drag and an unstable shadow to be seen when the subject moved around. Also, it could be easily undone if his body was shaken abruptly for any reason. Even though, the spell was still useful, being much better than nothing when approaching a hostile environment. The apprentice had some experience with it, he used it previously when engaging the orcs and it worked flawlessly.

Flying a few feet above the treetops, he approached the camp to observe. Once at visual range, he saw that the orcs made no effort at all to hide their location this time. It seemed strange to him the unusual and unbalanced number of fires within and around their camp. It was by far the biggest fires he had ever seen. The orcs used whole tree trunks in their fires, stacking them by the dozen, and had uprooted so many trees that a large clearing had been opened beside the trail where they were camped. There was so much light there that everything was visible for a long distance, making the shadows long and telltaling.

The fires are too well kept for that time in the night, and too many for the number of warriors, he thought while studying their camp. *It is almost like they want to be seen.*

The apprentice was intrigued, enough to hesitate. So he stopped over a treetop at the top of a hill to spy a little before taking his assault position.

There are so many more of them this time, but still, too many fires. There are just too many, his investigative mind continued to make remarks.

They even brought siege weapons this time. They must be confident, he thought. *And look at these massive beasts they are using to transport their equipment. I think they are Grey Mammoths. Nice, I had never seen one of them before,* he thought.

Gosh, I need to get out of that tower more often. He made the mental note as he caught himself digressing in his own geekiness.

Indeed he really needed to get out more, because if he did, he would know that in the Dire Woods the owls don't peep that late in the night.

Well, time to do what I came here to do, he thought, trusting his routine.

Flying low, he moved to weapons range, just as he did last time. After he reached the range limit of the fireball wand, he found a spot where he could oversee the camp's perimeter, as he did last time. He then searched for the most advantageous position over a tree branch, prioritizing target acquisition and area coverage, as he did last time. When everything was ready, he exposed himself a little bit, just enough so he could freely bombard the orc's tents with his first salvo, exactly as he did last time. The moment he started energizing the wand, a glimpse of light came from its tip, shinning like a lantern in a dark winter night. Seconds before he shot the first fireball, an orcish bola hit his torso with great energy and precision. Almost at the same time, and with great synchrony, another one hit his feet. Both came from totally unexpected directions, not really as it did last time.

Caught completely by surprise, he only began to understand what was happening when he was being brought down to the forest floor by several pairs of mighty arms. A third bola hit his thigh, causing the invisibility spell to collapse completely. Visible and exposed, he was now going down fast, and real panic took hold of him. He tried to reach his sword to cut the ropes, but as soon as his hand touched the wrist of the sword a fourth bola hit his arm. The rope quickly rolled over his skin and flesh, pressing its grip to the bone. When the round rocks on the tip of the device ended their lightning spin, they hit him in the face, breaking his nose, making his eyes water – things were not looking good for him.

Though the apprentice learned to fight with his mind, he had never deployed his own magic powers in such a dire situation. Thus, his reaction time was relatively slow, especially now when the orcs managed to achieve a masterful surprise. However, when he was getting close to the ground, something dormant woke inside him.

'If it's a war that you want, it is what you'll get!' he said, gathering his courage and igniting every single fire inside of him.

Cornered, the apprentice conjured magic projectiles on the ropes that were keeping him from moving. Fury materialized, and as if hit by dwarven pistols, the main knots were blown away into a cloud of its own pieces, raining in waves around him.

Freed, he jumped out of the cloud spinning like a cat. After the second spin he was already holding the fireball wand in his hand. Finding himself in a wrath he couldn't even conceive, he swiftly shot one fireball in the direction of each rope while performing evasive maneuvers.

The magical fire of the explosions from the first fireballs lightened the forest even more, shedding enough light to an almost daylight intensity. And then, he understood he had made a mistake.

It took him just a glimpse of the orcs positions for him to understand their plans. He was surprised at how natural it was for him to think tactically and even strategically, even in the midst of all the confusion and violence. The orcs had surprised him, but war was seeded deep in his blood and he would see it through.

When the first fireball illuminated the forest around him, he noticed he'd been surrounded, front and back, left and right, above and below. There were spearmen in the tree above him, too many for him to escape. They were all well camouflaged and immobile, they'd been patient and skillful.

It was now obvious that the orcs used the camp as bait to ambush him. They did this by hiding a network of watchmen and hunters where they imagined he would attack. They were good hunters, but what gave the apprentice away was his disregard for his opponents and the repetition of the same tactics. The apprentice had underestimated his enemies and was about to pay the price, the full price.

It was clear that he was now too deep inside the orc's trap to just turn his back and fly away. He had lost too much altitude and was only about twenty yards from the ground, the hunters in the trees above him could, and certainly would, attack him with bolas, arrows, and spears before he could stand off their reach. While barraging the orcs with fireballs to keep them in the defensive, he correctly calculated that his only way out was through their ranks.

In between fireballs, the apprentice drew the magic projectiles wand that Eliaroth had packed full to the brim with his own powerful magic. With one wand in each hand, he lighted the forest and the orcs on fire.

He was smart about his defense too, flying around the trees in a zigzag pattern, jumping from one branch to the other, getting as much partial coverage as he could while hitting groups of enemies in the ground with fireballs and lonely catchers in the trees with magic projectiles.

The fight was intense and brutal, with most of the orcs and the creatures that fought on their side dying victims of Eliaroth's supernaturally devastating fireballs. Their heat instantly incinerated wood into a cloud of ashes, evaporated the orcs' flesh into a stinky vapor, and melted weapons and armor into a fused puddle of hot metal.

The destructive power of the wizard's spells never failed to impress him. Eliaroth's talent crafting fire magic was beyond the things the apprentice imagined possible, surpassing the standard parameters described in all the manuals he had access to until then. The only thing he could compare it to was the feats of the legendary wizards of old. However, even though under an unrelenting barrage of certain death, the orcs responded. As best as they could, they came out of cover to throw spears and shoot arrows. And, although the apprentice kept flying fast and had protective magic conjured over his body, the sheer number of hits claimed their price.

The orcs were numerous and so were their arrows and spears. They overwhelmed the magic shields conjured around the apprentice. Soon, his clothes were reduced to rags and there was not a single spot in his body that was not sore or aching, for although the magic protected against the penetration, the saturation diminished its inefficiency against the blunt of the impacts. However, the more they hit him, the more furiously he attacked back, letting out all his long-repressed hostilities and all the magic he had available. The forest became a flaming nightmare and an ash storm integrated the landscape. Even some rocks were glowing red with the collateral heat from the magic fire.

Wave after wave, the orc's forces pushed the attack only to die in the blazes of the apprentice's fireballs. The fight continued until anger, fury, and magic were almost completely consumed into a wicked ritual of death. When the apprentice's wands were dimming weak with its last spells, most of the orcs lay dead or dying. It was in this moment that, for the first time, the apprentice saw himself exhausted by the expenses of his wrath. When he came back to his senses, he considered leaving, an orc's reserve approached from the East. They were advancing quickly for a final push.

The apprentice noticed that this time the orcs' commitment to the battle was remarkable and that everything indicated that they would fight to the last orc. Also, their strategy and coordination had improved greatly.

An experienced war leader must be around, he thought.

As if his thoughts gave life to some prophecy, the war leader presented himself. The apprentice's sharp eyes saw him among the last advancing company of warriors. Personally escorted by two heavily armed ogres and a vile-looking hobgoblin archer, Trosh finally presented himself to the battle.

Without second thoughts, the apprentice shot the last of his fireballs in their direction, hoping that it would cover his necessary retreat.

'Now!' Trosh screamed with a guttural voice.

The hobgoblin jumped over a large rock with the agility of a mountain lion, drawing a white arrow from his quiver almost as fast as an elf archer. The arrow had a very unusual crystal tip and impossibly colorful feathers. With great power and precision, he shot it from his thick and sleek bone bow. Nearly at the same moment it left the bow, and as if stimulated by the acceleration, the white arrow flicked and sparkled. In the middle of its trajectory, it transformed itself into an energy pulse as if the entire material elements of the arrow had transmuted into some kind of plasmatic energy. When the energy pulse and the fireball crossed in the air, the fireball vanished, dispersing into the air as an ordinary flame. Even so, by reflex, the orcs next to Trosh and the hobgoblin ducked, dodged, and hid, trying to protect themselves as much as possible from the spell.

Dispel, thought the apprentice in the split second before the pulse hit him.

He was right. The pulse passed through him as a blow of a strong wild, leaving no physical effect. In his spirit, though, he felt the void of the counter-spelling equations that the projectile contained. Instantly, the energy of the enchants and magic objects that he was bearing disappeared completely, leaving behind nothing but a loud silence. The cape that allowed him to fly failed, but luckily he was next to the forest's floor at that point and some of the reminiscent snow absorbed the impact of his fall.

As he got up, the rest of the orcs were finishing enclosing a security perimeter around him, keeping a respectful distance from him as they prepared their final strike. The apprentice assessed his situation and rationalized his options. Looking around, he realized that he was doomed. Surprisingly, however, that thought did not make him give up or despair. His courage did not fail him, on the contrary: they were boosted by the atrocious logic that is in the certainty of hopelessness.

A very pessimistic vision of his own life surfaced through his mind. In it, he accepted that, outside the tower and even in it, he had absolutely nothing to live for but emotional debt and suppressed anxiety. Notwithstanding his newfound passion for magic, all the suppressed feelings of a life in isolation and his past emotional traumas were pouring out of him as a river. He bitterly concluded that his life was a joke, and that no one cared about him, or, worst, no one loved him. He found himself almost desiring for the whole thing to be over. All his feelings added to his anger, which now burned at full strength.

It was then that he stepped forward. He did not try to escape, he stepped forward, and not only physically but also emotionally. He faced the orcs with a high chin, pouring his whole soul into his wrath. His heart was ready for his final stand. With great detachment and no reserve, he started to cast spells of his own doing. He started to throw magic projectiles in every direction, hoping he could take as many as he could before he fell.

One by one, Trosh's soldiers were cut down by the blasts of magic as they advanced. The war leader observed the human with admiration, seeing in the human's eyes the essence of an enclosed beast and a profound warrior's spirit.

A worthy adversary, finally, Trosh thought.

170

When the charging warriors were in melee distance, and his mind was too exhausted to conjure any destructive or dazzling spells, the apprentice knew it was the end. He then drew out the sword he had brought and prepared to see it over.

Before the orcs could get in melee with him, he had time to drink a small recovery potion that he always carried with him, but he never had to use it before. As it went down his throat, his muscles were instantly relaxed and all the tension and wear from the extensive combat were gone. He felt his strengths completely renewed as if he just woken up from a good night of sleep. The wounds he had sustained all over his body were still there, though, he could not avoid showing the discomfort the pain brought him as he gave it all in his final stance.

The orcs approached slowly now, savoring the moment. He looked at them without blinking. They would easily overpower him, for the orcs were very fit folks, and were owners of great strength and endurance.

Suddenly, a monstrous burst of magic energy flowed thru his body to the point of momentarily enlightening his eyes as lanterns. The dispelling effects of the magic arrow ceased, and all the enchants, whether from his items, or the ones cast over him in Eliaroth's Capacitator, got back in full power.

The surrounding orcs also felt the wave of energy and were taken by a momentary fear, stopping their murdering advances and stepping back as his arms regained the strength of four men, the dexterity of a cat, and the constitution of a bull.

The apprentice still recalled crudely the fighting lessons from his younger years. After all, he had spent most of his youth defending himself from the older kids, which was not an easy task, as they were all very athletic and trained.

It had been a long time since he had to dodge a blow coming his way, but he still remembered how to measure distance and when to strike and when to retract. It was true that the orcs were much larger than Westgate's aristocratic kids, but so was he also much larger than his ten years old self. In addition, the magic cast upon him gave him physical powers that, added to his strong body, greatly surpassed the charging orcs.

The first orc to attack jumped from the tree that was covering the apprentice's back. He came down screaming like thunder, throwing himself at the apprentice. Using his enhanced agility, the apprentice reversed his feet,

171

steadied his base and pierced the orc with his sword while the creature was still in the air. The blow went through the orc's skull as if it was an apple, and the impact between the fallen orc's and the magically sharpened sword was so energetic, that when its forehead hit the sword's guard, the head broke in two like a coconut.

With a quick defensive turn and great speed, the apprentice severed the arm, chest, and neck of the two unlucky orcs who tried to get to him fast, hoping that his teammate's bold plan would work. However, the three of them were defeated so quickly and brutally, that the apprentice was actually encouraged by it.

The magic sword he was wielding cut through armor and bone as if they were soft green summer twigs. But before he could realize the power of it, he stroke another orc trying to advance on his right flank. After, another on his left. A third one came in so suddenly after, that he only had time to redirect his sword from his defensive hook to another, even more wretched defensive hook. This time though, he had to place the blade vertically in an almost improvised attempt to avoid the third orc's attack.

Making a tremendous effort with his legs and twisting his body as much as he could, he landed the blade on the orc's helmet. He was hoping it would at least knock him down, however, what his counterattack ended up doing was vertically cutting the stout orc in two, scaring the apprentice and his attackers.

Although it was the first time he ever used that sword in battle, he had studied its history. The elves who forged it imprisoned in its matter hateful and cruel spirits that loathed the orcs. The apprentice knew all that, and it was for that very reason that he selected it for this particular mission, but he was not expecting it to be so brutal and sinister in its ways.

The enchanted blade shook with its willingness when engaging the orcs. Upon feeling the faintest hesitation from the apprentice, it started feeding him with its fury. He eventually stopped resisting and facilitated the flow of that hateful energy through him. Once filled by it, he momentarily reached higher levels of power, being overcome by a state of mind that allowed him to visualize nothing but victory.

The captain of the Pegasus Guard had used that precious weapon during the last elven war, centuries ago. Its blade was slightly curved and supernaturally sculpted in the form of a Pegasus' Head. One big emerald was fused on the blade from side to side, resembling the horse's eyes. The gem casted light whenever one of the weapon's powers was used. The handguard was in the shaped of golden wings and its pommel was made of a beautifully polished bone in the shape of a horse's foot. The weapon was so meticulously crafted and so full of details that an observer could not endure believing it was balanced before swinging it, but it was, in fact, perfectly so. It felt incredibly good to wield it, and it was easy, even for untrained hands, to gain and recover momentum when swinging it. The sharpness was so acute, that it could cut off a fly's wings, in mid-flight. It would never lose its edge and it never rusted. Except for some spots and scratches produced magically during its intensive and long fighting career, the sword seemed new just like in the day it came out of the forge who knows how many centuries ago.

The ground fight continued and the orcs fell one after the other, proving they were no match for the apprentice and his elven sword. Whenever he hit, the sword made sure that it would cause a fatal wound or at least a total disability. With its powerful ancient magic, the blade would whisper in the Ether, "telling" the apprentice when to attack and where to attack. Truly, the sword was wielding him more than he was brandishing it. Either way, he found himself being a better warrior than he had ever hoped to be. Although the apprentice had already killed before, violence only became truly intimate and personal on that night. Only then it had become a fixed reality in his life, never to be separated from him again.

The blade devoured its enemies as if its existence depended on it. When it touched the orc's flesh, a flare would burst into a sparkly explosion of rage, carving deeper cuts into the orcs's bodies. Any remaining wound from the blade would be filled by the sparks that would vilely burn and corrode flesh and bone until, eventually, a member fell off or a cut in the abdomen tore its body in two.

After two dozen more deaths, the orcs lost courage, therefore momentum, therefore initiative. The apprentice managed to break their attack, but that didn't come without a price. He had been hit a couple of times and when the orcs hit, they hit hard. However, the powerful spirits rooted in the sword had been transferring energy in the form of stamina and healing magic, helping him with the heavy blows he sustained. It was in the interest of the sword to keep its wielder alive so he could kill more orcs, but as the combat progressed, the limitations of the blade's power began to show and its Mana reserves started to fade. As a consequence, its healing became weaker and weaker.

The frenzy of the combat, nonetheless, increased evermore. The apprentice attacked and chased his foes with the blind determination of a demon. The sword partially took control over the apprentice's mind, and the furious feelings that were flowing from it had excited him to such a murderous degree, that he started openly ignoring danger, taking avoidable hits just to end lives. Ignoring the apprentice's best interest, the sword kept using its human handler to cut and pierce until all orcs's troops were dead, all but one.

After a chaotic and violent battle, silence reigned absolute around the gushing blood and the burning fires. As giant torches, the trees lighted the clearing where he was. The black smoke completely blocked the light from the moon and the stars. It was dark in the edges of the flames. Smoke, vapors, and ashes were all around, and everything surrounding him was dead and burning.

Slowly, the background noise became louder than the poundings of his heart. The snow and ice on the tree branches were melting, creating a kind of irregular rain that poured over everything. The apprentice's senses were vibrating into an unimaginable degree. He trembled when the crackle of burning wood, the dripping of the melting snow, and the whisper of the cold wind hit the flames reached his skin.

The heat from the sheer number of successive fireball explosions had cleared the forest's floor of snow, twigs, and leaves, consuming them in the blazing supernatural fire. The bare ground exhaled numerous strong earthy odors and the air was paradoxically filled with humidity and sparks.

Around him, as a crescendo, an elusive but very present tension was growing fast. The air was suddenly filled with expectation, as if all that just happened was only a prelude and that the true spectacle was about to begin.

The apprentice's body was hurt, but his mental disposition was at an all-time high. With a puffed eye, a bloody nose, and almost giving up to the weight of his own head, he raised his sight to watch fearlessly as the terrible orc approached. His heart was in the right place, and he wouldn't care about what would happen next, in his mind, he had already won all of today's battles.

He pushed himself to all of his limits, and beyond, almost celebrating the fact of being brought to the edge of his strengths. Over the last years, he discovered how much he wanted to create, but now, on that night, he unveiled to himself how much he wanted to destroy. How much he wanted to kill, and precisely how much he wanted to die.

With his eyes wide open while pressing his teeth against one another in a sick smile, surrounded by bodies and covered in blood, he was finally able to manifest the retribution he felt the world deserved. He looked at the approaching orc straight in the eyes, letting him know all that. Letting him know his discovery, letting him know this deepest and most intimal truth.

The healing energy of his sword was depleted by now. He grabbed a healing potion from his belt, but his fingers were not working. They were bloody, broken, and with missing bits. When he realized that his hand was not responding to his commands, and noticing that the orc continued to approach him, he instinctively feared, dropping his sword to the ground to use the rest of his functioning limbs to open the lid and drink the potion.

'Don't worry, wizard. Take your time,' surprisingly respectful, the orc assured the apprentice with his deep voice.

The warrior solemnly stopped at a good distance, making his word good. He calmly released the golden buckles of his heavy fur cloak, carelessly letting it fall on the ground. His chest and facial hair were white as snow and he was clearly advanced in days – a rare thing among such a bellicose folk.

From his yellowed broken tusks to his bony hands, everything about this tired warrior was seasoned. Signs of a lifetime of fighting and survival were visible all over his body. His wrinkled skin was full of scars of many sizes and shapes. He was blind from one eye and was missing a few other pieces of his body here and there.

He had a strong, athletic built and it was still hard to find a single ounce of fat over his extensive muscle mass, but it was also clear that his days were almost gone. An old, now blurry, but always proudly worn Red Claw tribe tattoo decorated his right arm. It was beautiful how it stood as a registry of all the things passed in his clearly long, and probably incredibly adventurous life.

He was carrying a stunning old axe on his right hand. The weapon was full of the runes of deep wood magic, mostly on its rustic but razor-sharp blade. Its pole was made from a single piece of Blackwood and it ended in a connection to a small blade in the shape of a sickle. The marks on it told the tales of its dire battles. Half a dozen little totems were strapped over it, revealing his superstitious old ways.

On his back, still in its sheath and with the hilt pointing down, he had a Valkarian two-handed sword that he wielded defensively in his off-hand as if it was a long sword. His overall broader orcish bone structure allowed him to do it so, and so he did, fighting with both weapons to a devastating effect.

The apprentice, with a heroic effort, managed to open and drink the potion, and all his wounds were cured instantly. Then, he gave the orc a second look, who was casually stretching and warming his arms and legs for the unavoidable incoming fight.

The human faced the orc and the orc noticed it. In his own brave way, the warrior expressed satisfaction and faced the human.

The apprentice knew what the orc wanted and was willing to give it to him. He started conjuring all the reminiscent protective magic he still could.

The orc took off his breastplate and his helm and started to simulate short attacks in the air. When the human finished with his enchants, the warrior saluted him slowly and reverentially.

'I'm Trosh, The Roar, from the Red Claw tribe!' he announced full of pride.

'Your sword took many lives?' Trosh respectfully asked. His voice was extremely hoarse, naturally throaty and clearly powerful, revealing the reason for his title.

'It was used in the last elven war by a great elven captain. It certainly killed many orcs.' The apprentice returned the Trosh's respect.

'Mighty orcs?' Trosh asked with the direct curiosity of an honest person who had nothing to lose.

'Yes, I guess so,' the apprentice answered calmly.

'This is Grash, my axe,' he presented his enormous axe. 'He killed many warriors from all tribes. Men, elves, dwarves, orcs, all. He battled against many warriors from your tribe. I have taken this sword from the most noble of them,' he said while smoothly drawing the great sword in reverse grip with his left hand.

'She brought me a lot of luck,' he added, as if he was contemplating the blade's flawless lines for the last time.

The apprentice knew that the orcs were prone to superstitions, but it was strange to him to experiment it first hand as Trosh oddly exposed his esoteric emotional connection to his weapons.

His now refined and trained magical instincts allowed the apprentice to read the simple and sincere spirit of the orc as an open book. In it, he saw that Trosh's spirit was strong and that there was a powerful living energy in him. For a second, he admired the condition of the orc's soul, and the courage and the bravery of whom had spent his whole life swimming through a sea of battles, and seemed to have now arrived at a beach.

Watching his foe's mannerisms from that close gave the apprentice a much different perspective of the orc folk, one far from the mindless beasts described in many stories about them.

With that in mind, he decided to give Trosh some honor and therefore space, waiting patiently as he gathered himself. At some point, however, he started having difficulties controlling the elvish sword, who categorically disagreed with his goodwill. Sensing the fight ahead, the blade was flickering and bursting for orc blood. It shook abruptly and randomly, even causing the air around it to break with furious magic energy.

'I saw you in my dreams, stargazer,' said the old warrior unapologetically. 'They now pass through you,' he solemnly raised his weapons in the apprentice's direction, 'for justice and for destiny.'

The apprentice didn't understand what Trosh was talking about, but the orc's presence of spirit was such that he let him continue.

'This I say unto you: when the time comes, treat my people with honor,' said Trosh.

'You still don't know…' he added when noticed the insisting expression of doubt on the human's face.

Trosh then lowered his head, gathering his thoughts. After a few instants, he nodded positively and raised his gaze again. In it, a wild rage sparkled from the bottom of his eyes. He was ready to give it all, one last time.

'Defend yourself, wizard!' he shouted and charged the human while skillfully spinning his weapons.

The apprentice raised his sword but kept his stance. Trosh leaped in the last yards of his charge and landed feinting. He skillfully attacked with his axe first, then feinted again and attacked with the great sword from the reverse grip. Then he feinted yet again and attacked with both weapons at the same time. It was an impressive offensive sequence, but the apprentice had his dexterity and stamina enhanced magically and the elven blade was "hinting" him on where the attacks would come from.

Even though Trosh clearly had a high level of expertise and a huge reach from the adding of his large frame and longer weapons, he did not manage to score a hit. Despite this fact, his intense aggressiveness made him able to keep

177

the initiative, readying himself to deploy the tricks he used when fighting spellcasters.

After the first clash, many things were realized and updated, and they started to circle each other and study each other. Concluding that his only advantages were his reach and strength, Trosh executed a front attack again. Yet, this time he would reduce the human's escape options.

Spinning his two weapons in the air at a different angle in every spin, Trosh unleashed an exemplary storm of blows over the human.

Finding no space to dodge, the apprentice had, for the first time in this fight, to block one of the attacks to disrupt the momentum of Trosh's terrible outbreak. And a second before he ran out of options, the apprentice blocked one of Trosh's low angle strikes frontally. Even though he was not a weak boy anymore, being, in fact, quite a strong man with a great bone structure and exemplary muscle mass, and even with his magic enhancement strength and resilience, the formidable blow from Trosh's magic axe shook the apprentice from head to toe. He barely only managed to stand up, doing so only because the elven sword was propelling him greatly against the orc with fluid equations of great power.

Their geometries rejected each other so bitterly, and both weapons had so much energy behind its motives, that when they clashed, a magnetically aggressive disengagement manifested in reality causing a dry forceful explosion.

Most of the bursts came out of the human's sword for it contained far more manifestable spells. Nonetheless, Trosh's axe was enchanted with enough Mana to withstand the vibrations and the energy levels of its attacks.

Sensing that it would not win by brute force, the intelligent and active spirits in the elven blade used the millisecond of material manifestation on one of the hits to spray a flash of liquid light right in the orc's face, burning his remaining functional eye and blinding him for good.

Trosh, however, was far from defeated. Not even for a second did he allow the thought of defeat to even touch his courage. The old orc was used to fighting in the dark against astute wild beasts far more dangerous than the apprentice.

His strength was leaving him because of his age, but his ears were still as acute as an owl's, and he knew exactly where the human was. When the time was right, Trosh invested in that direction, unleashing an even faster and more penetrating sequence of blows. He was trying to ambush the human again, covering an even greater area now, rotating his weapons with open arms in a great display of balance and harmony. If it wasn't for its sheer violence and aggression, Trosh's movements looked like an aggressive well-orchestrated dance – whirlwind of strokes.

Even with his enemy blinded, the apprentice was finding hard to avoid the series of quick and hard attacks deployed by the orc. He barely managed to escape a dozen, and he knew that soon he would run out of luck.

He tried finding space to attack the orc though, but he truly had no option but to stay on the defensive, for the reach of his long arms and large weapons was too encompassing.

The orc's technique was excellent. Trosh was so martial in his ferocity that he smoothly dominated the fight until the end. He was always three or four movements ahead of the human, never put himself in a vulnerable position, and always had a follow-up plan. When the apprentice tried to surprise him, or break his balance with a trick, he moved as he saw that coming, and adapted his stance instantaneously – a seasoned warrior indeed.

In time, the human started to run out of options, and Trosh knew that. The orc had been on too many battlefields throughout his life to know it. For him, now, after so many years of war, to sense the fight was more of a gut feeling than a rational thought.

Progressively, he wearied the human and studied him. Although blinded, the orc dominated the duel, but even then he could not manage to decisively defeat the human. This impasse prolonged for quite a while. In time, the apprentice and the old warrior started to get tired. Both were now fearful that a mistake would lead them to certain death.

Struggling with hopelessness and at the same time rejecting defeat, the apprentice decided to use his most powerful weapon: his brain.

When they had disengaged from one of their many skirmishes, the orc immediately tried to locate the human through his heavy breathing. The apprentice struggled to be furtive, then discreetly started to create a small wheel of solid ice on his left hand by freezing the air around it with the rest of his forces.

The orc perceived the hiss of the spell and threw a fresh sequence of blows to halt the human's concentration. He knew that the wizard was using a magic trick, but he was not aware of what it was, and the apprentice took advantage of that.

As soon as Trosh finished this new round, the apprentice started executing his plan by attacking the orc and seizing initiative for the first time. The apprentice knew he had to act fast because he couldn't resist Trosh's counterattacks; therefore, he advanced toward the warrior, who, not exactly caught off guard, took a defensive stance. In the last second before they engaged each other, the apprentice let the ice wheel roll to the right of the orc. It worked perfectly, and it rolled over the leaves and branches of the forest floor, creating an effective distraction. At the same time, the apprentice stepped in a log and jumped with all the energy his legs could give him to decisively attack the orc's unprotected flank.

His plan worked, but Trosh would never have reached that age if he would play with his luck so carelessly. Without even thinking, and already suspecting some nasty trick, he was very careful into adopting his guard and positioning his weapons.

His axe hit the ice wheel, crunching it out of existence. However, in a movement that truly exposed the greatness of his technique, he kept his sword in an offhand position, revealing it at the last moment in a counter-attacking move that was borderline genius, and effective, but it was not enough.

The apprentice, giving everything he had left, jumped in the air while spinning his body to gather impulse to reach and pass the orc's long guard. The elven blade dragged him through the air while it buzzed in pure joy as it flew in the direction of the orc's exposed neck. Trosh's head hit the ground way before his body did.

Flabbergasted by the image of the orc's head rolling down the forest's floor through an unreal atmosphere of fire, blood, ashes, and snow, the apprentice ignored the sharp pain he was feeling in his chest and watched it all in shock.

When his legs failed him and he was unwillingly brought to his knees, he could not ignore the pressure and the pain anymore. He looked down and saw the massive great sword plunged in his torso.

With surprise in his eyes, he stared at the large blade so deeply hammered into his body. It was then, and only then, that he contemplated Trosh's last move.

The shock of the wound depleted him of control over his emotions, and he could not avoid feeling his most deep-seated hopes leaving him. His insistently inquiring mind, however, could not help but go back and forth, rationally admiring the orc's deed and realizing the violence in his body. He laughed, kind of.

Good one, he thought, slightly smiling and slipping into total hopelessness.

The insanely sharp blade went through him easily and relatively painlessly. It was inexorably fixed in his lower chest and spine bones, and although he was not sensing or controlling most of his body anymore, he could feel the cold metal inside of him. He lost all hope.

This is it, he thought.

He went beyond his own limits, and there was nothing but a dark abyss on the other side. He gave up his life as blood flooded his mouth and shock blocked his brain. He could not think or do anything. He could only bleed, feel an atrocious nausea, and suffer the anguishing pain. His presence was just there, in a state of total passiveness as he died alone in the forest.

Some of his muscles spasmed and he collapsed to the ground, increasing the size of his wounds. He involuntarily burped blood and was embraced by an impossible cold as the world under him started to spin. For a split second he thought about his life, but before he could form a sense out of his feelings about it, his conscience went away.

The Valley of Bones

'The Valley of Bones.' Bastian wanted to sound inspired and emotional as if he was theatrically citing a verse or a poem.

From a rock on the edge of a canyon, he looked down while Lucien and Klunk drank fresh water from a Rocky River's small affluent on the lower part of the canyon. They drank a lot of it, enjoying each gulp of that refreshing and light tasting water.

After Klunk finished drinking, he looked at Lucien, who was beside him. Lucien filled his canteens first and was only now drinking his share. Klunk then changed his expression from general distraction to a mischievous child who was struck by a naughty idea. Once Lucien inclined his head to take another gulp, Klunk pressed the human head into the water, getting him drenched and causing a lot of water to enter his breastplate.

Klunk laughed while pointing at Lucien figuring he would take it in good spirit. However, when he saw the anger in Lucien's eyes, his expression changed to a frightened child. He then quickly ran to seek refuge behind Bastian, fearing Lucien's revenge.

'It is nothing like I have imagined,' said Bastian, ignoring the mishmash between his two companions happening around him, 'and I have fantasized a lot about this place.' He breathed in the air as if it would help him connect to that place.

The differences between the version of that place that he projected in his mind and the reality that was now upon him, motivated him even further to know the truth. An urge for discovering the real history was being born inside of him. It was a strong drive, and it got stronger as it burned in his heart ardently in a way that it was so far unknown to him. His projections about that place, the source of most of his anxieties, were destroyed by what he was seeing. They were now outdated and untruthful, and, above everything else, he hungered for the truth. He was willing to find out what really happened in the hopes he could be at peace with all the illusions he allowed to grow in him to ease some of his pain. He now felt strong enough to face the facts, all of them. In the end, he found out that this was precisely the urge he had in his soul, though he was not able to verbalize or to isolate it between the fog of his young heart's emotions. Truth, rather than an object; redemption, rather than a sword, was, therefore, the reasons why of his quest. Deep down, Lucien knew that and admired Bastian for it.

This new perspective restored and recovered Bastian's strengths. Before, the journey to that place existed only in his mind, occupying a significant part of his inner life, dragging him with its mixture of anxiety, duty, and fear. Now, watching the Valley of Bones, he felt as if his motivations had matured, as if he had really achieved something. Getting to that place gave him the impression that he could hold the whole world in his hand and nothing was out of his reach.

By witnessing the real valley, Bastian overcame some of the most negative aspects of his memories and, therefore, of his personality, leaving his sorrows and melancholy behind. He tasted these new sensations with flavors of excitement and detachment while casually walking through the valley, crossing the creeks jumping from rock to rock. He was feeling cured of an emotional illness that he didn't even know he had. He felt whole, renewed, and full of enterprise – a more complete person.

He looked back in his short life with great courage and had a true epiphany. Smiling to himself, he perceived that the fact that they got to the Valley of Bones alive was in itself wonderful. He felt grateful and satisfied with his existence as he would rarely feel. He was now his own personal hero, although he was no hero at all, yet.

It is getting late, he thought, realizing he had spent too much time wondering, distracted.

He went to gather Lucien and Klunk so they could focus their efforts to scout the entire place methodically. As they explored the valley's rocky terrain up and down, it didn't take a long time for them to form a clear picture of what happened in the Battle of the Cursed Stones.

Rather than having one, The Valley of Bones was a collection of waterfalls. Its landscape was composed of large, sharp depressions where numerous cascades gathered to pour their water in a monumental display of nature's glory. The waterfall's galleries were impressive, but not just for their number, but also for their variety. There were many kinds, each made unique by its differences in heights, depths, width, and volume.

In the lowest parts, where the water lost speed and the river split several times in two, there were several pebbled beaches. Down there, in one of the conversion points, there was an ample space between the two main river's arms. This long and wide bank formed a sort of island that was as large as the valley itself. Its pebbles were all dark and smooth, and that created a lot of contrast between them and the huge amount of bones that covered it. In many points, the bone layer was so dense, it covered the pebbles completely, tainting the whole place with a morbid and cruel aspect. In the end, the beauty of the magnificent waterfalls and the ubiquitous colorful succulent flowers that embraced the water bodies were overtaken by the terrible open-air graveyard theme of the surroundings. So much so that it changed the name of that place, for the current name of Valley of Bones was adopted after the Battle of the Cursed Stones as a testament of its ferocity.

When Bastian and Lucien were still children, precisely on that pebble island, an entire reinforced infantry battalion from Westgate was ambushed, surrounded and decimated by the minions of a rogue wizard named Kestos. Both sides consumed themselves in that terrible battle, filling the valley with the bones of heroes and villains alike.

Although far from being the most powerful, Kestos entered history as one of the most astute emissaries that the Dragoness ever employed. He always resented the Valkarians and their empire and long before the War of the Flame heated up, he offered the Red Legions his detailed knowledge of the areas around and of the people within Westgate in exchange for gold. Xshisrahil, however, counter-offered, demanding his full commitment to the war as her lieutenant in exchange for his life. He accepted it, becoming her emissary in that region.

Supported by one of the world's biggest powers, the wizard had no shortage of resources. He used them to hire specialized mercenaries, buy powerful artifacts, and get famous assassins to accomplish his cruel bindings. The endless flow of money, plus his cunning, allowed him to do a lot of damage long before the imperial authorities could understand his actions or even track them back to him. When that finally happened, Westgate commanders found themselves outmaneuvered and with limited options.

During his accession, Kestos knew that his would be a war of attrition. It was clear to him the futility of clashing his forces against Westgate's walls or even to randomly ransack or lay siege to a Valkarian city in the region. He knew well that he should only openly engage the Valkarians when he was able to present an advantage of at least five to one in the battlefield. However, long before he shot the first arrow of his guerrilla, he skillfully waged a silent war of intelligence and counterintelligence throughout his area of influence.

Before becoming an Xshisrahil acolyte, Kestos had spent several years venturing between the cities of the western frontier of the Valkarian Empire. He became exceptionally competent in collecting vast amounts of information about everything and everyone that mattered there.

During his first years of adventure around Westgate, he presented himself as a sellspell and explorer. He was particularly interested in the ancient ruins located deep inside the Dire Woods, venturing over there on every opportunity he had. People knew him for his cleverness and useful magic, but also for an eventual megalomaniac and delusional drunkenness at the local taverns. He was an enchanter by trade, selling his magical items and solutions to many influential people in the region, winning their favors and keeping their secrets. In time, he played with his influence, becoming a persuasive agent of his own interest. As his magic powers grew, many of the most prominent local families were eager to gain his unorthodox favors, reaching for his counsel in many matters.

People from Westgate's most powerful families and influential local officials were indebted to him. As a result of the power struggle between the lords of Westgate, some were willing to make secret deals with the magician to fulfill his blind ambitions. Kestos understood his position perfectly and learned to use every part of it to his advantage.

Therefore, many years before he launched any attack under Xshisrahil orders, Kestos already had built a vast network of spies and informants. His net was so effective that he managed to hide his true agenda, and even his identity, until the very end. His sphere of influence permeated many facets of the local society, going from criminal guilds to dodgy noblemen. His leverage went so far that he had open channels to some imperial politicians even after his plots were revealed.

Kestos stopped at nothing, he bribed and bought favors and information with much more than gold and silver. His specialty was blackmailing, which he played with a particularly deadly persuasion, always playing for keeps.

The wizard cheated, deceived, made deals he never intended to fulfill, and all kinds of dirty measures to get what he wanted. The sneaky enchanter proved to be ruthless, capable of doing anything to achieve his goals. His relentless will, boosted greatly by his sociopathic mind, forced his talents into a distorted greatness, turning him into an exceptionally dangerous individual. His house of cards endured way past the values of his own selfish interests and the immature expression of his ultimate vanities. Too young for his powers, too brilliant for his background, and too reckless for his world, he was largely deemed unworthy of his desirable gifts and his rare luck. He became an agent of chaos, an evil that stubbornly propagated himself through a heavy cost of pain and grief. For a time, he prospered unchecked and undefeated. And by the means of his high intellect and his effective magic, he always got away with the Valkarians' attempts to "contain" him.

Through lies, assassinations, deceptions, and an apparently infinite amount of financing, he managed to gather a considerable number of troops and resources under his command. What he organized in the peak of his power was not even close to set siege to Westgate, but a formidable shock troop nevertheless. Numerous, powerful, and agile enough to create considerable turmoil across the whole region.

Through the spread of rumors and falsehoods, Kestos resurrected old feelings of despise and revenge among orcs toward the Valkarians. He gathered dispersed clans, subduing them under his leadership, forcing them to side with the Dragoness and to wage war against the empire.

The wizard had an expansive knowledge of many different subjects, and his approach to his military operations included a number of smart decisions when building his forces. From the beginning to the end, his forces were a patchwork of various races, tribes, and motivations, but his iron discipline, the victories under his belt and his ample rewards made it work.

Although he preferred to let each troop elect their own chiefs, he extensively used able mercenaries in leadership position. From the worst of the worst, Kestos hired the best, placing them as overseers and commanders. Many were directly from the top of Westgate's list of wanted, all were unscrupulous individuals competent in the works of violence and perversity.

The wizard chose the orcs to compose the core of his infantry, paying mercenaries to teach them to move, hold position, and attack as a unit, turning their companies into considerably more menacing forces.

The plentifulness of hill goblins in the Dire Woods was astounding, and the wizard managed to gather a gigantic horde of this obstinate little creatures. He supplied them with a forest of specially designed throwing spears, and the nasty little creatures would embed its sharp tips with nasty poisons and infectious diseases. In battle, they would throw their spears in massive quantities, managing to create a barrage that strongly argued against the goblins' total uselessness in the battlefield. In melee, on the other hand, they relied basically in deploying their overwhelming larger numbers, always pushing for a flank maneuver followed by an attempt to overrun their enemies' columns. Largely, they were mostly used as an occupying force over an extensive territory, spread out in small mobile platoons. Their restless temper meant that they were always on the move, covering large areas with their patrols, and their treacherous nature caused them to install traps, alarms, and ambushes wherever they went. Overall, they could slow advancing enemies and kept "information" flowing through the chain of command. Their reports were not always composed of the most precise intelligence, but nonetheless enough for one to discern that something was wrong.

With deceits and made-up promises, Kestos managed to get the support of some of the most vicious and resented Barbarian clans. Although they were not willing to join the wizard into direct battle, especially if siding with orcs and goblins, they served mostly as scouts and guides, trades mastered by them.

An entire reinforced battalion of hobgoblins sappers armed with steel longbows and siege weapons were also under the wizard's command. They were exceptional archers, fast on their feet, highly professional and loyal to their contracts. They were trusted to organize the most important assaults and ambushes directed by Kestos's field commanders, seldom failing.

Kestos employed dozens of trolls sourced and recruited from the deepest and darkest places of the Dire Woods. They lived to eat, being slaves to their magically cursed appetites. The wizard used that fact in his favor, allowing them to eat whatever they wanted after each battle.

Some giants and many other obscurer and wilder creatures were enchanted into magical servitude by the wizard, greatly reinforcing the wizard's forces.

In the depth of his secret slave mines, away from the reach of his enemies' spies, he forged swords, plate mails, spears, shields of steel, and all kinds of tools of war, arming his troops well.

When Kestos concluded it was the right time, he risked his first operations, hitting and running and then hitting and running again. The wizard knew where to attack, choosing only the battles he could win. The wizard proved to be very competent in maintaining the initiative, always surprising, slowly tiring, and evermore restricting the Valkarians' maneuvers.

His kinetic strategy had several phases. First, he expelled all the unwanted presence from the Dire Woods for many miles north and south of Westgate. His objective was to establish dominance over the forest, making it his withdrawing place. This would allow him to move his troops more discreetly, attacking the Valkarians anywhere within the central-western border with surprise.

Initially, he sent small war parties to destroy and terrorize woodsman lodges, hunter gatherings, and the occasional lonely men and women who lived in the forest to free it from potential informants in order to move their troops undetected as he pleased. During this phase, it was paramount for the wizard to keep his identity and objectives in secret, avoiding early countermeasures from Westgate. He obtained success in doing this by placing the orcs at the forefront of his actions, giving the impression of an opportunistic uprising of a few tribes. Systematically and quickly, he attacked strategic points, being very careful not to leave witnesses and clues behind. He was very elusive when commanding this first phase, and his presence in the field was always veiled and covered very thoroughly.

After he was able to use the Dire Woods as he planned to, and his forces and wherewithals reached levels he deemed acceptable, the wizard started launching attacks on the Emperor's Road, farms, and small villages spread all over the territory. With that, he isolated and limited the reach of any imperial reaction.

When the Westgate men were finally convinced of a mastermind behind his action and started understanding the full extension of the wizard's plans, it was too late to reclaim the strategic initiative. By that point, Kestos had already established what he had intended to and they were pretty much playing the wizard's game then. He could move faster, concentrate his forces, and surprise, while the valerians had limited knowledge of their enemy.

The second phase of his plan started with him trying to maximize those small attacks with the extensive use of high magic, cutting off the larger populations' centers, therefore creating further distraction and chaos. His mission was, ultimately, to survive and thrive while forcing the local troops to spread thin and stay local, not allowing them to head north to support the real fight that was taking place between the Lava Peak and the Capital.

For a while, Kestos's plan led the Valkarians to chase their own tails. He seemed to foresee all imperial reactions and knew precisely how to respond to every single one of them, always thinking ahead. Through his insightful strategies, merciless tactics, wealth, refined information warfare, and his powerful magic, he achieved his goals one by one.

His genius really came to life with his intrinsic tactical maneuvers. He devised his attacks in many sectors locally, breaking the logistical lines, and denying the movement of small Valkarian patrols in the open. He intensely and methodically attacked the lesser strongholds and villages in the region, always making sure his troops would retract in time before they could suffer an effective counter-attack. At the same time, he opened inventive venues for leading the Valkarians' counter-attacks into desirable directions.

The wizard never ceased to insert untraceable disinformation, to promote displays of fake weaknesses, and use magical illusions to demoralize the Valkarians, attracting the imperial troops to consecutive frustrating futile operations.

The wizard went over huge risks and efforts to hide the true size and nature of his forces and his reserves. They used high magic and mundane tricks to look much more numerous and terrible than they really were, inspiring hesitation into the Valkarians' commanders, causing them to be full of precautions and maintaining a defensive posture.

He took many measures to always fight against the imperial forces from a massively advantageous position, but nevertheless his effective and often fantastic efforts, a decisive victory was impossible to be reached against the Valkarians at that point. Kestos knew that, and was quite aware that it was all a game of cat and mouse designed to buy him time. Still, the wizard's uproar caused confusion, strain, and distraction throughout the whole period he had operated in that region. He fought a losing battle, but that didn't stop him from fighting it vividly until the end.

Kestos knew deeply the hearts and minds of the Valkarian commanders and, due to the high number of misinformation and the implanted false strategic notions, it took time for the Valkarian commanders to agree between themselves what Kestos's true final objectives were. That hesitation caused enough problems to keep most the imperial troops of the region to be redirected to the northern battlefields, making the wizard strategically victorious.

Even though late, the Valkarians ended up apprehending the spirit of his plans and, together, decided to act decisively. Kestos knew very well that it would be the end of him if he allowed the Valkarians to take the initiative, even if for a brief moment. With no choice, he executed a risky plan he had been working on for quite a while.

With the help of the best assassins Xshisrahil could supply him with, Kestos infiltrated Westgate and quietly killed its field commander. He then replaced him with a doppelgänger spy. The doppelgänger, acting and arguing over carefully planted false information about the wizard's location and numbers, ordered the formation of a reinforced battalion with the most willing Westgate's soldiers to be sent ahead of the main force to confirm the location of the wizard's sanctuary. Once positive about it, a bigger force would quickly join them with the use of magic, attacking and destroying the Wizard and its minions.

Although seemly despaired, Kestos's move was justified. He was adamant, and had scarified a great deal over the need to discourage all Valkarian activities in the Dire Woods. Nevertheless, he provoked the Valkarians to venture there to accomplish two things: 1. Destroy the most formidable warriors in Westgate, demoralizing the imperial army; 2. Eliminating the possibility of future Valkarian campaigns inside the Dire Woods, keeping the strategic initiative on his side.

Also, Kestos was perfectly aware that the empire's leadership had the tendency to be very hands-on when it came to combat. The battalion that headed out to hunt him would probably be no exception, composed of many great names from Westgate's powerful houses. Depending on the level of his success, the magician calculated that his plans could evolve to be a beheading operation, rather than a castration. However, he did not include in his calculations that Valkarians necks were thicker than he thought.

By this time, Kestos had complete control of the parts of the forest that interested him, and before the battalion reached the Dire Woods treeline, an ambush had already been set up. The Valkarians were lured deep into the woods and were provided all sorts of false clues to convince them that their maneuver was being invasive and was causing complications to the Wizard's plans. When their march took them to the pebbled beach that Bastian and Lucien were now exploring, Kestos, using a powerful magical artifact, discreetly severed their connection to the outside world, placing the entire valley under an isolation dome of anti-scrying meta-magic spells.

From the shadows, orcs jumped against the Valkarians shields. From the canyons around them, giants threw rocks large enough to disrupt their formations. The goblins, made insane, hysterical, and suicidal from the delirious magic potions brewed by the vile wizard, advanced like a massive and unstoppable wave of stinking flesh. They buried the Valkarians, throwing them on the ground by their combined weight, and then poking them with their poisonous spears. Hobgoblins using small and very efficient high-quality dwarf catapults launched acidic bags in the center of the Valkarians' defensive circle, limiting the flexibility of their defense line drastically while corroding their equipment. The few Barbarians fighting for Kestos launched heavy spears against the Valkarian, killing many of them.

Unable to receive reinforcements or retreat, trapped in unfavorable terrain, and outnumbered ten to one, everything seemed lost to the Valkarians.

Initially, Kestos was amused by the success of his deception. However, the wizard made a mistake in underestimating the strength and resistance of the Valkarians in open warfare.

The tenuous training and the constant battles imbued into the Valkarians a collective and highly effective martial reflex. When fighting in groups, as in a collective unit, the Valkarians were able to take advantage of all their tactics, optimizing their defensive and offensive capabilities. The collective use of shield formations and other heavy weapons had been developed to an almost artistic level by the Valkarians. Their high level of discipline gave them the capability of executing smart maneuvers, defending themselves and neutralizing the enemy's advantages with great speed and efficiency. When they noticed that a link in their line had been broken, they quickly realigned their shields in a "U" shape, rushing the pressing enemies inside their perimeter, getting then the reserve troops to surround and destroy them. In this manner, the flankers became the flanked, allowing them to dilute attacks from larger enemy formations.

The end result of their fighting style was a giant mass made of flesh and metal. Their experience in this sort of military feats was decisive in diminishing the shocking effect intended by the overwhelming pouring of troops over their positions during Kestos' ambush. Although they were not able to alter their final fate, their abilities made all the difference in the Battle of the Cursed Stones, causing their enemy to pay the highest price for their "victory."

The battle started in the late afternoon and continued throughout the night, lasting for many gruesome hours. During those, the Valkarians committed countless acts of bravery and heroism. Among them, it is told that Lankan "The Strong" broke formation and advanced in a killing spree until he reached the cliffs from where hill giants were throwing boulders in their front line. He, alone, killed them all, stopping the rain of rocks over his companions. Exhausted, he was overwhelmed by the enemy, dying on that cliff after being stabbed in the back by treacherous trolls.

Although many heroes tried desperately to change the outcome of the battle, eventually the sheer number of enemies, Kestos's magic, and the disadvantageous terrain got them all.

Except for very few men, the whole battalion was lost. However, in their bravery, they consumed the entirety of Kestos's troops. The few surviving creatures deserted in fear, hiding in deep places inside the Dire Woods. Kestos himself left the fight magically spent and seriously injured. At any rate, that was the last time he was seen.

The brutality of the battle was such that even after almost two decades the marks of the incredible violence could still be seen and interpreted on the valley's floor. It was possible to see that the eventual spring flood and the pillage of the forest's creatures had removed many of the signs and remains from the battleground, but most of the scars were still there.

Almost every tree had arrows still plucked on it. The moss that covered them formed green sculptures that testified of past brutalities. Spears entirely covered by small blossoming flowers were deeply tucked in inaccessible places over the cliffs. An eventual lonely and melancholic Valkarian helmet could be spotted right beside a brutish orc axe under the translucent running water of the stream. And bones – hundreds of thousands of them, everywhere. By their quantities, their variety in sizes and shapes, and their state, Bastian and Lucien could only imagine the savagery and the disheartenment of the battle.

All the elements and marks around them testified of what had happened there. Through the impressions gathered in that place, they reconstructed the fight in their minds. They became horrified by what they projected, for they could not even imagine that kind of destruction and slaughter was possible. In spite of the intense morbidity, every single one of those lost objects represented to them a clear picture of a past glory of some beloved deceased countrymen. In their eyes, the remains were a collection of pieces that testified of bygone acts of courage in the face of certain death. For them, the entire valley was a massive registry of millions of expressions of bravery brought together simultaneously in a stupendous, and therefore even more dignified, work of art. Befuddled by the enormity of what they were witnessing and overtaken by their own curiosity, they explored every inch of it. With restrained reverence, Lucien and Bastian went on examining evidence on the ground, searching for any random clue that could lead them to their objective.

'Cursed stones,' said Bastian to himself while holding one of the black polished pebbles in his hands. 'They could not stabilize their shields,' he continued his lament, correctly guessing the reason why the Valkarians were ultimately entrapped inside their lines, ending up being pressed into death.

'Blanket!' Klunk said it to Lucien on the other side of the valley while painfully nudging the human's shoulder.

Lucien was happy to ignore Klunk, hiding any sign of pain.

'Bl'll'llaaan'ket!' Klunk tried to nudge Lucien's shoulder again with his massive index finger.

This time the Valkarian dodged it and set some yards between him and the irritating brute. While doing that, he stumbled on a rock, revealing a golden arrow tip that immediately called his attention.

'BLAAANNKEET!' Klunk was plainly shouting now.

'What?!!' surrendered Lucien.

With the golden tip in his hand, he looked back at Klunk demanding the meaning of this new interruption. Lucien clearly had no more patience left in him.

'Blanket.' Klunk, now satisfied with the attention he finally got, calmly pointed to an approaching dire bear.

The beast was drooling enough saliva to fill a bucket. His open mouth was a clear appeal to his present appetite and a display of his massive teeth.

Among all the land animals in the world, one of the most fearful is the dire bear. They were plentiful in Dire Woods, and as dreadful as anything there. With all four legs on the ground, the creature's shoulders could easily reach ten feet in height. When it raised itself on its two back legs, they were as tall as a small watchtower. Their claws could grow to be as long as short swords, their teeth big as daggers and their stomachs large as dwarven barrels. Altogether, they did resemble the exact measure of a certain death.

In general, they behaved as ordinary as any other species of bear. They were omnivores, basing their diet on meat, and human flesh was not off the menu by any means. They were not known for letting pass any meal opportunities. Owners of great appetites, they ate all the things that crossed their way, including rotten carcasses and other bears. Their hide was highly prized in Valkar, for they were not easily pierced, even by steel blades. Although the bones of their heavy frames were heavy and dense, it was common knowledge that they could outrun horses in an open field. Few managed to escape their ambushes, as they had enough athletics in their massive bodies to run as fast on the forest floor as in an open field.

However its enormous size, agility, and stamina, what made these deep-wood predators terrible and treacherous threats was the nose. Many renowned hunters consider them the best trackers among all animals. They could track trails that are weeks old for days and could sense fresh blood from miles away. An adult male could hold a territory ten times larger than an ordinary grizzly bear. Besides being a voracious animal, they were also known to have an intellect above its lesser cousins, making them one of the most elusive and dangerous game to hunt.

The wood elves were the only race capable of creating magic penetrating enough to tame these terrible animals. They use them mostly to conduct long patrols over large border territory, but also ride these giant bears into war as cavalry. Carrying long, shiny silver spears, only the strongest and most courageous of their warriors proudly ride bears in battle.

From a stone-throw away, the beast was looking straight at Lucien. Its ears were down and its mouth was foaming a white viscous liquid as he slowly approached them. Its intentions could easily be read over its eyes: to have lunch.

'Klunk, attack. I will cover you,' whispered Lucien as he smoothly drew a javelin.

'Hum?' asked Klunk, distracted.

Klunk was looking the other way, at a passing butterfly. He seemed to have forgotten the approaching giant bear and was devoting all his attention to his attempt to capture it. The tiny colorful thing, however, continuously escaped the traps he was setting with his huge hands.

'Klunk, A–ttack! Me co–ver you!' Lucien whispered with a trembling voice. Lucien's hands were steady, but started to sweat as he could feel the giant bear flavoring the moment as he approached them.

'Bye! Hehehe.' Klunk laughed as he said goodbye to his butterfly friend. Lost, he kept a big and sincere smile on his face as he imagined how clever the little thing was to escape his palm so many times.

Suddenly, the bear started to growl terribly. Abruptly, it transformed itself into a deafening, guttural roar that shook the whole valley. He turned back with a jump and started running in the opposite direction. It was then that Lucien saw Bastian's javelin nailed deep in the bear's back, right in the middle of the rear hip.

The bear's silhouette was so wide and tall that it was only when the bear jumped and turned that Lucien could see Bastian across the pebble beach, by the river.

Instinctively, and using all his body's weight, Lucien also shot a javelin at the creature. To everybody's surprise, the animal jumped in the air in pain and, turned, and start heading again towards Lucien and Klunk. This time, however, the bear was not simply irritated, but made mad by the pain of their well-placed shots.

'Klunk!' Lucien cried despairingly while aiming at the bear's massive head.

Klunk, apparently oblivious to the whole situation, was mesmerized by his own reflex on a small pond. While he watched himself on the still water, a long filament of saliva ran from his thick lips. The fat saliva drop was almost hitting the ground after the lengthy, slow, and disgusting descend it took to get there.

The two friends were alternatively attacking the beast, making it ever more furious with every hit. Confused by the pain of consecutive attacks, it changed the direction of its charge every time a spear or arrow plunged into its flesh.

Lucien and Bastian were hitting the bear as much and as deadly as they could. Some of their spears and arrows managed to go through its thick hide, but no major incapacitation was reached. At a certain point, the bear decided whom to charge, committing to Lucien. Anyhow, Bastian had already spent all his javelins and had nothing to distract the bear now.

The bear ran over the shallow waters of one of the affluents, throwing an immense amount of it in the air as he hit it with its powerful legs and belly. The splashes it created were large enough to produce a fine mist downwind. It was an impressive and furious demonstration, but the beast would not add to its calculations the valley's secret weapon.

The relatively thick layers of sleek pebbles and slippery fragments of bones was deep enough to make the towering animal slide and lose control at the end of his attack. It was out of balance just enough to miss its bite on Lucien's head.

With a loud snap, it closed its mouth, moving its attention from its prey to its lack of balance. Its attack failed in eating Lucien, but it was successfully tactical, for it knocked Lucien to the ground.

The bear's situation worsened as it was unable to stop or restore any balance, sliding free over the sleek stones. Considering the amount of energy and fury it injected in its charge plus adding its weight, the bear slid for a comical period of time until it was able to stop itself.

Lucien remained on the floor, half-covered by black stones and made unconscious by some random blow from the chaotic ran over. He was an easy target now, and on seeing it, the bear attacked him again as soon as it was ready.

The creature seemed to be now even more enraged and willing to kill Lucien because of its shameful skidding.

Bastian was now running to the fight with his sword high in the air, desperate to protect his friend from certain death, but the damned black stones took a toll on his speed too, holding him back a great deal.

'KLUUUNK!' he shouted from the top of his lungs in utter panic after he concluded that he would not make it in time to save Lucien.

Upon hearing Bastian's cry, Klunk woke up with a jump as if he was stoked by surprise. He raised his club in a defiant stance while turning his whole body in Bastian's direction. Then he made a serious face and slurped his saliva right back to his mouth. After swallowing every single cold drop of the long slurp with a big gulp, he put himself in an even more attentive posture. Theatrically, he focused on Bastian. He made a surprised face when he saw that the human was running in horror in his direction. Then, he looked at Lucien in the ground. After that, he looked at the incoming frantic bear. Next, he looked one more time at Lucien. Then, to Bastian again. Then, to the bear. Then, he finally looked at Bastian and raised his arms in the air and made an "I don't get it" face with the sleaziest smile ever.

'Bear! Attack! Now!' cried Bastian with the rest of the air he was carrying in his lungs while he slipped and fell for the hundredth time.

As quick as lightning, and with an incredible dexterity for his size, Klunk leaped in the air and ran directly to the bear's direction, intercepting the beast on its path. The animal readily put itself over two legs to strike with its front claws and stop the brute's sortie. Without any hesitation, Klunk, with the fluidity of a perfectly executed singular movement, jumped over Lucien in a huge arc, falling with his right foot exactly in front of the beast. Even before he landed, he started a feinting maneuver with his left foot to avoid the monster's claws. Then, effortlessly, he threw his body in a low arc over the bear's left flank. He quickly and precisely made it to the bear's back, escaping the animal's fury entirely.

Grabbing the beast's fur with an iron grip, Klunk climbed to its neck. Then, with the naturality of someone who had done it before, he used his other free hand as a lever to put his massive club inside the bear's open jaw. Before the bear could understand what was happening, its destiny was already sealed.

When the animal started to react, trying to get rid of Klunk and his club, the brute had already grabbed the other side of the club with his other hand and was already crossing his feet over the bear's soft belly, setting an unbreakable grappling anchor with his legs.

The initial amount of pressure was quite considerable, impeding the bear to turn his head and claws to hurt Klunk. The beast was also instantly forced to go down to its four pawns to lever his strength to shake Klunk out of its back, but it was too late.

On their way down, Klunk flexed his arms with great strength and precision and a loud and clear snap was heard. The bear's head turned ninety degrees in the wrong direction before its front paws touched the ground. Other snaps followed as his spine was brought to an unnatural angle by Klunk's efforts. The bear's eyes instantly became void, and its massive tongue fell heavily from his open mouth. Titanically, the beast hit the black pebbles.

Klunk raised himself up while oscillating like a naughty child. He took his club from the dead creature's mouth, cleaned his nose with the back of his hand and then with his tongue, and approached an astonished Bastian as if nothing had happened. Swinging heavily while dragging his club, he stopped in front of Bastian and opened such a broad smile that Bastian took a step back.

'Klunk help!' he said happily.

A "Man" of Few Words

Slowly, his eyes opened. It took him a while to get a grasp of reality and completely take hold of his faculties. Even after his mind was completely in synchrony with reality, the apprentice just stood immovable for several minutes while trying to understand what had happened to him.

As he remembered the pain and the trauma, he instinctively raised his hand and touched his chest. The acts of moving his arms and feeling his chest's skin felt strange, as if he had never done it before.

He felt good. In fact, he felt relaxed and rested in a way he hadn't for a long time. Still feeling all sorts of awkwardness within every move and every touch, he sat down and saw that he was in his bed, in his room, without the slightest idea of how he got there. Without an explanation, he could do nothing but suppose. With nothing else to do, he went to the kitchen for some tea.

Everything looked normal and perfectly regular in the kitchen and in the tower. However, couldn't take his mind off what had happened and what was happening now. His eyes were lost while he mindlessly set the kettle on the stove. Suddenly, Eliaroth entered the kitchen and sat down at the table.

Moved by an abrupt anger, the apprentice turned to face him, finding the half-elf seated, casually waiting for some tea while reading a book printed in a gelatinous sort of skin. The material of the book's cover was unstable, and it kept flicking in and out of the physical reality. The apprentice got distracted for a second, frowning by the stove but still curious about the surreal compendium.

'Two sugars please,' he said to the apprentice without taking his eyes off the book.

It infuriated him that the wizard was acting as if nothing had happened. The apprentice was changed, however, he would not internalize and deal with it on his own this time, he was now overcome with anger and the overwhelming feeling of going beyond everything that restrained him, and that included Eliaroth's "authority."

With a grim, but without saying a word and feeling a little dizzy, he did as he was told. He acted out of pure reflex because his heart was now regurgitating uncontrollably the bitter mix of emotions and thoughts that had surfaced during his latest incident.

The furious things that he had unrooted and had then manifested revealed themselves to be seductively insisting and overwhelmingly tasteful. The second he revived them, they were not willing to depart from his heart and from his soul. It was part of his nature and emotions, and he liked it.

When he grabbed the kettle's handle, his hands were trembling with desires of ire and death. When he stood beside Eliaroth to serve his tea, his hand froze. It was too much; his feelings overcame him. He lost his composure and started pouring everything out, except the boiling water.

'You know what?!' he blew up. 'I'm done!' The apprentice dropped the kettle abruptly over the stove. It hit the ground immediately with a disturbingly loud noise, but Eliaroth's expression didn't change. He was completely undisturbed and did not even look at the apprentice.

The early abandonment by his parents, the years of isolation, of solitude, the pressure, the traumas, the cold distance and partial silence of his master, the recent battle, everything surfaced at once. It was too much for him to either bare or handle.

'I'm tired of how you treat me!' he dared. 'I'm not invisible or a slave! I'm not your servant either! Whatever agreement you may have made with my heartless father, it was not signed by me,' he was now openly shouting.

'I'm not here to clean your shelves and cook your food!' Tears started rolling down from his eyes.

Strangely, although he was taking a stand against Eliaroth, he felt like he was hurting himself instead.

The wizard continued to ignore him.

'You know what? I will do you a favor and leave! Before you get tired of me and do condemn me to the same horrible destiny as the other apprentices!'

The apprentice felt like he had just removed a huge weight from his chest, but also that he had gone too far. He had waited for years to say those words, but they felt empty and underpowered now.

Strangely, Eliaroth kept his eye on his readings while eating a corn cookie. The apprentice lost it.

'I give up!' he said carelessly while aggressively taking his apron and throwing it on the ground. 'I quit!' He immediately went to his room to pack the few belonging he still could call his. He had no home to go to, but he was determined not to stay in that tower one more minute.

'You are wrong,' with a calm but frank voice, the wizard declared it, while still examining his strange book.

It was enough to stop the apprentice on his track. He stopped at the hallway and then returned. By now he had been blinded by a burning anger that was almost becoming blind hatred. The intensity of the apprentice's emotional aggressiveness was so intense, that two candles in the wall were lit as he passed by on his way back to the kitchen.

'I'm sorry, what?!' he furiously demanded an answer as he stood right in front of Eliaroth. With that, he crossed all the lines that there were to be crossed.

Eliaroth stood up. Not slowly, not fast, he just stood up. He closed his book and stared right through his apprentice. Then, the human saw in the wizard's face an expression that he would never forget.

'I've always treated you with the respect and the seriousness that US wizards should treat ourselves.' Eliaroth's tone was severe enough to break through his pupil's emotions, but it contained just enough mercy to pick up the pieces.

'The very nature of OUR dealings demanded it so. ESPECIALLY, in the relationship between an apprentice and its master.' The wizard stopped to let the energy he carried in those words be absorbed by the Valkarian.

'If one day, you ever feel willing to be any of those two, it is best for you to start practicing.'

A different sort of tear was running down the human's cheek now. It wasn't rage, instead, coming to himself, he was smart and sensitive enough to understand what was about to unfold.

'Your power is already considerable, and will naturally grow,' Eliaroth stopped to consider, 'maybe limitlessly.' He stared gravely at his apprentice demanding he understood the implications of what he was saying.

'You have been awakened. It is an irreversible process now.' He stopped for a brief second and made sure that his pupil was on the same page as him.

He was.

'My dear apprentice,' Eliaroth restarted, but upon listening to these words the Valkarian started sobbing uncontrollably in grief and great guilt, 'if you could be anything, what would you be in that day?' he proposed.

'I will tell you that: above all, be yourself the changes that you want of the world,' the wizard said.

'Clearly, we are both individuals that appreciate the privacy of our contemplations. And, for now, this must remain. For it is only in silence that one can hear more than words. Silence allowed you to listen and learn a language that you will use for the rest of your existence in this place. Maybe even beyond.' The emphasis Eliaroth gave to his words dignified them, and their fairness made them irresistible.

'My absence is justified in the limits of my interests. And those demand the most of my time, and my energy. Nevertheless, if you enhance your sensibilities, you will perceive that I have never prevaricated in my tutoring activities. Especially due to any kind of private interest or selfish reasons.'

The timing Eliaroth chose to justify and explain himself to him for the first time was perfect. It served to remind the young man of his position and his degree of maturity. In doing so, Eliaroth showed him several things he still had yet to learn. It put things into perspective for the human, ending and opening a new phase of understandings for him.

Now, and only now, the apprentice could see that Eliaroth was and always had been deeply and truly ethical, and very serious about his duties as his teacher. He now comprehended that the wizard had guided him all the time and taught him more with his unorthodox, silent, and subtle ways than anyone could have with a million words. He had conducted things throughout all those years with a greater understanding and a larger compassion. Eliaroth had always been there, even when he was not.

It was in that moment, when all things came together, that the apprentice saw how deeply the wizard accepted him and how far Eliaroth took him with his tutorage. Although he communicated it differently, the fidelity and constancy of the wizard made him a great master. The apprentice now finally faced how he was deeply wrong in his reactions and all his assessments regarding the wizard over the years. Eliaroth's geniality had become obvious, and so was the apprentice's immaturity. He felt ashamed.

'If you may be missing vain tavern conversations, then maybe this is not the place for you,' Eliaroth pressed on.

'The tasks I entrusted to you during your first day were designed to develop your corrupted sense of discipline, as now you see that order is fundamental to what we do. When they stopped being a necessity, I likewise stopped demanding them. Why haven't you contemplated that fact?' His question was fair and the apprentice had no answer for it.

'Don't you know that in most places of magic it is forbidden to train an apprentice in the age and state of consciousness that you had when you arrived at my doorsteps?' he said.

In a rare moment of hesitation, the wizard stopped himself and gave his pupil a second look with calculating eyes. He narrowed his eyes, checked something on his mind, and only then continued.

'And there is a reason for this forbiddance. You, today, are living this reason,' he said and he was right.

'Haven't I gotten the magic means to create all the food I desire? Haven't WE by now?' he provoked, sternly. 'So why do you cultivate the garden and cook our food?' he mercilessly challenged the apprentice to answer him.

'You do it because you are following your heart. Not due to a command of mine. To say the contrary is an injustice,' the wizard's tone gave away shades of sadness.

The half-elf paused as if reflecting on his own words. His face could not hide his disgust, and this showed the apprentice how high his master's morals were. Again, the apprentice became ashamed of his own small perspectives.

'The courtesies that I have asked from you were accepted by me because I believed you made things with a willing heart, as any good student should ever do. If that wasn't the case, I would not have allowed that exchange to occur,' Eliaroth said.

'If you consider yourself my servant, you are either not a good apprentice, or think that I am not a responsible teacher. Therefore, either you are irresponsible, or you are attributing to others the moral responsibilities for your actions. That, by its terms, denote weakness of purpose, which is the very shadow of fear. And fear comes from blindness and immaturity. You are not ready,' he concluded rationally, but not as coldly as usual.

A few grams of disappointment could be felt weighting on his voice. Being disapproved when evaluated to a high standard brought mixed emotions to the apprentice's heart. He felt failure, but also a strange feeling of achievement, for it was the first time he saw himself as a responsible object of interest. Even if the conclusion of his evaluation was a scandalous defeat.

'Now you call yourself my servant, when, as a brother, I share my residency, treasures, and table with you. You watch over my sleep, oversee my sustenance, are trusted completely and regardless, and still you call yourself my servant? No, my dear apprentice, I have no servants. But if one day I do have them, they will not be as foolish as you insist on being,' said the wizard.

Commotion and shame were the right words to describe a fraction of what the apprentice was feeling now. Eliaroth's speech fused a higher humility and a wise hesitation into his spirit. His soul was opened by it, changing some of his perspectives forever.

'Your father paid a high price for you to be under my tutelage, and after all those years, after all you have seen, after you hold the testimony of what I do and what tools I have in my disposition, do you really think I need, desire, or look for gold? I tell you to make it clear what you supposed to have clarified yourself: I am searching for something far more valuable. I search for an apprentice – for teaching, and also learning.' The wizard was now opening himself. His purposes and inner thoughts were now being displayed.

'I have been breathing this world's air for seven hundred and eighty-five years now. You won't believe how far I have to go to learn a new thing,' he said looking away.

'Learning is the single most precious thing to me now.' The wizard looked back at the apprentice to make his point across. His momentous approach denounced that the wizard was about to bring forth a new revelation.

'I am in search for an apprentice, youngling. And I have sincerely accepted you as mine,' he said.

'"Master the above and you shall shape the below,"' he respectfully and solemnly quoted one of the greater laws of the magic.

'How deep can your heart go? Where will it linger?'

The wizard took a step back, breathed in briefly, and raised his chin without taking his eyes off of his apprentice.

'Conversely, be sure that you are free to leave according to your will. I shall regret that fact, though, I sincerely believe that you would, eventually, become a great wizard,' he nobly confessed.

'This will happen and start the day you fully accept yourself,' Eliaroth prophesied.

The apprentice was now crying a cry without blinking. Tears streamed from his eyes and fell on the kitchen table. They would dry out on their own, as no mercy was offered in return, for they were tears of real change. Right there, at that moment, he grew up and his shame disappeared. He now, and forever, carried a greater understanding of himself, of his own purpose, and of his own perspectives.

'Moreover,' Eliaroth was not done, 'and finally: to defend myself from your foul accusations, I shall declare to you the reasons why all your previous precedents ended themselves while guests in this tower.'

The wizard was not surprised or changed by the fear and embarrassment on his apprentice's face. Rather, instead, his expression revealed that he knew about his fears all along.

'The reasons included pride, vanity, disobedience, recklessness. For a while, I thought that you would rise above them, but I may have been wrong.'

Eliaroth seemed tired, consumed by that conversation. He inclined his head back, looking up as if old memories were being projected high on the kitchen's ceiling. He then turned his eyes back to the now and to his pupil. He stared sharply at the apprentice and restarted with a remorseful tone.

'I have accepted you, I have received you in my house, I have guided you, I have taught you, and I have tested you. You failed,' he said conclusively.

'You have underestimated an enemy and was defeated. If I wasn't around to rescue you in proper time, you would be beyond healing now,' he said.

The wizard was willing to continue, but he stopped after noticing the huge interrogation mark lying on his apprentice's face.

'What?' the wizard asked slightly impatient.

'In the woods. Were you aro –?'

'I am ALWAYS around,' he interrupted the young man abruptly.

'Accept, learn, and walk your walk,' Eliaroth ended his case.

By noticing his facial expression, the apprentice deducted that the wizard was not very satisfied with him, but he was still considering his tutelage.

'Furthermore: go wash and neaten yourself. You smell almost as bad as an orc, and you are most certainly starting to look like one. I will not allow you to be such a disgrace to the art. Cut your hair and trim your beard, and put yourself presentable. You have a long road ahead of you,' said the wizard, turning to his meal once again.

'Please, master, don't expel me!' he begged in sudden despair.

The apprentice now valued his life in the tower as he had never before. It was the only happiness he knew, it was the only world he knew.

'Expel you?' The wizard stopped and raised his left eyebrow and kept it high.

'Not before you retrieve the values of my Cloak of Flight. You do remember it, don't you? The one you destroyed in your irresponsible skirmish,' he said, still very serious.

'But…but…' The apprentice was out of words.

'I don't care what you do, or how long it takes. I want a cloak just like that. I trusted you and it was destroyed due to your miscalculation. Your training will only continue when and if you bring me another one, thus settling this debt that you have raised on yourself. You can leave as soon as you're ready,' he said.

'Yes, master,' transformed, the apprentice started to get ready to leave the kitchen.

'I have two advices that you may find useful,' the wizard said before his pupil could reach the kitchen's door.

The apprentice turned quickly. He was not nervous at all, but still a bit confused about where to put his hands.

'The sword and axe of the orc warrior you killed are made of Star Ore, a very precious metal, as you should know. They could be sold or traded. It can be a solid starting point for you.' Eliaroth looked ready to resume the conversation.

'And try not to sleep against the wind whilst in the Dire Woods,' he said lastly.

'Yes, master,' the apprentice answered.

'And one more thing,' the wizard restarted.

The apprentice stopped at the kitchen door and patiently returned.

'In the future, I will not tolerate that you raise your voice to me again. Be advised,' he said deadly serious while biting an apple and returning to his examination of the alien book.

'Yes, master.' This time, the apprentice knew exactly what to say, and he did it truthfully, solemnly, and without hesitation.

The Moon Lake

Their scouting over the Valley of Bones was largely a waste of time. They noticed that the west side was particularly crowded with orcs and traces of their presence. On account of it, they decided to invest their efforts in that region, maximizing their chances of finding a lead.

The tip they received from the goblin on the plateau about the Red Claw tribe over the Moon Lake seemed to have some substance, and as they raided the western portion of the Valley of Bones, getting closer to the Moon Lake, they encountered more and more orcs from the Red Claw tribe. No "big warrior with sky sword" though.

As patrols and hunting parties were all over that place, in their first scouting they tried to go silently. They planned to set traps and ambush the orcs to capture some of them for interrogation, but they soon realized that it was impossible to do something like that with Klunk.

When they moved, or did anything actually, Klunk made so much noise that it was virtually impossible to surprise anyone. He broke young trees with his elbows while walking, and sneezed loudly enough to be heard from miles away. Sometimes he simply shouted out loud or started singing an incomprehensible song when he saw a new kind of flower or a colorful bug.

When he lured the orcs toward them, an ambush was the best option they had, but that would not work either, for Klunk was chronically unable to endure the orcs. When he saw them, he charged regardless of the number, the presence of a dangerous shaman, or any other factor. On top of it all, he would do it ignoring any notion of tactics, simply running and smashing them from the closest to the further until they were all dead.

He would not give them a chance to question the orcs, ignoring any appeal or explanation from Bastian and Lucien about the importance of talking to them. When they managed to capture a living prisoner, Klunk would forcibly take him away from Bastian and Lucien as if he knew better, and then quickly, and often horribly, destroyed the poor creature.

The good thing about Klunk though, was that up until that point, nothing had been capable of resisting him. Not even organized combat parties reinforced with War Wolves and ogres. Klunk was almost as big as a Hill Giant but fought with an unbelievable agility and speed, and nothing they would throw at him was able to stop him.

Bastian and Lucien could not make any of their tactics work while Klunk was with them, they had to adapt their strategies to whatever Klunk's "style" would bring. His careless attacks cut the orc's formations like a hot knife through butter, and they could do little to get away, guarding Klunk's flanks and covering his advance by shooting their arrows and javelins.

The amount of trouble Klunk put them in was massive, and they quickly acquired extensive combat experience, getting ever more comfortable on the battlefield. Although they were trying to find and keep prisoners, they were invariably contaminated by Klunk's "motivation" and eventually obeyed their gut filling by surrendering to the warrior ethos deeply seeded in their hearts. During those weeks of relentless fighting, they were somewhat forced to mature the soldier inside of them.

Because of Klunk's blows and the boys' courage, they managed to survive semi-unscathed against the several attempts by the orcs to hunt them down. Being so deeply infiltrated in the Dire Woods and therefore knowing that they could not resist such attacks, made the two friends even more daring. They became bolder in their explorations, always penetrating deeper and deeper into the endless forest.

Trusting that Klunk's escort would keep them safe even if they were attacked by an entire company of orcs, they risked coming closer to the Moon

Lake – the place of origins of most of the patrols from the Red Claw tribe they were encountering.

The closer they got, the more orcs they found. However, they had the impression that, for some reason, orc patrols suddenly became weaker in numbers and in strength. Now they seemed to be made up mostly of inexperienced warriors and young hunters.

At the end of an afternoon, they heard a great noise of drums and war cries coming from far away, in the direction in which they calculated that the Moon Lake would be. At night, when Klunk slept heavily, they scouted in that direction. Once there, they quickly understood why a proper combat patrol was not sent to deal with them.

From the discrete observation point they had settled, it was possible to see, even late at night, the wild and ancestral beauty of The Moon Lake. The mirror of its water was perfectly aligned with the moon's orbit, making its dark waters reflect the moonlight like a bright beacon all along its banks.

There, upon its rocky beaches, the orcs built their huts and strongholds. At night, for an epic effect, the golden flame of the orcs' torches contrasted with the vivid silver light of the moon and the amusing multicolored constellations of the stars.

They saw that the rumors and screams they had heard in the past few hours were due to celebrations and rituals of a great war party leaving to war – fortunately, not in their direction.

They were armed to the teeth with many siege weapons, and there were plentiful provisions loaded over the giant beasts they tamed. With their spirit fed by their guttural war cries and carrying torches in their hands, they left the orc city while the drums played into the night. It was a grander scene to watch and, dominated by a sense of curiosity, Bastian and Lucien watched it for a while, forgetting what they were doing there in the first place. It was strange to watch the orcs from that close. Being so deeply in their territory and seeing them in their intimacy, somehow connected them to their enemies.

When comparing the number of torches that were leaving with the ones that remained, they concluded that most of them left with the war party. For a moment, they wondered who they were fighting with.

After seeing what they needed, they returned to their hideout. It was mid-morning when they arrived at the base camp, and they found Klunk still sleeping and snoring heavily, as usual. So heavily, in fact, that many small colorful birds were playing with the air current generated by his breath. Some pushed their luck too far, getting sucked by his powerful inhalation, remaining stuck in his big nostrils for a few seconds before being expelled as small, feathery, gooey cannonballs.

During the following days they kept a close watch over the Moon Lake. By doing so, they noticed that their patrols ceased in the area and that there was very little movement from their part elsewhere. They took advantage of this strike of luck in their favor, and used that time to search the area for more info about their objective. By capturing an orc, they found a few more hints about the "great orc warrior with sky sword." During the brief interrogation, they received confirmation that there was a warrior from the Red Claw tribe that was known to bear a Valkarian-made Star Ore two-handed sword.

Needless to say, although this news seemed shady and doubtful, they had renewed Bastian's hopes. Lucien, in another hand, saw it as a reinforcement of Bastian's paranoias, considering in his intimacy that the sword was surely lost forever. That it was now rusting in some river's bed or under the forest's grass. Although, for sake of seeing this whole thing through, he was still willing to keep adventuring. At least until Bastian's faith would die and he finally come to his senses.

One night, they decided to get close to the city to capture another orc to interrogate. They left Klunk at their camp sleeping, and made their way through a different path, settling on the border of the city, waiting for some random opportunity.

As the night was ending and their patience was stretching thin, they decided to sneak in one of the most isolated huts to see if they could snatch one of them. The two friends had become bold like foxes by now, pushing their great luck to its edge.

When they were about to step outside their hideout and proceed with their plans, both felt a massive pressure on their shoulder and the ground leaving their feet as they were raised into the air.

'Shiiii. Dangerorr,' said Klunk after he landed the humans, pointed to the orc city and shushing them with his other hand.

'Klunk!' Bastian shouted in silence when his blood came back to his lungs. 'How did you...how could you...when...aw never mind,' he said, resting his case.

'What…how?!' Lucien blabbered, trying to process a bunch of info while still unsettled by the brute's surprise.

It has been some time since Lucien gave up trying to understand Klunk, but he was now completely perplexed about how he got there in complete silence and, moreover, how he found them in that darkness. He looked at Bastian for help, but, in the precise moment they crossed their puzzled eyes, a blast of heat hit their faces, and then another, and then another, and so on.

They ducked and sought cover instinctively. Once they felt safe, they raised their heads to watch the spectacle of the fire raining down from the sky while the city was being bombarded, shaken, and burned by the magic fire.

The majestic visions of destruction, the godlike power of the explosions, and supernatural radiation of the heat overwhelmed them. They could not think or do anything but watch while the huts, the rustic towers, and the forts were mercilessly blown into oblivion.

Soon after, however, they could no longer watch. They had to hide their faces from that unique display of wrath, as the intense light from the explosions was blinding and the heat dried their eyes. Although they were fairly out of the way of the destruction, the heat of the explosions lit the moss on the stone wall behind them on fire.

The barrage of flames passed next to their position as a mad hurricane. It lasted for quite a while, leaving nothing alive behind its path. Some explosions lighted the night with such a splendor, that it turned it into day for brief moments.

The rumors of cracking trees and crumbling stone walls were terrifying. The scream of the burning orcs added a dark tone to it. Although Bastian resented them deeply for their part in his father's death, he found no pleasure in their dying cries.

Picturing the massive battles of old when they read about them in books had not prepared them to live through the real deal. They had never imagined how such a destruction and such a sudden and vast amount of deaths could be unleashed in such a brutal and sudden manner. The terror therein marked their souls and the experience stood in their minds afterward, increasing their respect for magic.

When the explosions ceased, they stretched their heads out of their cover. They had a scared, impressed, and confused expression on their faces as they emerged from the protection of their trench. They were sweating inside their armor, some of their clothes and hair had been burned, and their mouths and eyes were completely dry.

The Moon Lake was now a colossal torch that illuminated the hills around it. Everything was burning. There were only two colors to be seen around them, the glowing red from melting hard matter, and the pitch black from everything else that had already burned.

All things previously alive were dead or dying. The dead were either burned to their bones or to dust, and the dying were screaming, wailing, and running in the hysteria of their last moments. It was an apocalyptic sight, with no consolation to be found anywhere.

'See, Dangeoourr,' Klunk said, smiling optimistically.

His self-satisfaction was in complete contrast to the awkwardness of his ash-covered face, his burnt hair, and his still-burning fur cloak. Bastian and Lucien looked at him, and at the bizarre panorama he embodied, without knowing what to think. Then, they helplessly observed their surroundings, but no sense or answer would come of it either. They exchanged looks, searching in each other consolation and direction, but neither found none. They were not sure what to feel or do now, and their minds suffocated under a pile of doubts upon doubts. They tried to ride the wave of their fantasies and live this adventure, but now reality came knocking with such strength that it shook them to the core of their reasons. Perplexed, they couldn't connect with the moment, feeling distant and a little bit lost. From that moment on, it was not fun anymore, and the adventure started taking its toll on them.

When everything that was dying died, the only noise that remained, beside the burning trees, was Klunk playing with the now ubiquitous black ash. It was then that they finally discerned the absurdity of their situation. It was then that they realized that maybe they had come too far to find home.

Leeroy's Coat

The sun was rising as the apprentice finally and lastly put on his blue wool coat. He stood up all night finishing it.

When he first got to the tower he was just a boy, now, however, he had developed the body of a full-grown man. While growing up, the apprentice had no option but to develop a set of skills to repair the clothing he had and make new ones when needed. Although he sew by necessity, he enjoyed it very much. Luckily, he had access to plenty of quality fabric from the other apprentice's trousseaus, and access to a magic needle from Eliaroth's possessions.

He had permission to use the magic needle, but, as all the other magic items in the tower, he had to organize, contain, clean, and sometimes educate it well. The last part, though, was a bit hard.

Ancient and brilliant, it was a very dedicated and skilled needle, but it had the most irritating sense of humor. Often, when she wanted to celebrate the completion of a job, or when she managed to get out of its box, the little thing enjoyed sharing its happiness with the apprentice with a pinch on his behinds. He always managed to surprise him completely, adding to the pain and the frustration the poor boy dealt with daily during his early years in the tower.

Nevertheless, in time, he learned how to understand and communicate with it, and since them, they had shared some projects together, becoming good friends. Out of all the projects they worked on together, the one that both were most proud of, was his magic enhancer/outdoor/travel wool garment.

As Eliaroth was entrusting him more and more with outdoor activities, he felt the necessity of sowing a field coat that would serve him as a protection layer and as a way to carry stuff during these missions. With his late interest shifting to magic and the ethereal, the project was abandoned and many of the design aspects remained on paper. Now that he really needed it, he went back to find the pre-cuts and the main model ready. However, they were only partially complete, still missing most of the work and all the details.

The first thing he did was to collect his drawings and notes and revise them. Before the whole thing was over, he had made many personal modifications and improvements that gave a deeper sense of exclusiveness to it.

He gathered everything he needed by collecting only the very best materials from his and the other apprentice's stuff. This was a fundamental point for him, after all, he did not allow himself to take anything from his master's treasure. His debt was already too high, and he felt he had to rely only on himself for this one.

He started it by selecting the best wool he could find. And he could find some exquisite wool among all those rich kids' blankets and coats. He cut what he needed from a dark blue cover made of a mysterious woolish fiber that excelled in many aspects. It was incredibly warm and very breathable for its thickness, and the texture of its blue tonality was very peculiar.

He also chose only the finest silk for the lining, taking a portion from a bright and vivid gray silk sheet. From all the quality fabric he had at his disposal, this one called his attention the most, for the aspect of the color was very similar to starlight when dimly illuminated.

The first thing the magic needle did when he took it out of its box was to prick the apprentice to show him its dissatisfaction with the years of inactivity that it suffered while locked in its dwelling. As soon as peace was agreed between them, they began working on the coat again.

The night was too short to contain all the happiness they found while finishing it. They both shared the same feeling and worked as one, completing and supplementing each other's crafts. When the sun was rising, they had a sleek, warm, and durable overall coat in front of them.

It was the result of minds spared the pollution of external influences, becoming full of innovations and exclusive features. The whole garment had a style of its own, and its refinements made it worthy of most assemblies without losing any practicality. It was self-contained, comfortable, and most importantly: made to support and increase the speed of his spell-crafting.

The apprentice learned that when facing the reality of doing magic in the field, the handiness of its ingredients and the capabilities of putting them into action quickly and efficiently, were the most important things. This set him into sewing many kinds of specialized pockets and supporters in many unusual areas and at awkward angles all over his coat.

The hyper soft and flexible silvery Giant Silver Back Spider silk lining and the mysteriously elastic blue wool had a major part in its overall look. Everything was overbuilt, and even contained a repairing kit with extra sewing threads, textiles, and buttons hidden in an unusable space. It provided total hip and leg freedom, which he thought was very important in any situation. The coat preserved most of his agility and was so exceedingly comfortable that he felt like it was an extension of his own body, and, ultimately, of himself.

Since he had learned what he personally classified as "field magic," he put himself into thinking how to safely keep, quickly bring, and promptly employ his ingredients and magical resources. The ingredients for self-defense and tactical tricks were all next to his wrists for ultra-fast deployment. For obvious reasons, almost all pockets were "hidden" pockets, except for some necessary external cargo pockets.

Aesthetically, it was a big leap for him, being used to the loose and practical shirts he usually dressed in the tower, the coat empowered him in a revolutionary way. The cut highlighted the masculinity of his presence, making him more aware of his own manhood, giving him some pride for the first time.

In a strange manner, he felt what he had accomplished was more than just a coat. A piece of him, rather than just pieces of cloth; a personal statement, rather than just a useful garment; a uniform, rather than just a jacket. It wasn't only just about a coat, it had to do with his perspective on life, on his personal spell systems, on how he would project his powers, and, eventually, on the kind of wizard he would end up being.

A defining epiphany hit him when he looked at himself in the mirror while wearing it for the first time. With incredible speed, his now exceedingly sharp and matured mind brought many aspects of his life together, and a thunderous idea stroked him. He realized many things at once, and many old doubts and insisting reasons were nullified by the immensity of his conclusion.

He and only he saw it: his vision was his own. He discovered who he was, and the perspective of himself changed forever. The powerful and elegant man in the mirror made him forget the boy he once was, consoling him with the thought that he might have a chance to do something good with his life after all.

He then looked straight in his own eyes for a long time. He did it without knowing what he was looking for, watching, analyzing, searching in the profound of his own soul. There, for his surprise, he now found absolutely no hesitations and no questions. He only found will and drive. Then it hit him, and he discerned. He knew exactly what to do, he was now as sure as one could be. He nodded to himself, took his things, and left.

Crossroads

Klunk spent the whole day trying to fit a stinking pointing skull of an unfortunate giant flying reptile into the tip of his weapon. Apparently, he was attempting to modify his mace into some sort of pike. His insistence on the seemingly impossible task would drive Bastian and Lucien crazy, if they weren't already.

At a forgotten crossroads in the middle of nowhere, the boys were hanging on the edges of their sanities. They were now many weeks wandering into the wild and things were starting to get out of control.

The merciless reality of the Dire Woods dictated that everything was constantly and continually trying to kill and eat them, day and night. However, because of Klunk's prowess, they survived these encounters, but the attrition from the endless fighting eroded their will. None was willing to admit it though, but they were now tired beyond themselves.

Their appearance was a long shot from what it was when they had left Bastian's stables. Their beards were long and dirty, their faces thinner, and their eyes way more desperate and much less innocent.

They were dirty beyond hope for they had stopped cleaning themselves a long time ago. Approaching and staying next to water was too risky, for giant and hungry beasts always lurked around it searching for preys.

Their scent was the most popular thing for many miles. The smell from their own wounds and the unwashed fluids from the creatures they killed to eat or to defend themselves stood in their clothes, hair, and skin, carrying a variety of blood fragrances that proved to be irresistible for the forest's beasts.

Their clothes and armor were torn and mended to their physical limits, with some parts missing or hanging by a tread. A day with two serious battles was a calm day, and it was a miracle and a testament to their fighting talents that they managed to keep themselves in one piece up until then. Although Klunk's inexorable club had a lot to do with it.

When he was not distracted, the brute was able to destroy most things that came their way relatively easily. Despite the boys being annoyed with him most times, they had learned to appreciate his help and knew that they would have never come this far without him. In the end, the three of them reached many understandings about each other, and, without noticing, they became a team.

Klunk could not be trusted to keep guard though, so the boys were doing only five to four hours of sleep per night each. Which was not nearly enough to recover from the adrenaline rushes and the wounds of all the battles they were facing. They had ditched their tents and sleeping bags long ago, resting in any place they could find that would protect them from the surprise attacks of the creatures and dwellers of the forest.

Among all the difficulties they found themselves into, the worst was the lack of proper food. Because they wanted to maximize the search and scouting time, they would hunt and grab anything they found handy. A short preparation time was essential to keep their meals fast, so nothing far from the very basic was being done. Bread was just a sweet memory now. As well as anything but a quick plain rabbit, semi-raw deer, or some occasional wild berries. Wine, potatoes, coffee, eggs, fresh vegetables, bacon, beer, butter, and corn were completely out of their reach during the day. They would, however, taste them at nighttime, in their dreams.

Lucien and Bastian were a fine sample of the best of the Valkarian youth. Strong, brave, resilient, full of drive, and with a stomach for it all, but the high intensity of the encounters and the constant fights were weighing in heavily. Bastian was considering giving up on the quest.

At least for now, he thought. *Until next summer. Maybe,* he said resentfully, but sincerely accepting his weariness.

The only one who was having fun throughout the whole thing was Klunk, never complaining, ever happy, good old Klunk. But today, even he stood frustrated with the apparently impossible retrofitting of his weapon.

Lucien was still in the quest, but hanging on mostly on his pride. Exhausted, he rested his weight on Klunk's side, almost falling asleep. Klunk's rustic bear cloak was beginning to feel like a very soft and wonderful bed. "If Bastian can do this, so can I," he kept telling himself for the last weeks, when things started getting real harsh. Now, however, he had forgotten about it for a minute and was comfortably slipping into a deep sleep over Klunk's cloak.

Without changing his embittered face, or even the direction of his stare, Klunk was pounding lightly on Lucien's back, just like a mother will do for her baby, inducing his sleep to an even deeper level. Lucien started to smile, he was dreaming; deeply dreaming now.

Ignoring all that, Bastian was examining the crossroad, trying slowly to make sense of it all. With dried, broken, and trembling lips, he was scrutinizing the very old rock signs. It was full of inscriptions, but they were written in an unidentifiable language. Looking through the sights and babbling like a properly deranged person, he was acting more out of instinct than of proper rational action. And that was why he couldn't believe his own eyes when he saw a man coming down from the North.

However, the most important thing in that moment was not that he saw a man, or even that man in particular, or even his many particularities. The most fundamental thing for the understanding of what was happening was the state of Bastian's mental process, and how his own circumstances had altered his perspective. Thus, the most important thing was HOW he saw this man.

Although Bastian had not entirely lost his mind just yet, he saw this man walking down the road as a person who was lost beyond all hope in a desert or in a wilderness of some kind would suddenly see a man dressed for a luxurious party walking by. The differences of their realities increased the absurdity of the encounter. For the first time in his life, Bastian thought he was going crazy.

The abrupt shock of perspectives was the last drop in Bastian's insanity bucket. It overflowed it, and he gave up. He did nothing, and he thought nothing. He did not even allow his mind to go or exist in any way or direction. He just stared at the approaching figure with his mouth open and a numbed gaze.

Sensing the approach and his friend's reaction, Klunk stood up and went to stand right beside Bastian, imitating his dazed face, thinking that it was some sort of welcome ritual.

Lucien, who was leaning against him, fell from a good dream directly into the cold ground, planting his face hard into the thick layer of dust and the nasty little sharp rocks that laid over it. At first, he could not understand if he was still dreaming, or if the good dream he was having had suddenly became a bad one. But after his tired mind mumbled some unstable thoughts for a little bit, he came to his senses and concluded that they were being attacked again – which was basically the only thing that had happened to them for the last several weeks. Instinctively, and looking somewhat drunk, he jumped to his feet, pulled out his sword, and came roaring, shouting, and kicking like a completely demented man. He arrived where Bastian and Klunk were with a great and despaired fury in his eyes, he was raising his sword high while searching for targets.

'What?! What?!' he screamed, looking around with neurotic crazy eyes while spitting through his dirty and overgrown beard.

After fruitlessly browsing the horizon, he laid his troubled and turbid eyes over his companions, looking for clues. Then, he noticed Bastian and Klunk's dead glances. Salivating and jerking his head he slowly followed them, setting his eyes into the focus of their strange hypnoses.

'Ah, this...' he barely whispered. His shoulders dropped heavily, his sword came down involuntarily, his face became just like his friends' and they reeled together numb in the heat.

Crusader

Deep inside an endless mountain range, which was lost within another lost endless mountain range, buried in the depths of one of its desert and inconspicuous peaks, inside the dark corner of a discreet cavernous junction, between two terribly vertical walls, hidden by the most acute wisdom and the highest magic, was the Hidden Temple.

It was conceived and built to be inaccessible by all means, and so it was. The temple was not only veiled from searching eyes but also from the reach of preying minds. Its very existence was a secret, which meant that only a handful of beings knew about it, even fewer knew its location, even fewer knew how to get to its location, and even fewer could really get there.

There was no visible pathway in or out of it, and no trail for countless miles in any direction. Its only purpose was to remain hidden, but nothing that happened around it was random. Things were kept that way by someone, with a purpose, and for a reason.

Its architecture was impressive, ancient, slightly militarized, and very sober. Around its front wall, over its gates, and after a relatively small empty courtyard, there was nothing but tens of hundreds of yards of free fall in the perennial darkness of a steep vertical valley below.

An observer looking from the fortress gate could easily be dizzy with vertigo, for, beyond the top of the towers, the gray wall rose for hundreds of meters at an unnaturally acute angle until it kissed the sky.

The landscape was dramatically colorless in every aspect around the entrance of the structure. Everything was composed by the same sterile gray tonality, and there was almost no light to be see. The visible part of the fort, the one that was projected out of the mountain wall, was in a place of eternal penumbra. At daytime, it was never directly illuminated by the sunlight. At nighttime, it was never in total darkness either.

In and around it, there was an ever-present soft frozen white light that emanated from the temple. It was subtle, barely there, only enough to keep the fortress from darkness. It mystically embraced its rocks with patient resolve.

217

It was a calming and peaceful light, like an aura of quietness and hope. At first, it could seem scarce, but it was certainly there – humble, strong, sufficient.

The unfathomable restfulness and tenacious silence mascaraed any sign of its inhabitants. An external observer would straightforwardly tell that the place was abandoned. Its enormous towers, galleries, and hallways seemed deserted and depleted of life, but it wasn't.

In a certain afternoon, snow was falling quietly over the gray granite walls of the temple when a rare wind of transcendental agitation blew over it. It gently shook the snow over the tower top. Suddenly, the wind got turbulent, changing course and blowing over the stained glass of one of the windows with a muffled pressure. The old dust that covered it cleared, and a dim light was spilled in the massive entrance hall inside the temple. From there, quick passes were heard coming from within. Two monks, dressing heavy gray wool robes were crossing the long entrance hall heading directly to the main gate.

The entrance door was a relic. It was made of a forgotten type of silver alloy, but now thick layers of mountain dust covered its glow on both sides. When the two figures reached the sealed gate, they stopped.

'It is time,' one of the figures said solemnly.

He lowered his hood, revealing the head of an old man. His eyes were full of sincerity and truth, showing a soul clearly burdened by the heavy load of a lifetime of duty. At the same time, his face radiated the resilience and the plentifulness of true love.

'Yes, master,' answered the other monk from the darkness of his broad hood.

Like a hunchback, his large frame was abruptly curved by the neckline. He sounded young, profound, and slightly electric. Somehow, his voice carried even more weight than the old man's.

'Your hour has arrived.' The old man stared at the tall hunchback, trying to inspire him with courage, but his own eyes were humid and his voice trembled. The old man had on his face that unique mixture of fear and hope that a lovely father would have when sending his son on a dangerous venture.

'Yes, master,' the hunchback answered serenely, not totally unmindful of the old man feelings.

'Our enemy is lurking at the frontiers of this world once again. Once more he found allies that are willing to perform the necessary rituals to bring him back. Soon, he will reveal himself. War is imminent,' the old man said.

'Any news from the East?' the hunchback asked, hoping for a good answer.

'No. Nothing yet, my son.' The old man lowered his gaze and most of his hope left his eyes.

'I will find them,' said the tall man willingly.

'No,' the old man interrupted. 'First, find the fountain and gather the chosen ones you may find. Do what you need to do. Do what you must do,' he said and started to take something out of his collar. 'This will help you find it. It will help you find anything.' The old man removed a collar from his own neck and gave it to the hunchback.

The hunchback examined it for second in his hand. He handled it as if hesitating to accept the gift. The collar was a thick platinum chain that held a circle of pure gold, crusted with massive diamonds. The pattern of the diamonds' disposition was a geometrical mystery, and it was there where its magic lay. In the very center of the diamond formation there was a dark silvery blue nugget of an unbalanced and deformed brute stone. Its aspect was of uniqueness and roughness.

'And remember:' the old man said. 'the most important thing of all is that you shall not reveal yourself until your time comes. Act like your brothers before you. Hide yourself in the shadow of the morning light,' he said, filled with the sadness of the imminent farewell.

'Walk the path, but don't be revealed yet. It is not OUR time to be revealed,' the old man insisted while staring above as if grasping a prophecy or reading the signs of the times. 'Not just yet,' he repeated himself emphatically. 'Look for your brothers if possible, but pursue mostly your mission, that is; in secrecy, reopen and prepare the way,' he said as he closed the hunchback's hands around the necklace with his own, insisting for him to accept the offer.

'I will be here preparing The Order. Go, my blessings goes with you.' The old man put his hand on the hunchback who instantly knelt in a solemn gesture.

A pale light, very similar to the one surrounding the fortress, came out from the old man's hand and shone for no more than a split second. As the old man prayed, it gradually flooded the hunchback's robe until it was shining around him. When it covered him completely, the old man opened his eyes and raised his head. The light was then absorbed by the hunchback's frame and undoing itself sublimely, left an out-of-focus electricity behind.

The hunchback then raised himself and took another look from inside his hood to the necklace. This time the lower part of his face showed from inside his hood. The expression over his pale skin revealed a greater hesitation.

'Master?' he asked purposelessly, but uncertain.

'It is time, Hanamanaruil. It is time for you to become what you were raised to be. Your heart will find a way!' The old man grabbed him gently by the shoulder. 'It will find a way to the light through whatever darkness you may find. You won't fail, that I promise you.'

'Yes, master,' the hunchback said, his voice still had a regretful tone.

'Remember this: in your darkest hour, when you may be confused about what you are, just remember WHO you are. For, even the strongest lights cast shadows,' the old man spoke with authority and wisdom.

'Yes, master.' The hunchback expressed the will to be confident in his mission, but the old man could see through people's souls as if they were translucent glass. His eyes pierced beyond their projections and ego's theaters.

'Who are you?' the old man asked unexpectedly and energetically.

'Master?' The hunchback was clearly off guard.

'WHO – ARE – YOU?' he insisted, demanding an answer.

'Hanamanaruil Cuthamarú, a monk, a faithful server of The Order,' he replied, uncomfortable with the pressure his master had suddenly placed over his shoulders.

'Monk? No, you are no monk!' the old man said with a slight despise.

'Master?'

'I'm the guardian of this order, and, as such, I am responsible for keeping all of you on the path of light. I have guided tens of thousands into such path. You, Hanamanaruil, do not walk as one of us. No! You are no monk!' The old man's voice accelerated in tone and pace, speaking in a dryer and grander way now.

'I have trained countless monks in the arts of war and saw how you fight in spirit and with a sword, for faith and with a shield. You do not fight as a monk. No! You are no monk!' he continued.

'In your long concealment, I have been watching you. I have meditated deeply on you and your destiny. Not for a moment I have seen you as a monk. No! You are no monk!' His words were progressively gathering momentum and volume.

'I have looked at the bottom of your eyes and saw the radiance that they emanate. I have contemplated your soul. You do not possess the soul of a monk. No! You are no monk!' The deep truth and the spiritual intimacy of the old man's words touched the hunchback.

'I have heard you pray and felt the potency and the shape of your faith. I have seen your light. You are not like a monk. No! You are no monk!' Hanamanaruil felt like the old man's words were a burning blade gradually penetrating deep into his soul, but instead of causing pain, it filled it with relief and fire.

'I have read your heart, saw your strength, and I have understood your essence. No! You are no monk!' the old man was now openly exclaiming.

As sudden as the whirlwind of words had started, it finished. It had no anchor in reason, or even in emotions; it was a spiritual dispatch, a truth bound to strengthen the soul. It worked.

The old man started to look down, exhausted, but he slowly restarted. This time with more energy and decisiveness, letting every word fall into place.

As he raised his head, he let his stare fall onto the hunchback, but this time his eyes were away as if he was looking through him, contemplating something elusive that only he could see.

'Even now,' he said with great tremor, 'with all these shadows brought by this oppressive darkness, I can see the tracks of your destiny.' He paused for a few seconds, fighting the moment.

'YOU – ARE – NOT a monk!' The Temple trembled and the dust was mystically shaken from the silvered door. Its light reflected upon them both.

'You will never be one,' he whispered. His voice was filled by many other things than words and breath.

'Master?' The hunchback's voice was trembling with a fearful modesty, but through the extent of his wisdom, and not from a rational fear. He was humbling himself, but deep down he had understood the importance of that revelation.

'You are, my brother, the first of your kind in more than eight hundred years.' The old man talked slowly but with an overwhelming pride, as if he was struggling between the truthfulness of his words and the earthquake they were bringing in the Ether.

'You are the fury of justice. You are the river of light that cleans and purifies the filth that is upon the face of the abyss. What you will begin, many will finish. What you will sow, all will gather,' the old man said, resolute.

'You are the sparkle that lights the fire that burns the world. You shall punish, and you shall flail. Evil shall tremble at the very sight of you. It shall fall over the dust of your feet. AND YOU SHALL STEP ON IT!' the old man said it in a spirit of greatness and true justice.

Hanamanaruil gathered all the strength he had to ask the question he knew in his heart that he needed to ask.

'Who Am I, master?'

'A CRUSADER!' the man revealed it vigorously. His voice echoed through many dimensions in very subtle ways. An elusive but present blast of hope was heard through the faces of the Ether. The conversation ended there, and no more words were said.

Campfire

'So that is why we are here in the middle of nowhere, looking like well-armed beggars,' Bastian closed his case and shoved another spoon of the unbelievably tasty smoked meat stew down his throat.

The wizard said nothing.

'This cake is so good it should be illegal. It is wrong,' said Lucien almost crying in a rare glimpse of satisfaction.

'That, in fact, is bread that I baked two days ago. But I still do have some carrot cake here, if you feel like having some,' said the wizard politely, offering more food.

The way the wizard was dealing with the strangers impressed himself. It made him proud. He had come a long way since the last time he had contact with civilization or other humans. He was a completely different person now, and he felt as if he was above many things.

'I'm used to putting blue grape jam in them, instead of elven corn icing, but I don't have any now,' said the wizard, apologetic. 'If you don't mind, you can have it,' he said, offering the cake.

'I forgive you,' said Lucien rolling his eyes with pleasure after the first bit.

'Here, I have some sweet wine. It will compensate and balance de flavor.' The wizard was completely unaware of the high standards of precision he was used to judging himself by, and the overwhelming impression it was causing on Bastian and Lucien.

'I'm loving this guy!' said Lucien to Bastian frenetically and sincerely as he pointed to the wizard.

Bastian was lying on the other side of the fire pit. He casually noted without undoing the massive smile on his face. He was determined to enjoy the digestion of the very best meal of his life.

'Well, I suppose you guys can use some help now. Regarding your quest, I mean,' said the wizard diplomatically. 'If you allow me, I may help you. At least with what I can.' The wizard looked around, gathering his thoughts. 'Besides food, let me see if I can offer something more,' he said, putting on his "calculation face" and starting to consider. 'Well, the place where I was is not mine to offer anyway. So, there is just the road ahead. This road is almost straight-lined to east. The passage to go west can only be found, or not lost if you prefer, by ways of magic. There is a powerful enchant on it indeed.' He looked above, moving his fingers as he made plans. 'However, the ways to Valkar are mostly free of those things.' He looked down and faced the two friends, as if he had found a solution. Or, at least, got to a conclusion.

'If we wish, and follow this road, we could reach the forest limits in a week or so. By then, we will be close to the cities north of Westgate. I need to go to Rocksprings. I have business there,' said the wizard, forcing the terminological limits of his words. 'I need to trade some stuff,' he justified. 'You are free to join me. I mean, if you care to.' The wizard let his last words sink for a moment. Although they had not noticed, his words were calculated.

Bastian and Lucien, now reestablished by the exquisite food that the wizard had provided, exchanged looks but no words.

'Regarding the beasts and the hungry animals,' continued the wizard, correctly reading their stares, 'I can cast some spells for protection that will give us better nights of sleep,' he said.

After these words, all the chewing and relaxation quickly ceased among the two friends. Both warriors had their eyes fixed on the wizard immediately and no smiles could be seen on their faces anymore.

Most Valkarians use magic very indirectly, having contact with it mostly through magic items, healing potions and pre-made enchants. They would even admire the Battle Mages, the Water Monks, and any other spellcasters that were close enough to them or was institutionalized enough to be above reasonable doubt, but, in general, they are very jumpy around an unknown spellcaster. Bastian and Lucien were no exceptions to that rule.

The mention of magic made them suddenly realize the danger of their situation by accepting food and suggestions from a total stranger that had appeared in the middle of nowhere. Even, and above all, an inoffensive looking stranger who was now talking about magic.

Although he looked very familiar and brought a ton of relief to their senses, they both suddenly realized the fact that they did not even know the name of that strange gentle man or his agenda.

'Hey, buddy, where do you come from and what were you doing here, in the middle of nowhere, anyway?' Lucien could barely hide his new distrust, his wariness. 'You look familiar,' he added, buying time for his hand to find his sword.

'Yeah, maybe too familiar,' Bastian looked with a glance to Lucien while semi-discretely grasping his own weapon.

Aware of what was happening and rapidly projecting the direction of things, the wizard knew it was time to make a move.

'I can cure you, you know,' the wizard said, pointing to some wounds in Bastian's arm. 'For a price, of course,' he counter-balanced, managing to keep his emotions and intentions out of his face.

'How much?' asked Bastian, biting the bait. Lucien though, was still looking right through the wizard, ready to kill him in a blink of an eye.

'Well, I can do some now, but the bulk of it should be done tomorrow,' he said. 'I'm tired from the road and there are other magical details that you don't need to know,' said the wizard, ignoring Lucien's stare and believing in himself.

'How much gold?' asked Bastian.

'For the complete restoration of your health, huumm...let's say...10 gold coins each? And tomorrow morning you both will be like new, even the pain in your feet will be gone,' said the wizard.

The temptation was too great, and the wizard's proposal was almost cowardly placed, considering the terrible condition of their bodies.

Bastian looked at Lucien, who nodded before his gaze even reached him. They agreed with the deal, but continued to scrutinize every detail about the young wizard throughout the night.

Ignoring their suspicious gaze and their tight grip on his sword, the wizard understood that he needed to openly establish some trust.

'Let me start right now,' he said as he got up and sat next to Bastian.

The wizard gently took Bastian's arm and conjured the enchant. Bastian felt an overwhelming sense of relief go through his bones, while most of the cuts and bruises on his arms disappeared before his eyes.

Seeing this, and realizing that what the magician had accomplished fitted his understanding of "normal" and legitimate magic, and yet only after he had certified that Bastian had not become an irrational zombie controlled by the magician, Lucien relaxed his defenses.

'OK, it is my turn now,' he said, getting closer to the wizard. 'The one by the knee please, it has been killing me for a while now.'

Again, the wizard performed the same procedure. And again instant relief was the result.

'Awww. That is sooo good.' Lucien's eyes rolled into his sockets as the spell liberated him from some of his pain.

'We will pay you in the morning when the rest of the healing will be done. Right now, I'm done,' said Lucien as he settled over the fire and hugged his sword like a pillow.

'You had the first turn today,' he said to Bastian, and before he could protest, Lucien was fast asleep.

Klunk, who was close to Lucien, did the same and hugged him, falling into a deep and heavy sleep before Bastian could say anything.

'So, wizard, what is your name again?' asked Bastian, trying to start a conversation to keep awake.

'My name?' The wizard sounded surprised.

'Yes, your name. You do have one, don't you?' Bastian insisted as he leaned against the fire, struggling to stay awake.

'You need to give us one so we know what to call you, right?' said Bastian, too tired to go beyond obvious logic or to be suspicious.

'Yes, I suppose I do,' answered the wizard while offering a mug of strong black coffee to Bastian.

He accepted without questioning where the mug or the coffee came from. Bastian immediately drank the deliciously sweet and warm liquid as he curled up on his blanket.

Silence and peace took hold of the place where they were. The fire pit was now mostly consumed, what was left of it was nothing but a large brazier. A gentle wind dispersed the clouds away surprisingly fast. The stars and the moon presented themselves with great boldness, illuminating the night and everything around them. The sky became white with stars, to a point of which one could even tell the depths of the constellations. It instantly composed a majestic view from the edge of the cliff where they were camping. The stars immediately attracted their attention, but especially the wizard's. Who, disconnected, quietly laughed with himself while admiring them?

Bastian was also touched by the vehemence of the moment, connecting himself emotionally with their beauty. Having gone through a lot lately, he gave himself a moment of peace, admiring their greatness while drinking his coffee. However, noticing how the wizard stared at them, Bastian was under the impression that he would never see, feel, or understand them in the same dimension that the wizard could. Thinking about it, he forgot about the stars and set his mind on the wizard. He kept studying his strange and unusual person, on how different he was from him, and what he had to go through to become what he was and learn what he knew. Looking at the intensity of his passion while he read the skies, Bastian became increasingly curious about the wizard.

'And?' Bastian asked.

'Stargazer,' the wizard's gaze smoothly drifted down from the stars directly to Bastian. He had a smile of real joy upon his face. 'You can call me Stargazer.' Still with the same smile on his face, he looked at the stars once again, finally accepting himself.

Beyond Heaven's Stairs

The Empire's End was a massive tavern. It was located exactly in the middle of a sympathetic hill that over-watched the triple frontier between the Dire Woods, the Valkarian Empire, and the Fire Mountains.

A few miles southeast of the tavern, the high and sharp walls of the Blackspear were part of the horizon. The city-fortress was the landmark that marked and maintained the northwestern flank of the empire. The spearhead shape of the city walls made its silhouette very distinguishable in the skyline, and the crystallized black granite contrasted sharply with the green fields around it. The physical and transcendental aspects of the city made it a bastion; a testimony of the vigilant presence of the empire and its commitment to its borders.

The Empire's End itself was a large, rectangular, and rustic building made of big boulders and gigantic logs. It was built over the foundations of the first ancient forts that once guarded the northwestern crossroads. The whole hill was actually artificial. It was made of the debris of dozens of destroyed fortifications that piled up on that exact location. They were destroyed and reconstructed there throughout centuries of wars and invasions, until the empire finally built Blackspear. Human activity, pluvial erosion, and thick grass made sure the hill looked natural, convenient, and unsuspicious for the untrained eye.

The structure of the tavern was simple and very sturdy. It's every detail was built to resemble the frontier houses of past days. It had large windows, thick walls, and huge fireplaces that produced good hearty food all year round.

The ground floor of the tavern had a famous messy hall, kitchen, deposits, and other facilities. The sleeping quarters and private gathering halls were located on the upper floors.

Empire's End was no ordinary alehouse, being as worthy of tales and legends as any other famous locations of the empire. Its relevant position attracted a huge number of exotic customers. The place was so multicultural, big and busy, that it had its own security team. In addition, certain peculiarities of the frontier people that constituted the bulk of its customers also created a demand for a special type of housing and treatment. Looking for attending all sorts of folks, it contained many special features that set it apart from a regular pub.

On a certain night, the moonlight poured over that part of the northern border was so intense that it flew through the tavern windows like a silvery sun. The light was prettier and smoother to the eyes, but more discreet and less intense in its reflections. One could even see the small bugs flying across the night air in the open fields without the help of any other source of illumination.

Even though it was late, many guests were having their supper in the main hall and the place still looked fairly agitated. The atmosphere, however, was relatively peaceful and light – it was business as usual.

Some folks were arriving slowly, tired from the road. A few were diligently leaving, apparently fully committed with the risks (and advantages) of traveling at night.

The dispositions of the many windows on the south wall, that faced the only road that conducted to the hall's entrance gate, allowed everyone there to watch who was arriving and leaving through it. Since the place existed, it had been a sort of tradition for the people who sat inside to eyeball who was arriving and leaving through those windows. Many did it out of habitude, staring at the comers and goers without even thinking about it while they chatted and sipped their cups.

The air was too still to be noticed when an uncommon thing happened. No one had passed outside the windows, but the gate doors opened anyway.

Many, consciously and subconsciously, through the senses of their flesh or their connection to the Ether, noticed the incident, pausing their cups and forks midway to their mouth to watch out for the imminent happening.

When Hanamanaruil entered the gate, he immediately felt their eyes over him. He could not hide his hesitation and his legs froze. After no more than two steps, he stopped by the entrance of the main hall and timidly observed from the inside of his gray hood. However, a second after he entered the place, half of the people who were watching lost interest in him. Mainly due to the fact they thought he was a beggar from the road. Although most observers went back to their business, the hunchback stood still, midway to the counter, absorbing the huge amount of uncomfortableness the self-awareness caused him to feel. Even from under his thick mantle, his body language denounced he was taken by an odd guilty tension.

Eventually, he held on and renewed his intention to be as discreet as possible, but it was clear that some people noticed his mysterious figure. When he went to the counter looking for a table, he saw that some eyes remained tracking him, especially those of the most sensitive races. A prudent group of recently exiled high elves kept looking straight at him, making him uneasy, but in general, folks lost interest and went back to their own business with nothing more than a mental note about it.

In the end, Hanamanaruil's appearance was just another relatively ordinary incident at the Empire's End. That tavern was, and it always has been, crowded with odd people. The place was not a hidden unfaithful's wine saloon, but it was not a commoner pub or a simple pirate's den either. It was an iconic meeting point in the middle of one of the most important intersection in the world. All sorts of traders formed its clientele as there was a great variety of risky and profitable enterprises to be conducted in such a strategic location. Not all businesses there were legal and few were pedestrian; thus, the majority of the people there were dangerous, and the minority was very dangerous.

The huge saloon had all sorts of adventurers in it. Mercenaries, hunters, knights, spellcasters, and businesspersons from all corners of the continent and beyond. Many different races could be observed there as well. Some were common like half-elves, dwarfs, and gnomes, others much more uncommon, like panther-men from the Green Valley, and Urubaia, a four-armed multicolored-skinned folk that lived on the south coast.

Since its foundation, the inn hosted some of the most famous (and infamous) adventurers of Elaroth. As a result, the staff was extremely open-minded and tolerant – at least by Valkarian standards. And that is why the employee who attended the hunchback at the counter paid more attention to the authenticity of his silver than to the mannerisms of how he conducted himself or the details of his person.

After ordering and paying for a meal and a room, Hanamanaruil waited for his food sitting at the smallest table he could find, in the darkest corner in the depths of the tavern hall. His plan was to eat, passively absorb some local information and gossip, and then head out for a good night of sleep in a proper bed.

They served him a bow of beef stew, a big loath of the house's famous thousand grain bread, butter, fruit, and a huge double pint of milk and honey. Although he needed less rest than most men, after his meal, Hanamanaruil was ready to go to bed. Nauseated with all the different new things he was experimenting at once, he felt all the weariness of his long road hitting him at once. When he was about to get up and go to his room, he noticed three heavily armed and armored human warriors coming toward him. They seemed to have come out of nowhere, and before he could assess the situation, they were upon him.

'Can we sit down, please?' asked the noblest of the three, using a very diplomatic but somewhat unsure tone in his voice. 'We mean no harm,' he added, humbling himself.

Hanamanaruil said and did nothing. Under loud protests from the chair, the tall man sat down, but he and the other warriors kept their heads and faces covered by their hoods.

'Someone sent me,' he carefully talked in a clam and straightforward manner. 'This someone asked me to come here and take you to him, so that you may speak to him directly.' The warrior paused, waiting for a reaction. He got none. Hanamanaruil did not move or made any sign whatsoever.

'He cannot be here because he cannot be seen here,' the warrior continued. 'We will, however, provide a secure place for you to meet,' he said in a volume barely high enough for Hanamanaruil to listen. 'It is imperative that the meeting must occur in private and it must happen tonight,' he warned.

No reaction came from Hanamanaruil, who remained still and unresponsive.

'He also asked me to show you this.' The warrior took a necklace from his pocket and placed it in the middle of the table. The jewel was exactly like the one his master gave him before he left the temple. The only difference was that the rough stone in its center was white, instead of blue.

Clearly surprised, Hanamanaruil inquiringly inclined his body in the direction of the pendant to exam it. Moved by fascination, he even reached for it, but stopped halfway, and, unsure, retracted his big and muscular hand.

'So be it,' he said softly, and if his voice hadn't been so decisive, it would have been a whisper.

They left the saloon as discreetly as possible and went to the second floor. The room they got into was warm and welcoming as all Empire End's rooms were, but this one was bigger, as it was designed to accommodate a larger group of travelers. Apparently, the warriors had previously moved all the furniture to one side of the room, giving it a sense of openness. Everything was carefully stacked on the north wall, where the windows were, purposefully blocking the view from the outside.

With a high degree of professional military discipline, the two escorting men guarded the entrance from inside the room. Very seriously and attentively, they positioned themselves on both sides of the door. One of them quickly locked the door's mechanical mechanism once everybody was inside, then the other one placed a small rock over the lock and started pronouncing some mystical words. The little thing trembled and burst silently, expelling a contained light from the rune that was drawn on it. It magically melted into the lock mechanism, and its light-filled the contours of the doors and windows of the room, sealing them all shut with magic.

The warrior who had spoken to Hanamanaruil took off his hood, and then he removed his simple but dynamic full-faced helmet. Hanamanaruil instantly felt a sense of familiarity coming from the man's noble face. The hunchback was surprised by the fact that he somehow could not verbalize or explain his feelings circa his first impressions of the man's appearance. For a moment, he could not translate his feelings into thoughts. Then, the others also removed their head gear. They all looked alike. They were all obviously closely related, most likely brothers.

Rationally, Hanamanaruil could not make sense of the situation, aggravating his edginess. However, there was something more in that room that the eyes could meet. Forces were acting there and energies were looking for balance. In the instant he tried to explore these sensations looking for answers about his circumstance, he caught himself discerning that these warriors had powerful and pure souls. Somehow, he felt safe around them, as if their nobility overflowed the immediate mater of their flesh. He didn't become surprise with the substance of that direct revelation, but rather with its dynamics. The blast of their aura's energy was very sudden. So sudden, that it led him to correctly deduce that, in fact, their helmets were magically hiding their true presences.

Then, the speaker (that also seemed to be the older brother) took off his cloak, disclosing a very sturdy built. He was wearing a high quality unmarked full plate mail armor and bearing high-quality unmarked steel shield.

The others did the same and Hanamanaruil noticed that they were all armored and armed in the same manner. They all had hand-and-a-half swords, short swords, and large fighting knifes on each of their metal boots. They were purposely not bearing any discernible coat of arms or symbols that could identify them – a rare thing for a Valkarian warrior.

'Don't be afraid,' the spokesman said to Hanamanaruil.

He then closed his eyes and started doing something that resembled a quiet prayer. Shortly after, he started whispering.

'Father. Father,' he called out placidly, as if he was dreaming a good dream. 'We've found him,' he kept talking to the air. 'He is here with us now.' He said and then paused for a couple of seconds. 'As you wish,' he agreed.

He raised his head, then lowered it again, and then opened his eyes. They had changed into another man's eyes. There was a different color as well as a different soul behind them. Clearly, it was a mightier and fiercer soul.

The standing warrior still had muscular control over most of his head, but not of his eyes. It was as if they had become independent of their face and were being used by someone else. The bizarre changing of the eyes' colors from a bright blue to a dark brown was unsettling enough, but its independence from the head created a nightmarish atmosphere of absurdity. Although, in general, it still looked like the warrior's face, some expressions changed to correspond to the new consciousness who took control of his physiognomy. A few physical aspects, however, transcended through whatever magic was being used, prevailing over the features of the embodied, creating, likewise, a strange scene.

The eyes moved quickly, observing the surroundings, as if measuring the place. The alien eyes closed shortly after. The man then leaned forward his body, almost passing out from what seemed like a sudden exhaustion. Hanamanaruil jumped ahead and seized him by sheer protective reflex. When he grabbed the warrior, Hanamanaruil instantly felt his heart heavy and extenuated. When Hanamanaruil touched the man's arm, the commotion of the moment capacitated the deep mercy that the hunchback had in his heart to pour out, flowing from him to the warrior. He could not control it. It just went through him like an involuntary pulse of energy, materializing as a transmission of physical vigor. The pulse was received with great surprise and fear by the warrior, but not because he didn't know what it was (for he did), but because of its intensity.

With great sincerity, the warrior's eyes transpired all that he felt, and many things were said without a word. After the warrior had recovered his strengths and could stand on his own, Hanamanaruil let go of him and retreated to a more defensive posture next to one of the room's corners.

After that incident, the hunchback saw that the warriors looked at each other with a growing doubt and anxiety. Reading the reaction in their eyes, Hanamanaruil perceived that he was a mystery to them in the same manner that they were to him. He also felt that he had an unknown connection with these strangers. It echoed in the deepest levels of his being, and although he couldn't fully understand it, he knew that it was good. The mystery of that connection, both in purpose and in nature, was quickly discerned by them as a spiritual interaction. Surprised, they understood they were all men of faith.

The look of surprise and wonder over that fact was still in the warrior's face, when, in the middle of the room, a light brightened and flickered. Then, a surreal warping noise invaded the room. The light reached its peak with a blinding intensity, and then faded away quickly. As it drew back, the form of a man was left behind. As it diminished its acuteness, an epic knight appeared before them.

Every single detail about him was majestic and surreally extraordinary. His grand figure was fully covered with a massive white full plate armor that looked fantastically robust. His head would touch the ceiling, and his shoulders were abnormally broad. His giant body was the body of a champion in his prime, but his face was the face of a well-kept old man. His hair, beard, and eyebrow were crispy white and his face was exceedingly distinguished and honorable, perfectly stained with a smooth black tonality of his skin. Behind his back, he also had an immaculate white cloak, a large white metal shield, and a monstrous magnificent two-handed sword that an archangel would be justified in bearing it. In his war belt, he had a very thick bladed golden longsword on his left side, and a splendid silvery war hammer on his right side.

Hanamanaruil could feel a tremendous magical power coming from Oberan's person, from his weapons, and from his magic items, however, what touched the hunchback the most was the knight's invisible and poignant aura of righteousness. He had seldom felt such a powerful pulse of disruptive energies, and as far he was concerned, he was looking at the Emperor of the Valkarian Empire.

'Hold thy peace,' he said to the hunchback. 'My name is Oberan Kriton, server of the Emperor, first of the White Knights. These men are sons of mine,' he said with deep humility, and his voice had that unique tone of strength and wisdom that could only come from a tired soul who has gone through a lot.

Hanamanaruil noticed the clear physical resemblance between Oberan and the warriors, although there was an extensive gap in size and glory between them.

'May I please see your face?' the White Knight pleaded as he gently moved his hand in the direction of the hunchback's hood.

Hanamanaruil turned away slightly. Oberon retrieved his hand politely.

'Are you a newcomer?' he asked.

Hanamanaruil hesitated and did not answer it.

'Do you have something to give me?' the knight tried again, and silence was heard again.

The knight shook his head, frowned his forehead, and decided to open it.

'The reason why we are having this encounter is still an enigma to me.' He let his words sink in for a second. 'However, I have lived enough in this world to know that all good things start with a mystery,' he said.

'We have not been receiving enough news from the temple to know exactly what is going on,' he continued. 'Yet, taking into consideration the source, I will openly talk to you.' He tried to spot a reaction but found nothing under the inexorable barrier of the hunchback's gray hood.

'I had a vision yesterday. The person on that vision was someone from –' he interrupted himself, evaluated his words more carefully, and only then continued '–someone from the past. Someone that I deeply regarded and trusted. This…someone, showed me this place and showed me…you,' Oberan said, completely overcome by the humility brought by the mere memory of that event. 'She told me that you have a gift for me, for us,' he clearly was struggling with his mature and powerful emotions – powerful emotions from a powerful heart. His presence filled the room.

'I have nothing to give,' Hanamanaruil finally gave something.

'Who are you? What is your name?' demanded the knight, anguished.

'Hanamanaruil Cuthamaru,' he said.

A great silence followed as the knight digested the hunchback's words.

'"The strength of the morning light,"' translated the knight.

'I did not…know that,' said Hanamanaruil, restrained.

'No one does, not anymore. At least no one from this age,' lamented Oberan. 'It has been a long time since I have last listened to this language. A long time except for last night,' he said.

'Are you from The Order? Have you arrived newly?' Oberan asked, but was answered with nothing but persisting hesitation. 'You have nothing to fear,' he assured the hunchback. 'Even before I've stepped into this room I could feel WHAT you are. Yet, I need to know WHO you are,' declared the knight. His voice was filled with honesty and intension.

Hanamanaruil put his hand inside his cloak and exposed his necklace.

'How isolated are the men in the Hidden Temple?' Oberan asked the instant he saw the jewel. 'Any word from them?' the second question followed quickly. Despite his wisdom and experience, the knight could not hold his anxiety.

'Isolated?' Hanamanaruil shot back.

'Some time ago the way back to the temple was…lost. Its location was protected by magic and secrecy. Unable to find it, the enemies of this world amplified the spells cast over it, hiding it until no one can find the way back,' Oberan said. 'We feel this relates to another important fact.' He stopped to make sure the hunchback understood or even accepted his words.

He did.

'We have intercepted many disturbing reports,' Oberan continued. 'An old enemy has awakened recently. They are connecting with someone or something,' he hesitated for a few seconds, 'on the other side,' he revealed.

'Communicate? We?' inquired Hanamanaruil.

'I have been in the Hidden Temple. It was a long time ago. The Emperor was with me. It happened before he became The Emperor,' the knight said.

'Impossible, it is forbidden,' Hanamanaruil was very tacit about it.

'Yes, I know,' replied the knight. 'There, we have learned about the possibility of reaching the higher planes and many other things about it. We were there on a desperate mission to find a way to the higher dimensions. More specifically, to the Fountain of Mercy,' said the knight with great solemnity.

'Impossible, the way is shut for mortals.' Hanamanaruil was clearly intrigued.

'Yes, I know,' said the knight again. 'But when forced to the utmost of our love, mortals can commit to immortal deeds. That is what mortality is all about.' Oberan's eyes looked suddenly tired.

'Around that period, I got to know your master too,' said the knight. 'He taught us about the purpose of The Order and blessed us with a fervent wisdom and a profound knowledge over the Ether. We ended up using all that many years later,' he said.

Hanamanaruil commented nothing.

'Heironeus was one of the most prominent heroes of the empire and already a sworn enemy of the Dragoness by then. In those days, we pursued mostly personal goals in our adventures. After learning the costs and the risks to reach the heavens, we decided not to. Though, we kept the knowledge. Destiny made it terribly handy later,' Oberan lamented.

'The history of one of our greatest endeavors started years after our visit to the Hidden Temple,' the knight regretfully started to tell a tale. 'The Dragoness, unable to strike a direct blow to Heironeus' rule, devised maybe her most terrible plot that we have yet to know,' he said, disgusted by the memories that his own words brought back to him. 'She infiltrated the Steel Citadel, and, through strong magic, she shifted herself into the likeness of the Empress, spending a night with the Emperor and later conceiving a son of him.' It was dreadfully clear how those remembrances caused havoc in the old warrior's heart. His face mirrored his despise. 'Using the most despicable and cruel strategy to destroy the empire from within, she tried to drive the emperor mad, leaving their baby child in the empress' chambers.' He paused, trying to withstand the violence. 'A terrible curse indeed. We were all sorrowful as the destiny of the empire was at stake, for a tainted descendent of her would now have a claim to the throne.' He nodded his head in disapproval. 'An offspring of one of the vilest creatures who has ever walked this green world would for sure be destined to evil. An evil that would, by entering Heironeus' lineage, contaminate the empire, and, thus, us all,' he paused.

'And so, it was. I saw it myself. I will never forget the fiery power of the child's fury when I held it for the first time. I have fought her many times before, and I knew well her wrath – it was planted deep in the child's flesh and soul. He surely was his mother's son.' The knight looked away as if he regretted to have lived through it all.

'What a terrible day, the day I held the end of the Valkarian Empire in my own hands.' His words trembled while he recollected his memories. 'The Emperor would never raise his hand against a son of his, no matter what. She knew that, the whole world knew that,' he said. 'All the Emperor's sons were at risk now, for they were the next logical targets. To make things even worse, there were also many unsettled internal conflicts regarding Heironeus' position on the throne. In those years, more than a few powerful men contested his right to it,' he said. 'The situation was critical from all fronts. The dilemma imposed on us all by Xshisrahil's wicked feat consumed everything around us, especially our priceless hope,' the knight meant every word. 'The emperor knew that the empire, his position, his family and, ultimately, his own life were at risk. All the people that loved Heironeus were also under a living torture, and the ones who would not recognize him would use the opportunity to fuel their unjust hatred. Action needed to be taken,' Oberan justified. 'It was at this

236

decisive moment that the emperor showed his true self.' The knight's eyes started shinning again. 'With the courage and the love of a thousand kings, he took the half-dragon baby and set off into one of the most dangerous and desperate adventures ever lived,' he said, looking up as if he could see it in his mind. 'How could I fail him in his most painful hour?' Oberan asked rhetorically. 'I didn't, I guess. Certain of our deaths, I've joined him.' Everybody in the room were now taken by the knight's tale, even though they all knew it very well, except for Hanamanaruil.

'I was there, boy,' the old knight looked straight to Hanamanaruil, 'beyond Heaven's Stairs, in the Fountains of Mercy, where love is born,' he said, almost crumbling under the power of that memory. 'It was there that a solution found us.' His wet eye shone brightly with remembrances that transcended what words could tell.

'In the final moment, however, we learned that the purification process could kill the child. The result was unpredictable by any means or knowledge we possessed,' he said. 'I knew the Emperor since before he had grown a full beard and I assure you his courage had never failed, but the decision finally overwhelmed his heart and the horrendous uncertainty froze his will.' Oberan paused, remembering. 'Even a man like Heironeus had his limits.' The White Knight meditated over his own words. 'It was in that moment that one of his servants arose and, moved by the direst madness that affliction is able to curse a man's soul with and blind in his purpose by an overwhelming caring love, took the child and bathed him into the fountain.' Oberan's eyes looked distant while he revisited the moment. It was visible that every word touched him deeply.

'The newborn's essence changed and overpowered his physical body. He didn't die, instead, his soul was redeemed and its geometry redesigned – his whole purpose was modified by the transformation. His body though, stayed as one of a half-dragon.' A resonating joy exploded inside the knight's eyes. 'He was altogether a renewed soul. Blessed with a wonderful new essence, his spirit became bound to love and goodness. He was not a child of fire and hate anymore, he phased into a creature of love and good will.' Oberan smiled the most satisfying smile, his eyes were shinning with his held tears. 'The curse became a blessing,' he said. 'A fair counter-move from the Emperor's part if you ask me. For, in this manner, the Emperor humiliated any claim that the Dragoness could manifest and withdrew any legitimacy of her dominium or political actions. He turned the tables on her.' Sheer happiness, drenched in the sincerity of a true champion, sparkled in the knight's eyes. 'The Dragoness, now turned deranged in her fury, fielded all her armies and challenged the Emperor for open war. In the Battle of Broken Bones, over a huge cost for the empire, she not only lost her army and many powerful allies, but most of her disgraced progeny. Wounded, she fled, swearing revenge.' He restrainedly savored his words.

'The infant grew in strength, in kindness, and in every good virtue. A fair Valkarian prince he became,' said the knight. 'Later, we discovered that the blessing of his fate held more secrets than we first thought.' Oberan paused, as he apparently tried to summarize all his thoughts. 'He possessed healing powers,' he said conclusively. 'Real healing powers. The likes of the ones narrated in the lost days,' he continued. 'And now, even as we speak, many other unique enchants and wonderful things are flowing through him,' he said with pride.

'We understood that those powers resembled the powers of a very old, almost forgotten, class of warrior.' He looked straight to Hanamanaruil. 'These warriors fought in the past for the cause of goodness and justice,' he said. 'True goodness,' he concluded in his inspired fashion. 'They denied the idolatry of a name or a title, hence they were called the Paladins due to the mere facts that their armors were made of palladium – a lost alloy of the old days,' he said.

'It was easy to find out about the Paladin's deeds. However, it was very hard to raise specific lore over the Paladin's true source of power,' Oberan continued. 'After a lot of secret field researches involving many of the most powerful people of the empire, we concluded that the only way a soul could receive their powers was through the waters of the Fountain of Mercy. Later, when we eventually reached it, we were made sure that we were the first mortals who had ever been there. That fact led us to discover that, in ancient times, the dwellers of the heavens themselves redeemed the mortals by bringing cups of the fountain's water and pouring it over the ones who found grace upon The Light of the First Creator,' he said.

'Unfortunately, the modes of our existence are such that the powers of light only bring interference like this when destruction first manifests itself in the material world. There is a balance in this world that lingers in stances beyond our reason, there is little or nothing we can do about it. Every single drop of the fountain's water is the direct result of a bucket of blood. Every blessing comes to mend a suffering,' he lectured.

'One thing we do know: the stage of the world today is settled in a way that will certainly allow evil to get in once more,' Oberan said. 'Ignorance and suffering are everywhere, this balances everything toward favoring chaos, but order will naturally prevail in the end,' he was deadly serious. 'We must haste that end. We are warriors of the end,' he concluded.

Although no one could see, the hairs on Hanamanaruil's arms raised and he felt a rush of blood to his head.

'Throughout history,' the white knight continued, 'since unmarked times, here and there, some men and some institutions were granted a gift. They were, from time to time and according to the world's needs, presented with a certain quantity of the precious water. In time, every drop was used to spend every manifestation of evil and destruction. We are living in an age in which a relative equilibrium was artificially created by the Paladins. But the winds of change are coming, I can feel it.' For a few moments, the knight's eyes remained lost in a horizon of his own making as his faith stared at the future.

'Unwilling to break the balance,' he said while his mind came back to the room, 'and thus causing suffering upon the world, the skies shut. No more water would break through the heavens and thus no more blood would be spilled on the ground. At least not in an amount that could be generally perceived as unbalanced,' he said. 'The acquired powers, though weaker in every generation, passed through the bloodlines of the blessed ones. Stimulating balancing disgraces upon this world. That is why The Hidden Temple was built – to hide the last descendants of the Paladins outside the boundaries of this world, preserving the remaining bloodlines and the blessings thereof, and at the same time sparing the world of any justified evil. That is why the temple's design creates a temporal distortion – to isolate and conserve the blessed mortal flesh,' he clarified. 'And thus, the objective of The Order is to oversee the world's balance and to preserve and protect the good that Eternity has shed upon us.' It was clear to everyone in the room that Oberan was now lecturing his sons and not the hunchback any longer, as most of this information seemed to cause no reaction on him and all kinds of impressions of surprises on them.

'Through millennia, they actively conducted periodic probing missions to raise information on the world's status quo. Regretfully, when they left the temple, they aged normally, and after patrolling the rotation established for long centuries, many had died of age in the process. Many more perished in their tours of duty never to be seen again.' He reserved moments of silence in condolence and respect for the fallen.

'The ones sent in my lifetime, at least the ones that we could find, were hidden and organized by us in secret, but we are very few. We have supported, assembled, and hid newcomers like you, especially now that the way is closed,' he said. 'I know you are aware of most of what I just told you, but I need you to understand our side of the story because we need you to help us with one thing: we need to communicate with the High Priest. There are many new issues that are called to be settled. We have to reopen the way,' said the knight sternly.

'I was sent by the High Priest to find the fountain, and reopen the way,' Hanamanaruil finally opened up, showing some trust.

Oberan gave the hunchback a second look. Within it, newfound respect. Shortly after, a distracting conclusion came into the knight's mind.

'Then our worst fears are true,' he said, taken by a great fear. 'He is raising an army again. The High Priest can feel it too.' Oberan's face became distorted by the disturbances of his wariness.

'My lord,' the hunchback humbly intervened, 'this…war, will never see an end,' Hanamanaruil spoke in truth.

Oberan raised an eyebrow and looked sideways, bitter, regretfully agreeing with a tacit momentary silence.

'If the High Priest trusted you that mission, we are bound to support your efforts,' the knight said, willing to take his mind to a more objective subject. 'We have managed to gather some of the holy water, we also possess considerable resources and political reach inside the empire and the lands around it,' he said. 'Go now. Keep secrecy and misdirection always with you. Use the name Hanam from now on; otherwise, you are at risk of being identified,' he said. 'Go south to Westgate. Use the Emperor Road, it is safer this way. As far as we know, no one has heard of you yet, you can hide in plain sight. I will send for you,' said the knight.

'Remember: my identity as the organizer of The Order inside the Valkarian Empire must be preserved at all costs. My name must never be mentioned.' The knight looked straight down at Hanam to see if he had understood the true importance of what he was saying. 'Do not worry about your brothers, they are as safe as they can be with us. Take this gold with you for your travel expenses.' Oberan gave him a bag full of gold coins from various sources and mixed dates.

'The way must be reopened,' Oberan concluded. 'It is imperative that we reach the High Priest now,' he said.

'What about the fountain?' asked Hanamanaruil.

'The linear path was removed. What we have done to reach the fountain in the past is impossible to be repeated now,' Oberan answered. 'Only what is part of heaven comes from heaven, and back to heaven can return. Only a celestial being can have access to both worlds now.' Oddly, Oberan's eyes pierced Hanamanaruil's hood, as if he could see what was inside its shadows.

'Earthly flesh can't withstand well the rigors of true righteousness,' the knight added. 'Truth is too broad a perspective,' Oberan said, lamenting every word. 'The servant that took the prince inside the waters of The Fountain of Mercy had his whole body covered by it, almost getting himself eternally obliterated for the wickedness of his own human nature,' he said with distant eyes. 'Somehow, because of a higher grace or a hidden purpose that is yet to be revealed, the servant managed to get back to this world with his body and sanity intact.' Oberan's eyes were far away, filled by brawny feelings that disturbed his stable demeanor.

Every level of the old knight existed into a frequency far above and beyond most men's. His sentiment had such a range, that quickly his sons fell into distress and worries. Oberan's sons were all seasoned and wise men, but they resembled children when around their powerful father, for the charisma of Oberan's presence waved the very air around them.

'Funny fact about that servant and his clumsy destiny,' the knight continued with a lighter tone in his voice, 'is that he found that his magic pockets and his enchanted canteen were all filled with that water once he came back,' Oberan said with a smart smile on his face. 'In time, he discovered that just a few drops of the living waters could turn a man into a Paladin, embodying him with fervent cosmic inspiration and great healing powers,' he said. 'And through this servant's work, many were transformed, becoming a true bulwark of justice as in the legends of the old days,' he said and granted himself an amusing, slightly satisfied, and deeply humble smile of fully accomplished happiness. It was an expression in the kinds of which only a rare

241

breed of man would convey, for it contained victories that solely he could understand its true value and extent.

'What happened to him?' asked Hanam.

'Who?' replied Oberan distracted and a bit confused.

'The Emperor's servant who entered the fountain?' the hunchback asked.

'You are looking at him now,' said Oberan with a crushing humility.

Silly Road Chat

After the first quiet full night of sleep in a very long time, and a breakfast with bacon, eggs, sausage, sweet cornbread, fried bread, honey, and the most amazing coffee they had ever tasted, Stargazer finished healing the two friends.

Being restored with magic showed Bastian and Lucien how hurt and drained they really were. By experimenting the gift of instant reality transformation, they realized that magical healing had the power to positively and suddenly change their perspectives on how they did things. That experience brought them a greater respect and a terrible want for it. It was too convenient, forcing them to appreciate the mysterious strider's help and accept him among them. They now felt so immediately renewed and unburdened that it seemed that everything that had happened to them in the previous weeks had been nothing but a dream.

The wellness and security that they were now feeling even allowed them to risk misusing a few hours of their time by a nice little pond for some must needed shaving and washing. Bastian and Lucien were so dirty by then that, after they finished their bath, a thick crust of dirt, hair, dead skin, and soap foam covered the entire surface of the pond's water, hiding its beautiful translucent shine. The pond was still little, but was surely not nice anymore.

As they retook the road, they experienced that all of Stargazer's spells worked flawlessly and they accepted that he was a real wizard. Since they met him, they had not been bothered by predators or beasts anymore. Stargazer's enchants were now masking their scent and footprints, making them almost invisible to the animals. The sheer comfort and relief that this brought contributed for the two friends to trust Stargazer even more. The benefits of having the wizard with them were overwhelmingly greater than any possible suspicion they may have had about him only hours ago.

Bastian and Lucien's reality was now completely different from what it was less than a day ago. The sudden change was unnatural and hard to process, it made them feel as if they were living a totally different life now. Their bodies would not feel as if it was theirs, for their minds would still register the wounds that were healed. Most importantly, their environment changed without changing. The forest was now pacified through the wizard's protective spells, and, in the most surreal way, the trees around them would not feel as the Dire Woods they experimented for the last several weeks. They had been totally renewed emotionally and physically in such a short time window that they felt like everything around them was dreamlike. Yesterday's sufferings and anguishes, so tangible hours ago, seemed to be now recluse in a distant past, even forgotten. It was an appalling feeling as their minds were not prepared to absorb so many drastically artificial changes at once.

The joy of their relief became so prevalent in their minds that they had become childlike in their thoughts and feelings, abandoning all responsibility and judgment. Forgetting why they were there in the first place, the two friends followed the wizard through the ancient forest road heading east.

Relieved and light-minded, Bastian, Lucien, and Stargazer chatted happily. Klunk followed them even happier, utterly affected by their new misty optimism. As they strolled, Klunk was forcefully and clumsily trying to emulate a casual pace. He upheld his mace over his shoulder, plated a smirk on his lips, laid his head back, and walked with his legs open, theatrically pointing his knees sideways with each step. He also gave an exaggerated positive sigh from time to time as the conversation progressed, although nobody was ever really asking his opinion on anything.

After many hours, they found themselves tired of talking and spontaneous silence took over. In it, some conclusions set into their minds. Bastian finally conceived that his quest was over. He felt a little disappointed and sad, but he now knew he had tried until the limits of his abilities.

There is always a next summer, he thought briefly, finally deciding to let it go.

In peace, Bastian accepted that the whole thing was over. Lucien saw this and was happy for his friend. Well-fed and pleased, they relaxed and forgot about themselves for a second. There wasn't a constant rush anymore. No more tension now, just the road ahead. The morning was beautiful, they felt fresh, and everything they had gone through now felt as only one more story to be told. They were actively not minding their futures, and not focusing on any self-imposed burden, however little it might be. They were really enjoining and focusing on the gift of the present, and for a long-time things were kept this way.

Eventually, however, their minds wondered, and slowly but surely the big question at hand grew into Bastian's and Lucien's heads.

"What now?" they both thought.

Lucien's cynicism caused him to give up thinking about it before Bastian did. With nothing else to do, Lucien started to really consider how strangely unusual the wizard was. He started reflecting on all suspicious things about Stargazer; on how he had appeared out of nowhere, how awkwardly generous he had been with his free gifts, and how he carried himself gently and spoke in an unexpectedly soft manner. The wizard was just too well kept for a traveler from that parts; he had pale skin, clean hair, and his eyes were full of rest and trust. His tailor-made garments were remarkably divergent, almost alien, and his priceless Hashanian cotton shirt, although high-end, was incredibly outdated. His blue wool pants matched his coat to fashion and style, and an artisanal multi-pocket leather belt loaded full with god-knows-what hung from his waist. His tall leather boots looked ancient, but they had almost no wear marks on them, not even in the soles. He had no backpack, instead, he was carrying a small messenger leather bag filled mostly with his exotic foods and magical spices. Crossed over his back, he had two large long objects wrapped tightly in bedsheets. At first, Lucien thought that it was the wizard's camping equipment, probably some kind of tent or shelter, but that idea was dismissed quickly and the mystery remained.

Noticing the investigative stares Lucien was throwing at Stargazer, Bastian started having thoughts of his own. By studying the wizard, he thought that the most intriguing and disturbing thing about him was the fact that he had no weapon at all. Bastian became alarmed, for who in the world would be wondering in the Dire Woods unarmed?

Does he trust his own spells that much? Bastian thought. *How powerful is his magic? Can he use it against us? Is he already using it?* he questioned himself.

When Lucien saw Bastian's face, he instantly knew what was in his mind, deciding that it was time to take action.

'So, wizard,' Lucien started, 'you are a piece of work, aren't you?'

'What do you mean?' Stargazer answered casually, without showing that he knew quite well what was going on.

'Out of nowhere, amazing food, magic...no weapon.' Lucien winked at Bastian.

Bastian was quiet but supported what Lucien was doing. He decided to stay out for now, playing distracted.

'Well, I AM CARRYING weapons,' Stargazer said emphatically but not aggressively. 'I'm just not BRANDISHING them,' he explained calmly while artificially distracted, pretending he had not noticed Lucien's agenda.

'You mean the big bulky roll you are carrying on your back?' asked Lucien, openly suspicious. He knew how to be relentless when pressing someone.

'Yes,' answered Stargazer. 'Do you want to see them?' he said as if he didn't mind showing them the weapons. However, he did mind. He would rather do it some other time over a different situation, but he was now under pressure to build some trust with them.

Without waiting for an answer, the magician took the roll off his back, lowered the volume on a large flat rock at the hips that was conveniently on the side of the road, loosened the two belts that held everything together and casually unrolled the leaves, revealing their contents.

'See,' Stargazer started, 'although radically different in styles, making, and alloy composition, both weapons are made from the same rare metal called Star Ore.' The wizard enjoyed every opportunity to share knowledge. 'From what you told me before, I assume you know this metal, its outstanding characteristics, and, of course, its denouncing blue color. However, I must...' Stargazer stopped his lecture abruptly as Lucien's trembling hands reached for Bastian's dagger.

Lucien pulled it with such a nervous strength that he snapped the dagger out of its sheath clean off. Lucien's eyes frantically searched for Bastian's family crest engraved in the dagger's palm, and then looked at the two-handed sword's palm. Then he looked at both again, comparing the symbols in total disbelief. Then he did it yet once more and madness took over his eyes.

Bastian's head was following Lucien's sudden and dramatic actions by sheer reflex. He was not really aware of what was going on for he was still focusing most of his mind on the issue of the wizard. Finally, Lucien looked straight in his friend's eyes, and the sincerity of his tears injected an explosion of thoughts and fears in Bastian. Bastian did not deviate his glance, not even to rest his eyes on the sword. He didn't need to. What he saw in Lucien's eyes told him everything he needed to know. Everything they had lived together, especially in the last several weeks, was there. Each struggle with faith and hope, each doubt over an act of degrading violence, each drop of blood shed in fear for their lives – everything was there.

In their souls, that moment stretched on forever. They said nothing to each other, still it was one of the best conversations they had ever had. When they finished it, both looked at the wizard at the same time.

'What?' Stargazer asked, fearing the powerful feelings newly awakened in the warrior's eyes.

Although the wizard had prepared the moment, the intensity of their reactions caught him off guard. He instinctively took a step back, stumbling over Klunk, who managed to sneak up behind him somehow. Startled, Stargazer turned and looked upward, finding a giant's smile of true and innocent happiness on Klunk's face. The brute's wet eyes contained a concentration of gratitude and satisfaction that Stargazer hadn't imagined possible.

The Healer

Rocksprings had been conceived by the Valkarian Empire long ago to serve as a guarding post monitoring the navigation over the Blue River. It was located a hundred miles north of Westgate, laying amid softwoods, waterfalls, scenery plains, and multi-colored wildflowers.

The oldest building in the city was centered right in the middle of the extensive rapids that marked the birth of the Blue River and the beginning of its slow descent across the Valkarian's central plains. The river was not immensely large at that point, but it was deep enough to be navigable by considerably large boats and barges. Its waters left Rocksprings with a respectable volume, fatted by the gathering of small forest streams that came down from the Dire Woods, the lazy creeks the descended from surrounding elevations, and by many generous springs that poured out from the abundant hefty rocks in and around the city area.

In the beginning, Rocksprings was little but a bridge and a relatively small fort built over a large boulder in the middle of the river bed. The building structure was shaped like a thick, tall, tubular watchtower and its foundations were merged with the bridge's.

The bridge was built integrated with the deep canals and the large lagoons around the crossing, housing on its stone decks around its pillars as many ports as order would allow it. The bridge and the fort functioned as a continuum of systems of checkpoints that controlled traffic on land and over water. The entire city grew from them.

The Old Tower was still there during the days when Hanam entered the city. Its facilities were still used by the local guard in the same manner they did centuries ago. Rocksprings's relevance, however, grew extensively since the time of its inception, and all of its structures expanded with it. For the imperial authorities, the city's main objective remained the same – to guard the river's access, avoiding deep infiltrations of spies and ill-willing interests to the empire central plains. Nevertheless, as the Blue River had smooth and slow waters along its entire course, and traveled all the way from the western border with the Dire Woods to the eastern sea, commercial navigation was not just possible but also very profitable. With the occupation of the central plains and the pacification of the tribes and the end of the perils that block the Blue River waterway, commerce boomed. Attracted by it, waves of migrants from as far as the word could travel turned Rocksprings into a rich and colorful place. Somehow unexpectedly, the city became the largest multicultural, diverse, and interesting hub in the entire empire.

Since the day the first bargeman profited going up and down the river, the city's economic growth had never stopped. In time, it became an irresistible source of revenue for the empire. The authorities, however, remained very concerned about the military implications of its position, investing most of the taxes produced locally to build walls and fortresses as the city expanded. The people of Rocksprings had always resisted the need to transform its city into a fortress-city per se, and although it was less protected than other same-sized urban centers of the empire, its defenses were still pretty much dense and robust, composed by seven layers of walls.

A long time ago, a visionary Baron used the combined surplus wealth of the local families to inaugurate an arcane library and a magic study center. As the number of magicians in Valkar was (and still is, actually) relatively low, the Valkarians that dealt with magic suffered the stigma of been atomized, seeing in the city's libraries and thinking gatherings as an opportunity to concentrate and to interact. In this manner, Rocksprings became a meeting point for everyone who was willing to exchange experiences and knowledge in the realm of all things magic. Spellcasters from all over the empire transferred their residencies to the city to exchange knowledge, to work, and to be together. Some were indeed foreign wizards of renown, but most were second sons and first daughters of rich Valkarian families. Regardless, they all brought their fortune and influence with them, enriching the city's structure, culture, and brain pool even further.

However, all that prosperity came at a price, and many corrupt and undesirable people, attracted by the possibilities of high earnings, established their roots in Rocksprings. Organized crime, smugglers, and resilient thief guilds became a never-ending headache for the locals. Although Rocksprings has become one of the wealthiest cities in the empire, it has also become the most crime-ridden region thereof. The place's incredible wealth has always been stained by the misery and violence of the apparently unsolvable systemic crimes.

Hanam had walked south through the Emperor's Road since his encounter with Oberan. He was still using his gray wool cloak and was still barefoot, but had carved an oak staff for defense as the perils of the road taught him a lesson or two. Therefore, when he heard the gossips concerning Rocksprings, he had mixed feelings about crossing it. He anticipated that it would be a hard place to pass by unnoticed, considering that there would certainly be more than common eyes watching him there. However, he decided to risk it anyway, for he needed to press south and heard that the situation was even worst along the city's surrounding areas, leaving him without the option of going around it.

After carefully considering his plans, he decided that, once inside the city, he would inconspicuously join the next large commercial caravan set straight to Westgate, his final destination. When he was just a few hours north of the city, he sensed a disturbance coming from the woods on the right side of the road. Normally, he would ignore any trouble and just continue to walk down his road, but in that day he was overcome by a harsh sense of danger and decided to investigate it. His feet were quick and silent for someone his size and he managed to sneak through the brush until a point where he could see without being seen. When he was finally able to see what was happening in the clearing, he witnessed a scene of violence.

It looked like a deal had gone bad, really bad. Apparently, three men had just wounded and captured a woman. A scar-faced man with long and scruffy oiled black hair and dead eyes seemed to be commanding whatever that was. He was dressed in black leather armor and was holding a serrated longsword in his right hand and a mysterious masked woman in his left. He was slowly choking her to death, and enjoying every second of it. His physical strength seemed unnatural as he easily managed to keep all her body weight high in the air with just one stretched arm.

The woman's eyes started to turn inside her head as the last vigor left her body. She had the left side of her back pierced at least twice by crossbow bolts. The wounds were foaming a toxic green and vivid orange foam, indicating the use of a very toxic poison. The acidity of the poison's oxidation and its resulting agony could be felt even from where Hanam was.

The other two men were not as wicked looking as the tall one, but were far from being angels and were thoroughly armed with longswords, daggers, and black crossbows (probably the ones they had used to shoot her). Hanam noticed that they all carried a symbol of an awful gray rat on their chests. One of them had it tattooed to his face, terribly close to his rotten teeth. As the woman squeaked in agony, they begged for their captain to leave a "piece" of her for them. They were sadistically laughing deep in their throats, and Hanam had ever heard such evil before.

'Told you I would get you, Sahafira!' said her tormentor in a voice so deep it sounded demonic.

His Coronian accent was almost caricatural. He sucked some saliva that was overflowing the festering sores in his lips. All his attention was directed to the pleasure he was achieving while murdering the woman.

'The poison in your veins is Mummy Dust, you elvish whore,' he said, not holding the slightest portion of his rage toward her. 'It will block your magic powers and keep you quiet, but you will feel and remember all the little things we are going to do with you before I slowly cut you in half,' he confessed to her ear.

She lost consciousness and Hanam decided it was time to act.

'First,' said the wicked man, 'let us finally take a look at your pretty little fa–' the moment he dropped down the woman's mask, a light took the whole glade. All three men instantly fell to the ground, and were as dead as someone can be before they hit the dirt.

Hanam, moved by an uncontrollable urge to preserve that woman's life, jumped out of his hideout with amazing dexterity half a second before the man removed her mask. He was mid-air when he saw her light, and if the Universe were ever naked, and if the revelation of its intimacy would ever be in the form of a chaotic symphony of countless strings vibrating and colliding against each other at the same time in the most all-encompassing and overwhelming song, her face was silence. Her beauty was all things still, full of what is in the end.

Instead of being harmed by it, the lethal light fed Hanam. Propelled by its magnetism, he crossed the distance between them faster than he calculated, managing to grab her body before her head hit the ground. The elastic cloth of her mask retracted to its original form, covering her face and hiding her light immediately after the man's fingers sloped out of it. The mask was made of a flexible dark violet silk that acted alive and could not have been made by the skills of hands.

Hanam noticed that she was lightly dressed, and her whole body but her eyes was covered in soft leather and silky fabrics, mostly dark in tonality. Her clothing was functional and reinforced, but it was not armored to a visible degree. She had very high leather boots that came the whole way onto the middle of her thigh. She also had a short cloak with a small fixed hood and two long daggers crossed over her waist. Half of her outfits were not human, and she had many minor direct and indirect magical items discreetly attached over her garments. Her overall appearance was very cosmopolitan and refined, it was an interesting mix of the high elfish and the high sea styles.

Through her fitted garments, one could see that her body was abundantly feminine exactly where it needed to be, and that her bone structure was probably of a half-elf. Even though her face was almost all covered, it was possible to see that there was a nearly mystical beauty gushing out of her. Her eyes had the most wonderful blue-greenish color Hanam had ever seen – it seemed hypnotic to him. The moment he touched her, he felt how special her essence was, and how imperative it was to preserve her life. Deeply moved and feeling an instantaneous and spontaneous fondness for her, he allowed many of his emotions flow to her. Hanam did not reconsider, pouring out his affection profusely over her. He held her tight, letting her have the full extension of his transmission. Instantly, the bolts were ejected from her flesh, the poison expelled to the ground, her wounds closed, and her intoxication sublimated.

When she recovered control over her body, the first thing she did was look right through the darkness of Hanam's long gray hood. By the expression of surprise on her face, he knew that she had looked directly into his eyes, as if her wisdom and vision could look beyond the darkness of his hideout and see him. He avoided that quickly, turning his face down and breaking the spiritual connection with her. He then encouraged her to stand on her own feet only to promptly distance himself from her.

'What are you?' she demanded to know. Her eyes were full of a great amazement, and her voice was as dazzling as her gaze.

'Hanam, The Healer,' he said.

When Hanam first started finding populations centers, and was therefore forced to interact with people, he figured out that he needed a disguise, a persona to satisfy people's curiosities about him. It was easier that way and he learned to use that title every time he was asked who he was. Besides, it was the truth.

Since he had left the Hidden Temple, and in spite the need for secrecy and the urgency to stay out of trouble and to focus on his mission, Hanam could not stand aside when people called for help. In time, he saw it was easy to declare himself as a traveling healer, which was relatively common, socially desirable, and perfectly acceptable. It was much easier to go by as an ordinary (and inoffensive) poor sellspell who made a living healing folks in need. It had been working flawlessly, and he managed to conduct himself out of many situations without further complications. He got in, he healed, got what he needed, and left. Sometimes he was obliged to receive payment, when that happened he just kept it in his pocket and gave it to the first poor family he encountered. Sometimes he just left it on the porch of a house, or inside a beggar's bucket.

'Well, Hanam, I am Sahafira,' she said. 'You saved my life. I am in debt with you now.'

She stared at him with her eyes full of fascination, completely ignoring what happened and what almost happened to her a minute ago.

'Not at all,' said Hanam, avoiding her inquisitive stare.

'Do you know how long until Rocksprings?' he tried to change the subject smoothly, preparing himself to leave.

'Too far for you to reach until sunset,' she said, giving the hunchback a second look, trying to read his strange selfless actions and understand his hurried disengagement.

'Come, be my guest tonight,' she said, not ready to leave him be. 'Shelter and supper are not enough payment for what you have done, but I pledge you. My house is not far from here. Stay with me tonight. It is the least that I can do,' she said, still trying to process his person.

Another thing that Hanam discovered during his travels was the fact that staying in the commoner's farmhouses, barns, or homesteads was far more discreet than in an inn, a tavern, or any public facility of this nature. When the sun started to set on the road, he would start looking for a sick child or a herniated old farmer to acquire the favor of that family and spend the night with them. That was why Hanam hesitated when Sahafira proposed that to him. Plus, it would be good to avoid Rocksprings. For he knew the city would be full of spies and people he would like very much to avoid. Above all, the reason he accepted Sahafira's invitation was the reason he used to guide him in every good deed that came out of him – his heart. He sensed a great deal of goodness and a deep-seated love coming from her. The instincts that he learned to trust his life upon were now telling him he could trust her, and so he did.

'I accept your offer,' he said with a calming and secure voice.

Although quieter, she seemed even happier than the other folks he had encountered so far. It was then that he was sure that she knew something about him. He was not sure what it was, but he saw that she definitely was convinced of something.

'Lead the way, please,' he said, and they disappeared into the forest.

What Now

They were still looking at the wizard, completely and utterly astonished. Nobody, besides Klunk, could believe what was happening. It took a long time for them to digest their thoughts.

'Can I handle it?' Bastian asked politely and with a moving voice.

Lucien felt his heart weighing in his chest. Stargazer could not resist the momentum of the moment.

'Please?' Bastian insisted, trembling.

Stargazer moved aside, utterly out of words, making it clear through his body language that the mere request constrained him. Lucien was speechless and without action – a rare thing.

When Bastian touched the blade, he rapidly retracted his hand in pain after a sharp static shock hit his finger mercilessly. It was not enough to discourage him though and he tried again. This time, there was no discharge and Bastian took it out of its sheath so he could see and touch the blade. The first thing he felt was that the whole weapon was strangely hot. It was not a radiant metallic heat, but the kind of warmth that comes from a person's body. It gave the blade an awkward presence, as if it was alive.

It was a masterfully crafted sword. The design was very sober and the blue steel was magnificent. Although big, it was perfectly balanced. Overall, it was simple but elegant, easy to swing and quick to push – a weapon made for the sole purpose of winning battles.

Its condition was very good, as Star Ore does not age like most metals. Besides a piece no bigger than a man's finger was missing from the blade, it was otherwise flawless.

'It is a Blood Blade, you know,' the wizard said.

'What do you mean?' asked Bastian without taking his eyes off the sword.

'It is truly connected to your lineage. Magically, I mean,' said Stargazer.

'That much I know,' said Bastian while slowly swinging the sword in the air, feeling its balance.

'Interestingly, however,' interposed Stargazer, 'I cannot sense a lot of magic power radiating from it,' he said while looking at the sword as if staring at a mirage. 'Besides the fact that it has the foundational enchant of a Blood Blade,' he added. 'At least not in a surface level.' He looked at the blade sharply, reconsidering.

'Still not getting you, wizard,' said Bastian.

'The sword reserves a lot of potential to be enchanted,' Stargazer explained himself. 'With the right amount of money, of course. It was your grandfather, right? I mean, the one who forged the blade?' he asked.

'Yes, it was him. I told you before,' said Bastian, forcefully deflecting his eyes out of the blade and onto the wizard.

'Why haven't you told us about the sword before?' Lucien asked the wizard with initial signs of anger.

'So...wizard,' interrupted Bastian, ignoring Lucien's question. 'We need to talk,' he said, looking at Stargazer straight in the eye.

'Of course,' said Stargazer, seizing the opportunity to put in place a plan that had popped into his mind since the moment he met them.

Although he had done his calculations well, Stargazer knew he would need to buy more trust from them first. The only currency he could use to do that was information. However, the most important thing was that he had now confirmed beyond any doubt that these people's story was true, and that he could now trust them enough so his plan could work.

'Earlier this week,' the wizard started, 'I got involved in a nasty fight with some orcs from the Red Claw tribe. There, I killed an orc named Trosh, The Roar. He was the possessor of these two weapons you are looking at.'

'You defeated him?' Bastian asked impressed.

'Yes,' answered Stargazer.

Bastian and Lucien gave him their respects.

'But he killed me too.' The wizard paused, checking Bastian's and Lucien's reactions.

The two exchanged confused and doubtful looks between them.

'OK, maybe not,' Stargazer said, noticing that the warriors raised their shoulders and hands in a sign of absolute doubt.

'Well, the reality is that I don't know,' the wizard finally admitted.

Lucien grew in mistrust, but Bastian was wise enough to sense Stargazer's honesty and to sort of comprehend from where the wizard was coming from.

'Magic healing of some sort?' Bastian supposed.

'Yes,' Stargazer thanked him. 'Anyway, I was rescued by my master. During the battle, however, I have destroyed one very valuable piece of property that belonged to him. He then sent me on a quest to reclaim the value of these items and pay for my debt,' said the wizard.

'And how much do you think they are worth?' asked Bastian.

'Well, I thought about that for a bit,' said the wizard, somewhat glad Bastian asked. 'The sword, besides the magical connection with your family, it is just a sword for the rest of us, so it costs its weight, times two, plus the value of an excellent sword, which is a total of around five thousand gold coins on this part of the empire,' Stargazer reckoned. 'Now the axe has more than double the amount of metal, but it is made of a much more diluted alloy and has very specific and special magic powers imbued in it, so I estimated it will be worth around fifteen thousand gold coins. Both combined maybe will generate enough gold to pay for around half of a Cloak of Flight, which is my master's lost item. If, of course, I somehow manage to find someone selling one of those.' Stargazer said, but his words were responded only with silence. Long and thoughtful silence, for the values were too high. High beyond all hope for them.

'The sword belongs to his family,' protested Lucien, restarting the conversation. 'It is his heritage. You cannot make him pay for it,' he said. 'And even if he is willing to pay, selling his family farm and all his possessions, he still won't have enough money,' he said.

In a rare display of empathy, Lucien was showing that he was perfectly aware of how relevant all that was to his friend and how important and personal this cause was now for him too. Bastian quietly collected and kept this in his heart, even forgetting about the sword in his hand for a second.

'Yes, but he cannot ignore his master's debt either, Lucien,' Bastian said, trying to do the honorable thing. 'The sword is part of his war spoils, which makes him entitled to a compensation,' he added.

'We need to sort something out. Something fair,' proposed Bastian.

'Well,' interjected Stargazer as if he was waiting for that moment, 'I think we could arrange something,' he said. 'The situation is this: you cannot buy it, but you must claim it,' he pointed out. 'What about earning it then?' proposed the wizard.

'I am listening,' said Bastian.

Lucien disapproved, but was also listening.

'I did the math,' said Stargazer. 'Look, it will take me years of selling low-level scrolls and healing services to get near the kind of money I need to pay my master. Therefore, I'm also in a dead-end situation myself,' said Stargazer.

'Still listening,' said Bastian.

'Well, I figured it out even before I met you guys that I could go to town, sell that stuff, arm me to the teeth, hire some mercenaries, and go after some serious GMG!' said the wizard.

Lucien raised an eyebrow, interested.

'What is GMG?' asked Bastian.

'Gold, Magic, and Glory!' Stargazer liked how energetic those words came out of his mouth. He could feel an agitation growing in the warriors. It was so intense that he wondered if he had cast an indirect spell without noticing.

'This guy is a genius,' said Lucien emphatically, pointing at Stargazer.

'Yeah, but how we sort the sword problem?' asked Bastian, interested but skeptical.

'Well, I told you I will be needing some mercenaries,' said the wizard. 'You could be my bodyguards,' he proposed, and then looked at Klunk adding, 'You all could if you want to,' he said matter-of-factly.

'Friend!' Klunk agreed, nodding sharply and then turned back for the enduring puzzle of his club and the flying reptile skull.

'I mean, you guys made it all the way here alive!' Stargazer pointed out. 'You have got to be a tough team. Let us make it tougher,' he said. 'Besides, this is what you are already doing now. Sort of,' he said.

The wizard's argument made sense, finding place in their hearts and minds. They stopped to reflect on it a little just for the sake of it, but the young wizard's patience was still short and he decided it was time to push it.

'What will you do when you come back home?' the wizard asked. 'Back to your farm?' he looked at Bastian. 'Or to your boring aristocratic family?' he looked at Lucien. 'Are you going to sell your abilities to a fat merchant for breadcrumbs? Join the freaking army?!' Stargazer knew that he had their attention now, so he decided to go for it. 'If you join the army, you could pass years washing stables without seeing any action, you know?' said the wizard.

Bastian looked at Lucien, hoping for advice, knowing that Stargazer was right.

'Don't look at me,' Lucien said to Bastian. 'I'm totally in!' he affirmed with an excited smile on his face.

'That soon?' asked Bastian, disappointed at Lucien for his lack of willingness to at least put some thought into it.

'Sir,' Lucien turn to Bastian, 'he totally got me with the GMG thing.' He laughed and nodded.

'What about money?' Bastian asked the wizard. 'How much are you going to pay us?'

'I'll cover Klunk's expenses, as he clearly does not value gold but eats like an infantry platoon.' Stargazer unleashed his plan with great sagacity. 'I'll pay Lucien the fair amount of five gold coins a day, plus all travel outgoings. And for you...' He paused, assessed the situation for a few seconds. He looked at the sword and then to Bastian, and then to the sword again. He bit his lips and then went for it.

'I tell you what: serve me for a thousand days or until I die, and the debt is paid,' he said dead on. 'As for the sword in particular, if you join me immediately, she is yours. As of NOW,' he said, knowing that he could not resist that.

'Aha!' Klunk screamed suddenly, before Bastian could respond to Stargazer, scaring them all out of their socks.

He had finally managed to fix the skull in his club. Full of pride, he pointed at it, turning his head to his friends and back to the club feverishly, showing them his accomplishment. His tongue was sticking out of his mouth. On his face, a silly smile of sheer contentment.

Inevitably in a Nutshell

They'd found her house a few hours later. It was a nut farmer's hut deep inside a former plantation. The plantation itself was wrapped around an inconspicuous and obscure pathless forest. There were no roads, pathways, or even a single rustic hunting trail connecting that forest with the rest of the world. These and other highly uncommon features of the place increased the mysteries surrounding Sahafira's circumstances. As Hanam followed her through the forest, he felt the vegetation impenetrable and suffocating. Those woods had their own spirit, and he could sense that all matter there had been slightly altered somehow. The changes were invisible to the eyes however, but palpable to the soul nonetheless. A raw and unusual agitation was present in all things there, and the air tasted like old magic. It was as if that place was still suffering the consequences of strange and chaotic spells, insistently conjured and re-conjured over each other ages ago. Even the dust over the rocks and leaves seemed to express uncanny elder motives that agitated the forest composition. Hanam was certain that there was nothing fundamentally tainted or evil there, but the alien electricity of that forest brought his mind into apprehension and alert.

There was no easy or clear way to go across it. They moved on slowly, dodging low shrubs, branches, and all kinds of obstacles and debris. They did this until they reached the outer limits of the plantation. Once under the impenetrable shadows of the nut trees, they found no path forward but the straight, precise, and tight space between them. The maze-like disposition of the trees was so symmetric and persistent that Hanam felt slightly disorientated at first. The trees were too numerous and had been planted and artificially kept too close to each other, giving the place a haunted claustrophobic atmosphere. The light there was affected, dimmed, and muffled, even during the day. The densely packed nut trees were uncared for and there was overgrowth of all kinds everywhere. The somber neglect caused a worsening in the sense of danger that the place radiated so profusely.

Hanam could not help noticing that there were a great variety of nut trees, and that they were so productive and abundant that the ground was piled with rotting unpicked nuts. There was also an excess of movement and life everywhere he looked at. He couldn't keep track of the number of different animals he saw crossing their way. The whole plantation seemed overcrowded by squirrels, mice, rabbits, small deer, nut-eating birds and many other species of forest creatures of magnificent colorful constitution. Many of them were of a rare kind, all were made fat and robust by the abundance and variety of food that place provided.

Hanam was amazed when he saw Sahafira's hut for the first time. It was right in the middle of the only opening they met over what he recollected as endless miles of closely packed nut trees. Her house was right in the center of the glade and there was a small crystalline creek going around it. The floor was completely covered by a silky, vibrant, and perfumed yellow moss. The main structure of the hut itself was a giant fossilized nutshell. Only half of it was above ground and there was no sign of the gargantuan tree from which such fruit had sprouted.

Overall, her little abode was adorable. It was simple, but nothing about it was distasteful or uneven. It had a gracious chimney, a couple of tiny round windows, a small door, and a beautiful water wheel that spun at the lazy speed of the stream. Everything about it was perfectly and thematically integrated with the background, its harmonious colors and shapes naturally mingled with the environment. Its walls consisted of a rock-solid material, being also very thick. Sahafira explained to Hanam that she purchased the land and the hut from a family of "unusual people" who moved east several winters ago.

Hanam was surprised by the suspicious concentration of colorful bugs and small woodland creatures around the hut. The critters were just standing there, as if waiting to salute Sahafira. And as soon as they approached the door, a baby dwarf deer approached to greet her. Next, a few rabbit families and birds groups joined the reunion. Hanam noticed in wonder how the creatures seemed remarkably relieved and happy upon her return. Sahafira made sure she paid attention to all of them individually, regardless of their numbers. In quiet admiration, he witnessed Sahafira engaging them one by one, using their own unique and rustic forms of expressions. He could feel that something about that place and that woman had a magnetic appeal to those animals, a mystical connection of sorts. When he spotted the presence of some Woodland Fairies and other timid mystical creatures that gradually came out of their hiding places, he understood that he was right.

When they entered the hut, Hanam could not believe how fresh the air inside of it was. Its crispness was almost cold and breathing was incredibly easy. The decoration was very cozy and the objects and micro-environments inside the house were boldly adventurous and unimaginably full of life — everything had movement. Magic colorful herbs, enchanted singing flowers, and a tapestries of beautiful living things could be found everywhere.

Hanam was offered a chair to sit on and accepted it gladly. While resting his legs by the fire, he observed that however gracious Sahafira moved and did things around the place, she still somehow looked like a guest in her own house. Esthetically, the colors, shapes, and textures found there were completely opposed to her personal style. He realized that there was something more profound about this dissonance, but the hunchback kept this and many other impressions about that place and that woman to himself. Sahafira was much quieter than an average person and he was instructed to be highly discreet in his dealings, therefore he enjoyed the silence and the obvious personal secrecy she shared with him.

'Going south?' she finally broke the silence while they were having pumpkin soup and nut bread by the fireplace.

'Yes, for now,' he avoided.

'The men,' she said, 'from today. There are more of them, and they are as vicious as it gets. The one with the scars was one of the captains of the River Rats, a band of criminals who operate in this area,' she said.

Hanam didn't say anything, he barely moved.

'They killed my friends, so I followed them to their hideout and notified the local authorities. The city guard then busted the place, killing and arresting most of them. The rest spread out in search parties, looking for me and revenge. I am no longer safe here, I'm thinking about going south too,' she concluded.

Hanam kept silent.

'They have divinators in their ranks. I calculate that they are already aware of what happened to that party,' she said. 'I have protection,' she pointed to her boots and one of her rings. 'That is the only reason why I'm still alive, but it won't last forever. If they find their way to better magic, they will track me down,' she said. 'In the meanwhile, they will think I have run north, and they will think I have done it a few hours ago, so they will go look for me in Rose Creek, which is the next little town to the North. But I will break their direction and timing,' she said.

'This place is safe. No one knows about it and I have ways to hide our tracks. I will cross Rocksprings tonight and set south. It is my best chance,' she concluded.

'Why are you telling me all that?' Hanam asked gently but sharply.

'Fair enough,' she said. 'I may not know who you are,' she paused, 'but I know WHAT you are,' Sahafira said it confidently.

Hanam became clearly uneased by her answer and his chin, the only visible part of his face, moved in the door's direction.

'Don't worry,' she said, 'your secret will always be safe with me,' her voice was sweet. 'Are you from The Order?' she asked eagerly.

The hunchback placed his bowl of soup over the little table in front of him and retracted his shoulders and hands, signaling with his body that he was about to leave the hut.

'It's all right,' she assured him while she restraining herself from touching him. 'My father was from The Order too,' she added.

He instantly changed his posture. Hesitantly, he turned his face toward her again, but said nothing.

'I didn't meet him, nor my mother. Both were killed shortly after I was born,' she said. 'I was raised by an old elf hermit deep in The Realm,' she said.

'I'm a spellcaster by trade, but I don't manifest evil magic. My mother was a Nymph, that explains my mask and what you saw back there,' she said.

Hanam kept perfect silence.

'There is nothing left in this city for me. Can I go with you?' she asked.

He said nothing.

'If we travel together, it will be less likely that the River Rats will find me and that someone else will eventually unmask you. The city is full of spell caster and spies of all interests, including in the guard. They will certainly notice you,' she pointed out. 'Besides, I know this region really well. There are many robbers and contrabandists down these roads. I could help you avoid them.' She lowered her soup bowl and waited for an answer.

'I am used to traveling alone.' Hanam's voice indicated hesitation. He was tempted by her proposal as he would probably need a hand to keep out of trouble at the checkpoints ahead.

'Once we reach Rocksprings' south crossroads, we can go further for a few more days; after that, we can depart, if you wish to,' she argued.

'I agree,' he said.

Although their perilous situation, they went on designing their plans with contained enthusiasm. It was obvious that they were both feeling glad they had met, although none of them could still say why. Two hooded figures that hid themselves in plain sight. Two odd creatures, who, in spite many or profound mysteries, could reach a long-desired trust between them. It was almost as if their meeting was guided by things much higher than their eyes could see or their minds could interpret. Things they somehow knew were part of the very composition of their beings. Things they'd learned to trust and even depend upon during their whole lives.

They found each other in the parity of them both being special creatures with mysterious origins and pasts, far too disconnected from this world to properly operate in it. They were both distinct, harmonious, and unique.

Something tangible came to be when they "saw" each other. And now, just a few hours later, that moment had established itself as a present truth in their hearts. There was no erotic attraction, impersonal charity, or rather any egocentric admiration between them. They were also connected by the pain of the concessions they made to exist in society. They could now finally relate to someone else the silent and hurtful isolation they felt by existing in the dying world that surrounded them. They still didn't know what they had, but they knew it was precious, for they had now found a peer, a partner in their rare destinies.

What they were, how they felt, how they did things, and all of their whys, could not be easily grasped by the common and apparent logic that guided most folks, as they lived inside and through a higher vibration. They were of a larger perspective and, therefore, quite aware that the world would never understand them, and that it would even oppose and oppress them in many different ways. For that and other deeper reasons, Hanam felt that it was just and right to help Sahafira out of her troubles. He decided that it was fair to protect her until she was safe enough and, in silence, he made his heart about it.

She would not show or tell much about herself, but there was an overflowing sincerity in her that told Hanam many things. The more he was with her, the more he was convinced of the deep pain and the great solitude that poured from her essence. By sensibly reading her *sutil* expressions and metaphysical scars, he found himself even saddened by the thick coldness she raised to protect the true beauty of her true spirit. Hanam could not resist the strength of his defending heart, and he had learned that it was better never to do so. He was overcome by a sudden compulsion to care for that woman.

When the stars were out, they initiated their evasion plans. Extra weary, they stepped into the night, minding every breath. In total darkness and silent as a night fox, they advanced through the most unusual trails and over many abandoned places. After a dense and exhaustive advance, they arrived at Rocksprings. It was the middle of the night when they started crossing the city. Nervously, they jumped from shadow to shadow, following unconventional routes whenever they could. The streets were deserted, the only things moving were an occasional stumbling drunk or a sneaky cat. Once deep inside the city, across the fourth gate, Hanam stopped and held Sahafira with his arm. She looked at his hand, then she looked at him, and then she looked toward the direction he was staring at. There, out of nowhere, a dark silhouette appeared in front of them, popping slowly (even graciously) from behind a shadow. Then other, and other, and other until they were completely surrounded and very much outnumbered. They looked around, there was no escape.

The Fellowship of the Sword

'We need a name,' said Stargazer.

'I have a name,' joked Lucien.

'No,' the wizard cast an impatient stare in Lucien's direction. 'I mean we need a name for our purpose,' he said.

'What's that?' asked Bastian.

'If we want sophisticated people contracting us for lucrative missions, we need to position ourselves as the expensive mercenary companies and the famous knight's orders do,' Stargazer explained.

Bastian's eyebrow lifted, he was definitely listening now.

'The Gold Diggers? The Behind Kickers? The Glory Keepers?' Lucien joked again.

Bastian laughed and looked away when he saw how angry Stargazer was getting at Lucien's constant cynical interruptions. Bastian was actually relieved that now he wasn't the only one who had to deal with Lucien's bad side.

'Look at all those high towers and large mansions in that city,' said Stargazer as they watched Rocksprings on the horizon. 'If we want to be given some credit by these people, we need more than what we have got now. Otherwise, we will end up hunting wolves for local farmers.'

'Nonsense, we have everything we need. Even our own giant!' Lucien patted Klunk on the back, who returned a friendly smile, unconsciously projecting his tongue between his teeth.

'I think we will be bound together for a long while, and we are going to make our names during this time,' Stargazer pointed out. 'We need to decide now what we will be, while we can still control it,' he said.

Stargazer's words had a greater impact on Bastian, who began to seriously meditate on them.

'Or we die before anything gets done,' Lucien said.

'We must start with a winning statement of our own,' continued Stargazer, ignoring Lucien.

'Look at us,' the wizard continued. 'We are not exactly green in our expertise, but no one has heard about us. No tale, no song,' he said. 'I lost count on how many times I've read that not-exceptional, if not plainly talentless, wizards made fortunes because of sheer fame or charisma. Even when they were simply the wrong guys in the right place at the right time,' he said.

Stargazer looked at the horizon, immersed in his thoughts. Bastian was quietly considering the wizard's point.

'Damn it!' he snapped. 'We will always be in the wrong place and at the wrong time if we are not the right guys,' he energetically lamented.

'Goodness, wizard, give us a break,' said Lucien, too afraid to show that he was considering what Stargazer was saying. 'No one will be given ridiculous names here,' he said, trying to end the conversation.

'He is right,' said Bastian conclusively, looking at Lucien.

'You too now?' complained Lucien.

'We need a name,' Stargazer resumed.

'Well, when I was a child, I spent the summer nights reading about great orders, guilds, groups of adventurers, and brotherhoods,' remembered Bastian. 'I agree with you, Stargazer.' He was actually being fairly serious about it.

'There we go with childhood dreams again,' said Lucien sarcastically.

'I have my share of reading through those stories too.' Stargazer gave Bastian a warm smile. 'I noticed that most of the time they called themselves by something they had in common,' he continued. 'It was almost always about something they shared, something that kept them united and that gave them purpose. Sometimes it was an ideal, sometimes a mission, it could be even a person or an object,' he explained.

'"The Klunk's Victims" then,' interjected Lucien.

Klunk gave him a grimace.

'What are we?' continued Stargazer. 'What do we have in common? What is keeping us together?' asked Stargazer.

Everyone was silent for a while, and even Lucien was thinking about the echoes of the wizard's words. All at once, their minds came together and they looked at each other. It was one of those moments of true connection when they felt that the answer that they were looking for was right in front of them the whole time, but only now they could see it. Everyone was hit by the same epiphany at the same time, and, together, they turned their heads to Bastian's back, where his father's sword was.

The Man under the Hat

'Sleek, but predictable Sahafira,' said a feminine voice coming from the dark silhouette right in front of them. 'We have guarded all the outer roads. Our eyes are everywhere,' the voice said. 'You are a fool to think that we would not track your stinking snitch scent from miles away. We still have friends downtown,' a woman all dressed in black stepped out of the shadows while all the hardened thieves that were with her tightened their siege around them. 'You may pull out this cheap cloak now, we know it is you,' she said.

'Marah, The Shredder,' said Sahafira. 'We finally meet.'

'We finally meet,' Marah said.

'Let us pass. We want no quarrel with you,' Sahafira said.

'Oh, but we want a quarrel with you.' The woman stepped into the dim light partially revealing the front portion of her body.

Marah had the same corrupted appearance as the man that assaulted Sahafira in the woods by the North Road. Her face was beautiful but scarred by steel and hate. Her hair was black, dense, uncared, and oily. She wore a black cloak over a fitting scuffed out black leather armor reinforced with metal on the vitals. In her hands, eager to attack, she was firmly gripping two sharp heavy sabers. Her weapons were deployed, ready, and her eyes were burning, vengeful.

'I will smoke your pretty head and wear it on my chest,' Marah promised. 'Then everybody will know what happens with the ones who mess with the River Rats!' she cried.

Excited by the eminent killing, the thieves stepped forward from the shadows, drawing their weapons. The tension in the air increased massively, and just before it exploded, only half a second before the thieves shot their crossbows and attacked with their long poisonous daggers, a sequence of paced hisses were heard as half a dozen bolts fell from the sky over Marah's men. The loud, muffled crack that the projectiles made when they hit the thieves' bones gave the impression that each munition weighed two hundred pounds. The damage they created was unusual and very graphic, they reached their targets as if a ghost of destruction followed each one of the flechettes. With a terrible energy, the bolts punched and crushed the thieves to death rather than pierce them into it. The shock of the violence was extreme, enough to reduce some of the attackers' momentum.

Almost at the same time, with a quick gesture of her highly sensible defensive instincts, Sahafira pointed her finger into the air and cast a protective shield over herself. The dome of protection was visible for one second then vanished. Milliseconds later, bolts were hitting the invisible wall around her and falling to the ground.

Hanam, putting himself between the two women, raised his oak staff to protect Sahafira. He adopted a combat stance, but went no further, choosing to stay in a completely defensive posture.

Marah hesitated a bit for she was now worried about the origin of the rain of death quickly killing all her companions. She raised her sabers, putting herself in a defensive position in order to carefully assess the situation. She was a professional at hiding in the shadows and ambushing from there, so it wasn't long before she figured it out what was going on. When a third salvo came and took another big bite of her troops, she was able to see where the shots were coming from.

'The warehouse's roof on the east side!' she shouted to her remaining men.

The remaining of River Rats immediately ran to where she pointed out, and Marah herself attacked Hanam and Sahafira with great fury.

Sahafira swiftly sent a thin ray of frost particles a few yards in front of Marah's pathway. For a good part of several yards, the ground froze instantly and profusely when the spell touched it, causing Marah to slip. However, with supernatural agility, Marah managed to control the direction of her fall, even using her newly gained speed to her advantage while she slid through the slab of ice. Like a cat, she passed between Hanam's legs. He tried to hit and/or block her with his oak staff, but he simply could not keep her tempo and missed her by a good amount. Marah was being so much more agile in comparison to the hunchback, that he looked like an old man struggling with a house mouse.

Still propelled by the same thrust, and with just a single movement, she raised herself while slicing Hanam's heel tendons mercilessly. He never saw it coming and screamed in agony over the terrible pain. The blow was so precise, that it completely severed his tendons to the bone. He lost control of his feet, immediately kneeling down.

Immediately after she was standing up, Marah faced Sahafira with a terrible blinkless stare of pure hate. Sahafira, compelled by the rapid and brutal violence and a sense of greater danger, threw her hands and her emotions in the air, hastily casting a destructive spell at Marah's direction. She was consumed by that manifestation of her scared fury in the form of two ice daggers that materialized and zipped through the air. Guided by a small contained magical explosion, they were faster than arrows and far more lethal.

With an impossibly fast and admirably powerful blocking blow of her sabers, Marah shattered them into two small clouds of tiny pieces of ice and unstable magic dust. With a jump, a feint, and a crushing blow, Marah closed the distance and kicked Sahafira in the chest with the sole of her boot. Sahafira lost all control over her body, immediately falling to the ground where she remained stunned by the lack of air in her lungs. When she managed to focus her eyes again, she looked up trying to find Marah, but she found only the thief's blades crossed around her throat. Sahafira gathered courage and looked up to face Marah one last time before she did what she would certainly do.

'This is for the Rats,' said Marah when their eyes met.

Marah's face was utterly corrupted with hate and despise, and the intensity of her expressions gradually became graver as she grimaced even harder and set her blades in an even more cruel angle. However, before her arms' muscles exploded, finishing the decapitation cut that her shoulders had already started, Marah was hit by a quickly consecutive number of blows.

They went through her body as if she was made of wet paper, and although her physical strength and her resilience was fairly altered by magic, the multiple impacts were able to push her back. That first salvo were not, however, enough to end her life and her eyes remained fixed at Sahafira, burning with the same intense hate as before. Barely controlling the body, Marah stepped forward, eager to finish what she started.

Without taking her vengeful eyes away from Sahafira, she raised her sabers in the air once more, trying to block incoming shots, but her body was too damaged to be fast and responsive enough. A handful of bolts hit Marah's body once again, smacking her flesh into pulp. The projectiles not only pierced through her, but they broke bones and ripped organs wherever they landed. The barrage was so intensely violent that it was able to divert her attention from her profoundly wanted revenge and focus it on the source of the attack. However, it was too late for Marah, for she had been hit too many times to survive.

Overwhelmed by her injuries, she finally knelt, leaning on the remaining sword and leg. The barrage of shots stopped. The amount of blood streaming from her mouth demonstrated, beyond any doubt, that she was alive only by the supernatural powers of her will that were being channeled through her manifested hate.

Stunned, with blood gushing from everywhere, she raised her eyes to stare at her approaching nemesis. A man walked out of the shadows. His face was mysteriously hidden by the very wide brim of his leather hat. Strapped on it, a long bloody scarlet silk ribbon flew in the night wind. With a sudden mechanical clank and unbelievable speed, the figure recharged the ammunition box of his huge ram-faced dwarf-bronze crossbow. He stopped between Sahafira and Marah. Then he aimed his weapon toward Marah's head. With a back and forward action, making a striking and characteristic noise, he loaded the weapon and shot the thief down.

The shot made a hole as big as a large orange on Marah's head. The bolt's shaft completely penetrated the ground behind her, raising a long tail of dust in the air and disappearing under the ground entirely.

The night was silent again for a second, but then it was not. Many lights and noises could be heard coming from all sides, announcing that witnesses and city guards were rushing in.

'Are you alright?' the man asked, briefly checking Sahafira before returning a few paces to do the same with Hanam.

'Yes. Hanam.' she answered the man under the hat and pointed at the hunchback.

With difficulty, she raised herself and rushed to help Hanam, but to her surprise the hunchback stood unscathed.

'We cannot be reached by the guard,' said the man under the hat. 'Come, I know a place,' he said, collecting his mind far too quickly from the grave situation he managed to take them out of.

'We did nothing wrong,' protested Sahafira. 'We finished the River Rat Gang. We are heroes!' she said.

'I know, sweetheart,' the mysterious man said in a different and surprisingly comical tonality as he took control of the situation. 'But we need to protect Hanam's identity. There are higher things at stake here. Come now,' he said.

Guided by him, they retreated to an alleyway and into the night's shadows. They managed to navigate the night quickly and discreetly as they were all light-footed, fast, and highly resilient individuals. Sahafira was impressed with the man's vast and detailed knowledge of Rocksprings's streets and buildings. Under his guidance, they quickly and smartly advanced over a large portion of it, arriving at their destination. It was the most improbable place of all; it was the most dangerous place of all; it was that man's favorite place of all; and it was a tavern – The Cat's Horn.

The Bard

It was not exactly early, but definitely not late at all when they entered the tavern. Most of the creatures there were so drunk, or otherwise intoxicated, that they wouldn't be able to remember what happened that night even if an

268

ancient dragon had entered the bar wearing underwear asking for a mug of the house's best ale.

Sahafira knew the Cat's Horn. It was the most popular place in Rocksprings for wizards, artists, bohemians, and all Rocksprings' colorful things to gather together. The tavern was one of the city's oldest facilities, and it had been exposed to drunk and drugged spellcasters for such a long time that it now contained a frightening number of magical abnormalities and paradoxes in and around it. Some of these unavoidable magical conundrums were of simple effect, but some, however, were impossibly complex and somewhat unique. Most of them were inoffensive, but there was definitely a very present, unstable, and dangerous minority of out-of-control phenomena. The locals were afraid to even come next to the tavern, and they were right in doing so. There were many tales of customers experimenting strange and terrible things, like in the case of some who shrunk to the size of a fairy after sleeping in one of their beds. Reports stated that people had entered the tavern at night to only exit the next day looking much older, claiming they had been lost inside of it for decades. There were even stories that talk about endless corridors, walls altering their color and shape, and rooms that changed position inside the building once the door was closed. Rogue animated objects full of ill intent, ghosts of terrible personalities, and wailing spirits had also been spotted harassing customers all over its halls. Among some of the worst stories was one of an instant teleportation to a dragon lair after an unfortunate guest closed the toilet door.

'Night, Fofo,' the man under the hat saluted the grumpy gnome on the other side of the counter. 'Put it all on my tab, including the "I've seen nothing" fee,' he said and winked and pointed at Fofo as they passed hastily across the room.

Fofo just pointed to the enormous and ancient "NO REFUND" sign swiveling slowly behind him. The gnome did not react, flinch, or say anything; instead, he acted as if it were business as usual. Keeping the same face he wore for centuries (a unique and perfect mix of boredom and tiredness), he took the multicolored pencil that was stuck in his huge dusty ear and wrote something on a piece of paper. He then looked for the wooden box under the counter with the name Mr. Dealonson written on it and jammed the bill inside of it. Then he put the pencil back on the right ear and continued to grumpily stare at nothing.

As quickly as they crossed the table of the saloon, they also climbed the stairs to the third floor.

'Don't worry, I have a room here,' said the man.

When they arrived in the strangely shaped corridor that conducted to the room, he saw over ten beautiful young ladies sleeping in the corridor by the doorstep of his room.

'Sshhhiii. Quiet now.' The man hushed Sahafira and Hanam when he saw the women. 'Damn it.' He silently cursed his luck.

Sahafira was under the impression that he seemed really tense with the situation. Careful not to step on one of them, he made it to the entrance. He meticulously opened the door and entered, then, he called for the other who repeated his procedure.

When Hanam started to cross the corridor, some heavy-handed guest (probably a dwarf) opened and closed one of the floor's doors loudly, waking one of the women. When she spotted the man with the hat, she instantly started shouting and pointing at him hysterically.

'The door! Now!' he shouted in absolute panic.

Sahafira and Hanam, even without completely understanding what was going on, jumped out of the corridor and into the room and helped contain the flow of arms, legs, and insane promises of eternal love that fanatically rushed into the room and desperately tried to squeeze through the door, trying to get in. With great effort, they managed to keep them out and closed the door.

'What was that?' Sahafira demanded to know. 'Are those women under some kind of spell?' she asked, weary.

'Hum. Some are, some are not. I don't know. Who knows? I'm very charismatic. I can't control my ego, nor my magic. They've blended a long time ago,' the man said casually.

'Who are you?' asked Hanam.

And the man took out his hat and revealed a perfect face. He was almost mystically handsome, aesthetically flawless, and everything about him seemed out of place. He was unique in his traces and features, spoke with no accent, and his clothes gave no clue as to his origins. He did not look like a Valkarian, or a Coronian, or a northerner, or of any other nationality. He barely looked human and Sahafira could see that he was not an elf either. It was overall very hard to classify him within known and normal parameters. His entire person made no sense, but he was also incredibly acceptable and his charms flowed through reality perfectly aligned. He had a satisfactory aura of mystery pulsing around him, seeming to belong nowhere and everywhere at the same time.

'I am Taalen Dealonson, at your services,' he said and bowed solemnly. 'I was sent here by your friends from The Order,' he continued, strangely addressing both of them.

'THE Taalen Dealonson?' Sahafira asked, really impressed, even a little scared.

'Yes, milady, the one and on...well, I can't actually say it...it's a long story...it involves a girlfriend...some cloning magic...huum...never mind,' he said.

Sahafira was now realizing that he looked confused, or a little drunk, or maybe a little crazy, or a mixture of all these things.

'Are you saying that you are THE Taalen Dealonson?' she insisted.

'Something like that, my lady,' he said as he bowed, blinked, and smiled at her at the same time.

His gestures had an unreal aspect to them, they were somewhat magnetic in a captivating way.

She noticed that he was indeed truly charming and wondered if he was casting a spell on her.

'Taalen Dealonson, The Bard?' she asked again, knowing she may sound stupid. She just could not bring herself to believe it.

'Yes,' Taalen said cheerfully. 'Wow, this thing is heavy,' suddenly distracted, he relaxed the sling of the monstrous beast and awkwardly took it off his back, leaning it against the wall.

He is definitely drunk, Sahafira thought, smelling the liquor and whatnots in his breath and perspiration. *If he could take out all of those hardened criminals like that, imagine what he could do sober,* she considered.

Ignoring their thrill, Taalen tossed himself in the chair right next to the window, carefully watching the street below while emptying the booze from a steel flask he took from his coat pocket.

'It is a nice weapon though,' risked Hanam. 'It carries a powerful punch,' he said.

'Yes, it does,' answered Taalen, sort of happy that Hanam had brought it out. 'The original project was from Torgren, The Mechanic himself. Smartest dwarf I have ever known.' Taalen allowed himself a more casual tone.

Still without taking his eyes off the streets, the bard poured a glass of wine from a bottle of the cabinet under the window.

'These weapons are very rare nowadays actually,' he continued to enjoy the conversation after a sip. 'They've made five of them if I am not mistaken,' he paused for another sip. 'And I'm usually not.' For a second he met Sahafira's gaze, winked at her, and directed his eyes back to the street.

'Multiple shots, enhanced magical throw, automatic loading mechanism, double enchanted bayonet, the whole shebang,' he cheered, raising his glass. 'You know, it comes handy from time to time.' Taalen hit the weapon slightly with his left hand. 'The dwarf bronze makes it as sturdy as an iron mace, but the best thing about it are the spells cast on this particular exemplary,' he said and sipped. 'It must have cost the duke a real fortune.' Without looking back, he passed a bottle of elven wine to Hanam, who, without drinking, passed it to Sahafira, who, also without drinking, immediately leaned it on the small table again.

'The Duke?' asked Hanam.

'Yeap. The Duke of Squinaria. He was serving as the Coronian ambassador in the Golden Ring when I…met him.' He sipped a big sip this time, emptying his glass. 'My goodness, that man was rich! Well, a little less now,' said Taalen with an unavoidable smirk on his face.

Taalen sipped from his cup with one hand and passed a glass to Hanam with the other. Hanam instantly passed it to Sahafira, who also returned it to the small table.

'How did you manage to be trusted with such a valuable weapon?' Sahafira asked suspiciously.

'I didn't. I won it from him in a card game.' He answered and passed a second crystal glass to Hanam, who passed it to Sahafira, who returned it to the table.

'Why didn't you meet me in Westgate as agreed?' Hanam asked.

'Because some things have changed,' he said, pouring more wine into his glass. His eyes were continuously fixed on the street below.

'Can you please tell us again who sent you?' Hanam was not taking any risks.

'In front of her?' Taalen said, turning his whole head to face Hanam and capture his answer and expression.

'No offence, honey.' He smiled sympathetically toward Sahafira, winking at her again.

272

'None was taken,' she said. 'I would get out for a bit, so you can have a private talk, but the women in the corridor would charge in here in a blink of an eye,' she said.

Taalen pressed and bit his lips and nodded, agreeing with her. He then gave the shoulders and emptied his glass.

'She can be trusted,' said Hanam. Sahafira instantly looked at the hunchback, surprised.

'Just say the name,' Hanam demanded.

Sahafira smiled a little under her mask, but only Taalen noticed that.

'Oberan,' said Taalen, not sure if it was a smart move but willing to earn their trust as fast as possible.

Kriton? Sahafira thought. *Wow, these people are high level,* she exclaimed to herself.

'OK, what is to be known?' said Hanam.

'You have no need to go to Westgate for now,' said Taalen. 'Instead, you should go west, to the Dire Woods. We have found a clue on how to fix the "entrance" problem. To the Twin Peaks, I mean. You know, the hidden place,' he said, emptying his glass with a big gulp and turning his head to the window again.

'Continue,' said Hanam.

'I have a trustworthy map with the location of the lair of a powerful rouge wizard. He lived in this region some time ago, but is now believed to be deceased,' Taalen said, pouring himself another full cup. 'Just before his disappearance, he was the possessor of a mighty artifact.' After filling his glass, Taalen passed the wine bottle to Hanam again, who passed to Sahafira again, who placed it over the table one more time.

'That artifact could help your cause,' continued Taalen. 'It is a very large crystal sphere. It weighs almost as much as you, depending,' he said to Hanam. 'You won't miss it once you spot it,' he said, then reached to his pocket. 'Here are the maps. In the back, there are instructions on its probable location of the entrance to the wizard's den. Attached, there's also a copy of an ancient plant of the lair itself, although it is likely that during his occupation, the wizard redecorated, changing a thing or two,' said Taalen.

'The Dire Woods is very dangerous,' Sahafira pointed out.

'I know,' said Taalen. 'You will be needing help, Hanam. All the help you can get,' he said. 'You need to hire some mercenaries and a great guide,' he sipped from his wine, smiling, as if he knew something they didn't.

'I can help you with this one, Hanam,' Sahafira said. 'Besides, I owe you my very life,' she said.

'Thank you, Sahafira,' Hanam said, humbly. 'I really appreciate it, but it is not necessary. You owe me nothing,' he said.

'I'm going with you,' she insisted. 'I was raised in a forest and I have done plenty of scouting in the Dire Woods before.'

'I cannot accept it,' Hanam said.

'You will be needing more than your healing magic in there too,' she said, 'especially dealing with mercenaries. I'm going.' She made sure her point was final.

'Well, in that case, I accept your help. But I will be paying you as a contractor,' Hanam said.

'We will need many more hands.' Sahafira already started calculating and making plans.

'My resources are limited,' said Hanam.

'Don't worry,' Taalen intervened, 'there will be plenty of gold and other valuable things in the place where you are going. Use that as leverage when negotiating with the mercenaries,' he advised.

'How do you know all that?' Sahafira inquired.

'I knew the guy…from before…you know,' Taalen sounded disappointed, bitterly emptying his glass once more.

'Before what?' she asked.

'Well,' he scratched his chin and refilled his glass, 'before he became so boring, and, you know…evil,' he said, looking even more depressed.

'After he fielded some tricky crafts, he caught the attention of some "important" people,' said Taalen. 'Then I was sent here to keep an eye on him. Shortly after, he disappeared and the war ended,' he said. 'Anyway, boring stuff,' he said, emptying his glass yet again with another big gulp.

'His lair's precise location was buried under the powerful magic he used to hide it, but recently I have come across solid information about it and drew this map,' he said, pouring more wine. 'But after the Battle of the Cursed Stones, we were all very tired of war and no one believed he would attack again. We hoped for silence and silence came,' he said with his eyes locked on the warehouse across the street and his glass always close to his lips.

'Plus,' he continued, 'there were a lot of jobs to do in the north, so I was called off.' He took another massive gulp. 'It was a very confusing time after the war, but I have always kept an eye and two ears on his whereabouts, hopping that later I would have some answers. Well, "later" has arrived, I guess,' said Taalen, stubbornly sipping his wine and staring at the warehouse.

'What will happen if the mercenaries ask for money upfront?' Sahafira worried.

Taalen did not answer. Instead, he kept staring out the window in silence, completely immersed in his thoughts while meditating on his intuition. He was a man of instinct, having made extensive use of this over the centuries that he spent avoiding Fabula's perils. He knew his feelings well enough to sense when a revelation was imminent. It finally hit him a few moments later, just as he had anticipated. He then suddenly realized that the key to it all was in what his eyes were subconsciously staring at since the beginning. In his epiphany, he found himself thinking about the new wooden panel above the entrance of the abandoned warehouse across the street. He remembered it wasn't there the day before and was then immediately made aware of how cheap and feeble it was, how horrible was the handwriting on it, and how poorly it was nailed to the wall. As the night breeze gushed, the pathetic thing was bluntly bashing against the warehouse's portico. Taalen then smiled, squished his eyes maliciously, and took a small sip of his Strong Wine.

'They won't,' he whispered.

Wait

Stargazer came back from a supply run in the city market when he caught Bastian and Lucien arguing under the loose board sign by the warehouse entrance. The light blue wooden plate had "THE FELLOWSHIP OF THE SWORD" written on it in white letters. The light colors contrasted with the disastrously old blackened wood framing of the warehouse. The plate was now hanging from just one side and everything about it was so precarious that it couldn't stand a light breeze. The thing was making them crazy, they couldn't make it work no matter what they did. When they managed to mend the rusty chain, the rotten wood gave in, and so on. The situation characterized well the state of the old warehouse they rented.

'Did you sell it?' asked Bastian.

'Yes, the metallurgists almost fought for it! Amazing,' said Stargazer. 'I went to The Forge, which is a whole street dedicated solemnly to metal work. When I offered one of them the axe, the others popped up like vultures over a carcass. They all started giving me offers. I picked the best one. It was a good price,' he said. 'Next time, let us be together, for security reasons,' he added.

Bastian and Lucien nodded, agreeing.

'What happened here? Why are you arguing?' asked Stargazer, willing to change the subject.

'I told him it will not hold. The whole thing is rotting. I can't believe you rented this, wizard,' complained Lucien.

'The location is very good and this is one of the town's most traditional area, you can find rich contractors just a few streets away in all directions, it has doors big enough so Klunk can get in and out with no problem, and the rent was a real bargain too,' Stargazer explained again.

'Have you wondered why?' asked Lucien impatiently.

'No, and to be honest I don't care that much. I have more important things to worry about,' said Stargazer.

'Like what?' asked Lucien nervous.

'Find us a job,' the wizard said it calmly, looking at the tavern right across the street.

'Yeah,' said Bastian relaxing his shoulders, 'I am ready to have some lunch now.' He was not yet fully recovered from the hardship he suffered at Dire Wood.

'OK, I will get Klunk,' said Stargazer. 'I think this place across the street will have us all,' he pointed to the Cat's Horn with his chin.

'Of course they will,' said Lucien. 'It's The Cat's Horn. They would take a lich for supper,' said Lucien.

'Do you know that place? I thought you'd never been at Rocksprings?' asked Bastian, surprised.

'This place is known way beyond Rocksprings' borders,' said Lucien as he stared at the building's distorted walls.

'Known for what?' asked Stargazer.

'For its…eccentricity,' said Lucien.

After trying to understand what Lucien meant by that, Bastian took another look at the place and started to have a bad feeling. The wind blew a little, just enough to creep them off and to lose the nails that held the rotten wood panel on the front wall of the warehouse. The whole panel board fell, slamming the sign against the porch and breaking it into two pieces.

Wait

'OK, the one with the nice coat has returned. Let's go there and talk to them now,' said Taalen.

'Why them?' asked Hanam.

'There are many whys. One: they are young, therefore cheap, but by the wear in their armors show they have some experience. Two: they are new in town and in the business. I mean no one with a minimum sense or self-respect would rent that pile of rubbish across the street, much less carve such excessively bold absurdity as The Fellowship of the Sword in that silly unstable wood board. Three: I reckon they pack a lot of luck and they even have their own little giant, which is precisely the sort of thing you need right now. But the main why is because I have an overall good feeling about them, and about this," answered Taalen.

'What is the plan then?' asked Sahafira.

'We go there and straightforwardly say that we have this map of this wizard's lost lair and that we need partners with their "profile." Since we have no money to pay them in upfront, we offer to divide all the valuable goods equally, but it is imperative that we keep the orb,' said Taalen. 'We give not too much information, but enough to convince them,' he added.

Hanam and Sahafira looked at each other and nodded.

'They are resupplying fast,' noticed Taalen. 'They spent the whole morning shopping and selling. And fixing that damn sign. Their clothes and armors were so torn when they arrived that they had to buy new ones. I'm pretty sure they would be ready for another job soon,' he said.

'OK, before we go over there I need to show you something, Hanam.' Taalen turned away from the window and untied a little suede bag from his belt. It was green on the outside and blue on the inside. The suede seemed to be of a very high quality, and it had a golden cord wrapping it closed.

'Check this out.' He smiled like a child and stretched the bag way beyond its natural size. He put the entire crossbow in it and the weapon disappeared inside of it. The bag then retracted to the same size and weight as it was before.

'This is a very useful magic item and it is also expensive. So you have to return it to me when you're done. Preferably, with the sphere inside it, okay?' said Taalen while casually taking out the crossbow from the bag and putting the massive weapon into another similar magic bag he had in his belt.

'You are not coming with us?' asked Hanam, alarmed.

'No. I have things to do overseas. Plus, I am more of a messenger than a doer, you know,' he said, excusing himself with a charming smile while raising his cup filled with wine to the brim. 'I will come back here in four weeks, maybe five. We shall meet here, in this tavern.'

'OK,' Hanam agreed.

'Now let us talk with them before they disperse again.' He hurried Hanam and Sahafira.

They hushed down, went through the saloon, passed Fofo, who was still looking tired and bored over the counter, and left. The instant they stepped outside, they very suddenly met Bastian, Lucien, Stargazer, and Klunk in the middle of the narrow street. Both groups immediately stopped on their feet. Everybody was surprised, almost scared. A tension abruptly stuffed the air around them. The moment held too much for them to process. Even Taalen remained reactionless over the face off. They all felt simultaneously hit by a stroke of destiny. All but Klunk, who smiled knowingly, as if he knew exactly what was going on and everything that would be.

Go

There was a general lack of words, and it was an overall awkward situation. Luckily, however, Taalen was there to break the ice.

'Gentlemen, we need to hire your services,' said Taalen.

An uncomfortable silence followed. Pressed, Stargazer steeped in.

'How…?' he asked.

'Your sign,' Taalen pointed to it and smiled gracefully.

They all looked at the "Fellowship of the Sword" wooden board. When they did, it fell again, breaking into pieces when it hit the ground.

'Shiiit,' whispered Lucien, looking covertly at Bastian who met his gaze and dropped his eyes.

'You're a group of mercenaries, aren't you?' asked Taalen.

'Yes, we are,' said Stargazer boldly, trying to draw attention away from the incident.

'Great!' Taalen facilitated. 'Can we go to some discreet place to talk? Maybe your nice little shop...warehouse...place...whatever?' he asked, pointing his finger to the crumbling building, unable to hide his disdain for it.

'Yes. Sure,' said Stargazer, not knowing where to put his hands.

They got in and sat around a huge round cordage roll that served as a table. There was no chair for everyone, so some sat on old wooden boxes. Klunk sat on himself.

'Here is the deal.' With a precise, dry, and casual movement of his wrist, Taalen unrolled a large map over the "table."

'This is a map of a place full of abandoned prizes of all kinds,' said Taalen. 'It used to be the abode of a powerful wizard that's been missing since the end of the War of the Flame. It is located deep inside the Dire Woods.' Taalen put it out very objectively, and since there were no questions or interjections, he continued.

'It should be an in-and-out simple job. Four weeks top. Once there, you will retrieve a special object to me. It is a large crystal orb of unknown coloration. The map is very detailed and accurate, and you will be well guided.' Taalen looked at Sahafira, everybody followed his eyes.

'OK, here is the deal.' He cleared his throat. 'I've got my overseer.' He pointed to Hanam. 'I've got the guide.' He pointed to Sahafira. 'I need some security, no questions asked.' He pointed at the rest of them. 'Can you do it?' he asked directly.

'I believe we can,' said Stargazer optimistic.

'OK then, questions?' asked Taalen.

'Here, yes, me,' said Lucien, raising his finger childishly.

'Has someone ever told you that your high boots, your leather trousers, this half-open loose cotton blouse, and, above all, this bizarrely large gypsy hat makes you look like a bad imitation of Taalen Dealonson?' Lucien challenged Taalen.

Stargazer looked at Lucien with piercing eyes. Hanam and Sahafira became tenser. Bastian was still thinking about Taalen's proposition. Klunk was nodding like he was getting everything.

'Yes,' said Taalen with the most shameless smile a man's face can bear.

'He is Taalen Dealonson,' Hanam said.

'It can't be,' said Lucien incredulously.

'What?!' asked Bastian, falling from his thoughts in the middle of the conversation.

'What about the money?' asked Stargazer.

'He really is,' confirmed Sahafira.

'It is an "all in bet,"' answered Taalen.

'Ahan!' pointed Klunk, nodding as if he was getting what was going on.

'He can't be Taalen Dealonson,' insisted Lucien.

'What you mean?' asked Stargazer.

'What you think doesn't alter the fact that he is,' said Sahafira.

'You will divide among yourselves all the treasures you find as reward. I just want the orb,' said Taalen.

'And if we find nothing there?' asked Stargazer.

'THE Taalen Dealonson?' Lucien was shocked.

'You will. Maybe more than you can grasp.' Taalen's thoughts went away as he looked to the East.

'Ahan!' pointed Klunk, nodding as if he was getting everything.

'Yes. Obviously.' Sahafira gave Lucien a little of his irony back.

'I trust him. The prizes should be plentiful payment,' said Hanam, pointing at Taalen.

'This is a big joke,' scorned Lucien.

'So everything divided by six, except the orb?' asked Stargazer.

'Maybe they want to kill us and take our money,' said Lucien.

'Five, we know old Klunk here has no use for money,' said Taalen.

'What money?' provoked Sahafira.

'Ahan!' pointed Klunk, nodding as if he was getting everything.

'He drank ten gallons of milk for breakfast today. He sure can use some gold,' Stargazer countered.

'Don't act like you don't know what I'm talking about,' answered Lucien.

'How in the world do you know Klunk's name?' asked Bastian.

'I just need the orb, you can divide my share among you,' said Hanam.

'I think you are being paranoid,' Sahafira decided to be blunt.

'What does this orb do that makes you value it so much?' Stargazer asked strategically.

'If you were a man, I would teach you a lesson or two or swordsmanship,' dared Lucien.

'Ahan!' pointed Klunk, nodding as if he was getting everything.

'We may accept the term but we need some guarantees,' negotiated Stargazer.

'Lucien, calm down,' interceded Bastian.

'As Taalen said: "no questions asked,"' reiterated Hanam.

'There is no need for a man to learn your lessons, child.' Sahafira was finding the human obnoxious, she decided to give him nothing but her cold stare.

'We are not a Coronian bank, kid,' said Taalen. 'We can't give you guarantees.'

'Is there or is there no gold there?' asked Bastian willing to end it before things (meaning Lucien) got out of control.

'Yeah, right, but yet you are hiring me because you cannot handle a gang of goblins in the woods,' provoked Lucien.

'Ahan!' pointed Klunk, nodding as if he was getting everything.

'We are interested, but need to sort some things out first,' said Stargazer.

'We told you: we don't know for sure, but probably there is some, and possibly a lot,' answered Hanam, trying to be as honest as possible.

'You would be amazed at what I can do with my bare hands, child,' Sahafira was being serious now.

'OK, last offer: all the gold for you four, orb for Hanam, and any other magical objects divided by five equally, considering the division will be done accordingly with its market value. Take it or leave it,' said Taalen and stood up ready to leave.

'I bet I will.' Lucien was smiling at Sahafira with the corner of his lips.

'Wait…hum… What is this "wizard's" name again?' asked Stargazer, trying to think fast under pressure.

'Kestos,' said Taalen. 'You are going to Kestos's Lair,' he said.

A shroud of absolute silence fell around them.

'Ahan!' pointed Klunk, nodding as if he was getting everything.

They were all shocked by what they'd just heard. Klunk, however, was smiling, satisfied.

Void

Dreak was a cold-eyed killer. A soulless man that traveled from town to town doing the only thing he knew, doing what he did best. His nomad lifestyle gave him the nickname "The Highway Horror." Although he was the epitome of a psychopath, he did not consider himself wicked. In fact, the whole concept of evil escaped him entirely, and that was precisely the root of his difficulties.

Dreak had never, during his whole life, even considered things like good or evil before acting. He was not a rebel, he simply never contemplated himself over the light of these values. He just pushed forward, doing things according to his needs and stubbornly surviving the resulting dangerous life one day at a time.

In his emptiness, everything was a direct cause and effect. In him, there was no "why." There was nothing but his needs and the now.

Like the placid waters of a large lake of nothingness, he kept undisturbed. He was always calm in his dark peace. He felt no empathy, no love, no pleasure, no sadness nor rancor or regrets. He felt nothing. His heart was void.

There was no voice inside his head. Nothing telling him "no" or "go." There was no shame and no rest. He was blindly trapped in his lack of consciousness, for it kept the desolation inside of him unchecked. As a soulless shadow of something that never was, he just kept going – he was a true horror.

It was difficult for a sane person to understand him, or even accept the fact that he existed. In his mind, he missed the place from where someone else would collect their emotions and morals. He was not corrupt or malevolent, he was just not there.

His appearance told people his story. His uncared hair and his expressionless frozen face were only less worse than his dead, blank eyes. Folks that interacted with him immediately got the chills by simply looking at them. He had the kind of demeanor and presence that would frighten a person deep within its most primitive mind the same way a horse would scare by an approaching unknown predator in the night. Whenever he was near people, they instantly knew that something was wrong with him. He learned to avoid that by always covering his head with a hood, rarely staring people in the eye, and interacting the bare minimum.

His uncontrollably profound calm and constantly unalarmed behavior did more to call attention toward him than to make him pass unnoticed. For that reason also, he was always on the move, going from town to town, trying to escape authorities and trouble. Somehow, he always failed.

Normally, types like him, possessors of this kind of mental anomalies, would be killed by local men as soon as their first evil deed was discovered, but that was not his case. Dreak's luck, sharp mind, and talent for violence, made him successfully survive persecution for decades.

His absent moral compass contributed for him to hastily become a terribly effective killer. From a very young age, he learned to kill his way out of most situations. Quickly, killing became the only world he knew, it came to be the world he ever lived in – killing was his life.

When he murdered for the first time, it was an accident. The episode set him on a sequence of events that brought him to become what he became. Persecuted, he lived on the road, forced to sell himself as a mercenary, and although people found it difficult to tolerate his techniques and his loose limits, he proved to be extremely effective at it. In time, his reputation and deeds forced him to a more underground life as a robber and a thief. Eventually, the world decided that cut-throating was his niche market.

Over the years, he had established a considerable reputation for himself, enough to encourage other adventurers to track him in search of the multiple and considerable rewards offered for his head. At some point, it became such a problem that the vast majority of its victims came from the persecutions he suffered and not from his contracts. Much more blood was spilled trying to capture him than for his crimes. His awake time was an endless Armageddon, and his days were dense and dangerous. If his life were transcribed into a novel, only a year would fill an entire bookcase. He was indifferent to the fact that his life had become an intense daily game of survival, escape, and evasion. He belonged nowhere, he was related to no one, and he lived tense under the shadow of death. He'd been around, seen a lot, and murdered most.

Dreak dressed discreetly, mostly in black and dark tonalities, always making sure he would pass by inconspicuous not giving away any clue about his identity. With the continued improvement of his arts and treasures, and as he had no addiction, nor inspiration, nor family, nor land to spend the money he made, he invested all he had in his gear. His profession demanded that he would carry a large variety of trinkets and gadgets, and he did it on a discreet, slim magic backpack under his dark cloak. But the most expensive magic items he had, besides his weapons, were the ones that provided him with protection against magical detection, divination, and scrying. For that, he had a pretty good setup, but he would always invest in more every chance he had. He learned very early in his lawless life that it was exceedingly hard to get some sleep without those. Without any magical protection against scrying, every third class sellspell in the world would be able to find him easily.

Some of the most powerful items he had were stolen or claimed from his deceased victims. He acquired his best weapons in his last job. It was the most profitable and dangerous one he had ever had. He was sent to kill an empire's Baron along with a wicked sellspell that was an infiltration specialist. They managed to reach the Baron's room at night and caught him by surprise. After silently killing the nobleman, his wife, and the wizard that protected them, Dreak found among the Baron's treasures the Emperor's Swords of Speed, a famous combat set composed of two swords. One was a slightly curved bastard sword and the other a thick double-edged straight short sword. These old weapons were once gifted by a powerful guild of mages to the Valkarian Emperor. Its enchants were unique and its value was incalculable. Both blades worked together for great magical effects in regarding speed and cutting power. They were beautiful examples of magical art, indeed worthy of an Emperor. Both blades took part in the Battle of Broken Bones, where they were stained black from the fire of Xshisrahil herself. Magic objects, specially of the caliber of that set, were built to withstand much, but dragon fire contained destructive equations far more powerful than mere heat.

Dreak recognized their value the moment he spotted the set, promptly taking them for himself. If only he was capable of it, he would regret that decision later, for his life would suffer a major shift because of those magnificent blades, and not for the best.

He kept his old sabers high in the center of his back, setting his new set crossed over his back. He placed the short sword on his lower back, pointing down, over his heavy war belt, and strapped the bastard sword over his right shoulder for a quick draw.

Before he killed the Baron, he predicted fairly accurately the considerable drawback it would cause him. Although Dreak was incapable of caring, he was not stupid and he planned to go underground for a long time until the dust settled. Hence he prepared a multilayer comprehensive escape plan. In the end, infiltrating the castle and taking the Baron's life in his sleep proved to be the easier part of it.

The bounty for Dreak's head was already one of the highest by then, but after the Baron's assassination and the stealing of some iconic national treasure, things would be pushed to a whole new level and they would come for him with everything they had. This time, he thought, he had to be very careful not to leave any witness or clues of his involvement behind.

After he evaded the castle, he immediately went to a house he had previously rented through unknown third partners, where a paid, inexperienced, and disposable young spellcaster was waiting for him. The nervous young wizard was supposed to use a scroll that Dreak had bought previously with the objective of opening a dimensional portal to the location where he would meet his contractor to receive his reward. When the portal sustained itself in the air and was stable, Dreak cut the wizard's head off with a clean blow of his new sword. He then took a thin glass jar full of Ansan Beetles from his backpack and dropped them close to the body. They were magical creatures, carnivorous, and owners of a wicked metabolism. When the flask hit the ground, it broke into a dust indistinguishable from regular house dirt. As soon as the beetles were free, they started devouring the corpse, starting with the severed head and the pool of blood around it. They ate through clothes, blood, and bones. They ate without ceasing until they grew to a point where their shell would burst, giving birth to two or three of them. As the magic that kept them alive was dispersed when the flask was broken, they would usually die a few minutes after food ran out, leaving nothing behind besides their own dried carcasses that would turn to thin dust after an hour.

After the last one of the Ansan Beetles disintegrated, Dreak went through the portal, arriving where his contractor was waiting for him. Once there, he made sure he was paid, then he killed him and burned the place up with a grenade of Dwarf Plasma. The fire did its job, consuming everything in the remote wooden lodge where the negotiation occurred. Even personal items made of metal like jacket buttons, belt buckles, swords, and rings were completely melted, becoming unrecognizable pools of mixed metal.

After this, he used a charge of one of his strategic magic items that he reserved as last resort, to teleport himself to an unsuspicious location several hundred miles far from there. When he arrived at the small and quiet fishermen village over the Valkarian coast, he immediately went to the hideout he had prepared in advance. It was a camouflaged tent, inside a dense bush, away from any trail or hunter's path on the village outskirts. The place was masterfully hidden and had minor spells summoned over it, so that none of the locals could find it.

The fishing village was perfect for his immediate objectives. It was absolutely inauspicious and had almost no imperial presence. Its small port was enjoyable and had a good flux of unmarked foreigner boats that ported for fresh water resupply.

It was still night when he got there, so he decided to hide and keep a low profile until a foreigner's boat left in the break of dawn. Luck, however, was not on his side this time, for no boat had ported there in the following two consecutive days. In addition, strange things started to happen to him. Ordinary tasks always seemed to go wrong and everything was turning for the worst. He was used to being extremely light-footed all the time, however, now he tripped over everything; branches, roots, rocks, every single object that crossed his path. A deer died inside the small lake he had planned to use as his water source during the period he would stay there. It irrevocably contaminated it and he had to risk trips to a nearby creek to fill his canteen. He could not surprise or hid from the animals he found, and everything he ate was tasteless. All colors seemed to become even paler for him, and he felt as if he was under some hallucinogen's effect – a bad one. He knew something was really wrong when, for the first time he could remember, he cut himself while he was casually manipulating one of his daggers. It was a bad wound, and it became infected no matter how much he took care it.

He could not understand what was happening to him, but after only a couple of days he was drained and feeling tired. By the end of the second day he was starting to feel restless. His instincts were now ringing in his ears like annoying bells, causing him to be unable to concentrate or focus on perceiving any danger.

Just before sunset on the second day, he went to the rocky hill where he had set a spotting place to oversee all movements in the village and on the small bay. He got into position behind a bush he previously trimmed and raised his head. If he had any emotions in him, he would have cursed, for he saw that no ship arrived at the port yet. When he set his eyes on the village a second time, a rush of blood rose violently to his head. His whole being struggled with what he saw for a few seconds, denying it and not allowing any emotion to be born inside of him. Almost aroused into fear, he forced the comfortable, conscienceless void he had inside himself to process what he was seeing as a simple cause and effect. Out of nowhere, like foam coming out of a pressed sponge, with great energy and in disciplined formations, several imperial troops started pouring from between the village buildings in all directions. They were at least a company strong.

A hunting party, he thought, knowing beyond any doubt that they were there for him.

They were a mixed troop, all mounted for speed. Dreak discerned that among them there were Fast Hunters from the central plains armed with long stocking spears, and exotic mounts; and also Northern Rangers armed with strong steel bows and fast horses. Dreak knew that each and every single one of them were hardened men, trackers of experience and renown that would stop at nothing until they got their mission accomplished. However, what almost disturbed Dreak out of his calm was the fact that they were led by at least six White Knights.

Every boy in Valkar fantasizes about being a soldier in the Imperial Army. The end goal of every good professional soldier is to become a knight. The dream of every knight in the Valkarian Empire is to be chosen to be a White Knight.

Elected by the Emperor and his closest advisers among the most trustworthy, talented, and dedicated men, they came from several different origins and backgrounds. Recruited from mighty lords of renown, honored champions, giant killers, and dragon slayers, they were all heroes of great feats, and their names sat among the most respected knights in the empire. To be above and beyond the best of the best was just a basic requirement to apply. Many famous heroes did not make the cut, and many infamous villains died under their blades. Their duty was first and foremost to guard the Emperor in times of peace and to ride by his side in war. Although, in special cases, they could act as overseers of the Emperor's will in a particular matter. Their numbers were maintained in five hundred, but only five of them could stop most armies.

Drake now had six on his tail, and that was how he knew he was in real trouble and that this time the imperial authorities really intended to end him.

When he felt he saw what he needed to see and that his plan was done, he immediately took action. Swiftly, and crouching over the cover of the bushes, he ran in the opposite direction of his pursuers, mixing his figure with the long shadows of the ending day. Before he got anywhere, he saw that the riders had already cut him from most of his exit accesses. Constrained to act quickly, he calculated that the best chance he had was to lay low until the sun was out, so he could take advantage of the night and use his magical equipment to jump from shadow to shadow, and, if necessary, silently "poke a hole" in their siege, escaping into the wild. Although, he would avoid any sort of contact with them, for even if he was incapable of feeling fear, he knew better than to fight a White Knight in the open.

Dreak was using a pair of magical boots that left no markings on the ground and neutralized most of his scents. It was very hard to track him, even with dogs. In addition, his apparently ordinary and worn-out black cloak was the work of dark sorcerers minding dark purposes. It was sewn with a special mix of fabrics, tempered with obscure powers. This allowed the user to blend in with the darkness, jumping from shadow to shadow in complete silence. With it, Dreak could pass in front of a farm dog without being detected. Over the years he had mastered the use of such cape, and the combination of it with other items he had allowed him to own the night.

He went straight to a close-by homestead he had spotted in his many nightly scouting runs around the area. He remembered that in it there was a well that he intended to use as a hideaway until it was dark enough. When he arrived at the edge of the tree line that bordered the homestead, he could hear the riders coming in his direction. He could see the well from where he was, but the path from his positions to it was through many yards of open space and there was still too much daylight. He stopped for a second to see if there was anyone around, but pressed by the coming soldiers he gave up his examination too soon and went for it. His approach wasn't as stealthy as he had wished it would be due to his hurry and his recent bad luck. The noise he made called the attention of a little boy that was leaning toward the other side of a nearby tree. The boy was resting and wandering against the cedar tree after he had completed his duties in the homestead. By his feet, a bucket full of water that he probably took from the well for his family, for the night. The young boy, probably the farmer's son, was no more than eight years old. He was an innocent kid from a decent family, raised in this small community his whole life, unaware of much from the outside world besides what he spotted in the colorful ships that ported in the tiny bay. Maybe he was wondering about it on that afternoon under that tree. Maybe he was dreaming he was a pirate or a ship commander in a far and wonderful sea, living glorious adventures and facing terrible monsters. Little did he know, a monster had come to his doorsteps.

When he got up and turned, he faced Dreak directly. Dreak, completely caught by surprise, stared back at him as he hesitated from the edge of the well. They both looked at each other for a few seconds. The boy then smiled at him with sympathy, and, imagining he was there for a gulp of water, offered Dreak the one he collected for his family. With great effort, he raised the wooden bucket and the cup tied to it in Dreak's direction.

Dreak looked at the boy, and then he looked at the dust being raised in the main road through the dusky horizon and its blood meridian. He knew that the dust indicated that a large party of the riders would be there at any moment. He considered he had only seconds now before he was their line of sight. He had no time, therefore, to deal with any witnesses. He looked at the boy again, calculated his odds, and jumped confidently inside the well.

Surprised by the inexplicable move from the strange man, the boy instantly dropped the bucket and the cup and ran to see what had happened to him. Ironically, he was moved by innocent thoughts of heroism and hope that he would save the man from any harm. In the end, the boy was dishearteningly right, for as soon as he leaned over to look inside the well, Dreak jumped out of the shadows like a trapping spider, grabbing him by the nape and taking him in. He brutally broke the boy's neck on their way down. The child died before they reached the water.

The Fellowship of the Orb

'Urrgh,' the road thief died making a grueling sound. His bleeding heart exploded as Lucien took his arrow from his chest. He casually cleaned it on the thief's clothing and put it back into his quiver.

There were twenty plus bodies on the ground and dozens of bits and pieces spread all around the battlefield. No casualty was counted on their side and no serious wounds either. The battle was won fairly easily.

The very day they left Rocksprings, going up the East Road, a big band of bandits charged their encampment, no questions asked. Apparently, the band was tipped about the companions deciding to attack them. The criminals assaulted at an inconvenient moment while they were having lunch, successfully taking them by surprise.

Sahafira had warned about the dangers of the region and of the roads around it. "There is a lot of money going up and down here. Whole nets of spies and organized crime have ears and eyes everywhere," she pointed out. "No matter what the city guard does, unlawfulness never stop here. Be aware," she said to them before they left Rocksprings, but they let their guard down on the first opportunity anyway. And although they had wiped this large group out, they were scared straight to never lower their guard again, wherever they were.

That same night, next to the fire, they recollected the afternoon battle. It was the first time they fought together and they debated on their impressions, determining strategies for the next one. When accessing what they had learned, Bastian and Lucien became convinced that having spellcasters in their ranks was a massive combat multiplier. They were plainly excited with what they saw and what magic could do for the effectiveness of a combat team. They went on for hours talking about how light their armor and weapons became after Stargazer increased their strength magically. They were thrilled by how their blows simply shred their enemies' bodies apart with very little effort, and by how far they were able to throw their spears. The instant healing powers of Hanam allowed them to keep a hundred percent of their momentum, breaking their adversaries' energy and coordination by protecting Klunk's flanks while he carved his way through the enemy's lines. Lucien even make his peace with Sahafira afterward, for, in the middle of the battle, she cast a spell over him that doubled his speed and agility to a point of "nearly taking all the fun out of it" according to his own words.

The whole road to their destination ended up being a workshop on how to effectively fight as a team. Motivated by the successive easy victories over all the obstacles they'd found, they pressed forward with confidence and a high spirit. Guided by Sahafira's knowledge and mystical intuition, healed and restored by Hanam's powers, supported by Stargazer's magic in every need, and often saved by Klunk's mighty pike, they successfully destroyed everything in their path. On it, they discovered many things about the world, but mostly they matured themselves on the knowledge of their own.

Bastian fell in love with his father's sword. He was not sure if he was being biased, but he felt as if the weapon was made for him. It was heavier than what he was used to, but he adapted quickly, strengthening his arms and grip. Inspired by his legacy, he used the blade at every opportunity, and in every single one of them, it cut like nothing he had ever seen before. At some point in the adventure, he managed to kill a Dire Bear with his sword. The beast tracked them for days and charged their group in the middle of the night. They ended the battle when Stargazer distracted the beast with a trick as Bastian picked up speed and jumped from a rock, stabbing it in the chest. The long, double-edge blade penetrated the creature's body the whole way until the handle, shattering its heart. The only thing he could compare it to was Sahafira's magic dagger. Although the two weapons were divergent in their magical nature, with the effectiveness of Bastian's based on the properties of the composition of its metal and Sahafira's on the disturbing aura generated by the alteration spells cast during its manufacture.

Hanam was very sober in combat, never fearful or passionate. He seldom attacked, always choosing to hold the center and aid the flanks with his healing powers. Although, when needed, he would sometimes press forward with the warriors, saving them from any trouble they may find themselves in. Eventually, he was not capable to hide from the others his warrior skills. But as he always conducted himself very discreetly, and was the source of much-desired healing magic, they saved him from their questions and doubts, leaving him out of their spotlight. Besides, his quiet and gentle manners alone were enough to make the hunchback everybody's favorite.

Another thing that he was not able to keep from them was the fact that Hanam was abnormally strong. In one of the several encounters they had, forced by a situation, and with no magical aid, he blew an orc chieftain's head and helmet with a single blow of his staff, impressing everyone. Eventually, because of the intensity and constancy of the fighting, carving new staffs out of hardwood branches became impractical. In the first opportunity he got, he commandeered a thick, hollow metallic spear shaft from one of their defeated enemies. The weapon's body was very heavy and oversized for a regular human, being clearly forged by and for the Barbarians. Its body was of decent steel and Hanam broke the clumsy, improvised spearhead that had been installed by the orcs, turning it into a perfectly balanced war staff. The weapon managed to endure much more than the oak staffs he had been carrying before, and, forced by the growing intensity of the battles they faced as they got deeper and deeper in the Dire Woods, it improved the offensiveness and effectiveness of his strikes to a scary level, ever more exposing what he tried to hide.

On one night, pushed by the urgency of defending his friends from the surprise sortie of a Giant Owl that only he felt coming, he grabbed his new metal staff by one end with his two hands, and hit the diving owl. Swinging the staff like a bat, he hit the owl with all his strength exactly when it reached the fastest point of its attack descend, maximizing the intensity of the impact. It was an unforgivable, extraordinary dry blow that sent the considerably large creature's body back to the deep darkness of the woods like a gaming ball. By the smashing noise it made, the hit probably fractured every single bone of the owl's body, leaving behind a tragic cloud of feathers and a brutal spray of hot blood. After that incident, and contrary to his wishes, he received respect and a slightly fearful awareness from the others.

Later on that same night, while most of them were sleeping and no one but Stargazer was discreetly watching him, Hanam noticed that his staff bent during the incident, so he straightened it using his bare hands. Pretending he was sleeping, the wizard contemplated all he had witnessed. Few things escaped his attentive watch, and he was very good at keeping his thoughts and impressions to himself. The wizard was very successful in letting them all think he was the most aerial and inconspicuous of their group, when, in fact, he was the one who truly was observant of them all. Stargazer carefully kept a detailed mental archive of every single thing about their individualities, and their potential. He meditated about their talents constantly. No one was really able or interested in "reading" the wizard or mapping his intentions, but he needed very little to understand the meaning and the depth of many details of his companions' personalities. One thing he had concluded so far: they were a group composed of the most improbable individuals, therefore fate was on their side. That fact comforted him somehow and he made plans for them. All the time, in silence, he made plans for them.

Stargazer would not waste any opportunity to try and apply the spells he learned. Every day he went to sleep feeling empty and exhausted from all the spell-crafting, but his efforts paid off as he was now learning at a very quick pace. He discovered that Eliaroth's influence on his formation made him a highly aggressive spellcaster. The practical experience he was having made him realize that most of the spells content he had been in contact with during his time in the tower was actually highly destructive magic. His combat spells, even in the beginning when he was still slow and not proficient with them, were as sharp and precise as Lucien's arrows or Bastian's javelins. His energy rays, poisonous clouds, and fireballs were as devastating as Klunk's pike, if not more. Sometimes he would even impress himself with the result of his magic. The power under the control of his fingers was growing every day, he liked it and feared it at the same time. By the time they were almost reaching their destination, if the terrain provided reach, he was capable of softening an advancing Barbarian's hunting party, to a small group of half-burned survivors.

His quarter-staff and sword skills were being put to the test too, as many times, because of their reduced number, close combat reached him. When the enemy approached, because of his Valkarian instincts, emotional repression, and a dormant will to prove himself, but truly for a complex mix of all those things, he charged with the warriors, preferring to fight in melee rather than to support them from a distance. He used his staff and his sword much more often than a wizard should. But again, Stargazer had always found a way to do things differently.

When they camped, he would sometimes train with Bastian and Lucien, who learned to respect him, not only for his impressive magical feats of destruction, but for his keen insights, bravery, and overall fitness. They eagerly and voluntarily shared tips and tricks with Stargazer helping him improve his fighting skills while the wizard explained the secrets of his art. It was during those days that they developed connections that would last a lifetime.

Lucien was pleased with the almost daily chance of getting some. He felt more and more that he was born for the battlefield. Every day he improved his tactics, increasing his risk and refining his abilities. He was increasingly letting the sword and shield go and was getting deadlier using two swords. Audaciously, even irresponsibly, he risked new moves all the time, paving his way to quickly becoming a master in the art of sword fighting. Propelled by security of the supporting spells, he craved ever more to be in combat. Even when he fought against the robust and terrible Barbarians, he charged them fearlessly and aggressively, regardless of the outcome of their actions.

Although she was very experienced and wise, Sahafira was also getting a lot more combat knowledge from the harshness of that particular adventure.

She had a slim frame compared with her extraordinary companions, but her magic was as strong as Stargazer's, she was as tireless as Hanam, as strong as Bastian, and faster than all of them. However, they took their skills for granted and she was very reserved, speaking very little or nothing about herself and the origins of her powers. She kept her space and through her coldness she indicated that she had no interest in trespassing others. In every opportunity she had, she helped her companions as much as possible, but also always made very clear with her actions that she appreciated a certain distance. Even though, the dire situations where they constantly found themselves in forced them to lower their emotional defenses and to tear down their walls from time to time. The adventure invariably brought them together, creating a kind of forced intimacy between them. This, while avoided by some, connected them on some level. In the end, they were comforted to find support and emotional shelter in each other, even if in small acts of mercy or companionship. Their growing intimacy was an irresistible consolation for everyone, but it was also true that even if to a greater or lesser degree, or in one way or another, they all wanted to hide.

Sahafira tried to hide her natural gentleness, but she failed on that intention. As they were all pushed to their limit often, she sometimes slipped and let some graceful expression out, mystically directing their admiration to herself. Soon, they agreed that Sahafira was a sweet creature – true feminine spirit. She was passionate, kind, and strong in love and in compassion. Although she tried to hide it behind a barrier of coldness and distance, her good nature and beauty spilled through the corners of her loving deeds. In time, even Lucien was subject to her natural subtle grace. However, it was Bastian who rested a special gaze upon her, discovering in himself a secret happiness that he felt only for her.

Sahafira was quick to pick up Bastian's growing feelings for her, but at this point she was convinced that it was just a typical transitional human passion. She could sense he had a good essence, but her answer to his stares was motherly condescendence and graceful patronization. After all, he was a child to her, for although they looked the same age, she was almost ten times older than him. No matter how fiery Bastian's pretensions were, her ice walls were too high for a young human like himself to surpass.

Klunk was having the time of his life. He was always in a good mood, constantly and widely smiling, even during combat, while crushing entire companies of orcs three at a time. It seemed that he had never had so many friends before and, to their despair, he was trying to give equal attention to each one of them. He did everything he could to help his new and old friends. From making a huge mess on the trail uprooting entire trees just to offer a small flower to Sahafira, to putting a handful of perfumed leaves inside Lucien's mouth while he was sleeping to help him relax. Once, he threw Bastian across (very much across) a small creek they were crossing, so he would not risk wetting his feet.

He was loving all of it, and making sure everybody knew that. He loved his new friends, the outdoors, the wild honey he occasionally stole from giant bee hives that ended up chasing all of them while he could not understand why his companions were running because his skin was too thick for the bee's sting to transfix – he loved it all.

To make sure everyone really understood how happy he was, he composed a rhythmically rudimentary, repetitive, simple but brilliantly irritating road song and sang it all the time – all the time. At some point, Stargazer was considering using his magic to mute him, but decided not to, for he noticed that the wild beasts would not attack them while Klunk was singing it. They would actually enthusiastically run away from the sound of his "music."

Growing with their acquired experiences, learning about themselves and each other, and annoyed by Klunk's song, they pushed forward. Being what they were, becoming what they would be, they went on. After many nights under the forest trees, heading westward almost in a straight line, cutting their way through old forest roads, deep trails, and dangerous ancient forests, facing many forest tribes and strange deep wood monsters, they reached the heart of the Barbarian Territories.

From the many things that opposed them in their advance, the worst, by a long shot, were the Barbarians. Keen, possessors of incredibly muscular frames, and as resilient as wild beasts they were to the Valkarians what the Valkarians were to the Coronians. On average, they were ten inches taller than a Valkarian, had a considerably heavier frame, and packed much more muscle. Individually, they grew to be tremendous warriors, but they lacked synchrony when fighting in formation. This absence of military discipline in most tribes was caused by their tendency of mixing warfare with hunting, a vital, daily activity for them. Their metallurgy was less than ideal, seldom wearing heavy armor. Also, they did not grasp the concept of profit through commerce, highly limiting the amount of personal and collective possessions and wealth among them. They were tough and very territorial. Even the orcs respected their borders and landmarks most of the time. When enraged, an animalistic fury would raise to the surface, and their spirits would burn like fire. All that fought against them or by their side could feel the heat.

Their radically divergent ways, persistent isolation, and foreign physical characteristics caused many to consider them an entirely different species. The reality, however, was that the growing distance between them and the "civilized" peoples was due to the lies with which manipulative and evil creatures contaminated both sides and the resentment for the many wars that followed.

During their long infiltration, The Fellowship had countless tense situations and even a few battles with the Barbarians, but managed to avoid most of their hunting parties through Stargazer's and Sahafira's rich variety of cloaking and protective spells. Relatively preserved by their magical concealing, they traveled a great distance inside their territories until they reached the Dead Cliffs, a continuous collection of brownish rock cliffs that spread in the horizon until the eyes could see. The very first time they broke the treeline and stared at the deep, rocky cliffs below them, they knew that they'd gotten somewhere, for even the air there seemed to belong to a different age, and they could not avoid the unsettling feeling that they had come across the forest, reaching a whole new land – a land beyond.

'That is it,' said Sahafira. 'Here we are. Careful now, this is the territory of the Phoenix Tribe,' she warned them. 'They are the proudest, most elusive, and most powerful of the Barbarian tribes. What we saw until now is nothing in comparison. These warriors use well-made enchanted metal armor and weapons, and are far more powerful and organized than the other tribes, but equally ruthless,' she said. 'They said they guard the last Phoenix on the top of that mountain.' She pointed to a lonely distant peak in the horizon.

'They also are the only tribe with the authority to call the others to war, so if there will be a talk, let us try not to get us or the Valkarian Empire into trouble,' she warned them, looking at Lucien.

'Our destination is over here somewhere,' she said, comparing the terrain with the map one more time. 'The entrance must be on the other side of that round hill.' Convinced, she rolled the map into her bag and jumped on the trail.

They arrived at the round hill Sahafira spoke of after a slow advance through the rocky and crumbling terrain. They had to practically climb their way there, for someone or something had destroyed the access road to the cave that ran from the border of the forest. They found a fairly sized cave entryway exactly where she indicated, but the cave was sealed with a gargantuan boulder.

'Now what?' asked Lucien. 'Not even ten Klunks could remove this rock,' he said leaning into a rock to rest.

Klunk stared at Lucien with an unconvinced grimace.

'This rock did not match the local texture and color. It was brought here. By which means, I do not know,' observed Sahafira.

'But we will,' said Hanam, pointing to the horizon.

There, contrasting with the light of the setting sun that spilled from behind the lonely peak Sahafira warned them about earlier, they saw several dozen gigantic white birds of prey approaching. They were rode by brown-skinned, blue-eyed, black-haired, seven feet tall men.

They flew straight for their location in a glorious attack formation. The mighty birds descended and landed on the border of the circular cliff with appalling speed and precision. Before they could help themselves, the adventurers were surrounded by more than a dozen of them.

In contemplating the warriors of the Phoenix Tribe in all their glory, The Fellowship understood how isolated and hermetic their society was. They were equipped with shiny golden steel breastplates, armbands, and greaves that left their massive bronze arms and tights exposed. They all had golden circles ornamenting and holding their straight, heavy, and thick black hairs. They were dressing in a short tunic made out of a perfectly white silk under their armor, and white, silver, and golden feathers decorated their outfits. They bore heavy bastard swords, war knives, and golden halberds. The majestic white raptors were decorated with gold and jewelry, and their claws were covered with a sturdy, razor-sharp gold alloy.

Their highly refined, almost ceremonial, garments, and their more composed manners, differentiated these from the other Barbarians The Fellowship had encountered so far. However, that did nothing to appease them, actually, it made them far more scared.

'What do we do now?' asked Bastian, uneasy.

'Nothing,' said Sahafira. 'We do nothing,' she said, afraid.

A Bigger Fish

Immediately after Dreak reached the water, he immersed himself into thinking about his escape plan, utterly ignoring the boy's body, leaving it to float carelessly in the very water his family drank.

In the dark, while his eyes got used to the low light on the well's bottom, he applied himself to think of how he could survive that situation. When he could see better, he noticed that there was a black arch in the stone wall right in front of him. He wondered what it was, but was not willing to risk a light. Instead, he drew the Emperor's Sword of Speed and tried to poke the black stain so he could have a notion of how deep it was.

To his surprise, the blade's tip found nothing but air. It was a cave of some sort. It was high enough for him to enter it, so he carefully advanced a few yards into it, groping the stones in the dark. After several steps in, he decided to risk a little light. For that, he grabbed a dwarf torch from one of his secret magical pockets. The object was basically a club made of a light bronze alloy with a Dwarven Fire Stone fixed in its head. It was balanced and shaped like a weapon, and for all measures it was, but its true main intent was to shed light. He activated the device, but only enough for him to inspect the place. By raising the torch in the air, he saw that the tunnel was narrow, no more than two men could walk it side-by-side. Dreak noticed that contrary to the well's walls, the passageway walls and floor were not finished with cemented stones. The walls were incredibly smooth, almost polished, and although they were clearly artificial, they showed no signs or clues about their builders. There were no discernible construction techniques, no torch hanger, no markings, no directions, nothing. It was of a strange making, but he was confident that he knew what had shaped the earth and the rocks that way. Used to navigate through the dark corners of the world, Dreak had been underground many times before and had seen a number of different dungeons, sewers, and caves, so he knew that this tunnel was shaped by magic transmutation. Who, or what, and why was what he needed to know, as that would help him answer the real question in his mind: where did that tunnel lead?

Knowing that he would have little chance of escaping on the surface, and still having some time until the sunset, he decided to explore the tunnel further. Walking a few more yards, he noticed it went up until it made dry land. Soon after, it started to go down again until the path became a slope with a very dangerous angle. After he headed down many yards, he decided to risk more light. By now he knew that it would be impossible for anyone to see him from the well's head due to the horizontal "neck" in the tunnel. He did not risk much light, as he did not know who or what used these tunnels. He settled the emitting output of his dwarf torch accordingly to what he thought was suitable and continued his explorations.

The tunnel's ground soon became leveled after a couple dozen yards. He walked for a long time in this even, dry ground.

"Three miles to the South," he reckoned by his step count.

Dreak was not as good as a dwarf miner regarding subterranean navigation, but he had developed a good sense of direction and a decent technic over the years of his burglar life.

It seemed to him that he had been walking in a straight line since he left the well. Still with no visible indication or apparent architectural motives, suddenly, the unruffled tunnel ended.

All dimensions, in all directions, became abruptly chaotic as the tunnel unapologetically connected itself with a natural and ordinary cavern formation. The ground was now full of gravel of all sizes and it was filled with a soft mixture of dry, old bat guano and ages of dirt. Stalagmites and stalactites were all around in many sizes and shapes, giving the place an alien aspect. Antagonistically to the many caves Dreak had wandered into before, these caverns' tunnels were dead. Nothing moved and he could not hear or see any sign of any life form in them, which he thought was never a good sign.

Not much after Dreak had explored the tunnels, he spotted a light coming from a rocky corner. Without taking his eyes off it, he immediately deactivated his torch and activated his cloak, silently jumping from shadow to shadow until he went around it and could spot what was the source of the light.

From a distance, he saw a silver gleam coming from some sort of entrance. Its walls had the same characteristics of the one from the well, and that made him even more weary. He observed for a while, studying the place before advancing. When he was satisfied, he carefully moved forward, getting closer to the entrance so he could identify the source of the luminosity. When he got there and looked inside the corridor, however, he couldn't. It had no central source, apparently pouring from the walls itself. By how it shone over the tunnel he understood that it was being generated by magic. Dreak knew all too well that artificial magic light radiated peculiarly. It formed different shadows and gave an altered contrast to textures and colors. It could have a more intense brightness than other lights, but, at the same time, had shorter rays, limiting the way it traveled through shadows. Benefitting from his large experience in the subject of darkness and light, Dreak could read that there was a lot of meaning and purpose in the way in which light was enchanted in certain places. He knew it reflected very intimal aspect of the mind who created it, for it was literally a visible suspended alteration implemented in reality.

Looking inside the tunnel, he saw that the light became growingly brighter, although the brighter light was limited in range, and its short radiation would not disturb the darkness inside the cave – it was very controlled. For some reason, Dreak always found himself interested on how that particular molded light worked, hence, he lost a few minutes watching it, fascinated. He was sure that the light he was seeing now was made by a higher intelligence with an idiosyncratic aesthetic sense, probably not human.

As there was no sign of usage on the floor nor on the walls, he considered that the place could have been abandoned for many years, or even centuries for what he knew, and after a while he decided to explore it a little further.

Like a startled feline, he advanced slowly and cautiously through the illuminated tunnel with his sabers drawn, his cloak down his face, his knees flexed, and his ears ready. He decided not to use the big bastard sword he just acquired, it was too big for a fight in a tight place like that. Instead, he chose the agility of his proven old sabers.

After walking only a few dozen meters, he found a large room full of strange objects that would have made him have a bad feeling about that place if only he could feel anything. There was not much to be said about the room, besides the fact that it was large and tall, but the devices Dreak found inside of it were a different story. They were too many to be counted, too strange to be understood, and too terrible to be described.

After a furtive and quick examination, Dreak knew three things about that place: it was probably a magic user's lab of some sort, where bizarre experiments involving many deformed life forms inside big glass tanks were being conducted; whoever possessed that dwelling was nearby; and their intentions were probably not the best as it had buried its lair deep underground.

He observed it for a while from the corridor, trying to identify possible traps, but found nothing or any signs of movement. After some time, he decided to scout through the room to better understand what was going on there and what kind of experiments were being conducted.

The second he stepped in the room, all lights went down and the place became completely and utterly dark except for an almost blinding cone of light that was shining over his head and followed him wherever he went. Before he could think of a way to deal with it, a pair of enormous reptile hands appeared from behind him, grabbing his arms with an iron grip and completely immobilizing him. The cone of light shrank and faded over his face as his expressionless eyes disappeared into the darkness while the demonic hands carried him away.

No one heard Dreak yell. And no one could have, for he didn't. Even when in a forgotten cave, deep beneath, beyond all hope, dragged by an unknown evil to an unknown hell, he felt nothing. Not even there, not even then.

The King Barbarian

'Who are you? And with what purpose have you entered my lands?' asked the human epitome, waiting for an answer from his throne of pure gold.

The king's accent was as thick as his wrist and as heavy as his jawline. His deep voice was in the likeness of his splendid aspect. On his head, a golden crown in the shape of a Phoenix. Laid on his lap, a huge golden two-handed sword casually unsheathed and ready to use.

'We are of several different trades, my lord,' said Hanam using all the grace he could amount. 'What keeps us together, and have brought us here, however, is the will to reclaim an artifact that lies in the cave where we have been found in.' Hanam's tone was very diplomatic and surprisingly well suited.

'That cave is sealed,' said the king, 'it is a traitor's tomb now. The one who sealed it is the only one who can open it,' he added solemnly.

Then, after giving a second look at Hanam, he leaned forward over his throne and his aspect became agitated and tense as if some invisible advisor was whispering something in his ears, something that made him uneasy.

Hanam wisely waited for the king to declare himself, the others wouldn't dare interfere. It took a while for the king to speak again, for the Barbarians lived and expressed themselves at a different pace.

The magnificent silence of the king's meditation made the very crackling of the burning wood in the golden pyres around the throne room to be heard as giant boulders falling from flying mountains. All the many mighty men and women of the court that assisted in the king's presence were silent, even the exotic giant beasts and birds that served as living trophies were soundless. His dominion was complete and uncontested. His will, the law.

The immaculate room was made of a beautiful and unique polished marble. So polished, it resembled a dark mirror. Floor, columns, roof, and the many golden artifacts shined intensely, reflecting the pyres' light and giving the whole place a splendid atmosphere. The Fellowship was so overwhelmed by the majestic presence of the King, his terrible court, and the throne room that they resumed themselves to the figure of spectators.

'You have entered these lands unmarked,' the king restarted, 'wishing to take something from it. Are you denying my claim, Haskshemi?' he asked gravely, staring directly at Hanam with his chin high.

The hunchback was the only one that had understood the intricacies of what the king was really suggesting. The imperious, manly tone was, in fact, a proposition. Hanam decided to risk it.

'We are at your service, oh king of these lands,' said Hanam and kneeled.

The others followed. Klunk laid down over the polished marble floor.

'Give us an opportunity to serve you and, by your name and authority, we will prevail and see your will done,' said Hanam, and hoped for the best.

The king stared at them while meditating over the subject, then he gave out a terrible smile.

'Deep in my lands,' he started, 'always in the vilest dark corners, lives the father of all wild beasts: The White Behemoth,' the king said. 'Its awakenings have cost my people dearly throughout the centuries. Many have successfully hunted it, but this Behemoth has the blessing of the Phoenix. Every time it is killed, it turns back many suns later,' he said. 'It is time to cleanse the land from this aberration. The High Oracle has prophesied none of our people will complete this hunt. It is written that only a Haskshemi Shastameni with a sky sword would destroy this evil,' the king said.

He then looked at Hanam and then slowly transferred his gaze to the sword on Bastian's back.

'Hunt the White Behemoth down and I will open the tomb and fare you goodbye in peace,' he said. 'Avoid it, and face the penalties of your trespassing and your admitted thievery,' decreed the king.

302

'Show us the way, my lord,' said Hanam promptly. 'We will see your will done or will die trying, oh king,' said Hanam solemnly.

None of Hanam's companions were willing to say something, but the "die trying" part kept echoing in their minds.

Vanity

'They are coming for you,' a powerful but well-adjusted voice shredded the silence like a dragon's claw would shred through a wall of thick glass. And like a dragon, every time Razec spoke, people around him were hurt by the fear of his voice.

By the sound of that voice, Dreak aroused, driven from an inner darkness to an outer darkness. He had no memory of how he came to be there. In his mind, there was no interval between the moment of the engulfment in obscurity to where he was now. He felt confused for a second. In addition, no matter where he looked, he could not locate the source of that voice. He started thinking that he was having his first nightmare, but then the darkness was suddenly removed from his sight and he could see again. He then understood that he wasn't previously in darkness, but had been made blind by some dark spell.

The first thing his mind processed when he was given his vision back was that he still was in the same laboratory from before. The second thing was that he was tied by thick steel bands over a vertical table, wearing nothing but his undergarments. Finally, he noticed that there was a terribly beautiful and disturbingly intense elf right in front of him.

He had the most vivid and strong black hair that fell straight until his waistline, the facial features that looked as if sculpted by a cynical artist, and the stance of a king. His skin was pale and unblemished, and his eyes were acutely hypnotically as if they existed in an uncanny agreement with reality. He was dressed in clothes as black as his hair, made without seams or buttons and discreetly but elegantly decorated with dark diamonds and light pearls that few mortals had ever seen before.

Dreak instinctively noticed that he was unarmed, and he could not avoid the thought that he had never seen rings like those he was wearing.

'They are coming for you,' Razec said again. 'We have no time for me to ask you all my questions, nor the time for you to select what you will tell me

303

and what you won't,' the elf said it with a light hint of humor. 'I will have to read your mind to see if you can be of some use,' the elf said to Dreak while raising his hand in his direction. 'Do not try to resist me. It is useless, and if I have to spend extra time on you, I may deliver you to your stalkers,' he said while lowering his face as if his head was a weapon and he was aiming it at Dreak.

'I see,' the elf said satisfied a few minutes later.

Drake passed out from the violence of the mental rape he suffered. Even though he had the stamina of a champion and was overall an incredibly tough man, the intensity and the invasiveness of Razec's will almost brought him to a comatose state from shock.

The elf, however, seemed indifferent about the condition he left the human in, but was rather giving him an unusual gaze, considering his own interests and many other things. Razec had forcedly uncovered all Dreak's most intimate thoughts, busting his mind and completely exposing his being in the process. Having read every single memory the assassin possessed, he was now determining what to do with him.

The tranquility and calm puzzlement on Razec's face was surprising and a very different reaction from what one would expect from someone that had just seen the totality of Dreak's crimes, villainy, and the whole extension of his abysmal soul.

'I am going to use him,' the elf said decisively.

'Bring me the old jar,' he ordered the dark figure waiting behind the raised table.

The half-dragon half-man creature obeyed at once, walking straight to one of the overbuilt wood shelves and grabbing a rustic glass jar almost as big as himself.

The jar was a testament to what was inside. It was made of rough crystal and had an oxidized old copper seal. Both, the seal and the jar, had enchanted runes all over them. The runes were active, slowly but constantly changing shape and position, sometimes even mingling among them.

Even empty, the jar was too heavy for three men to raise it. The six hundred pounds dragon-man had to stretch his wings to balance himself while carrying it. The care and solemnity with which he moved while holding the recipient revealed how precious the liquid inside was.

'Hurry, Draco,' the elf said firmly, but with patience. 'They will report back to their prince any time now, and when that happens, they will find this place.'

Doing as he was told, Draco approached Razec and was about to put the jar on the floor in front of him when the elf, who had not deviated his sight from Dreak not even once since the whole thing started, made a sign with his left hand indicating for him to bring the jar even closer. The dragon-man approached Razec and raised the jar with both arms and considerable effort. The elf picked it up with his left hand effortlessly as if it was made of dry, thin twigs.

Razec spun two of his fingers through the air and the lid's runes became truly activated, aligning, rotating, and opening the jar. The nimble multicolored liquid substance relentlessly tried to disperse itself in the air around it, but the elf promptly used his power to contain it. He inserted his hand inside the jar and dipped one of his finger tips on the strange substance. Then, he passed the jar to Draco, who, despite having massive steel tendons, picked it up with considerable effort. After he set the jar in its place over the shelf, Draco himself closed the lid using his own magic, but with considerably more effort than Razec.

Razec's eyes were serious and focused now. He was looking at Dreak as if he could see right through him, and he could. He touched the killer's forehead with his wet finger and the bizarre substance was instantly absorbed by Dreak's skin as if it was a fierce worm that was eager to accommodate itself by crawling inside the body of its host.

Razec started to summon a series of spells and after many incantations, in a procedure that could be accurately described as an invasive soul surgery, Dreak woke up again. He was feeling normal and his eyes were less hectic. He felt no dizziness nor pain. Razec snapped his fingers to Draco pointing at Dreak. Draco went on to a huge trunk and picked all of Dreak's gear and his weapons and brought it to him, leaving them at his feet. Then, the dragon-man unlocked the magical runes that kept the steel bands together, freeing Dreak completely.

'Gear up and don't ever take the black ring off your right hand or your pursuer will instantly find you,' said Razec emphatically while he gave his back to Dreak and went back to his tasks on the other side of the lab. 'Come on, Draco, offer the man a welcome drink,' he said and immediately the dragon-man disappeared over an entrance on the East wall.

As soon as Dreak touched the hilt of his sword, his hands froze and his feet immediately felt like they were glued to the ground. He could not draw it and stab the elf on the back as he had desired ever since he had recovered his conscience. He simply could not do it. There was something in his being now that would not allow him to do anything that could menace Razec. His reality was now tenaciously not providing the solution he wanted for the moment. Confused between his instinct to murder everything out of any situation and the forceful contours of his new reality, Dreak knew no better than to continue and try to impose his will against the absurd curse cast over him.

Razec, who was now busy around the lab gearing himself up and getting ready to leave the place, without even looking toward Dreak, raised his head and contracted one side of his lips as if he had regretted something.

'I thought you were smarter than this, Dreak,' he said while turning around and walking back to the corner where Dreak was.

When he got close enough, the assassin was drooling and breathing heavily without any concern to hide his intentions toward the elf while wretchedly trying to draw his swords. The more Razec got close to him, the more desperately he forced his will, but he simply could not do it.

'I will be as straightforward with you as I can,' said Razec, stopping in front of him. 'For your own good, I hope you make peace with your new destiny as soon as possible,' the elf said it while his mind actively imposed his will over Dreak, making him stop trying to kill Razec and starting to listen to him. 'You are now bound to my will. You are an instrument of it now. I have put a spell on you that very few can undo. And none of them would do it for a person like you,' Razec said it with a cold distance.

'You are a dead man walking, Dreak,' he continued. 'The people who are looking for you would have found you easily even if you have hidden inside the belly of a Leviathan. They have powers that greatly exceed the magic you wear. What you had was only delaying the inevitable. I have provided you a second chance, but I am not unfair. I will arrange for your hiding and protection while I see your services fit my interests. It is in your interest, thus, to do as you are told.'

'You cannot do any direct or indirect action to harm me,' Razec explained. 'Don't try it or I will cancel the spell that is hiding you from the powerful scryers that are looking for you at this very moment. I would even collect the money offered for your head to tell the truth. That, of course, although profitable, would be a shame due to your expertise,' he said unapologetically.

'You can, and you will obviously, in time, think you have come up with a great, smart, and workable plan to kill me or escape. That is why I am going to be forced to demonstrate to you, now, why this is not a good idea,' he said gradually changing the tone of his voice to a profound dreadfulness.

Draco, who had just came back from the other room and was no coward by any means, hid behind a thick stone pillar after listening to those words.

The elf moved his right hand's fingers in the air and something that could only be described as a small explosion of vivid dark brightness came out of it and hit Dreak's forehead.

'As of now,' he said, 'the spell I had cast upon you is not working. You may try to kill me now. Do not attempt to escape my presence or I will cancel the ring's enchant and the prince will find you and send his White Knights. They will kill you at sight. Evidently, there will be no negotiation or second chances from my part for you either.' Razec sounded bored as if he was reading from a manual.

Like a cornered leopard, Dreak looked at the elf full of suspicion and enmity. He grabbed and geared up the rest of his kit while his unblinking gaze was set on Razec.

The elf was not moving at all, he was just casually waiting for Dreak.

After he finished arming himself, Dreak, now completely focused, slowly drew his blades.

Razec slightly raised a corner of his lips in a relaxed manner, almost offering a respectful smile.

A dark and filthy tension was rising on the laboratory. A kind of tension that only came around when two evil creatures fought each other. The air was now carrying a taste of violence deprived of glory, of drive destitute of honor, of will damped in greed and unholiness.

When Dreak felt he had it, he charged the elf. Fast as a wicked cat, the assassin jumped forward with amazing speed. With only a few thrusts from his powerful legs he covered the distance between them. Razec remained motionless. When Dreak's swords were almost in range, he then jumped into the shadows and instantly materialized behind Razec. His large blade came out of the darkness first, forward, precise, and mighty, already set for the base of the elf's neck. The short one he kept on his left hand, reserving it for the defense with a reverse grip.

At the last moment, with a speed that surpassed Dreak's reflexes by a fair amount, Razec turned to face his opponent. The elf's right hand instantaneously holding the Emperor Sword of Speed by its tip.

Drake immediately released his captured blade and spun, using the other sword in a lower attack to pierce the elf's abdomen. Even so, this second attack ended in the same way, seized effortlessly by Razec's left hand. A translucent pulse of energy came out of the elf's chest, blowing Dreak and his swords away and they traveled in the air as if they were leaves blown by an autumn wind. The sudden acceleration and the landing in the rock-solid wall broke major bones across the assassin's body.

With a single consecutive gesture of his hand, Razec made body and weapons stop in the air. The elf opened his hand in an explosive gesture and Dreak's body stretched out like a starfish, breaking a few more bones and tearing joints apart. In a corrupt, vile, and phantasmagoric crucifixion, Drake's arms opened in the air, his legs stretched, his neck overextended almost about to break. The two swords stood suspended, slowly swinging in the air with their blades shining under the lab's golden low light.

With another gesture from Razec's fingers, the two swords began to slowly move in the direction of Dreak's neck. Their blades crossed like a scissor right in front of him. The Highway Horror could not move a muscle, having little to do besides suppressing that growing feeling inside of him that was definitely not, but incredibly similar to complete panic. A self-preservation instinct, an irrational tremor of a dying creature who could do nothing to stop its own death, nothing but watch. And in fact he watched as his swords, crossed in the air by the elf's cruel will, hacked slowly and painfully around his neck, slowly severing off his head.

While the act took place, Razec, also through his bottomless magic, caused Dreak and his swords to approach him until they were close enough to count the hairs in each other's eyelashes. The elf kept Dreak's eyes in contact with his during the whole time, showing him during the entire excruciating suffering the full extension of the hell he held inside his being.

When the swords ended their chop, Razec, with yet another discreet gesture from his fingers slowly removed Dreak's head from its body, bringing it even closer to his face and their eyes met in a terrible intimate experience.

Then, through his high magic again, Razec showed the unimaginable prospect of having complete control over Dreak's reality, not allowing him to blink or bleed to death. The elf then invaded Dreak's mind one more time, communicating a dense amount of dreadful understandings to him. So dreadful, Dreak thought them a thousand times worse than the pain that he felt while his head was being ripped off.

Razec made sure Dreak never lost consciousness and that he was hyped and well awake during the whole ride, feeling every induced misery and pain. The climax of the Dreak's suffering happened when their eyes met and certain aspects of their minds connected. Razec wanted to be there and wanted Dreak to know that he was there too, inside his soul, witnessing his pain, and crushing any subconscious consolation or refuge the assassin may retrieve himself to, guaranteeing, therefore, the completion of his worse hell possible.

When the assassin was about to die by sheer blunt trauma due to the lack of will to carry on existing, Razec arched his left hand's fingers, bringing the man's body forward to where his head was. The elf then connected both again and healed the neck's wound with his magic. The healing spell was so powerful that Dreak's body was completely regenerated in a matter of seconds, and his head was reattached to his body as if it had never been removed.

Finally, the elf released Dreak from the magical grip and Dreak instinctively rubbed his now perfectly healed neck as if his mind was still receiving pain impulses.

Razec politely and serenely approached the killer and offered him his swords back. After giving himself a few seconds, the human amenably took his blades and sheathed them smoothly, but he couldn't face the elf, for the intensity and the contrast of what had just happened were so overwhelming that even Dreak could not bring himself to look at him. He kept his gaze fixed on a spot on the floor, but the elf stood in front of him waiting, inescapable, silently demanding that the human engage him. Eventually, Dreak regrettably and haltingly raised his eyes.

'NEVER allow yourself to think that you understood what I am,' said the elf when their stares met.

The King's Will

Although the beast was as formidable an adversary as an adult dragon, its fight dynamic was much simpler. The most experienced among the Barbarians explained that the monster had no magical powers nor apparent intellect. Their translators described it in a broken common language that it was "just" a furious hill made of tough leather, muscles, and claws.

The Barbarians had been passing the knowledge on how to fight the creature throughout generations. The king's hunters told everything they knew about it on their way to the creature's pit. Its weak points had already been identified long ago, and the Barbarians had become proficient in killing it by now. On their way to face the beast, they explained to the foreigners everything they needed to know about it, and plans were made.

The hunt for Behemoth was considered a festival despite the fact that when the creature appeared somewhere random within the territory, it would kill many (including elders and children) before it could be killed.

Among the Barbarians of the Phoenix Tribe that marched with them most were newcomers willing to prove themselves. As far as they knew, the king had not given the hunters specific orders about helping the companions, but none of them agreed to be excluded from the hunt either, and tradition was the Barbarians' true sovereign. They were a courageous and hardened people indeed and even the mention of being kept out of such adventure was an offense to them.

The hunters instructed them exactly where to hit and in which sequence and what to avoid. They told The Fellowship many things, including the fact that the Behemoth fur was to be taken into consideration, for arrows were mostly useless against it and it took a full blow of a strong man to penetrate it. Their first priority, thus, must be the eyes. Then, they said, they would go to the leg tendons and arteries. After that, the arms tendons and arteries thereof. Then, the hunters who were alive and still in the fight would go for the back of the neck and head.

The companions made plans and established upon their strategies carefully, but when they started to approach the lands devastated by the Behemoth's fury, they began to second guess their tactics, for desolation around to the creature's lair was unrivaled by anything they ever saw before. By the sheer number of large animal carcasses, one could see that its appetite was supernatural. After arriving on the edge of a low ravine, the unbearably smelly hole in the ground was pointed by their escort as their final destination.

Mounts of rotten and infectious manure higher than Klunk's were everywhere. The creature's discharges made that forest reek like the deepest layer of hell. Most trees had died from the chocking toxicity and some had melted away from the acidity of the creature's urine. The whole place was a giant desolated latrine. They all covered their faces and Klunk clogged his nostrils with a handful of leaves and was walking around with a nauseated face.

'Geee, we should receive the king's favor just for being here,' said Lucien.

'The Behemoth has a very fast…metabolism,' said Ianckhan. 'Yes, I believe that is the right word,' he said with a heavy accent.

'That's actually very good,' said Stargazer. 'And accurate,' he reinforced the compliment, honestly impressed with the Barbarian's unexpected sharpness.

'Where have you learned the language?' asked Stargazer politely. 'And the science?' he risked a little more.

'Bad story,' said Ianckhan. 'Went too far on a hunt. Was captured by a witch. Was forced to help him for many moons,' he said, then he cleared his throat and spit on the ground as if the mention of that memory had left a bitter taste in his mouth.

Stargazer stopped asking questions but made a mental note about it.

They left all the travel equipment in a camp a mile away from the hole and prepared themselves for combat, advancing by foot to the entrance of the pit until they were into position. When their final approach began, The Fellowship took center stage in the troop deployment scheme. They adopted their classic triangle formation, with Klunk on the tip, Bastian and Lucien in his flanks, Hanam in the middle, and Sahafira and Stargazer on the outer flanks a little further behind. Their plan was to leave some distance among them and the creature, so they could alternate their bombardment of damaging spells into the creature's eyes and face, hopefully blinding it during the first moments of the combat, or at least distract it while the others incapacitated it.

Sahafira and Stargazer used all the scrolls, potions, and spells they had at their disposal, casting over their companions and over the Barbarians all the enhancing magic they could. Even though, most of the Barbarians approached Hanam instead, paying their respects and asking for his blessings and even kneeling before him in reverence while he prayed for them. When they advanced to face the beast, the most valiant warriors among the Barbarians formed a wall of flesh around the hunchback, clearly favoring and protecting him. Bastian and Lucien thought that the Barbarians certainly appreciated healers into their society, which was true to some extent, and therefore nobody really minded the hunchback's unforeseen favoritism, nobody but Stargazer.

The hunters made a circle around the hole and pointed their massive golden spear throwers at it. There was a lot of tension in the air, knees were flexed and weapons were drawn. Then, Ianckhan, who was the most experienced of them, started shouting battle cries of defiance. The others repeated in unison the loud, guttural, and impressive "roar." It was one of the manliest things that they had ever see. Even Bastian and Lucien who were raised in Valkarian warrior culture were impressed. They all felt contaminated with that growing energy and started to feel their blood boiling. Klunk was shouting and grumbling like he had lost his mind. He was senselessly shouting, entirely out of compass and rhythm, but he was still very loud and the Barbarians respected that. He was serious and had a very grave "I'm pissed off" grimace on his face.

Suddenly, the earth trembled. A terrible growl reverberated not only in the air but in the rocks, in the dead trees, and in the enormous piles of shit around them. The way the vibration traveled through matter gave the impression that the very earth under their feet had become enraged. All birds within many miles flew away, creating living clouds of chaotic speeds and textures in the sky above them. The Barbarians were not intimidated and did not lessen their cries, but instead increased the volume, now screaming from the bottom of their lungs, making it immensely loud.

They started entering a state of sheer ritualistic and hypnotic rage. Their faces were now made mad by the evoked fury. Their eyes were red, and their strong-bronzed necks and arms were popping thick veins. They were ready.

Out of the unseen dark abyss came out a colossal grayish white furred beast. It stood like a fat ogre, but much more animalistic with its arms bouncing from its heavy shoulders. The arms were thick like an old tree, ending into three great claws that could reach the heart of a fully grown dragon with one hit. It had a mouth like of a hog but with many more lines of sharp teeth. Its tusks were bigger than Sahafira.

From positions beyond view in the gorges that surrounded that forest, four golden darts of solid metal came whizzing through the air. They were twice the size of a man, and thick as a warrior's arm. They all hit the target at the same time as the hunters' spears.

The synch was not bad, thought Bastian and Lucien at the same time.

Only two of the ballista's projectiles hit the chest of the creature for a good effect, and only one eye was really blinded by one of the hunter's spears. Now they had lost the surprise effect and needed to fight the giant creature directly until the ballista reloaded.

After the hit, the Behemoth immediately emitted a shout and started to punch everything on its way with its mighty claws. Boulders, trees, soil, and warriors started flying through to the air as the fight degenerated into controlled chaos.

They all fought well. Stargazer's fireballs and energy missiles obliterated the creature's sense of smell, the rest of its vision, and half of its hearing capability. After that, he was exhausted and incapable of mining resources to cast spells relevant enough to have an impact on that fight. Thus, he retreated to a safer position looking for spears to throw.

Sahafira's conjured big ice spikes and accelerated them into the creature's soft spots that were opened by the warriors. In doing so, she worked the tendons and increased the depth of the wounds and the profuseness of the bleedings, but soon in the fight she was taken out of combat when a rock, propelled by one of the creature's strokes, hit her in the stomach, sending her unconscious body many yards away.

Bastian, Lucien, Klunk, and the bravest of the hunters were the first to enter in melee with the creature, bashing and dodging and doing all that was possible to incapacitate it and make it bleed as much as they could. They all fought smartly and bravely, but it was not enough, and even after almost senseless, and having a leg and an arm incapacitated, the aggressiveness of Behemoth pressed against the adventurer's luck.

Lucien and Klunk were articulating, with Lucien piercing a hole in the creature's extremely thick skin, and then Klunk hit the hole with his pike, nailing it deep in the Behemoth flesh. That strategy miraculously worked twice, but they were both knocked out by an instinctive blow that sent them away.

Bastian had got good results with his sword. It was entirely by his efforts that the left leg got incapacitated. His sword cut deep, very deep through the beast's skin, flesh, and even bones. At a certain point, when he went for the monster's heart, running and jumping over a fallen log, he managed to pierce the creature's flank profoundly. Feeling the sting, the Behemoth instinctively bounced in his direction, pressing him against a large tree. His body was shattered, breaking dozens of bones and squashing his organs, leaving him minutes from certain death.

The Barbarians also fought bravely and fiercely, but most of them were blasted into the air with every revulsive blow from the agonizing creature. Some, however, were still in the fight, opportunistically hitting the tormented beast and dodging of its counter-attacks the best they could. When the second wave of golden harpoons came, once more only two hit the target proficiently, for the creature, made crazed by pain and despair, was moving around madly and randomly, knocking down and smashing to dough everything it touched.

In that moment of chaos, Hanam saw that even if the Behemoth died from its wounds in the next five minutes, his friends could be squashed before that. In its dying frenzy, the monster was now going in the direction where a seriously hurt Stargazer was numbed over a rock while trying to heal a dying Bastian before it was too late. And so it was without delay that he saw the creature begin to move quickly toward them, destroying everything in its path.

'Stargazer!' he shouted at the wizard as he exploded with surprising acceleration, running to their rescue.

'Bastian's sword! Now!' Hanam shouted from the bottom of his soul, pointing to the sword still hanging from the creature's left ribs.

Exhausted, but still sharp as a razor, Stargazer immediately understood and raised his trembling right hand in the direction of the blade. The blade shook for a while but stood in place, increasing the madness of the monster.

'Now!' shouted Hanam again as he dangerously approached the Behemoth unarmed and the Behemoth dangerously approached the helpless humans.

Stargazer then took a longer breath of air and drained himself out of his last drop of vigor to cast one last spell. Strong and truthful, the sword flew through the air right into the hunchback's hands, who grabbed it powerfully and wielded it with surprising skill.

The effort was so costly for the wizard, that even before the sword reached the hunchback's hands, he collapsed unconscious in the fetid mud. His face hit it as he bled from his nose, ear, and mouth.

Hanam accelerated, charging faster than one would say a man could. He propelled himself from a log and jumped into the air, hitting the creature in the head. The image of the hunchback figure flying through the air in such a fast and aggressive arc while holding his bright and large two-handed sword with both hands pointing down was the last thing that Bastian saw before he was engulfed by the darkness of his failing body. Later, remembering the situation, he got the impression that, for a moment, in the middle of the air, when the extreme and sudden movements of the hunchback retracted his robe revealing part of his body, he saw a light. And it was the most delightful, comforting, and purest light he had ever seen. He kept this to himself, however, blaming his delirious mind.

Bastian's sword went through the creature's skull until the guard touched the skin of the forehead. The Behemoth dropped immediately, and a mystical vacuum started to suck in the air with a great noise. A magical explosion with more noise than actual damage ensued, and the immense carcass disappeared as if magically sublimated from reality.

'Victory at last!' shouted the men from the Phoenix Tribe when the dust settled.

Afterward, when all the wounded were treated and stabilized, Hanam and the Barbarians found a wood elf in the middle of the hole where the Behemoth's carcass burst. He had a long, deep, and dense brown hair. His muscular built was covered by the olive-brownish skin tone typical of the wood elves. He was laying down naked and covered in dirt.

'What is this, Haskshemi?' said Ianckhan, getting closer to Hanam while pointing at the elf.

'An old curse was removed today,' said the Hunchback, relieved.

'This never happen before,' said Ianckhan, admiringly.

'It's bad destiny,' Ianckhan sounded resentful. 'We burn it now,' he said.

'That is enough for one day,' said Hanam. 'The ancient evil that took hold of him has been banished, never to return,' he said, kneeling over the elf to pray over his body.

'Who was him, Haskshemi?' asked one of the Barbarians after Hanam finished praying.

'You mean who IS him,' corrected Hanam. 'He is still alive,' he said.

The Barbarians looked at the elf with great surprise and trembled in fear of those words.

'We need to kill it,' said Ianckhan, pulling out his huge field knife.

'No!' cried Hanam, protecting the elf's body with his own.

The Barbarians looked at him and then to Ianckhan, who was confused with the situation.

'I don't know why he was trapped in that curse, but he is free now,' Hanam said with authority, and even though he was a foreigner, no one challenged his words.

'Take him into custody if you will, over chains if you must, but take him alive,' said Hanam with authority. 'Enough death for one day,' he said. 'Life is precious,' he added in a lower tone, drained. 'All life is precious,' he whispered quietly, to himself.

Greed

Jane was a true rebel. Even before she became one of the empire's most wanted criminals, she was a rebel. And even long before she was nicknamed the Red Viper, she was a rebel. She was not rebellious, however, against what the world was, but a rebel against what the world allowed her to control. She was an insurgent of her own cause, a revolutionary out of her own greed. The red-haired woman had a tainted spirit inside her that made her insatiable. For her, there had never been enough gold, silk, or men.

She was the late daughter of a retired mercenary and a relatively famous tavern "dancer." Her father was somewhat successful in his career. Not reaching heroic fame, but being proficient enough for a warrior (and lucky enough for an adventurer) to have survived the Battle of Broken Bones. He was also good enough a lover to have seduced her mother into retirement.

He was strong, dexterous, and capable, having gathered some respect and a considerable treasure during his years of adventure. Gold wise, it was enough to buy a good farm and to keep some of his wife's luxuries at bay. Still, he was a distant and selfish man, not interested in giving enough love to tame and guide Jane's carnal heart and her immense wants. He was not a cruel person, but, because he spent his entire life in the business of violence and gain, he ended a little "ethically flexible," passing on his lack of values to his daughters, leaving Jane without any moral guidance.

Her father was the strong person of the house and his personality dominated them all. Although Jane was not particularly fond of the thought, she mirrored and measured herself to him more than she wanted to admit. She had always had a special connection to her father, mostly silent, but still very much in the air between the two of them. He died when she was still young and it broke her heart, for he was the only part of Jane's world that she truly admired.

Her mother was a proud woman, satisfied by her husband's attentions but embittered by the many humiliations of the acts of violence and the exploitation she suffered during her intense pre-marital life. She had a gorgeous appearance, a rare mix between one of the Coronian lineages and a somewhat diluted sea elf blood. Her exiguous elven features were just enough to make her complexion light and delicate. They were not visible in her ears or in her bone structure. In general, her external features were very Coronian in aspect, but the ones who got close enough to her could sense the mysticism of her elven ancestry pouring out of her through her mannerisms. Therefore, the legacy suppressed on her outside abounded on her inside, and her musical talents were beyond human natural capabilities, and, during her tavern days, the number of men paying her to sing was almost as high as the ones paying for her other talents.

She loved Jane, but when she started seeing certain strengths blossoming in her daughter, her jealousy played in and she began alienating Jane emotionally, raising a wall of passive-aggressive antipathy to contain her. She was too proud to love her daughter the way they both needed her to, and as the days went by, she saw that her love could not overcome her prideful resentments caused by her anger-infused vanity. Jane's mother ended loathing her daughter in the same way she detested the worse things about her own self.

With no emotional safe haven to relieve herself, no love to hide herself within, and an enormous hunger for life, Jane was set to disaster. To make things worse, her roots gave her the energy, the beauty, the talent, and the guts she needed to get whatever she wanted from whomever she wanted. Eventually, she learned that she could not be controlled, and she decided to let the sinful fire she carried inside burn freely.

That exceedingly strong consuming transgression was the only thing she felt she could trust, the only thing she eventually found herself with, the only thing she knew to be truly hers. She never talked about it since the early years of her self-discovery, but as she matured into a woman, the loneliness, the shame, and the pride forced her to decide to just let it burn. And so it did, becoming ever-present in her body, alive in her soul. It fueled her, unsettled her, burned her, never departing from her spirit until it became itself what she believed to be her soul.

As she fed her fire, the prosperous farmlands on which she was raised quickly became incapable of satisfying her. The strong and vigorous sons of the farmers became boring and insufficient to her at an alarming rate. The dresses and jewels sold by an occasional passing hawker were quick to become dull, limited, and gray to her taste. She spent most of her youth waking up and going to sleep unsatisfied. On some occasions, the boredom she felt was so intense that she screamed alone in the darkness of her room.

When she was not much more than a young lady, she was already known in the local trading village to be actively bartering her body and favors with the passing travelers and local studs. They give her whatever jewel, magic item, or amount of money she asked for, and, in exchange, she would give them whatever they wanted at the local inn.

Jane, however, was not a common prostitute. She was not a woman deprived of control over her life or sexuality. She was not a woman with an empty mind, or a frozen heart, or even a senseless body. Although likewise self-destructive, Jane was in control of her uncontrollable fire, voluntarily enjoying each and every flame. Nothing they could do to her could take her pleasure away, for she decided to be the one who would press the depths of any transgressions they engaged in, even in violence, even in filth, even in absurdity.

Jane had powerful emotions and her body was the very representation of a quintessential female. She was tall and imperious as someone fit for feats of passion, and of a wild complexion of fast and firm shapes as for her intensely sexualized person.

Sex for her, at every step of the way, was completely devoted to her borderline fanatical pursuit of pleasure and control. To Jane, the reward was a way of satisfying other appetites, but the act itself, the ritual, was what really fed her demons. And every time she met her walls, it never took too long for her to lose her attachments and press forward in the exploration of her limits. She was never satisfied, always pushing for more, and more, and more.

The simple people around her failed to understand that Jane's sexuality and seemingly anti-existential behavior were connected to the fact that the flesh suffers the consequences of the spirits and the ideas it manifests and confesses. Their cumulation also caused distortions and re-alignments on the soul, much

318

more so in Fabula, where sheer will can change the objective reality in drastic ways.

Jane came to be such a slave of her own transgressions that, in time, her actions finally vanished her remaining few moral senses, aligning the novelty of her discovered experiences to terrible potential wickedness. Without perceiving or caring, she became addicted to her vices, and they consumed her until the cumulation of her self-imposed repressions and the lack of structure to exist in her own uniqueness, made her act entirely boundlessly, and, when the opportunity presented itself, evilly.

The path she took was a complex and evolving fervently damaging situation, for she could not hold herself responsible, but couldn't ignore her objective guilt either. In the end, it all affected her in the deepest levels of her being, and, detached from any truth that could redeem her, feeling abandoned in a reality she couldn't completely understand or ultimately control as she wished, and trapped in a body full of consequences she couldn't tame, she found herself propelled by a deep will to destroy everything until the whole world was on fire.

When she grew tired of her local routines, she ran away with a handsome rogue mercenary called Dupas Bracco. He taught her how to fight, how to steal, and new ways to please her appetites, for he was a notoriously famous lover that was able to keep her satisfied for a time. However, the real reason why she teamed with Dupas and regarded him some trust, was because he taught her how to kill.

Fascinated with the act and its effect on people, she pushed forward the barriers of her sins and became addicted, searching evermore for opportunities to end lives.

They both shared a profound insatiability for it, partnering in that intent. The gluttonous transgression of having power over life and death became the source of their every inclination. Deciding to deliver themselves to such ultimate passion, they created a wicked necessity that abode beyond reason, and sanity. Propelled by it, they become exceedingly good at evil.

Before she left her home, she stole her family's most precious possession: her father's magical Belt of Strength and Protection and his rare weapons. This gave her a notorious advantage "on the road," facilitating her fanatical dispositions in the direction of her wrongdoings.

They traveled around doing as they pleased and taking what they wanted regardless. Quickly they developed a reputation for themselves. "The Dark Serpent and The Red Viper" was what was written in the wanted posters all around the empire.

After his execution by the Valkarian authorities, she established herself as an enemy of the empire and every organized civil society. Vengeful and terrible, she would bring harm to the world in every opportunity she had.

Shortly after Dupas' death, she went straying in the Fire Mountains for some time. There, she discovered an isolated community of half-ogres. In her maddening bitterness, she left herself to be captured, and the whole tribe raped her for many days. When she got bored of it, she killed them all. Sparing only the six among the strongest to serve her. She personally trained and equipped them, and as she poisoned them with her venom, they became her loyal guardians and frightened lovers.

The level of commitment they were willing to exercise for the Red Viper, and the skill set they achieved under her tutelage, made them by far the most dangerous of her many resources. She used them as her bodyguards and shock troop, and upon her return to the edges of the civilized lands, the people scourged by their actions nicknamed the six half-ogres The Helpers. Together, they were the terror of the outskirts of Blackspear, causing the roads to be unsafe for dozens of miles in all directions. There, she came up to full-grown maturity as a criminal, establishing her den on the northern outskirts of the fortress city.

Due to the suicidal intensity of her marauding operations, she became evermore hard to catch, and the fame of the Red Viper spread across the empire. Dupas Bracco had taught her well, and she knew exactly when to engage and when to run, and, most importantly, how to hide. All efforts from the empire to capture her failed, and every time they tried, she only ended up becoming more experienced at escaping them.

She specializing in raiding the many valuable caravans that passed through the city's numerous roads. She claimed an extensive criminal territory around that corner of the empire, enforcing herself as the uncontested leader. If a pocket was picked there, she either received a cut or someone would be cut. Ruthless and competent, she swiftly grew an extensive grid of minions and agents, even some of the most notorious thief guilds that operated in her area paid her tribute and "protection." Eventually, her hand stretched so far that she placed herself in the profitable business of selling information. She knew that if she pushed the empire far enough, she could not escape them, so she also utilized unconventional strategies to seduce and persuade many authorities to leave her alone. Half a dozen of Blackspear captains, warriors of renown, and knights of importance were in love with her. Somehow, she would even find time and energy to pay regular visits to many other men in positions of power to mitigate her demise and have some fun. Nevertheless she became a true crime boss, setting herself on the top of her "profession," deep inside, she was still the same insatiable rebel girl from her early years. And, although the half-ogres were bestially vigorous on their disposition, she easily got bored of them, considering them as a mechanical knockoffs of real lovers. Also, passionate about the bohemian life, she enjoyed the risky politics, constantly executing bold night raids in search of worthy lovers that could also provide her with favors all around that region. But eventually even all that became monotonous to her, and one day, overwhelmed by her boredom, she decided to raid the road to Ironclad, for she knew that by this time of the year the flux on that road was intense enough to highly improve her chances of finding a sizable bounty and a fair fight. However, she also knew that caravans from Ironclad were too heavily armed and well protected, so, besides ordering the Helpers to gather and arm themselves, she also summoned a dozen of her best ravagers.

She took them to a location by the road where she made arrangements for the ambush, and after she was happy with the preparations, they camouflaged themselves and waited in position.

After some time, as expected, a party appeared on the road.

A slow single black wagon pulled by a single black horse appeared on the road. The wagon and everything on it was taken by an uncommon darkness. The wood itself was as black as a night without stars, unbelievably old, wholesomely ancient in aspect and sound. Yet, the carriage was in a perfectly serviceable condition, it appeared very stable and sturdy as it was pushed forward. The black horse was unmarked, and it was very silent and unusually serene. There were only three figures over the open carriage. One at the front, mutely guiding the horse, and two seated in the back of the cart, with their legs dangling with the occasional bump of the road. They were all from different body shapes and sizes, but were all dressing the same kind of black cloaks, and their faces were completely covered by their black hoods.

The silence, stillness, and apparent apathy of every detail about the wagon and its occupants made them a discrete bunch. Too discreet in fact, for both the horse and the cloaked figures had an aura of detachment from their surroundings, a differentiation, a quieting uniqueness that floated around them. There was a loud silence following the wagon as they approached the place of the ambush. Birds would stop singing and farm dogs would hide as they went down the road. The Red Viper noticed it, and whatever they were, they now had her attention.

By this point in her life, she knew she had keen instincts, and knew how to read them, and how to use them. Right now, they were telling her that something about that caravan was the challenge she was looking for. She got very happy and excited about it, so much so that she could not keep from touching herself while she waited for the slow wagon to trigger the ambuscade.

When the right moment came, she gave the signal to her minions that she had targeted the approaching vehicle.

'Maybe they have a plague,' whispered one of her lieutenants that happened to be by her side. He looked disgusted by the cart's occupants' appearance.

'Do you really think so?' she asked, falsely interested in his opinion.

He nodded positively, not noticing what she had in her eyes. She nodded too as if mocking his head movement.

The lieutenant's head flew across the air, landing by the horse's hoof. The horse steadily stopped, unalarmed. Hastily, as the professional thieves that they were, they all closed into position. Behind heavy shields, eleven men pointed huge double crossbows to the wagon, four from each side, and three from behind. The Helpers advanced with heavy armor and massive siege shields and heavy swords, blocking the road and protecting themselves and the Viper.

She presented herself to the figure that drove the wagon, and at the same time, she used the opportunity to get a closer evaluation of the peculiar driver.

'I liked this man,' she said and pointed her sword at the lieutenant's head under her red leather boot. 'He was a good warrior and served me well, but he bored me to death.' She laughed freely at the hooded figure.

'His death, of course,' she added.

The figure remained silent and motionless.

'Do not bore me into your own death, please,' she said with the seductive charm of the powerful woman she was. 'Get out of the wagon and lose all your belongings. I may let you live,' she said it joylessly, as if it was an obnoxious protocol that she regretted.

'We have nothing that shall be of the concerns of such remarkable a lady,' the driver said. His voice was smooth and firm and delivered the sentence with an almost imperceptible tone of debauchery.

The Helpers, more animals than men, felt a hard coldness of screaming instinct climbing up their spines. The Red Viper noticed their reaction.

'We are keeping everything,' she said ironically, starting to consider killing them.

'Search it,' she ordered her men.

Instantly after her order, the driver calmly leaned the black reins by the wagon's side into a wood support made for it and raised himself. In perfect synchrony, the two figures stepped into the road and remained stagnant. The thieves hesitated.

'I cannot allow you to do that, my lady,' said the figure. Although unemotional, the momentum of his voice made the Helpers grunt and sweat. They hesitated, looking at her from the corner of their eyes. She hesitated too.

'Let us pass in peace and your life will remain yours,' he said it placidly.

'I'm the Red Viper of Blackspear,' she said, excited. 'If you resist me, this will be a lot funnier!' she said, touching the hilt of her sword with one hand and herself between her legs with the other.

Aroused by the slaughter that would certainly follow, her mouth was open in a kind of voluptuous smile that only a woman who is about to climax can perform. Her tongue was unconsciously suspended in the air as she sucked her breath through it.

'Well, in that case…' Razec lowered his hood, revealing his spotless and severe elfic face, '…your life WILL be mine,' he said, smiling, and his voice was sympathetic, objective, and conclusive.

Sparks of exploding light, thunders of tearing darkness, showers of blood, and clouds of pulverized bones were seen in the following second over the reflections of Jane's beautiful, terrorized, and orgasming green eyes. She was not sure what to feel, yet she wouldn't even care to know, for she was finally no longer bored.

The Seed of Destiny

The hunters and Klunk were singing, playing drums, and dancing by the campfire. The Behemoth was gone forever and many who had had mortal wounds had been healed. All of it was thanks to the Haskshemi Shastameni, as the Barbarians shouted the whole way back.

They celebrated merrily, proud that they had managed to accomplish such a magnificent task. All smiled in the camp, all but the elf, who was now conscious and in chains. He kept his head low all the time and he still looked stunned. He had not eaten, slept, or spoken nothing. At some point, Stargazer, Sahafira, Hanam, and Ianckhan came to talk to him.

Sahafira talked in elven, as Stargazer and Hanam were able to understand it.

'Can you please tell us who are you?' she said with a sweet voice, although she wasn't sure why she decided to use this approach.

'The dreamer of a thousand nightmares,' he said it in perfect high elf while still keeping his head down.

His words were piercing and intimidating to them, and his pronunciation was clear, and his grammar very elegant. The elves' tongue, when spoken the way he spoke it, sounded like a melodic song. Every phrase looked like the quoting of an old beautiful poem with all the words falling into the right place.

'What do you mean?' asked Sahafira. 'Please explain it to us,' she said, trying to stay on the subject of their doubts.

'I mean...' he raised his head and looked at her. His eyes shined with hundreds of lives, '...a thousand nightmares.'

Stargazer took a step back, losing his balance for a moment as if the elf's gaze hit him in the chest.

'Why were you cursed with such a gruesome torment?' asked Hanam with a reassuring and steady voice.

The elf suddenly looked fiercely at the hunchback. His big dark olive eyes pierced Hanam as if the elf was questioning his reasons why.

'I know,' said Hanam. 'We know.' The hunchback's tone was so irresistibly sensitive that he managed to make some progress. The elf's body language changed, his resistance diminished and he looked away.

'I can't remember clearly,' spoke the elf. 'We were at war with the orcs. We were winning. The war was coming to an end,' he said it as if he found pain in every unburied memory.

'I was a part of a major assault on their last stronghold,' he continued. 'They were not alone, there was also…darkness with them, within them. We managed to get to the portal, the filth portal. The great shadow cursed me and one of my companions teleported me away before I could devour them all,' he held his head as if it was about to explode.

'Trapped in this tainted monstrous body I have never found my way back to sanity. Everything was blurry, and hateful. There was nothing but this burning, raging, and endless fever – a true nightmare,' he whispered with much effort.

'The Elf-Orc Wars were more than a thousand years ago,' said Stargazer, startled. 'It was even before the First War, although their root causes are interconnected,' elaborated the wizard. 'The elves fielded such an army, that all kingdoms were brought to their knees and the orcs never rose again as a nation. Dark times, dark times indeed,' he said. Stargazer worried.

'Can you remember your name?' asked Sahafira.

'Semereth,' he said, confused. 'I can remember Semereth, but I'm not sure. It is the only thing I can remember,' he said, tangled in his own thoughts. 'I don't even know why I can remember that,' he said in sorrow. His nausea increased.

'He needs more time to recover from the transition,' said Sahafira.

'We don't have more time,' Stargazer remembered. 'Soon he will have to face the king,' he said. 'Now is the time to gather information and help,' the wizard insisted.

Regretfully, Sahafira and the others agreed with the wizard.

'It was like a dream,' he continued. 'I have found myself locked into this body for so long, and there was this rage…feeling inside of me. And all this hunger and this drive to destroy,' he said, terrorized with his own thoughts. 'I remember eating peo…' he stopped himself. The weight of his sorrows was palpable.

'Rest now,' said Hanam. He signed for the others to leave him be, and they did.

The celebration continued among the Barbarians. Sahafira, Hanam, and Stargazer went to a far and quiet corner of the camp to talk about the information they had just mustered.

'His history is lost in time,' she said. 'His memory is too damaged. He was trapped in that cursed body for dozens of lifetimes,' she lamented in horror.

'Yes,' agreed Stargazer, 'and this kind of curse could render a mind insane. It is amazing that he can even make conjectures and talk with us after all this time,' he said. Then he paused, considered, and then exposed a thought he kept. 'He must have an unnatural resilience. I do not believe he will ever retake his mental health after this without serious help. At this point, his memories are buried under a sea of somatic debris. Only with very powerful magic he will be able to reorganize his mind and completely remember his previous life. And even if he does, will it be worthy? The world has changed so much...' Stargazed ended the exposing of his reflection of what he could deduct from all he knew about the history of the last thousand years or so.

'Do you think what he is saying is true?' asked Hanam, checking Sahafira's and Stargazer's gut feelings.

'If it is, he was one of the greatest warriors of his time,' said Stargazer.

'I agree,' said Sahafira.

'What do you mean?' asked Hanam.

'My master's collection of historical books had a particularly higher number of works about this period, and about elven history. I loved reading about it, I read most volumes more than twice,' said Stargazer, thrilled. 'A lot of stuff that is part of our lives today came from that era, you know?' he asked rhetorically, looking at the others who were definitely not sharing his enthusiasm for history. 'But I digress,' he said, considering their reaction. 'If he was assaulting the last Hell Portal, it means that he was no regular conscript for sure. He probably was fighting side-by-side with the royal houses – a great honor for a wood elf,' said Stargazer. 'And very unlikely,' he added.

'He must have been more than a great soldier. We are talking about an epic warrior,' said Sahafira.

'To say the least,' confirmed Stargazer.

'How can you be so sure?' asked Hanam.

'Well, I'm not,' said Stargazer, 'but the assaulting of the orc's Hell Portal was an epic battle, common warriors would not even make it to the battlefield there. Plus, if he was there, he had survived throughout the entire Elf-Orc War, which was no easy task considering the devastation and intensity of the campaigns,' he said as if reading from a mental archive.

'It is perfectly possible that a wood elf would have taken part in that battle. It is, however, very, very unlikely.' Stargazer second guessed himself as he was clearly fixated on this clue. He knew instinctively that this fact mattered somehow for the understanding of that situation.

'That fact is noticeable because of how the elven society works and what I have acknowledged from my studies,' he continued. 'I have mostly read about the great wizards and warriors of the high houses of the moon elves and sun elves.' The wizard wandered after his own words.

'Could there be more divisions among the Elves than what outsiders would notice?' asked Hanam.

'Not exactly divisions,' Sahafira interceded. 'It is hard to explain their culture to outsiders,' she struggled. 'The elven kingdom or The Realm, as they call it, have been divided into three castes, or families, for thousands of years. The wood elves are the warrior clan, who guard the borders and are very physical. They have brown hair, brown eyes, darker skin, and very muscular bodies. The sun elves are the "worker" clan, they farm the Flow and are the ones with golden hair, light skin, and leaner bodies. Finally, there are the moon elves, the most powerful clan, they live in cities deep inside the elven realm. They are the ones who guard the Mana Vortexes. Those Mana Vortexes are used to keep the great dangers of the world away from their lands. They have black, purple, or even dark blue hair. They are the most ancient of them, and the most royal also. They are the descendants of the first elves and it is rare to see a moon elf outside the borders of their own domains.' She paused as if considering a final conclusion. 'They have rather different ways of living their existences, but they are all together for the purpose of defending themselves against any higher menace. They consider themselves as cousins. They are different, but intrinsically united as different colors in a colorful gem,' she managed to explain in her own gentle and inspired manner.

They all stood quiet for a time, reflecting peacefully over Sahafira's words.

'What now?' asked Stargazer, holding an answer to the question on the tip of his tongue.

'Will the king execute him?' asked Sahafira, worried.

'Probably,' said the wizard. 'The Barbarians are not really evil per se, but they do believe in redemption by blood, and by death,' he said.

'We need to do something!' she argued.

'Well, by what we saw and heard,' Stargazer pointed out, 'they have a lot to redeem. There were so many villages destroyed, so many lives lost over the centuries...and even if we could do something, I'm not sure we are in a position to negotiate his destiny.'

They went silent for a while, considering things in a completely different mood from the people around them. The camp was now a full-on celebration as an intense and passionate energy took over the place. Bastian and Lucien were completely drunk and were knuckle fighting the Barbarians for gold, and losing it. Klunk had caused a major crisis by starting a barbecue with one of the sacred beasts used to pull the heavy golden siege weapons. The three of them observed it all with a heavy heart. Finally, Hanam raised his head.

'My soul tells me that there are many things in balance in this matter. Things that are beyond our reach now,' he said, hesitatingly under the weight of the many things he was considering.

Sahafira and Stargazer noticed that there was an uncommon regretful tone in his voice.

'His destiny, it is not for us to decide,' Hanam said, revealing more of his face than he would normally do.

Even by the light of the Barbarians' fire and still half-covered by his hood, they saw that the depth of the hunchback's eyes was remote, as if he were reading deeper into an invisible reality.

'Not now,' he said, and the words of the healer's conclusion weighted so much, that they eased their consciences in a formidable way, and they all considered the deal closed and never talked about it again. Sahafira, however, kept her sorrow, and Stargazer kept thinking about the possibilities if the elf joined them.

Translation

The celebrations had quieted now. Most of the folks were either drunk, or sleeping, or both. The most vigorous enthusiasts were still chanting low-tone melancholic songs in the edges of the camp with their husky Barbarian voices.

Klunk was the only one still eating. He lively consumed huge chunks of roast wild hog while making loud noises with his inspired chewing of the soft, greasy meat. Every now and then he stopped biting and swallowing to methodically and thoroughly lick his finger one at a time. Although his hands and mouth were passionately occupied with his endless consumption, he kept his eyes fix over his friends. He would not turn his gaze away (not even for a second) while he attentively guarded Bastian and Lucien's mushroom wine-induced heavy sleep.

Ianckhan was away from the others. He was silently drinking and staring at the fire in a detached fire pit on the extreme border of their camp. His sincere and weathered eyes brightened, reflecting not only the firelight, but memories of rustic love and epic bravery. Clearly softened by some honey wine, his shoulders were leaned down a bit and he was struggling to keep his eyes opened.

'Strange,' said Stargazer while sitting by his side and helping him to stare at the fire.

The wizard was holding a drink and pretending he was drunk too, but the reality was that he had carefully chosen the right way, time, and place to start that conversation. Although his mind was intrigued by questions, he knew that he needed to be discreet and reserved on certain matters in particular.

'You know...' Stargazer pretended to take a sip, 'when the king said the Behemoth can be killed only by a..."Haskshemi with a sky sword," I had assumed it was Bastian,' he said.

He got no answer from the Barbarian, who continued to drink and stare at the fire.

'What Haskshemi mean?' he asked Ianckhan, faking informality.

'Foreigner,' said the Barbarian with a grave voice. 'Special foreigner,' he added with his heavy accent.

'Ah, I see,' said the wizard, as if he didn't care.

He took his time, during which he drunk many fake sips from his cup, waiting until he felt it was the right time. But immediately before Stargazer made his next question, Ianckhan fondled his beard with his fingers and led his head to the side while considering his own answer.

'Foreigner, but not from land,' he said, spontaneously deciding to explain himself better, 'from...above.' The old hunter was forcing his drunk brain into the conversation. He blinked slowly and heavily while trying to formulate his ideas.

'Like a spirit?' inquired the wizard, spitting in the fire and looking away while pretending disconnection and ignorance, but knowing exactly what he was looking for.

'No, not like spirit,' corrected Ianckhan. 'Not from this world. From…other side.' The Barbarian waved his hand in the air carelessly and unintelligently, trying to describe what he was failing to say. He gave up the gesturing soon after, for his mighty arms and austere mind were confused and weakened by the Barbarian's Strong Wine. He resumed his drinking and took another long sip, almost passing out before he could finish swallowing it.

'Hum,' Stargazer discreetly exclaimed. *Ele foi cuidadoso com sua voz, sendo alto o suficiente para manter Ianckhan acordado, porem preservando o segredo de suas intenções.* 'And what does Haskshemi Shastameni mean?' he pressed on.

'Foreigner that bring luck, bring light,' said Ianckhan chewing a piece of roasted wild chicken.

'Bring light?' asked Stargazer.

'Yes, like when children afraid darkness, we say a Haskshemi Shastameni come to save,' said the Barbarian.

'Like a…hero?' asked Stargazer.

'No, not like hero,' the Barbarian rejected the wizard's deduction.

He leaned his head down, closing his eyes slowly. Stargazer's eyes, though, were quite awake, running from side to side as his brain tried to process that information and make sense out of it. He knew now that he was running out of time, he had to formulate a question that would give him the answer he needed before the Barbarian collapsed in a heavy sleep.

'Like…Haskshemi,' Ianckhan added when he suddenly opened his eyes and bounced his head forward as if he had forgotten to tell Stargazer something.

That obviously didn't satisfy the wizard, who, disappointed, was about to leave the place to get himself some rest.

'Angel,' said the barbarian, waking from his delirium. 'Yes…like…angel,' he said, and finally gave in to sleep, ducking his head back and instantly starting to snore heavily.

Barbaric

'Take him now and throw him into the bottomless pit,' said the king.

'Nooo!' the elf cried with such a loud voice and deep despair that the king's great hall trembled over the reverberation of his anguish.

One of the king's guards hit Semereth in the back of his head. The violent blow brought him to his knees, but so vigorous was the elf, it failed to make him unconscious. Incredulous, the mighty Barbarian second-guessed his weapon and his hands.

Sahafira stepped forward but was held in place by Hanam's insurmountable arm. When he touched her, her heart calmed down a little, just enough she would not have them all killed. Hanam's touch made the angry words she had ready in her mouth dissolve in her mind like the morning mist in a hot day, and the rush of blood in her head flowed back to her legs as a quick summer shower.

'The rest of you may go to your fortunes,' said the thunderous king. 'We now know that the hand of destiny is with you,' he said, and his voice seemed to be coming from the very walls of his magnificent hall.

The Fellowship, however, had problems dealing with the king's decision. They all felt a bitter taste in their mouth for having to witness such a brutal sentence. It was a grueling feeling of impotency over what they felt was a great injustice. It took them a long time to stop resenting it, and a bitterness lingered in their tongues over it. For them, the execution of the clueless, and as far as they knew guiltless elf, felt more like a sacrifice to some tainted god of justice than what they would call a real pursuit of righteousness.

Later, reflecting on it, they concluded that on that occasion they had a taste of the true meaning of the word Barbaric. They lamented the excessive superstition and the lack of rational reflection in such decision, and became saddened thinking about what that sort of imposition (for them rather tyrannical) could bring to the individual – it was a cultural shock for them.

It was also not clear how much the king knew about magic and cursing, and how much he could understand what had happened. They as well considered what they didn't know about it too. Maybe the king knew or felt something that they did not. Plus, they were in no position to negotiate, and none of them were willing to risk his own death and the death of their friends.

They felt incredibly lucky to be leaving that place alive, but, still, a sense that a great injustice was being committed clouded their hearts.

There was indeed nothing that they could do, although Hanam had risked some words of mercy when presenting the prisoner at the king's presence. He knew that, at that moment, he had to make their hearts known to the king even if very lightly, so he could take hold of his companions. Because he knew that their youth, innocence, or heroism could get them killed easily. He saw that none, besides Stargazer, had seemed to have grasped the fragility of their position.

Stargazer was puzzled on how the king had been unbelievably merciful to them. That was very uncommon, however, he also knew that his favor could change in a blink of an eye, for the Barbarians were far more unstable on their moods than other folks, and they endowed circumstantial emotions far more than other "civilized" societies. They had all learned that the Barbarians were more gut than reason, trusting their instincts way more than their rational thoughts.

'We must do something,' said Sahafira while they were being conducted out of the king's hall. Her eyes were full of awe, as she could still see the look of despair on the elf's poor face. He was being taken in the opposite direction, under chains, escorted to a certain and cruel death.

'There is nothing we could do,' said Stargazer looking at Hanam in search of support, knowing that it was a risky moment.

'We cannot allow him to be condemned to such a destiny without a proper judgment,' said Bastian remorsefully.

'We just saw the Barbarian notion of a proper judgment,' insisted Stargazer, worried that they would all be killed.

'He will get killed like an animal and he is probably innocent,' said Sahafira, anguished.

'Even if his story was true, and he is indeed a victim of an ancient curse, we could do nothing to stop the sentence,' said Stargazer while walking, making sure none of the guards was listening to him.

'How they can be so cruel?' said Sahafira with tears in her eyes.

'The Barbarians have their own ways of feeling things, and they express themselves differently too,' Hanam tried to mitigate.

'Feelings?' Sahafira almost shouted.

Lucien and Stargazer apprehensively met a suspicious gaze coming from one of the guards of their escort. After noticing what she had done, she looked to the guard to read his reaction and then lowered her voice.

'How they could bring a life to an end without further consideration?' she said with much more control over her tone.

'Well,' started Stargazer staring at the nearest guard from the corner of his eyes, 'the elves and most of the civilized humans consider a lot of incidental factors when judging someone's crimes. The Barbarian don't. In their culture, the actions are much more relevant than other factors, like, for example, intentions. They believe in fate, they are a destiny race,' said Stargazer. 'This is how they are, and they had been like that for thousands of years. There is nothing we can do,' he said.

'Above all, we must not judge,' complemented Hanam. 'Remember, we are intruders here, and the king is no fool. There is much more than our eyes can see in him,' he said, nodding to Stargazer from his hood. 'He is entitled to many sensibilities that we are not. We should not retain ourselves in their matters. We must accept that he is the supreme overseer of his people's destiny, and of their land's justice,' he said as they went down the corridor leading to the main gate.

As they left the mountain, they were all quiet and weary. It was not a happy end at all. Their sense of security was completely erased, and they all now feared for their lives and their freedom as the realization that they were alone in their notion of justice in those lands sunk in. They were alone in their understandings of what was right and what was wrong, feeling isolated and oppressed as they were obliged to comply with the will of that king. To kill a monster or an evil doer on the battlefield was one thing, but to forcefully comply with an injustice execution was another. They understood that the frontiers of their worlds were narrow and that there were differences out there, however, to experience such realities in first-hand corroded some of their hopes and dreams, making their world forever grayer – a foreign land indeed.

An Improbable, Lonely, and Harmonious Chant in the Heart of an Empty World

From nothing, his mind was awakened into awareness.

Normally, when a consciousness is awakened, it resumes from its last memory. From there, it instantly travels back in time to further and further past memories, setting up the conjunction of information that forms what many call "personality," "identity" or "the self."

In this man's case, however, there was nothing. There was not even the idea of a remembrance to come back to. There was not even a shadow of a self in him, or a single drop of a cultural north – nothing.

In the beginning, his mind just stood there, suspended in his brain, in silence, pure and neutral, not willing to manifest itself. Then, an urge to overrule this first reaction started to push him into expanding his problems.

After that, he realized that there was no direction to go. There was no way to restart because his cognizance was empty of all references. He was nothing more than an instinct suspended in infinite nothingness – an awareness falling forever.

As his mind was not an option, he was naturally forced to take hold of his body, and the slow and progressive process of accepting to sense the world around him felt like a reincarnation. Once again, everything was a first, and, although some things felt familiar to some extent, all things were alien and strange.

As he was being reborn with an adult mind, he was pressed into the long way through the re-acknowledgment of the flesh wrapped around his conscience.

His mind was so alone and detached from his body, and in such a unique state of existence, that a long time before he could even establish he didn't know who he was, he had to realize WHAT he was.

As his mind was slowly expanding and taking control of his senses, he slowly felt the earthy, clingy, sandy clay in which his abdomen, torso, arms, and head were glued on.

It felt like he was trapped in an enormous mold, and he could not grasp any sense of direction. For a second, some nausea kicked in, and it appeared that the earth was crushing him, pressing its weight over his lungs.

After sensing his "trap" over his upper body, he found strange that he was not feeling much from the hip down. As his hearing was coming back, he heard a light swell of running water. And, upon feeling a minor pressure over his ribs caused by a variation in drag, he knew his legs were underwater. He then remembered water, and how it felt. Then, he understood weightlessness once again and comprehended a little more about the world he was in.

As he continued his embodiment, he started feeling his face against the strange mix of fine sand and soft clay that framed his face and composed the dark beach his body lay upon.

The first thing he tried to move was his fingers. Since his hands were buried in both halves, he still felt how incredibly soft and silky the soil was. Like a child, he played with his fingers, feeling the textures and learning the consistency. It felt good, although it seemed he had never used his hands before. In fact, he felt he couldn't even remember what it was like to have hands and fingers.

As more of his senses came back, he felt the same novelty for every single function of his body. Gradually, slowly, and one by one, he took control of his muscles and joints.

Slowly he unplugged himself from the earth, raising his muscular torso from the ground. His arms followed, and, abruptly, he brought his hand over his head instinctively, trying to contain a sharp pain that trailed through it like a lightning bolt made of blunt razors. He had no option but to stay there and take it. And he did. And it hurt badly.

When it was bearable to do anything else, he got his legs out of the water and tried to open his eyes. He failed. Then, as a blind man, he started to fumble his way out of there, wherever "there" was. With no distinctive direction where to go, and answering to sheer impulse, he crawled in the opposite direction of the body of water he had emerged from.

When he was just a few yards out of the water, he noticed a pale ghostly radiance coming from ahead. He stopped, fighting the sharp pain in his eyes that came and went from his head.

Initially, he thought that his vision was coming back, but then he noticed that his eyes were already open and that they had been so for a while now, but he did not remember when and how he opened them.

The light grew little in shine and still seemed timid at that distance, as if oppressed by the darkness around it. He sat there and studied it with sincere interest, even though he couldn't remember if he had ever seen anything like it. After a while, he continued to crawl until he got close to it.

When he was within arm's reach from it, he stopped to look at the gleam again. The object from which the light was coming from was metallic in texture and slightly rectangular in form. Its curves were polished and had strange and zestful shapes. It was small as a thumb, and it appeared to be suspended in the air at hip-high.

There was a manifested noise pulsing from it that propagated through the dark air like a living radiation. The air that surrounded it vibrated in its rhythm, creating a subtle wind turbulence that spread at its own speed. When he was by the water, he thought it could be some sound from the environment itself, but when he approached the light and had distanced himself from the watery roar of the river, he noticed that the ghostly object was, in fact, emitting it.

The noise was somehow connected to the light and they both were being oozed in synchrony. He could not explain it, but after observing the delicate waves that came out of it, he felt that both the light and the noise were alive together, manifesting themselves simultaneously in front of him.

Hypnotized by its uniqueness, he marveled at the fact that there was a growing, dancing harmony in it. The more he minded it, the more the theme made sense to him, and after some time, it seemed as if the object's singing was partaking the innermost corners of his being.

That was not, however, a selfish commanding song. It was a chant of forgotten glory and new hope. It was a magic tune that spoke directly to his spirit, carrying a poetry loaded with much more than words and melodies. It was completely external to him in relation to its source, but perfectly adequate in content in relation to what he needed to hear.

He could only resist for some time before he reached and touched the object. When he did so, he realized it was warm and not cold as one could expect of something made of metal. He could feel it was, in fact, physically vibrating to the tune, and, instantly, a warm feeling took over his whole body and his health was immediately improved with a wave of heartfelt joy and goodwill that deliciously flowed through him. His head was healed and all of his aches and nausea vanished, even the ones he was not even conscious of.

The light unexpectedly intensified with a micro-explosion of a high-pitch note. Scared, he jumped behind in horror of what the darkness kept from his eyes. A skeleton of a man-like creature stood right in front of him. It took him a few minutes to slow down his heart and realize that whoever or whatever that was, it was long dead. The creature was humanoid, but its bones were strange. It was dressed in what used to be fine clothes, and it was holding a beautiful sword in its hands. Only now he saw that the rectangular piece of metal that was emitting light was, in fact, the pommel of the sword, and the whole weapon was shining now. The radiation was so potent, that the fluid glitter from the blade was overflowing the sheath, and the faint nuance that was being emitted earlier was now a loud and clear note. He felt that in its echoey predetermined geometrical language, the object was clearly making itself present, revealing itself to him.

He stood there, captivated by the spellbinding music, ignoring the dead body, the dark suffocating cave around him, his total absence of reference, and everything else related to his situation. His amnesia-induced innocence brought him to a state of profound fascination over the subtle beauty of the blade's melody. He stood there, just a pair of engrossed eyes over a dirty face, a mind in the middle, all forgotten in the depths of an unknown reality as the sword sang for him, sang in him.

Kestos' Lair

As soon as they left the mountain of the Phoenix Tribe, they headed for the round hill, near the canyons, exactly where they were initially captured by the Barbarians several days ago.

To their frustration, when they reached the plateau, they saw that the immense rock was still blocking the entrance to the cave as before. The king's guards told them before they left to camp there and wait.

There was no smile, music, or celebration that night. The Fellowship set up camp and went to sleep. Around midnight, during Bastian's watch, he saw an orange light coming from the top of the mountain where the king's hall was.

Initially, he got scared, think it was a volcanic eruption, but then he dismissed the idea for there was no earthquake or roar. The light went straight up with furious acceleration, illuminating the clouds that were hidden under the cover of the darkness. Its light spread for tens of miles in all directions, literally turning night into day. As everything in the visible horizon became clear as midday, Bastian could see the flocks of birds waking up from their sleep and flying away in fearful confusion for miles and miles all the way until the mountain and beyond. One by one, they also woke up.

After the light went up above the clouds, it came straight into their direction, crossed high above their head, and disappeared through the blind angle of the rock cover above them. The light intensified its glow over their camp until its reflection on everything around them was barely bearable and they were all protecting their eyes from it with their arms and hands.

It was a fascinating light, full of grace and song. It was immensely shinning and multiform, it shimmered with many tonalities of white, light yellow, and a soft, unique orange. The intensifying light floated in the air as if it was persistently keeping separated from it, dancing around them like a living golden cloud. Surprisingly, they all became happy with its presence, feeling safe and, above all, inspired.

Stargazer noticed that the few magical objects they were carrying were affected by it, activating by themselves and increasing the pulse of their output while the source of that light approached the rock ceiling above their heads.

Shortly after the intensity of the light reached its apex, partially blinding them, they started hearing the beat of gargantuan wings mixed with the sound of trees being ripped off from the ground with their roots and all and flying away and falling all around them. Then, they heard and felt a tremendous noise that shook the land beneath their feet and everything else up and around them. Contradictorily, a comforting heat hit their skin.

Gently, but purposely, a giant golden bright claw with talons as big as Klunk appeared from behind the rock ceiling. The very way how it moved was dream-like, a vision from another world, difficult to accurately keep in memory or represent it with words. It grabbed the rock that was blocking the entrance of the cave. Magnificent creaks and sharp breaking sounds made them all deaf and actionless, and they feared the rock wall above them would fall onto their heads and bury them alive. The adventurers started looking for cover and dodge the falling boulders as they crashed around them. When the boulder that sealed the cave was removed, a dark tunnel was revealed.

'Now!' shouted Stargazer. 'Into the cave!' he was as loud and imperative as he could, for he understood what was going on.

Willing to avoid the raining stones that were pouring around them, and deprived of alternatives, the adventurers ran into the darkness of Kestos's Lair.

338

Once inside of it, they ran until the limit of the light, grouping in a corner under a low slab.

'Where is the wizard?!' shouted Hanam trying to top the deafening sound of the falling everything.

Before anyone could answer him, the giant boulder was returned into position by the mystical claws, sealing the cave entrance again and leaving them in complete darkness.

When the world stopped shaking and the rocks stopped rolling down the walls, they started to light their oil lanterns. After they had lightened the first one, and were trying to light two more with their trembling hands, an intense light illuminated the whole cave. It was Stargazer.

He appeared out of nowhere, and his magic seemed stronger and easier than ever. His mood was different from theirs too, for he was the only one who didn't look ruffled by what just happened. Instead, he was walking decisively and boldly while approaching the others.

Sahafira had the impression she saw the orange light from before faintly shining upon the wizard's eyes and the fingertips of his right hand. She looked at Hanam to check if he noticed it too, but she found nothing on him but a careful hesitation.

The wizard picked a rock from the ground and mindlessly enchanted it with light, passing it to Lucien, who looked at it puzzled.

Klunk projected his face in front of it, watching the stone, thrilled like a child with a new toy. Seen that, Stargazer touched Klunk's nose, lightening it up with his magic. Startled, Klunk immediately tried to get rid of it, rubbing it so vigorously he lost his balance and fell, tripping over himself. Stargazer smiled.

'What was that?' asked Lucien, still disturbed by what just happened.

'I don't know,' said Hanam. 'But it made the king's words true.'

'Was it a...Phoenix...bird?' asked Bastian, stumbling over his own words, clearly uncomfortable navigating such subject.

'Probably,' said Stargazer with an uncontrollable smile on his face. 'Almost certainly,' he said, and his eyes shone as he could not refrain the enthusiasm inside of him.

Sahafira had her gaze straight at the wizard, scrutinizing his every expression. She was surprised at the thought that maybe Stargazer was not sharing everything he knew or did with them. Suspicious thoughts were popping on her mind. Thoughts, that whispered to her that, maybe, the human was not to be trusted after all.

'I did never imagine it so beautiful.' Sahafira purposely changed the subject, willing to fish something from his answer/reaction.

'Yeah, right?' Stargazer gladly agreed. His happiness was so out of place that it even caught Lucien's and Bastian's attention.

'Come, we've got work to do,' said Hanam, discerning the situation and preemptively defusing any problem before they even manifested.

It took no time for their confusion, suspicion, and happiness to die off inside the tunnels, for the atmosphere inside them was oppressive, the air was full of old, filthy things and death was everywhere.

After cruising a large lake of rubble and dust, they reached a flat ground made of stone blocks with walls built in similar fashion. The architecture was unfamiliar to them, but the tunnel dimensions were impressive. With at least thirty yards large and twenty yards high, the tunnel was big enough to move an army of giants through it.

They found old torches in the walls and tried to use them to light their way in, but Stargazer insisted on the use of his magic, which was particularly plentiful that day, generating more than enough light for them to navigate safely.

As they progressed, they had discovered that the place was, in fact, an ancient mine, modified to hide Kestos's legions, war parties, and who knew what else. It had an endless continual broad corridor with side entrances for larger rooms. Some were carved in brute rock, others were more elaborate, built with a running water system and septic tanks. The rooms were large as storehouses, diverse in design and function. They were populated by a variety of huts decorated with many emblems of different sizes, shapes, and materials. Clearly, Kestos had faced the necessity to separate their multi-raced troops and mercenaries. He probably learned that one cannot mix orcs from different tribes without having them fighting each other the whole time, and that the hobgoblin mercenaries are far more demanding about the quality of their installations than hill goblins.

As they went deeper and deeper, exploring the never-ending galleries, they slowly started to understand Kestos's schemes. The first rooms had probably lodged the goblins. There were hundreds of them as there used to be thousands of those creatures under the wizard's command. Unfortunately, the chambers still smelled of goblins even now.

After that, came the livestock and pack animals chambers, then the hill giants, then the orcs (divided by tribe, of course), and so forth. The more they advanced inside the mine, the more the chambers improved in quality and in odor.

The Dragoness emblem was everywhere, and by the number of facilities and preparations that were being built there, whatever Kestos' actions had been up to the moment of his defeat, they clearly represented only the beginning of what he really planned to do. By the sheer size of the infrastructure found there, it was clear that the wizard was projecting to bring the war to the entire western portion of the empire.

Eventually, they got tired of investigating the huge forges, countless deposits, and piles of the incomplete works that lay around the tunnels.

'I think I have figured out Kestos' guerrilla tactics,' started Stargazer, breaking the dark silence of the tunnels. 'Somehow he obtained all this complex and detailed maps of the Underworld beneath the Dire Woods, he would then direct his forces through access tunnels in perfect secrecy, striking suddenly the Valkarian border whenever he pleased,' he talked while they explored.

'By what I can understand from the instructions and orders we have found,' he continued, 'his retract point was the entrance cave from which we came. Purposely far away from the empire's trackers and rangers,' the wizard deducted. 'By the means of his surprise attacks and by denying his opponents of a hard target for a possible decisive blow, he left the Valkarian leaders apprehensive, causing them to move when they shouldn't and, in this way, keeping the initiative to himself. The commanders here were reluctant to send more troops to the North, weakening the Emperor's position,' he said. 'He was a good tactician, but this strategy was clearly designed and established by his boss in the North,' he said.

'Without the Dragoness' support, he was nothing but an overrated mercenary,' ranted Bastian.

'I don't know about that, Bastian,' said Stargazer diplomatically. 'He got some proper magic training in Mezaron. Plus, he spent many years adventuring in the dangerous northlands,' said the wizard.

'Regarding his works here,' he continued, showing a deep knowledge of the local history, 'he was advised and helped by some very experienced taskmasters, spies, and much worse things sent by Xshisrahil.

'One thing is certain, he is no fool.' Stargazer nodded.

'Was,' corrected Bastian.

Stargazer said nothing.

'What?' Lucien asked Hanam suddenly, surprised by the hunchback's abrupt apprehension.

Everybody stopped and looked at both of them. The hunchback was completely immovable and was looking up to a corner of the tunnel's high ceiling.

'What?!' Lucien asked again.

Still no answer from the Hunchback. They all started drawing their weapons silently.

'A shadow,' Hanam finally said. 'Up there, in the darkness,' he whispered uncertain as he pointed up in the direction of the left corner that conducted to a large gallery to their left.

Stargazer shot a small ball of light in the direction Hanam was pointing. When the fast, spinning spark hit the wall the whole area was flooded by a bright light. Their anxious eyes, however, found nothing but empty space and flustered dust.

Lucien frowned at Hanam while everyone else lowered their guard and continued to explore. From then on, however, they all kept their weapons drawn, ready.

The more they spent time there, the more they found strange things that they could not understand the purpose of or explain the intricacies. One thing was sure, none of them could clarify what had really happened to Kestos and the remaining of his troops. In fact, they had more questions on their minds now than they did before venturing in those dark tunnels. With the exception of an occasional hungry troll lurking in the dark here and there, they had found no one and no trace of what transpired there. After they had killed and burned the trolls as they progressed, they sensed the air getting colder and an odd sensation was growing in their guts. At the pace of some evermore certain but yet unknown remaining evil, an uncommon fear crawled through their stomachs as they got deeper and deeper into the caves. At some point, exhausted by the constant tension of their search and the weariness their attention suffered from the unheard echoes of past foulness, they felt the need to rest for a bit more than the usual six hours of sleep they would normally allow themselves. With that in mind, they selected a room built within the main tunnel that was next to a sort of rampart pass. It had a thick lockable oak door that was plentifully reinforced with iron, and, most importantly, it smelled better than the other places they had found so far. It was reasonably furnished with a large table with some benches, a few large chairs and a small rack with some books and scrolls still on it.

They all accommodated themselves around the table. Stargazer went directly to the rack and started to analyze its contents. With a casual pointing of his finger, he magically lighted an oil lamp without even looking at it and brought on the magical wind he always summoned to remove the dust from surfaces and to take away any malicious odor from the air. The lamp was over his head on the right side of the wall, when it was lit, it lit up the whole room.

Lucien and Bastian sited on the bench. Lucien pulled a little bottle of Barbarian's Strong Wine, sipped from it, and offered it to Bastian.

'Still?' Bastian asked, wondering how Lucien managed to stretch the bottle this far.

Lucien ignored his question and Bastian said no to the wine with his hand. Lucien took another sip, put the bottle in his pocket, and started to lose his armor's belts.

Klunk and Sahafira leaned against the wall close to the small fireplace. They were getting more and more affiliated as Klunk sympathized a lot with the ways of her gentle dispositions. When she put her legs up and stretched them on the ways of the elves, he comically imitated her and almost broke the ceiling.

Hanam was tenser than they had ever seen him be. He guarded the door immediately after the last one of them entered. He locked it, blocked it, and spent the torch next to it. In silence, he stood guard there, listening to the darkness outside.

For a moment he thought he saw the same shadow from before, lingering in the dark next to the ceiling. This time, however, he took his time to study it. For a moment he thought he saw two red eyes looking into his direction.

'Stargazer,' he muttered.

Nobody answered.

'Stargazer,' he muttered again.

Sahafira raised her head.

When the wizard finally agreed to spare a second from his readings and regretfully looked at the hunchback to see what he wanted, he found Hanam pointing to the oil lamp above him and making the universal sign of decapitation.

'Lights,' the hunchback hurried him.

Grumpy for being interrupted and using only half of his attention, the wizard made a casual arch with his hands while immediately returning to his analysis of the books and scrolls he found. Before his finger completed the arch he established for it in the air and landed once more on the page of the large tome he was reading, the amount of light that the lamp was emitting decreased drastically to no more than a faint glimmer.

Once the light was low, Hanam looked again to where he thought he had seen the movement, but the shadow was now gone. Unconvinced, he stood there, watching and wondering what it was.

'Stargazer,' said Bastian, trying to keep it down.

Irritated with another interruption, the wizard looked at Bastian blinking and strained. Bastian pointed to the table and excused himself with a half-smile. Stargazer waved his left hand and a delicious buffet materialized on the table and Sahafira couldn't help notice how the powers of the young human were growing admirably out of his impetus' momentum alone.

Bastian, Lucien, and Klunk took places over the table and attacked the feast with great speed and agility, diving over the large portions of exquisite stews of many varieties, the mounds of incredibly soft steaks, the piles of grilled turkey, into the baked pig that was surrounded by caramelized fruit and pyramids of bacon-wrapped potatoes, and the entire collections of creamy chicken pies, the dozens of enormous loaves of freshly baked bread of all kinds, through the oversized wheels of the yummiest, sharpest cheese, among the arrangements of chocolate-covered fruits stacked by the dozen, amidst the heaps of apple and lemon pies filled with cream, and much more.

'That's a spell you aught learn, woman,' Lucien tempted Sahafira, pointing a half-eaten turkey leg to her while speaking with a half-full mouth.

Bastian laughed and hid his face in shame for finding Lucien's joke funny. Before she could answer it, Stargazer magically vanished the food in the center of the table and dropped a large map over it. Bastian and Lucien, already accustomed to the wizard's ways, managed to quickly save a few of their favorites from Stargazer's dispelling.

'OK, listen up,' said the wizard gathering them around. 'Apparently, I have finally found some plans of these facilities and a few trustworthy maps,' he said still reading the tomes and scrolls in front of him.

'OK, by my calculations we are no more than three hours of his personal quarters,' said Stargazer. 'So let us rest well now, and push for it tomorrow,' he said, but he couldn't hide his concerns.

They all noticed it.

'What?' asked Sahafira.

'I've got good news, but also bad ones,' he sighed.

'The good ones first, please,' said Lucien, overburdened but still sarcastic.

'Some of this place's exits are relatively close from the empire border, so there are pathways with the potential to take us home,' he said, and the concern from before was still on his face.

Sahafira's eyes lost their brightness and they could see from the visible part of her face that she paled. She knew exactly what the wizard was about to say. Bastian became terribly worried when he saw her expression. Lucien followed when he noticed Bastian's.

'What about the bad news then?' Lucien pressed, incapable of masking the anxiety in his voice.

'The bad news is how we access those exits,' said Stargazer, swallowing dry.

Sahafira closed her eyes and faced away, as if not willing to listen to what she already knew he would say.

'And how is that?' Lucien asked, struggling as he forced out a sarcastic laughter.

'Through the Underworld,' said the magician, quivering, and their faces paled.

Strange Hands

When he felt his heart's courage returning, he went for the sword. After raising his hands, he immediately retracted them. Illuminated by the new light, he could see them clearly now. They scared him.

He stared at them fiercely, but he couldn't bring himself to recognize his own hands. He thought they had a strange aspect, seemingly alien and irreconcilably unfamiliar under the blade's nimble light.

By inspecting them, he reckoned that they had robust tendons and solid bones, and were also very muscular and exceedingly strong. The skin was olive-colored and was still suntanned. He had no memory, but he was no fool either. He remembered the sun and connected some dots there.

It took a while for him to accustom himself, seeing them every time he reached for something. After observing them during long moments of reflection in which he would not trust his reality, he decided that he had to work with them for now, and, forcibly, he made a temporary peace with his innermost instincts. Nevertheless, a bitter distrust and a sense of wholesome unfitness grew in his heart, and, with it, fear and anxiety dibbled their seeds in him.

As if remembering or realizing (he couldn't tell) the precariousness of his condition, he leaned back and looked around. The light from the sword returned just enough for him to form an idea about his surroundings. He took his mind off the sword and the corps for the first time as he stood up and looked around. The cave he found himself into was colorless, outlandish, hell-like. The distortions of the undisturbed underground location where he was were radically different from anything else. And although he had no memory of what else was, he instinctively repelled the overall appearance of that place, repulsing its alien aspect and its suffocating confining features.

The ceiling was low, barely enough for him to stand up, and there was no apparent exit but the waters' cave. It was not more than a bubble of air inside a rock holding a forgotten beach. The grotto seemed designed to make one claustrophobic, and its general grayness and lifelessness gave it a tomb-like aspect. So much so that even he, someone who did not remember being anywhere else, still felt oppressed by that place.

When he had enough of it, he turned his attention to the skeleton that was leaning against the rock. The most noticeable legacy of the deceased was that it was still firmly gripping the sword's sheath, making it stand straight in the air like a cedar tree. The way the mummified, bony, and unusually small hand was strapped tightly around the sheath, revealed how the blade's wielder must have pressed it tightly till its very last breath.

Where, how, when, and why this swordsman came to be there, was something that puzzled him greatly, but it also gave him hope. He felt that at least now, in some illogical way, he was no longer alone. And, as morbid as the cadaver looked, and as present the terrible struggles of death still made themselves real in the carcass's gruesome details, to him, that corpse was a token of release in the absolute desert of nullities he woke in. It was a sign of some sort, a reference, a starting point – something at last.

Intrigued, he analyzed the remains carefully. The more he did it, however, the more everything about it became a mystery to him.

The first thing that caught his attention was that the bones and part of the skin crystallized, turning into stones like the bones of ancient creatures in dry valleys, notwithstanding the cave was very humid.

The second thing was that even though everything pointed to the fact that the remains were there for a long time, a few of the objects were not damaged or spoiled by time or weather or a combination of both. Some disintegrated when he tried to handle them, others instead were unbelievably untouched, even by dust. The sword in particular looked distinctively polished, as if its perennial vibrating undertone repelled all particles but the ones of its own composition. The difference between the preserved and the dilapidated artifacts had such a contrast, that he quickly identified the items that were intact and still useful, setting them apart and ditching the others. From the serviceable things, he found an armored battle belt, a set of reinforced fighting armbands, a gold collar with a clear emerald as big as a cherry, a few beautiful rings, and a leather bag that was in perfect condition.

After he carefully displayed the items by the shadow of the sword light in a crude organizational manner, the brightness of its light intensified as if she was motivating him to investigate the items.

When he handled the leather bag, he felt that it was packed, and decided to take a look at its contents first. After opening the retention strap, he inserted his hand into it. By groping with his fingertips, he noticed that there were several tiny objects inside the bag. For its size and its great diversity of shape and texture, he first thought it was a bag of mixed candy, but when he pulled out one of the mushy little bags by grabbing one with his fingertips, and the tiny object reached the leather bag entrance, it became heavy and increased greatly its size. The little package felt like it was as big as a grape when inside the bag, outside though, it manifested in its original dimensions, growing until it weighted no less than fifty pounds. To his surprise, it was a sackcloth full of provisions of an abundant variety and fresh and wonderfully tasty. He put the sack back in the bag and counted the others with his fingertips, calculating that there was enough to plenty. The smell of the food made him hungry and he took one of the sacks out of the leather bag again and, after a very brief analysis, he consumed a great quantity of it. He ate as he had never eaten before, but even then he could not remember.

The food, in regarding its content, flavor, and recipes, looked like it belonged to a different era of the world. He somehow felt that something about it was out of place as if it did not fit the air around it. The food made him wonderfully full, for it was plentiful and everything was very nourishing. He ate with pleasure but in terrible silence and awkwardness, for the place was oppressive and the company gloomy. When he was done, he felt direly odd to have that kind of need fulfilled that way in such an unfit place. Even an amnesiac mind like his could understand that and he felt desperately compelled to leave.

He geared himself up with the items he collected and left the riverbank, using the sword's strange light to guide his way. He examined the walls more closely and found a small passage behind a rock. The ground was still freshly revolved around the passage, and from the drier hue of the earth around the opening he deduced that it had been opened recently, probably by some sort of landslide. When he got closer, he felt an airflow coming from it. He figured out that if the air could come in and out, so could he.

When leaning on the rocky archway of the entrance to jump over the small pile of rubble on the floor, he saw his hand on the cave's wall and hesitated for a second. He then looked behind, and saw that there was nothing to stay for. He looked ahead, to the dark tunnel, and feared there was nowhere to go.

He inspected the hand on the wall one more time. He couldn't recognize it still. He then decided to use it to hold the long hilt of the sword. He gazed at the dark and drew it. The beautiful, untainted blade sung a crispy melody of steel through the air. Its light took possession of the spaces around him, subduing every shadow. It was then when something inside of him spawned the courage to move on. It was a crude and strong instinct, a simultaneous urge to do and a need to be. It was a senseless confidence born from oblivion. Renewed and encouraged by it, he fed on the energy of the weapon until his eyes glistened with it. He stepped inside the tunnel and pushed ahead. The sword's light lit his way.

Bits and Pieces

Beside Klunk, who slept the whole "night" for he could not be trusted to watch, all of them had watched through one candle each. When their resting was done, they ate breakfast and raised camp. They knew they had a decisive day in front of them, and although they kept silent about it, they could feel it in the air that something was imminent.

When they returned to the tunnels, they were impressed (and a little scared) by what they started to see. As they approached the wizard's deepest, most laborious installations, they began to discover his most secret activities. The number of preparations, the industrialization of the whole process, and the size of the raw material stocks they found led them to believe that the magician planned to transform his guerrilla war into an open war shortly before his disappearance.

By the projected number of siege weapons alone, they glimpsed the wizard's ambitions. Bastian understood now why his father had sacrificed himself in the risky and necessary mission of finding and attacking Kestos's Lair. If the wizard was given more time, he would develop a force of such agility and shock power that he would certainly be able to destroy all the small to medium-size cities in the region, completely isolating Westgate eventually. The loss of life would be unbearable, and even if he wasn't sure of how much his father knew about it, it was a calculated assumption that they were at least suspicious that, by the wizard's growing power and daring, he would finally try something like that.

Watching the endless production lines of weapons, Bastian received a new understanding of things past in his life, things he took as unmovable, but were now placed in a different perspective by a crushing reality. He could now almost feel the sense of urgency around the need for stopping Kestos. Not out of self-interest, however, but out of becoming even more inspired by the higher greatness of his father's sense of duty, patriotism, and heroism in the face of certain death. He learned how heavy were the chains of true sacrifice, of his father's sacrifice. He was terribly surprised when he finally received that the feelings of the men from the battalion that marched against the wizard were not light by the opportunity to achieve glory, but rather burdensome with the weight of their responsibilities to others. Bastian now realized that the men knew that it was the wrong decision to come to the forest, but they came willingly anyway. They gave everything away, defending their beloved with their very lives. And now, it was up to him, and by facing that, he understood that the life of a true warrior is indeed fought to the last drop of blood.

It is not about a sword, but mostly a shield. It is not a liberation, it is servitude, he reckoned in his heart.

He was thinking about it while looking down when he felt a hand on his shoulder. It was Lucien. When Bastian looked at him, he pointed at the great wall in front of them. The whole wall was filled with hundreds of short chains that ended in small shackles. Still strapped to the shackles in horrid convulsive poses, hundreds of small, dusty skeletons laid against the wall, and the ground was littered with numerous piles of tiny bones. By the colorful clothing and the stature of the figures, Bastian thought they were children. He was so horrified that he stopped as his heart sank.

'Gnomes,' said Sahafira, guessing the look in his eyes. 'Specialists enslaved, sequestrated, and brought here to work for the wizard. Probably to "help" with the magical siege weapons.' She allowed herself to touch his shoulder gently to encourage him to move on.

'They got dwarf prisoners too,' said Stargazer, dusting off a skeleton's leather cap revealing dwarf runes. 'From the North,' he added. 'High north,' he added more.

'How were they brought here?' asked Lucien.

No one answered.

Passing the mines, they reached the work pits and then the forges. Finally, they arrived at the labs and the enchanting areas. Now guided by Stargazer, they entered into a larger room with a bronze altar in the middle. The altar was as big as a barn and was full of inscriptions and symbols of high geometry around large jewels embedded in its metal.

'Bastian, Lucien, take the gems from the altar,' Stargazer asked. 'They might worth something,' he said.

'That's an emerald,' said Lucien. 'You bet it will worth something,' he said, eagerly drawing his knife and going to work on it.

Beside the altar were a large amount of siege weapon projectiles. There were many kinds and they all looked of excellent quality. Stargazer pointed out

350

that most were magically enhanced and that the altar was part of a mechanism for enchanting them in mass.

'Such things were not built by a fool,' he said while examining one of the projectiles.

'Neither by a poor man,' added Sahafira. 'A very powerful energy fountain is needed to do this,' she said looking at the wizard. They both nodded in agreement.

As they examined the facilities further, Stargazer's attention was unexpectedly drawn by a heavy and aggressive ballista missile made with a surprisingly light black metal. It had a glass container imbued in its head with a pale purple light pulsing from its interior. The wizard picked as much as he could and strapped them to Klunk's backpack.

'For later,' he said. 'You never know.'

When they were about to leave the place, Stargazer stopped in front of a very large and deep wood wardrobe as if struck by a sudden suspicion. He used a shaft of one of the inactivated weapons to bust the old rusty padlock. Inside of it, he found hundreds of half-pint sized glass containers with the same pale purple pulse inside of them.

'OK, let's take those too. They will be quite useful. Make sure you have some on your belt too.'

'What are those?' asked Hanam.

'A powerful class of Dwarf Grenades,' said Sahafira.

'Yes, but these are improved by magic,' said Stargazer. 'Make sure you throw these far from you. I can sense a lot of destructive power flowing from them,' the wizard warned them.

'They have a type of chemical gas that only the dwarfs know how to mine and brew, but this one is much more powerful, and can receive extra enchants too. The glass is thick, so it won't be breaking even if you drop them, you need to throw them really hard,' said the wizard.

In their exploration of the area, they collected many other types of grenades, enchant runes, weaponized scrolls, and a variety of other items still lingering around. Because of this plentiful loot, they now advanced carefully, investigating every corner for valuables. The more they did, the more they found. Most of what they found were things that only Stargazer praised as having some worth, but as they learned to respect the wizard's knowledgeable mind, they put in their pockets, backpacks, and magical sacks everything he pointed them to, trusting the wizard would provide a future advantage for them.

Hanam was quiet and watchful. Little interested in all of that, always standing next to the door when they entered a room. Worried, he kept a ready stance the whole time, and his apprehension did not pass unnoticed by the wizard.

'What's the matter, Hanam?' asked Stargazer in a reserved manner.

Sahafira kept a discreet and distant attention to their conversation.

'We are being followed,' Hanam said directly and quietly to Stargazer.

'By who?' Stargazer asked.

'By who or by what, I don't know. But we are being followed since we have entered these chambers,' he said, looking bleak.

'Let us all keep both our eyes open then,' the wizard said, trying to bring some comfort to the hunchback. It didn't work.

As they got closer and closer to Kestos's chambers, there were much more things to see and collect. Moved by the incredible treasures they were finding here and there, they agreed that they needed to cover all the chambers they found and cover them well. They were not missing a thing, and although they were ultimately looking for the orb, they happily gathered all the gold and magic they could find and take with them.

'Maybe there is something here,' said Stargazer while increasing, with a wave of his hand, the potency of the light emanated from the magical light crystal he had found a few hours ago.

He wrapped it around his forehead with a piece of cloth and another one in the tip of his staff and sealed both with magic. His "staff" was improvised out of the best bolt shafts he found. He removed the fins and used it upside down, with the sharp side of it pointing to the ground. It was a little too big for a quarterstaff and made of a rare magic wood (the main reason why Stargazer chose it). It was light, strong, and incredibly susceptible to magic enchants. The spear point had a broad and razor-sharp blade made of some light elven alloy, although it was clearly forged by dwarves. On its other end, it had a metallic space for a Dwarf Grenade, it was there where he set the light crystal. He made a few field modifications and casting a handful of minor enchantments, and it was enough to turn it into a useful wizard's tool. In the end, he became proud with the result of his customization and it was happy how it worked just fine for him.

'Oh yeah, Iron Golems,' Stargazer smiled like a child in a toy shop he had never been to as they entered an entirely different room.

The light of his staff illuminated the room which was big enough to host an entire production line of enormous metal statues as large as Klunk. The place was packed with machinery, ritual altars, ore ingots, spent forges, tools, and parts. Like many of the rooms they searched before, this one looked suddenly abandoned and full of half-finished things and processes. Unfinished golems laid all around them, many were missing arms, legs, and heads.

'Are these automaton?' asked Bastian. 'I mean, like the famous Dwarf Steel Warriors?' he said curiously.

'Kind of,' answered Stargazer. 'They are tough and hard to kill. One or two of these would probably be enough to defeat us,' he said as he checked the runes on the mechanism inside one of the incomplete metal statues.

'Well, let us hope they stay quiet then,' said Bastian.

Precisely when Bastian finished his sentence, they all jumped into the air crazy scared by the sound of a metal arm falling to the ground. When they looked up, they saw a line of arms like that one hanging on the wall next to a few high windows. The line of arms was still swinging, and one of the windows was open, but there was no wind there. Lucien looked to Bastian with a scold grim. Bastian noticed that Lucien's hand was already on the hilt of the sword and, even without understanding what was going on, he grabbed his own.

'Stop abusing our luck, boy,' said Lucien.

'What have I done?' asked Bastian, unhappy with the blame Lucien was attributing him, 'and it is not like some of them can came to life to fight us, right?'

As before, immediately after Bastian said this, the eyes of three of the Iron Golems shone with a yellow light that quickly turned to blood red. One was very close to the only exit door and when he got up, animated by some invisible magic, his first action was to hit the door with his leg, closing it.

'You…' With a lot of anger in his grim, Lucien drew his sword and advanced in Bastian's direction. He charged in with such a momentum, that he confused Bastian into a reactionless state. For a second, Bastian thought Lucien would strike him, but he passed right by him and attacked one of the golems on the other side of the room.

Dark Inferno

There is only so much loss and suffering a soul can take, only so much before forever losing its gist, its ordination, its sanity. There is a point of break in every mind that, if trespassed, it impedes the consciousness from going back to its former geometry. If breached, it leads to a stage of degradation and decay that would not allow any return to its previous form.

One interesting fact about the Underworld is that there is not a lot of food there, especially for the ones who have no idea where and how to find it. Although it contains a great number of species and even entire civilizations in the countless forgotten corners of its depths, most caves are empty of life and sustenance is scarce. Even water is mostly hard to procure and incredibly inconstant in its availability. Nevertheless there are deep lagoons that stretch to the world's core and an infinite number of underground rivers, many tunnels go on for weeks without crossing a single course of water. Dying of thirst is not uncommon among unskilled travelers of the deep realm.

The inhabitants of the depths are the stuff of nightmares. Because of the scarcity of resources, and also the fact that it has been used as a hideaway by every dark creature since the beginning of time, there is no other environment apart from the Hell itself, so populated by vile and corrupted life. All living and non-living beings there, and even the plants, are hazardous, to everything including to themselves. Perennial hunger, cannibalism, autophagy, and madness are everywhere. Most creatures that live in its dark not even sleep, crawling from the moment of their conception to the moment of their demise with no objective in mind but to feed their insatiable appetites, spending their whole existence exclusively to devour whatever pass their dark tunnels. Deeper you go, worst it is. For the most part, they are insectoid or magical abnormalities of bizarre shapes, forms, and natures too vile and ugly and terrible to live in the surface. Although some possess incredible intelligence, most are mindless, never failing in being despicable and cruel.

It was in this environment that the lost man and the singing sword lived for what now seemed like an eternity. They fought so many disgusting and soulless creatures together, that they both became experts in killing them. Although forced to do so, he was still surprised to discover that he was a natural when it came to violence.

The songs of the blade were mighty. In combat, he emitted terrible symphonies of destruction that could cut through steel like rotten wood. The more powerful the enemies were, the sharper its notes throbbed through the air and through them. It never failed to destroy whatever crossed their path.

The combination of the powerful magic items he collected from the corpse on the riverbank worked well for him. He found that the bracer and the belt he was bearing magically increased his strength, agility, and stamina, amounting to a devastating effect on his targets. One of the rings caused his wounds to regenerate prodigiously fast, almost like a troll. This, above all else, made him very hard to kill.

Even though he had started rationing, his cache of food was running dangerously low. His water storage was not better either, and he was always at the peril of hunger and thirst. However, in spite of all that, the worst thing he was facing was the effects of the many magical paradoxes that exist in and affect the Underworld. Those, combined with the claustrophobic surroundings cause a syndrome called Cave Madness. A disease of the mind, originated by longtime exposure to the Underworld. It was especially worse over the ones that become lost, and, although he was able to keep his body from death, his mind was being slowly undone.

His sense of space and all his perception of time eventually escaped him, and he became lost in many ways. He still had no recollection whatsoever of any memory before his awakening in that dark beach. The obscure pestilence took over and made him lose all sense of purpose and continuity of thought, everything was the same. Everything became pure instinctive and he lost control. All things were conveying to a terrible feeling of claustrophobia and animality. For all he knew, he was dead and this was hell. A never-ending dimensional prison full of horrors where there was no escape. His hyped mind and constrained spaces made him feel as if buried alive all the time, and the ensuing despair plagued his mind with hallucinations of such magnitude, that no hope could survive them. Heavily infected by it, he was daydreaming all the time, sleeping over his cumulated anxieties and trapped in this eternal horrific senseless, futureless, hopeless prison. It got so bad that he didn't know when he was awake or sleeping, for it was altogether a horrible nightmare. The sword light was the only thing keeping the last pieces of his sanity in him. It was the only thing that gave him hope that there was something else somewhere, but even so.

His panic attacks stopped being the exception and started to be the rule. He had become a freak of fear, no less psychotic and vile than the creatures he fought. His whole world was the few feet of light ahead of him, and it was not enough. He lost his mind.

Long after his food ended, and even though their meat was foul and natural and certainly poisonous and bitter, he decided to hunt some of the dark monsters for eating. He decided to follow the tracks he found in a random cave, tailing it until they gathered with an unusual amount of other traces. They all came and went from a particular direction. Wary, and made half insane, he followed them.

After entering a round cave through a small tunnel he heard the sound of running water. Although he knew that water bodies were the most dangerous places, he quickly went for it. In his madness, he was not minding or fearing anything anymore.

As he passed through the narrow passage that led to the water he heard, his instincts started shouting something in his ears that he was stubbornly ignoring, or was not able to process any longer. Made crazed also by thirst, he jumped to the water line as soon as he saw it, drinking profusely from it. His weakened body could not hold the shock of ingesting all that water, and he threw up all of it and convulsed violently over the dark sand. When he was done with his spasms, he drank again.

When he felt satisfied, the tactile sensation of his fingers caught his attention. He pressed the soft sand with both his hands and remembered the feeling of silkiness from before. In panic by what his mind was revealing to him, he grabbed the sword he had dropped in his rush to reach the water. He raised it in the air, illuminating the sand. He felt the sand in his palm again. With a sudden movement and a manifestation of his will, he increased the blade's light. He saw the body, and he recognized the cave, and the dark sand, and the river. It was the place from where he came. He cried in agony, spending all of his remaining forces in a shout of pain. As his last strengths left him, his legs failed and he involuntarily kneeled over the riverbank. Even with the magical implements, his body, mind, and soul were made too weak from the lack of food, rest, and hope. His eyes were blank, his spirit completely and finally surrendered.

Over the gloomy light of the sword he saw something moving in the river, something organic, complex. He looked at it casually, hoping that whatever it was it would kill him quickly. But the thing did not kill him, for it was his own reflex on the water pool. It instantly was waved away by a tender current disturbance, dismantling the picture of his desperation.

Slowly, all movement ceased, and the water in the small rocky pool became a perfect mirror, dark and deep. His interest in it increased, the blade smartly adjusted the light so he could see it better. The reflection of the blade was the only thing telling him that the face he was seeing was his. He instinctively raised his hand and touched his own visage on the water. The elfish face he was looking at was completely alien to him. No memory of it came to his mind. Still, he stood there, looking right through it with his empty stare as his unblinking tears rolled down his cheeks and chin. He stood there until the light of his eyes faded away.

Kestos's Abode

'It does not make sense,' said Sahafira. 'We sprung no trap, and none of us could have activated it without the Charm.'

'Charm?' asked Bastian.

'The artifact that controls a golems.' Stargazer explained. 'More often than not is a gem or some of crystalized matter.'

'The window,' said Hanam looking up. 'Before the attack,' he said.

'So, whoever was following us finally decided to play a card then,' said Stargazer. 'Well, at least now we know something about him.' He smiled sarcastically.

'What do we know?' asked Bastian, curious.

'We now know that, whatever or whoever it was, it can activate golems,' the wizard pointed out.

After Stargazer preemptively deactivated the last remaining combat ready golem, they decided to stay in that room and rest for a while. Although they had survived, the battle completely drained them of their energies.

Stargazer went on longer, collecting as many high-energy artifacts and tools from that room as he could. He was so excited about the potential of what he was collecting that he was barely able to sleep. He stayed close to their small fire making plans for the future. His mind was so busy and stimulated with the possibilities he projected, that he had to prepare for himself a green rose tea to make sure he could get some rest.

In the next "morning," as they called the time after the fifth candle had burned, they continued their exploration. As the tunnels and rooms now presented a fairly streamlined and architecturally elaborated structure, culminating the progressive design that improved gradually since they entered that forgotten place, they could deduct that they were close to the wizard's quarters. They were extra careful while they advanced now, and their attention paid off rather frequently, as they started finding more wonders and terrible traps. Slowly, they gathered what they could and disabled what they should as they pressed on. When the higher solemnity of the chamber's decoration became obvious, they knew they had arrived.

The Fellowship now progressed meticulously and painfully until they finally arrived at the entrance of the long and broad stair. After they defeated the animated sentries that guarded those steps, they continued up them. The stairs ended in a long rectangular room. On it, there were two lines of thick pillars; across it, a double door; beyond it, the obvious expected but still unknown.

They wearily crossed the pillar doors with sword in hand and watching their flanks as if they would be attacked at any moment. When they arrived at the double door, they scanned it extensively for traps and curses in every way they could possibly imagine. Finally, Stargazer opened it with a stick while the others ducked behind some pillars. After a click, without any incident, it opened wide.

Once inside, they found what you would expect from a living room of a megalomaniac wizard. It was full of the Kestos's plunders, incredibly detailed magical maps of many important places, rare books, and most of his original notes on his researches and developments on enchanting objects with magic. Several of his unfinished projects lay around, immediately catching the attention of Stargazer's eyes, who ignored everything else to collect those.

'This man was an Enchanter,' he said decisively while loading his pockets and backpacks with everything he could grab. 'And a fairly talented one,' he added after quickly examining a block of colored crystal full of runes.

'What he enchanted besides orbs and golems?' asked Lucien while still holding his drawn swords in guard, watching his surroundings tensely and defensively.

'Everything,' said Stargazer. 'Apparently, he was working on some pretty interesting projects,' he said distractedly while reading some runes in Arama that were imprinted in a small altar made entirely of soft gold.

'Like what, specifically?' asked Bastian, standing in the same defensive posture as Lucien.

'For starts: some pretty nasty siege weapons,' summarized Stargazer while inspecting a masterfully crafted and heavily armored adamantium constructor.

'The magic he used, while powerful, it was not uncommon,' the wizard pointed it out. 'My question is: how he acquired so many resources? I mean, this whole thing right here is made of fairly pure adamantium,' he said while tapping his finger on the golem's chest plate.

For some reason, Bastian noted how the metallic sound that came out of it was harmonically crispier than other metals.

'Either he was immensely rich, or the rumors that the Dragoness was backing him up are very true,' said Stargazer, imagining a way to take the golem with him.

'There is no way he could gather some of these toys here without a ton of gold, a considerable political leverage, and a lot of power backing him up,' argued the wizard. 'From this quantity of adamantium alone, you could imply he was doing business with the dark elves,' he said. 'But if so, who in the world could be his guarantor while dealing with them,' he shivered.

'Do not talk about them out loud,' reprimanded Sahafira, as if the very mentioning of the dark elves would bring a bad omen.

'Among these maps here, and the other ones we found before, there are a lot of details of Underworld passages and the location of certain "places,"' said the wizard. 'It is only possible…' he suggested.

'Any sight of the orb?' interrupted Hanam, addressing his question to everyone.

'I can feel a lot of magic energy coming from behind that door.' Stargazer pointed to the massive steel door on the other side of the room.

They all approached it carefully.

'It is magically sealed and my powers are not complex enough to open it,' said the wizard after a thorough analysis.

Noticing their interest in the steel door, Klunk started studying it quite curiously. He bumped it with his knuckles, directed his ear to hear if any sound would come from it, smelled it, and even tasted a little bit of its dust and spider webs with his tongue. Irritated with the object inactivity, he took a large booger from his nose and glued to it when nobody was looking.

After lighting the room better by igniting some bronze pyres, Lucien noticed a small piece of blue metal crimped in the back of the Adamantium Golem's left shoulder. With the help of some of Kestos's enchanted tools he commandeered and a copious amount of force, the wizard removed the piece of metal. After analyzing it against the firelight, he called Bastian.

'Give me your sword,' he said dryly to Bastian, who, surprised and scared by the sudden and rare anxiety on the wizard's voice, quickly handed him his weapon.

The fragment of metal extracted from the constructor matched perfectly the bit that was missing from Bastian's sword. Instantly, a thousand questions grew on their minds, especially Bastian's, who was clearly shocked.

'Does that mean that he managed to come all the way until here?' he asked the others with tears in his eyes.

'Apparently, yes,' said Stargazer. 'As far as I can tell, this golem is not fully operational yet. The hit was probably an accident while trying to strike something or someone else,' said the wizard. 'Whoever was wielding your father's sword, fought his way until this very chamber,' he said and directed his gaze to the sealed door. 'Maybe beyond it,' he speculated.

'What a hit, hum?' said Lucien awkwardly. 'It shattered a Star Ore sword,' he said, willing to take his friend's mind over his anguishes and doubts, but clearly lacking the social skills for it.

'Indeed,' said Stargazer looking at Lucien and trying to help him in his intent. 'It looked like your father was a heavy-handed man,' he said, smiling at Bastian.

'It is possible, even likely, that remnant survivors from the Battle of the Cursed Stones followed the wizard here, destroyed the rest of his troops, and killed him,' said Stargazer. 'By what is said, and by what we saw here, Kestos was relentless and would not run away,' he nodded to the sound of his own words. 'One thing is sure, someone or something stopped him,' he concluded.

'We can always count on the Valkarians' bravery,' interceded Hanam with his calming voice while he placed his hand over Bastian's shoulder.

'Yeah, but many things are still unknown,' Stargazer added. 'I believe we are going to find many answers when we meet Kestos's remains,' he said.

Hanam looked away, thinking about what Stargazer had said concerning Kestos's remains. He had this insisting gut feeling that unveiling the story behind the wizard's final destiny would be somehow fundamental to locating the orb. While searching his feelings, he rested his gaze instinctively to a more discreet part of the chamber. There, among a few mixed objects, there was what looked to be an ordinary painting hanging on the wall. It was nothing more than a quite ordinary portrait of a melancholic landscape of a small castle over a green pasture and a few trees. The frame was positioned at eye level, therefore it was only natural that Hanam's eyes fixed on it while his mind drifted away. Suddenly, he saw movement coming from it, enough to catch his attention. He saw some sort of black spot, probably a bug, crawling over the painting. Then, as it moved, it shape-shifted in a manner totality different from anything he had ever seen. With his attention was completely directed to it, he slowly approached the painting eager to define what was that.

No one but Sahafira noticed this change in his behavior.

As he approached, the light from the torch he carried illuminated the painting, which became terribly clear. It looked abnormally alive. Its trees moved, stirred by a portrayed breeze. Its birds flew, crossing the horizon, and the figure of a man dressed in black from head to toe walked on the tall grass. He was walking straight into Hanam's direction, making the painting look a bizarre window to another world.

'What is that?' asked Sahafira, who followed Hanam with the corner of her eyes, and was now witnessing the living picture over his shoulder.

The others approached quickly.

'Wow! That's a magical painting!' said Stargazer excited. 'I have never seen one in person, but have read about it.' His eyes shone with excitement. The others looked at him confused and a little frustrated that he wasn't getting to the point.

'It is a portal to another dimension,' he said, noticing their expressions. 'Let me see.' He studied the frame and the scene on its back that now looked entirely alive. 'Hum, this one seems to be stabilized. The disposition of space there looks fine and synchronized,' he said, amused like a child. 'Quite nice actually,' said the wizard, completely immersed in his fascination.

'Well, this one doesn't look like it is the dominant side. That's great news for us, right?' he said and laughed freely. He stopped when he saw that his anecdote only made sense to him.

'Dominant?' asked Lucien, already struggling with his nerves.

'Yes,' replied Stargazer matter-of-factly. 'It means that this dimension's space captured in the frame was created from ours, not the contrary,' he said, convinced that this was very important. 'That is the first and most important thing to establish when dealing with these things,' said the wizard, nodding to his clueless friends.

'Of course, it was made from ours. From where else?' mocked Lucien.

'Not necessarily,' noted Stargazer. 'Who can say with security that our world isn't a creation of someone from another world?' he proposed. 'Or even our whole creation was created elsewhere and the door or the "painting" now resides in a world created in that first world?' asked Stargazer.

Klunk scratched his head and blinked hard.

'That's complicated,' said Bastian, trying to keep up.

'Not really, it is just a matter of access to energy and transmutational talent. Time can be accelerated or decelerated to the extreme, but never stopped. So it is just a matter of measuring and containing everything using the original world parameters, or altering things if you are into it. There is always a portal. Creation is a portal,' he said, perceiving that his words made little or no sense to his companions.

'From the conscious state it is difficult even to imagine it, but from the perspective of the Ether, the geometries are just there to be molded and unfolded accordingly. It is not really different from active dreaming, really. Anyone can open and play with a separate reality, you just need the training. And the right amount of focus and energy of course,' said the wizard.

'Did someone ever try?' asked Sahafira.

'Tried what?' asked the wizard.

'To find the original world?'

'Oh, of course. Sure. Hundreds of people. Some are still trying. Most have died or got trapped in undesirable places,' said Stargazer.

'Undesirable places? Like what?' asked Bastian.

'Hell,' clarified Stargazer.

'THE Hell?' Bastian asked anxious.

'Well, also,' answered Stargazer.

'So why people would be stupid enough to adventure outside our world?' asked Lucien.

'The Flow is different in intensity and shape. It ranges from a world to another, and, although variety and change may exist, all of the worlds are fundamentally connected,' said Stargazer.

'So?' asked Lucien unsatisfied.

'So there are many artifacts and resources that could be gathered in other worlds that have a tremendous potential in this one,' answered the wizard. 'An idea, or a concept in a certain dimension can manifest as an angel, a demon, a Vortex, or an object in ours, and vice versa. Do you ever hear about the Sword of Fury?' he asked.

Bastian and Lucien were fast to shake their heads in a positive sign.

'It was forged in the world located just two dimensions higher than this one,' said Stargazer. 'Higher you "go," more strings you can pull on the planes below. That is why so many ambitious mages tried to get to the higher worlds,' said the wizard as if that information was supposed to be commonplace.

'Did someone ever get there?' asked Sahafira returning to her original question.

'The Original World? Well, our dimension's most famous plain traveler was a wizard that lived not so long ago actually,' Stargazer answered. 'He managed to get back to our world and shared in his publications his memories and experiences collected along the way. He became very famous, but vanished shortly after he published his writings,' he said.

'What did he say?' asked Bastian.

'He wrote hundreds of books and described thousands upon thousands of places and non-places,' Stargazer said looking up, gathering his knowledge from his memory. 'He wrote about the Original World too, and he was strangely and unusually very succinct about it,' he said. 'His exact words were: "It is not for us to be there, not just now." And: "The end is the beginning,"' said Stargazer, pausing to consider his own words.

Everyone in the group seemed involved in some level by what the wizard said.

'There is a lot of mystery and verbosity when we try to explain or define these things, but I think that in this case, if you do not understand something, you are not supposed to,' said the wizard, sounding very satisfied with his formulation.

'Some claim he was a fraud, but by the size, depth, and validity of his published works, one can see he was a serious researcher and the bearer of a mighty mind and a wise heart.' There was a certain melancholy in the wizard's voice now.

'Well, I guess we will never know.' Stargazer looked down, as if he was lamenting that probability.

'Well, maybe we will,' interfered Lucien. 'But, right now, we need to know who is this man who is waving at us from inside a freaking painting,' he said pointing at the portrait.

They were all dragged out of their distractions and looked at it shocked. Collecting himself, and for everybody's awe, Stargazer simply got the painting out of the wall and held the frame with his hands while he analyzed it one more time.

'Let me see,' he said. 'Hum,' he pressed his lips together.

'It is a simple, limited, one-way stabilized parallel dimension,' he said while aligning his sight with its vertical horizon and seeing things that were apparently invisible to the others. 'This thing is a trap. And a prison,' he warned his companions.

'This man here was probably trapped by Kestos,' he said while he shook the painting and observed the effects on the dust around it.

His words immediately stirred everyone up, and they looked at each other worried.

'Can we take him out of there?' asked Hanam. 'He can answer one or two questions. He may help us figure out what really happened here,' he said.

'And what if he is hostile?' asked Sahafira.

'Good, I haven't killed anything alive since the morning,' Lucien replied with a sneer and a wink.

Stargazer looked around for consensus. When he got it, he stepped back, and all the others did the same. He raised his hand over the painting, focusing the whole of his mind on it, he then uttered some unintelligible words while twisting his hands and fingers in the air until a manifestation of a spray of light and sparkling magic dust unapologetically extracted the man from the picture. He came out as fast as a lightning bolt, abnormally decelerating until he was delivered, safe and sound, into their world. With a calculated and industrial violence, the man was fiercely thrown by the mechanisms that transferred space between the two worlds into a corner.

He was shorter than Bastian and Lucien but was better built, which meant he was very muscular, but not enough to lose an overall dynamic mannerism. He moved gracefully and his feet and hands were light and fast.

Nothing in his appearance denounced evil or corruption, but he was dressed in black from head to toe. He looked like someone who knew how to handle himself well. His clothes were still holding up but were very worn, and everything about his equipment seemed loaded with purpose.

Strangely, he was wearing a mask, and his boots were made of a very soft rubbery black leather. In their tip and in the knuckles of his black leather gloves, there were thick and sturdy spikes that resembled lance points, but curved. He had a very distinguished hand-and-a-half western sword and dagger, their sheath and palms were completely matte black. The only thing he was carrying beside that was a small velvet black sack by his hip.

'Greetings,' he said in perfect Valkarian while removing his mask.

What they saw was nothing short of surprising. He was a western man. His face had very sharp traces and was very proportional. His long and straight black hair looked made of silk, and his black almond-shaped eyes were perfectly set with his slightly pointed ears.

'My name is Shunto Fang,' he said solemnly and respectfully, bowing with his hands by his side in a western manner.

'What were you doing there?' interrogated Lucien, pointing to the depiction.

'I was imprisoned there a long time ago by an evil sorcerer named Kestos,' Shunto said.

'What were you doing here?' asked Lucien.

'I was sent by the Emperor of Valkar to...neutralize Kestos,' answered the western man.

Bastian and Lucien were impressed right away and they all exchanged stares of awe among them.

'How do we know that you are not lying?' asked Lucien.

'He is telling the truth,' said Hanam.

The others looked at him astonished by his unusual bold declaration and precipitous judgement.

'I know,' he affirmed himself, implicitly asking for their trust.

And they give it to him, for the hunchback had used his healing powers to save every single one of them from certain death so many times, that they now relied on him with their lives.

'I was born and raised in The Capitol. I'm the son of two prominent ambassadors stationed there. I've been on adventures since I can remember and have spent many years training to be a Steel Fist, but then my path turned to a more…discrete direction,' said Shunto openly.

'Do you still serve the Emperor?' asked Bastian.

'Always,' Shunto answered promptly and energetically. His answer bewildered and inspired Bastian at the same time.

'This rouge spellcaster,' Shunto continued, 'was an evil man who has aligned himself with the Dragoness, waging war against the Valkarian Empire on her behalf. His evil cunnings cost us dearly. We lost a lot of good people due to his actions, not to mention the innocent victims of his recklessness and cowardice,' he said, disgusted.

'My mission was noble,' he raised his head high. 'Kestos was an evil man, you must believe me,' he pledged to them.

'We do,' said Bastian, giving him respect.

'When were you imprisoned?' Stargazer asked.

'I'm not sure, time is counted different there, the days are far too long, I believe. I think it was around twenty years of your time ago,' said Shunto.

They were all flabbergasted by Shunto's story. Even Klunk seemed intrigued with the tale. He took possession of the painting and was now analyzing it with the curiosity of a toddler with a new toy. He peeped at it while turning it quickly, he shook it, poked it, smelled it, licked it, but nothing could satisfy his curiosity.

'So you were all that time inside that paint?' asked Bastian, honestly shocked.

'Yes,' Shunto answered. 'I thought I was supposed to die there, forgotten by all, but then I saw your light,' said Shunto.

'It must have been sooo tedious,' said Lucien disgusted. 'What have you done during your time there?' he asked, digressing.

'I have trained the whole time.' Shunto left the others looking at each other, imaging the proficiency level that he must have achieved now. 'The place is not that bad, actually. The weather is very good and there is plenty of good food,' he said.

'I've had some help from some empire's operators to infiltrate myself here so I could complete my mission,' Shunto continued. 'I was in Westgate preparing my sortie when, out of nowhere, a decision was made to launch a spear point battalion to hunt and destroy Kestos' hiding place,' he said, and Bastian's eyes widened.

Lucien looked at his friend from the corner of his eyes.

'I've followed the battalion very discreetly, and I did not engage in any of their fightings directly or openly, as my mission would not allow me to,' he added. 'I was sent for a decapitation operation, which proved to be very effective against other captains and lieutenants from the Lava Peak, but it must be executed in a certain way. Anyway, her servants tend to keep a lot of power and control in their personal hands. This kind of actions have worked good for the war effort, overall. So, the decision was made and I'm here. I've failed,' he said.

No one was able to say a word.

'How is the war going?' he asked.

'We won,' answered Stargazer.

'But not without losing first,' said Bastian, staring at the western man right in his eyes.

Stargazer looked down slightly ashamed, Lucien looked away unwilling to engage or see what was in Bastian's eyes.

'As in all wars,' Shunto lamented, his eyes were bursting with emotions too, but he still reserved space for Bastian's pain as if he knew exactly what he carried in his heart.

'And her?' asked Shunto with repugnance all over his face as if he suddenly had a bad taste in his mouth.

'Disappeared. Location unknown,' answered Stargazer.

'Cursed be her name,' he said, spitting on the ground.

'What happened here after the Battle of the Cursed Stones?' asked Hanam.

'The story we heard was that the only few survivors made their way back to Westgate,' Bastian added, uncontrollably anxious.

'They thought they would lose and sent messengers before the battle was over. I helped the runners escape the best I could. It is a relief to know they made it,' Shunto said.

Bastian and Lucien immediately exchanged stares and nodded.

'The fighting still went on for a while and it was horrendous, it really was,' Shunto continued. 'Luckily, Kestos' arrogance made him understand too late that his ambush had turned into an open battle, and a price is always paid to fight the Valkarians in an open battle,' he said. 'In his fury, the proud wizard exposed and consumed most of his best resources and troops. When he finally admitted that the field was lost, he furiously called a retreat,' he said.

'When they disengaged, the remaining Valkarians were so deeply grieved by the death of their brothers, that they swore vengeance against Kestos among tears. They left the corpses of their companions behind, collected only weapons and provisions, and followed the wizard and his remaining lackeys here,' he explained and formally paused out of respect for the remembrance.

'Those were true heroes,' he said, 'Valkarians of great tenacity if you asked me,' Shunto said with a spark of pride in his eyes.

Bastian was quiet and contained.

'They systematically destroyed the troops that the wizard sent to meet them. In the end, the wizard's craftiness won the day,' he said, 'and he finally managed to defeat the remaining men here, in this very room,' Shunto said still angry with the result.

'I could not reveal myself or join the final attack as my technique demanded that I study the target for longer,' he said regretfully.

'How did you manage to stay here unnoticed in the middle of all that?' Lucien asked.

'I have…ways,' he said.

'Why didn't you join the fight and help those men?' asked Bastian barely holding his growing distress.

'Although I'm trained in direct combat, my approach to this kind of situation is more…hazy and…definitive,' Shunto replied as he looked down to recover some lost memories, but not really.

'Please be more clear,' said Bastian 'because I am starting to think you let those men die,' he said threateningly, showcasing a rare display of anger.

Hanam smoothly landed his hand on Bastian's arm, to calm him down. Bastian looked at him and saw that he was exposing more of his face than usual. The surprise of the evident rarity of the moment caught Bastian's attention and took his mind out of his rising wrath and the mutiny it issued against himself.

'What troubles you?' asked Shunto wisely spotting the reasons for Bastian's feelings through the devise of some hidden but now manifested wisdom.

'His father fought with the men you mentioned,' answered Lucien looking at Bastian and fearing that he would snap.

'Urien Starblade,' Shunto said gallantly.

Stargazer immediately raised an eyebrow for he knew there was more than logic on Shunto's correct guess.

'Even though he fought among knights, he was the last man standing – a great warrior and a true Valkarian,' Shunto praised Bastian's father.

'You looked a lot like him,' he said while giving Bastian a second look. 'I can see you managed to find his precious sword too.' Shunto pointed it out with an encouraging smile.

The moment was so intense for Bastian, that even though his face was straight and frozen like a stone statue and his gaze was firm and he was not blinking, uncontrollable tears spilled from his eyes and, as they fell down, they were the only things moving over his whole person. His stoicism was so deep that nobody could tell if he was angry, proud, sad, or happy. He was now completely out of his usually humble, accommodating self, and was using his whole being that emerged from the simultaneous and devastating gathering of all his emotions and beliefs. And they all saw him, and it occupied the air around them, and they felt it too, and they understood.

Touched, Sahafira and Lucien stared at each other and then away. Hanam pressed his hand against Bastian's shoulder in a display of emotional support. Klunk was capturing his immense tears with his massive fingertips and dripping them back into his eyes.

'I was looking for the right opportunity to complete my mission since the first time I met Kestos, but couldn't find one up until then. After your father's last stand, however, I finally managed to attack and poisoned him,' said Shunto satisfied. 'I used a poison so rare and powerful that even the powerful magic he had available could not save him. With a surprise strike I managed to contaminate his blood,' he said.

'So you did kill him?' asked Bastian out of his trance and ready to redeem Shunto.

'Yes and no,' he said, aware of the duality of his answer.

'His flesh is defeated forever. But Kestos was…guileful in his preparations, and the tools at his disposal exceeded what we envisioned.' Shunto looked ashamed of himself and stared at the floor. 'After my attack, and before the poison completed its effects, he imprisoned me in the painting so I wouldn't finish the job,' he said, and it was clearly hard for Shunto to tell tale of his failure.

'Death by Green Lotus is certain but relatively slow. He found time to transfer his soul to a Soul Stone,' he said.

'A Soul Stone?!' asked Stargazer, impressed.

'Kestos was becoming way more dangerous than what the people from Westgate were ready to accept or willing to admit,' said Shunto. 'Local politics were highly involved with the wizard's schemes even to a dangerous and treasonous degree. Many thought they could control or use the wizard, but when news arrived at the Emperor about the reality of the situation on the ground, he decided to intervene directly, and that is why I'm here in the first place,' he clarified.

'Were the local authorities really that weak and corrupt?' asked Lucien, oddly reserved.

'There was too much…compromise,' Shunto answered diplomatically, correctly reading the place from where Lucien was coming from, and transpiring that in the stare he gave him.

'But that was not all,' Shunto said, turning back to the subject of the wizard's destiny. 'After he transferred his essence to the crystal, he had one of his slave imbuing his essence in a powerful metal body. That one right there,' he pointed to the Adamantium Golem.

Klunk raised his club, taking a defensive stance against the dusty constructor.

'I witnessed everything from within the frame,' said Shunto.

'We have come here to recover a crystal orb that we believe was in his possession at the time of his death,' said Hanam, cutting straight back to business before anyone had time to process all they'd heard.

'I have seen it,' said Shunto. 'It is in his treasure room, beyond that door,' he signed to the small steel door they had inspected before. 'No one can open it though. Kestos was a talented enchanter and casted a mighty spell over it. The door charm is linked to his soul, and only he can open it,' he said.

'I'm pretty sure that if we can get his Soul Stone, I can open that door,' said Stargazer, guessing as he spoke.

'The Soul Stone is with his last remaining lackey, a demon called Ubaba,' said Shunto.

'He still lurks these halls. Haven't you met him?' he asked, looking around.

'Yes,' said Hanam.

The sudden bewilderment on their faces told him that they needed an explanation.

'The evil shadow that is following us since we've entered these caves,' he explained.

'Why didn't he finish his master's assignment?' asked Stargazer, avidly looking at the golem.

'Because I hate him,' a deep voice shouted through the air. Its perverted echo perpetrated like poison that infused their hearts with terror.

From one of the balconies above the entrance door, a dark shadow jumped in the air and landed on the other side of the room. It kneeled heavily over the weight of its tainted bones and by the impact of the hard touchdown of its landing. The oily texture of the black feathers of its crow-like wings shone a scary and deeply dark non-color. The wings were big enough to engulf the whole creature as a cocoon, and as they opened they spun and the ape-like creature rose. It emerged slowly and threateningly from the middle of it, much like some blasphemous blossoming from hell itself. Like a hunting viper, the movements its body produced were independent, smooth, calculated, proud. Its broad head and most of its very muscular body was covered with a despicable dark fur. His legs were short and his arms were disproportionally long, both were strong and terrible. Its feet were like brawny hands with six fingers in each, reptile scales over its palms, and terrible claws on its fingertips. His posture was menacing and his eyes were full of intelligence and purposeful malice. He was using no armor, but was carrying a leather belt full of pockets with several objects attached to it, a golden rope, a dagger and different potions and scrolls hung from his hip belt. He was armed with fighting spears and a particularly large and curved two-handed sword. His weapons were neatly strapped to his back in sheaths of black leather and his hands were by his side, free and ready. His sword was beautiful and colorfully decorated, looking departed from him in almost every aspect.

'I hated him then, and still hate him now,' said the demon monkey.

'So why did you serve him, Ubaba?' asked Shunto, touching the hilt of his sword.

'I had no choice,' he said, resting his eyes on Shunto's hand. 'The wizard and his raider destroyed my village, killed my family, and enslaved me with his magic. He had my body drenched with evil magic, making me miserable for decades while commanding me to do his cruel business,' he said with his angry, animalistic voice.

'Why didn't you leave after his flesh died?' risked Stargazer.

'Because the chains are still over me, for the wizard lives,' he said.

The Fellowship felt their blood freeze right there and then as if Ubaba had cast a gelid spell with those words.

The demon monkey then raised his arm and opened his hand and showed them a piece of rough crystal that pulsed with a yellow light.

'Kestos's Soul Stone,' warned Shunto.

'Indeed,' rejoiced Ubaba, and his eyes glittered with a confused lust when he looked at the stone.

He then looked at the companions and his expression changed.

'So,' he said, 'it looks like we have a dilemma here,' his voice malevolent. 'I have something you need and I need something from you.' He smiled, somehow pleased with the situation.

'There will be no negotiations with this monster!' declared Bastian with rare partiality while tightening his grip on his sword. Lucien pursed his mouth in a self-satisfied smirk. He drew his weapons and raised his chin and his killer eyes in Ubaba's direction.

'We have heard histories about him, we know his crimes,' continued Bastian. 'He was with Kestos from the beginning, and his crimes against our people are numerous. He shall be taken into custody for judgment. If he resists, he shall be put to death, here and now if necessary.' Much like an executioner, Bastian drew his sword. There was not a speck of hesitation in him. Sahafira and Klunk were stunned by Bastian's stance. It was new, unalike him, dangerous.

Ubaba looked at them with great suspicion and it adopted a defensive stance.

'Wait, let us listen to what he has to say,' said Stargazer, trying to control the situation.

'I know you have spellcasters among you,' said Ubaba. 'If you cancel the spell that enslaves me, I will give you his Soul Stone,' he said.

The companions looked at each other seeking agreement.

'He is not to be trusted,' said Hanam without deviating his gaze from the nefarious creature.

'After I'm free, I promise you I will leave,' he said. 'And I promise that I will have no quarry with you,' he leered slightly.

'I say we kill him and get the stone from his cold, dead hand,' said Lucien, stepping forward.

'No! He is a spellcaster,' intervened Stargazer. 'There are many ways he can escape and vanish!' he said. 'Let me talk this through,' he whispered at Lucien.

'I can do it,' said the wizard, looking at Ubaba. 'But I need access to Kestos's spell book first. Do you know where it is?' he asked.

'Yes, I have it right here with me,' said Ubaba, opening a rectangular brown leather butt pack and retrieving an enormous golden book from it.

'Kestos Grimoire,' the wizard murmured as an unusual light sparked from his eyes.

Without a second thought, Ubaba threw the heavy book at the wizard. The large and thick compendium flew through the room like it weighted nothing. Stargazer grabbed it with great skill and staunchness.

The Grimoire was indeed disproportionally light for its size. Its cover was made of a golden metal very similar to brushed gold. It had the shape of a hundred dragon fangs pressed against each other in an oddly morbid and corrupt fashion. On the fang's edges, there were tiny runes and magical inscriptions of many types and styles, all in the color red. The object was big, pompous, and flashy.

To pry into another wizard's Grimoire was Stargazer's favorite thing in the world. He was in love with the fact that a spellcaster's Grimoire is a reflection of that magician's entire experience, going, therefore, significantly beyond the inherently wonderful nature of magic, assembling a deep view on personal philosophies, insights, and limitations. It was a personal statement about a wizard's career as a spellcaster, its life's work as a contributor for the unveiling of things hidden throughout the universe, and, above all, it was a very comprehensive blueprint of its entire perspective — a rare thing to find anywhere else.

He could not avoid noticing that it was almost as thick as Eliaroth's, but after a brief analysis, he knew that Kestos's was made vast through the devise of the artificially accumulative pressure of greed and fanatic megalomania. It lacked altogether the deep artistic and metaphysical interpretation of the several centuries of contemplation that Eliaroth had on Kestos. It was a lesser work by any metric, but still powerful and drenched with insights nevertheless.

With a simple wave of his hand, Stargazer unlocked the book and started looking for a specific spell he deduced Kestos would have. His quick eyes were now scanning the pages at full speed. They became even more overburdened and neurotic with effort as he noticed that the book was full of rare incantation, many of which came from completely different angles and designs, being radically refined and very ingenious.

Stargazer was exercising an enormous amount of self-control not to show how thrilled he was by what he was reading and seeing, for he knew he was now experienced enough to risk using such magic, and couldn't wait to try it. For him, the adventure was over. In the back of his mind, he was only thinking to get out of that place and study that book until exhaustion. With a tremendous power of will and self-control, he managed to ignore so many side interests and distracting things from the book itself and focus on the task at hand.

'Can you do it, wizard?' asked Ubaba, impatient.

'Yeah, yeah,' he answered. 'Let me see… Oh yes. Yes, I can,' he said.

The wizard opened the Grimoire wider and leaned it on a stand that stood nearby. The others raised their guard.

'Here it is,' he concluded satisfied, still staring at the book.

There was a moment of silence and the wizard searched his feelings and instincts and considered their opinions about Ubaba. He hesitated and looked at Ubaba one more time.

'Are we doing this or no?' Ubaba asked them all, but with his mouth directing the question to the wizard and his unquiet eyes awaiting for an abrupt answer from Bastian and Lucien.

'He cannot go unpunished,' insisted Bastian pointing his sword at Ubaba. Lucien was in the same spirit, ready to go. His legs nervously bouncing around and his hands readjusting his grip on his sword's hilt as if to release his over overflowing aggression.

'Bastian, our mission here is the orb,' the wizard reminded them, discerning the imminent risks that the moment carried. 'Remember that is entirely possible that he did the things he did on the behalf of the wizard because he had no chance of resisting that man's evil spells,' he said, carefully minding his words and his voice tone. His mouth was directed at Bastian, but his eyes wouldn't leave Lucien.

'So why he has not destroyed the Soul Stone and freed himself?' asked Bastian.

'Kestos was no fool,' promptly advocated Stargazer, 'it is highly probable, almost certain, that the spells he used to enslave Ubaba would not allow him to do it.'

'The young wizard is right,' said Ubaba.

'Silence!' shouted Bastian in a rare expression of rage and authoritarianism. 'This monster killed women and children during the war,' said Bastian without moving his new terrible gaze from Ubaba.

'He is right,' said Shunto.

'Who's right?' asked Sahafira.

'Both,' said Hanam, and they all went silent while considering.

'If we have his Soul Stone, we can destroy Kestos once and for all ourselves, and have access to his treasure,' said Stargazer. 'Then, we can honor our word to this adventure and you will have enough money to pay me for your father's sword,' he went beyond what he felt comfortable trying to leverage Bastian. 'About the other...subject...we can always deal with it...later,' the wizard whispered.

'I say we kill him FAST and get the stone from his cold, dead hand,' Lucien updated his original plan.

Stargazer gave him a disgusted stare. The wizard always tried not to judge their actions or act directly against them, but he didn't need Lucien's recklessness then. Especially when there were so many things in balance. He, who always saw ahead, calculated things that the others couldn't.

Although Stargazer made his point clear, they were all looking at Bastian, waiting for his decision. His face, as sincere in his anger as in his compassion, portrayed precisely the internal conflict he was experiencing.

'Can you destroy the Soul Stone?' he asked Stargazer without taking his eyes off Ubaba.

'Yes,' the magician said firmly, not allowing a single hesitation to show in his voice.

'Will Kestos be removed from this world forever if the Soul Stone is destroyed?' Bastian asked, ripping the rest of his selfishness out of his heart as he did so.

'Yes, never to return,' assured the wizard.

'Do it,' said Bastian.

Lucien shook his head and bit his lips in disapproval.

'But know this, monster,' said Bastian, pointing his sword at Ubaba. 'The deliverance of the Soul Stone does not erase your crimes. You will answer for them. And if you try anything, I will hunt you to the extremes of the earth and the seas. That I promise you,' he said, and they all believed in him.

Ubaba's eyes shone dark lights of deep and bitter hate, but he said nothing.

'You may need to take cover now,' said Stargazer shortly afterward and without thinking twice, willing not to let the opportunity pass.

He signaled to his teammates where to hide while hurriedly beginning the redesign operation. They were all quick to take his advice and looked for cover as they could, for they knew not what to expect from this magical novelty. Klunk hid behind a tiny table that could not even protect his foot.

The ritual went without incidents, and after a long and fussy cumulation of rites, where the wizard conjured commanding words of power and summoned mighty energies, a light was thrown on Ubaba's body and then vanished in a windy violent spark.

Completely drained of his energies, Stargazed fell to the ground. He was caught in the air by an omniscient Hanam, who appeared when no one expected him to. When the hunchback touched the wizard, he instantly felt restored, reassuming control over his failing legs fairly quickly.

When the turbulence and agitation of magic ceased, Ubaba was examining his hands and arms. Undoubtedly, he could feel that his invisible chains had been broken and that he was now free from long-kept bondage. His eyes were filled with an intense and selfish joy.

'Well, you gave me what I wanted,' he said, addressing them as a group. 'Now, I will give you what is due to you,' the tainted bliss in his eyes gradually shifted to a bitter malice and rotting hate.

They all watched the scene passively, all but one. Stargazer kept himself ready for all the possible outcomes, and when he read the changes in Ubaba's demeanor, he understood his intentions and guessed what was about to happen. He then discreetly started preparing a calculated spell.

At the same time Ubaba opened one of his pockets and exposed the Soul Stone again, Stargazer hid his right hand behind his body. While the lackey raised the glowing stone high in his strong ape hands, bits of magic dust began to pour out of the wizard's fingers. The dust flickered into the air with growing intensity as the wizard quietly moved his mouth and speedily and quietly pronounced words into a multidimensional language.

'As agreed,' Ubaba had a solemn tone in his voice and Stargazer increased the speed of his incantation accordingly, 'I give you,' he said slowly and sadistically, enjoying every word, and the wizard leaned his shoulder back and fixed his feet on the ground, 'Kestos!' the monkey demon shouted, moving wings first through the air in a majestic supernatural jump. Stargazer closed and opened his eyes, and the conjured energy on them followed Ubaba's movement as if it knew beforehand exactly what he would do. With great dexterity and skill, Ubaba ended the great arch of his jump in a surprisingly soft landing and, stretching his long arm he moved to press, with a dry blow, Kestos's Soul Stone into the Adamantium Golem.

'No!' Stargazer shouted while he threw the spell he prepared.

The concentrated spray of dancing particles released by Stargazer spread across the air and ground and ceiling, but gathered together as they reached the golem at the same time that Ubaba finished his attack. Just before the tip of the Soul Stone hit the silver receptacle prepared to receive it in the golem's chest, a magically conjured rabbit materialized in the space between them. The Soul Stone pierced the animal's body thoroughly and the air pressure of the resulting spell exploded in Ubaba's face, launching him to the other side of that great chamber.

Showing an unnatural physical resilience by forthwith overcoming Stargazer's sneaky trick, Ubaba flapped his black crow wings and leaped into the air, reaching the balcony in the blink of an eye. From there, he looked at the wizard with a wave of sour anger shining from his eyes and disappeared into the darkness from which he came.

When they looked at the rabbit again, it was transforming into an anomaly, a mix between a man and an animal. As it morphed, all the white fur fell on the ground around it, revealing a sickly pink skin, pale and sticky. The noise of broken bones, stretching skin, and growing organs could be heard as if the nature of both bodies, man and animal, were mutually rejecting each other and forcefully amalgamating at the same time.

The scene was altogether repulsing. It was the physical representation of the wizard's soul crushing the essence of the unfortunate rabbit and tearing its spirit apart while invading and possessing it. The poor creature's despair, agony, and distortion made Stargazer regret his action, silently promising himself never to use a living being in that way again.

The half-man half-rabbit grew unto a naked hominid little taller than a halfling. It stood up with its eyes wide open and breathing heavily and looking down as if it was getting used to its new body. The gem was still nailed to the creature's chest, now fused with its flesh and smoking with the intensity of the manifested magic.

Suddenly, it raised its eyes and looked around, and the intelligence in its stare was piercing, fiery, alive. It stared at each and every one of them. Finally, it looked upon its reflection on an old dusty silver mirror on the wall.

'Who did this?' awkwardly, the pink and deformed creature surprised everyone with its strong, slow-angered voice. Corrupted and powerful, it vibrated the air as if it was coming from another dimension, a bad one.

'Who put me into this body?' it demanded to know.

'This is pure madness,' babbled Lucien, shaking his head.

'Ubaba,' answered Stargazer.

'Good,' the rabbit man said, ritualistically blinking his new eyes, 'I will kill him slowly,' he said, then slowly lifted its eyes to face them all again. This time it was personal, and they started seeing the terrible fires of high magic growing ever hotter in his eyes. They feared, they hesitated, some stepped back involuntarily.

'You,' said Kestos, finally revealed through his malice, 'you, I will kill fast,' said the reborn wizard as a vengeful smile grew ominously on his pink, deformed face.

The Dark Elves

Collectively, the elves are considered the most powerful known race in Fabula. This was and still is mostly due to the fact that they have natural lifespans measured in centuries, rather than decades. Many even stretch their existence with magic, becoming living ancient artifacts full of lost knowledge, life-changing wisdom, and true magic.

378

Their incredible life expectancy, mistaken by many as immortality, define how they behave and live, both as individuals and as a society. The outstanding accumulation of experience of their people during their long lives allow them to reach incredible mastery over everything they do. What humans consider geniality is everywhere and in everything in their communities, and it cumulates through their generations, constantly inspiring them to greatness, forging, therefore, from the ground up, incredibly stable and strong nations.

They face time differently, thus, they deal with everything differently. Only when they reach one hundred and fifty years of age they are considered to have matured. By that time, they are introduced to all deeds of adulthood that they believe to be important. Their warriors train for a hundred years before setting their feet on a battlefield for the first time, their artisans fill everything with magic, their minstrels master melodies that can make rocks dance, and their wizards are a vision of glory.

In general, even the most ordinary and meek elf is far more gifted and sharper than most humans would ever hope to become. Owners of pointing ears, their whole bone and muscle structure is slimmer than the human's, but their body is incomparably stronger. They keep their vitality well within their final centuries and are far less susceptible to diseases and toxins than most races. However, their intense attachment to life is not only biological, but also spiritual, with their personalities being generally grateful, happy, and highly musical.

As a people, they were lovers of peace, haters of violence, slow in their anger, quick in their spells, and profoundly artistic. It is said around the world that art is the language of an elven heart. From music to painting, from poetry to magic, they placed a high value on all forms of utterance. They considered all their activities from the point of view of self-expression, pouring themselves into their labors to the utmost of their talents' reaches. Everything they did, therefore, was done as a form of sharping the edges of their souls. Their slightly larger perspective brought them to live their lives with an intense desire for boundless self-refinement.

Although their organized societies can project a lot of power, even establishing a considerable dominance, it was, at least in the beginning, not of their nature to pursue ambitious goals. During the first eras of their civilization their contemplative nature prevailed over their dominium desires, and they did things for the sake of creating novelty and beauty, not for vain upholding or tyrannical accumulations.

Being strong as they were, the only menace to their way of life could only come from within their ranks. Eventually, it did, for in ancient times, because of reasons that are now largely lost, corruption had contaminated enough of them to lead them into a terrible civil war when a group of powerful dissidents, believing that the elves were the chosen race to rule all others and that they were the chosen one to rule the elves, tried to take power over the known Vortexes and use it to establish a world empire, dominating all known creation.

The rebellion failed, but the rebellious would not repent and were cursed and cast away. The curse was terrible. Their skins were turned pitch black, as their sins against creation; and all their hairs were discolored to a pale white, as a remembrance of their destitution. Afterward, and forevermore, they were named "The Dark Elves," for in darkness they walked indeed.

Banned and hunted down, the survivors found refuge in the endless night of the caves under the earth. There, they built fortified dwellings in deep gloom, ever away from the green earth, the blue seas, the golden sun, the silvery moon, and the multicolored stars. There, they plotted revenge while refining their already dangerous and impetuous magic.

Centuries passed while they insisted on their failed goals. In the end, they turned on each other, becoming a cruel society of pure oppression and hatred. Consumed by their wrath and poisoned by their selfish magic, they drowned themselves and their social institutions with the worst in the universe, living in a state of constant collapse by biding their collectives in a position of perpetual war. Such was their ability, their passion, and their commitment to their evil path, that life in their cities came to be described as the antechamber of hell.

In their everlasting thirst for power, they went drunk on many bitternesses, gathering despicable things from the Ether that ultimately consumed their souls, fusing their beings with whatever evil gluttony that may advance their cause.

Belligerent, cruel, and destructive, they escalated their evil fanaticism until they became the perfect example of a fallen society. Respecting nothing but strength, their cities were the birthplaces of perfect psychopaths. They raised their children in an environment where they were destitute of any regard for life or compassion; where the only thing that mattered was to win, and to win big.

In their world there were no sculptors, or architects, or farmers because the whole fabric of society was corrupt and devoted to domination. It was a given that they were all trained in the arts of killing, with every single one of them coming to age as flawless assassins, raised to be nothing but the lords of an ever-coming Dark Elf Empire that would one day rule over the world.

Fortunately, the quarrelsome nature of their tyranny and the blind hatred of their disposition created a perpetual general lack of coherence between them, preventing the world from suffering the cataclysmic result of their united reprisal.

Their beloved pride, the consequent lack of interest in building long-term relationships between them, and their artificial lack of morals caused by their self-imposed spiritual pollution, made them extremely lustful. As a result, they were far more fecund than other elves, and although they even surpassed the humans in some cases, their hyper-violent lifestyle balanced their population.

Their destructive magic was the most powerful among of all the known races, allegedly even stronger than the wizards of the sun elves. Thus, they were formidable enemies in direct combat. However, their favorite tactics were sabotage, political treachery, and backstabbing. Plotting against the surface realms and each other was the only life they knew, and killing was their favored sport. The mere sighting, or even rumors of a sighting, of a single dark elf lurking on the surface, was enough to trigger a full hunt by local authorities and to give any wise king a sleepless night.

Full of an old and acid resentment, they did their evil deeds in the shadows. Masters of manipulation, they rarely exposed their hand, especially when dealing with surface kingdoms. Sponsoring turmoil everywhere, the dark elves lived only to promote chaos throughout the world, weakening the strong, destroying the rare, and poisoning the beautiful.

Though brighter, their flames burned quickly. Because of their dangerous lifestyle, most dark elves were young, rarely going beyond three hundred years old. As a result, finding a dark middle-aged elf was as common as finding legs in an oyster.

Linothana'reth Enamedel Dûn Azar was a middle-aged dark elf. His malice, scheming cunningess, and his prominent magical knowledge had taken him through six hundred years of blackmails, murder, and the entire comprehensive list of formats for the manifestation of unrestricted raw violence.

Linothan solidified his position as the overseer of Rak'hamon, a large city that controlled a few mines. He could be classified as a politician by outsiders, but he was, above all, a survivor – an astute, resilient, and absolutely lethal survivor.

He was a political genius, and his capability to do magic was infinitely greater than his proper understanding of it, which made him a very dangerous man indeed. In his rage, he could blast a young dragon in pieces, but his vision of how his powers worked was less than ideal. In fact, he was a walking and talking menace to himself, but he wasn't entirely aware of that, and that was, in the end, his great miscalculation.

It was not hard to understand Linothan's motivations, for his personality, as in most dark elves, was a result of his whole being trying to answer a simple question at every moment of every day: "How can I get more power?" This inquiry was in him since he could remember, and, now, its echoes took control of every aspect of his life, pushing him to commit something that he seldom did – a mistake.

Perhaps because he thought about it longer than other dark elves, he eventually placed himself under the impression that he had found a definitive answer to that ever-longing question. However, his sightless focus, fueled by his selfish lust for power, blinded him to certain aspects of the unabridged truth. Truth, in its many forms, is reality unfolded, therefore, he was inconsiderate for some aspects of it, missing the bigger picture of the pathway he opened for himself. In the end, he was right in concluding that he had found a possible answer to his deepest desires, but, as his thought process was tainted by vanity, he was unable to predict all aspects of what might happen.

Through his politically privileged position and his great luck, he had found the ancient formula for mixing blood. A formula developed by their sect millennia ago, before their rebellion. Using their prodigious magical powers and their already efflorescing bottomless ambition, they develop a way to mix the essence of different species. At first, they were mainly interested in improving their own bodies and minds, diligently attaching to themselves whatever characteristics other beings had that could benefit them. They experimented with many fleshy and spiritual things, incidentally populating the world with the successes and the failures of their tryouts. It was during those ancient days that they created most of the isolated pockets of hybrid species that now existed in Fabula.

In due course, they learned enough to successfully mingle their bloodlines with potent species and entities, enhancing their powers even more. Luckily, after the Elven Civil War, the secret of "The Fusion" was lost and considered really hard to be replicated afterward. By a struck of luck nonetheless, Linothan acquired accesses to the foregone formula, working on it in secret to replicate its ritual. His intentions were clear: to expand his own powers and use it to form an unstoppable army under his command, forcing the dark elves to stand behind him while he launched a campaign to take hold of the entire Underworld to build an even greater army and then conquer the entire world.

However, he soon encountered a major problem in his plans. Unexpectedly, and to his great agony, he found that he was unable to understand many parts of the profound magic involved in that process. Without alternative and betrayed his best instincts, he did something he hated and avoided throughout his whole life: he shared his plans and granted some "trust."

Saazireth was a young wizard. As her mother before her, she possessed the sort of talent for spell-crafting that only manifested once in a generation. It took her just a handful of decades to acquire a fearful reputation throughout the caves of the Underworld. Her intelligence and her understanding of magic surpassed the logically possible, reaching places and things that only talent could attain. Her powers were profound and she was not afraid to use them, yet what took her to the next level was the fact that she had a unique way of approaching magic. Her deep intimacy with it was the consequence of her being raised and trained in isolation by her own mother, who was a legendary wizard herself, and whose true origin was lost in time. Saazireth had a bold, fearless, and charismatic personality, but also a tremendous immaculate beauty, which she sometimes used to exert a better and deeper influence on her targets than her spells would.

For the jealousy of her brethren, who almost universally kept their hairs carefully fixed in complex and refined styles full of excesses and jewelry, Saazireth kept her silky hair tousled and casually fallen over her face. Although this may look as a minor fact for an outsider, this small act of cultural rebellion was a devastating affront to her rivals, who were constantly fighting for positions on their lethal social battlefield of their social norms. For the other dark elves, this was her way to publicly express her outsiderness, her privilege, and her deemed superiority. This was correctly interpreted as an arrogant sign of insubordination, a claim from her part that she did not needed to comply with the sacred social rules simply because she knew and was better. It was as implicitly huge as it was apparently insignificant, and they knew it, and she knew that they knew it, and they hated her for it.

Linothan, admiring her beauty and boldness, fascinated by her personality, and in great need of her powers, made her his companion, always keeping her by his side on public occasions and giving her many private gifts and public honors. Together, they worked on the necessary rituals to bring The Fusion to a satisfactory operational status, but to achieve his goals he found that they needed many uncommon foreign ingredients and a good quantity and variety of rare things. As raiding and stealing all those things was not feasible for it would raise too much attention, he came up with a slower but safer plan.

With his immediate objectives in mind, and already thinking about the future expansion, he promoted a major shift in Rak'hamon's activities, remodeling the city economy. He was very careful to hide his true intentions, gradually allowing and stimulating "commerce" in the city. With the excuse of enriching their local economy, he even created a kind of "guard" in other to pass some sense of security for whoever dared to visit their city and outposts. Discreetly but surely, the isolationist policy predominantly adopted by the dark elves communities was broken. Linothan secretly opened and secured a few trading routes and facilitated the attraction of "merchants" to his dreadful city. He purged or made pacts with some of the occupants of the higher galleries in order to protect the passing caravans. Most were thief guilds and other organizations that possessed a need for hiding, but at the same time were full of precious information and surface contacts. Softly, with bribes and favors, he took control of those tunnels, and they too became trading posts for Rak'hamon, and the hidden agenda was always promoted on the background of everything he did. He used agents to stimulate smuggling and black markets throughout the caves he controlled so he could enjoy the benefits of it, acquiring what he needed for his project. These operations became very successful in establishing an intelligence network that greatly increased his outreach and influence under and over the surface.

Linothan also took advantage of the fact that the dark elves loved art in all of its many forms and hence were willing to trade massive amounts of rare gems, precious metals, and magic items for it. Overall, he was successful in making the new aperture pleasing to the large majority of Rak'hamon's inhabitants. As the dark elves loathed the concept of money, devoting their minds exclusively to the pursuit of power, there were, indeed, many marvelous and precious things that were undervalued in their cities. It was not long before some brave merchants were attracted by the possibility of making a fortune and starting to do business on Rak'hamon's trading posts and even in its very own marketplace.

It was the right plan, at the right time, for the right place, for his self-righteous reasons. Everything worked flawlessly, and Linothan got what he wanted, up until a point. At that point, he went to see Saazireth at the secret location for there was news of breakthroughs and expectations that their intents had finally come to fruition.

'How are things, my love?' he asked her when he saw her standing over the large table on the other side of the laboratory.

Linothan entered the place taking dominium over all things. He cruised the large room with his typical haughty air, despising everything under his high chin. He seemed to even inspect the air around him from the bottom of his overbearing eyes.

It took a little while for her to answer him – a deadly crime for anyone else, but her. Apparently, she was very concentrated, working on something important over one of the lab's amethyst table.

With a patronizing smile, he got closer to her telling his colossal ego that she was probably immersed in something exceedingly complex while simulating admiration for her loyalty to his project.

'Everything is…prepared, my lord,' Saazireth finally answered him while she made the powerful magic dagger she was examining over the table disappear into the air over the palm of her hand. Her answer made it clear that she heard him, yet decided to answer at her convenience. However, Linothan knew better than acknowledge the potential offense, deciding to solemnly ignore it for he was now too close to get what he wanted. Her favors had become too precious for him, leaving him no choice but to conceive to her inconceivable things.

Only when he was directly behind her, and only then, she turned to receive him with an overwhelmingly charming and massively malicious smile – just the way he liked it. She read him entirely while looking at him with that smile. Saazireth was delighted when she noticed no suspicion over his face and no major changing in his geometry.

'I shall make you my queen,' he said while grabbing her by her shoulders after a long and violently passionate kiss. He used an unusual amount of strength to seize her body and, for the first time since she knew him, she could spot the nuances of a conflicting lie in him. However, she was not surprised or disappointed, but satisfied. His hesitation demonstrated that part of him was really on the emotional inclination she wanted him to be on. Among her many prowess, her best and most secretive trick was the one she was taught to master first, which was to hide her thoughts and final intentions so deep in her soul that not even magic could trace it. And, at the same time, read other's intentions with a depth that reached the very designs of their essences.

'And the world would soon receive a worthy ruler,' she said while looking at the ceiling as she was passionately watching it from her mind.

'Through what we will do today, the dark elves shall rise again and establish forevermore their rightful place among the nations,' she said, turning to him so he could see the fire of her lust burning into her soul.

Her fantasies overwhelmed her, taking control of her senses as her blood boiled in desire. Her natural charm gave place to an ugly power-hungry maniac aspect. Her eyes were filled with carnal appetites and were begging him to join her ecstasy. She kneeled in front of him with her tongue unconsciously out of her salivating mouth while, without breaking their eye contact, she frenetically started to open his fly.

'Calm now, my child,' he said, tapping her shoulder and ego-tripping through the fact that he could partially control his lasciviousness while dominating hers. 'Let us make haste of this endeavor,' he said, enjoying every word that came out of his own mouth. 'For greater pleasures lay ahead of us,' his tone was of a rare sincerity. Although his love for the flesh was great, even notorious, his love for himself and for power was far greater.

She was already delivered to unconsciously touching her own body, still, contradicted, she had risen from the submissive position she was in for, apparently, his words affected her higher passions too. When she was up, he pointed to the complex altar that clearly was the focal point of that facility.

'Through my powerful magic,' she said, 'I promise that I shall put you in your rightful place, my lord.' Her words still came out heavy from the breathlessness of her arousal.

She then left his arms and hurried to execute the final preparations. Together, they started the rituals activating the runes and casting many ancient spells from old Grimoires. The ritual was incredibly long and intricate, and after hours of engaging in the many necessary rites, they grew the magical crescendo to a point where the complexity of the equations kept the fullness of her mind bound to the higher dimensions. The excitement of the energies and the construction and organization of the equations took most of the time.

The Fusion dictated more than just understanding and power, it demanded a supreme understanding of all things, requiring certain artistic geniality to draw and integrate all the equations. The amount of information passing through her mind was so overwhelming, that it created the side effect of a tremendous quantity of energy pouring over her eyes. The portion of that energy that manifested itself in form of light was fiercely blinding, penetrating everything. Linothan was using special goggles to protect himself from it, otherwise, the intense radiation of the light would make any observer physically drowsy. He was also empty of his spells, for she instructed him to use all his extensive magic energy in the many steps of the preparation process to acquaint himself with the metaphysical mechanisms. When she felt satisfied with the way the geometries were set, and all things that mattered to her were in place, and while most of her mind was still on the other side, balancing and holding it all together, she signaled to him.

'The altar is yours, my lord,' she said with a deformed voice that seemed to come directly from the Ether.

He knew exactly what to do. As her mind was giving support for the new design, he opened a valve where the precious blood of a powerful trans-dimensional creature of their choice dripped profusely through the altar.

Linothan was weakened as never before. He could now barely stand. Trembling and with a lot of difficulties, he took off his robe and lay naked on the altar over the blood. His body and soul were so drained and damaged by the rituals, that bruises and ruptures were visible all over his skin, but the dark elf would not bleed out for his mighty heart was damaged and enfeebled almost to the point of failure. The dark elf felt frail and vulnerable, standing only over the visions of his ambitions accomplished. When he lay in position, she made a gesture with her fingers and a set of iron straps materialized over his body, binding him to the altar.

'What is the meaning of this?' he asked alarmed, barely gathering the strengths to talk.

'It is necessary, my lord,' she comforted him. 'Soon, all will be over,' she said, her voice was still terribly psychedelic for all the energized places in the universe that her mind was simultaneously connected to.

Saazireth closed her eyes slowly and purposely. When she opened them again, the bright light and the intense radiations were gone. She redid the distortion that made her float over the altar and landed by Linothan side. In a motherly manner, the young dark elf put her left hand on his forehead, as if consoling him. At the same time, she made a discreet gesture with her right hand and the strange black blood started to redraw back to its container before it touched Linothan's skin. While gently running her hands through his hair, she used her thumb to press a magic rune on his forehead, preventing him from doing any spell. Too decrepit to react or even protest, and bound by strong magic, Linothan could do little but to look at her from his sick eyes and express the emotions that he still could consciously manifest. He tried desperately to free himself, but his situation was hopeless. When he saw the knife materializing in her hand, he knew instantly what was about to happen. Tears of hate poured through his eyes, veins pumped all over his face, forehead, and neck as his agony came to a peak. He spasmed heavily, using all of his remaining energies in a despaired attempt to free himself. Saazireth pressed her thumb against his mouth sealing its flesh with another rune, preventing him from talking or screaming even though he had no stretch for neither. He was still crying through his throat and chick bones when she hacked his neck from ear to ear, slicing his jugulars wide open.

'I'm nobody's queen,' she whispered in his ears while his blood left his body. There was no violence or distraction in her voice. She was graceful, as if hoping he would understand and accept everything logically and peacefully.

Her golden eyes smiled frankly with pure pleasure as she held his bleeding head in front of her face.

The Cost

Kestos' chambers were utterly destroyed. The violence of the fight had spared nothing. There were pieces of rubble everywhere, the majority of the ceiling collapsed, most columns had crumbled, and half of the balcony had been reduced to a pile of rocks. Either by fire, ice, dwarven grenades, or steel, almost all objects around them had suffered damage from the intense combat.

388

It was the worst fight they'd had so far. They spilled a lot of their own blood, learning in the worst way possible what it was like to fight against a powerful and experienced spellcaster.

Without magic items or potions to help him, and although incarnated in his frail half-rabbit body, the wizard proved to be quite lethal regardless, coming very close to annihilating all of them. In the aftermath of the battle, even after deploying and depleting all of their considerable healing resources, The Fellowship was still in a pretty bad shape.

Stargazer was limping, barely standing. His outfits were completely destroyed, including most of his coat. At least a third of his body was burned to a good crisp, a few bones were shattered to powder, and he was missing an ear, part of his hair, and two entire fingers from his left hand.

Shunto proved to be a formidable warrior, but even though, he barely made it alive. He was able to do things on the battlefield that impressed everybody and really introduced Bastian and Lucien to the next level of fighting prowess. Without him, they would undoubtedly have been overcome by Kestos. Fighting with his whole body and making his weapons a fluid part of himself, Shunto would alternate his eastern style of sword fighting with terrible energy-filled blows from his bare hands and feet. Later, he would clarify to them that his father was the ambassador of the mighty Ansan Empire and her mother an elven princess from Aglorathan, an independent elven city-state at the Fire Mountains. He told them that he was taught the art of sword fighting by his mother, and his father introduced him to the silent arts, where he learned how to jump shadows. Growing up in Valkar's capital he had the opportunity to train with the Steel Fists, learning how to channel his mind's energy to break and disrupt matter barehanded. He mastered his technic to a point where he could integrate his mind and body, sourcing, much like a spellcaster, energy from the Ether and then unleashing it in fantastical physical feats like the one he used to end Kestos. When the fighting was in its most desperate hour, and they faced defeat, Shunto saw himself unarmed for the wizard had melted his swords with the power of his magic. He them jumped into the shadows and appeared behind Kestos, striking diagonally with his bare hands, he punched through the wizard's frail body from behind, extracting the Soul Stone from his chest through his thorax. With the violent detachment of the Soul Stone from the avatar body, it exploded, launching the wretched remains of Shunto's arms on his own face and neck, blinding him and reaping his body all over

389

with shrapnels made of his own bones. Hanam stopped his bleeding, but even so he was now still lying on a wall, unconscious, blind, disfigured, and helpless.

Bastian was still catatonic, swaying and shivering on a corner as he fought to stay sane. He was still suffering consecutive and powerful panic attacks as a result of the mind control spells cast on him. His body had suffered too, and he was still bleeding profusely from a few head injuries. He was being cared for by a mutilated Sahafira who was doing the best she could for him, but the pain from her missing leg was not making it easy for her. The last healing potion she drank closed her wound and stopped the bleeding, but would not regenerate her limb nor alleviate the pain from the nerve damage. She, as all of them, had most of her body, clothing, armor, and equipment ripped apart, burned, dissolved, and shattered by the many magical hazardous materializations of the chaotic fight. It was only later that Stargazer, with the help of Kestos's powerful Grimoire, would slowly repair their bodies and garments to a workable level, but they were almost totally unequipped to keep themselves safe on the tunnels.

Lucien was numb from the hip down. The broken pillar he was leaned against was an allegory for his broken spine. Through his smashed thorax, he tried to breathe, but his lungs hurt with every sip of air. Most of his weapons and armors, including his swords, were broken, melted or disintegrated. He was conscious and with no major external bleeding, but, having used all his healing potions during the battle, he could now do nothing to contain the growing fever that was burning through his body because of his multiple injuries.

When Hanam had just finished applying healing, bandages, and tourniquets on what was left of Shunto's arms and face, he went to check Klunk, finding him still trapped in the force field conjured by Kestos early in the fight. Although he had no major injuries, he was very upset with his enduring invisible prison. With a tap on his shoulder, Hanam comforted him, and with a nod of his head, he let him know that there was nothing else he could do for now. Desolated, Klunk frowned and let go a long-muffled moan. Hanam went for Stargazer.

'You got it there with you?' Hanam asked Stargazer while he applied just enough healing magic to stop the bleeding from the cracks over the wizard's toasted blackened skin.

Stargazer noticed that the tone in Hanam's voice was more direct than usual.

'Yes, I'm keeping it safe,' he replied, relieved, and then sat on a huge piece of the ceiling.

'Can we use it to open the door?' the hunchback insisted in the conversation.

'I don't think so. It is too dangerous,' lamented Stargazer, grimacing with pain.

'So it is all over then?' asked Hanam.

'I didn't say that.' Stargazer friendly smiled at Hanam, but a sudden sharp pain brought the grimace back to his face.

'What do you have in mind?' Hanam asked.

'I think I have the equipment here to destroy the Soul Stone,' said the wizard over his pain. 'We must ban him from this world first,' he said while painfully opening a flask of a special herbal ointment of his own making. 'Although,' he stopped all movement to gather strength to continue, 'I will need a few days to study the stone's architecture and maybe weeks to learn some of the spells from his Grimoire,' he said.

Hanam looked around, finally exhausted.

'Take your time,' he said, then slowly sat on a massive shard of the wall beside Stargazer. 'We are going nowhere,' he said while helping Stargazer open the flask and taking some of the wizard's ointment for himself.

Traders of the Deep

The unfaithful were half-humanoid half-octopus freaks created by the dark elves with the sole objective to be used as super-soldier in their megalomaniac wars of conquest.

Back when the dark elves were still truly united, they planned to spawn extraordinarily powerful armies by mass deploying these creatures in large formations. Through these armies, they would invade and take control of the surface world. They failed, and the history of their failure is the history of the unfaithful.

Ironically, the dark elves created them too powerful and too smart, and, eventually, they rebelled and fled the dark elves' domains. Most were hunted and killed for sport and revenge, yet a remnant found refuge in the deeper areas of the Underworld. There, they found themselves too intelligent and creative to remain lurking in those deep dark corners, but their nature was altogether too wicked to completely integrate with the peoples and institutions of the surface either. Thus, they ended up hiding in between them.

The unfaithful were created as quick learning, ruthless, and powerful spell crafters. Therefore they were the possessors of incredible magical sensibilities, especially in what regarded the affairs of the mind and thought reading. Even away from the dark elves' dominium, these gifts naturally and effectively developed into rare and useful abilities that invariably brought them closer and closer to the surface. In time they quickly discovered that trade between the surface and the deepest realms of the Underworld was the perfect fit for their social status and geographical position. It was very profitable, convenient, and it allowed them to progress their very questionable notion of a civilized life and finance their numerous despicable passions. Applying their sharp minds and magical talents to it, they ended up becoming the great merchants of the underground, working as the delicate connection between the surface world and everything below it.

"Peace" between them and their former masters eventually came about when the dark elves got tired of killing them and started tolerating their presence and using their business. Coexistence, thus, came ultimately from convenience and mutual interest, and for centuries the unfaithful went around trading whatever they could, expanding their routes while establishing for themselves a relatively safe reputation among customers and suppliers from the surface. Although the word "safe" should never be used to describe anything around an unfaithful, for, in their gargantuanly lustful and abysmally dreadful dreams of power, the dark elves forged in these creatures an uncontrollable appetite for the brain mass of sentient beings, condemning them to a terribly degrading parasitic, bestial existence. This sadistically implanted hunger was a supernatural curse that caused them to go through great lengths of risk to satisfy it. The intrinsic details of their vice were truly soul-crushing, especially because their will to eat people ran parallel to their deep understanding of the universe and their keen emotional sensibilities – they connected with people's emotions, they appreciated all the existence expressed in them, and they still wanted to devour them, brain first.

Vorlok was an unfaithful. He was a merchant by trade and a glutton by choice. He traded slaves, mostly surface people who got lost in the Underworld somehow. He was particularly good at his job for he had a talent for sensing fear. Like a shark with blood, he could taste terror at incredible distances. As the Underworld was seemingly endless and required complex three dimensional navigation, he built a net of spies and informants in his area of operation to increase his profits. For a fee, they provided him with info about any disturbances that could mean that there were lost people or soft targets around what he considered his territory. He then proceeded to capture his prey and sell it to the highest bidder wherever he could.

Recently, he has been tipped by some scouts that something or someone was leaving a trail of death by killing hundreds of creatures next to the eastern sector of some abandoned mines. After paying the scouts generously for their information, and for the "license" to "hunt" in that area, he immediately set on a chase.

From the very start he had a bad feeling about this one, but business was slow and he needed a good amount of quick cash fast. By the time he was warned about this new "job," he was so desperate that he was almost preparing for a surface raid to hijack some goods, which was a terribly risky thing and he preferred to reserve it as a last resort. Especially with the recent rumors that several groups of competent dwarf raiders were cleaning and trapping the upper tunnels for some unknown reason.

It is too deep, even for the dwarves, he thought. *Whoever it is, it is probably lost, but how have it managed to get so deep without being noticed?* he inquired, curious to his bones. *It must be a highly experienced adventurer,* he worried. *Probably got into the deeper levels with the help of magic and is now trying to get to the surface,* he speculated. *I will wear it down until the time is right,* he plotted, getting excited by all the evil things he saw himself doing.

Vorlok unleashed his varmints and started his hunt. After a few days, he found the tracks, but he was surprised, confused, and worried that they were of a male wood elf. Reluctant, he decided to play it carefully and take the time to study what was really going on before he put himself in any sort of risk. He had never encountered a creature from the surface alone at that depth before, let alone a wood elf. He followed the elf around for several days until he became convinced that all the dangers he feared were minimized.

The first thing he noticed was that he walked in circles, taking random directions with each step, not only looking lost, but disoriented. The second was that he was not exactly helpless. In fact, he managed to kill everything on

393

his way, and Vorlok found clear evidence indicating that he was carrying at least one magic weapon, probably a sword. The third thing he noticed was that, over time, his tracks became less and less deep and closer to each other, a sign of weight loss due to lack of food and/or sleep.

After many days Vorlok saw that the elf was increasingly lethargic by his tracks' patterns, and the unfaithful decided then that it was time to act before some other creature could snap him away, or eat him, or both. When Vorlok felt it was the right moment to put him into custody, he quickened his pace and found the elf unconscious over a tiny sand beach inside a river cave. He was struggling, but still alive.

The first thing Vorlok had to do was to use the utmost of his willpower to contain himself. When he smelled the elf's body from close, his whole being trembled over his greedy appetite. It took him an amazing amount of self-control not to devour the elf's brains right on the spot, for purebred elves tasted especially good for the unfaithful's palate. Wood elves were now uncommon anywhere because of the king's quarantine and extremely rare in the Underworld, this could be a once in a lifetime treat for him. To make matters worse, Vorlok could smell that this elf's blood matured in a different era, a time when the world was fresher and wilder. He had been salivating from his tentacle mouth for days while on the elf's trail, but now, approaching his fallen body enough to feel its warmth, Vorlok couldn't contain his acid saliva inside his detestable lips. It dripped all over the place, dissolving holes in everything it touched and releasing smoke as it fell over rocks and on the ground.

When he was about to break the elf's skull with his beak and eat "just a little bit" of his brain, his innermost survival instincts made him think of his outstanding debts with Saazireth. Then, he remembered the things she was capable of, AND willing to, do with him. Just a quick pick into that realm of possibilities was enough to end his fanatical appetite, and once he disengaged his mind from his stomach, he could face the elf with a higher interest and a rational set of eyes. Vorlok's curiosity took hold of him once again. He fed on the elf's emotions for so long while he followed him through the tunnels that he now believed he knew him somehow. Yet, he was wrong, and this was fascinating to him.

Examining his body and possessions, Vorlok noticed that everything about the elf was peculiar, and each particularity brought loads of corrosive interrogations to Vorlok's anxiously inquisitive mind. Worrying for his safety, he decided to pry a little bit in the elf's mind to evaluate how much he might worth.

After he was satisfied with what he found through the summoning of a powerful mind reading spell, Vorlok telepathically summoned the giant beetle he used to transport heavy loads and strapped the elf to its back. To avoid any surprises, he used an indestructible dark elves' Silk Rope to bind him in place.

'You, my most uncommon friend, will make me rich,' he said it while lightly tapping the shoulder of the unconscious elf.

He then stepped into the tunnel and commanded the giant bug to follow him.

Spoils of War

Following the battle with Kestos, they started a period of healing, in which Stargazer, Sahafira, and Hanam worked tirelessly to restore their bodies to a full health. They combined their magic to heal all flesh wounds, but they could not regenerate legs and arms, and fingers, and ears, and eyes. Stargazer, however, studying directly from Kestos's Grimoire, assisted by Sahafira, and using many of the magic altars, the equipment, and the capacitors he found there, was able to grow their missing body parts and complete the healing process.

Shortly after, the wizard sold them the notion that it would be very important not to leave behind all the strategic magic equipment at the disposition of an eventual new villain. Upon seeing their legs grow back and their spines regenerated, it was not hard to convince them of the benefits of having these resources at their disposal. They became truly committed to getting the most of it, but they had now spent too much time in the darkness of Kestos's Chambers and were worn out and ready to see home again.

Stargazer then set to learn how to use the trans-dimensional portal on the frame in a safe manner. While he did, he had them hauling everything they could into the frame where they found Shunto imprisoned. Following the wizard's recommendation, they set everything inside the structure portrayed in the picture. Shunto called it "The Small Castle," and the name stuck with them.

They systematically and methodically picked the tunnels and chambers clean of anything that had some value. Finished and unfinished magic siege weapons, entire production lines, raw materials, precious elements, parts, books, and manuals were all set up inside the Small Castle, virtually creating a vastly capable laboratory and potentially great workshops composed of the gear that took Kestos and his allies years to put together.

Stargazer also devoted his time to study the deceased enchanter's Grimoire, personal library, and memoirs. He, then, without knowing very well what he was doing, set up a destruction ritual in the same place the Soul Stone was forged. After a couple of failed attempts he achieved success, destroying the Soul Stone and sending the wizard's soul to the higher dimensions, finally banning Kestos from this world.

'So frustrating,' lamented Bastian, witnessing the boring and tedious conclusion of the ritual. 'I never thought it would be like this,' he said.

Lucien said nothing, he just stared at his friend.

'There is no honor in it,' Bastian added, unsatisfied with how things turned out.

'You should be glad that it's over,' said Lucien pragmatically.

He then turned his back to Bastian and followed the others that were moving to check the chambers beyond the steel door that unlocked and opened immediately after the Soul Stone was crushed.

Stargazer, Sahafira, and Shunto searched for traps by the entrance but found none. They had deducted the astute wizard must have deemed them not necessary or justifiable when such a powerful sealing spell was in place. Their eyes were now accustomed to the low light, hence, when the door opened, they had to look away for they could not stand all the light coming from inside the room. There were several stashes of gold and piles upon piles of silver. Jewelry, pearls, rare weapons and spellbound armor filled the rest of the spots.

'We are sooo rich,' said Lucien, gloomy with fatigue but still very happy.

In the center of the room, over an altar of marble, in a clear favoritism, there was a translucent sphere with a dark blue core carved from a single crystal. The orb was larger than a man's chest, and inside of it, in perpetual motion, there was a miniaturized storm breaking. It was hypnotically beautiful and they all stopped to watch it from a distance. Hanam, ignoring the gold and the silver, went straight to it. He took the little velvet bag Taalen Dealonson provided them with and engulfed the huge orb until it disappeared in the space inside the bag.

In an inconspicuous corner, there was a skeleton still dressed in a very fine wizard garment colored with a loud yellow and blue. The outfits were spotless, obviously magically preserved. All of the deceased's personal objects were preserved and unspoiled in the same manner. He still had his jewelry on. Rings were still on his fingers and a golden tiara on his skull. A thick leather belt full of pockets covered his whole abdomen, from his hip to his chest. His staff was still stubbornly gripped by his bony hand.

'Kestos's remains,' said Stargazer for the ones who were still in doubt.

He also ignored the gold and silver and was now shaking with excitement at the contemplation of the fallen wizard's kit. Although he was quite aware of Kestos's evil deeds, he admired his possessions solely as the magical marvels they were. His eyes shone with desire as he looked at them – especially the staff, for it funneled all the wizard's undeniable talents and vast vanities.

The staff was Kestos's most prized and beautiful work of magical art, expressing this idea not only mystically, but also physically. Among all his prolific works, the staff was Kestos's greatest creation. It was a masterpiece by any angle for the ones who could see and understand its dimensional geometries, and a dreaded object for the ones who would suffer its power. The staff could be described as a drop point short sword attached to a metal shaft with a flawless large blue gem on the other extremity. It was brewed with talent and embedded with the power drained from other ancient artifacts. It was crafted not by hands, but solemnly by magic will. It was not only a magic-enhancing device full of secrets, but at the same time a formidable weapon filled with rage.

They spent two days counting and dividing the gold, the silver, and all the gems. Shunto helped too, even though he would not claim a single coin for himself. He, in fact, was revealing himself as a real gentle and smart person, and, at this point, everybody was liking and trusting him.

After everything was counted, they transferred everything to the Small Castle. Stargazer made a list of all the things they found and displayed the market value on the side to facilitate the count. As there were some magic items, he explained first the function and powers of each one briefly and, after a lot of discussions, he managed to make everybody happy, including himself.

'Well, let us see what we have here,' he started, examining his notes.

'Hanam, you are getting the orb as agreed,' he said and Hanam nodded positively. 'And that is that,' Stargazer crossed out something on his list and moved on.

'Klunk is receiving his share of the gold, silver, and jewels,' he said. 'As he had no interest in any magical object, everybody should pay a fifth of whatever that person is taking in terms of the magic items according to the evaluation table we have all agreed upon.'

They looked at Klunk for confirmation and saw that he was distracted, failing miserably while trying to lick his own hair.

'I will take that as an OK,' said Stargazer, crossing his list again. This time twice.

'Sahafira, you are getting your share of magic items plus most of my gold to compensate for a trade on the Mind Ruby. Your selection of items consists of: his Defensive Ring, his Cloak of Fortune, this True Silver Fury Dagger and his Wand,' the wizard said, and by the tone of his voice, he clearly regretted not having the last one. Kestos' Wand was one of the most powerful wands Stargazer ever saw. Kestos imbued it with several rare spells and special tricks and merged different wands into it. In the end, the idea that Stargazer was gaining its share, plus the Grimoire, plus the entire structure for setting up a state-of-the-art enchanting laboratory, comforted him that he didn't have the wand, but still. Regretfully, the wizard crossed his list.

'Lucien, you are having your share of gold, and of silver, and precious stones. This dwarven made, magically enhanced, full plate mail; this very rare dark elfish pure adamantium long sword; and this old Knights of the Golden Order magical belt that increases the body strength and stamina. Crossed, crossed, and crossed,' he said.

'Bastian, you have decided to end your debt with me, so I will be deducting from your share of gold, silver, and gems the amount agreed for your father's sword, minus the days you serv...helped me,' the wizard corrected himself. 'And, as you requested, you will use the rest of your liquid values and your share of magic items, so you can have the magical weapons and armors from the other fallen Valkarians that we could identify from their family coat of arms.' Stargazer looked at him waiting for a final confirmation.

Bastian signed a resolute yes and the wizard crossed his list again and again.

'You are being so naïve, my friend,' Lucien lamented. 'You think any of them would ever do that for you?' he asked Bastian, looking irritated with his friend's decision, knowing very well what he had in his mind.

'And, finally, myself,' said the wizard. 'I will have my share of gold, silver, and gems; Kestos's Battle Staff; his Mind Ruby (that I have traded with Sahafira); his Lava Ring; and Kestos's very own Battle Belt of Physical Might and More,' he said, crossing his list rhythmically.

'There is, of course,' he said, 'the siege weapons and the unfinished Adamantium Constructor that we agreed to deliberate later, but, for now, I think it's time for us to do our last checks and prepare to leave,' said the wizard and they all agreed.

When they were ready, Stargazer put them all together in the empty treasure room that was now devoid of every single piece of gold and silver, and asked Hanam to put the orb back on its altar.

'What are you going to do?' asked Lucien, wearied.

'I thought we were leaving,' said Bastian, also wearied.

'We are,' answered Stargazer.

Using the same abnormal process of space suppression of Taalen's blue and green velvet bag, Hanam popped the orb back to the current world and placed it were they found it.

'I will show you guys a trick this baby can do.' Stargazer pointed to the orb and winked at them.

'This guy needs a girlfriend, seriously,' Lucien whispered to Bastian.

'Hold on now,' he said while closing his eyes and starting to wave his hand around the orb.

The wizard started disturbing the energies of the artifact, and the majestically alive crystallized patterns within it gathered speed. The elements that formed the reality inside the orb moved and flashed in pulses of increased intensity into a circular thunderstorm that glorified in a ballet of particles and energies subjected to an entirely different set of physical laws.

Suddenly, a second thunderstorm appeared, not inside the orb though, but on a corner of the room. Startled, Stargazer immediately stopped what he was doing and drew his weapons. Instinctively, they all did the same.

'What?! What?!' Lucien shouted, demanding to know.

The others were too surprised to say something.

'This is not good,' Stargazer said while his mind was going through a thousand hypotheses.

'No shit,' said Lucien pressing the hilt of his new adamantium sword.

'Someone, somehow, found us.' Stargazer concluded, becoming even more apprehensive about the possibilities that his own words might bring.

The vortex in the corner imploded in a dry vacuum crack and seven human figures materialized in the room.

'Iana?' asked Bastian.

'Father is mad as hell, Lucien,' she ignored Bastian and all the questions hanging from their faces.

'I'm telling you, between these guys,' she pointed to the huge professional warriors escorting her, 'the scryer, and the two expensive teleporting scroll, you caused a major bleeding in the family treasury.'

The whole scene was bizarre to them, and no one, not even Lucien, knew what to say.

Sahafira noticed that Iana was in full combat gear, with a light plate armor, a sword, and a dagger by her belt, and two wands attached to a leather bracelet by the sleeve. Sahafira has been in countless hard negotiations, and she knew better than not to maintain a defensive posture and procure a tactical advantage. She discreetly flanked the warriors while they talked. The huge men on Iana's flanks immediately noticed what she was doing, but maintained unflappable iron stances, moving little but their eyes.

Iana approached Bastian and checked him out from head to toe. Sahafira didn't like that. While still looking at Bastian, Iana pressed her two armored fingers on Stargazer's chest.

'And how the hell did you manage to cancel the espionage and teleportation shields?' She was being strongly authoritarian, but she couldn't hide her strong curiosity.

'We…ah,' Stargazer choked, 'we…stole them,' he replied, immediately regretting the way his words came out.

She looked at him.

'Many imperial wizards fought against these shields for decades, trying to find and breach into this place,' she said, intrigued about Stargazer.

He said nothing at first, but he immediately understood that once they placed the runes and magic equipment inside the painting, their effects were transferred outside this plane of existence, causing them to cease to exist here.

'Have we met before?' she asked Stargazer, giving him a second look.

'No,' he lied.

He recognized her the moment she teleported in the room. They were almost the same age and although he was homeschooled and elusive, he still remembered seeing her around Westgate. Although his body was completely changed by the years of ingesting the garden's super-foods and the fountain's magic water, Iana's could have identified him had it not been for the fact that her attention was now completely focused on his left hand.

'Is that…?' she hesitated.

'Is that?!' asked Lucien, looking at the altar and noticing that the orb was not there anymore.

Stargazer somehow was holding the orb with just one hand. It was so permeable to magic that he diminished its size enough so he could grip it.

'What are you doing here, Iana?' Lucien shouted at her sister.

'I'm here for you,' she answered her brother without taking her eyes off Stargazer and the orb.

'What?' asked Lucien.

'Do you think Father will let you run around doing whatever you want without keeping an eye on you?' This time she rested her gaze on Lucien, but not before letting Stargazer know that she knew what he was holding.

'We have been watching you since you left, but we lost you when you got into this place,' she said. 'When an opening appeared, I scried you and teleported here under his orders. This operation cost him a lot of money, and it is now time for you to go home. He has had it with your reckless adventurer fantasies,' she was impassive.

'I'm not going anywhere, but where I choose to,' said Lucien.

'I'm going to take you home one way or another,' she said and drew her wand.

At the same instant, with a scary discipline, the seasoned Valkarian soldiers drew their heavy weapons.

'OK, OK,' interrupted Shunto, 'put your wands and weapons down right now!' he commanded.

They did what he asked and the tension eased a little.

'Is Iana right?' Shunto asked her politely. 'Look, unless he is an outlaw, you can't force your brother to go anywhere he doesn't want to. Furthermore, they are here in the service of the Emperor,' he said.

'What?!' Iana immediately looked at Bastian and Lucien for an explanation.

'What?' They all looked at Shunto for an explanation.

'They are here under the guidance of Taalen Dealonson,' Shunto said.

'THE Taalen Dealonson?' Iana asked.

'Is there any other?' Lucien asked.

'Actually, last time I' checked there were like three of them,' answered Shunto. 'But never mind, this was a long time ago.' Shunto tried to remedy the impact of what he said. It didn't work, and The Fellowship continued to be confused for a while.

'Anyway,' continued Shunto. 'Is your father ready to explain himself to the Imperial authorities? Because he might if he interferes here,' he put it down.

Iana hesitated for a second, and then looked at Lucien one last time.

'Forget about it, I'm not coming,' Lucien answered her unspoken question.

'Look,' Stargazer decided to risk something, 'take these to your father as a trophy,' he said, giving her a small bag filled with the phylactery shards.

'What is this?' she asked.

'Proof,' he said.

'The pieces of Kestos's Soul Stone,' added Bastian, wrongfully thinking she needed further explanations.

Iana was surprised to her core, and that was exactly were Stargazer wanted her to be. He didn't waste a minute, setting to explore the advantage to the max.

'Take it to Westgate,' he said, 'it will help heal some of the wounds of its past. A lot of people will sleep better when they know that Kestos is finally dead.'

'How do you know for sure?' she asked, falling into the second trap he set. This one, however, he placed even before that conversation started.

'We killed him,' he said. 'I split the Soul Stone myself.'

Confused, she looked at the bag, feeling the pieces of the crystal inside of it. She then looked at Bastian and Lucien, and both of them confirmed the wizard's story nodding with their heads.

'Who are you?' she asked.

'I'm Stargazer,' he said. 'And this is The Fellowship of the Sword,' he pointed to his companions as he savored the prophecy drenched words.

The moment was suddenly made intense and they all inflated their chests with an air of newly perceived pride, for they all understood then the consequence to the outside world of their deeds in those dark caves. Iana stepped back, intimidated by their surprising results and their boldness. She gave them all a second look and sheathed her wand.

'Very well,' she said, and, whipping out a scroll, she began reading from it. A spot of light then shone under the center of her formation and a tiny whirlwind of distortions was manifested between her and her escort. The snap of the vacuum implosion was heard and they were gone.

'That was really good, boy,' Shunto wanted Stargazer to know that he understood what he had done.

Stargazer pretended he didn't hear it, instead, he changed the subject.

'Now, where was I?' asked the wizard while manipulating the orb physically and magically.

Promptly, and a little unusually overconfident, he set the orb to float in the air and restored it to its "original" size. Stimulated by Stargazer's magic powers, the transmutational process restarted, intensifying until it transcended the space inside the crystal ball, blowing Stargazer's hair with the winds of its agitations. The energy and vapors crescendo grew quickly, and it was not long before they were in the middle of a cyclone with the room's dust hitting their eyes, blinding them. The wind got so strong that they were finding hard to stay balanced on their feet. Lucien was not disturbed at all though, for he was now enjoying the added magical strength coming from his new magic belt. He stood tall and laughed at Bastian's struggles to stay up. In the end, he grabbed his friend by the arm and helped him, but not before getting into Bastian's nerves a little bit.

The wind started to distort the space around them and everything became fluid and dismantled like fresh ink from a fresco on a hot day. Stargazer crossed his finger over the horizon and a separation appeared. It started as a narrow-angled distortion, but soon enough the world outside the whirlwind folded and changed unexpectedly. Before they could completely absorb the altered landscape surrounding them, the whole air snapped with a decisive but harmless break and everything was made embarrassingly calm once again.

It took a few instants for their minds to get used to the new scenario. It took even more time for them to get used to the sharp sunlight that made their eyes hurt. Little they knew, what looked like a mid-summer noon was just a few faint rays of an autumn sunset. They hid their faces from them as they shone mercilessly from the broken ceiling and shattered windows of their precarious meeting hall at Rocksprings.

403

Insanity Market

If there was any trade in hell, what was happening in Rak'hamon's entrance plaza was a perfect rendition of it. The city's newly installed marketplace was now attracting a number of "merchants." They came down from many places, even from the surface, and none of them were less than evil. Their greedy, corrupt hearts brought their tainted business down to the underbellies of the world and there was no limit on their buying and their selling. Slaves were the least immoral things negotiated there, and the agonizing screams echoed throughout the caves high above the city as the diabolical bourgeoisie butchered all kinds of intelligent beings under their customer's precise demands on large wooden tables set in the middle of the "streets." Small children were also among those consumed, and there wasn't any kind of commotion and no empathy whatsoever to be found there. The city's very wall came alive to devour their remains. Vile beasts, dread worms, and immortal parasites crawled from their ancient hideouts to fight for a space to lick the blood in its gutters. Sometimes they would attack each other and eat each other, and then eat each other again in a devouring cycle faster than their chewing. They lived in the sewers and in cracks on the walls, fiercely feeding on anything or anyone they could ambush, making the city itself a deadly fiend.

In the insane market of Rak'hamon, when someone entered in a private dispute and was murdered (a fact that happened quite frequently), the deceased body would be shredded in pieces by those creatures even before it touched the cold marbled floor. Sometimes, the fight for cadavers and other 'leftovers' created more death and, consequently, more disputes. Occasionally, these disputes would grow into a frenzy, and a huge number of them would mindlessly jump out of their hideouts to join in, perpetuating their brutality throughout the entire city while devouring everything on sight in a wave of vile teeth and sheer madness. These cycles ended only when most of the creatures involved were dead and properly eaten or the city "guards" had laughed enough.

For an outsider, however, watching the chaos of the disputing hungry crawlers made mad in their spiral of death was something taken directly from the most inspired nightmares, or any known putrefied imagination. In its lunacy, greed, and disregard, Rak'hamon was alive. And its life desired nothing but to prey on the weak and, ironically, in the end, the dark elves found their realm.

When traders started to arrive in the city, they had to abide by the local customs. Therefore, any disputes and "culture clashes" were resolved on the spot, most commonly with death, severe mutilation, and/or magical disintegration. When Semereth was being conducted through the rocky streets, he saw an insect man having two of his four arms cut by a striking blow from a mysterious pale figure dressed in a pitch-black cloak. Out of nowhere, formless crawlers and other terrifying things leaped from the dark to grab his fallen limbs. The insect man had to fight the living terrors to retrieve them. He managed to get one half-eaten arm back, but the second one was taken apart and away to even darker places to be devoured.

Scared, Semereth could not bring himself to understand what was the cause of such explosive violence all over that horrific place. The only explanation he could muster was that he died and went to hell. But somehow he knew he was alive, and when he contemplated the great and terrible fortress glazed by a toxic and cursed purple light lingering alive and thick around its towers and walls, he knew instantly that he would be brought to an understanding before the day was over.

'Welcome to Rak'hamon, Semereth,' said Vorlok with a coward smile while feeding on the elf's terror. 'It will be your new home for today,' said the unfaithful. 'Maybe forever,' he added, licking the saliva from his tentacle lips as he tasted every fear his sadistic words generated in Semereth.

'Let us find a good place to settle our business so we can sell you for a good price, shall we?' he said, neurotically enjoying his power over the elf's life.

There were other slaves in Vorlok's cruel iron carriage, but Semereth had received the best treatment by far. He was fed good food and even received a bath. Vorlok visited his mind many nights and got into his dreams, transforming them into nightmares so he could learn more about the elf's resilience and past. With it, some memories came back, but they were disorganized and hard to understand, so Semereth was incapable of forming a whole picture out of it and remained lost.

By paying a fair amount to the dark elves that kept the "order" on the marketplace, Vorlok set his tent in a good spot. It was a privileged place and he managed to sell the few other slaves he had in a short time. Contradictorily, and for some reason that escaped him, Vorlok was having difficulties trading Semereth. The wood elf noticed that all the buyers were having a hard time paying what Vorlok was charging for him, or even believing in the stories he told about the elf in the strange language they used there. The unfaithful was stubborn about Semereth's worth and would not accept lesser offers, an intriguingly fact that did not miss the elf's attention.

Finally, when the already limited flow of dealers diminished, the city gates opened and their protective runes lessened their power while an entourage came from it. The security of the procession was oddly tight, being guarded by much more than dark elves in heavy armor. Saazireth came marching in gloriously through it all. She was majestically riding a gigantic arachnoid demon and the ooze that came from its collection of monstrous mouths was digging holes in the pavement as it dripped. Its thick natural armor was reinforced with magically crafted plates of True Silver and Adamantium fused into the creature's exoskeleton. On its armor and on its flesh, the beast was covered in pulsing runes of cruel and powerful magic.

The giant spider and its rider were the only things that had polished metals and bright things over themselves. The rest of the escort party had all their gear made darksome, and this was no coincidence being done under Saazireth's orders. Her intention was clear and obvious, and that was exactly what she wanted to transpire. Everything she did was for and with a purpose, especially in public.

Much before she killed Linothan, she had anticipated the steps she would need to execute her intentions in Rak'hamon. She was now taking those steps to openly establish her domain over the citizenry, who were already raising questions about Linothan's absence.

'My lady,' Vorlok saluted her, bowing in an angle that would make him stumble if he had a spine.

'Where did you find this wood elf?' she asked him as she climbed down her beast.

'Around, my lady,' he said, looking sideways. 'Around.'

'If you allow me, my lady –'

'No, I don't,' she interrupted Vorlok as she looked the elf straight in the eye.

Semereth stared back at her, amazed by her golden eyes and her astonishing beauty.

'…the most important thing is not where I find him, but what can he do,' Vorlok completed his sentence while he was trying to read Saazireth's strange fascination with the wood elf.

'What does his mind say?' she asked the unfaithful.

'He is a warrior of the ancient world, my lady,' answered Vorlok. 'A great one,' he said. 'He fought the orcs in the wars of old,' he bragged, overwhelmed by an anxiety regarding the value of his property.

'A mystery in time,' she said, raising an eyebrow. 'I see.' Saazireth changed her demeanor, appreciating the challenge of the exoticism.

'Nothing that could damage his value,' Vorlok was quick to cover his flanks. 'And potential, my lady,' he added, looking around at the watching crowd.

She had still not looked at the unfaithful directly, resting her gaze in the analysis of the elf, but she smirked when Vorlok mentioned the crowd.

'I suppose I can see my debts forgiven, my lady,' he pried. 'And, perhaps, more,' he said, greedy to his very bones.

'How deep have you been into his mind?' she asked him, completely ignoring what Vorlok said. Her expression and voice strangely denounced a sudden good mood, as if she had just made up her mind about something she saw in the elf's eyes.

'Not too much, my lady,' he said, 'but enough, I assure you, to guarantee the quality of this lot,' he said, suddenly distracted and worried by her mood change. 'There is such a powerful magic blocking hi–'

'Silence!' she cut him again.

Vorlok would not dare to disobey her, but his hate for her patronizing attitude toward him was getting hard to hide.

With a discreet and unnoticeable raising of her indicator finger, she instantly placed the elf into a deep sleep. With a circular wave of her left hand, she folded the heavy iron bars of Vorlok's enchanted prison coach as if they were soft gnomish rubber. She grabbed the air with her right hand and his body started to move, floating out of its cell. With her magic, she directed the elf's body and placed him in front of her. She then drew an arch in the air with her hand, opening a portal to his mind. With a spark of energy and a formation of a purple-lighted geometry, a small paradox was opened in front of his forehead. The small circle of bent reality used as a gateway to his mind and soul was like an unreal mirror. It was curved to the infinite in its borders and, although

407

Saazireth had her eyes closed, images and scenes of the elf's mind were being played and manipulated in the middle of it.

She really forced her magic into it. Warping reality around the elf as a heavy side effect, distorting Vorlok's iron carriage and many other nearby heavy objects beyond recognition. The reach of her power impressed and scared Vorlok and the observing crowd. Doing as she pleased, she surpassed many magical and biological barriers, finding, rescuing, and reassembling many things about Semereth. Some, she managed to keep in secret, but some she had to share with the elf, for the procedure forced her to allow a few memories to come back.

The spells and the incidents that caused havoc in his mind were indeed strong, but she was able to learn many things about him. Though she was not able to precise WHO had done the rare and complex magic that set his destiny, she knew exactly WHAT had unleashed the spell. Still, she kept everything to herself, her specialty.

When cold sweat was starting to form on her forehead, she had come to her senses and decided to investigate further in privacy, away from eyes that could be measuring the true extent of her power. She knew quite well that the unknown was far more fearful, and fear was what kept a dark elf leader in power.

She opened her eyes and all visible traces of magic disappeared instantly in a muffled implosion. His body fell heavily on the floor. Still under the influence of her mystical inducement, the elf kept sleeping heavily. While she turned to leave, she signaled slightly to her mount and the creature promptly launched a white web that grabbed the elf by many different retention points with unreal precision. With a pull from its claws, his body flew through the air and fell in the creatures forepaws, and with great ability and speed, it rolled him in a cocoon of soft and breathable silk. It then set the cocoon on its back, next to Saazireth's saddle.

'But, my lady,' interrupted Vorlok, 'my due fee,' he said as Saazireth climbed her mount.

She took her time, climbed the whole way up, sat in her saddle, grabbed the reins, and looked forward firmly, and considered. Then, and only then, she looked down to the unfaithful for the first time from the corner of her eyes.

'You may see your debt redeemed,' she said austerely, quite aware of the swarm of dark elves watching the scene.

She knew that most were there to take a measure of her, and their intentions were very much hostile toward her, for they were now starting to question the whereabouts of their longtime leader.

She could feel their hate toward her. It flew into the air like a cloud of poison with the weight of ten thousand curses. She felt it over her skin, it burned like an evil omen that oppressed her. It was as tangible as the rocks of the dark cave around the city. Even so, she counted on it. And everything that she did was made to place them exactly there. She not only wanted their hate, she needed it.

'Here,' she said with a detached and unusually lurid voice while grabbing a black silk bag attached to her saddle, 'something to show you my mercy and my generosity,' she said and threw the black silk bag over Vorlok's feet, her eyes fearlessly staring at the faces in the crowd.

The package hit the ground with a cracking noise, and it seemed heavy. Excited by the large volume and apparent weight of the bag, Vorlok rapidly grabbed and unfolded its content, hoping for good treasure. When the unfaithful took the content of the bag out, a great silence took the doors and walls of Rak'hamon. The only person above that silence was Saazireth. She stood high, feeding on it.

There was no treasure on the bag, instead, what Vorlok took out of it was Linothan's head. The distorted features of his face were a resemblance of a painful and dreadfully agonizing death. And as Saazireth designed, all eyes saw it.

Vorlok could not contain himself anymore. Defrauded of his gains, frustrated to his core, he didn't care anymore. He finally gave in to his maddening hunger and before anyone could say anything, the unfaithful started devouring Linothan's head, digging for his precious brain. With one good bit, he cracked the weakened skull and sucked its cerebral matter loudly and carelessly with a great appetite. The observing crowd was staggered, watching everything in absolute silence. Considering that they were all dark elves, their commotion was indeed a remarkable achievement on the part of Saazireth. The cracks of the skull bones and the disgusting noises that Vorlok made while he sucked, licked, and swallowed Linothan's encephalon were the only noises that could be heard in that great plaza. Nonetheless, Saazireth knew that those noises were talking rather loud to the heart of them, and they talked in a language that they understood well. Her action spoke louder and clearer than anything she could say in any speech.

With a solemn expression and smiling eyes, she stood tall, actively searching throughout the hundreds of faces one that could stand her gaze. She was letting them know, beyond all doubt, that she knew what they were feeling, and that she herself crafted that feeling intentionally and purposely, and that she mercilessly injected it into their hearts. She raped their status quo and she wanted them to know she knew how they felt.

Taking her time, she savored all the fear in their surprised and horrified gazes, making sure they all understood the message. Only when she was completely satisfied with the absolute clarity that no one would have the guts to say or do anything, did she pull on the reins of her hideous mount and returned to her new palace.

Crafting Magic

As soon as he could, Stargazer was going through all the things they commandeered on their last adventure. He was fully committed to organizing a functional laboratory within the Small Castle. And in a short time, he did.

He was obsessed, and his mind ran a thousand miles a minute. The wizard had now access to so many powerful and different artifacts, that he spent weeks feeling like a child inside a candy shop – a very, very good candy shop.

After a while, he went beyond even that, and his researches started bordering fanaticism. He could not sleep, was barely eating, and he caught himself perennially chained to his ambitions and immersed in his need to know and to feel the things of the universe flowing through his being. Stargazer could not help it, and his need for magical experiences overcame everything else in him. He had truly become a wizard. A purist even, considering his deepest reasons, as he did magic for the sake of magic.

After several weeks, he realized that his mind was everywhere, dispersed, and without method. He then decided to focus on Kestos's personal belongings, as these would be the ones he would use daily.

The staff was a formidable tool for a wizard. It was also surprisingly light for its size and unbelievably balanced considering its shape. Magically, its uses were endless, and Stargazer quickly unlearned how to live without it. He discovered that the blue crystal in one of its extremities was actually a rare magical sapphire, which was a great catalyzer to draw new geometries. The properties of its energies worked as a magical facilitator, multiplying the power of any spell summoned by it. Although the crystal was the catalyzer, but the staff was the conductor, working as a gate to manifest the magical tendencies that Kestos had decided to draw in the item. Because of certain aspects of its mystical architecture, it was very easy to shape magic with it, turning the conveyer into an instant meta-magician, a rare and very useful trick.

The sharp point at the other end was shaped more as a short sword than a broad spearhead, giving the staff an acute martial aspect. Overall, the blade's dynamic favored precision, being too slender for a dwarf job, but also too objective for an elf's work, and too focused to be extra-planar. It was indeed a piece that came from the mind of a human that knew the Ether well indeed.

It had legions of spirits bounded to it, and even when deactivated, the passive vibrations of its powers were rough on everything around it, slashing, splitting, deforming, and breaking the matter it touched. Sometimes Stargazer had to control its energies as if the staff was a wild and dangerous pet. In a melee fight, the sharp point could go through a steel armor easily. When he hit a target with the sapphire extremity, it unleashed a destructive smashing violence that came from a dimension above the laws of physics. It was, in fact, a BATTLE staff.

Even though the staff may be sold for a small hill of gold, Stargazer knew that the world was full of other treasures and perils, deciding to use it instead of trading it. He studied it for the longest time, unfolding its secrets and refining his handling of it. Eventually, he started to like how the staff operated, becoming his favorite weapon.

He discovered several minor tricks of immense usefulness and beauty "hidden" in the staff's magic. Most of them were not indicated in its physical body, but in its representation in the higher dimensions. They were written in the details of what the wizards called the existential geometry. Studying them, Stargazer learned that something profoundly genius, almost divine, was within the spiritual forms of the staff. The arrangements were unusual in precision and the myriad of schemes denounced a sort of limitlessness in the trigger of energy, a work too far beyond the conceptual capacity of a human mind. And it was then that Stargazer had an epiphany, and became suspicious of the high likelihood that Kestos had his intelligence dramatically increased through magic. He set out to inquire it, and after a brief analysis of the vast material he

411

collected in the tunnels, he confirmed his theory. Stargazer then finally understood why he was still unable to comprehend so many things, and was always feeling like his mind could barely grasp the concepts he was exposed to, and that he was not reaching the full extent of his potential in the art. The young wizard then decided to cast upon himself a few spells from Kestos's Grimoire that increased intelligence, the flow of Mana, and the mind's reach.

The experience took him in a different direction in relation to personal magical powers and revealed to him much more than he could have imagined possible. Before, the effects of magically enhanced intelligence were just tales in the books of some wizards who were able to survive their experiences with magic and themselves, but, now, they became a wonderful and alarming reality to him.

He was instantly brought to a new horizon as far as self-improvement was concerned. He discovered a whole new world at his fingertips, and he showed no reservation about grabbing it all.

In the first time he managed to perform these tricky spells, it was as if his mind had slept all his life and now he had finally woken it up. The first thing that became clear to him was that there was no limit to anything, including the concept of completeness and nothingness. Literally everything was open to the possibility of happening and that was surprisingly the scariest thing for the wizard.

When he saw himself on the stage of higher consciousness, while still within his rational thought process, he understood that his mind and its creation capability were also limitless, being regulated only by his own intelligence in what regarded focus and concentration, and this was somehow the most pleasurable conclusion for him.

The wizard entered a completely new realm of understanding of all things, changing his perspective radically as a tree that abruptly becomes a dog and now also grasped the notion of how things would be like if it became a human, but still held the wisdom of how it felt like being a plant. When he realized the things he was missing, he wanted them all, he wanted everything, including the unknown. By tasting from the same fountain as Kestos, his thirst for power took control of him.

When he moved his mind to the Ether to do magic under the effects of those spells, its outcomes were organically multiplied many folds, both in effectiveness and in extent. He experienced firsthand that the only thing that limited all of his possibilities, transformed into probabilities by degrees of focus and choice, to come to reality was energy, magical energy. In fact, he now completely received that the difference between a non-magical (or "normal" creation) and a magic creation, was only the complexity, integration, and stability of its geometry's designs in the higher dimensions. This difference was fundamentally in the variances of the energy vectors of a particular manifestation. These vectors behaved like pulling strings in the very large and semi-infinitely complex puppet show called reality. Being the puppets all matter, the rudimental spirits next to it, and all interactive materializable energies in between. Mana, or magical energy, acted as the most available and common form of strings. The mind, the most common catalyzer, was the key playing or creating geometries. The operator's ambitions and will alone were the determinant of what to be manifested.

In his experiments, Stargazer could expand his mind to levels that seemed boundless to him, and glimpsed a power equally large upon having the right fountain of energy to increase his mind's interactions with the higher dimensions until he lost himself. He could now see the magical geometry of all things and its connections with everything on an even deeper level. He then learned that through the understanding and the gathering of the right energies, he could truly shape all things and be boundless. He could even create new realities and new laws of existence out of nothing.

All those things certainly changed his career plans, and after reaching higher states and understandings of consciousness, he couldn't get totally back from it. His mind and his ways of seeing the world were never the same again. Consciousness never returned to the same size after being stretched. Not even his gaze was the same, and he stared at the stars in a totally different way now. His companions noticed how he became much more distant and introspective, sometimes touching a random object many times and listening to the sound of it, sometimes appreciating the air around himself as if invisible flowers were surrounding him, and sometimes squeezing his eyes to a particular direction as if he was seeing something beyond. "The wizard look" they called it, but whatever it was, Stargazer now had it.

He even began to talk differently, caring more about being precise and less about being understood. The Fellowship got used to it fairly quickly, but kept themselves worried about him as insanity was pretty common among wizards. Especially human wizards, for human minds were not made to live within two or more different perceptions of one reality at the same time. Humans were created when the world was already too deep into the falsehoods of carnal cultures. Humans are too flexible, tending to lose the anchors of their mundane values of good or bad, or both, particularly after spending too much time seeing things through their true spiritual geometry.

As Stargazer understood and felt that the process he was in now was dangerous for him, he took his time and started watching his every step, but it was too late. He had been exposed to too much power and was already hooked.

Many of Eliaroth's lessons came into his mind more often than he would like to admit during this period of his life, and the way they fitted perfectly always surprised him in a positive way. In the end, and through his internal yet tremendously real struggles, he accepted with his entire being that it took a lot of wisdom for a person, let alone a human, to do powerful magic without being consumed and corrupted by it. Alone, with no guidance but the echoes of Eliaroth's teachings and his reflections over the things he experimented in life until then, Stargazer kept pushing himself forward in the direction of the infinite he just found multiplied. He took a step back and was still smart and sane enough to know that all those newfound wonders were about to be put to the test, in him, and soon enough.

Game

Saazireth's ways were different from Linothan's, mainly in what regarded magnitude and impetus. While he has always worked in silence behind the curtains, her methods were as loud as they could be, on purpose. Saazireth was smart enough not to deny to herself the fact that she was not as skilled with politics as Linothan, and she knew herself enough to know that she would never be as nearly interested in that game when navigating or exerting power over the dark elves.

Created to govern, to possess, to destroy and, above all, to be herself, Saazireth's overconfidence sustained the strength necessary in her to do whatever she wanted in any situation. Regarding her reign over Rak'hamon, therefore, it was only logical that considering her person, she would almost inevitably shake things to the core.

The way she saw the city was quite different of how an actual mature dark elf leader would see it. She had little respect for tradition and stability,

414

considering them just excuses for adopting mediocre and stagnant policies, even attributing to them the blame for the demise of their entire race. And it was precisely because of these beliefs that she was interested in being as bold in her decisions as she could.

Saazireth had high ambitions, much higher them to rule Rak'hamon. Thus, she clearly perceived, or was willing to accept, that Rak'hamon was little but her house's garden, denying, in her neglect, what it really was. Although she was indeed powerful and insightful in many things, her young age, temper, and overconfidence made her rule the city as her personal property, as if Rak'hamon was an automatic extension of her subjections, and that was her first mistake.

Out of her necessity to enforce her new authority, she ignored the pledges of the prominent citizens who tried, in a very dark elfish manner, "reason" with her. Out of pure lack of patience, she demised the High Council ambassador, and this rash decision was considered a highly dangerous and risky measure by almost all senior members of the elder houses. Still, she did not esteem them, or at least considered their correct weight in her political calculations.

As too many citizens feared her enough not to openly move against her, Saazireth's opposition decided to wait. They were confident that the High Council would not allow these things to continue, so they decided to build up some strength before moving against her. Certain that she would eventually be neutralized, they waited.

Convinced it would aid her objectives in a decisive manner, she now openly promoted the commerce and integration that was silently encouraged by Linothan. He did things in secret because he knew he needed to keep the appearances and respect the dark elves' ways. This, he thought, was fundamental to retain his position to slowly but smoothly seed the things he would want to see grown in his future. Saazireth, instead, decided to step up things a great deal, doing according to her wishes, not even bothering hiding her hand, thus scandalizing many of the established leaderships in the Underworld, and on the surface too.

She openly promoted direct commerce with the folks from above, transforming the mines to real productive facilities instead of the refined torture chamber they had been for centuries.

With some of her most powerful servants, she opened new direct tunnels from the city to the surface. She employed a mix of engineering with group-magic to accelerate the works greatly, finishing in weeks what it would have taken decades to accomplish. This measure by itself outraged the dark elves, as, for generations, they had used the secrecy and inaccessibility of their cities as one of their main means of defense. She would even pay runners and emissaries to go to public markets and to cities under the sun, declaring that she would guarantee the security of anyone who was willing to descend upon her new entrance tunnels with the intention of bringing commerce to Rak'hamon.

Driven by greed, smart merchants came down to the city and found great profit there, especially with the trade of spell filled gems. The dark elves had little interest in most things from the surface and were quite self-sufficient as they generated all of their needs through their mighty magic, but many of them did learn quickly to indulge themselves with expensive pets, rare art, and new, highly interesting, magical ingredients.

Considering the city's disclosure (a blasphemy to their entire way of life) the vast majority of the houses' leaders could not bear any argument in favor of her rules, and the only reason she was not killed in an open rebellion after the tunnels were opened was the overwhelming success of her endeavor.

Things changed so quickly and so intensely in the dark elves' perspective, that most of them were late to understand what was going on around them. But when they did, most accepted that they had turned their backs to a peaceful life long ago, and that they were not ready to see order happening yet. Although they received benefits from it, and even some pleasure, their minds and hearts were so consumed by their hundred generations' vengeance plans that they could not withstand peace or promote prosperity anymore.

In addition, their extremely xenophobic nature prevailed, and the deep belief that any tranquil interaction with humans and other inferior surface creatures was an abomination won their hearts once again. In the end, when they began to realize where Saazireth's leadership was taking them, a great sense of revolt grew among the population, and beyond. Rumors and plots began to be whispered in many gloomy places, and a thirst for blood grew in the dark.

Feeling the pressure, and realizing she needed to act, Saazireth was swift into presenting a solution. She fostered a distraction that would ease their spirit, encompassing their cultural needs, and promote her plans at the same time. She served them a feast of emotions that would restore and nurture all the

416

desires of their dark souls by channeling their need for violence and their competitive energy into an ancient custom: The Arena Games.

Inside the walls of Rak'hamon there was an old stadium where, in the old days, the dark elves would settle their disputes publicly by fighting to the death. Although they loved the old custom, it fell into disuse, for they grew to kill each other wherever they stood centuries ago.

After a brief restoration, Saazireth would promote daily spectacles of violence in that arena. Her servants organized disputes that met the elves' needs for blood and sport, directing and isolating their anger.

Her success was massive, and they literally could not bring themselves out of it. The houses became occupied with the blood and the gamble, searching and electing their own champions, competing with each other in the vain pursuit of their gory glories. The canalization of their hopes and dreams of death increased their need for money and valuables, forcing them to do business in the local market, therefore improving the number and the refinement of its daily exchanges.

Her plan worked to perfection, they became distracted and Saazireth became prosperous. Things calmed down for a while, even if on a merely bearable level, and she could finally direct her time and attention to her true pursuits.

In a short time things shifted so much in the city that having a champion in the Arena, something totally ignored a short time ago, now carried a great deal of prestige among the elves houses of Rak'hamon. After most of her researches were done and when her plans had cumulated unstoppable momentum, Saazireth felt she was also in need of this political prestige and she would grasp as much as she could from it. She needed a champion now and she knew exactly where to get one.

She had many slaves, but her favorite was Semereth, the amnesic wood elf. There was something about him that was irresistible to her. She received him in her chambers the very day she bought him, and she would never again allow him to depart her presence afterwards. The wise among her entourage could see that there was a rare quality in Semereth, an old nobility that made him fall into her likings and quickly becoming her preferred, servicing Saazireth in all of her needs to her contentment.

To reward him for all the pleasure she took possession of during their interactions, she would bring great relief to him by occasionally plunging into his mind and letting a memory or two surfaces.

The enchantress was very comfortable regarding the methods of the mind, and had discovered Semereth's potential in the very first time she read him. When she dived into his thoughts now, however, she always tried to be as discreet and wary as she could, careful not to reveal too much, for she selfishly enjoyed him in the way he was now and understood the consequences of unleashing his potential.

In pleasure, therefore, and as the guardian of his secrets, she often drank from his deliverance lagoon, but always ended up spitting its waters back. Yet, she truly came to love his relative innocence and the exclusive secret of the ever-arrested potential of his repressed powers. For although the dark elves decided a long time ago to live in hate, they were no strangers to love. And as violent, possessive, selfish, vindicating, and sick their love stories were, they were also very much real and powerful.

He fundamentally was a sincere being, and despite his many traumas and shattered spirit, his soul resisted, truthful. He freely offered her his emotions, his energies, himself, and she could not resist caring for such a creature.

The warm honesty that he shared with her was almost impossible to find among the dark elves, and she found herself very fond of it. That sort of interaction was very rare for her to see or taste, and she learned to appreciate him for what he truly was, regarding him as a precious jewel and keeping him with a possessive craving and under great protection.

Considering her status, she enjoyed the wood elf a lot more than she should, but now she was under pressure from all sides, especially from within. The sadist in her liked to play with the weakness of his ignorance, but fate called her to a position where she needed his true strengths.

Undoubtedly, Semereth cared for her burning passions and became addicted to the way she drove herself when they melted together. Saazireth would not hesitate to use her powerful magic to enhance their carnal experiences. Sometimes she would even take possession of their minds and cause their ecstasies to transcend into something spiritual. Through her, he would learn a lot about the dark elves' powerful emotions to the point of believing he found in her some suppressed quality of greatness, a raw hunger for existing and for existence that was ultimately good and redemptive.

Semereth, for his part, was not insensitive; on the contrary, Saazireth found him the most intense lover she had ever had. What they allowed themselves to live healed him considerably and helped her to release the tensions within her thunderous heart, for she could not resist the notion of them together to any extent and she was the only life he knew. After so many dark days of despair and lack of direction, the things he experienced with her were the only things that did not taint his soul. She was the only pleasure he found in his memoryless life.

For a time, they shared what they shared, and, although they still called what they were and what they did by its proper names, and despite the cruelty of his situation, Semereth's position allowed him to have a unique perspective on her true nature. Saazireth knew this, admiring and responding to the loyalty he maintained even in the face of his calamitous adversity, and Semereth responded by making himself bound to her needs. Nevertheless, Saazireth was still what she was, and, when her situation changed, she acted as it was expected of her. Knowing what very few people knew, and able to do what few people could, she planned to unleash him so she could use him as suited her, and, for now, she suited a champion.

One day, after they had spent many hours sharing themselves in one of her beds, she felt it was time. She searched his attentions with her large golden eyes and, with a stare, let him know that she was about to do something serious in his mind. Reading her intentions, he immediately gave her unrestricted access to his body, thinking she would "heal" him with her magic, as she often did. This time though, it was different.

She leaned over him and did something that she had never done before. Saazireth gently kissed Semereth's forehead in an act of deep care in a prelude to the gift she would bring him. The demonstration of the kiss was so alien to everything they had lived together, that his emotions came forth like a windy storm. He instantly let his most inner guards go and felt that he should spit out all the words and promises that were popping into his throat, finally declaring himself to her.

By gently pressing her finger to his lips, she pointed out to him that it was not time for him to talk. With another look, she still restrained him, indicating that she was aware of his feelings, knew his questions, had his answers, and that everything was fine but that she still hadn't finished what she started.

Semereth trusted her, surrendering himself completely.

419

With total control, Saazireth touched his forehead and opened his mind. She unlocked the last chains and put down the last veils, revealing all things to him and letting his memories as naked as in the day they were made.

As if drugged by a powerful stimulant, he found himself standing and looking up at the high ceiling of the darkroom while mesmerized and in shock at the sight of the concept of his own self. He stared at the wall, but in reality he was seeing himself. He was watching his whole life unfold before his eyes as his own memories found their place in his mind's horizon.

He felt overwhelmed by the extremes of that strange and rare experience to return to what he was before, to become again what he stopped being once. His spirit was deeply disturbed as he watched his entire life being revealed all at once, and, as the information adapted to his mind as the process took over, his memories flooded him, completing his thoughts and filling his soul.

When he was done, he felt full and complete. Yet, an anger was ablaze inside him, and before he could organize his thoughts to understand why, he felt that the whole world was his enemy, his soul contaminated, foul. Compelled, he wanted to destroy something.

'I remember…everything,' he said, exasperated, sounding like a madman. In his voice, there was now a unique mixture of commotion and ire. His eyes were expressing and anguishing as if he had just woken from the most bizarre and confusing dream and was not convinced of the depictions portrayed in his mind.

'Good,' she said. 'Now, let's use it,' and her voice was loaded with decisiveness and a little humor.

'Use what?' he asked, his eyes still glassy.

'Your everything,' she said, smiling a terrible smile. Her expression was full of a burning greed, lust, and anger.

He finally looked away from his mind's images and engaged her utterance, for she was indeed his savior and he now desperately needed to comprehend what she meant, and not just her words, but all of her motivations.

'What –' the question died on his lips when he met the gaze she was offering him.

She kept the same intensity in her eyes, showing him that it contained everything he needed to know now. Her intimate, wordless act made it perfectly clear to him what she had in her heart and where she needed him to stand.

Their bond was now sensitive enough for him to fully comprehend all the intrinsic details of her will. Hence, at that moment, he not only understood where she was coming from, but he finally and completely connected with her, and, in doing so, he gave in a lot of himself, conceding to her love, receiving her greed, desiring her lust, and sharing her anger.

Fame

The winter would start soon and they had far too many personal interests to settle. No one was thinking about The Fellowship now, and they dispersed as a result, pursuing their personal agendas, each one doing as they pleased.

Alone, Bastian rode to Westgate to deliver the lost treasures for the families of the deceased. Rather than collect the glory for himself, he secretly left the items where the owners would certainly find them, using the cover of the night to conceal his identity. Most of the items were heirloom weapons from rich, influential, and/or noble families. Many were public figures of renown, so although he knew them, none knew him.

Bastian truly desired no recognition, doing it only for himself, exclusively because he felt it was the right thing to do. The city though had eyes and ears, and the word of his deeds ran the region. It didn't take long for people to connect the dots and his fame started to spring up.

After completing this self-imposed task, he went to spend some time with his mother. Although he would not admit it, not even to Lucien, he missed her very much. Seeing her was great, but having the honor of revealing her husband's final destiny was a moment of true greatness for him. It made him grow up inside, maturing his feelings as he overcame some of his heaviest emotions, setting old wounds to rest. When he felt the occasion was right and his heart was content, he set to meet his friends at Rocksprings. Now, as he left the farm, he realized that he was a totally different person than when he left the last time. He was a man now, and he would live by it.

Hanam spent his mornings in the slums curing the people who couldn't afford to buy the healing magic they needed. Soon, there were lines of poor sick people who could not afford magical healing at The Fellowship's front door. The Hunchback didn't care at all, working as hard as he could until his energies completely abandoned him. His deeds and name were getting around town and people was starting to talk about him and The Fellowship.

Hanam and Shunto eventually met Taalen by The Cat's Horn. Taalen was giving Hanam a bad time because he was late for a few weeks, but the bard gave Shunto an even worst time because he was late for many years. For Hanam's great surprise, he discovered that they were friends and had many adventures together in the past. Seemingly, they were members of a rather extravagant Malandro's Brotherhood, a not-so-secret society of bards and spies that kept an eye over the thuggery in most of Elaroth.

Hanam found that Shunto and Taalen could go on talking about their old adventures forever, drinking heavily while chatting about things that happened decades ago for hours and hours. Listening as Taalen updated Shunto on the news of the world, Hanam was impressed by the amount of inside information that both were in the habit of accumulating. Thinking about it, it occurred to him, now that he had a better sense of their personalities and a real feeling of their characters, that they had been and still were, above all, agents of the Emperor.

Although the hunchback was still uncertain about the kind of agents they were, if spies, unofficial procurators, unconventional diplomats, assassins, mercenaries, or any other kind, he was certain that they definitively possessed the right set of special abilities to get their job done. However, the way they presented themselves still left Hanam with certain doubts regarding their seriousness. There was something awkward about them. Their smart, humorous cynicism, typical of people who had been around for far too long to behave themselves differently, left an untrustworthy air around their personas, making them look far too disconnected and undisciplined to be formal representatives of the Valkarian Emperor. Hanam became impressed, however, by hearing how deep their involvement had been in the political overturns of the last seven decades.

Hanam found all that strange, for Taalen seemed younger than Shunto who seemed to be in his best years. The hunchback wondered how long both had been alive, where they got it from, how it influenced their accumulation of experience and lore, and also how far their ways were from a normal human being.

Regarding spiritual energies, Hanam felt a great mixture of confusion and uniqueness coming from them. They were all over the place and were of a rare, unidentifiable type. They had seen a lot and were exposed to far too much not to be altered by all the things that crossed their paths. They were, in a large part, the consequence of the abundance of surprising possibilities and scarring situations that their world had to offer.

They are the true children of Fabula, Hanam thought.

After many hours without touching the subject of the orb, which was the reason why they were meeting in the first place, Hanam, who was just listening from the beginning, finally decided to intervene.

Taalen, however, barely paid any attention to it. The bard just took the velvet bag and strapped into his belt and continued his exceedingly immoral stories involving one of the Valkyrie Sisters. Shunto looked very entertained by Taalen's story, and also did not give importance to the subject of the orb. Their presence and company were merry, but Hanam could not avoid feeling a little troubled by their unconcerned attitude. Instead of taking the orb somewhere, they would rather sit and drink and talk. And that's just what they did, they told old and new stories for an entire afternoon, and the whole night. When the sun came up, they were still drinking and talking and laughing, amused as if they had just started. After a terribly funny tale about being transformed into a toad, without a hot bath, any rest at all, and still very much drunk, Taalen simply declared he had to leave for the Capital.

Almost incapable of making sense of his words and stumbling upon himself, he asked for Shunto to stay put and "keep an eye on the boys." He blabbered something on how he would spread the word of Shunto's return and see if he could find a nice adventure for him.

Barely standing and still with a bottle of wine in his hand, he drunk climbed an old mining mule that appeared from nowhere. He then headed for the North Road, staggering under the scandalously large brim of his leather hat.

Not convinced that this was a good idea, dissatisfied with the debriefing, and full of consternation about the fate of the bard, Hanam decided to intervene, asking the questions he had been holding all night.

'What about us?' he asked. 'What do we do now? Any words from Oberan?'

'Yeshh,' said Taalen. 'I had almoshht fo–forgot,' he could barely keep himself conscious. 'He he he did shai somening to you,' he said, falling asleep over the mule.

'What he said?' asked Hanam, surprised and interested.

'Prepare for war,' answered Taalen, waking up in a reflex, swinging heavily out of balance, and almost falling off the donkey.

Hanam was hit hard by those words. He stood there, not knowing what to do. He looked at Shunto, but he was also too drunk to help.

'Or somemting,' Taalen added. He passed out and the donkey took him away.

Hanam entered the hall of The Fellowship and, without knowing what to do, he started training immediately. After his hangover was healed, Shunto joined him.

Without Bastian around to stop him, Lucien was turned loose. He dragged Klunk into underground sword fights and boxing competitions, and they were both enjoying themselves. In the boxing competitions, Lucien used his newly acquired magic belt to cheat, winning most fights. He also "persuaded" Klunk to bet some of his money on him, and the two became even richer. This attracted a lot of bad attention from a lot of bad people, and as soon as the mobsters who organized the fights saw what Lucien was doing, they set a price for his head, and it wasn't cheap. Many tried to collect the prize, but all failed for Klunk's escort was impenetrable and Lucien was becoming increasingly deadly with his blades. The more they failed, the higher the price became.

He did the same thing in the illegal underground fighting pits. There, the gain was higher but the fighting was to the death. Living fast and on the edge of his vanity, Lucien couldn't stay away from the killing and seemed obsessed with testing his limits and his luck.

No one cared about rules in those pits, and that was just the way he liked. Magic equipment and even healing potions were tolerated. The only thing that mattered was to win. As Lucien stubbornly managed to survive whatever they threw at him, soon enough he developed a reputation and a nickname in that clandestine world. When he started boxing, he was called The Giant's Son, for his demonstrations of incredible strength in the boxing matches and the constant presence of Klunk by his side. This nickname did not last much, for he was a completely different animal when he had a sword in his hands. In the lawless pits, the fame of his unstoppable adamantium sword preceded his, and he quickly became Black Blade.

Lucien's lack of consideration alone inspired fear in the hearts of the people who watched him fight, but what really amazed everyone was to witness his black sword at work. It cut through armor and shields as if they were made of cloth. The dark blade was a very rare weapon, born for attack, forged for a bold and disrespectful warrior, fitting Lucien perfectly. Few things in Fabula could block it, which gave Lucien a huge advantage over his opponents, making it possible for the young warrior to defeat fighters far more experienced than himself. Most of his opponents were not prepared to resist both, as the adamantium blade alone was a marvel of the magical metallurgy, but when added to Lucien's super-aggressive fighting style, they became irresistible. When the supernatural strength and endurance he was receiving from his belt and the excellent protection from the magically enhanced full plate mail he now wore was added to the formula, Lucien became a death machine. And he loved to show it, and the public went crazy with his morbid displays, and he developed a taste for it. A taste that sometimes-bordered cruelty, but he was hooked on it and there was no one around to tame his worst side. And so his name was made, and the words of his actions began to spread across Rocksprings, but rarely on the tongue of a good person.

Sahafira was utterly unsatisfied with the state of their hall. After buying the whole block, which was really cheap because of The Cat's Horn's constant problems, she set to build a proper place to host The Fellowship of the Sword.

She collected a share from everybody, with the exception of Bastian, who was away and had no money anyway. However, Lucien, who was now the richest of them all, paid his friend's share and the works began.

Although she sought his advice, Stargazer was never available to help. He was restless about activating the Adamantium Golem, doing little but to study the researches and materials collected from Kestos's hideout. Fortunately, Shunto, always gentle and helpful, showed himself to be very interested in developing The Fellowship into something bigger and better. He helped her the best he could, making himself available all the time, but apart from him, Sahafira had very little help from the others. She decided on the architectural plans, supervised the workers, bought the building implements and decided on the most relevant details of the project almost by herself, which was quite an undertaking.

On the bright side, Rocksprings was very prosperous and had many ongoing construction projects. In this favorable environment, she managed to find a very talented and experienced group of contractors and architects who brought to her attention the perfect design for their meeting hall. The architect's vision was basically an extremely secure, compact, and self-contained fortress in the classic Valkarian style. That meant an innate seclusion, thick doors, tactical windows, and double granite walls. The plans described a relatively tall squared building of solid stone with narrow windows made to fit and defend that specific city block in case of siege. It had all the facilities necessary for hosting an entire battalion in case of need. The city administration was happy to approve it, as it would make the city's defense stronger by transforming an entire city block that was a collection of old and decrepit warehouses into another solid piece of useful and defensible hardware.

Local contractors had long joined some of Rocksprings' highly commercial wizard guilds and had been able to offer many interesting extras. They suggested dwarf protection tokens on doors to prevent unwanted visitors, teleport-proof walls, stationary defensive Stone Golems, and more.

Stargazer liked the project and made some appointments himself, but let clear to Sahafira that he felt it was not the moment for most of the extras proposed by the contractors, for they lacked the money.

'We still do not have that many enemies,' he said.

'But we will, shortly,' she said.

He nodded, and then left the meeting they had regarding the issue, and then went back to the Small Castle and his studies.

The wizard was now spending most of his time frustrated with the fact that he felt he needed more time all the time. There were just too many things he felt he wanted to do, and his mind had now the conditions and the fuel in place to accelerate the growing of his powers – and that was precisely what he did.

The speed with which things were happening for him was scaring the young wizard when he stopped to think about it. Alone in the Small Castle, surrounded by the high magic of Kestos' life's work, he was manipulating a sort of power very much above the grade he had, by his own means, earned access to. Consequently, many projects were popping up in his mind, but he feared that he would simply not have enough time for all of them. On top of everything, his conscience kept reminding him that he needed to return to his master to pay his debt and finish his training. He was now continually drinking elven tea to deal with the constant headaches the newfound amount of issues was causing him. The special, personal blend was the only not magically created food he was eating, but it was not enough to bar the great anxiety brewing inside of him.

After months of research, he finally understood that, as of that moment, he did not have the skills and powers to finish the golem as he would like it to see

426

it finished. This was because the constructor was not of a textbook built, if such a thing ever existed. From the ground up, it was Kestos's own creation, designed to serve Kestos's own interests, but to fundamentally be unstoppable. In it, Stargazer noted, there were far too many custom geometries, and judging by the notes retrieved from his lair, Kestos worked on the constructor for a long time, and the thing seemed to be just the precursor, or the prototype, of something larger, something worse.

The builder was made specifically to host a Soul Stone and was too complex from the magical perspective to be inverted to function like a normal golem. With a closer analysis of Kestos's style, Stargazer perceived that the wizard was in the habit of crafting very refined and personalized objects. With a megalomaniac obsession for legacy, efficiency, and purpose, Kestos reinvented every detail of everything. That made him an exceedingly effective enchanter, but at the same time disrupted and blurred the interface within his creations. All that specialization and specifications bored Stargazer after a while, as he was used to seeing magic in much broader ways, and although he would never deny himself the use of any particular magical equipment, he still had his heart fascinated by the objective beauty of the magic behind it, not any individual statement framed on it. He loved all things magical, but was not inclined to become a sort of neurotic specialist, preferring to admire the charm of practical magic in his life and in the life of others than to capture it and sell it somehow.

With that in mind, Stargazer took his thoughts off the small perspective he had been using for so long, and, reclining over the chair he was sitting on and raised his eyes and placed all things he experienced in the last months inside his naturally broad frame of mind. He then accepted the fact that Kestos almost certainly had a magnificent source of energy, and that he did not. Logically, then, there was not much he could do now with what he had. With that conclusion, he made peace with himself.

I must stop looking at cakes and buy myself an oven, he thought.

Then, tired and tense, he stretched his back, pulling his arms up, and looked through the window at the perennial wheat fields outside the Small Castle. He then remembered that he couldn't remember the last time he slept. He couldn't tell what time it was either, for there was no night in the world of the frame and the sun never changed its position or its intensity.

He left the lab and went for a walk around the fields. He then realized that he had never strode through them or paid much attention to that world. As always, the temperature, the breeze, and the humidity were perfect. The sunlight warmed his skin tenderly while the breeze cooled it down gently. Filtering the observable around him with much scrutiny, he was struck by an instinct that told him that there was something in that world that was strange and out of place. Without a second thought, he set his mind to investigate it while walking through the plantation, distancing himself from the Small Castle.

Instinctively, while he lightly meditated about it, he snapped the head of a wheat shaft. To his surprise, another head instantly grew on its place. He snapped the same one again and it grew again.

'It never changes,' he said to himself, captivated and alarmed.

He then reclined his head and broadened his gaze with an arch, looking at his whereabouts with a wider perspective. It was then that he finally felt the cumulated exhaustion over him. Beyond tired, he let go, and his legs failed him, and he sat down in the middle of the field. Then, he lay down on a pillow made with bent wheat. He later remembered having a genial, brief, and confuse epiphany regarding flour, cake, wheat, and ovens, but he could not, for the life in him, hold on to reality then. The wizard fell into a deep sleep under the perfect sun of that painted world.

When he woke up, he wake up spontaneously and he felt as if he had a new skin. Searching his mind, he concluded that there was nothing left for him to do, but something different. Therefore he held the golem project on standby and decided to rebuild his coat to refresh his mind and humor.

This time, he took his time and retrofitted the whole project, taking what he learned in his experiments and adventures, using it to improve the design of his coat even more. He used plenty of his money, and most of his newly gained knowledge to enchant the thing heavily.

After many trips to the city market and long talks with foreigner merchants and hunters from distant lands, the young wizard gathered the best fabric and materials money could buy, and went to work on it.

He changed the fabric completely, finding a very competent weaver to prepare him a mix of Black Onix wool and Ansan Dimensional Spider silk. As he projected, he ended with a unique mix that was naturally very fire resistant and unbelievable stretchy and strong.

428

Leather reinforcements on the shoulders were not necessary because there was no need for a backpack anymore. The dimensional spider silk once manifested materially into existence by the spider that produced it could not be taken out because it contained a dimensional anchor that forever connected it to the Ether. Therefore, the coat was incredibly wear proof, in fact inherently magically wear proof for it regenerated itself constantly back to its original shape.

Stargazer fortified the elbows, neck, and chest with terribly expensive, and seamlessly indestructible, Gray Naga leather. As both creatures had very active and fluid dimensional anchors, it was undemanding to lay an enchant on both geometries, achieving a desired particular effect reflected into the tangible reality, making it possible to reinforce and upgrade the coat as Stargazer learned new magic and grew in power.

This time he made pants of the same fabric, the same protection levels, and same magic power. It was also reinforced with Grey Naga leather on the knees and on every vulnerable vein and tendon. He applied the same logic he used in the coat, ending up with a lot of pockets too, including two large ones on each side.

This time he enchanted the hidden pockets, making them capable of holding far more space on the inside then it looked from the outside, like Taalen's bag and the Small Castle painting. He would make his new spear/staff disappear into one of his palm secret pockets, adding no weight to it whatsoever and making draw and transportation very convenient. He could now haul all he needed in and out of places with no added weight and total discretion. Ironically, the ritual to establish that paradox in the laws of space included sewing. In that work, he used much of his gained abilities as a self-thought clothier. Although, for the execution of the magic trick, it was necessary the complex manipulation of different dimensions, the proper use of a trans-dimensional scissors, and the ability to handle a special needle and thread.

He made two copies of the garment, but enchanted only one of them. He kept the second in reserve in case he destroyed the first. He enchanted it with all the spells he could cast, paying contract wizards to cast others he couldn't. He even used the high magic in Kestos's Grimoire to integrate and adjust the pants into the coat's geometry, making them a single magical unity.

Although perfected, the overall design was structurally similar to the first model, only more refined. He kept the color patterns of blue, yellow, and light gray, but this version of the coat looked much less bulky and even more dynamic, which was appropriated considering the wizard he became and the life he now knew.

Even with all his efforts and the wonderful things that came out of it, he concluded the project unsatisfied with the result. Although it came out as a great piece of equipment, he could now see and feel that it was possible to do far more than he had done. A greedy feeling of wanting was ever-present in all he did now, nothing seemed enough anymore. Ignorance was indeed a blessing, he found out.

It was a cold afternoon when he finished his work. It looked like it was going to snow that night, the first snow that winter. He felt tired again and set to rest before the meeting that Sahafira arranged when he received news of Bastian's return. The Fellowship had not gathered together for a long time and the wizard did not take the occasion lightly. He had a proper meal and took a long and relaxing hot bath. He used expensive aromatic herbs and spices that he bought in Rocksprings's plentiful market. He put on a set of exquisite wool undergarments as a first layer, covering all his body from wrist to ankle, protecting up to his neck from the elements. On top, he wore a new, elegant, high-quality durable blouse, which was very fancy and worthy of any lord's gathering. After that, he dressed in his special trousers and strapped them with the best suspenders he could buy. Following, he tucked in a pair of thick wool socks and entered into his pair of Elven Speed Boots, tying all the True Silver buckles on it. He set Kestos's Lava Ring on his left hand and Kestos's Mind Ruby on his forehead, and both items instantly adapted magically to his head and finger, staying in place and fitting him comfortably. Then he adjusted Kestos's Battle Belt of Physical Might and More on his abdomen and started loading in it all the objects that he deemed necessary to be his every day carry or even his adventurer loadout, which were mostly things that he would need to keep with him at all times and things he might need at any time. His kit included many potions, herbs, ingredients that increased the flux and stability of some spells, two pairs of extra wool socks, some travel food, rope, a large cast iron cauldron and spoon, Kestos's Grimoire, his own Grimoire (which was an ongoing project), scrolls, a nice tent set, a blanket, pencil, pen, ink, paper, etc. Everything was previously and neatly set over a large table, and he loaded

430

each one of them on a specific pocket for convenience and quick draw. When he finished it, he grabbed Kestos's Battle Staff and took a look at himself in the mirror. He could not believe how heroic he was looking.

'But they better believe it!' he said, fiercely brave.

I am finally looking like Eliaroth's apprentice, he thought.

He set to the meeting with a clear idea in his mind. He knew exactly what he needed to do now. He knew what all of them needed to do now. He had spent too much time and applied too much of his being exploring the echoes of eternity not to know. He surrendered to the great theme higher than him that reflected upon all things, the sense and the direction behind every small particle of fate he would see manifest from time to time in actions and reactions, in the things that were and in the things that weren't, in the things he saw and in the things he believed into. It was time to become greater, he was certain, by conceding to the Universe a broader manifestation within his soul and his life. It was time to get things done, to break paradigms, to write stories, to gather fame, to be destiny.

The Small Castle painting was now ranging on the wall of The Hall, as they now called the main room of The Fellowship's old warehouse. Once he got out of it, he immediately felt eyes on him, and it was then that he felt the energies from the others confirming the higher planes that were echoing into his heart. He set his eyes on all of them, reckoning that they were all ready, and that they grew and changed once more in perfect preparation for this very moment. He figured that he was looking at a true brotherhood of adventurers, at least true enough to fulfill the notion that his mind transpired. Spending some time separated, the new perspective of this first assembly gathered a powerful subjective cloud of energy that surrounded them as individuals and as a group – everything was in the air, lingering from a thread. Stargazer felt it, he saw it on the Ether, and he knew that whatever that was, it fueled them to move ahead together.

The wizard looked around, noticing how different they were now, and yet, they were the same as before. Their armor, clothes, bodies, and minds had improved, but their eyes were still the same, and they were filled with a righteous and momentous measure of destiny in every single one of them. What Stargazer saw in them, passing any mystery, anxiety, fear, secrecy, anger, or insecurity, was the same thing he had in his heart. It was something that, although very subtle, they all shared and it attracted and bonded them together inexorably. They were natural born heroes, and, now, they were truly home.

Vain Arena

The competition level over Rak'hamon's arena was already too high when Semereth started fighting. Saazireth knew all about it. It was part of her plans. She needed to grow their egos, then subdue and/or destroy them, exalting hers in the process while giving them a real demonstration of what pride was.

Although, for her plans to work, she would need more than a champion. Hence, she invested all her powers, knowledge, and resources, to improve Semereth's fighting capabilities. She was a firm believer in destiny, and highly sensitive to its nuances. Thus, through her raiders and Vorlok, she silently recovered the magic items Semereth was found with. She gave a special recommendation regarding the chanting sword, for she felt that the blade would still have a part in Semereth's destiny. Saazireth went to great lengths to get the sword back, insisting on it for she understood that the magic blade chose Semereth and she had learned to respect the decisions that enchanted objects took, as their existence and motives were much higher than ordinary rational thoughts and schemes.

As the other objects were mostly rare items and the majority of them were connected magically, working their powers in conjunction as a set, Vorlok still kept the ones that were linked with the sword. He was willing to make more money by selling them as a complete kit, as, together, they could provide an extra edge on the dynamism of the geometries, enhancing all the power of all the items, giving a considerable advantage to the warrior that would bear them, and to his pocket. That fact, however, turned up to work against the unfaithful. For when Saazireth's emissaries demanded them, they paid a price that was well under what he was expecting to receive for them. Cursing his luck and the dark elves, he had no option but comply.

When Saazireth had the items, she gave them to Semereth. As planned, their collective power increased Semereth's capabilities a great deal, mainly because the abilities that he used in his fighting style were the same enhanced by the items' magic aura. Saazireth also added a few very powerful objects and weapons from her personal stash to boost him even further, providing him with her most precious enchanted gems. She bathed him in special oils of ancient formula, casting many unique enchants and rituals to maximize his physical prowess and mental resilience. Likewise, she made him practically immune to magic domination and very resistant to damaging spells and poisoning from any source.

When she openly showcased him with his equipment on, and his weapons ready for combat, she caused a great deal of gossip and hateful envy. Some even correlating that she replaced Linothan for this inferior slave as her lover and confidant. Although it was common for the dark elves to use slaves to tame their fleshly desires, the insinuation that was now upon Saazireth, was that she gave this slave an improper and offensive status. The rumor spread quickly and villainously, and many were deeply offended by her clear preference for the wood elf. Especially since Linothan's presence was still lacking, as his figure represented the dark elves in all of his ways. Semereth's, on the other hand, seemed a real and perfect target for all their hatred, as the emotional scars of their civil war were still very much alive among them and they had not forgotten that most of the surface elven warriors were from the wood elves' clans. Semereth's position hurt them where it hurt the most: their pride.

Saazireth's plan was working perfectly, for the fact that she chose, and was now openly declaring, Semereth as her personal guard, champion, and lover, was the final humiliation that many felt that they could not forgive, if there was ever a grain of mercy among the dark elves.

Nevertheless, she feared not. Maintaining a provocative stance while she advanced through Rak'hamon's great assembly hall while keeping Semereth close by her side. She stared as many as she could in the eye, to read and to be pleased and to laugh at their hateful reactions, letting them know she would not abide, bend, or break under their opinions. Truly, their repulse was all part of her designs, and she was willingly funneling their emotions only to throw it back at them, at the right time.

The members of her personal guard could not hide their fears over the shouts of indignation and furious murmurs of the crown while she took her place in the assembly hall. All the leader of the elder houses were there and they were absolutely infuriated by the shamelessly public confirmation of this new scandal.

'Blasphemer whore!' a dark elf shouted and charged her with sword in hand.

Many followed the elf in a burst of lasting hatred, and they all shouted words in their language that could not be translated into most languages as vile as they were. Their ferocity was so intense and true, and their numbers were so surprisingly high, that, for a moment, Saazireth herself feared for her life. But in the right moment, Semereth break momentum, deploying himself in her defense and countering the first charge.

Although she was an expert killer herself, trained in the utmost arts of combat, she had no idea of what the remembering of Semereth's old combat skills and experiences could really mean. She knew that he came from a time where his people had faced centuries of dire conflicts and had mastered violence, but to witness how he fought was shocking, even to her.

To the absolute surprise of every eye in the hall, with excellence, he alone destroyed several of the charging elves. And he did so with such talent, that it did not take long for the attackers to lose faith in their offense and hesitate.

Saazireth noticed how Semereth was in a totally different level from most warriors in that hall. His disciplined and focused ability was above and beyond them. Even though he was among dark elves, the majority of his opponents could not even follow his movements as his chanting sword disintegrated metal, skin, flesh, and bones, cutting with its vibration rather than with its edge. The spasmodic, keen, and terrible sounds of her slashes and piercings taught the terrorizing and brutal dark elves a lesson in fear and violence. And even before the first charge came to a stall, the floor was soaked in blood, guts, body parts, and agonizing elves. Many of the ones that stood down cheered frenetically, excited over the killing, masturbating, or even copulating through consent or blatant rape over the sudden splash of crude violence. They loved that they found themselves in the next level as the bloody spectacles of the arena tussles were brought to the open and to the collective, as if the containment was broken, and, in a larger and bigger sense, the chaos they venerated had transfigured to break the utmost of their social order and the violence they desired was now upon their intimal sphere. The reproduction of the shows of death that they were now used to watching and applauding in the arena was now around them. The massive and somewhat personal violence took the dark elves out of their habitual boredom, and they became inebriated with potent substance of their gruesome thrills. And they loved it. They loved all about it. This new and deeper taste of death and mayhem removed all authority and accountability, leading the whole city into a frenzy that was literally out of all control.

Saazireth waited until the right moment to intervene. She waited until the very last second before acting, for she needed to do what she was planning to do perfectly. She knew that her victory would be even more devastating if Semereth and her guard would win the brawl without her help, and he did. She saw far and her vision was fixed way beyond blades and blood, and even magic.

When she witnessed Semereth's surprising performance, she overcame her initial fear and sadistically smiled inside her mind, but did not allow it to transpire to her face. She stood with her head up while the killing happened as if she was above all that. When the fight got to a standing point, and Semereth and her guard had broken their enemies' initial momentum even without the need of her intervention, she raised her head even higher, maintaining a stern and unshaken face. Everything came to a stall and the skirmish demanded terms, and she delivered hers.

'I have assembled you here today,' she said, 'to declare my champion,' she was being as solemn and serious as a queen, remaining indifferent to what had just happened.

'But the rebels, the traitors, and the dead among you have declared him instead,' she said as if those words nauseated and hurt her.

'This treasonous usurpation I shall not forgive,' she simulated a false bitterness perfectly, but she was bursting with pleasure and satisfaction inside for her plans were being carried out flawlessly.

She looked to Semereth, who was waiting for her orders covered in blood and pieces of skin, as ready as a warhound. The love he had for her and the anger he now had for everything else brought his fidelity to a fanatical climax. She saw that in his eyes while his sword dripped the blood of her enemies. He was holding it in his hand in a perfect grip, and it trembled with its resonation as if it could feel what was to come. His eyes were directed straight at her, waiting in quiet discipline.

Although there were hundreds of people in there, and many had weapons on their hands and a killing wish in their hearts, an incredible silence reigned supreme. In a meticulously calculated move on her part, she looked down to him, surprisingly and deliberately transmitting, in front of all, a love they had only shared in private. With a sincere smile, the ultimate profanity for them, she openly and freely showed her feelings. She did not smile to him, or at him, but for him. And they saw it. And they could not believe the size and depth of the offense.

'Kill them all,' she commanded with a delicious smile full of genuine gratitude. Her voice, though, was as cold as the malice burning in her heart.

The crowd that had stood out of the rebellion stepped back and formed a circle around the ones that had charged her, promptly separating themselves from them, not allowing, in their terror of Semereth, any of the remaining defiant elves to escape his unstoppable fury and inspired loyalty. Some in the crowd did it so simply because they were addicted to their sadistic cruelty and were willing to watch the killing of their neighbors for the single reason of their own personal entertainment. Many did it because they were truly starting to admire the ruthless manner how Saazireth conducted herself, and were really willing to support everything new she signified.

There, on that day, Semereth drew a masterpiece in the art of violence. The fighting memories recovered by Saazireth's spells turned him into what he was: a blade master from the old days. He had fought too many wars, and had spilled so much blood, and took too many lives to be challenged by an assembly of rebellious dark elves. Few things over the face of the earth could have faced him and come out unscathed. The ancient warrior in him was finally brought forth, but now he was even more appalling, for his days in the Underworld had brutalized his sensibilities, and the dark elves' magic increased his powers greatly. Saazireth's influence had shadowed his heart and the memories of his old feelings. Through her irresistible manipulation, she achieved complete control of him, turning the elf into the dismal, stormy, and ruthless instrument of her will. He was now, in all respects, from his soul's bottom to the most material substance of his body, her champion.

The Winter Hunt

'I like the beard.' Lucien was ironic, but his smile was sincere.

He could not contain or hide the happiness he was feeling by meeting with Bastian again, and making fun of his friend's scruffy appearance was the only way he knew to say "I'm happy to see you." Bastian knew that and he hugged his friend as he entered The Fellowship's main hall. Although no words in that regard had been said, it was clear that Lucien had missed him. After so many adventures together, he got used to having Bastian around, and he was the only one Lucien could bare having a real conversation with.

'I have something for you,' said Lucien, pointing to a masterfully built breastplate armor with gauntlets, greaves, and helmet. 'It was crafted with classic Valkarian designs,' he said. 'Got your specs, tailor-made. Dwarf steel,' said Lucien discreetly but not escaping Sahafira's radar. It was the closest Lucien had ever got to praising his friend, or anyone else.

Bastian was wordless.

'Besides,' continued Lucien, 'I cannot stand the fact that we will be seen together, and I don't want people thinking that I have a beggar for a squire,' he said. 'It is not good for my reputation,' he smiled and was corresponded by a large smile from Bastian, who looked down to divert attention from his emotional face.

Lucien tapped his shoulder.

'Are you using your old clothes?' he asked, giving Bastian a second look. 'Have you visited your mom? How is she?' Lucien asked, genuinely interested.

'Fine, I guess,' Bastian answered. 'You know how she is, always in the garden or by Aunt May's house,' he said. 'I can see you bought Klunk a helmet too,' he changed the subject.

'Oh no, he bought himself,' said Lucien, and Bastian's entire demeanor was filled with suspicion.

'Long story,' he explained himself briefly while laughing at Bastian's shocked expression. 'Let just say that it is better for me and him not to be seen in the Wall Market for a while,' he laughed.

Klunk laughed naughtily and nodded, looking at Bastian from the corner of his smiling eyes.

'Let us say a lifetime,' said Lucien and they all laughed.

'Is it a real dragon skull, you know?' said Lucien. 'Tell you the whole story later over a keg, you're going to love it,' he promised.

'As if I'm going to love your boxing and fighting pits stories?' Bastian used the moment wisely.

'Oh, come on!' protested Lucien as his humor dropped subtly. He immediately gave Sahafira a sharp stare. She deviated her eyes from him, avoiding confrontation.

'Can't a man have fun?' he asked Bastian with a charming look, willing to ease the situation.

'They offered me money for your head on my way back here, Lucien.' Bastian was serious and was not giving up.

'So what? Let them try, more fun,' Lucien sounded bitter while pouring himself a glass of wine.

'We are gentlemen of Valkar, Lucien, we have a name to protect,' said Bastian, willing to give him no space at all, just like in one of their sparring sessions.

'Go dress in your armor and prepare yourself,' said Lucien, annoyed. 'The other witch will be here soon,' he said while diving into his chair holding his second glass of wine and staring at Sahafira with a grim expression.

He was right, and shortly after Bastian got ready, Stargazer got out of the Small Castle portrait and The Fellowship of the Sword was together again.

They watched as the wizard rolled up the painting and made it disappear in a pocket of his new coat, then he stared at them.

'Nice coat,' said Lucien, trying, but not sure he was being ironic. He only knew that he had to break the long wordless moment where they exchanged stares and smiles of satisfaction.

Stargazer smiled in his direction and sat around the big round oak table Sahafira have settled for them. The place was even messier than before. Dust was everywhere and loads of construction material and tools populated the corners around them.

'Here we are again,' started Sahafira. 'I am glad that all of you are here. I understand that it is a shared feeling that it is time for us to unite again and search for new adventures,' she said.

'Hello,' interfered Lucien, sarcastically raising his hand. 'Winter is upon us, don't you think maybe now would be the right time to settle down a little?' he proposed with a voice full of disdain.

'Well,' she said, 'I think we all know how you are settling down on the fighting pits, Lucien. Or should I say, Black Blade?' she didn't like to answer people like that but Lucien left her without any other alternative.

He leaned his body forward and looked at her furiously. She had him, and he knew it. Hanam put his hand on his shoulder calmly, encouraging Lucien to lean back in his chair. He did it, and he looked at Bastian for some support and received nothing but an "I told you so" face. He shrugged at the table, showing everyone his contempt and turning his attention to his wine glass with his usual cynical look.

Stargazer stood up and, with a gesture, politely asked Sahafira to sit down. As he had shown himself responsible on many occasions and always found solutions that would please everyone, she decided to give him a chance.

'Gentlemen, and lady,' he said, 'many of you, including myself, have depleted the resources gathered in our last enterprise. Mostly, by pursuing personal interests and by promoting the establishment of this hall – a necessity to keep ourselves comfortable, our valuables safe, and our ideals high.' The wizard captured everybody's attention.

'All this, nevertheless, will not come cheap,' he said. 'Winter is almost here, that's right, Lucien, but common wisdom says that we must listen first and then we must listen even more.' He politely addressed Lucien, who hated his patronizing tone, but was willing to listen out of curiosity and the respect he had for the wizard.

'What I propose will hardly exceed the limits of this city, but have no doubts, it will probably exceed ours,' he said and paused, letting it sink a bit.

'It will be a long-term operation, but it is the right place for it, it is the right time to happen, and we are definitely the right people to see it done,' he paused again.

'As you know, this thriving city is plagued by all sorts of crime, and the city guard and even the imperial authorities have never been able to get rid of it completely, and there is no indication that they will. Keeping it under control is the best result they can sometimes achieve,' he said.

'There is, of course, the financial side to this. If we stack all the rewards that citizens, independent guilds, and even the empire have established for some of the criminal's heads, be sure that we will be financially comfortable until spring finally comes,' he said with a smart smirk on the side of his lips that hinted his proposition.

'I have complete trust in your capabilities,' he said, 'and I know that, if we set in this direction, we will set for success,' he nodded, sure of his own words.

'With Sahafira's knowledge of the local criminal organizations, Shunto's experience in covert warfare, Hanam's wisdom, and you boys' battlefield skills, we are definitely settled for it.'

Klunk grimed his face and crossed his arms, hurt that he was not considered.

'Settled for what?' asked Bastian.

'Victory!' Sahafira spoke suddenly in a way that even Lucien appreciated.

439

'Against what?' asked Lucien skeptic, but listening.

'Evil,' said Hanam, showing an inspiring discernment.

Lucien and Bastian exchanged looks and raised their eyebrow. Klunk smiled. Sahafira nodded. Stargazer smiled discreetly, satisfied, as in the same way he saw it starting before it started, he could now see it before it all would end. He was so very much ahead of them and therefore knew what was going on in every mind and heart on that table. He had them, he had fixed them on the fate in which he himself was a partaken.

'It is about time to rid this city of all the extortion, murders, and worsts,' Sahafira added with a great passion. For her, it was personal.

'It will be our entering job,' Stargazer skillfully used the feelings Sahafira brought forth to sell them his idea. 'It will be our debut, so it needs to be complete and properly done,' he paused, the stern expression on his face said a lot. He looked into their eyes to make sure they had understood what "properly done" meant.

'So, I think we are going to arrest a lot of people,' said Bastian to break the tension.

'Hope they have space in the city's dungeon,' added Lucien, entering the conversation actually motivated and trying to be more practical than sarcastic.

Bastian laughed discreetly with his friend's conclusion, but he stopped laughing the second he looked at Stargazer. What he saw in the wizard's eyes scared him. Although he was staring in his direction, his gaze was passing right through him. The wizard had a cold and distant expression over his face that was different from all the things Bastian ever saw in his eyes. Stargazer started nodding slowly and sourly in a negative sight that disturbed them all, even Lucien. They all froze. The room was silent.

'We will not arrest anyone.' Although the wizard said it coldly, it looked like he was holding a sea of vengeful emotions. 'We are going to KILL. THEM. ALL,' he said as he seemed to embody a thousand judicators' desires of justice.

A long silence followed. In it, they stared in the flames by the wizard's eyes, absorbing his livid desire for reckoning.

'I'm in,' said Lucien, dead serious, raising himself from the table.

'When do we start?' asked Sahafira, raising herself and grabbing her bow.

'Now,' Stargazer immediately replied with the fiery grim still on his face.

They all felt a rush of blood taking over their whole bodies.

The wizard locked his gaze on the door and walked over to it with great self-assurance. Before reaching it, he materialized his staff in his right hand with a loud flash of energy and light. He didn't look back or say anything, but even so, they all followed him in a great rush.

The After Champion

First, Semereth killed the mercenary warriors that fought in the Arena. Then, the voracious and terrible monsters that the dark elves captured in the world's darkest places. Some were summoned by the use of the most vicious magic that reality could withstand without shattering and collapsing. Then, he faced the local champions, who were the dark elves of great reputation that fought for the elder houses. One after the other, unmistakably, he killed them all.

It did not matter how they tested him, trying to evaluate his strengths and analyze his weaknesses so they could develop tactics against him. He won every time. It seemed that he knew all the tricks in the deck, and was always ahead of them. This was not easy for the proud dark elves to take it, and they hated him almost as fiercely as they hated Saazireth.

Although Semereth appeared to be unbeatable, things were not free from drama. On more than one opportunity, death almost caught him. Many times, he left the Arena almost dead. However, he always managed to be resilient enough to consistently achieve victory.

Sometimes the clashes were clean and quick, but occasionally they were cruel and long. One thing was certain: they never failed to be bloody.

His sword had a part in his reputation as well, following him in every triumph. It reigned supreme on the arena, and its rare magic was part of the show. Its sonic vibration tuned itself to the texture of its target's matter, transfixing, disrupting, and melting anything it hit. Together, they were one. In each attack, in each battle, and in each death, they sang a song of doom – and the crowd loved it.

In one of the duels, a wealthy house presented an incredibly expensive and powerful magic constructor. The metal warrior was built with a surrounding field of anti-magic radiation, designed to immunize it not only to magic weapons but to most magic. It was a terrible foe, but the sword still had a trick or two to show, and shortly after the fight started, when all seemed already lost, the blade sang a new and wonderful chant. Semereth swigged the sword in the air, drove its sonic waves in the direction of the constructor, attacking the very structure of its matter not with the magic itself, but with the physical consequences of it. The entire golem shattered as if it were made of wet sand, and the dark elves learned to fear even the noise the weapon made when it moved through the air. They learned to fear and desire its hidden and mysterious enchants.

The experience of Semereth and the screaming sword grew with each victory, and Rak'hamon ran out of options to throw at them. Before long, there were no more challenges for them there.

When he had wasted all the city resources, in delight, Saazireth started to create bloody spectacles to keep her distractions working. She set hordes of horrible and irrational creatures drugged and enchanted into a killing frenzy to charge Semereth at once. She bought expensive and terrible beasts from all the corners of the world to fight him. She arranged many types of encounters and death shows, and she invested a lot of resources to spread the word of a reward beyond measure to anyone who could defeat Semereth. Occasionally, a dark champion presented himself for the challenge. When that happened, they never failed to put on a genial and fierce fight. Saazireth also created all kinds of shows and bravados, making extravagant bets on how quick the wood elf would win the skirmishes, pretending all too well to enjoy the spectacles and faking that those things really mattered to her when in reality, although it was true that she liked to see Semereth dominating everything they cast at him, her mind was always elsewhere, deep into her plans.

Behind the smoke screen she carefully raised, Saazireth was making very dangerous political moves. Even more dangerous and daring than the ones she implemented before. As she sent messengers to explain her ways and share her propositions to many places on the surface, she also sent emissaries to the dark elves' main cities with the sole objective to scandalize them and to provoke the High Council. Saazireth was keen to tell them, in the language they understood best, that her and her ways had come to stay, and that she would take orders from no one. Most of her messengers never returned, but her message stood clear.

During those days, the dark elves of the nearest cities learned that when Saazireth made a move, she always had at least three clear and perceptible reasons why, and a few veiled. Consequently, many powerful dark elves, willing to hurt her and reveal her plans, sent delegations and champions to Rak'hamon to fight in her arena. As they were silently supported by the High Council, the challenges became increasingly difficult even for Semereth to handle and, after a series of struggles with the rogue warriors who almost finished him, Saazireth decided that it was time to intensify things, as she saw that the time for the next phase of her plan had finally arrived. She knew (actually she expected) that many hidden hands would plot against her, after all, that was the very nature of the game they played. Therefore, wishing to expose her enemies and also to probe the reaction of the dark elves over one major element of her schemes, she acted swiftly and boldly and, one day, the enchantress disappeared with Semereth and her personal guard. They quarantined themselves in Linothan's secret chambers where she once killed him and where the core of her researches came to a fruitful conclusion.

With the help of some of her most powerful apprentices and loyal allies, she prepared the rituals of The Fusion. She planned to fuse Semereth first and then her entire guard, increasing their powers dramatically, and using them as a blueprint for her future army.

When everything was in place, she solemnly looked at Semereth.

'No one here can contest your loyalty or your might,' she said, gravely but distant. 'Although, we must face that the relatively small challenges in this city's arena are already overcoming your capabilities,' she said to him in front of everybody from her inner circle. 'My plans, however, go way further than the meek realities of this place,' she said and then breathed in, as if her lungs could filter inspiration from the air. 'How can we accomplish that if we are not decisive in our compromise to grab every chance in our way?' She looked around into the eyes around her. 'There was a time when the dark elves would stop at nothing to achieve what we believed to be our destiny. That time defined us and made us,' she said. 'Do not be misled, the challenges ahead demand a higher greatness. A greatness that can only be procured outside the barriers of this world. A greatness that can only be controlled by sound minds, powerful souls, and dense spirits. A greatness that can only be achieved with total compromise,' she said and paused.

Saazireth was surrounded by talent and ambition, and by already knowing the full extension of her meanings, some of the dark elves trembled with excitement.

'By feeling hate, we reduced ourselves to feelers of hate,' she restarted. 'By promising revenge, we became an eternal promise of a never coming reckoning. By filling ourselves with rage, we blindly turned against one another. And by merely using indiscriminate destruction, we have reduced our reach and demolished the very pillars of our society.' The fundamental veracity of what she had the courage to say shook her followers to the bottom of their dark hearts.

'Channeling those emotions and exploring its magical results gave us power. However, it limited us to the lesser rules of this reality, as it now contains many cyclical counters against our interests,' she said, and her words were conclusive, deep, and refined to their ears. The higher the power of the mages there, the more they became moved by her proposition.

'We need to transcend it. Transcend it all. To go further. To go beyond those laws that bind us. We need to reach out past this world and fuse ourselves with the higher beings that live where the essence of things are born. We need to sow ourselves with the fabric of their essence. We need not to use hate, we need to become hate. We shall not get revenge, we shall be revenge. Let us be no longer slaves of any rage, let us be known as rage itself. Let us transform ourselves into the destruction we need to see crowned in this petty world,' she said gravely, and the dark inspiration she summoned flowed from her lips to their souls.

'No more barriers or limitations,' she said. 'Let us not be used anymore, instead, let us use this world and everything in it for our benefits and glorifications,' she proposed, magnificently, and every single dark elf in that chamber felt their hearts stopping by the grandness of her vision finally revealed.

'No. More. Compromises,' she said, looking at them in the eyes, causing the dark elves to enter a megalomaniac and psychosomatic delirium of amusement and arousal.

Immediately, they started singing a new and powerful song of dread and hysteria. As in a hellish hallucination, they delivered themselves to physical pleasure to alleviate their overflowing desires, dancing in a dance of passion while desperately trying to tame their bottomless lust. Uncontrollably, they started touching themselves and each other, copulating while standing up, sodomizing the weakest among them by force, pressing excrement against their unhinged faces, doing everything they could to manifest what was overflowing from their souls. In abhorrent synchrony, they danced by the symphony of their own composition. And they manifested magic during the expressing of their utmost rebelliousness through the spontaneous and vicious orgy composed by their most inflamed voluptuousness.

'Come, my champion,' said Saazireth, turning to Semereth after dancing for a while among and above them. Her eyes were sparkling with the truest joy her perspective would ever bring forth, for her reign, and even her very self, was already the theme of that song. 'Be the first to transcend,' she proposed to him, offering her hand – a rare act on her part.

'Let your soul be filled with power. Arise!' she shouted as if declaring it to the world, and the rhythms of the elves changed to a faster frenzy. 'BE beyond,' she whispered into his ear, and licked it. Her eyes full of madness.

She pointed the altar to Semereth. He laid on it, naked and ready. Immediately, and in great fervor, all the present started the refined and complex rituals still through the trance of their dark opera.

Sparks of darkness and magic fire of many evil colors burst through the air for several hours until the magic came to completion. Over the altar, smoke, ghostly light, and fluid shadow poured into existence through Semereth's new body.

'Arise, my brave champion,' she said in absolute delight, and she marveled by the magnificent contemplation of her vision.

'Ascend! Victory is at hand!' she said crying with joy through her words.

Suddenly, a fraction of second after she said these words, the whole room shook violently. It shook in a way that it was not supposed to. It shook as if the walls were made of wood and a giant had just hammered it with a colossal lead hammer. Dust filled the place, and a massive crack was heard when and enormous piece of the ceiling separated itself from it and fell over one of the tables, causing a deafening noise.

Yet another bang and another shake. The whole cave seemed to be in convulsion now. The dark elves were reactionless. Many other pieces of rock continued to fall from the cracked ceiling and walls, causing further confusion among them. They exchanged looks and quickly understood that none knew what was going on, except for Saazireth. She was looking up, as if she could see what was happening at Rak'hamon through the dozens and dozens of yards of rocks and magic above them. Her tenebrous expression and pursed lips told them that something was impossibly wrong.

The Big Catharsis

After many months of direct and bloody combat in an all-out hunt for criminals, Rocksprings got rid of almost all of its illegal activities. The adventures and misfortunes that The Fellowship faced during this period could fill many books. It was a very dense period in their most unlikely lives, nothing shorter than a war.

Used to hunt feral beasts and terrible monsters, Bastian, Lucien, and Stargazer mercilessly rolled over against the city's thieves conclaves, and assassin guilds with a unilateral ferocity – no quarters were given.

Most of their combat experience came from all the time they spent fighting for survival in wild secludes, and that imbued the boys with a guttural aggression that unexpectedly gave them an edge in comparison to even the sharpest city dweller. It was a given to them, therefore, to face their enemies with a raw disposition and total violence. Just as domestic dogs cannot resist wolves, most of their urban targets, however vitriolic they were, could not resist the warriors of The Fellowship.

Sahafira, Hanam, and Shunto fought bravely too, but kept a different stand, a more mature and conservative one, thinking and deploying their powers not only tactically, but strategically. All and all, The Fellowship became highly effective, especially when working together. For the desperation of their enemies, they prospered into their enterprises with every single battle, resisting all the attempts against them and growing in experience and in strength. In the end, desperate and pressured, some targets tried to bargain and pay tribute to them, but it was all in vain, for under Stargazer's leadership they became focused and brutal.

One by one, the criminals fell and, in time, even the city's pocket pickers started looking for honest jobs. Stargazer's plan worked to perfection. Not only over the objective of being effective against the crime scene, but in regard to printing the desired legacy to The Fellowship. They became real local heroes, recognized, praised, respected, and even feared, everywhere in Rocksprings.

In the beginning, their raids were just a rumor, but the colder it got, the higher was the pile of bodies in the city hall. The considerable amount of money they won in bounties and rewards paled in comparison to the influence they managed to acquire. In a frenetic rhythm, they collected prize after prize, for the wizard warned them that, for his plan to work, they must not give any time for the criminals to reorganize or hide after the first blows. Hence, they kept a strategy of hitting first and hitting hard and hitting everywhere, leaving no one alive to tell anything. Their actions were so sudden, unexpected, and focused, that the momentum they needed was achieved masterfully and their extermination was downright accomplished.

As the impact of the annihilation of the enemies of civil society started to be felt, many of the previously oppressed citizens started to recognize and support their activities. Directly and indirectly, they did many favors to many people during those days, gathering allies and admirers in important places. The good people of the city were quick to embrace the hope that The Fellowship of the Sword represented, giving them their support in many different ways. Sometimes with precious information, sometimes with resources for the construction of their hall, and sometimes with open praise.

Much sooner than expected, they had their hall completely paid for, including all the extras they could possibly desire. With the support of Rocksprings's Traders Guild and the Coronian Bank (the two most powerful business forces in the city), who had, both, previously suffered dearly with the local crime for centuries, they gathered all the help they needed for their plans and their actions. On top of that, one after the other, the suppliers lowered their prices, sometimes providing the materials for cost value or even for free. And with all that, the works on their lair accelerated to a maximum speed, and beyond.

After they suffered retaliations that almost took the initiative from them, the commander of the city guard ordered an entire company to camp around their hall, and some guards even gladly helped with the construction during their spare time.

Common people, especially the hundreds directly victimized by local crime also volunteered, working day and night with great joy. Rich wizards, honorable citizens, and prosperous merchants helped as they could. Some did it for believing in The Fellowship's undeclared ideals, some because they foresaw the benefits of their actions, but, most, for the sake of watching evil men getting some payback.

At some point, The Fellowship killed a legendary local thieve and scattered his minions. On that occasion, they recovered a magical artifact that belonged to the famous Rocksprings's Library. When they freely gave it back to its previous owners, some of the sages and mages offered their help. With their magic, the construction work was accelerated and improved to a great deal. As a result, miraculously, The Hall, as they called it their place of assembly, was standing strong before winter was over, and the spells cast through the returning generosity of the city's organized wizardry made their fortress far more secure than Sahafira and Stargazer had ever hoped it would ever be.

After receiving aid from some of the Rocksprings's finest enchanters, Stargazer managed to modify and activate the Adamantium Golem they took from Kestos's lair. The constructor was a game changer for him and for the entire Fellowship. Its power was tremendous, way beyond their actual necessities then. It was an unstoppable and formidable war machine, far more resilient and controllable than Klunk, multiplying their strike capability by tenfold. Later, they would discover that its activation took place in due course, as soon after activating it, they struck what they learned to be their last and true opponent of their righteous crusade.

Throughout their war against the city's criminal organizations, they puzzled together that a small conclave of dark elves were the real masterminds behind the rampant and seemly perpetual violence in the city. Although they could not guess why the dark elves would bother doing that, they were astonished at how efficient they became in manipulating the sustenance of crime with the intention of destabilizing Rocksprings and its surroundings. In the end, they were amazed that such talented, beautiful, and brilliant creatures could devote their lives to such hateful and evil purpose just for sports.

Not without difficulties, The Fellowship managed to track them down and, after much preparation, attack their sanctuary. Aided by some senior and powerful citizens, and using the best of their resources, experience, and combat techniques, they managed to overcome the dark elves in a terrible battle where they almost lost their lives.

Afterwards, there was a clear perception on their part that luck was on their side, and they become quite aware that they could never have accomplished victory over the elves without their higher number and magical equipment, particularly the inexorable Adamantium Golem. The speed, skill, and killing sharpness of the dark elves were on an entirely different level, a much, much higher one. Most of them ended the combat unconscious and had to expend large amounts of their acquired wealth to receive all kinds of expensive treatments against the terrible exotic poisons, curses, and magical toxins with which the elves bathed their blades and themselves in.

Lucien lost an arm and his whole lower chin in that fight; Bastian, both legs. They only escaped, because Sahafira quickly cold burned their open wounds, stopping the heavy bleeding of such gruesome wounds. But even on the ground, legless, and with part of his body consumed by an acid discharge, Bastian would berserkly shoot arrows. And even with only one arm, half his head, and with his torso pierced severally, Lucien would bravely get close in and throw Dwarf Grenades on the elves' flanks.

The game they played was indeed a high risk one, and it took its toll on all of them, but The Fellowship only knew how to play for keeps, ultimately prevailing against their opponents. With the end of extortion, blackmail, and corruption, free trade was again a rule, not an exception. Consequently, the city profits increased considerably and the good news quickly got to all the corners of the empire, attracting even more business, prospering Rocksprings a great deal more. By the middle of the following summer, they were solid heroes, greeted with admiration everywhere, and holders of a trusted reputation in Rocksprings and beyond – all things were going according to the wizard's plan.

Deep Siege

Wise men say that it is in the depths of the Underworld that many of the world's greatest battles are fiercely fought and totally forgotten. The total annihilation of Rak'hamon was carried out quickly and devilishly wide-ranging, precisely in that spirit and honoring this legend.

They did not attack the city to seize it, they did not attack it for any prize or even to capture Saazireth. Instead, they chose to demolish it as zealots handling a profane idol.

Within and around the city, the High Council captains arranged their preparations and the city fell much before the first fireball was shot. Weeks before the attack, by taking advantage of Rak'hamon's new flux of visitors, they spied the outskirts and the insides of the city methodically. Not only selecting and preparing prime locations for their assault portals, but studying magical solutions to quickly deactivate the city's colossal magical protections. Ironically, their strategy ended using Rak'hamon's blasphemy against themselves.

The initial wave was composed of subversive assassins – a skill that the dark elves had developed into an art. They were infiltrated and oriented with the help of insiders, and once in position they silently neutralized any sentinels that might anticipate any defense. Then, a wave of enchanters came forth. Cloaked by magical invisibility and protected from detection, they quietly disabled many of Rak'hamon's key defenses. Totems guarding key points, automatons shielding shooting towers, golems protecting access to specific corridors, passive detection runes, and many other highly technical defensive spells cast all over the city were deactivated and neutralized with speed and efficiency. To that end, the attackers equipped themselves with mission specific magic that favored the accomplishment of their objectives in the quickest and quietest way possible.

They had dozens of decades, and in some cases even centuries of combat and spell-crafting experience, and they moved in perfect synchrony, operating like a single wave of independent refined mechanisms, for they were artists above and beyond any professionalism. All the actions, from the first to the last one of the raiders, were planned to be executed in a clockwork manner. Every assassin, wizard, sorcerer, siege weapon operator, beastmaster, and infantryman knew the timing and the tactical reasons of the objectives signed to them. Their initial schemes were successful and they kept the element of surprise on their side long enough.

Seconds before the third and the fourth wave started their attacks, the enchanters of the second wave, the elite of the High Council armies, using a powerful artifact, got together and covered the entire city with a very powerful force field. It isolated the city from the world, blocking any magic, whether a communication, scrying, or teleportation, to escape the dome. Making it impossible for Rak'hamon's defenders to call reinforcements, send messages, and, especially, to escape.

The third and the fourth wave were transported together by means of their assault portals to the outskirts, rock balconies, and caves around the city. It was composed of mercenaries (mainly depth dwarves) operating powerful siege weapons that could launch terrible magic projectiles. Their first shots were of dispelling spells, used to neutralize the strengthening magic imbued in the city towers and walls. Some structures came down just from the effects of the magical dispelling, for their stability depended not on architectural calculations, but in enchants that saturated the minerals of its compositions.

In general, the dark elves' architecture was very artistic and uncontrollably megalomaniac. Therefore, most of its fortifications were very expressive and impractical, more of a proposition than something useful, more of a statement than a home. They were conceptualized and built to affirm something and to scar reality rather than to be used in any defense or any other way.

With the timely rigors that would gain the respect of a dwarf siege master, the fourth wave of magic operators unleashed an insane barrage of explosive magic. Their salvos were synchronized with the dispelling of the third wave, reaching their targets milliseconds after they were weakened by the negating enchantments. This wave was formed mostly by lesser-skilled users of magic, minding, of course, the dark elves' high standard. They used prepared and relatively inexpensive magic items developed to be employed in mass. They attacked in groups, holding hundreds of plentiful wands, an abundant number of scrolls, and their terrible magic infused gems, creating an absolutely overwhelming volume of fire that, by itself, destroyed half of the city. The way the fourth wave operated was a classic example of the main component of most dark elf armies, trusting their energy sources and deep knowledge of magic to create large quantities of destructive devices and deploy them simultaneously and massively.

Even the most unskilled dark elf was considered highly erudite regarding magic. For them, manipulating a magical object like a wand was as easy and natural as a dwarf would use a hammer or an axe. A regular wand loaded with a dozen charges of "cheap" fireball, a common magic projectiles, or a lightning bolt was devastating when deployed in large numbers. On the attack on Rak'hamon, the several battalions of wizards systematically bombarded every inch of the city, blasting into oblivion everything and everyone who decided not to take cover, regardless of who they were. They employed such a high volume of destructive magic, that within minutes they released an unbearable amount of blasts, annihilating Rak'hamon's buildings to the last pillar. The battle was a scary demonstration of how magic could be masterfully used in a war, and long after they ended their bombardments, Rak'hamon's rocks kept glowing red. The intense violence of their fury was unmatchable, and very few races and kingdoms could replicate something like it.

After they had deployed their surgical dispelling, the siege weapons of the third wave smartly used magic munitions of several different varieties and applications. In conjunction with other troops, they were employed in a variety of stand-off tasks for good effect. They shot spells that turned solid rock into mud on the basis of the more robust towers, causing it to fall under many other structures and causing further desolation. They launched a swarm of enormous magic wasps through a fort window, expelling or distracting its occupants. They even froze an entire section of the exterior wall before some charging beast cracked it with its thick horns. They were also used strategically, filling entire fields with paralyzing spells, denying the city defense the ability to move troops tactically inside the city perimeters.

Under the initial heavy artillery barrage, dark mercenaries from forgotten kingdoms of the Underworld and the beastmasters unleashed their fury over the city, entering it and killing everyone in sight. The havoc they created opened the way to the main force that followed.

After a pause in the first volley of fire, an extra number of assault portals were opened and the High Council shock troops attacked the city. They were composed mainly of highly disciplined elven heavy infantry and organized into small independent platoons, each having its own organic healer and at least two dedicated protective sorcerers and two dedicated offensive spellcasters. Armed with heavily enchant adamantium full plate mails, some of the sharpest swords in the world, and a lot of dreadfully destructive magic, they brought the fight to a hellish melee.

While the mercenaries' mission was to start the mop-up operations by basically taking control of the city, the shock troop platoons took from there and stroke specifics rounded up pockets of resistance, destroying them systematically.

Nevertheless their operation was greatly facilitated by some of Rak'hamon's houses, they decided to make the city an example by sparing no one, and all in the city were killed or worse.

The momentum of the invading forces was masterfully kept until the end. When most of the city inhabitants realized what was going on, they were already fighting a hopeless fight. There was some resistance, but not organized enough and not in sufficient numbers. Divided and unprepared, they were easy prey for the hunting squads. Many surrendered, but only to be put to the sword on the spot or later, after cruel torture.

As the egoistic society, the dark elves concentrated power on the individual. Their military efforts focused on the power of the single elf. Mainly, in its ability to exercise violence and wrecking by magic. This fact increased the overall range and scope of the violence and the destruction of their clashes. Explosions and blasts in all directions consumed what was left of the inner city and the interior of Rak'hamon's palaces. Obviously, both sides employed this strategy, therefore, as the fight went on, the collateral damage rapidly transformed the city into a hill of dustified rubble, minced guts, and blasted blood. The vapors of the turmoiled particles of all the things disintegrated in the battle outspread throughout the air of the cave where Rak'hamon was, covering everything there. The telling mist of burned guts and demolished walls formed by the brutish act of tens of thousands of sadists was a silent testimony of all the violence concurred on that place.

On behalf of the High Council, the captains of the invading troops interrogated all the rounded up surviving elves. It did not matter what answer they provided under torture, in the end, they were all executed massively and ritualistic in the most painful and despicable way possible. Before they resumed the interrogatories and the killings, there was a creek of blood flowing down the valleys between the hills of debris that once were the city gutters. The pyramidal piles of heads were only smaller than the piles of rubble. The attack on Rak'hamon was not a siege, it was a ruthless raid.

Eventually, Saazireth and her guard presented themselves to fight, and they fought bravely. The dark elves were especially treacherous and dangerous when they were cornered, and she was no exception.

While very young, Saazireth was a true master of destruction, and as such, she was able to deploy spells of terrible effect. She also possessed access to some ancient artifacts that gave her enough power to face the invading army with some hope of escaping.

The resulting destruction of the fight she put out was worse than the first barrage, and the caves around them trembled and fell from the violence of their manifested fury. The raider's commanders were willing to sacrifice anything to capture the enchantress, for the high Council had instructed them in this manner. Although she put a hell of a fight, even killing most of their captains and crushing, burning, melting, freezing, and simply disintegrated many of their best units, Saazireth was eventually subdued and taken into custody to answer directly before the High Counselors.

The savagery of the battle was so intense that its tremors could be heard, and felt, for many miles in all directions. It was even worse than the siege itself. The hard rock cave systems surrounding the city produced an interesting phenomenon of sound propagation. The scary uproar of hundreds and hundreds of fireball, thunders, and all sorts of magical blasts striking the city walls viciously resonated all over the caves as if they were a gargantuan trombone blown by some buried titan of old.

Vorlok was traveling through some shortcut that he believed he was the only one aware of when he started to hear the sounds of the battle. Those sounds caused an impression on him, raising the hair on the back of his neck.

At first, he thought it was an earth tremor or some gargantuan creature waking from some ancient long sleep, but then he got mighty suspicious of it, for his instincts could identify inexplicable familiarities in the sounds he was hearing. Even though he could not explain the reason why, he was completely taken by it. He cursed his luck again for his mind told him to keep traveling and going about his business, but the anxiety to know what was going on was chewing his insides. He stopped and concentrated his psych sensibilities in its direction. He doubted his sanity when he felt nothing.

Knowing that Rak'hamon was just one day from him, he projected his mind astrally, concentrating in the city. Struck by an extraordinary void, his doubts increased and he hesitated. Immensely frustrated, like an addict who cannot end his vice, he finally gave up and, contradicting his best judgment, he went straight back the way he came.

Epilogue

Jackpot! he thought. *Jack freaking pot!* he thought again, cheering alone, to himself.

He did it as if by mentally repeating those words would increase the bliss he was feeling at that moment or stretch the duration of that rare pleasure he enjoyed.

Vorlok was lying down over the dark crystal throne that had once belonged to Saazireth. It was broken, scratched, and tilted sideways on top of a mountain of debris. Still, it was the most intact object for miles in all directions.

There was nothing around him but hills of rubble and piles of heads. Comfortably, he lay with his head over the inclined throne. He put his feet up and settled down while absorbing all the pleasure he got from watching the result of the city's total annihilation. The unfaithful was laughing to himself while he childishly moved his sickly skinny legs and his profane dark feet. Relaxed, he licked his repulsive tentacle lips between gluttonous and long sips of wine. He was feeling like all his dreams had altogether come true. He could not contain his gladness for the destruction of the city, the death of all dark elves (especially Saazireth, whom he hated the most), and for the great loot he found around the city ruins. But what was really making him happy were the contents of his stomach.

The fulfillment of his entire appetite was a rare event in his life. As such, it left him in a sort of a pleasure trance. And in this trance he was enjoying himself to the fullest.

In one hand, he had a disproportionally large goblet made of the purest amethyst. It was carved from a single stone and decorated exquisitely and lavishly with a soft gold encrust. The cup was full of the most perfumed wine, courtesy of so many destroyed cellars. He sipped the dark elves' wine, enjoying every gulp as he did it. His heart was full of the vile contempt and the simple happiness of someone who has witnessed the total crushing of their enemies. Satisfied, he lay on his throne of vengeance.

Vorlok had never, in his whole existence, ate that good. The Unfaithful had a powerful metabolism, and their bodies, although seemingly fragile, were strong and resistant. They had the strength and stamina of two men and could eat like four. Vorlok, in particular, ate like eight, and his belly was now full. Full to a point where he could not breathe properly. He was so full that he decided to do nothing but rest and celebrate until digestion did its thing.

His belly was bizarrely bloated, composing an even more distorted figure from his frame. Inside of his inflated stomach, there were the brains of several elves.

As the dark elves were not in the custom of burying their dead, and they also did not value gold or silver, upon searching the ruins, he found so many countless intact heads, precious loot, and many other rare items of his interest that he thought he was dreaming.

As the first hoarder, he was quick to follow into a satisfactory ecstasy while witnessing himself becoming a rich man. For the first time in his miserable existence, he was feeling larger than life.

After he had bagged and piled it all up, he felt weary and decided to treat himself to a feast. By choosing the most offensive spot, he took some of the best heads and the best wines he found and celebrated Rak'hamon's doom. He drank and ate like a king. A king of death, wreckage, ruin, and shadow, but still a king.

Alone, Vorlok laughed openly with excessive self-approval when he thought about the suffering and despair of the inhabitants of the city. He could still smell the fear of the inhabitants of the dead city in the air, and he inhaled it as if it was some sweet fragrance. He giggled when he portrayed the brutality and mercilessness of the High Council soldiers while they advanced on the streets. He was not a particularly imaginative creature, but as he sat there framing those things in his mind he found a fair amount of satisfaction.

He gathered a massive quantity of precious goods that would make up for all the losses Saazireth inflicted him, and for the first time in his life he was felling real lucky. Lucky that he had left the city before the strike portals were opened and the attack unleashed. Lucky for the fact that he thought he arrived at the ruins just when the last patrols withdrew, finding the remains still intact for looting. And lucky that they had left so many fresh heads behind for good eating.

There he was: happy and content with how things had turned good for him, and triumphant with his changing luck. He was lying carelessly over the crystal throne, thinking about his next step while he balanced a large shred of Darkwood as a toothpick between his hideous lips. With it, he was proudly and skillfully removing the last remaining pieces of skin and hair from his beak teeth.

When he decided that it was time to make hurry for the road ahead, he stretched his skinny body, sat, and stretched himself raising his hands into the air. Enjoying every second of his life now, he put his arms down and, while tapping his slender hands on his knees, decided that it was time to go. When he looked ahead, he froze completely. Before he could raise himself from the throne, his legs failed him, and he actually retracted into the crystal chair. The shred of Darkwood fell from his mouth and both his hearts stopped for a second. His expression changed in a blink of an eye, for in a blink of an eye he found himself accompanied.

Right in front of him, less than a yard away, stood a figure in a dark cloak. Behind him, other figures, also in dark cloaks. Vorlok was so scared by those presences that he started feeling the emanation of his own fear.

'Ca-can I help you?' he asked, cursing himself for his frightened mind could not think of something better to say.

He cursed himself again for he was not able to at least hide the fear in his voice. Vorlok was very dangerous himself, he knew that, but could not control the instinct saying to him that he was facing a bigger fish. A much, much bigger fish.

'What have you found here, Vorlok?' asked the hooded figure.

'Ra-Razec?' the unfaithful asked, trembling. 'I-is that you?' Vorlok was overcome by his fears and silently begged the universe to answer with a resounding no. He did not manage to hide or control what he was feeling now. He did not curse himself this time though, for he knew that the reverence of the panic in his voice would be justified if he was right.

The figure lowered his hood, revealing his face. It was Razec. Instinctively, Vorlok raised his left hand to his mouth when he saw the elf's face. The unfaithful leaned against a large piece of rubble as his knees failed him. He knew not how to react, and his mind was captured by the space between his worst dreads. He was paralyzed by doubt and panic, hesitating in an emotionless place, lost without knowing where to go or lacking the will to.

'What have you found, Vorlok?' the elf repeated the question rather patiently.

Completely self-aware he was transpiring tons of suspiciousness about the elf's intentions, Vorlok indicated a pathway down the rubble hill with his long dark finger. Then, like a dog, he submissively, politely, and scarily asked Razec to follow him.

He then conducted the elf and his followers down to a valley where he had hidden his iron carriage with his bounty. Once there, he found Razec's black wagon already parked in front of it, and, for the increasing of his bitterness, Vorlok noticed that Razec's "men" had already looted it clean. All the most powerful objects, including all of the dark elves' magical gems, were missing and the other objects were spread over the ground in a manner that absolutely enraged the neat freak inside Vorlok.

'What ELSE have you found here, Vorlok?' Razec calmly asked him one more time, reiterating himself rather humbly, but completely and utterly ignoring any implied claim that the unfaithful had made over his own property.

Vorlok did not answer it, for he could not. His heart was burning with bitter hatred and his mind was overloaded with a thousand maledictions. The vilest of which he was promptly employing in the privacy of his mind while hexing the entire elf race, swearing against them forever. Paralyzed by the sheer harshness of his destiny, he trembled with hate, blamed his fate, hated his life, and cursed his luck, for when he finally found himself free from a tyrant, there came another one and took its place.

Razec looked at the disgruntled unfaithful one last time and laughed slightly from the corner of his mouth.

'Search,' said Razec to his minions, ignoring Vorlok.

After their master's command, the other figures immediately spread out over the terrain, looking for something.

Vorlok was furious with his cruel destiny beyond any fear for his life. When Razec turned to rescue a half-buried compendium from the ground, he carefully drew a concealed long dagger while he kept his suicidal eyes fixed on the base of the elf's skull. When he went for it, he suddenly lost his equilibrium as the ground trembled under his feet. Before he could react he found himself perfectly out of balance when the piece of the slab under him quickly raised him into the air. He tried to recompose himself, but failed, ridiculously collapsing on his backside.

Living shadow and terrorizing flame rose from the ground in front of him. In danger, a common person would direct all of its senses to the perceived danger; Vorlok, however, as a psyche, directed his special sensibilities to whatever was coming out of the ground. His panicking mind needed desperately to find answers for what he was feeling in order to have a clear understanding of what was the source of the terror that overcame him. As a result, before his common senses transmitted an impression of the danger to his brain, his mind had passively received the true nature of the menace. The unfaithful had been around the worst this world had to offer since the day he start existing, but the intensity of what he felt now paralyzed him. Hate, transgression, and the destruction of a thousand nightmares boiled together in the utmost unbearable chaos right in front of him. It all came to him at once, as an insufferable punch to his soul's guts. His blood boiled cold, for his whole being was tasting the presence of the very incarnation of utmost abominable feelings. This, in all its maliciousness, was something new. It was as if the purest form of the deepest and most hazardous emotional traumas had come to life, and they were now raping all his notions by existing in the same reality as his mind. Not his subjective mind, but the objective materiality of everything he considered real and loaded in his head when he woke up. He felt oppressed in every inch of his soul by the magnificent intensity of what was in front of him. Whatever or whoever it was, hell was following it. Uncontrollably, and for the first time his life, tears came out from his eyes while he froze in an absolute panic. His dagger glued to his hand due to involuntary muscular contraction. On his lower thighs, a dark matter glissaded copiously down his long leather boots as he relieved himself without even realizing it.

The dark figure arose. It was tall and terrible. It had long horns, impure bat-like wings dressed in thick leather, deformed pointing elfish ears, and hellish burning eyes. When he moved his skin, fowl poisonous vapors were let out as if his body itself was a portal to the abyss. A shadow was always manifesting around him, as if attesting the heavy dimensional signature pressed on his flesh. When infuriated, a furnace burned inside of him, to the point that his joints, eyes, mouth, and chest glowed red, instantly igniting everything around him. And around him indeed there was a tainted air that radiated fear directly to the soul. By the sheer revelation of his unnatural forms and the disclosure of his presences, most people would flee in terror.

When Vorlok got back some control over his own muscles, he crawled, disheartened, behind a boulder, peeking from a corner what would unfold from that horrendous situation. He immediately recognized the chanting sword, the war belt, and other items that were being worn by the devil.

It must be Semereth, the whore's slave-warrior, the unfaithful thought.

The half-demon came close to Razec, stopping in front of the elf as if facing him. Vorlok was close enough to hear whatever they would say, but also far enough to run if a fight broke out. He began to hope that they would kill each other in a horrible battle so that he could take some revenge at last.

'Hello, my old friend,' said Razec, opening a heartfelt smile to the half-demon.

Vorlok clenched his fists miserably and cursed his wretched luck once again.

CPSIA information can be obtained
at www.ICGtesting.com
Printed in the USA
LVHW100745260621
690828LV00020B/96

9 781643 784267